THE STONE HEART

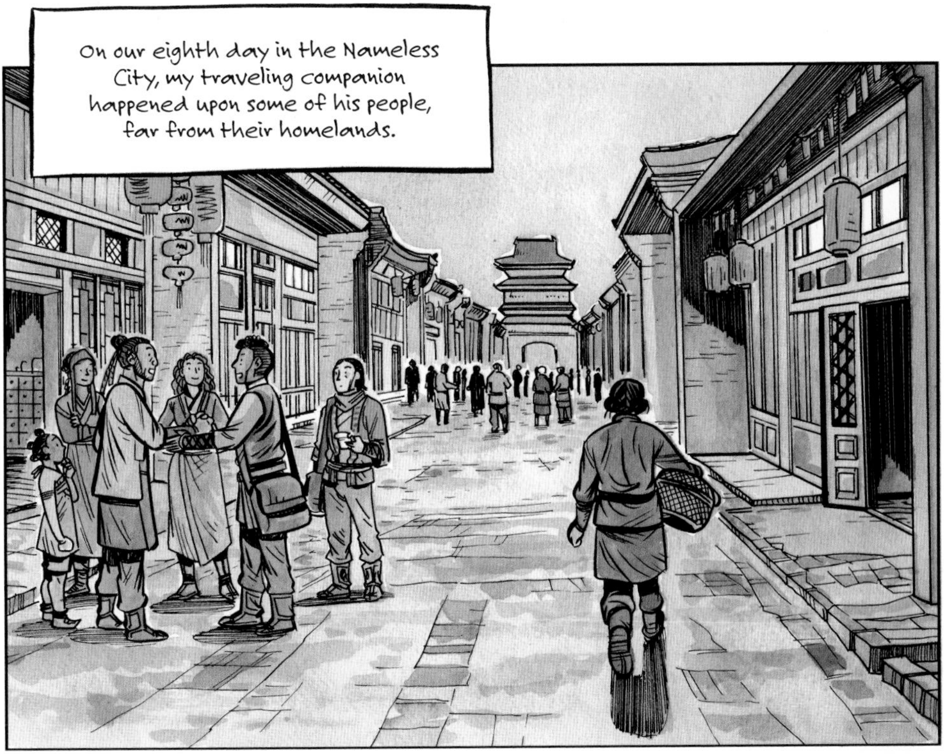
On our eighth day in the Nameless City, my traveling companion happened upon some of his people, far from their homelands.

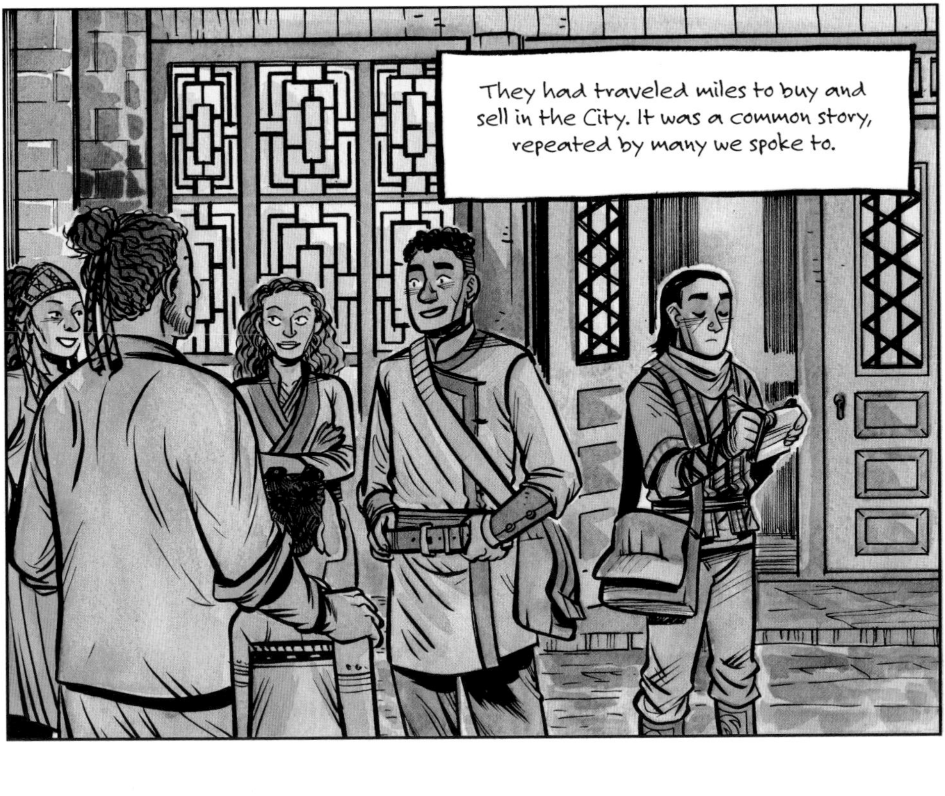
They had traveled miles to buy and sell in the City. It was a common story, repeated by many we spoke to.

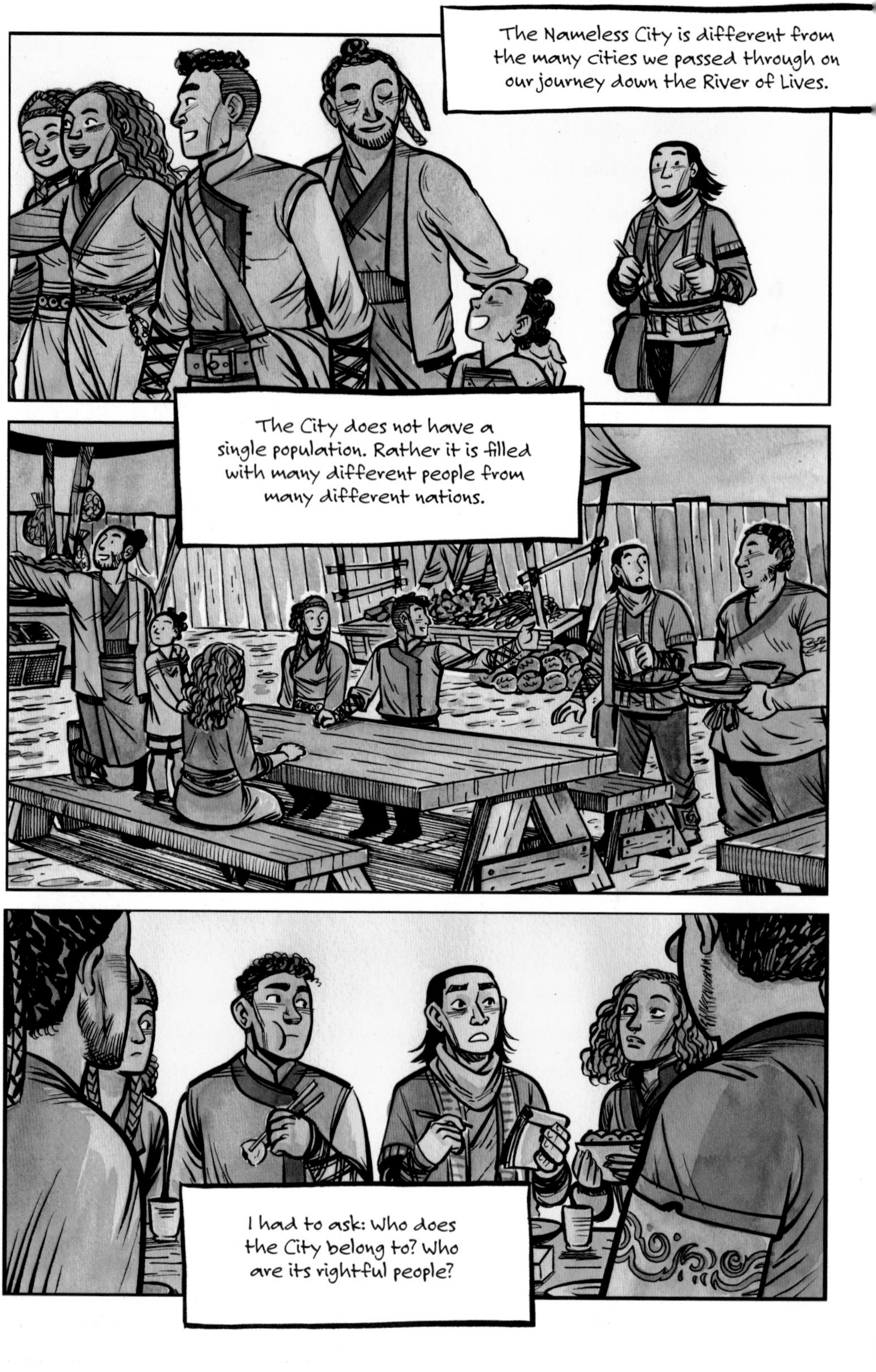
The Nameless City is different from the many cities we passed through on our journey down the River of Lives.
The City does not have a single population. Rather it is filled with many different people from many different nations.
I had to ask: Who does the City belong to? Who are its rightful people?

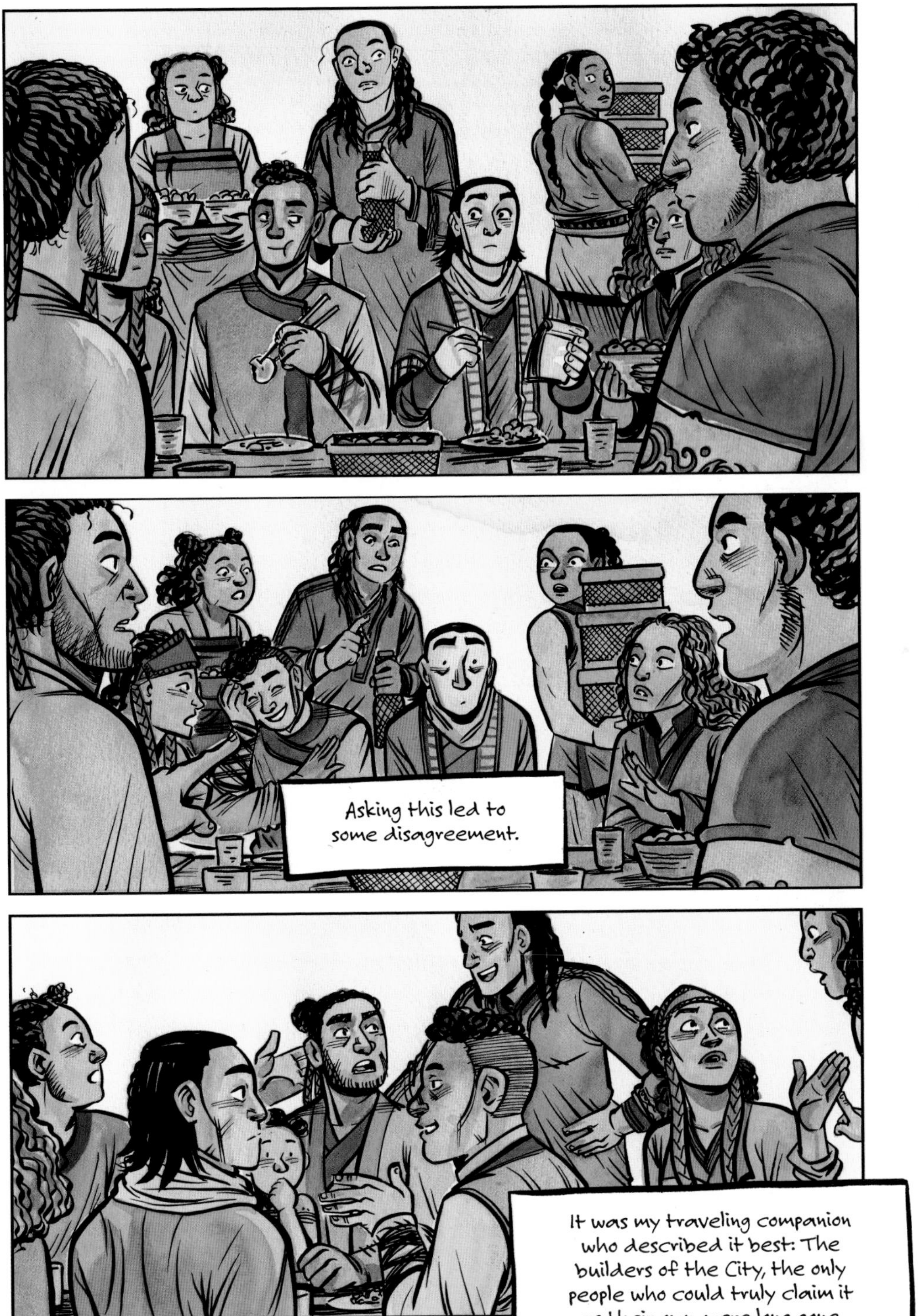
Asking this led to some disagreement.
It was my traveling companion who described it best: The builders of the City, the only people who could truly claim it as their own, were long gone.

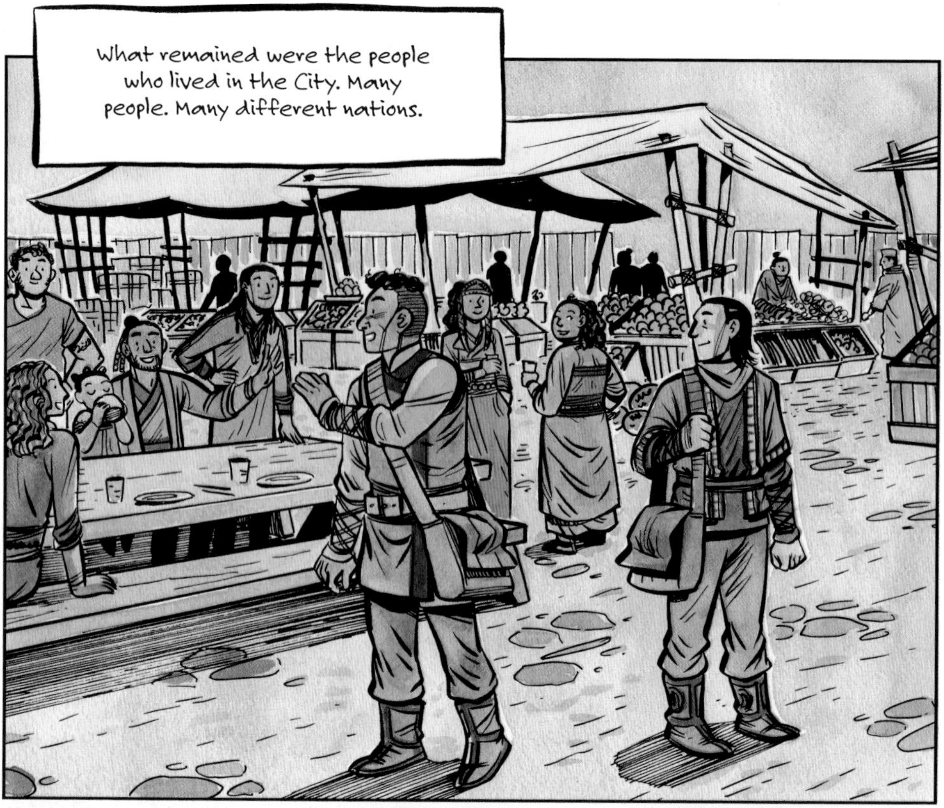
What remained were the people who lived in the City. Many people. Many different nations.

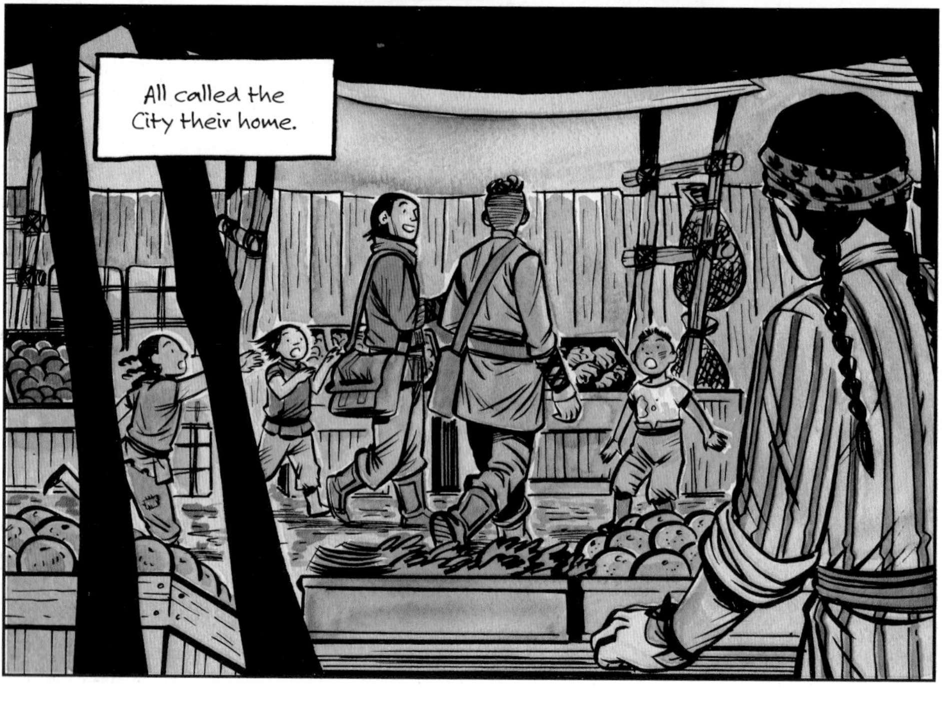
All called the City their home.

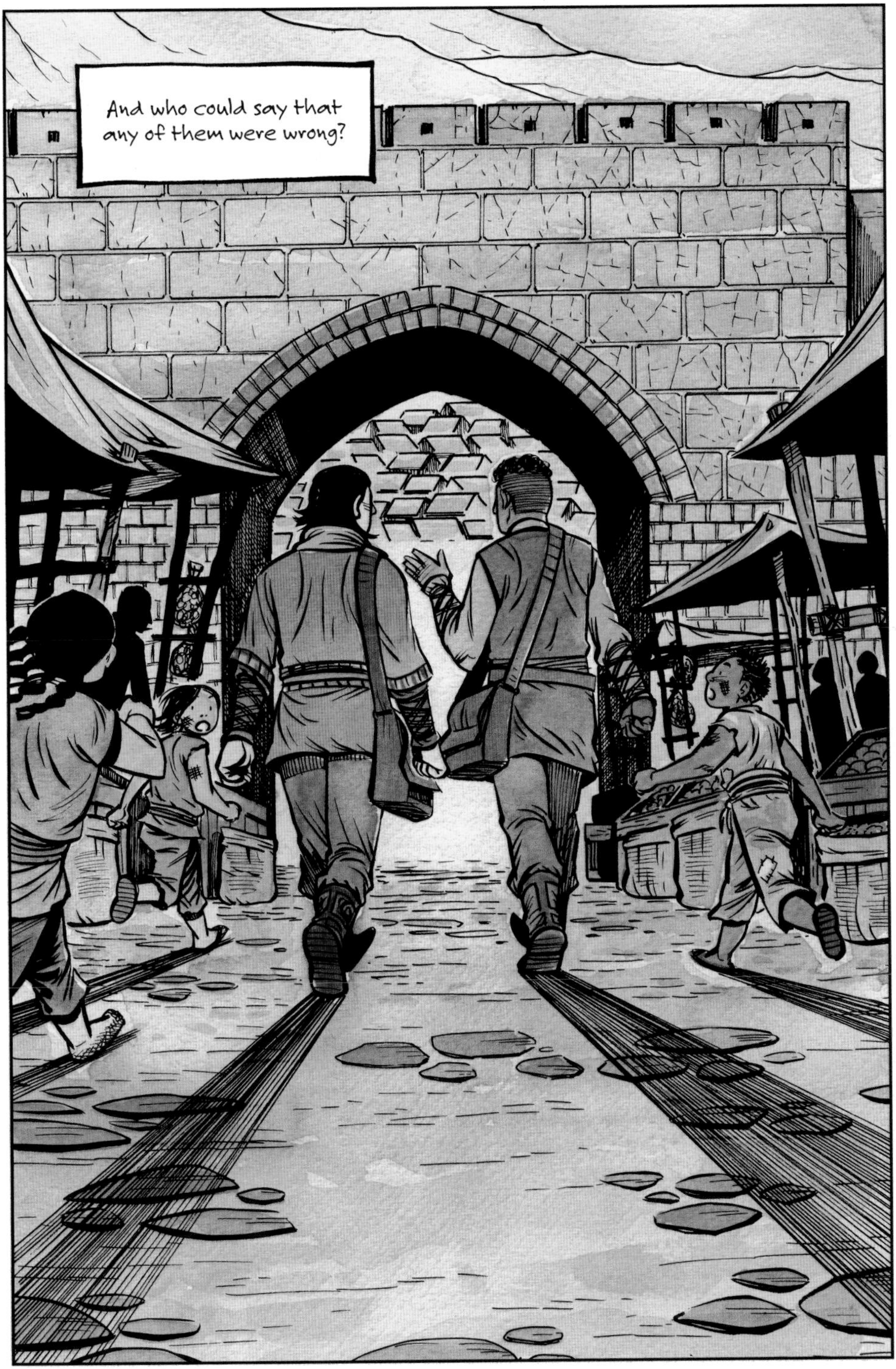
And who could say that any of them were wrong?

THE STONE HEART

THE NAMELESS CITY

FAITH ERIN HICKS

Color by Jordie Bellaire

First Second
NEW YORK

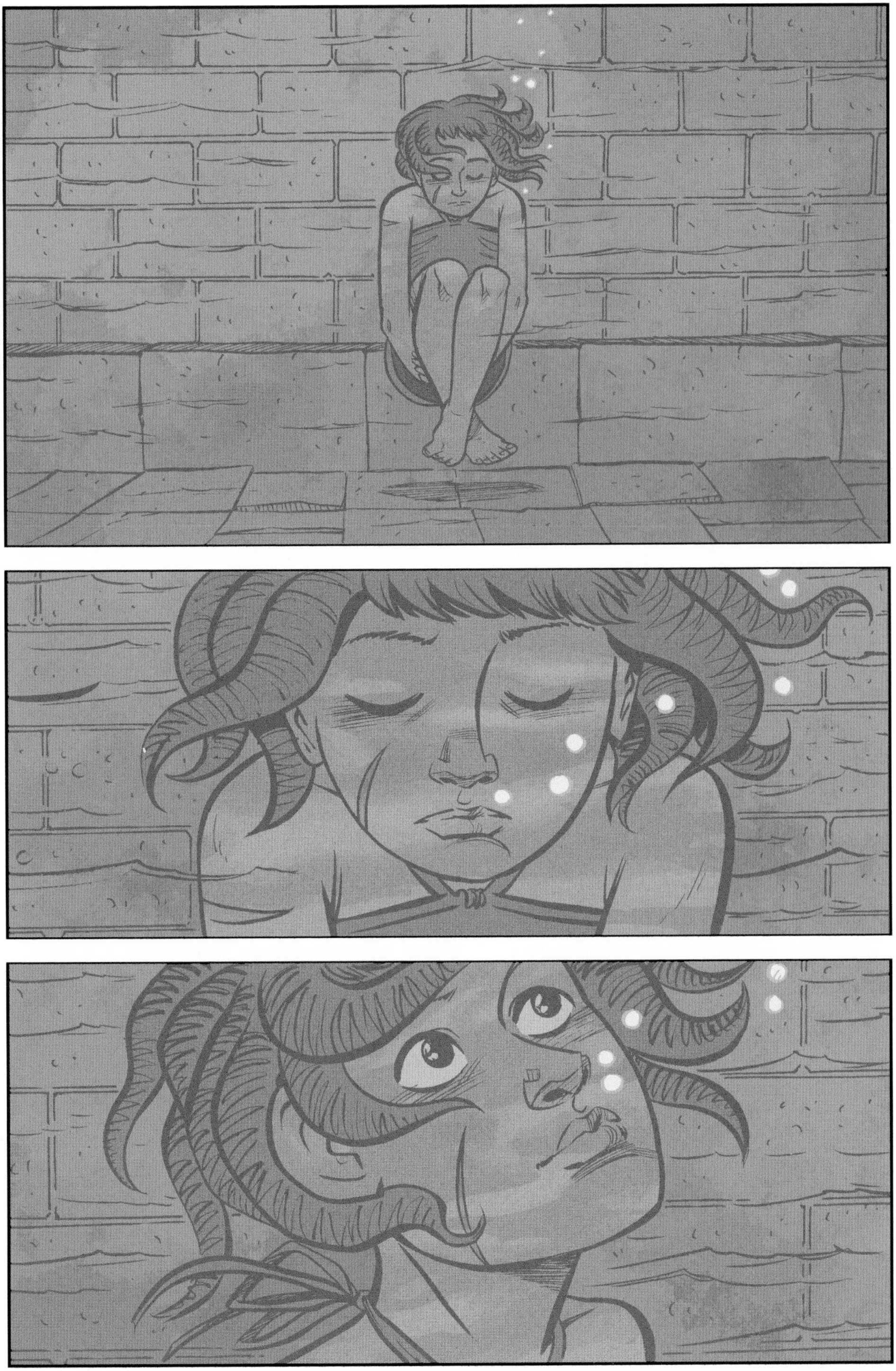

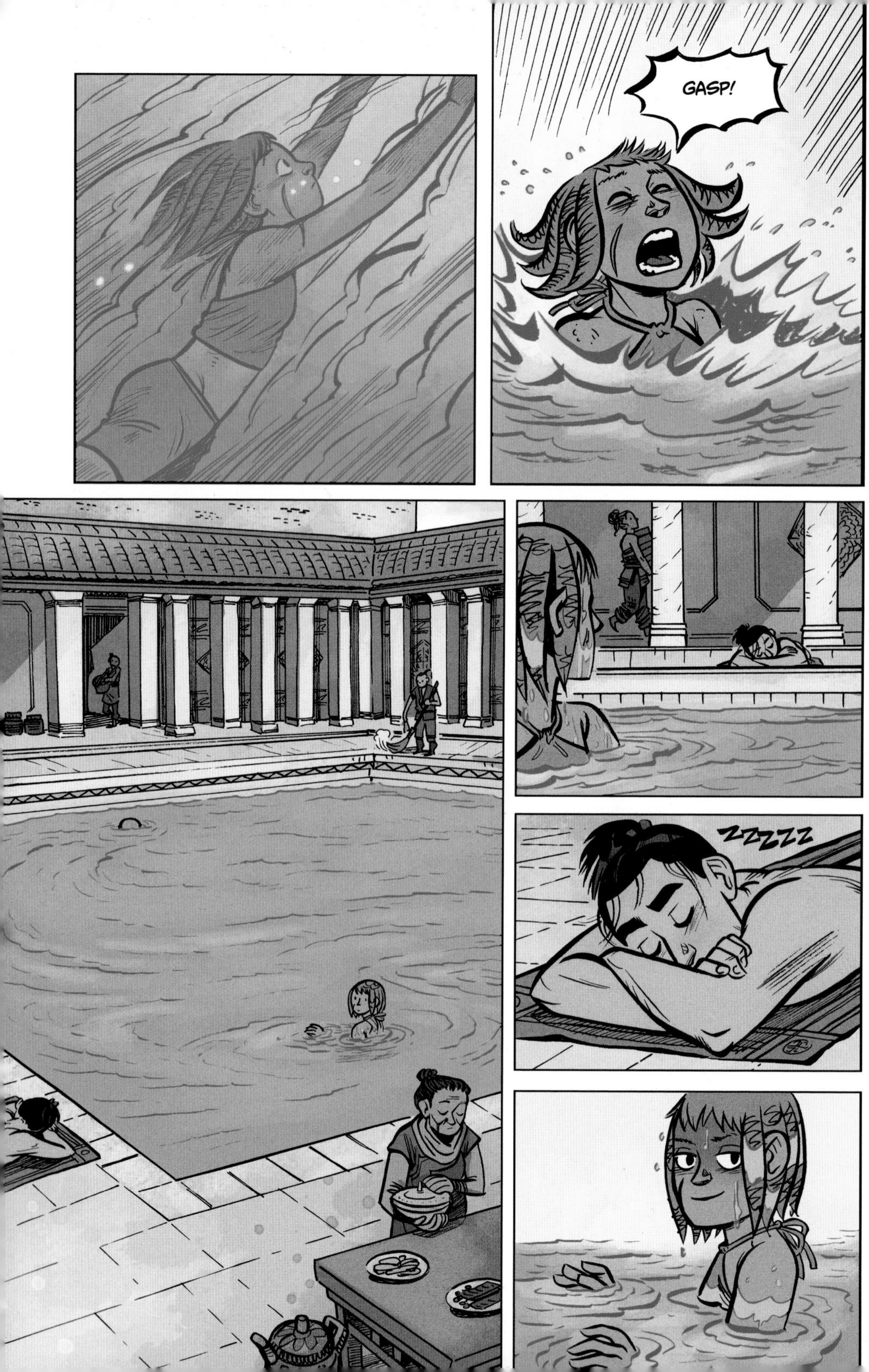
GASP!
ZZZZZ

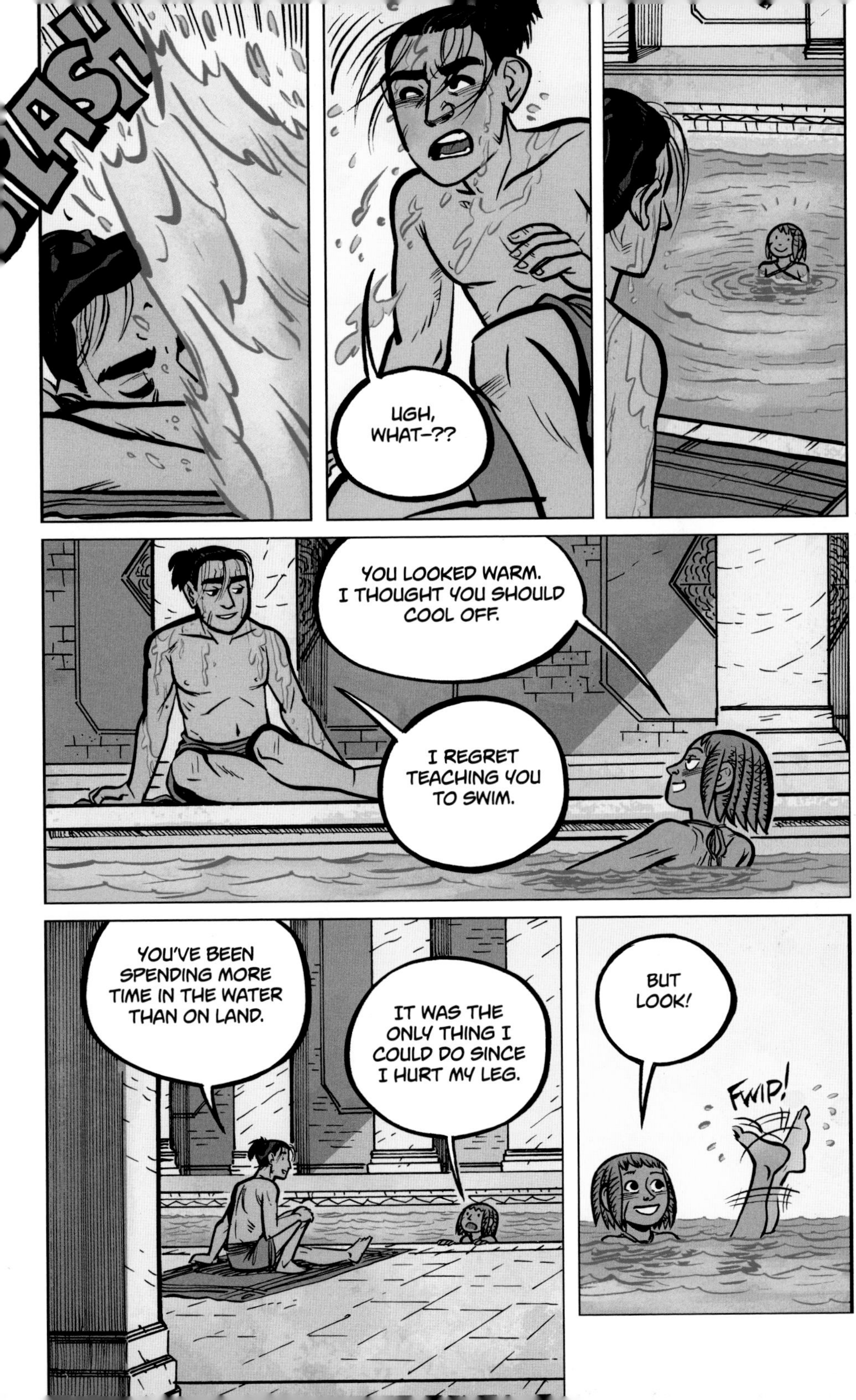
SPLASH!
UGH, WHAT-??
YOU LOOKED WARM. I THOUGHT YOU SHOULD COOL OFF.
I REGRET TEACHING YOU TO SWIM.
YOU'VE BEEN SPENDING MORE TIME IN THE WATER THAN ON LAND.
IT WAS THE ONLY THING I COULD DO SINCE I HURT MY LEG.
BUT LOOK!
FWIP!

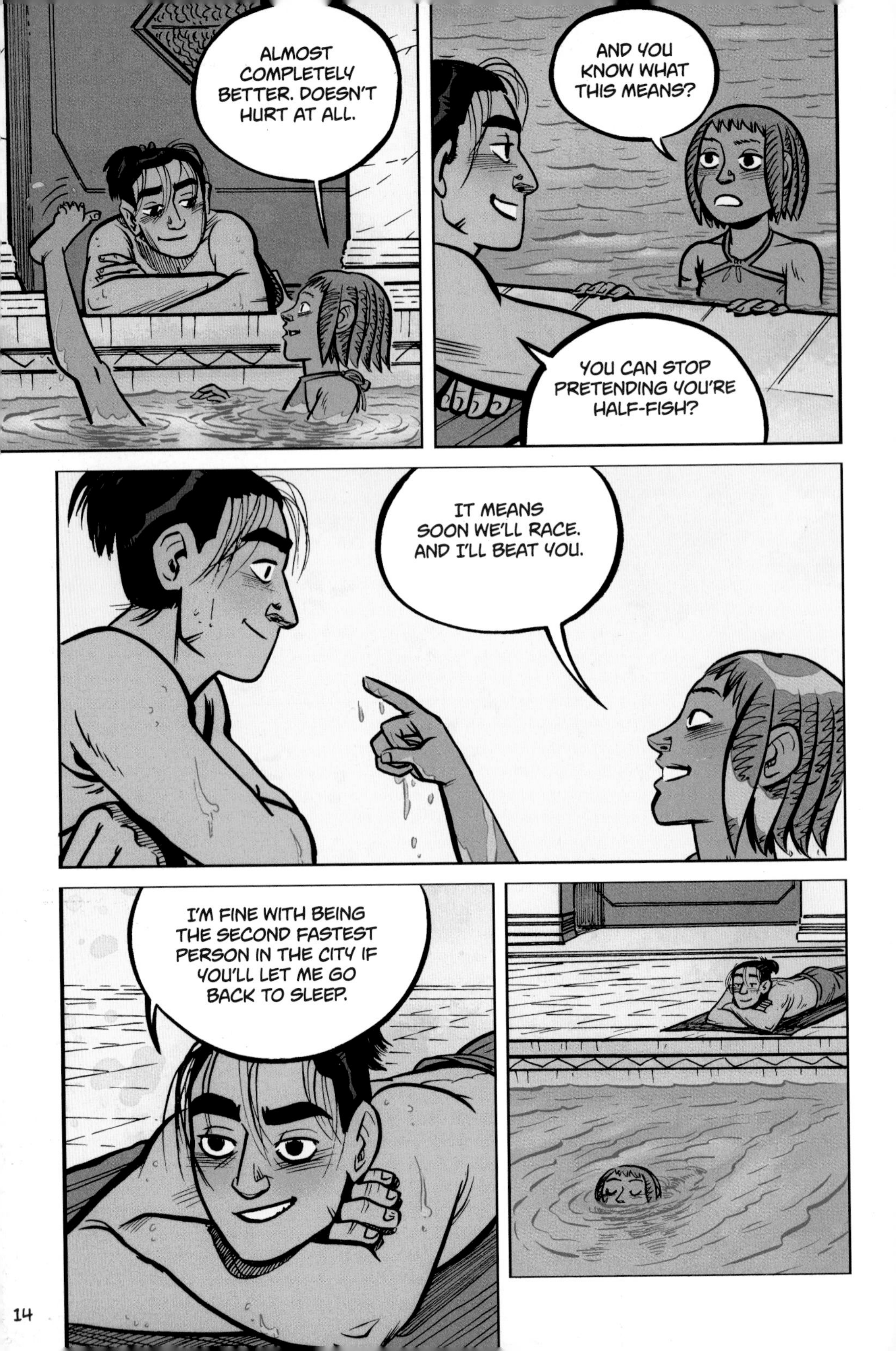
ALMOST COMPLETELY BETTER. DOESN'T HURT AT ALL.
AND YOU KNOW WHAT THIS MEANS?
YOU CAN STOP PRETENDING YOU'RE HALF-FISH?
IT MEANS SOON WE'LL RACE. AND I'LL BEAT YOU.
I'M FINE WITH BEING THE SECOND FASTEST PERSON IN THE CITY IF YOU'LL LET ME GO BACK TO SLEEP.

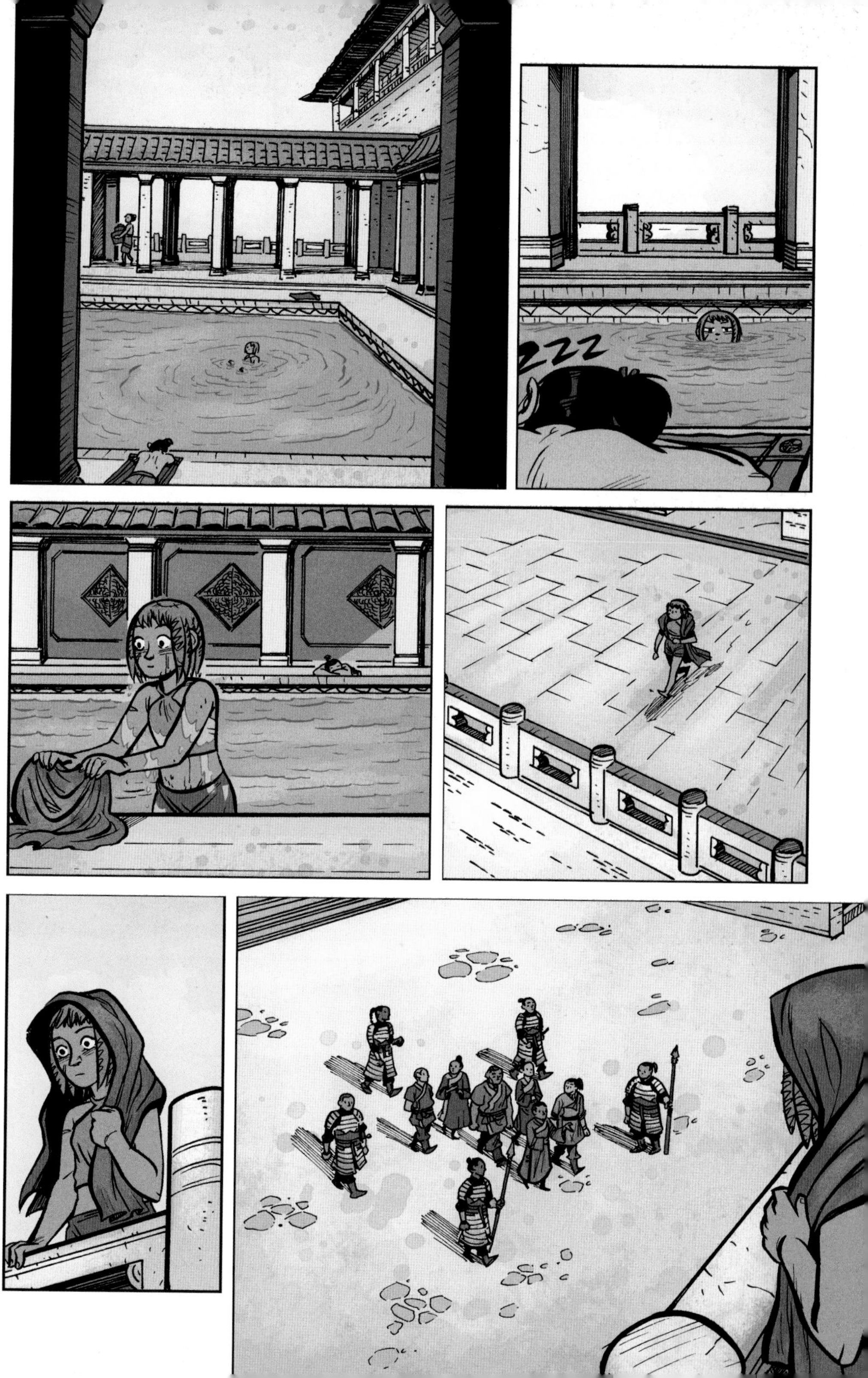
ZZZ

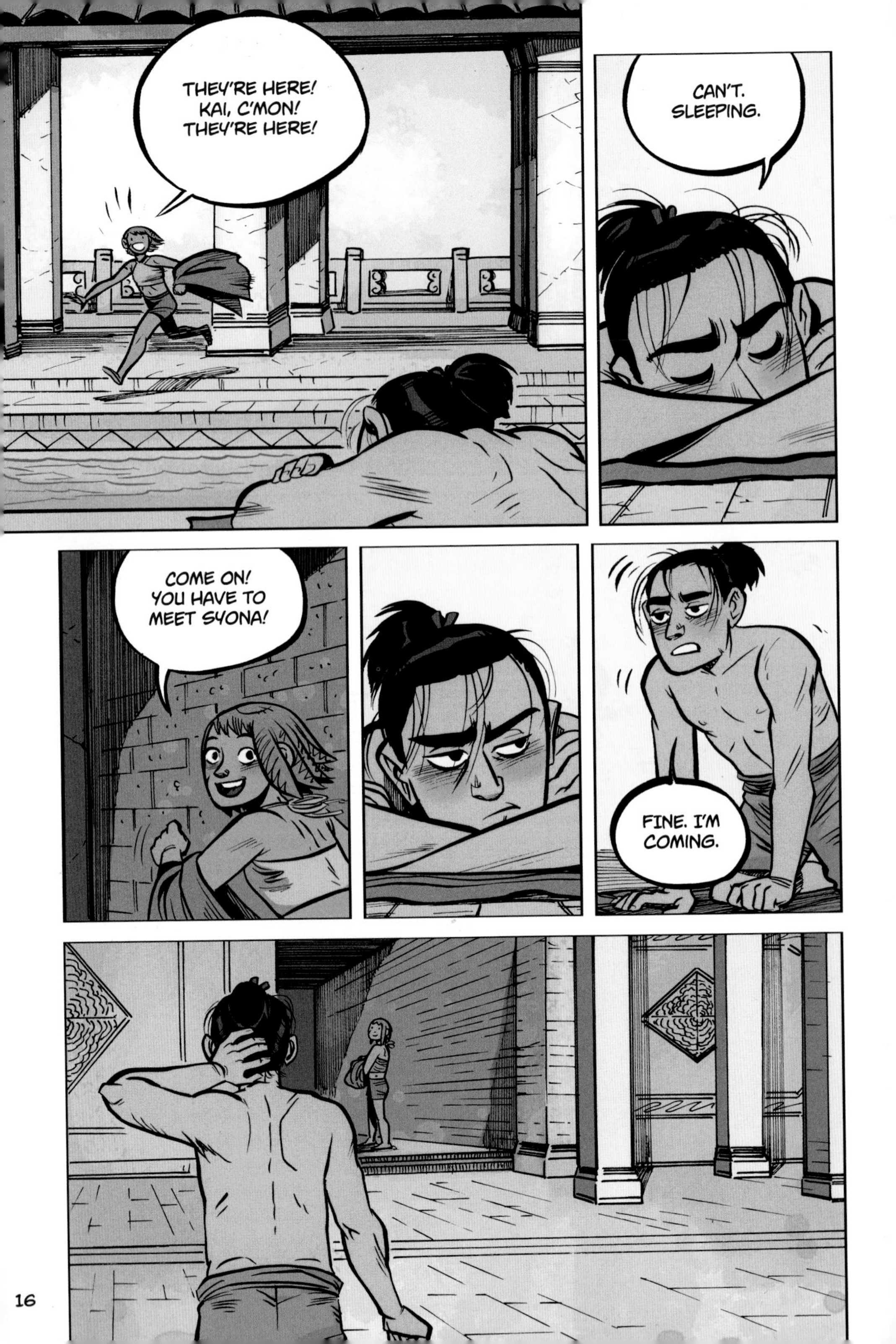
THEY'RE HERE! KAI, C'MON! THEY'RE HERE!
CAN'T. SLEEPING.
COME ON! YOU HAVE TO MEET SYONA!
FINE. I'M COMING.

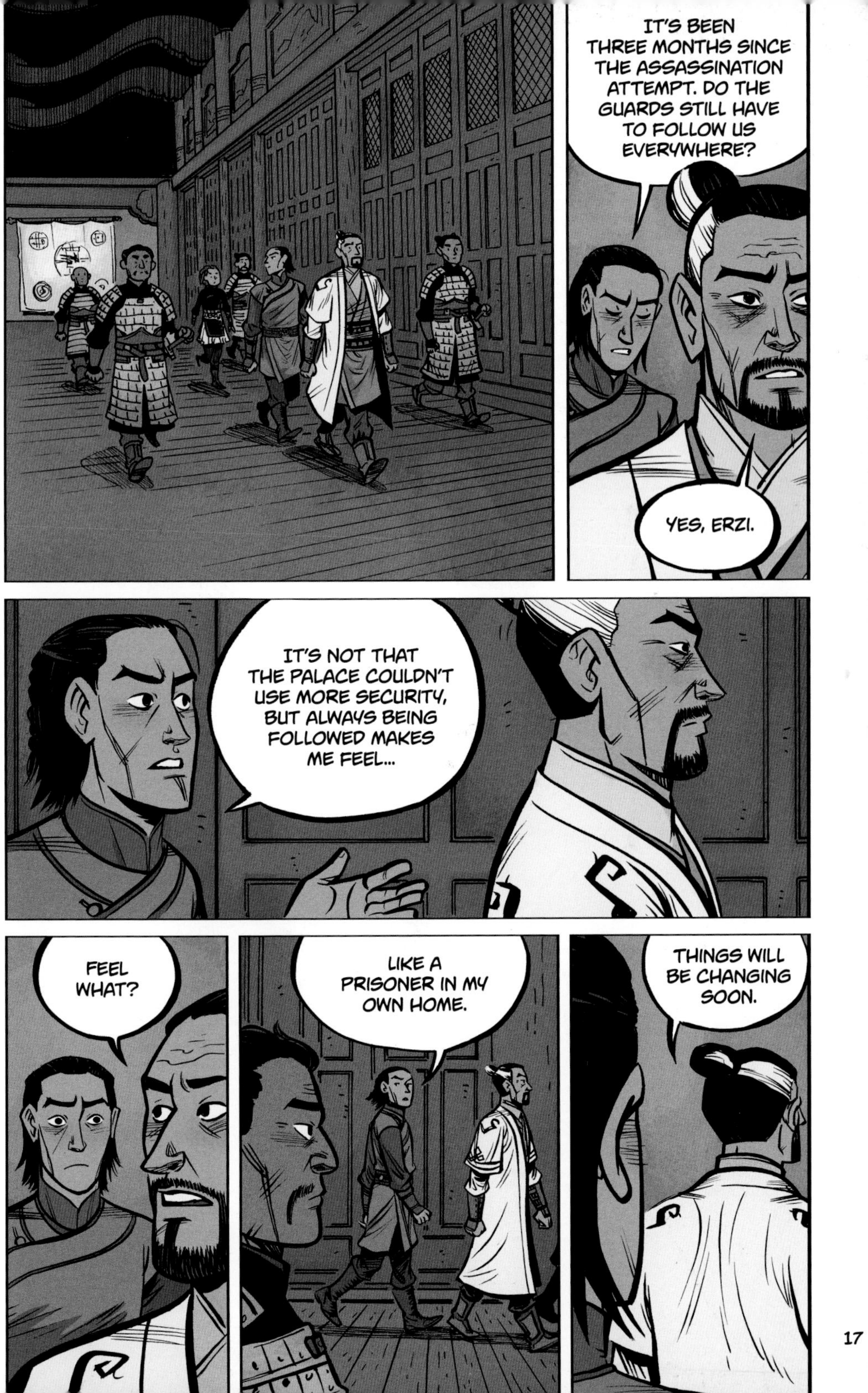
IT'S BEEN THREE MONTHS SINCE THE ASSASSINATION ATTEMPT. DO THE GUARDS STILL HAVE TO FOLLOW US EVERYWHERE?
YES, ERZI.
IT'S NOT THAT THE PALACE COULDN'T USE MORE SECURITY, BUT ALWAYS BEING FOLLOWED MAKES ME FEEL...
FEEL WHAT?
LIKE A PRISONER IN MY OWN HOME.
THINGS WILL BE CHANGING SOON.

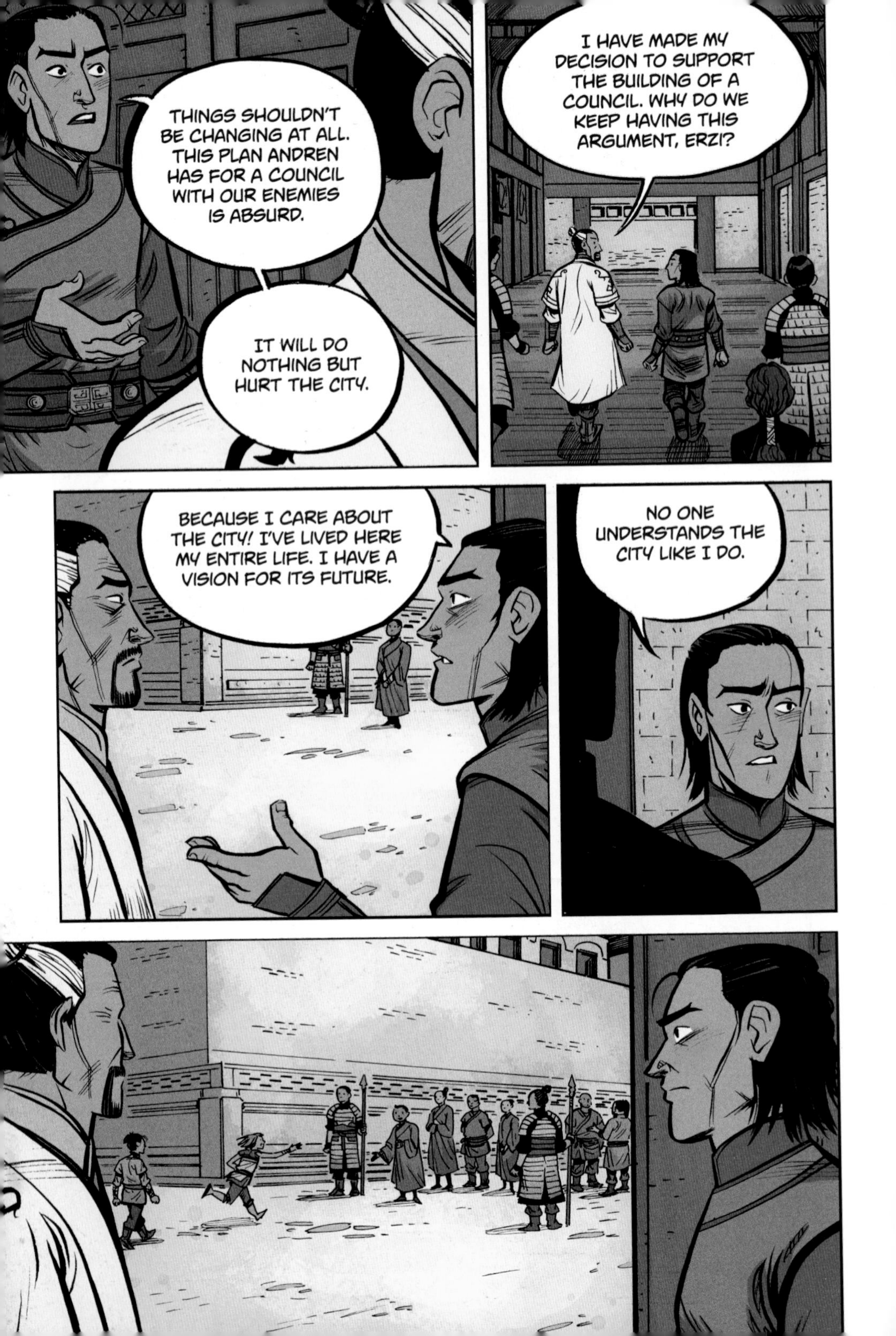
THINGS SHOULDN'T BE CHANGING AT ALL. THIS PLAN ANDREN HAS FOR A COUNCIL WITH OUR ENEMIES IS ABSURD.
IT WILL DO NOTHING BUT HURT THE CITY.
I HAVE MADE MY DECISION TO SUPPORT THE BUILDING OF A COUNCIL. WHY DO WE KEEP HAVING THIS ARGUMENT, ERZI?
BECAUSE I CARE ABOUT THE CITY! I'VE LIVED HERE MY ENTIRE LIFE. I HAVE A VISION FOR ITS FUTURE.
NO ONE UNDERSTANDS THE CITY LIKE I DO.

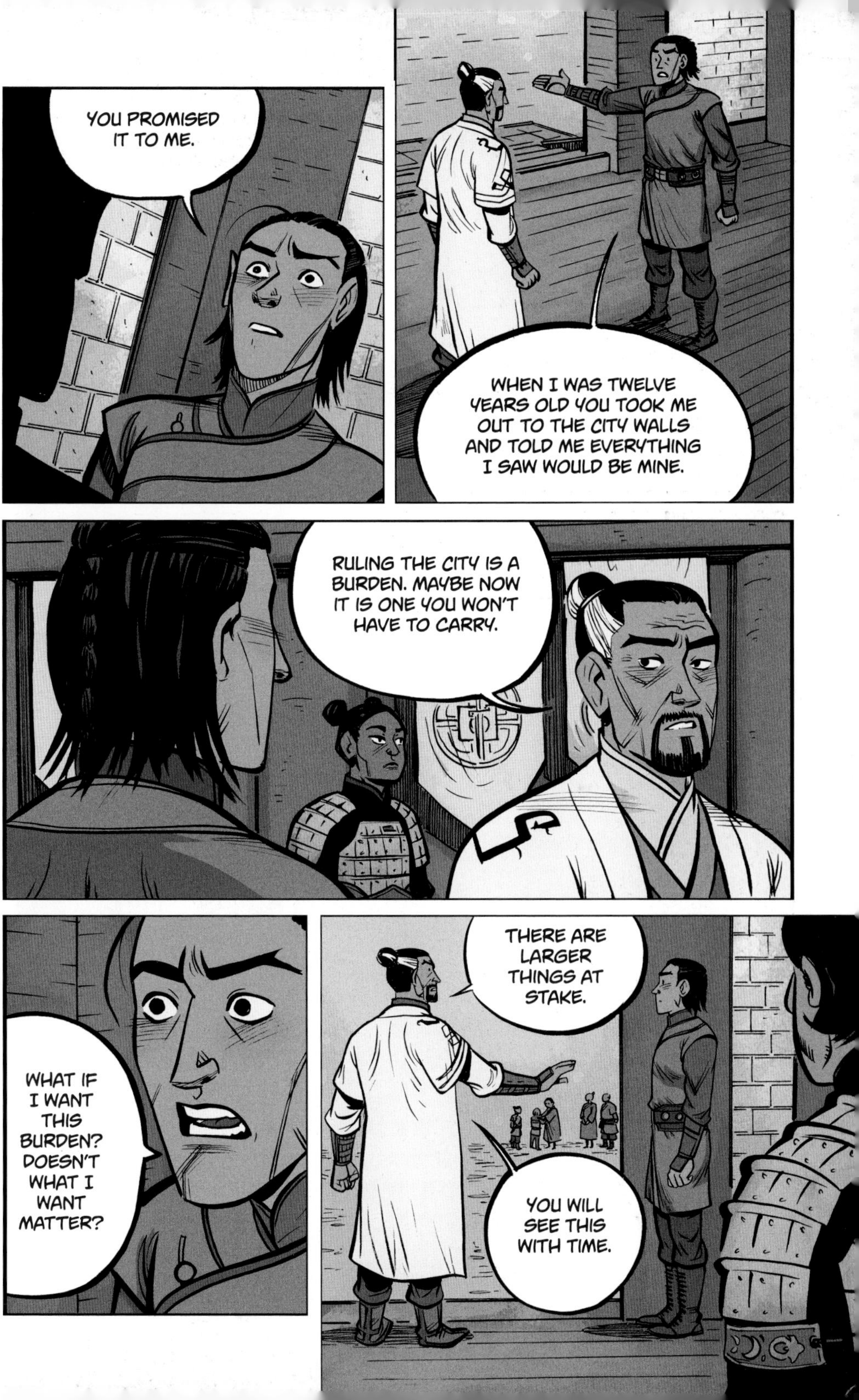
YOU PROMISED IT TO ME.
WHEN I WAS TWELVE YEARS OLD YOU TOOK ME OUT TO THE CITY WALLS AND TOLD ME EVERYTHING I SAW WOULD BE MINE.
RULING THE CITY IS A BURDEN. MAYBE NOW IT IS ONE YOU WON'T HAVE TO CARRY.
WHAT IF I WANT THIS BURDEN? DOESN'T WHAT I WANT MATTER?
THERE ARE LARGER THINGS AT STAKE.
YOU WILL SEE THIS WITH TIME.

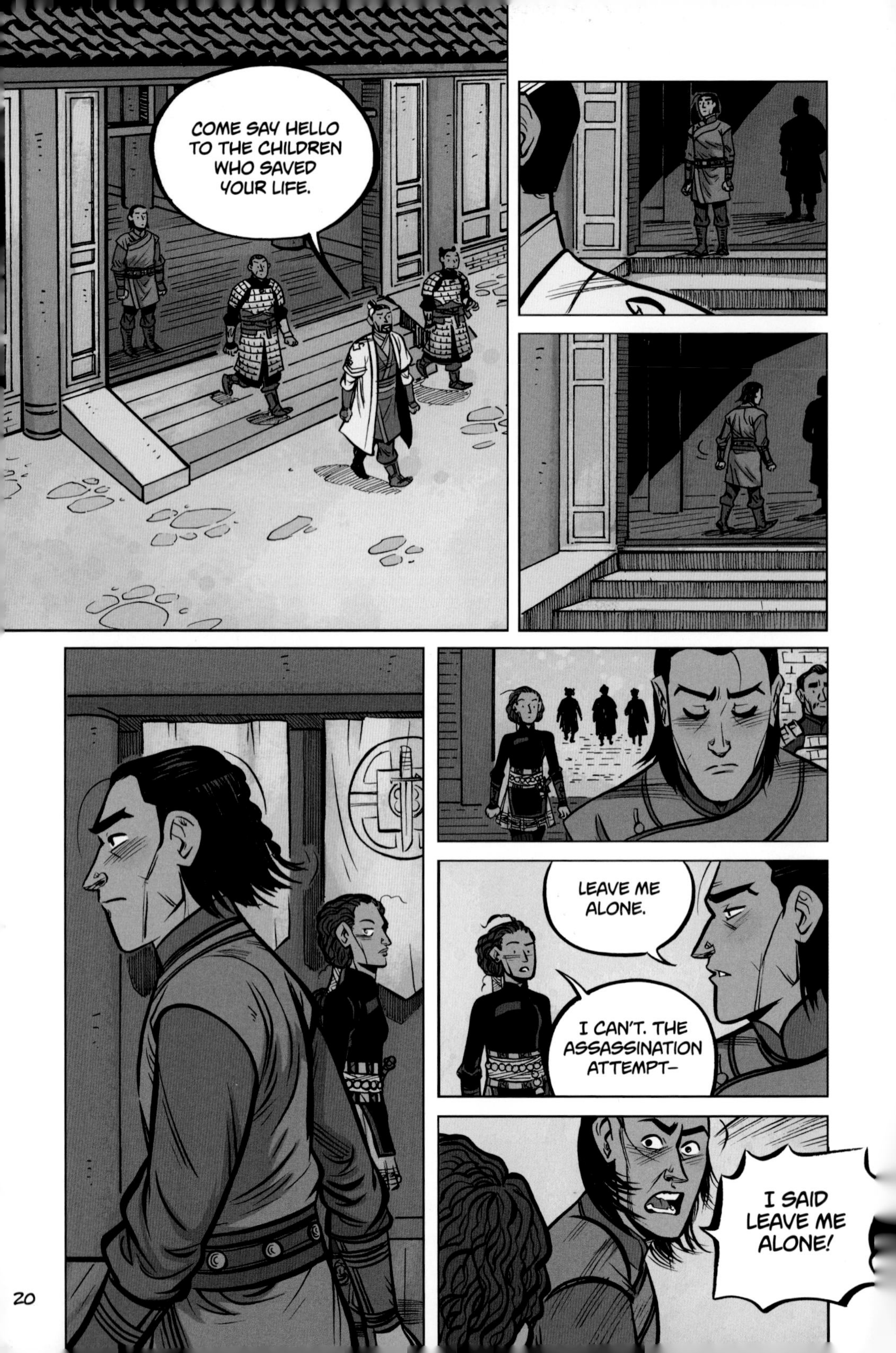
COME SAY HELLO TO THE CHILDREN WHO SAVED YOUR LIFE.
LEAVE ME ALONE.
I CAN'T. THE ASSASSINATION ATTEMPT-
I SAID LEAVE ME ALONE!

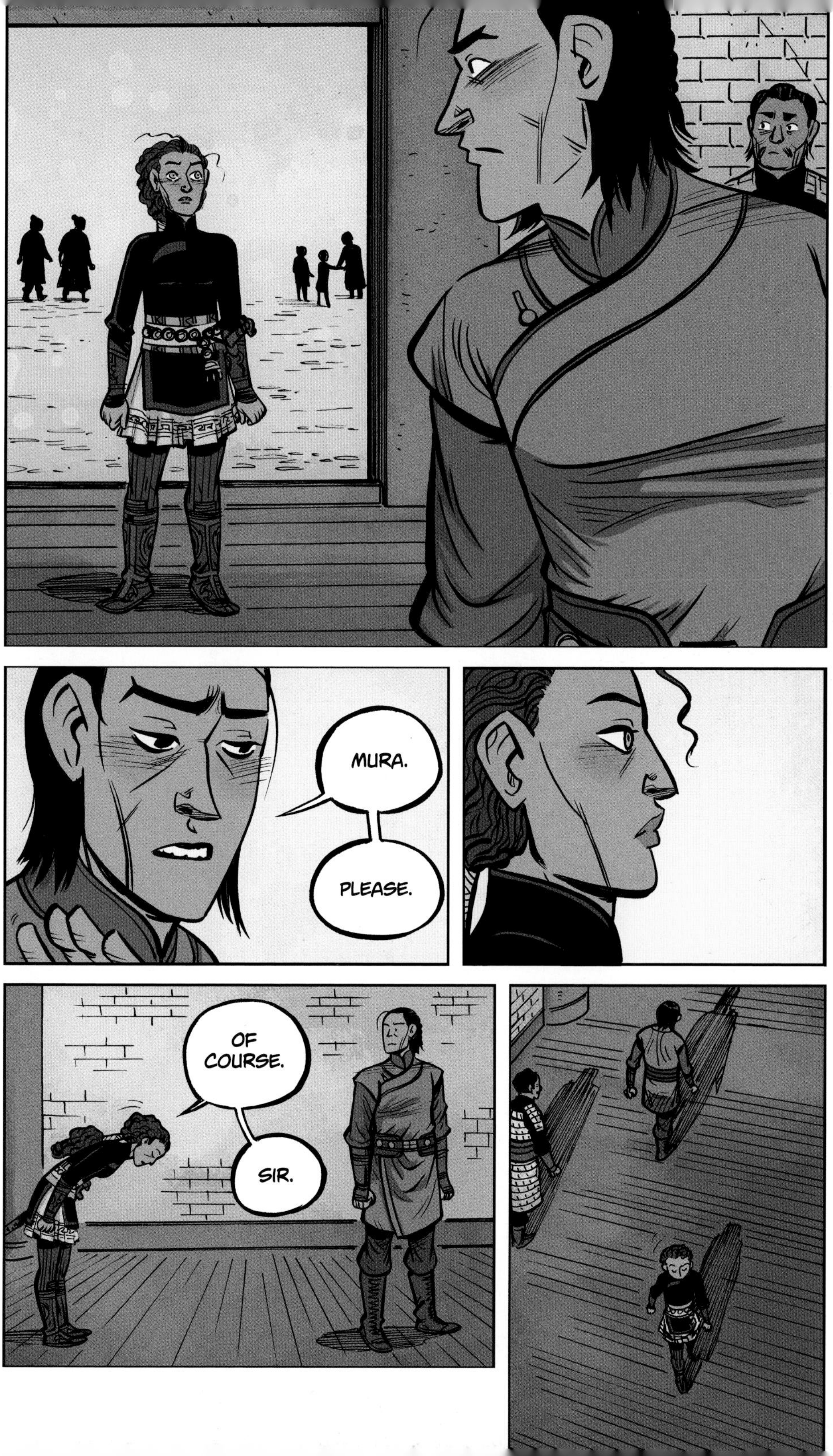
MURA.
PLEASE.
OF COURSE.
SIR.

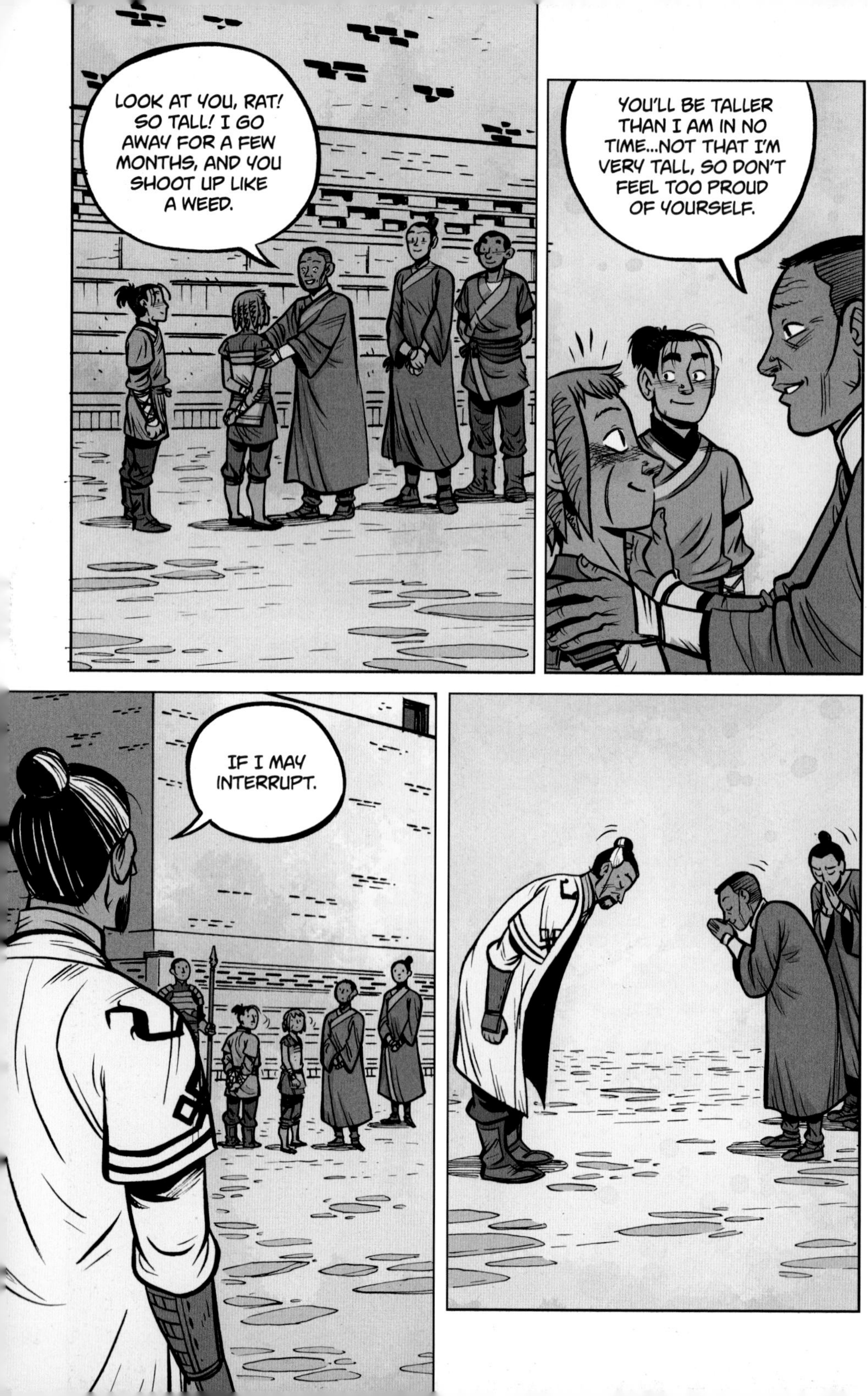
LOOK AT YOU, RAT! SO TALL! I GO AWAY FOR A FEW MONTHS, AND YOU SHOOT UP LIKE A WEED.
YOU'LL BE TALLER THAN I AM IN NO TIME...NOT THAT I'M VERY TALL, SO DON'T FEEL TOO PROUD OF YOURSELF.
IF I MAY INTERRUPT.

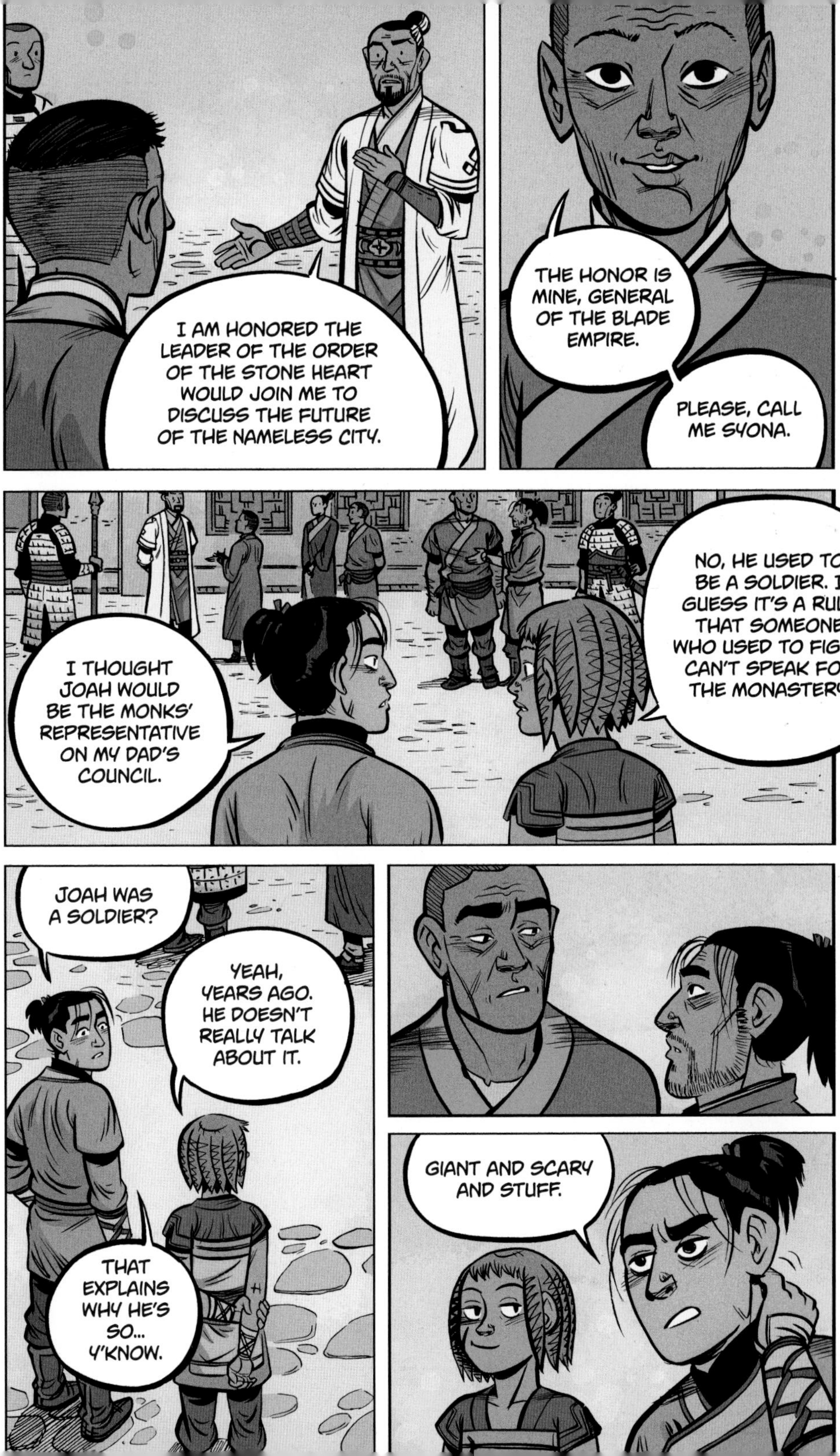
I AM HONORED THE LEADER OF THE ORDER OF THE STONE HEART WOULD JOIN ME TO DISCUSS THE FUTURE OF THE NAMELESS CITY.
THE HONOR IS MINE, GENERAL OF THE BLADE EMPIRE.
PLEASE, CALL ME SYONA.
I THOUGHT JOAH WOULD BE THE MONKS' REPRESENTATIVE ON MY DAD'S COUNCIL.
NO, HE USED TO BE A SOLDIER. I GUESS IT'S A RULE THAT SOMEONE WHO USED TO FIGHT CAN'T SPEAK FOR THE MONASTERY.
JOAH WAS A SOLDIER?
YEAH, YEARS AGO. HE DOESN'T REALLY TALK ABOUT IT.
THAT EXPLAINS WHY HE'S SO... Y'KNOW.
GIANT AND SCARY AND STUFF.

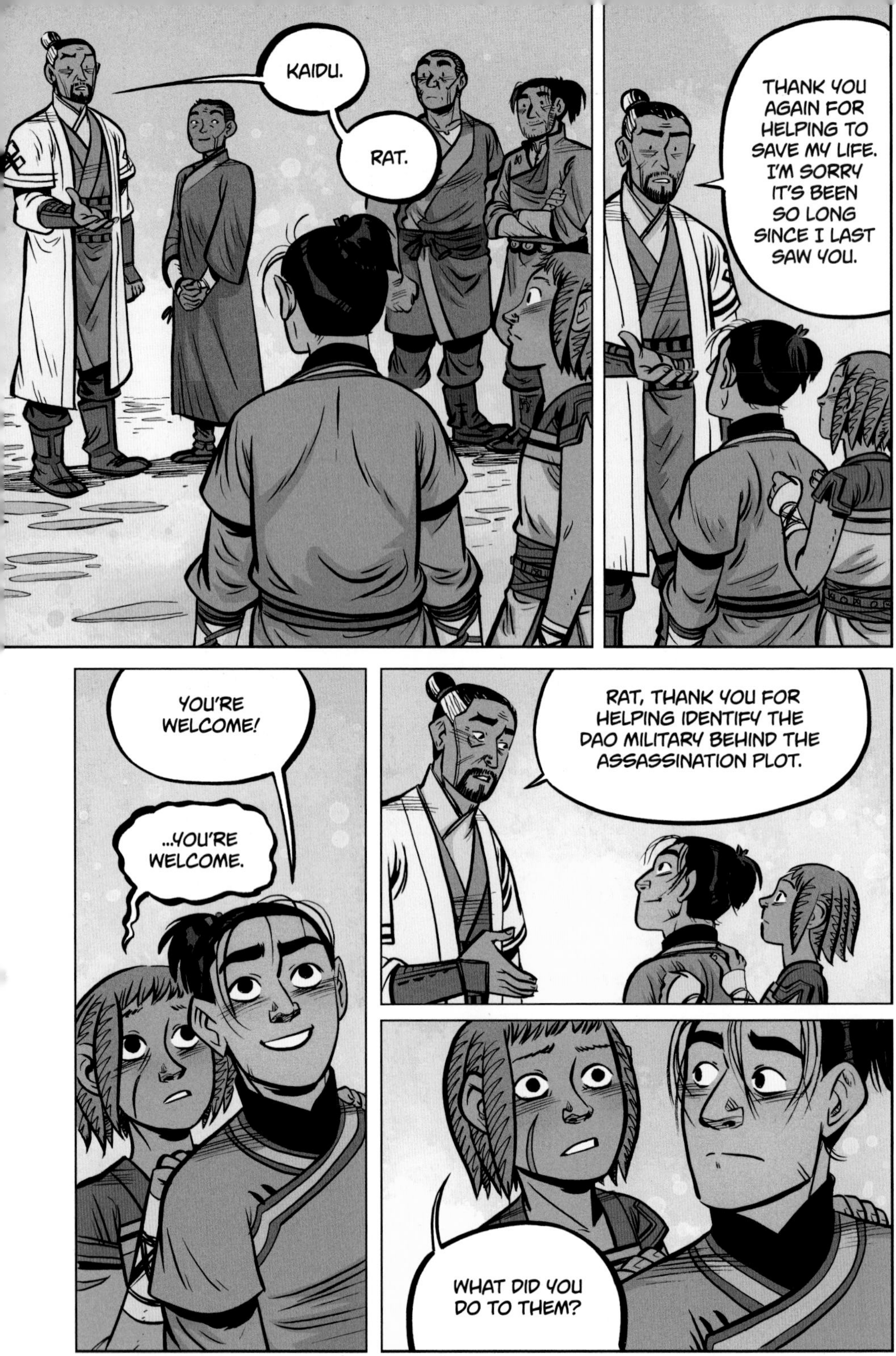
KAIDU.
RAT.
THANK YOU AGAIN FOR HELPING TO SAVE MY LIFE. I'M SORRY IT'S BEEN SO LONG SINCE I LAST SAW YOU.
YOU'RE WELCOME!
...YOU'RE WELCOME.
RAT, THANK YOU FOR HELPING IDENTIFY THE DAO MILITARY BEHIND THE ASSASSINATION PLOT.
WHAT DID YOU DO TO THEM?

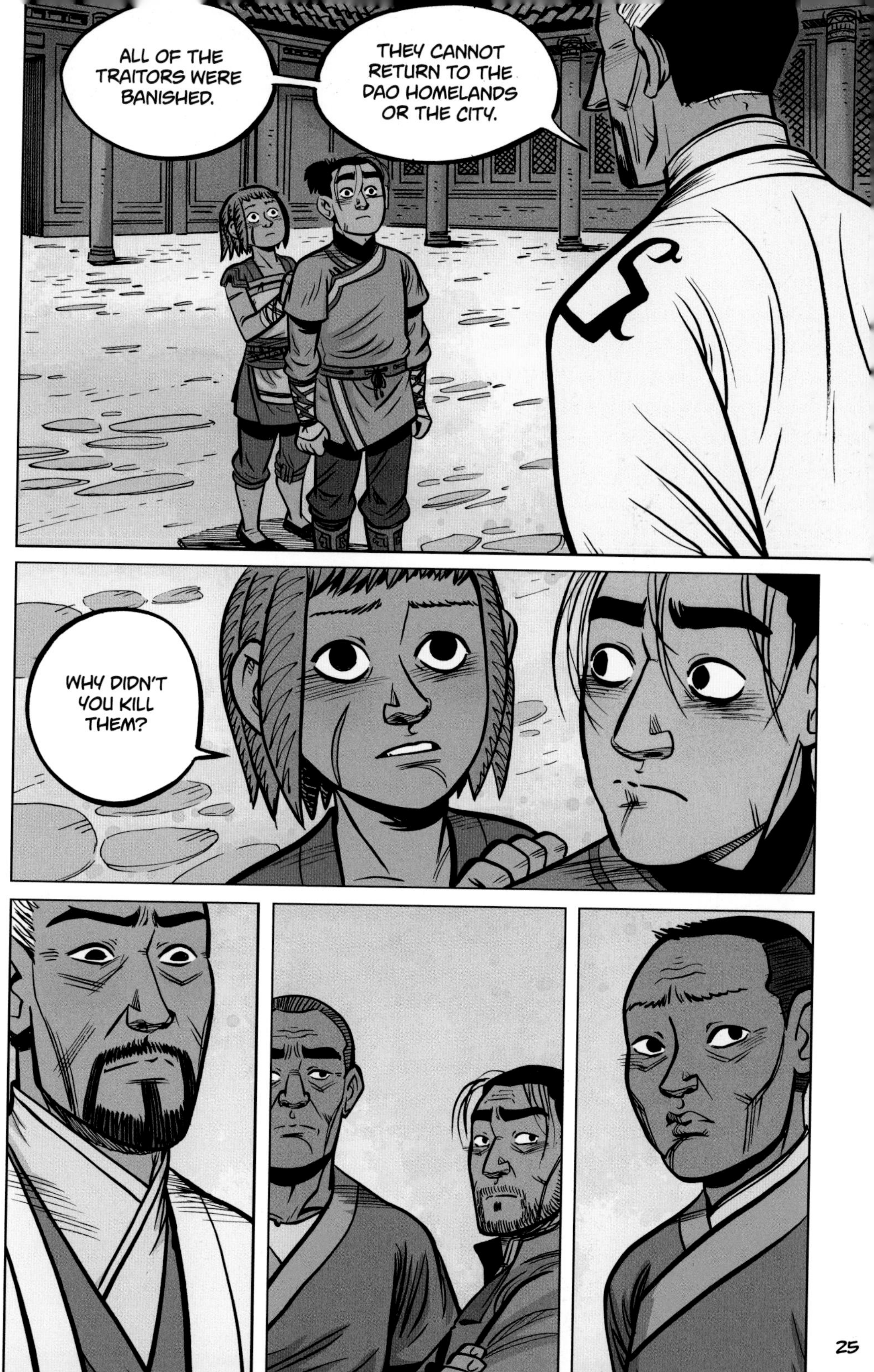

ALL OF THE TRAITORS WERE BANISHED.
THEY CANNOT RETURN TO THE DAO HOMELANDS OR THE CITY.
WHY DIDN'T YOU KILL THEM?

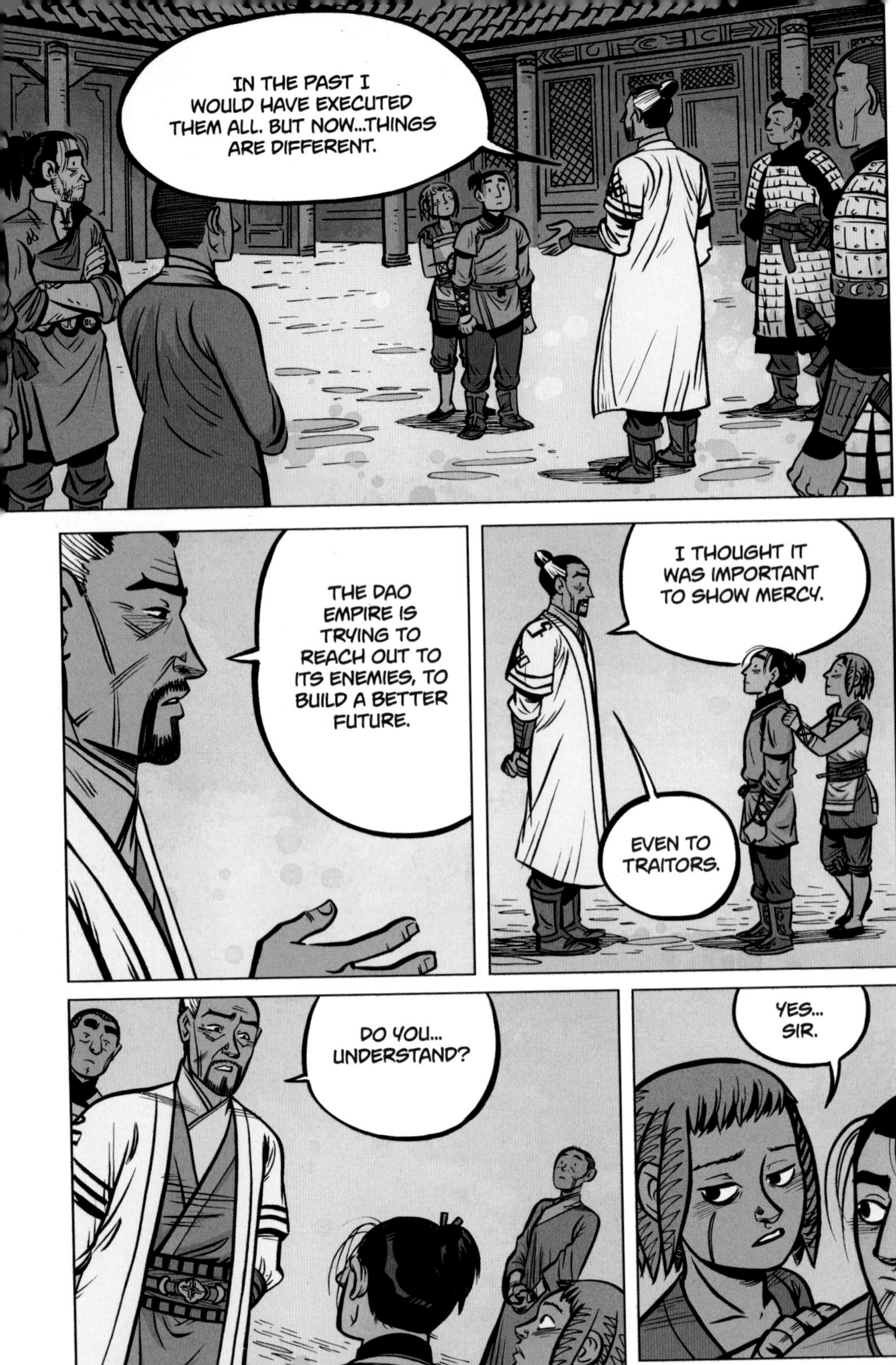
IN THE PAST I WOULD HAVE EXECUTED THEM ALL. BUT NOW...THINGS ARE DIFFERENT.
THE DAO EMPIRE IS TRYING TO REACH OUT TO ITS ENEMIES, TO BUILD A BETTER FUTURE.
I THOUGHT IT WAS IMPORTANT TO SHOW MERCY.
EVEN TO TRAITORS.
DO YOU... UNDERSTAND?
YES... SIR.

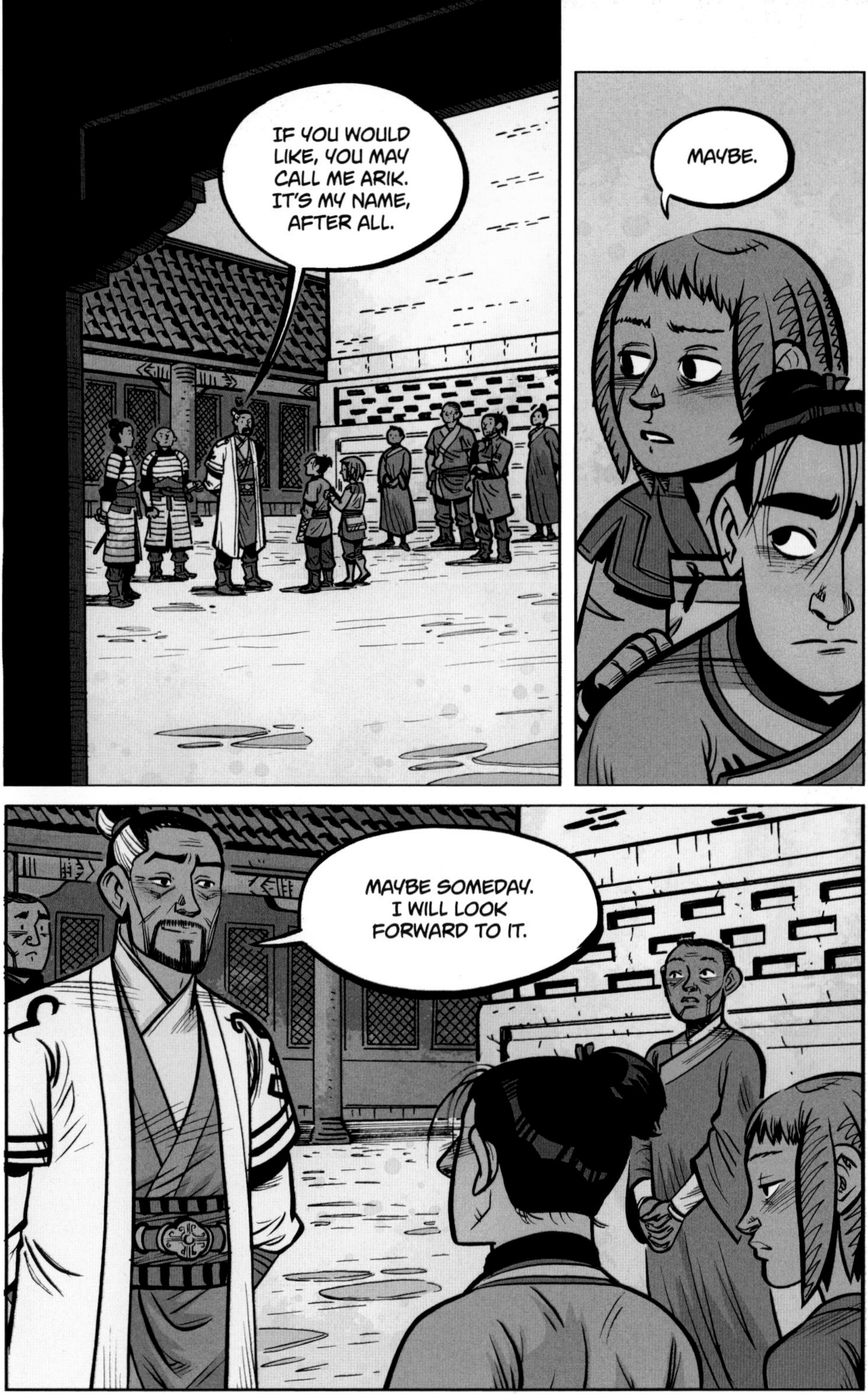
IF YOU WOULD LIKE, YOU MAY CALL ME ARIK. IT'S MY NAME, AFTER ALL.
MAYBE.
MAYBE SOMEDAY. I WILL LOOK FORWARD TO IT.

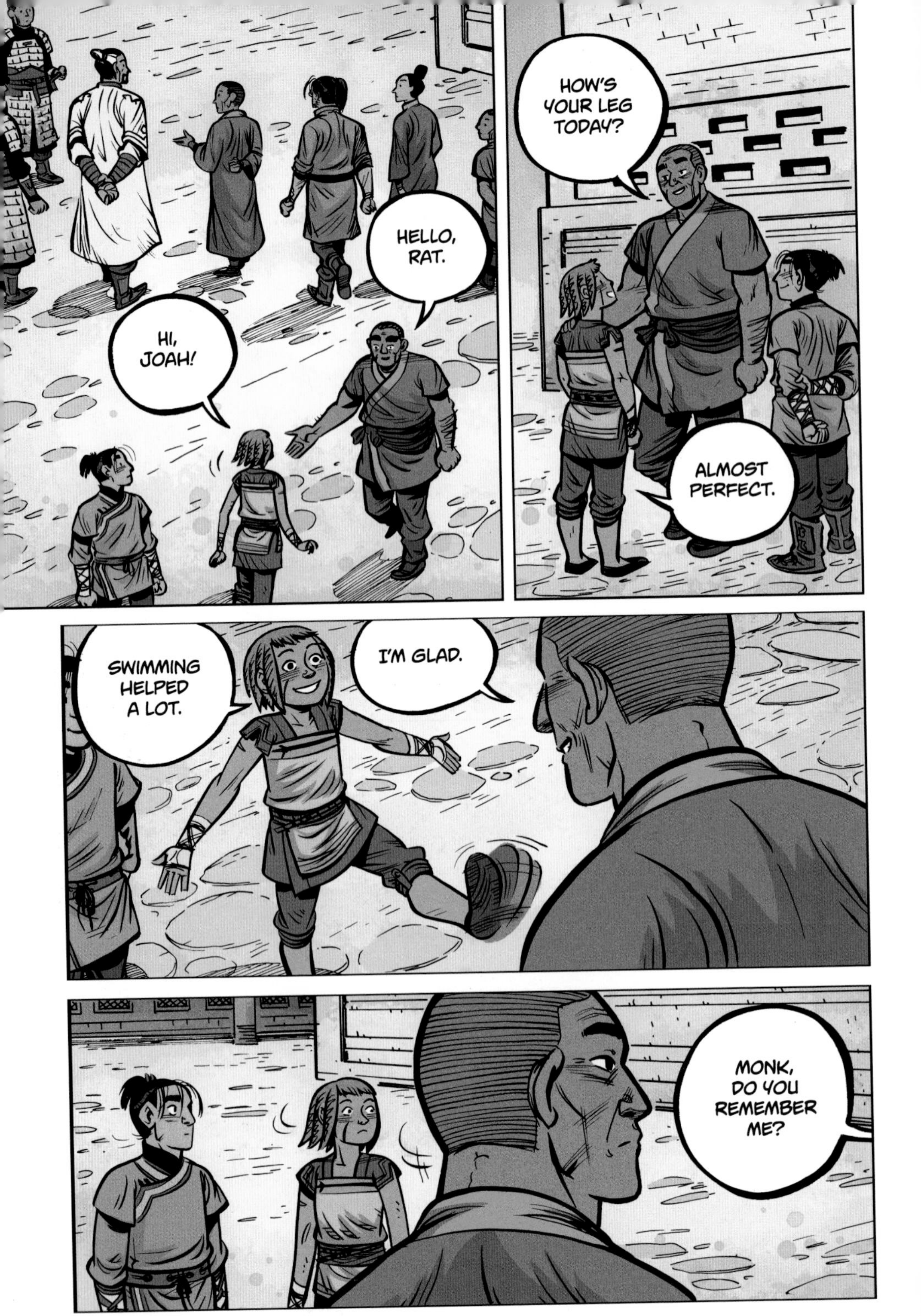
HELLO, RAT.
HI, JOAH!
HOW'S YOUR LEG TODAY?
ALMOST PERFECT.
SWIMMING HELPED A LOT.
I'M GLAD.
MONK, DO YOU REMEMBER ME?

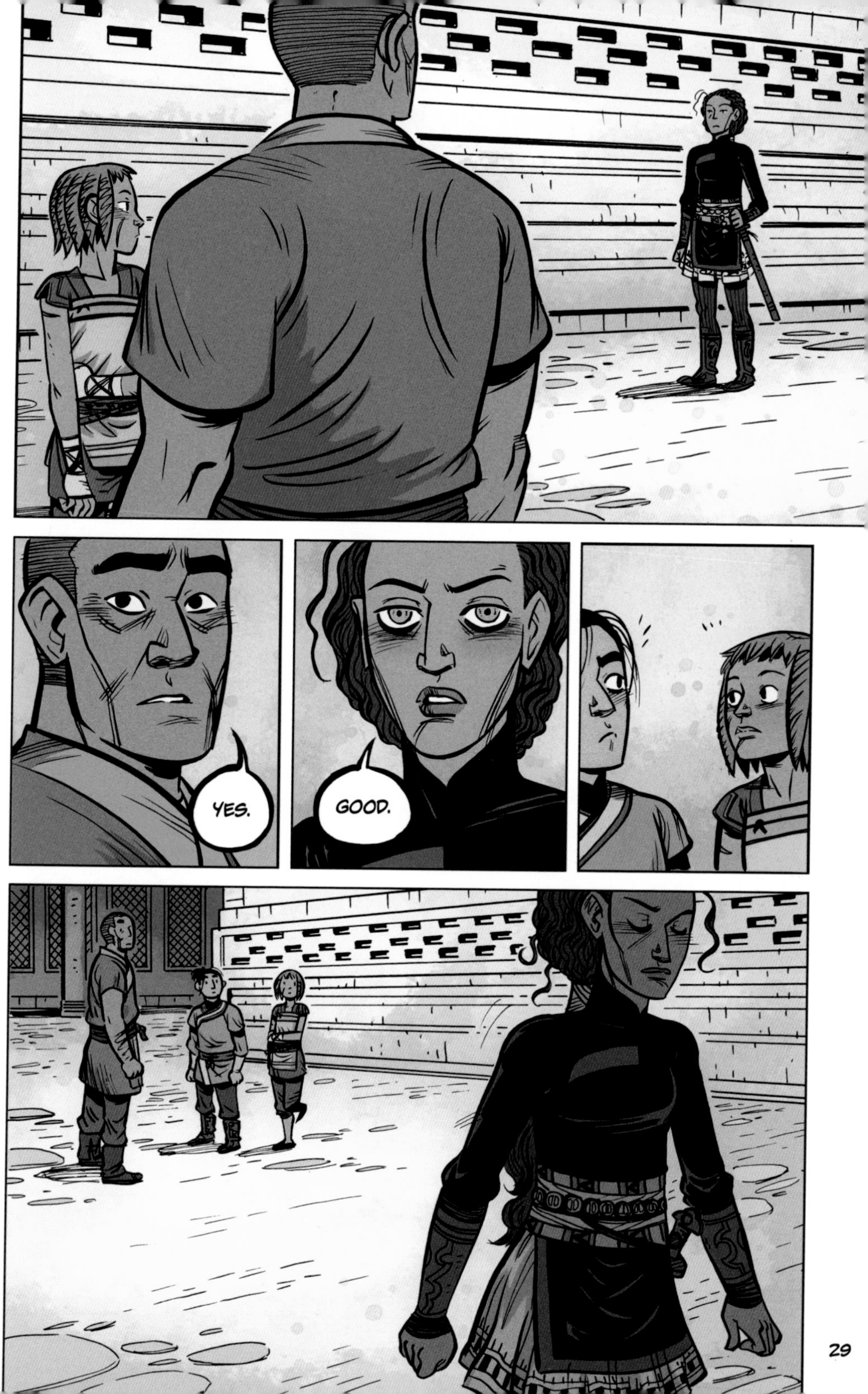
YES.
GOOD.

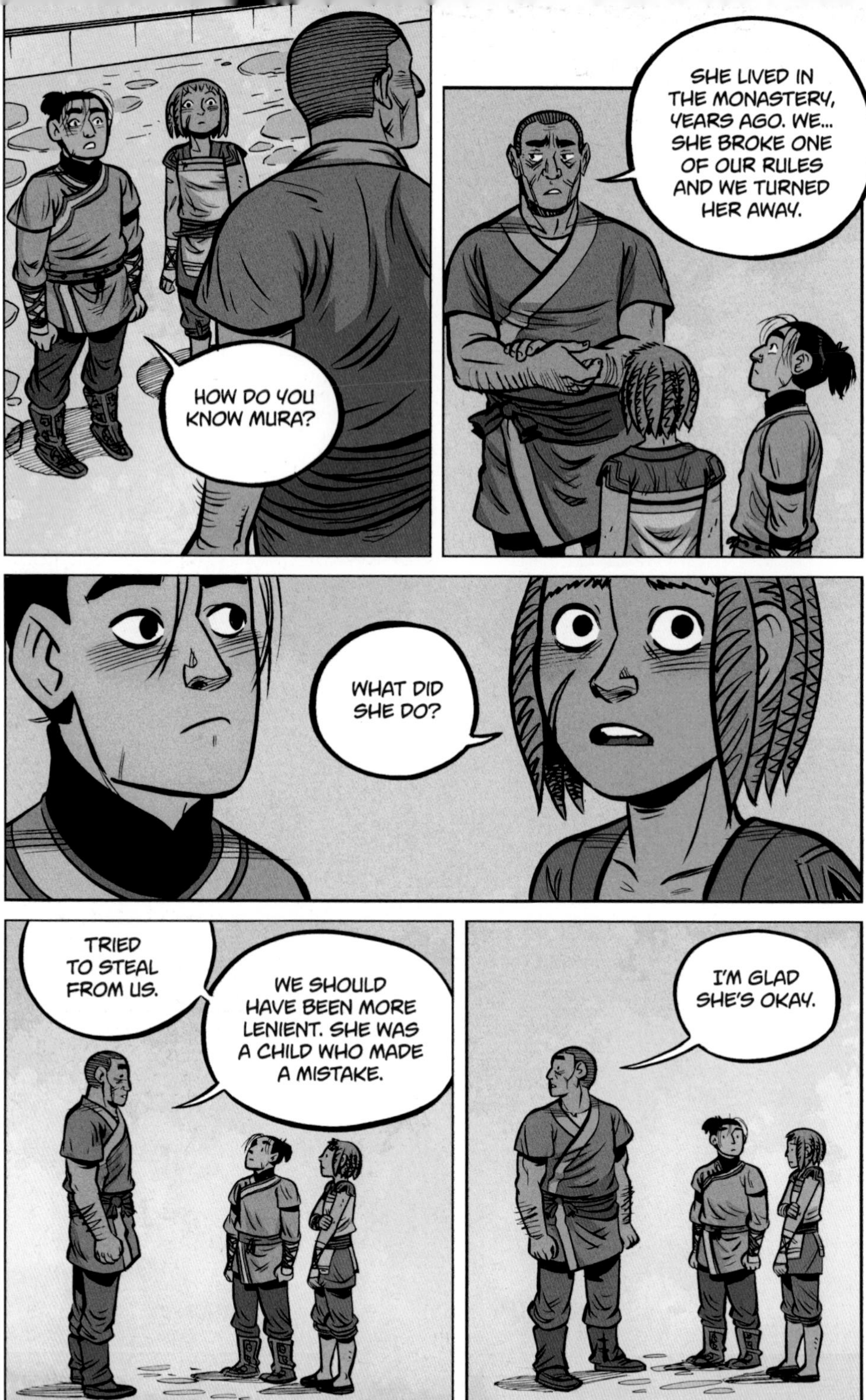
HOW DO YOU KNOW MURA?
SHE LIVED IN THE MONASTERY, YEARS AGO. WE... SHE BROKE ONE OF OUR RULES AND WE TURNED HER AWAY.
WHAT DID SHE DO?
TRIED TO STEAL FROM US.
WE SHOULD HAVE BEEN MORE LENIENT. SHE WAS A CHILD WHO MADE A MISTAKE.
I'M GLAD SHE'S OKAY.

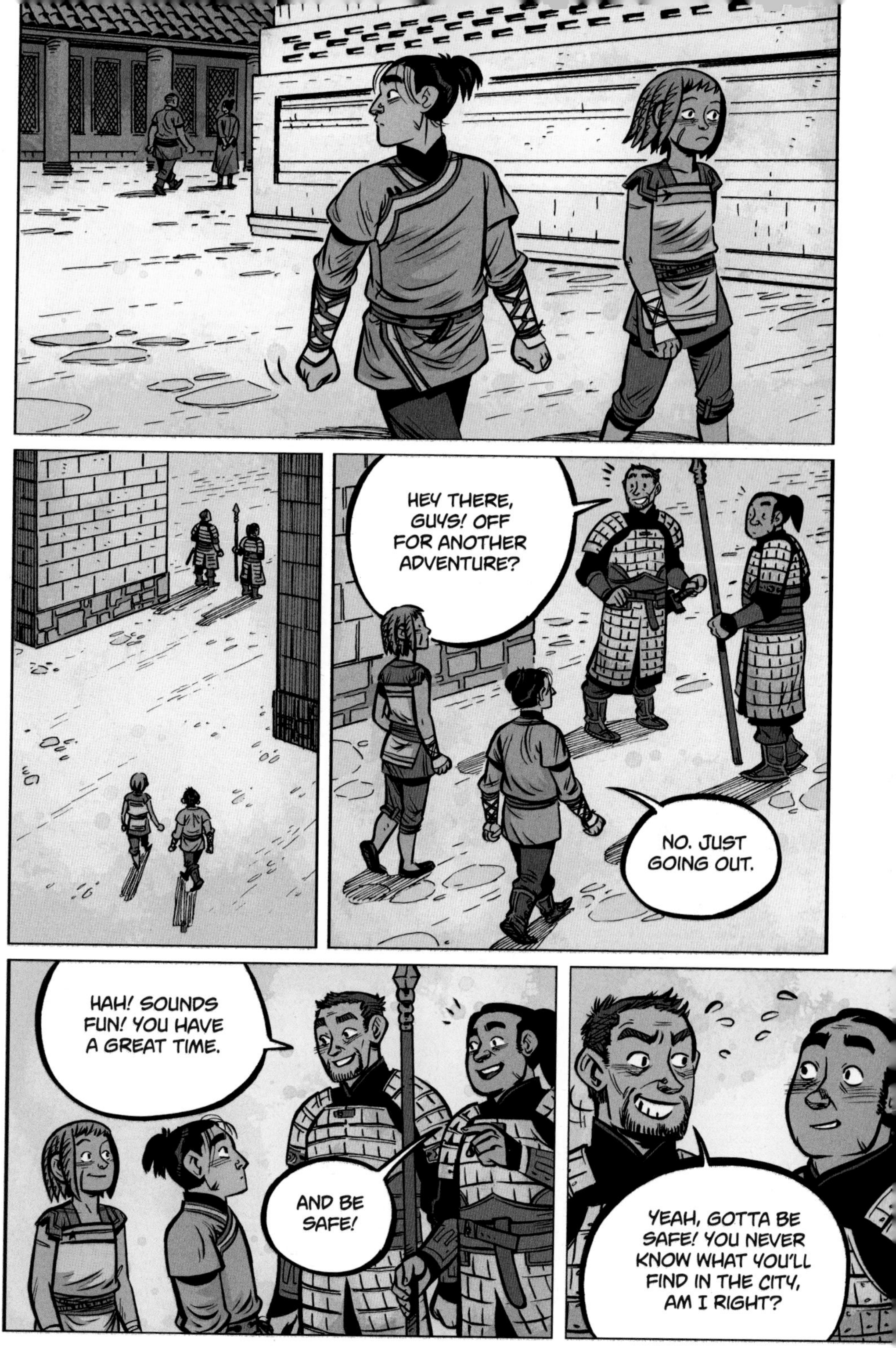
HEY THERE, GUYS! OFF FOR ANOTHER ADVENTURE?
NO. JUST GOING OUT.
HAH! SOUNDS FUN! YOU HAVE A GREAT TIME.
AND BE SAFE!
YEAH, GOTTA BE SAFE! YOU NEVER KNOW WHAT YOU'LL FIND IN THE CITY, AM I RIGHT?

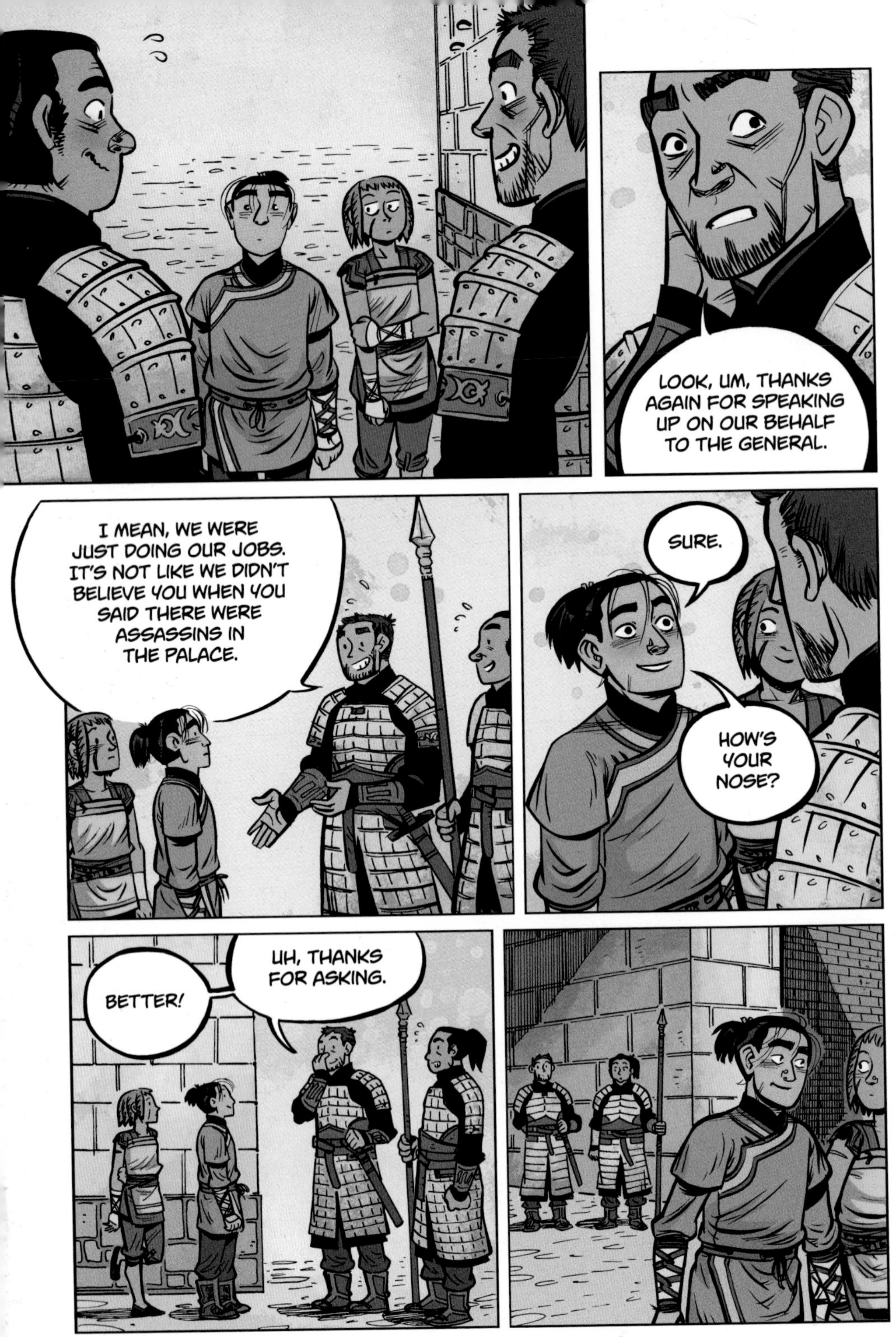
LOOK, UM, THANKS AGAIN FOR SPEAKING UP ON OUR BEHALF TO THE GENERAL.
I MEAN, WE WERE JUST DOING OUR JOBS. IT'S NOT LIKE WE DIDN'T BELIEVE YOU WHEN YOU SAID THERE WERE ASSASSINS IN THE PALACE.
SURE.
HOW'S YOUR NOSE?
BETTER!
UH, THANKS FOR ASKING.

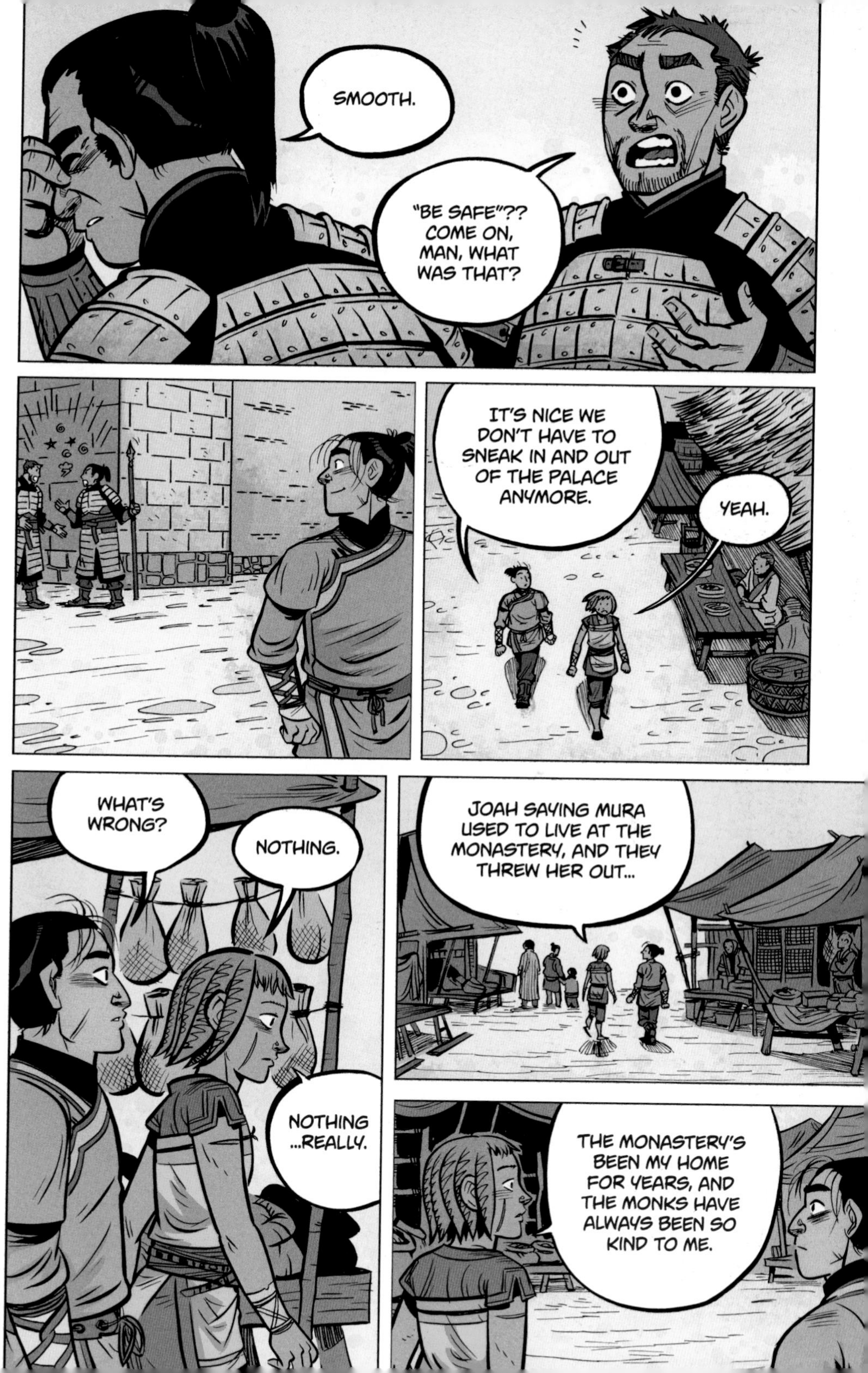
SMOOTH.
"BE SAFE"?? COME ON, MAN, WHAT WAS THAT?
IT'S NICE WE DON'T HAVE TO SNEAK IN AND OUT OF THE PALACE ANYMORE.
YEAH.
WHAT'S WRONG?
NOTHING.
NOTHING ...REALLY.
JOAH SAYING MURA USED TO LIVE AT THE MONASTERY, AND THEY THREW HER OUT...
THE MONASTERY'S BEEN MY HOME FOR YEARS, AND THE MONKS HAVE ALWAYS BEEN SO KIND TO ME.

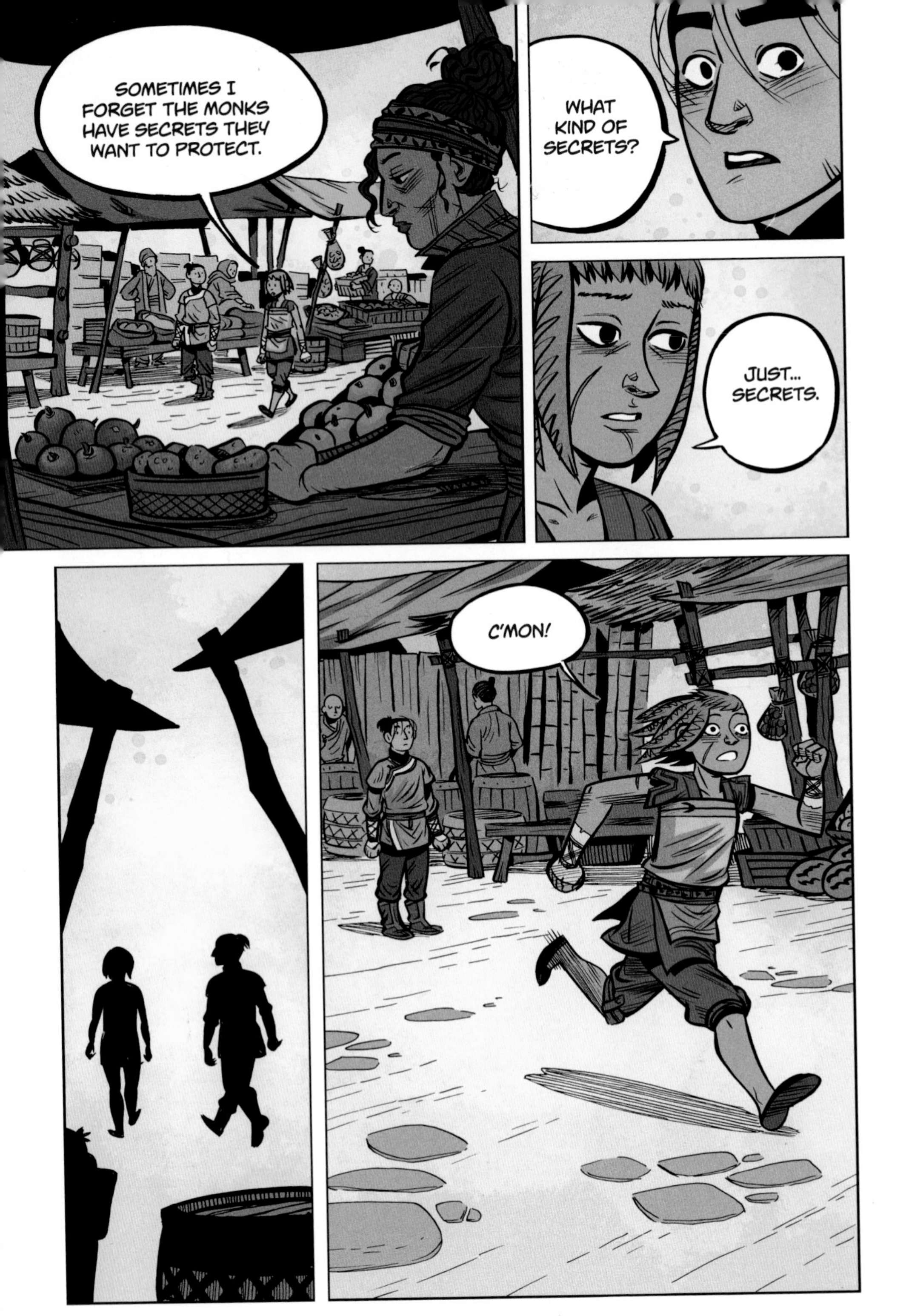
SOMETIMES I FORGET THE MONKS HAVE SECRETS THEY WANT TO PROTECT.
WHAT KIND OF SECRETS?
JUST... SECRETS.
C'MON!

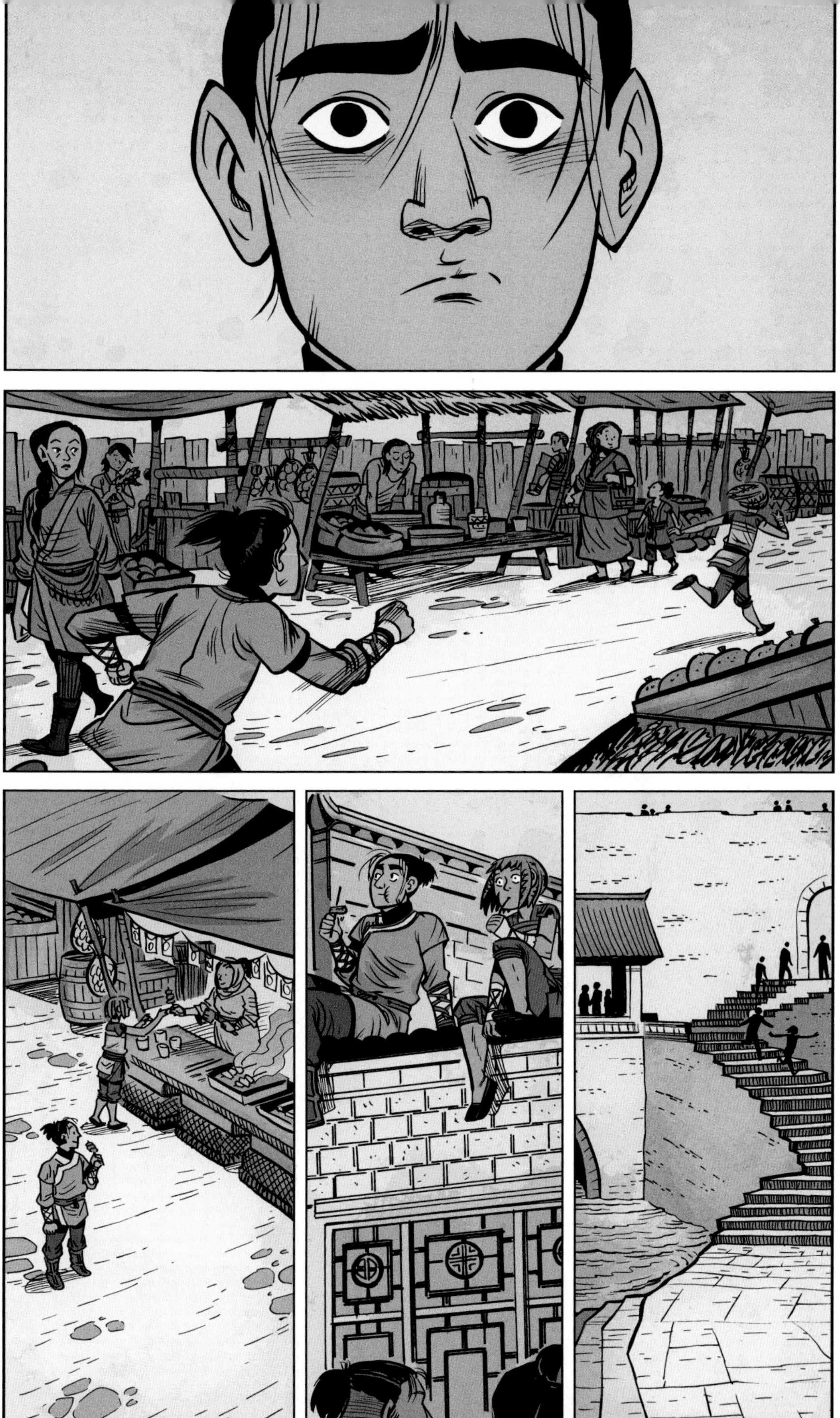

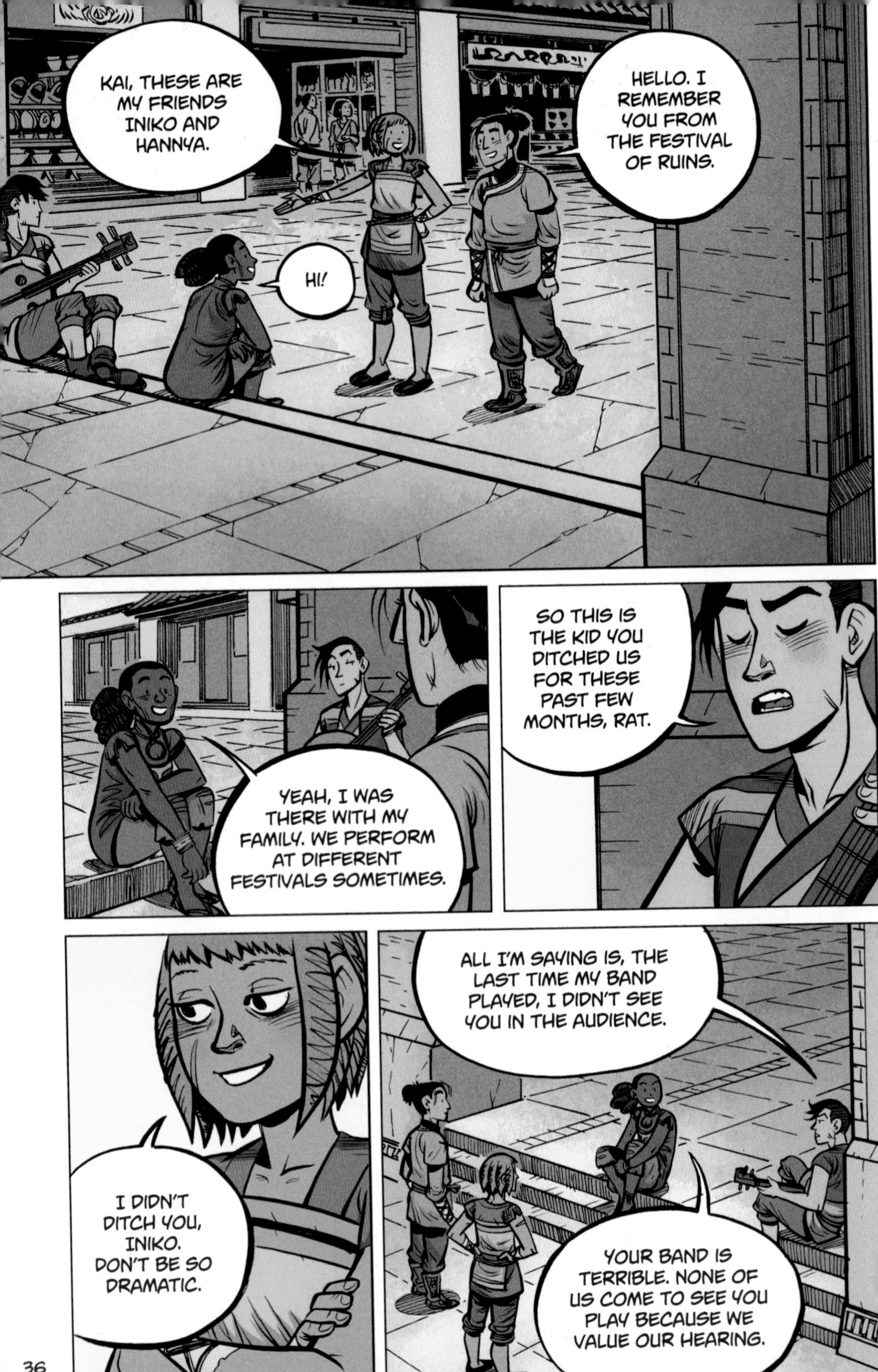
KAI, THESE ARE MY FRIENDS INIKO AND HANNYA.
HELLO. I REMEMBER YOU FROM THE FESTIVAL OF RUINS.
HI!
YEAH, I WAS THERE WITH MY FAMILY. WE PERFORM AT DIFFERENT FESTIVALS SOMETIMES.
SO THIS IS THE KID YOU DITCHED US FOR THESE PAST FEW MONTHS, RAT.
I DIDN'T DITCH YOU, INIKO. DON'T BE SO DRAMATIC.
ALL I'M SAYING IS, THE LAST TIME MY BAND PLAYED, I DIDN'T SEE YOU IN THE AUDIENCE.
YOUR BAND IS TERRIBLE. NONE OF US COME TO SEE YOU PLAY BECAUSE WE VALUE OUR HEARING.

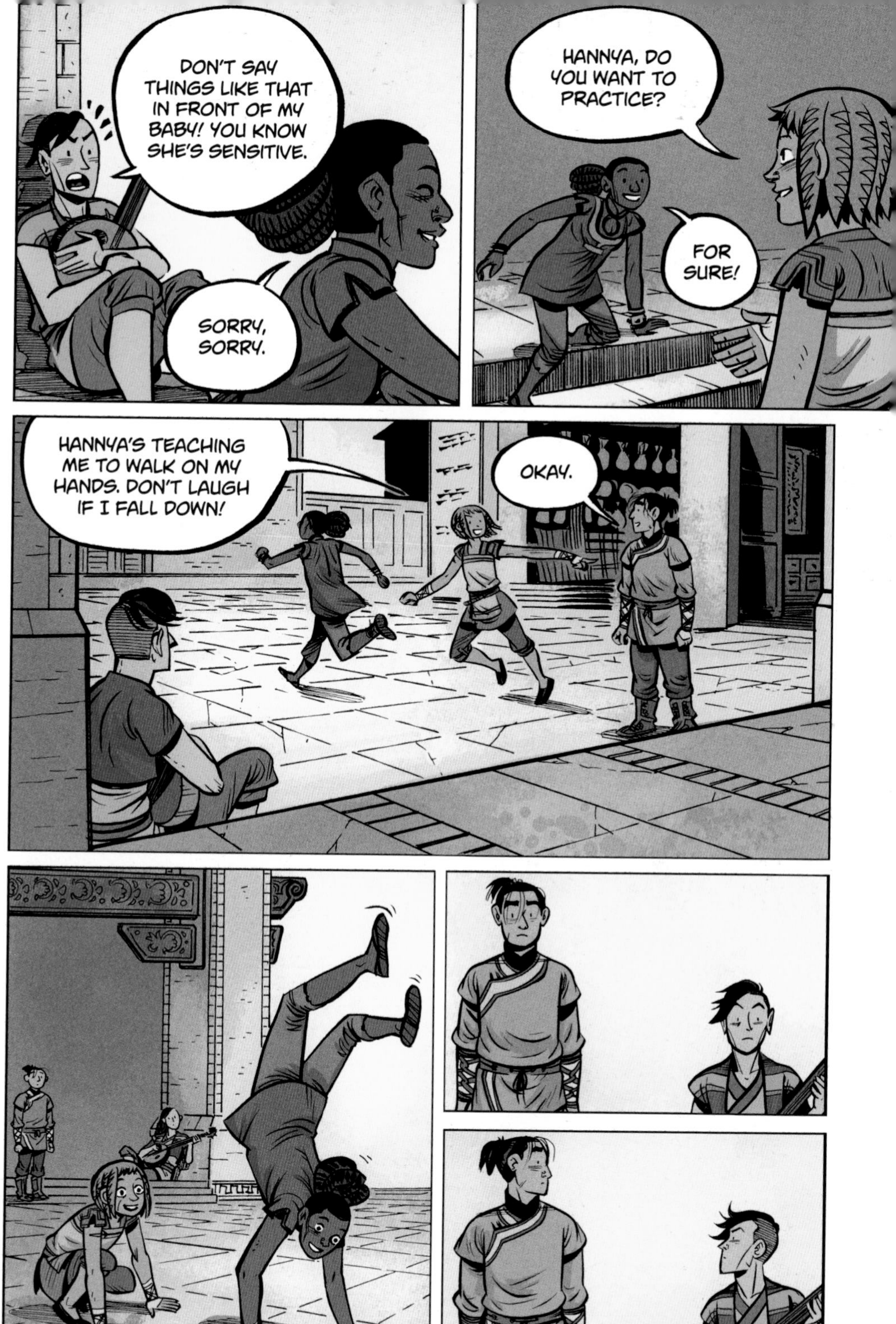
DON'T SAY THINGS LIKE THAT IN FRONT OF MY BABY! YOU KNOW SHE'S SENSITIVE.
SORRY, SORRY.
HANNYA, DO YOU WANT TO PRACTICE?
FOR SURE!
HANNYA'S TEACHING ME TO WALK ON MY HANDS. DON'T LAUGH IF I FALL DOWN!
OKAY.

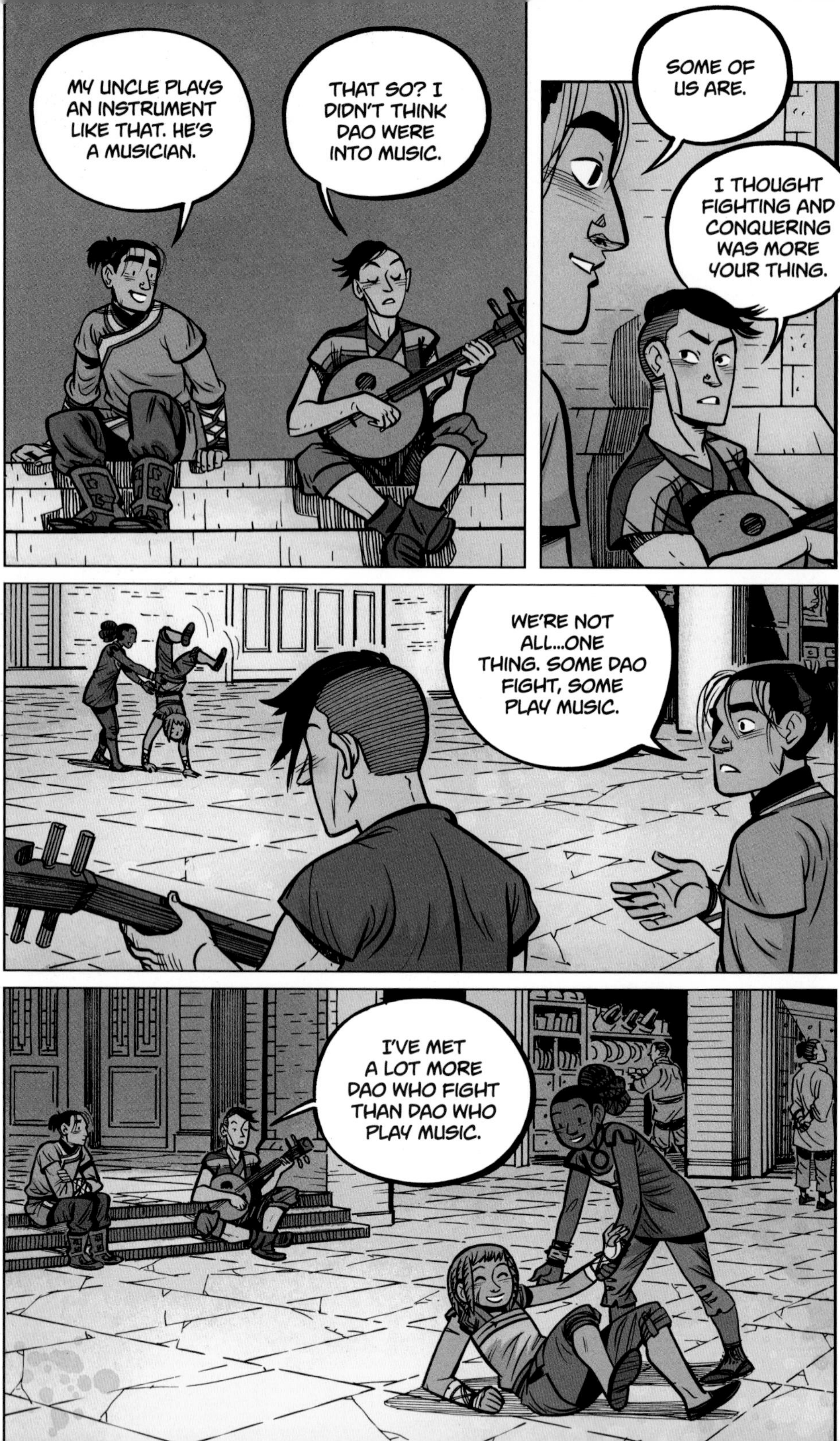
MY UNCLE PLAYS AN INSTRUMENT LIKE THAT. HE'S A MUSICIAN.
THAT SO? I DIDN'T THINK DAO WERE INTO MUSIC.
SOME OF US ARE.
I THOUGHT FIGHTING AND CONQUERING WAS MORE YOUR THING.
WE'RE NOT ALL...ONE THING. SOME DAO FIGHT, SOME PLAY MUSIC.
I'VE MET A LOT MORE DAO WHO FIGHT THAN DAO WHO PLAY MUSIC.

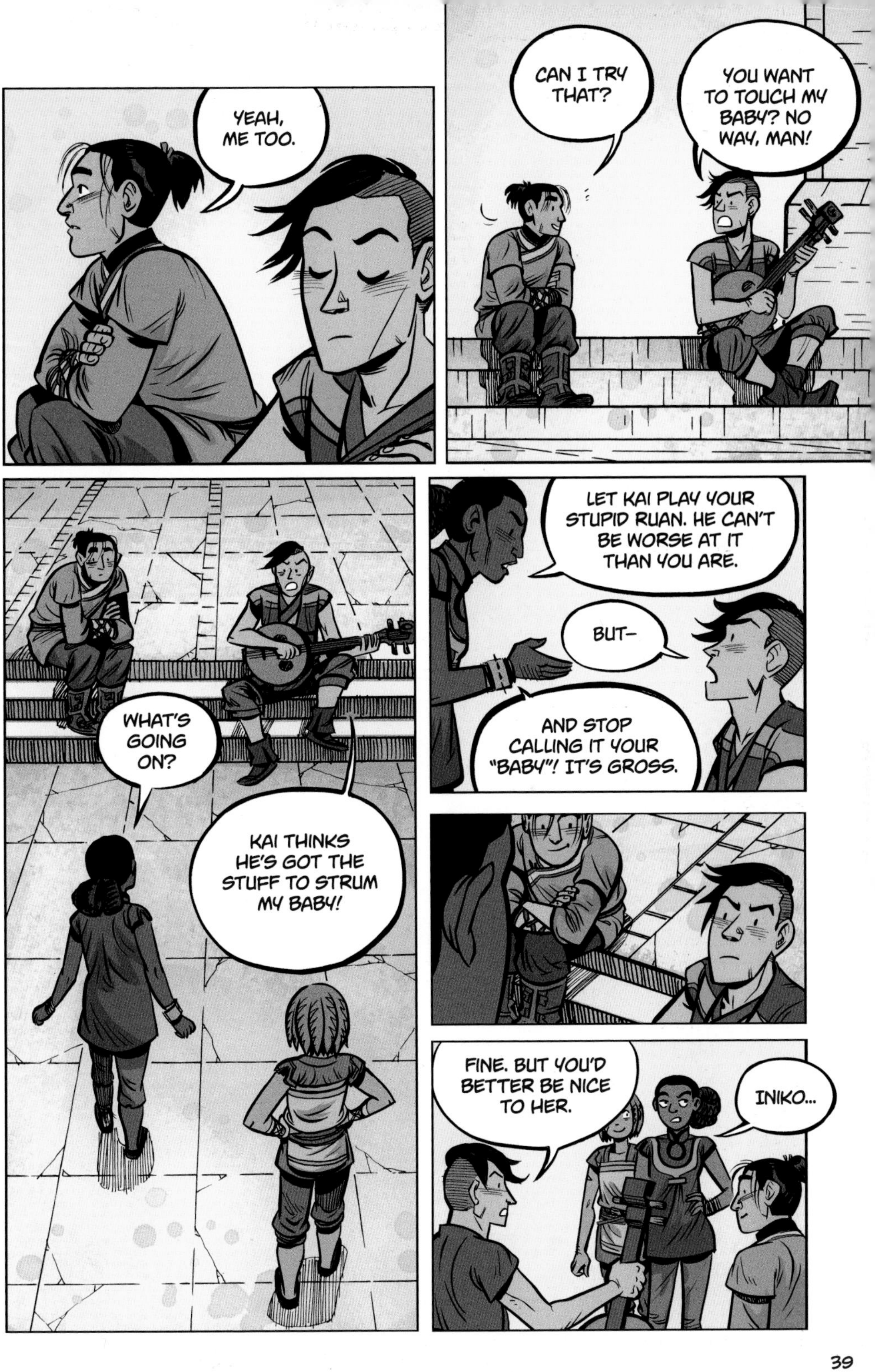
YEAH, ME TOO.
CAN I TRY THAT?
YOU WANT TO TOUCH MY BABY? NO WAY, MAN!
WHAT'S GOING ON?
KAI THINKS HE'S GOT THE STUFF TO STRUM MY BABY!
LET KAI PLAY YOUR STUPID RUAN. HE CAN'T BE WORSE AT IT THAN YOU ARE.
BUT–
AND STOP CALLING IT YOUR "BABY"! IT'S GROSS.
FINE. BUT YOU'D BETTER BE NICE TO HER.
INIKO...

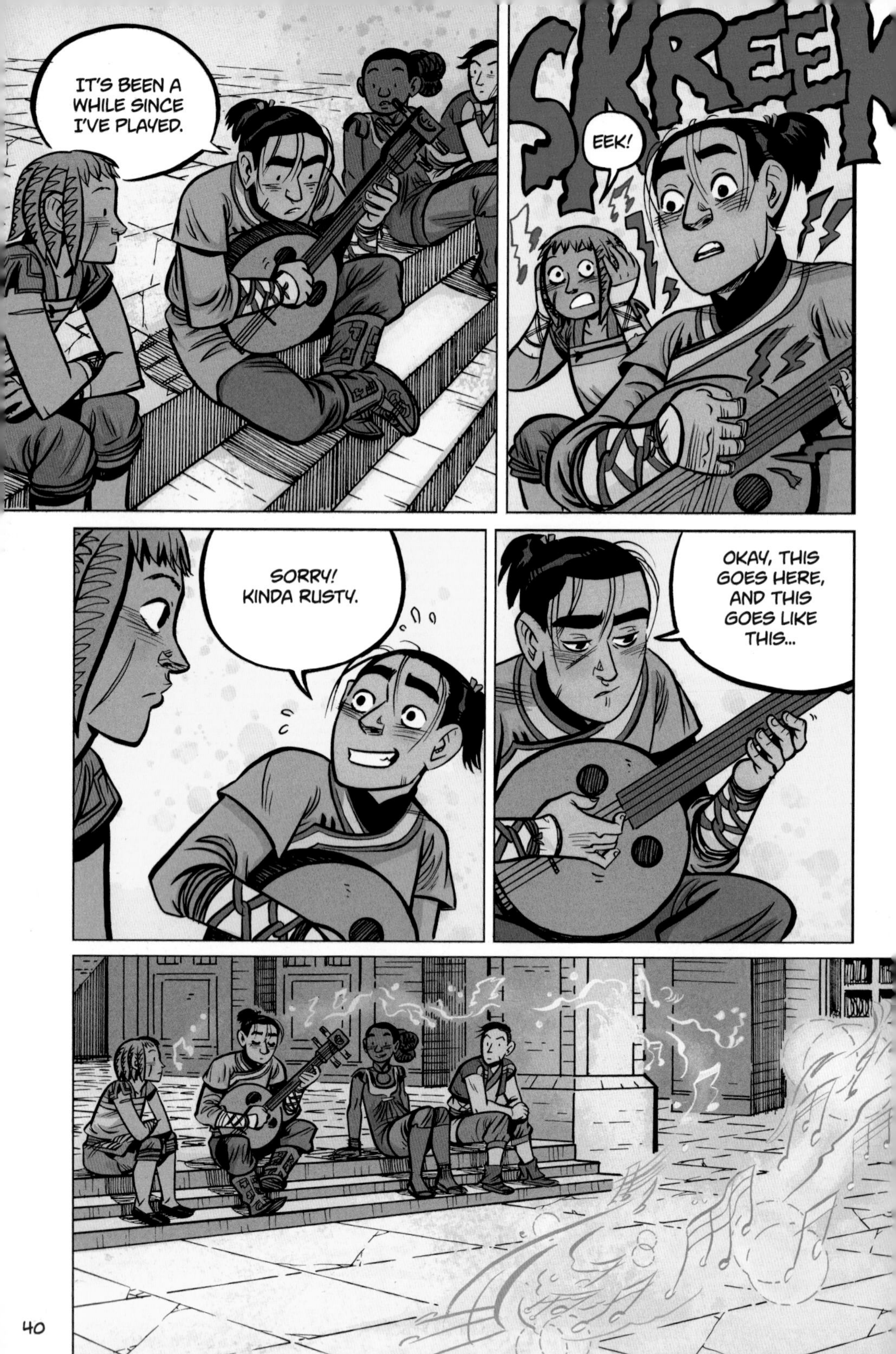
IT'S BEEN A WHILE SINCE I'VE PLAYED.
SKREEK
EEK!
SORRY! KINDA RUSTY.
OKAY, THIS GOES HERE, AND THIS GOES LIKE THIS...

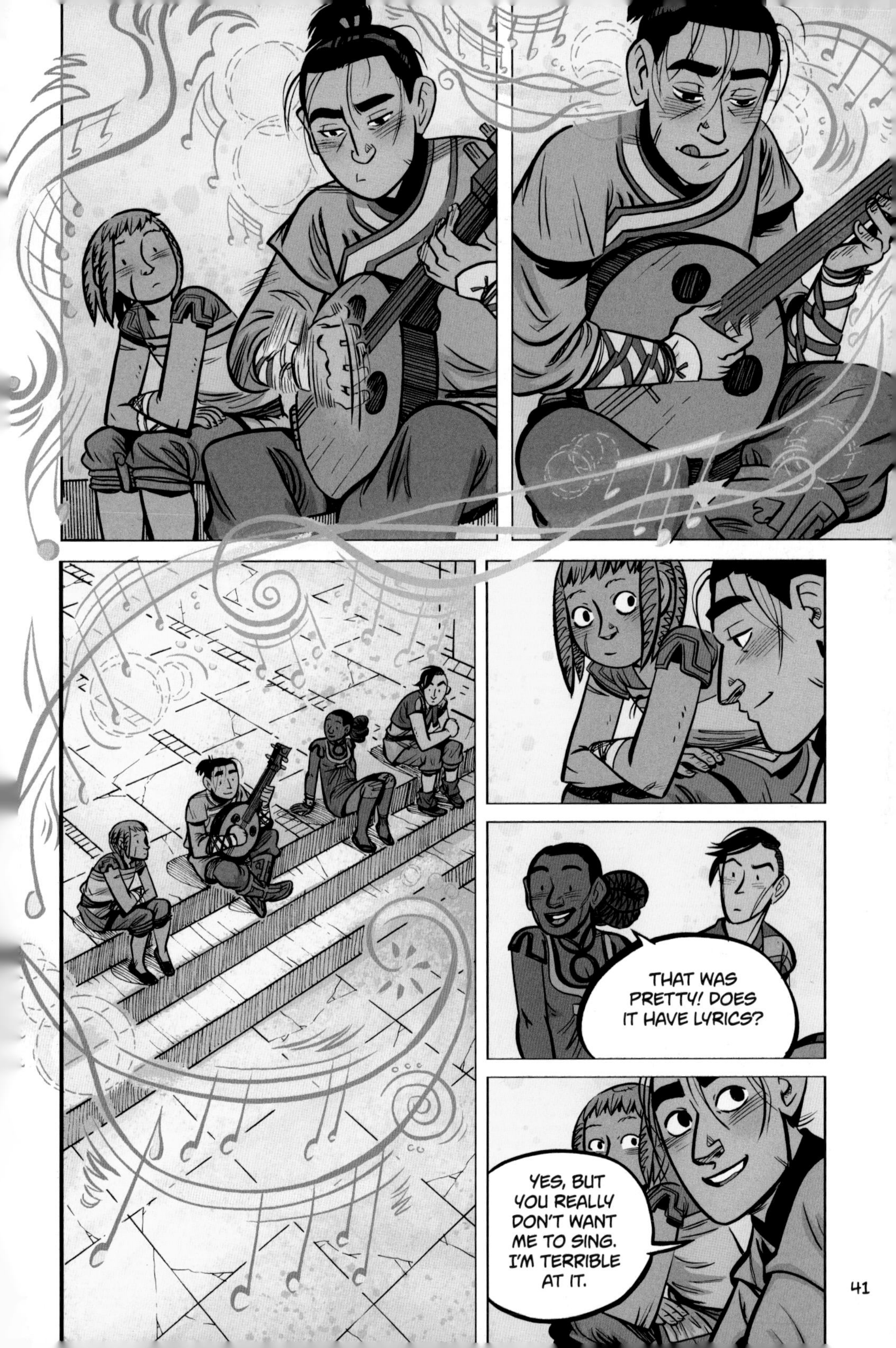
THAT WAS PRETTY! DOES IT HAVE LYRICS?
YES, BUT YOU REALLY DON'T WANT ME TO SING. I'M TERRIBLE AT IT.

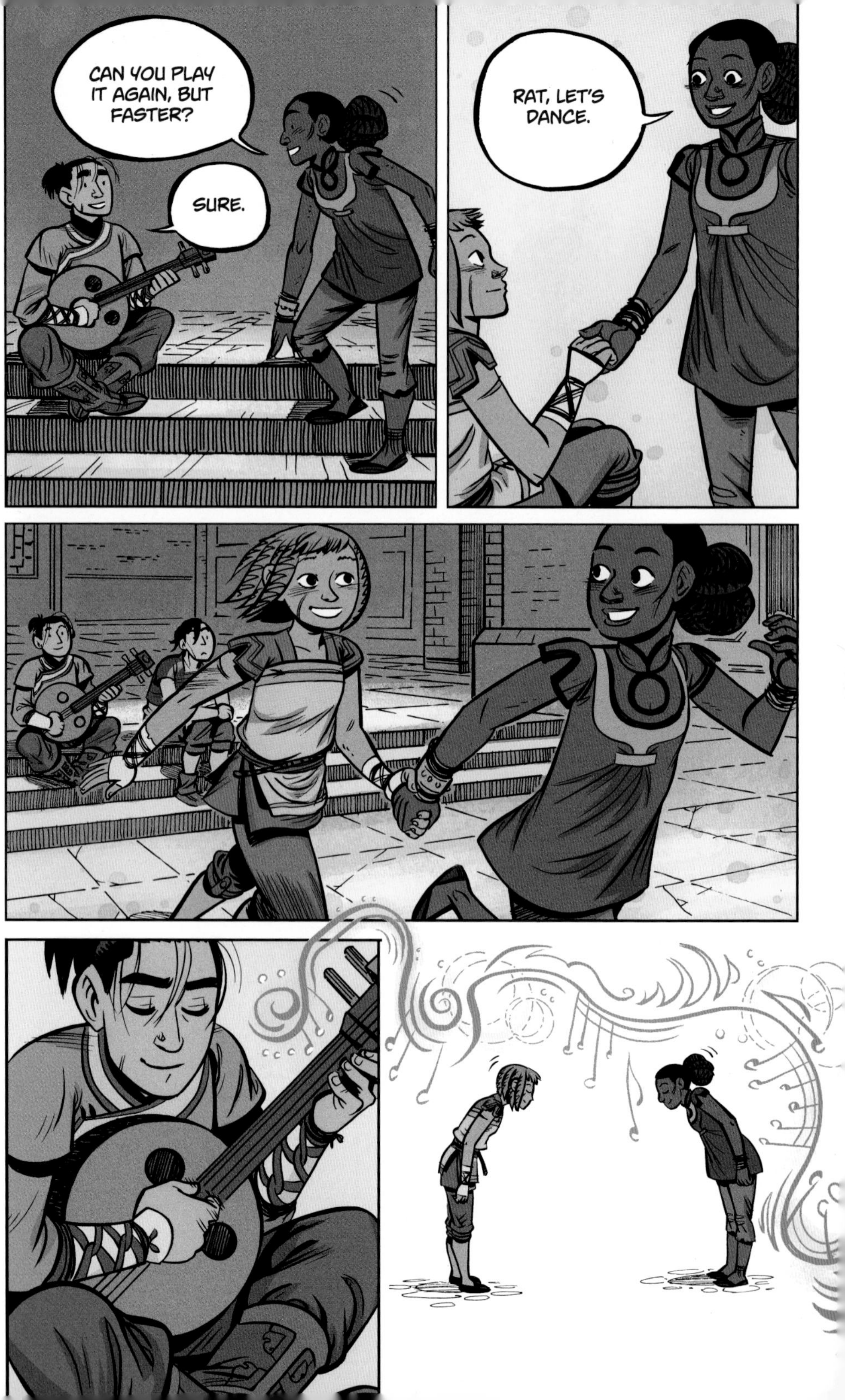
CAN YOU PLAY IT AGAIN, BUT FASTER?
SURE.
RAT, LET'S DANCE.

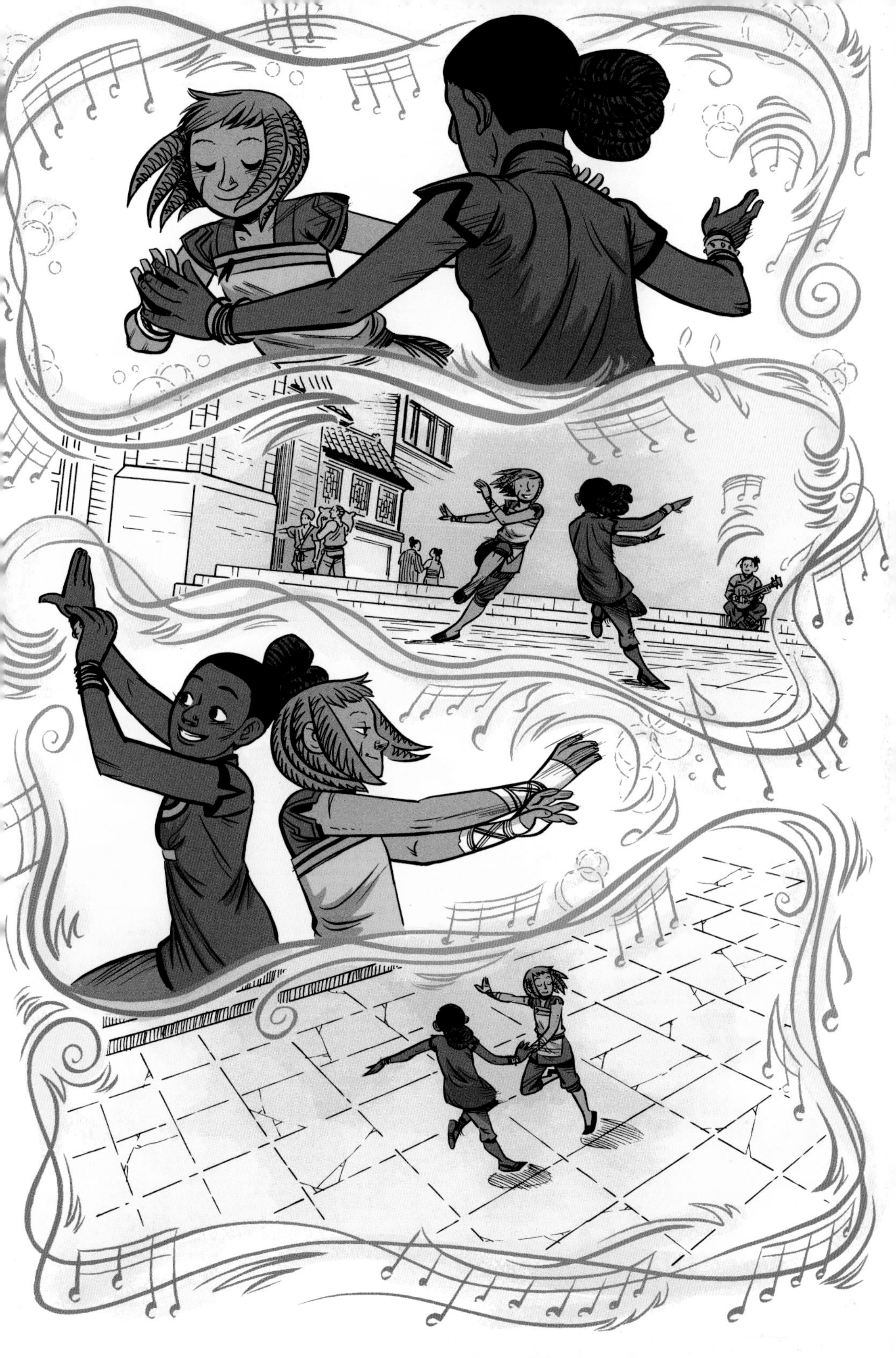

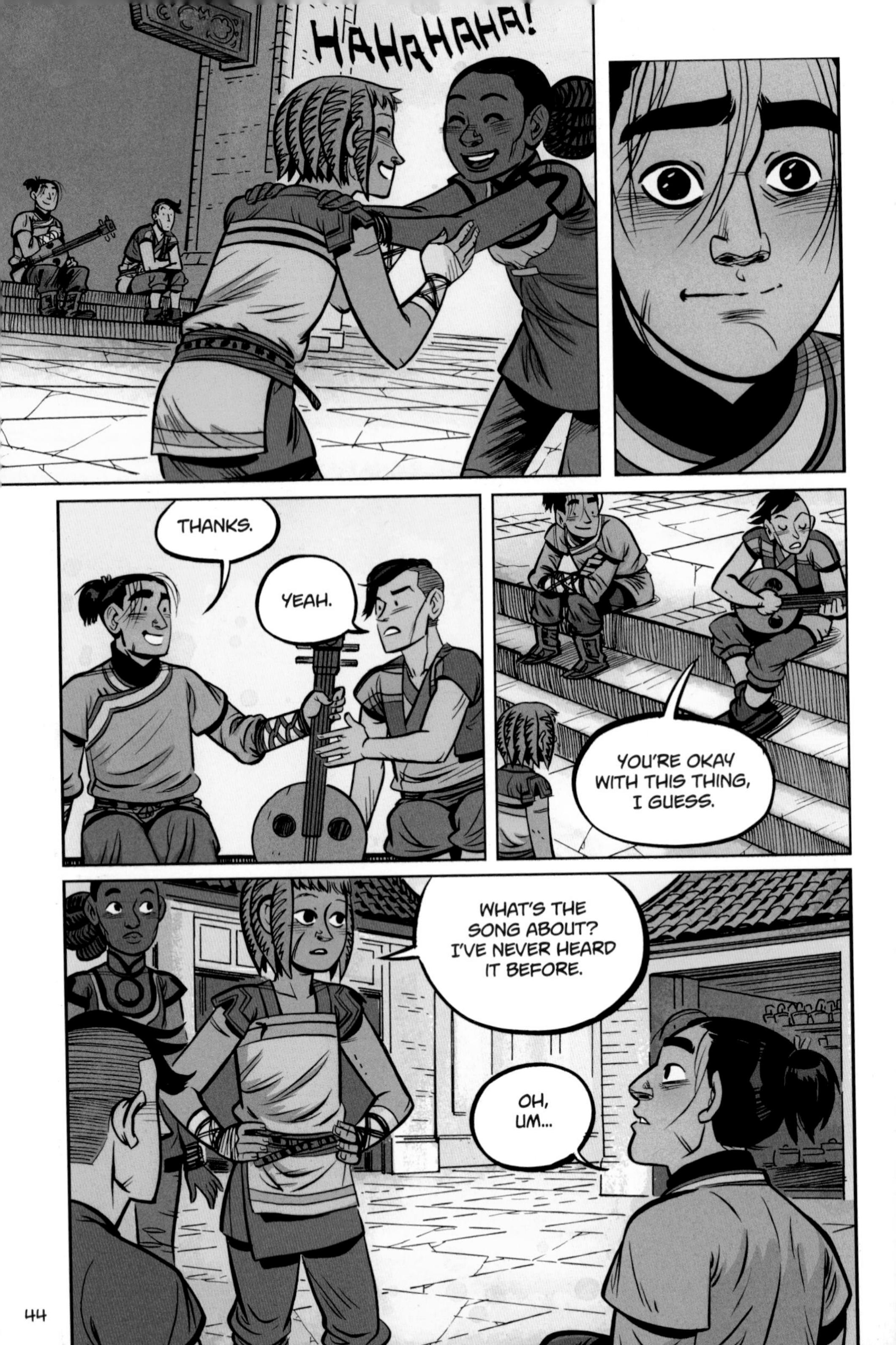
HAHAHAHA!
THANKS.
YEAH.
YOU'RE OKAY WITH THIS THING, I GUESS.
WHAT'S THE SONG ABOUT? I'VE NEVER HEARD IT BEFORE.
OH, UM...

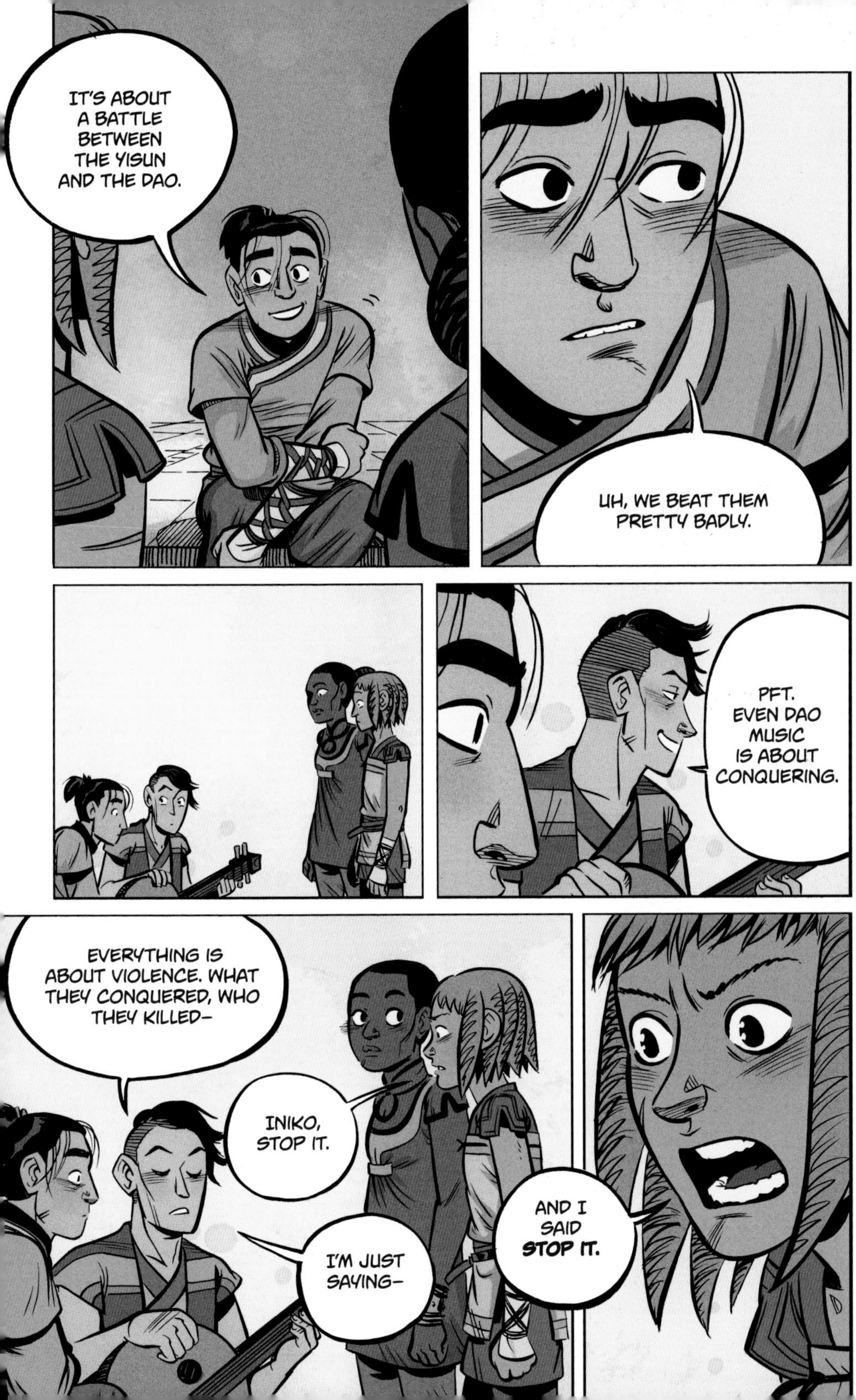
IT'S ABOUT A BATTLE BETWEEN THE YISUN AND THE DAO.
UH, WE BEAT THEM PRETTY BADLY.
PFT. EVEN DAO MUSIC IS ABOUT CONQUERING.
EVERYTHING IS ABOUT VIOLENCE. WHAT THEY CONQUERED, WHO THEY KILLED–
INIKO, STOP IT.
I'M JUST SAYING–
AND I SAID **STOP IT.**

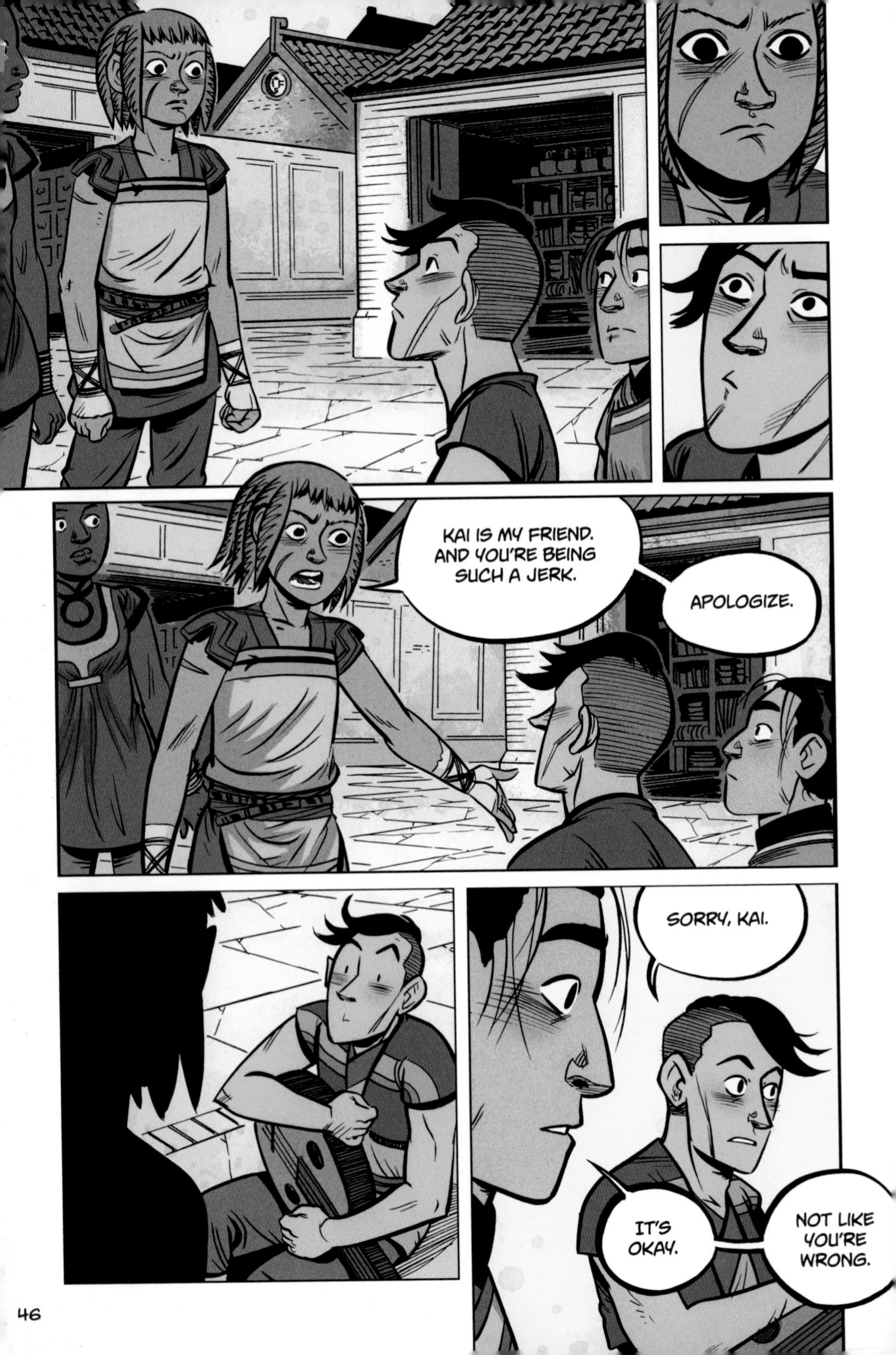
KAI IS MY FRIEND. AND YOU'RE BEING SUCH A JERK.
APOLOGIZE.
SORRY, KAI.
IT'S OKAY.
NOT LIKE YOU'RE WRONG.

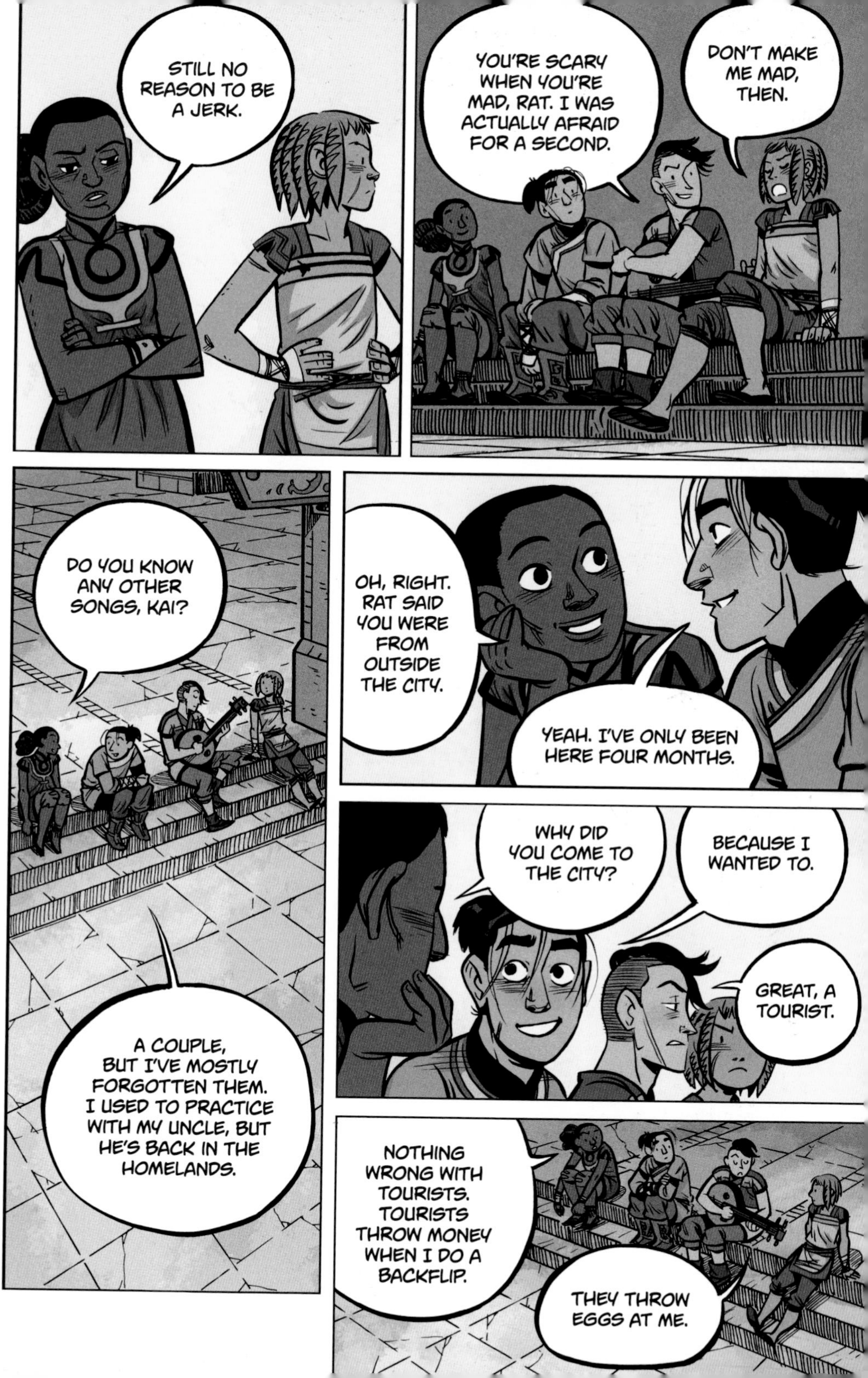
STILL NO REASON TO BE A JERK.
YOU'RE SCARY WHEN YOU'RE MAD, RAT. I WAS ACTUALLY AFRAID FOR A SECOND.
DON'T MAKE ME MAD, THEN.
DO YOU KNOW ANY OTHER SONGS, KAI?
A COUPLE, BUT I'VE MOSTLY FORGOTTEN THEM. I USED TO PRACTICE WITH MY UNCLE, BUT HE'S BACK IN THE HOMELANDS.
OH, RIGHT. RAT SAID YOU WERE FROM OUTSIDE THE CITY.
YEAH. I'VE ONLY BEEN HERE FOUR MONTHS.
WHY DID YOU COME TO THE CITY?
BECAUSE I WANTED TO.
GREAT, A TOURIST.
NOTHING WRONG WITH TOURISTS. TOURISTS THROW MONEY WHEN I DO A BACKFLIP.
THEY THROW EGGS AT ME.

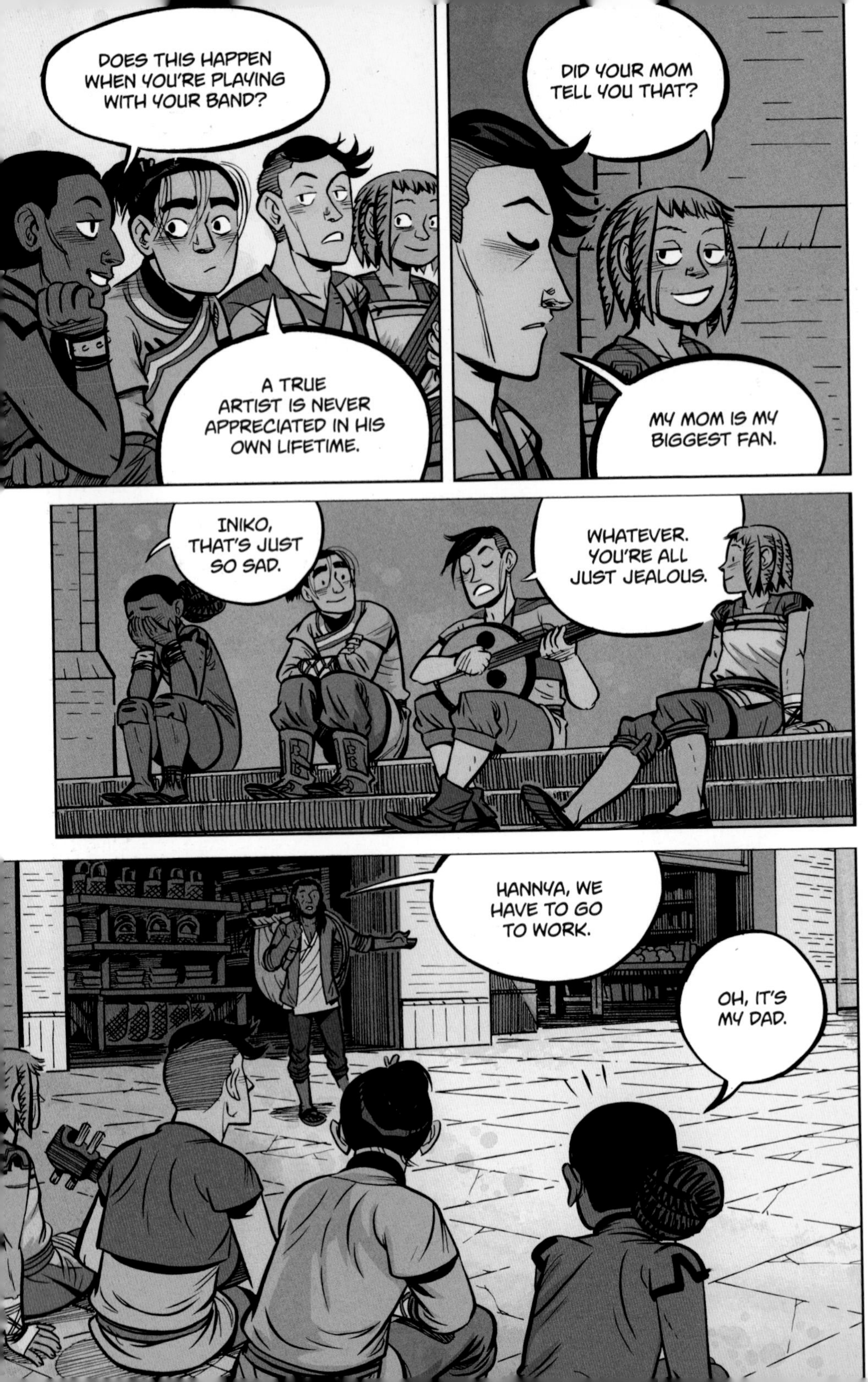
DOES THIS HAPPEN WHEN YOU'RE PLAYING WITH YOUR BAND?
A TRUE ARTIST IS NEVER APPRECIATED IN HIS OWN LIFETIME.
DID YOUR MOM TELL YOU THAT?
MY MOM IS MY BIGGEST FAN.
INIKO, THAT'S JUST SO SAD.
WHATEVER. YOU'RE ALL JUST JEALOUS.
HANNYA, WE HAVE TO GO TO WORK.
OH, IT'S MY DAD.

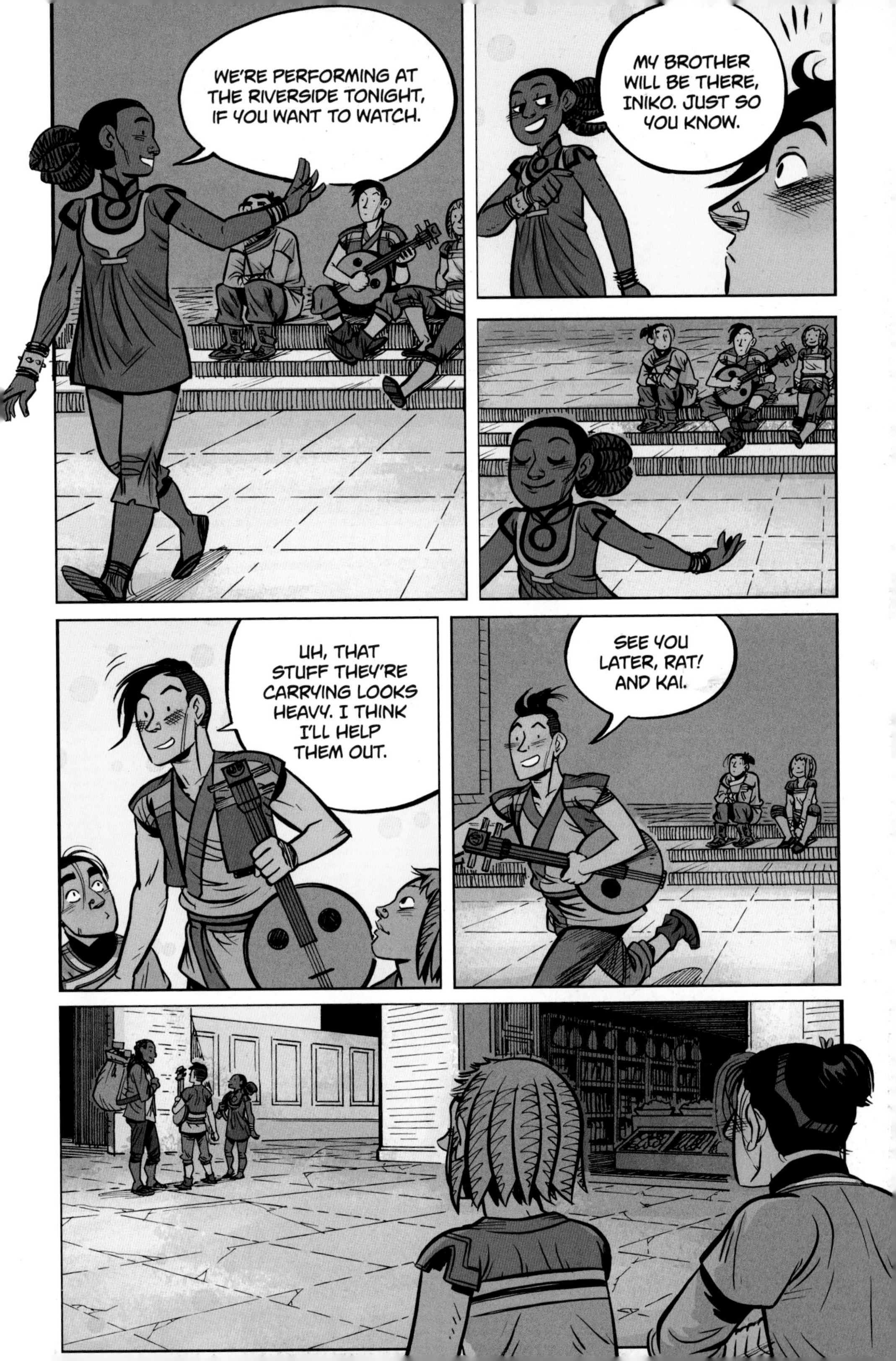
WE'RE PERFORMING AT THE RIVERSIDE TONIGHT, IF YOU WANT TO WATCH.
MY BROTHER WILL BE THERE, INIKO. JUST SO YOU KNOW.
UH, THAT STUFF THEY'RE CARRYING LOOKS HEAVY. I THINK I'LL HELP THEM OUT.
SEE YOU LATER, RAT! AND KAI.

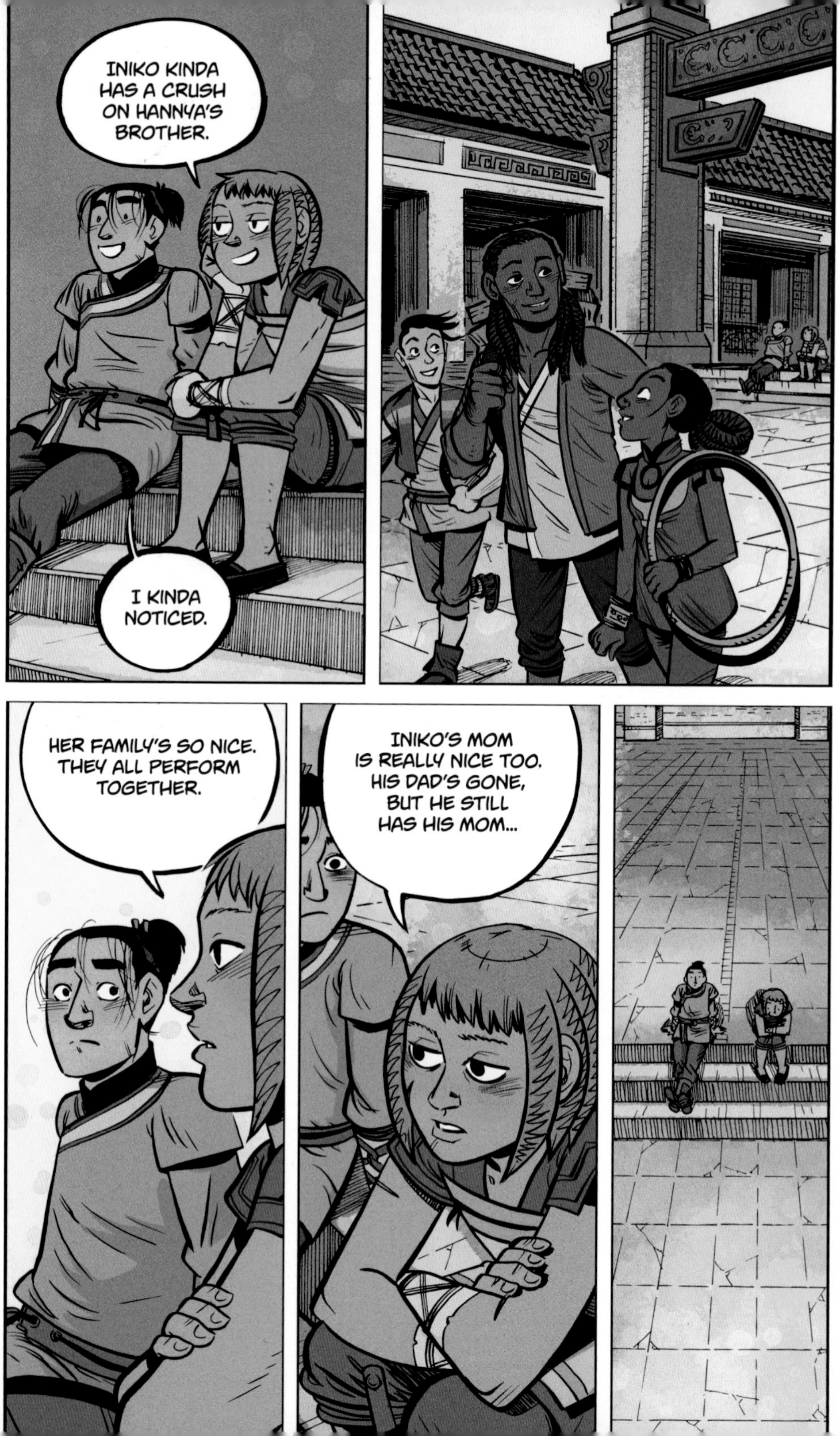
INIKO KINDA HAS A CRUSH ON HANNYA'S BROTHER.
I KINDA NOTICED.
HER FAMILY'S SO NICE. THEY ALL PERFORM TOGETHER.
INIKO'S MOM IS REALLY NICE TOO. HIS DAD'S GONE, BUT HE STILL HAS HIS MOM...

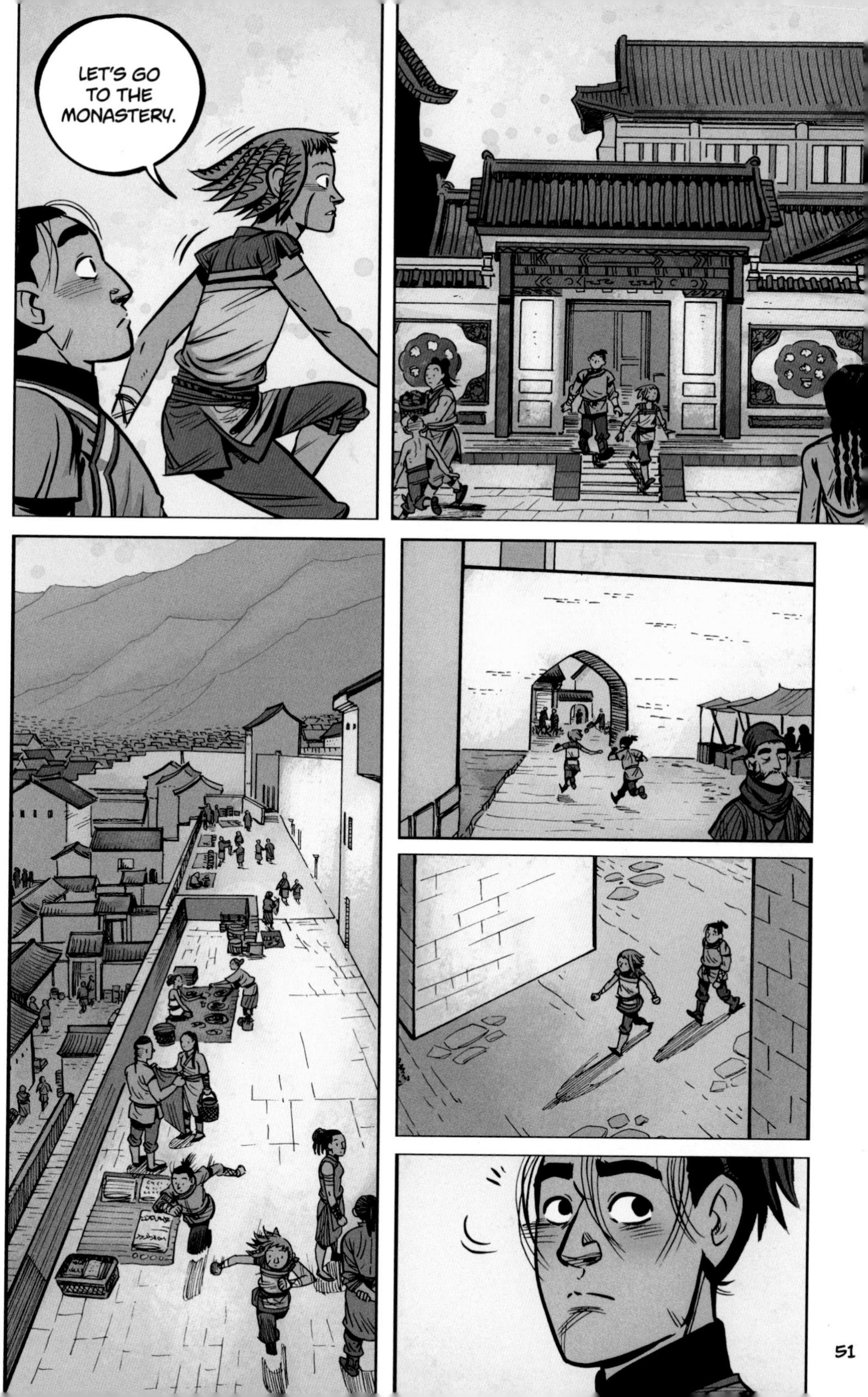
LET'S GO TO THE MONASTERY.

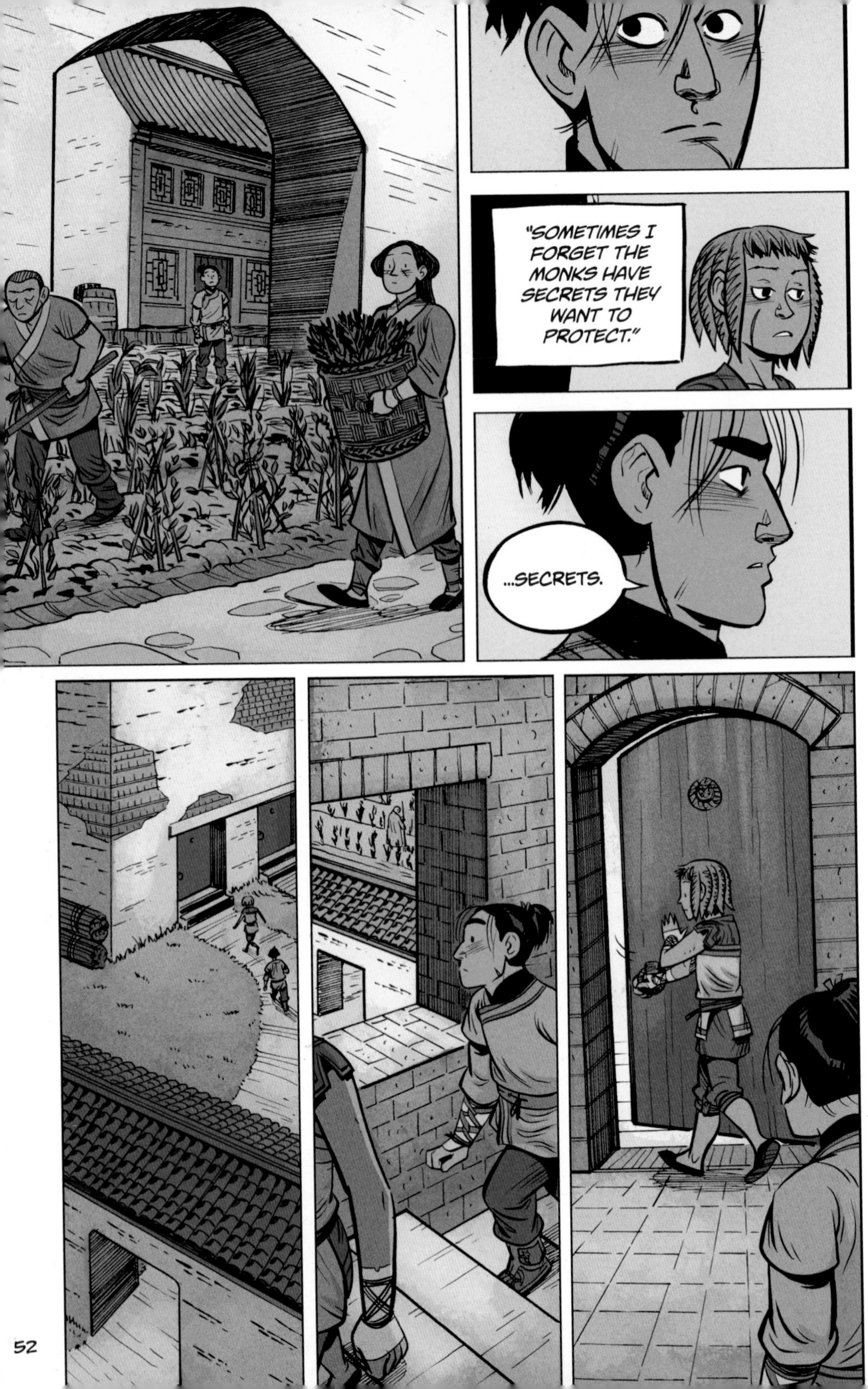
"SOMETIMES I FORGET THE MONKS HAVE SECRETS THEY WANT TO PROTECT."
...SECRETS.

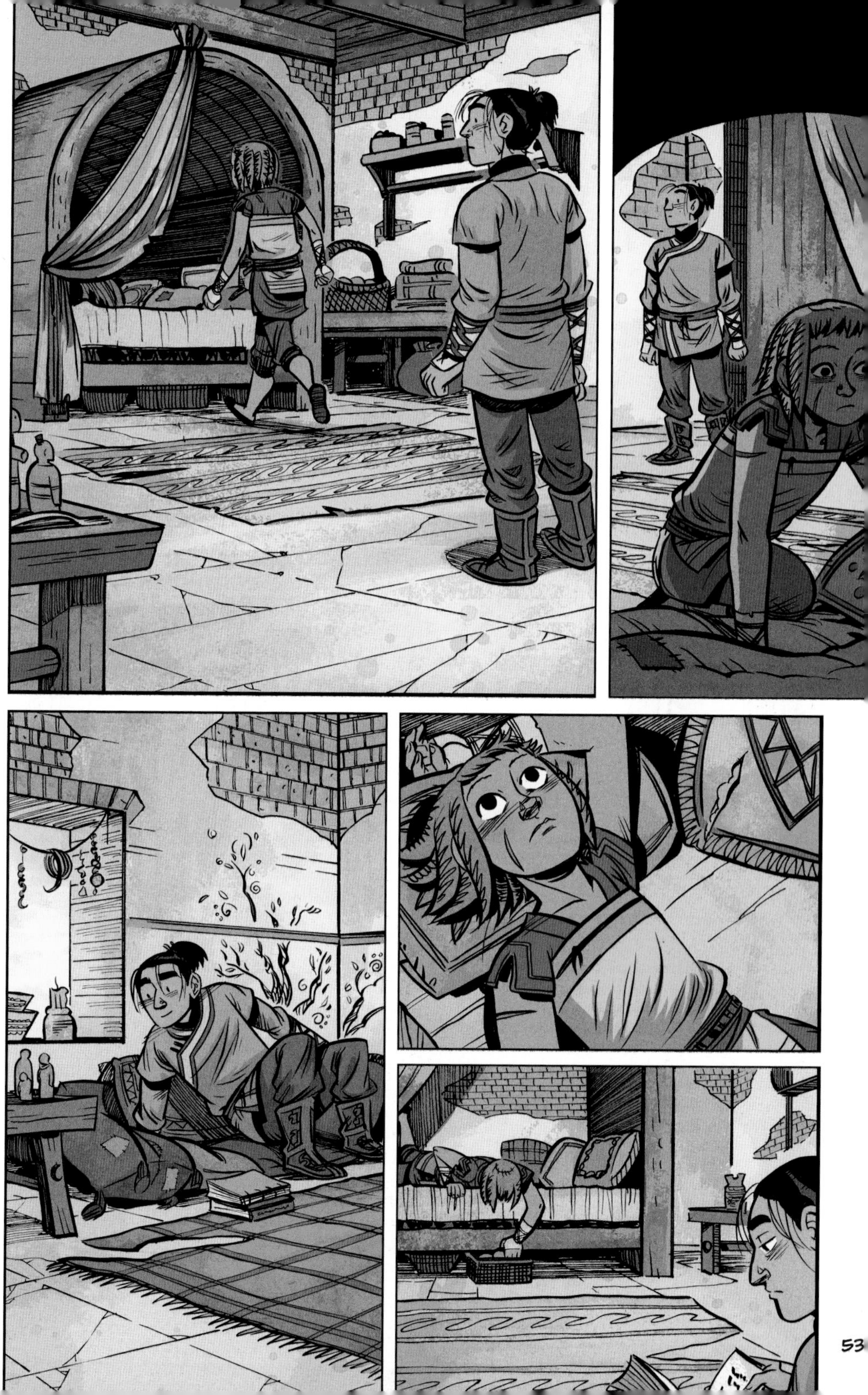

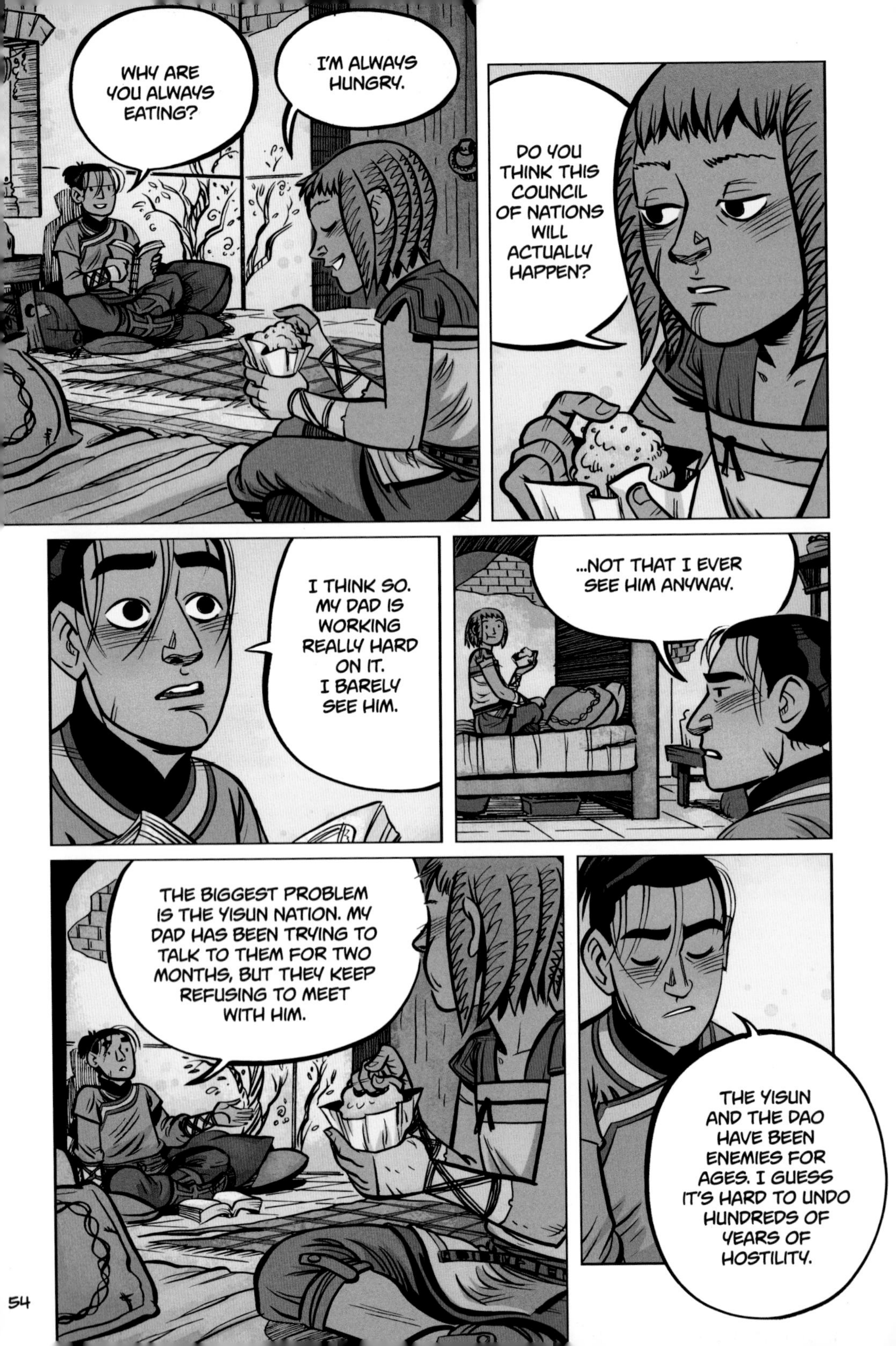
WHY ARE YOU ALWAYS EATING?
I'M ALWAYS HUNGRY.
DO YOU THINK THIS COUNCIL OF NATIONS WILL ACTUALLY HAPPEN?
I THINK SO. MY DAD IS WORKING REALLY HARD ON IT. I BARELY SEE HIM.
...NOT THAT I EVER SEE HIM ANYWAY.
THE BIGGEST PROBLEM IS THE YISUN NATION. MY DAD HAS BEEN TRYING TO TALK TO THEM FOR TWO MONTHS, BUT THEY KEEP REFUSING TO MEET WITH HIM.
THE YISUN AND THE DAO HAVE BEEN ENEMIES FOR AGES. I GUESS IT'S HARD TO UNDO HUNDREDS OF YEARS OF HOSTILITY.

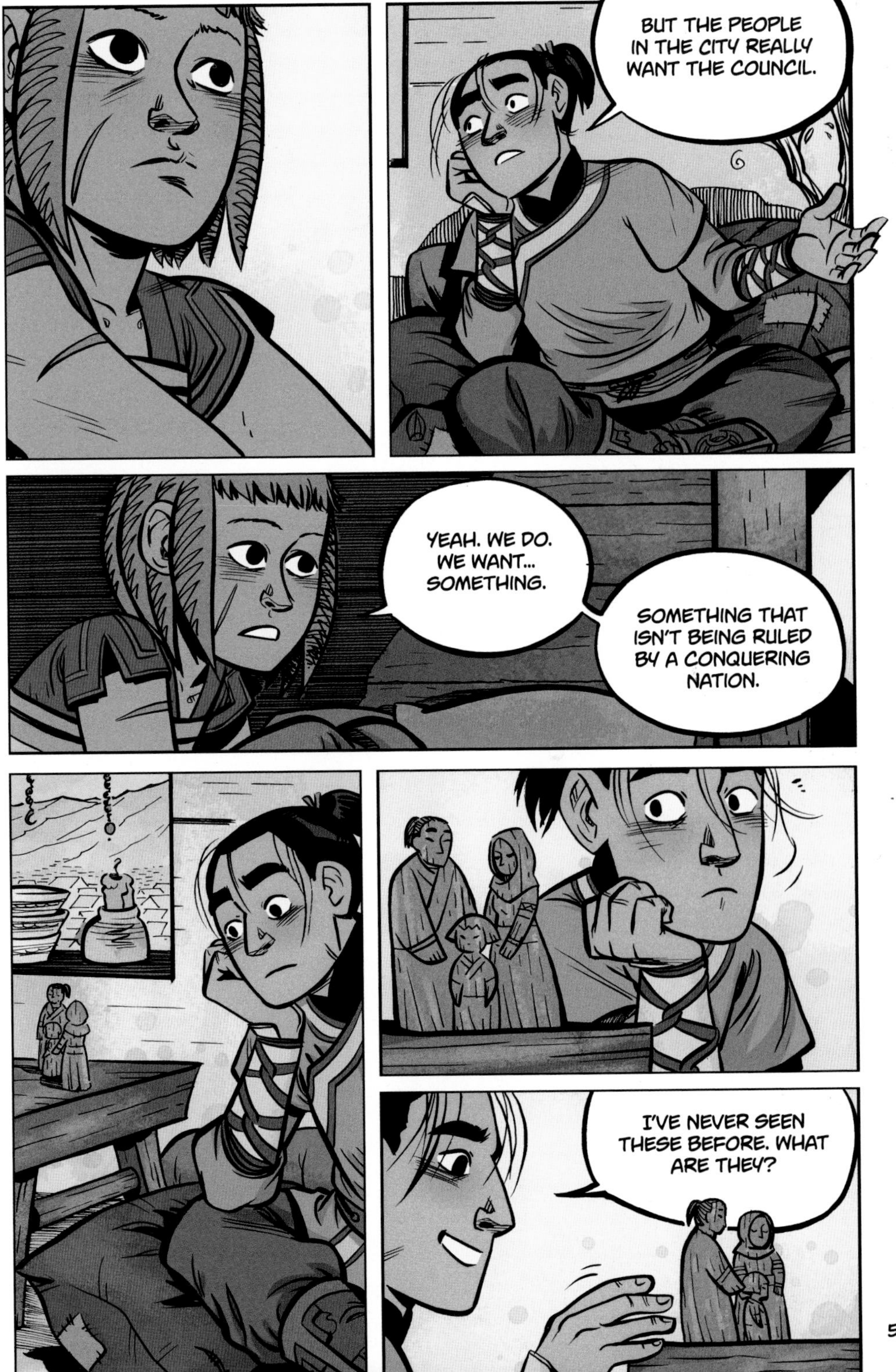
BUT THE PEOPLE IN THE CITY REALLY WANT THE COUNCIL.
YEAH. WE DO. WE WANT... SOMETHING.
SOMETHING THAT ISN'T BEING RULED BY A CONQUERING NATION.
I'VE NEVER SEEN THESE BEFORE. WHAT ARE THEY?

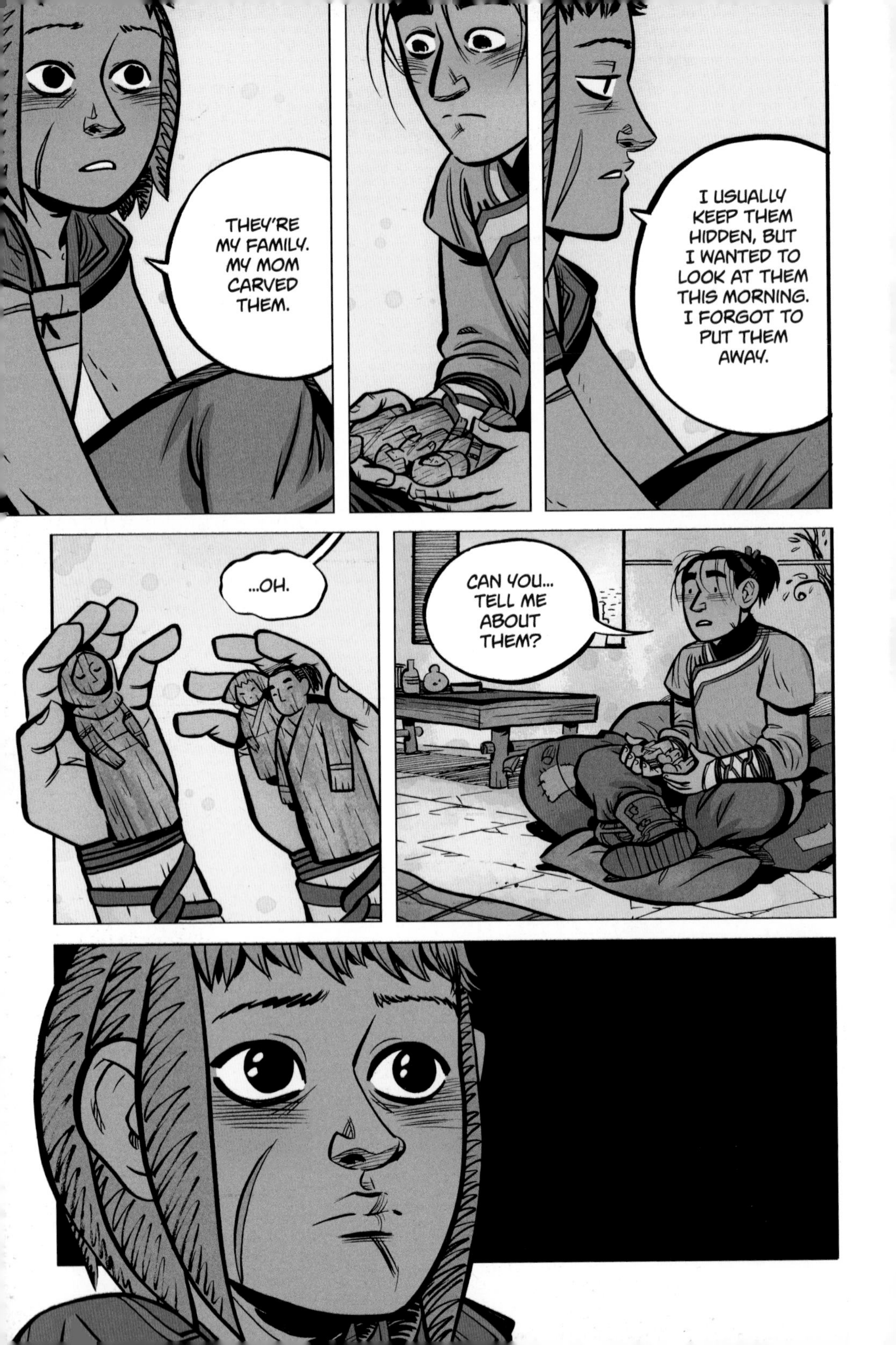
THEY'RE MY FAMILY. MY MOM CARVED THEM.
I USUALLY KEEP THEM HIDDEN, BUT I WANTED TO LOOK AT THEM THIS MORNING. I FORGOT TO PUT THEM AWAY.
...OH.
CAN YOU... TELL ME ABOUT THEM?

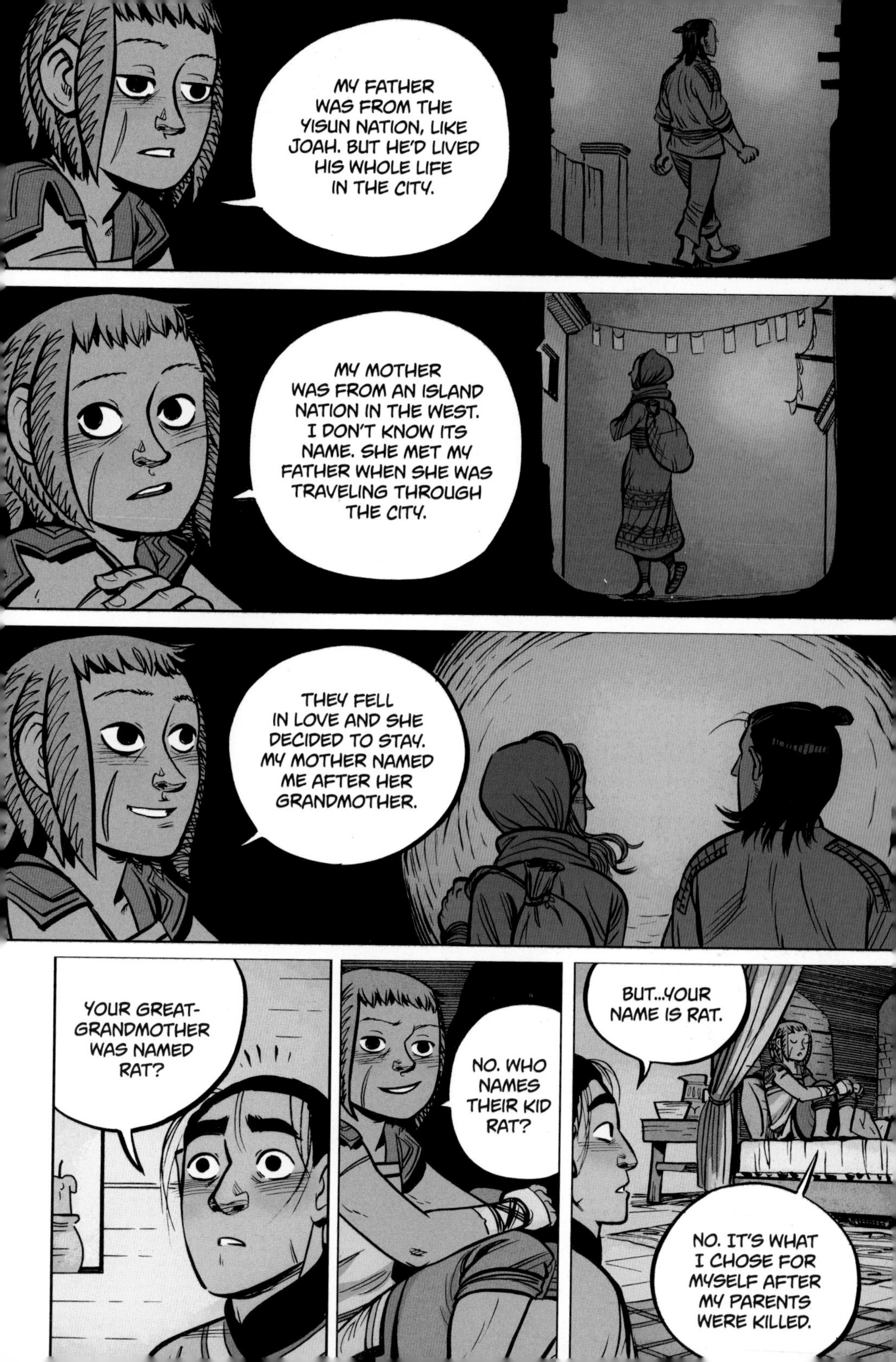
MY FATHER WAS FROM THE YISUN NATION, LIKE JOAH. BUT HE'D LIVED HIS WHOLE LIFE IN THE CITY.
MY MOTHER WAS FROM AN ISLAND NATION IN THE WEST. I DON'T KNOW ITS NAME. SHE MET MY FATHER WHEN SHE WAS TRAVELING THROUGH THE CITY.
THEY FELL IN LOVE AND SHE DECIDED TO STAY. MY MOTHER NAMED ME AFTER HER GRANDMOTHER.
YOUR GREAT-GRANDMOTHER WAS NAMED RAT?
NO. WHO NAMES THEIR KID RAT?
BUT...YOUR NAME IS RAT.
NO. IT'S WHAT I CHOSE FOR MYSELF AFTER MY PARENTS WERE KILLED.

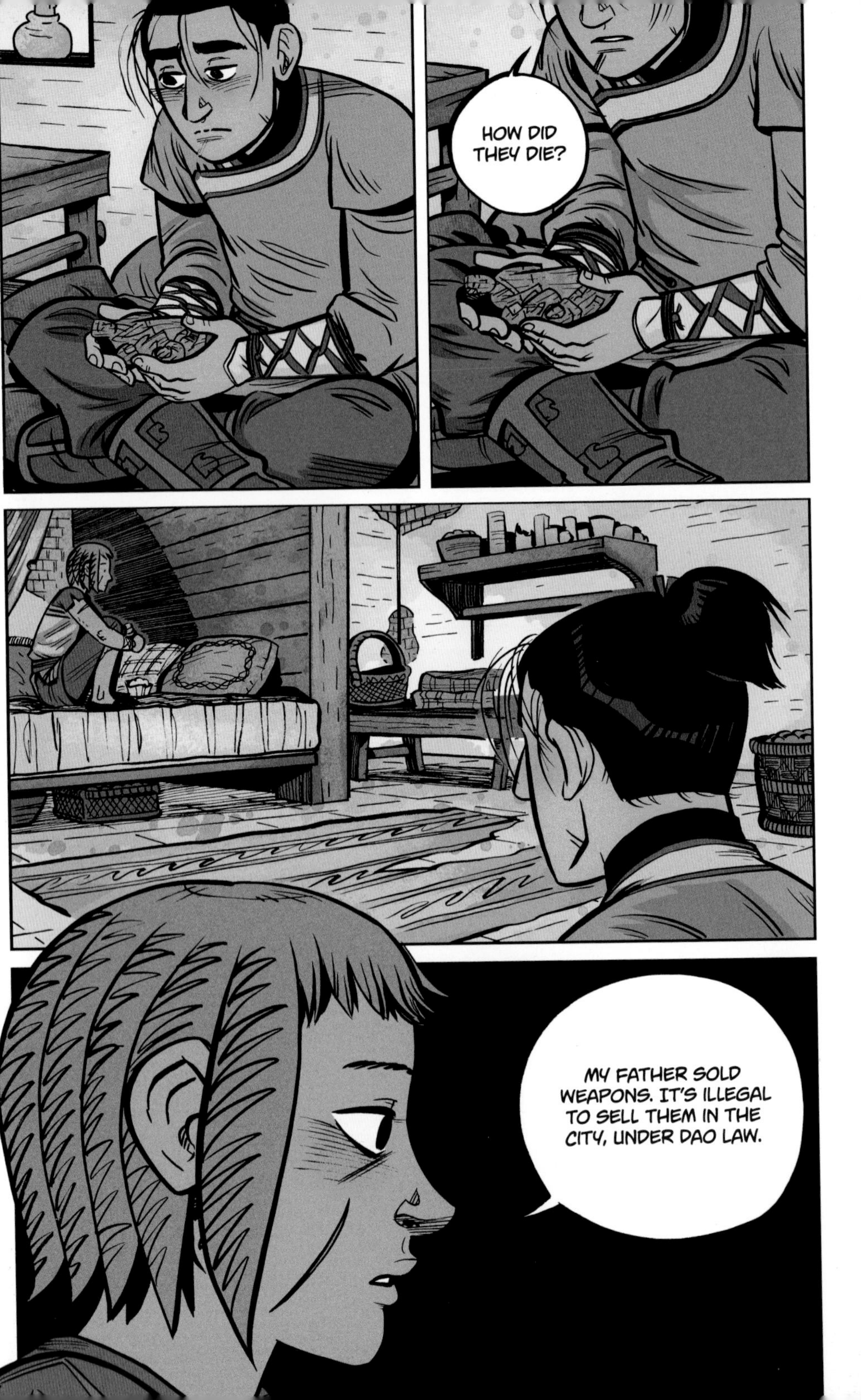
HOW DID THEY DIE?
MY FATHER SOLD WEAPONS. IT'S ILLEGAL TO SELL THEM IN THE CITY, UNDER DAO LAW.

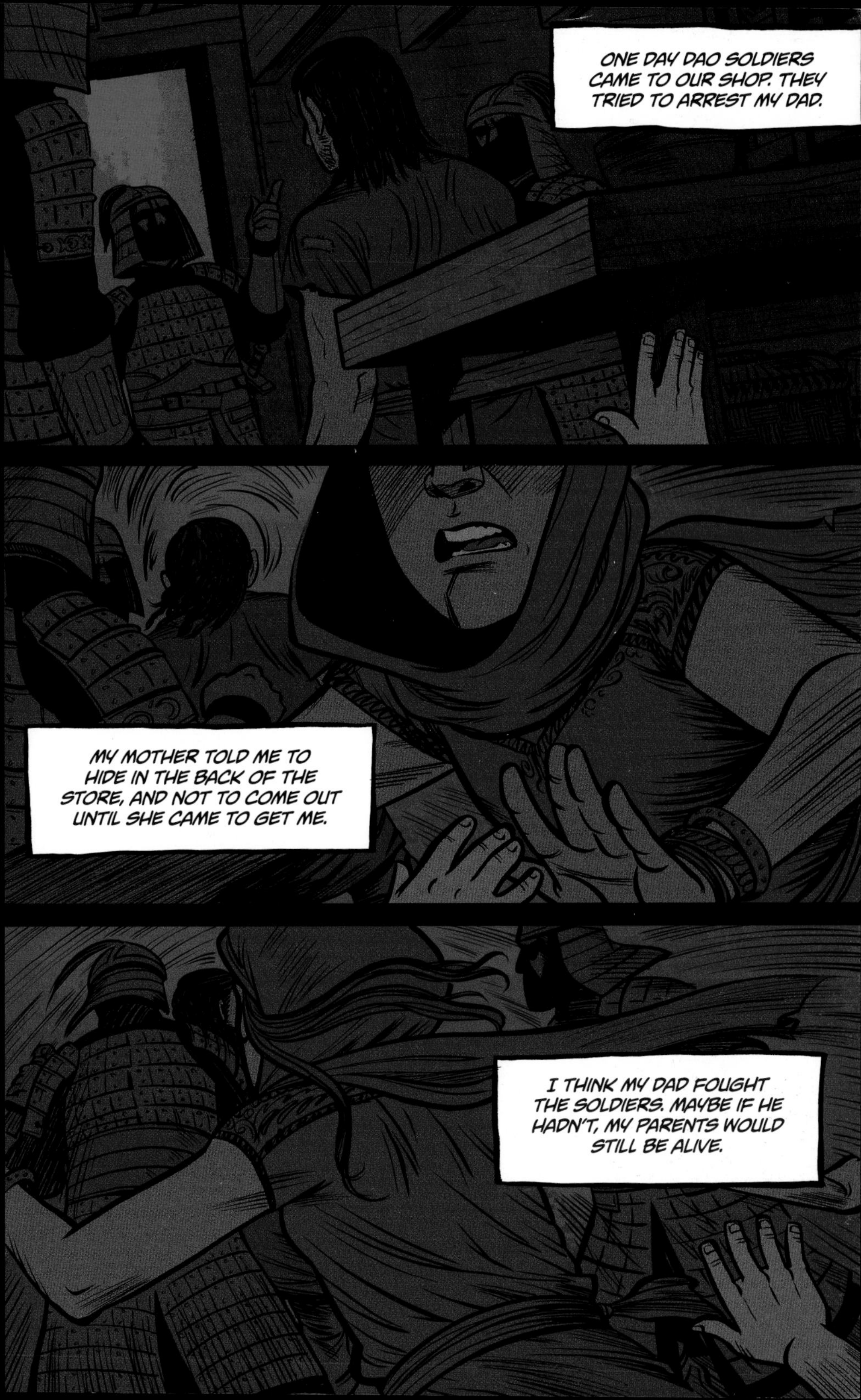
ONE DAY DAO SOLDIERS CAME TO OUR SHOP. THEY TRIED TO ARREST MY DAD.
MY MOTHER TOLD ME TO HIDE IN THE BACK OF THE STORE, AND NOT TO COME OUT UNTIL SHE CAME TO GET ME.
I THINK MY DAD FOUGHT THE SOLDIERS. MAYBE IF HE HADN'T, MY PARENTS WOULD STILL BE ALIVE.

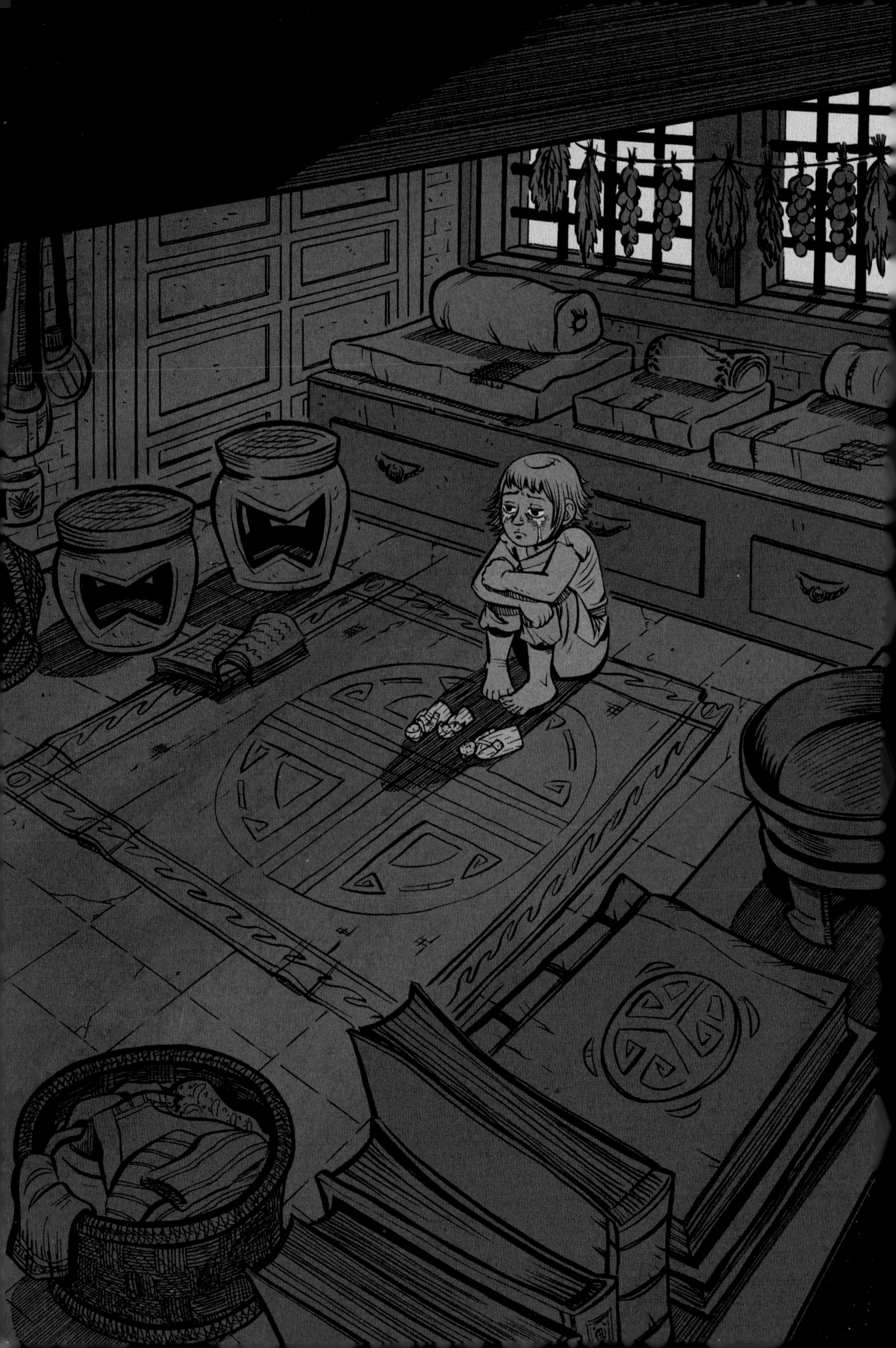

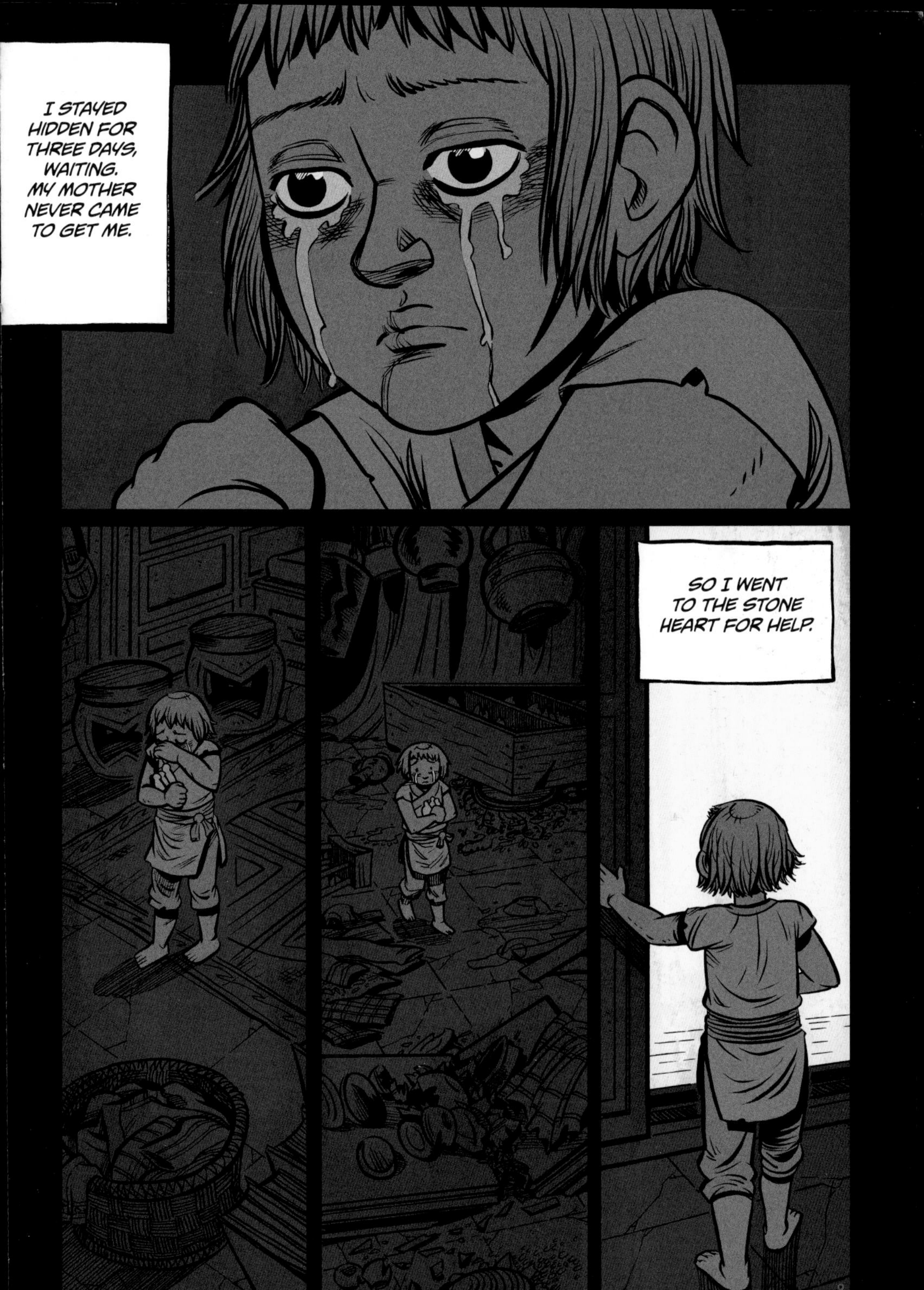
I STAYED HIDDEN FOR THREE DAYS, WAITING. MY MOTHER NEVER CAME TO GET ME.
SO I WENT TO THE STONE HEART FOR HELP.

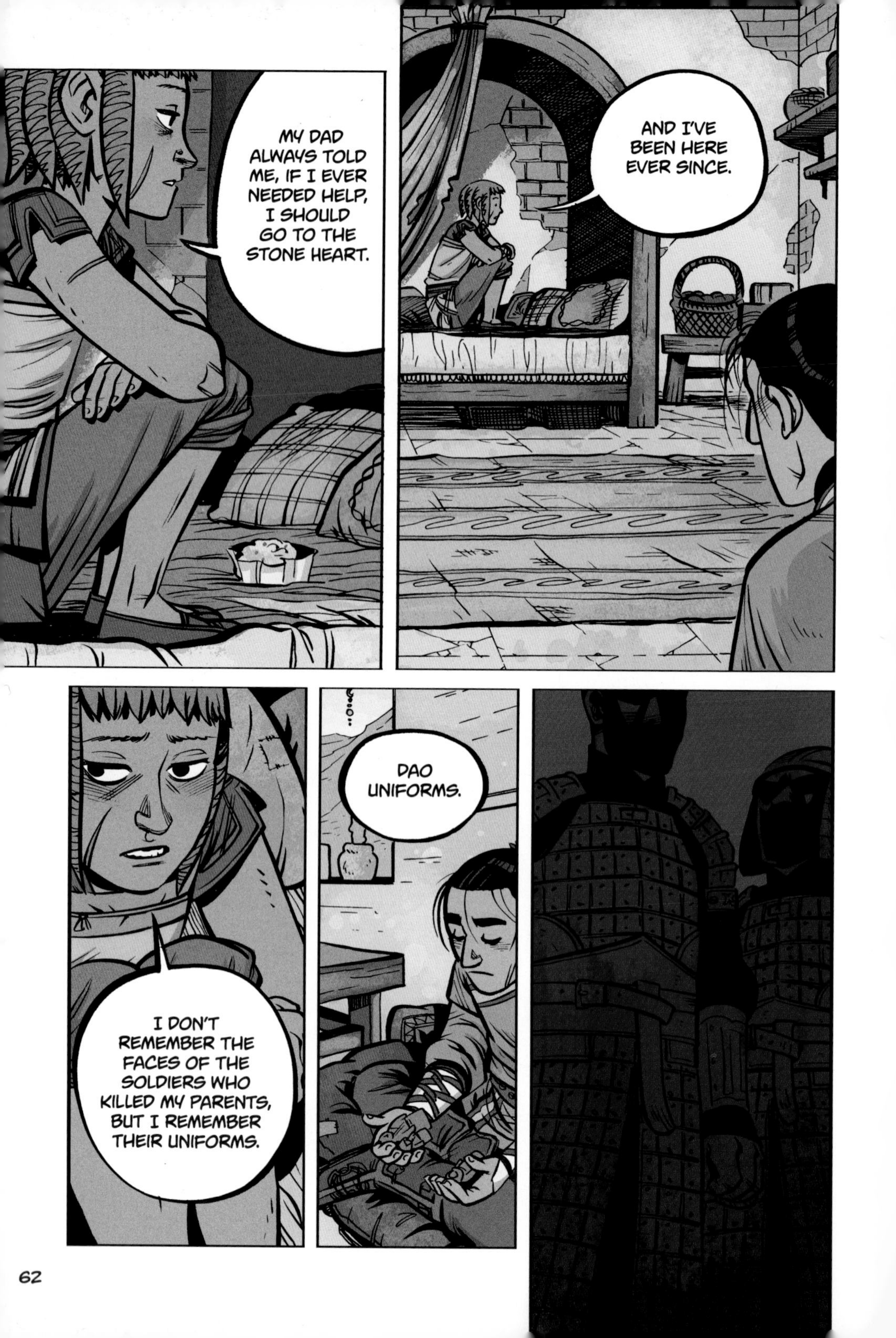
MY DAD ALWAYS TOLD ME, IF I EVER NEEDED HELP, I SHOULD GO TO THE STONE HEART.
AND I'VE BEEN HERE EVER SINCE.
I DON'T REMEMBER THE FACES OF THE SOLDIERS WHO KILLED MY PARENTS, BUT I REMEMBER THEIR UNIFORMS.
DAO UNIFORMS.

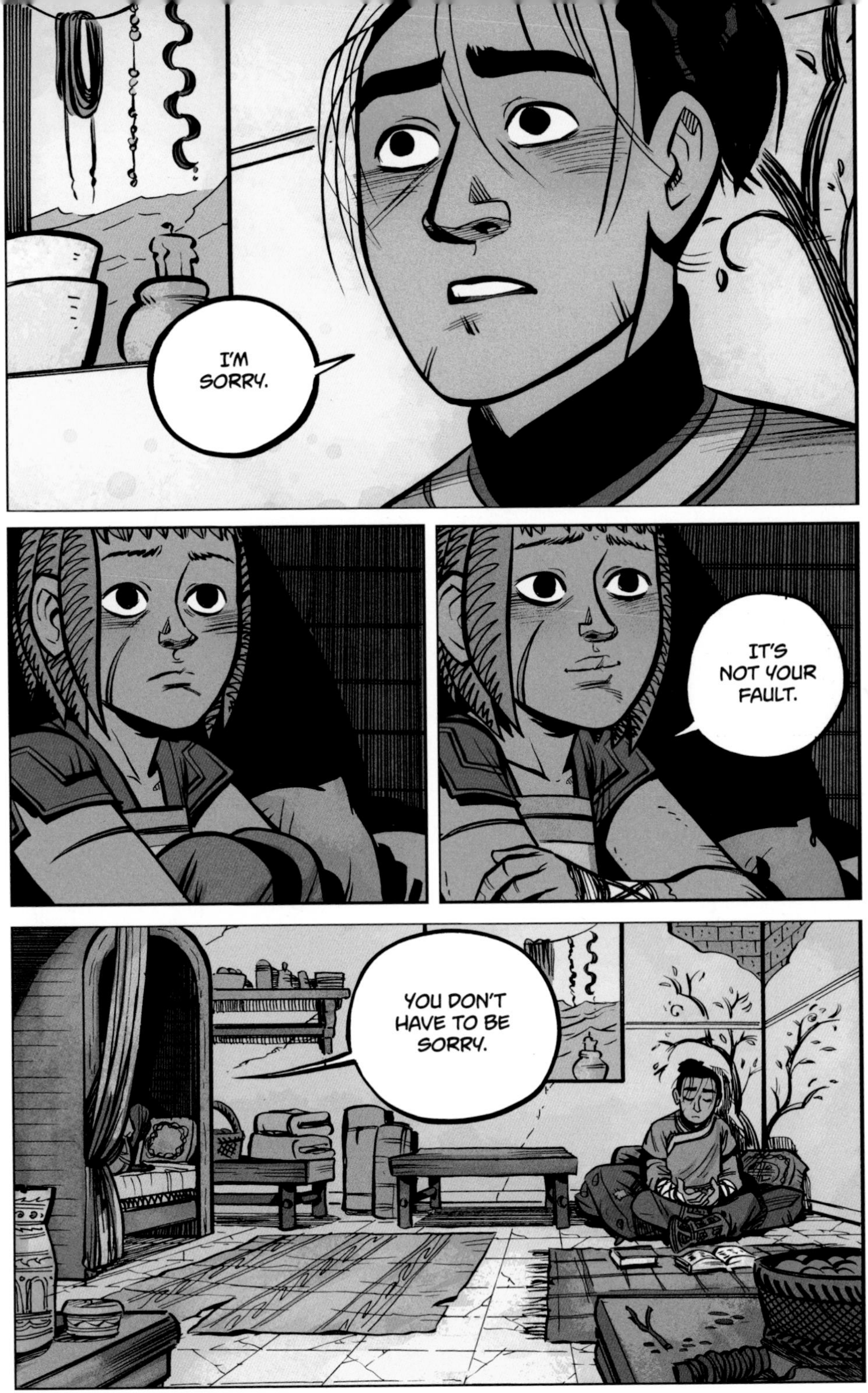
I'M SORRY.
IT'S NOT YOUR FAULT.
YOU DON'T HAVE TO BE SORRY.

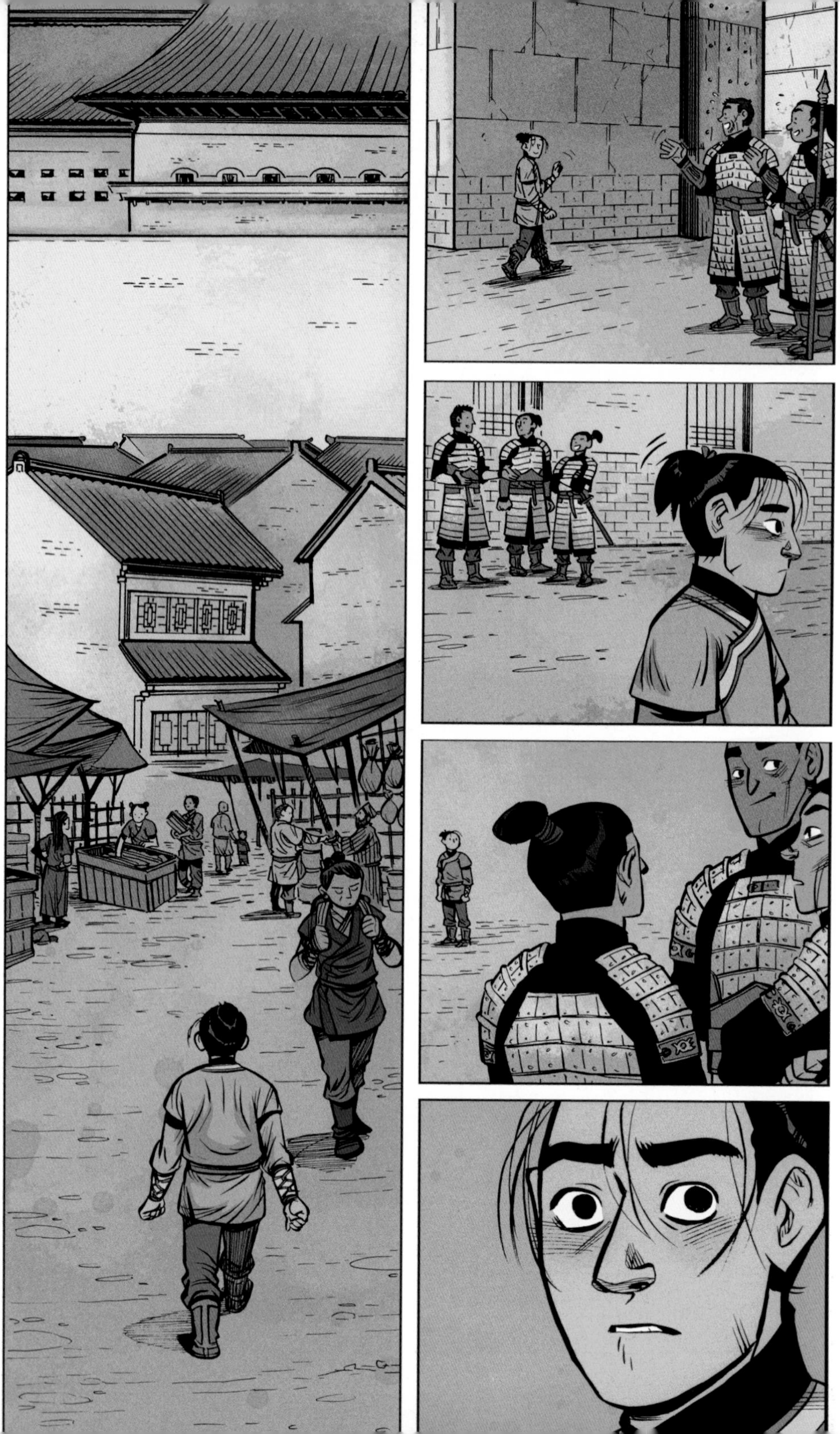

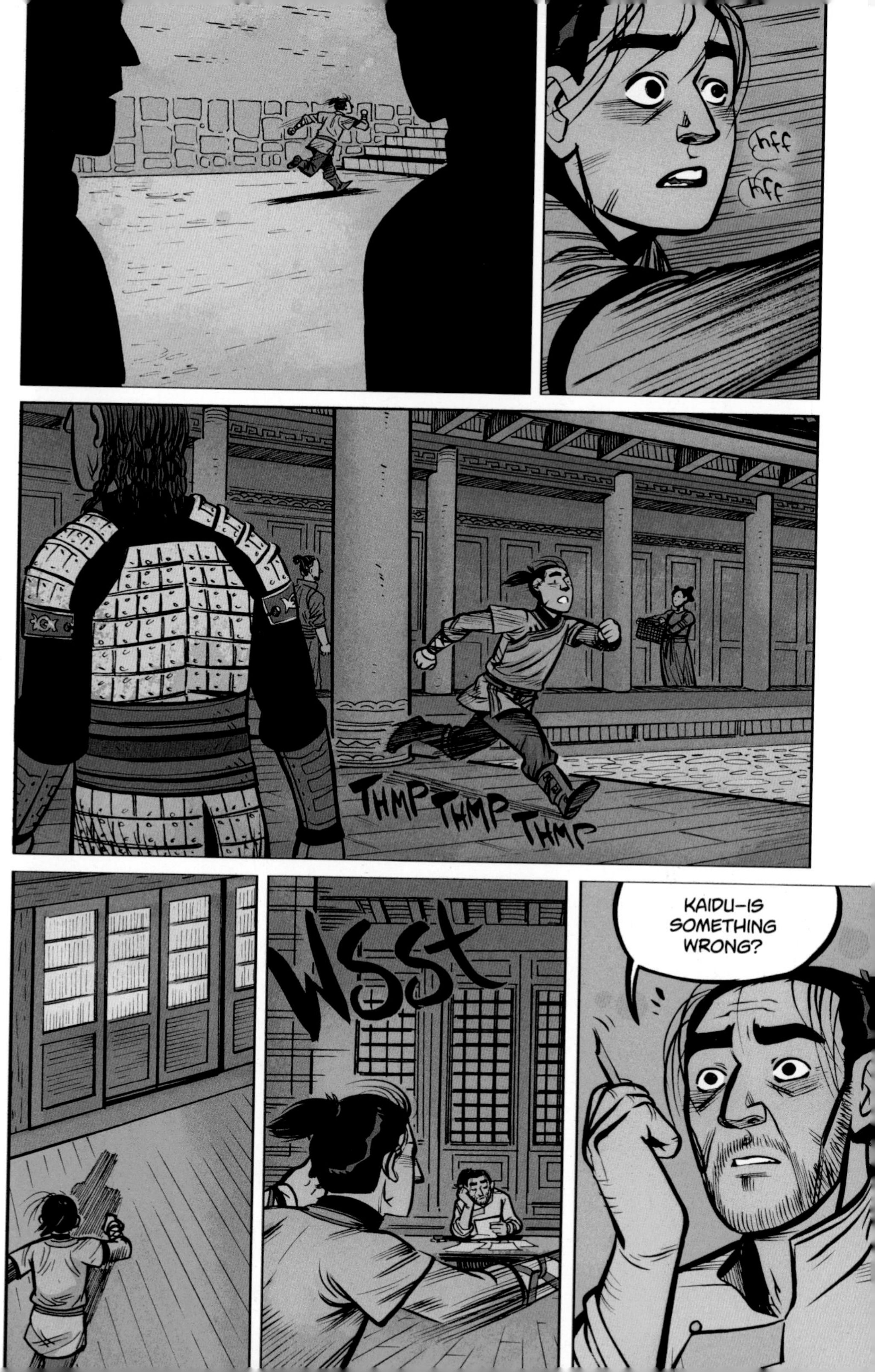
hff
hff
THMP THMP THMP
WSST
KAIDU—IS SOMETHING WRONG?

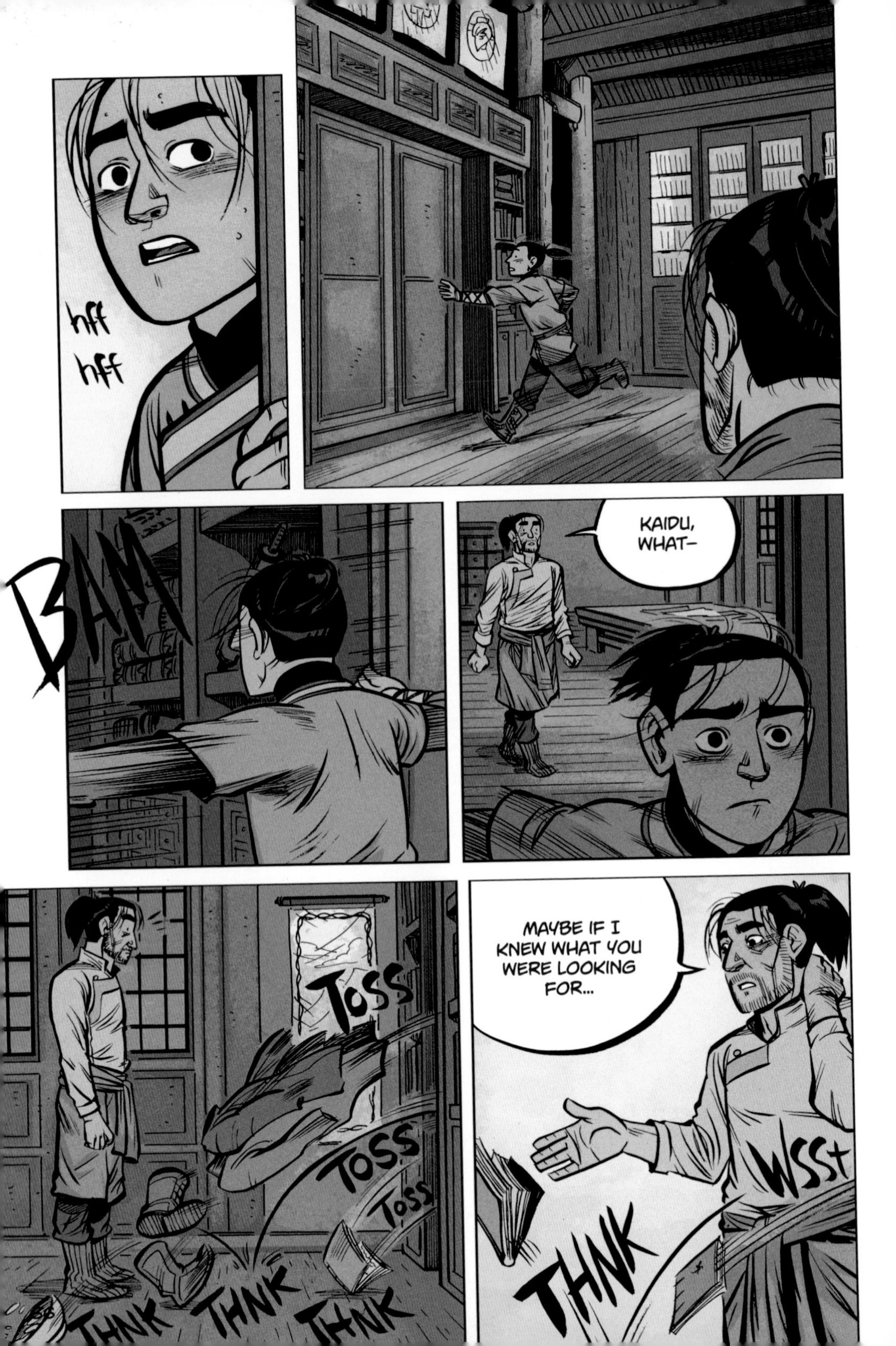
hff
hff
BAM
KAIDU, WHAT—
TOSS
TOSS
TOSS
THNK
THNK
THNK
MAYBE IF I KNEW WHAT YOU WERE LOOKING FOR...
WSSt
THNK

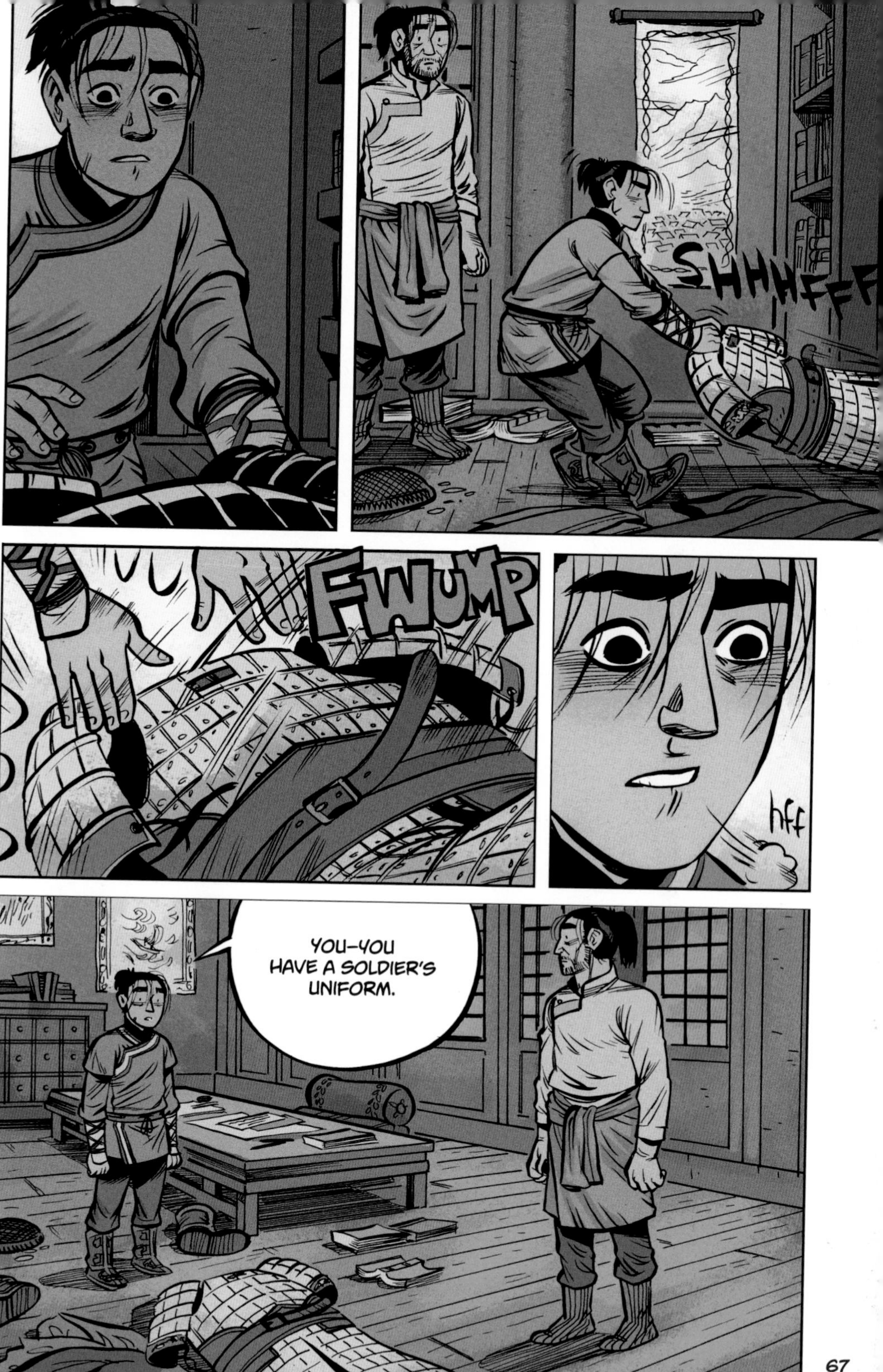
SHHHFFF
FWUMP
hff
YOU—YOU HAVE A SOLDIER'S UNIFORM.

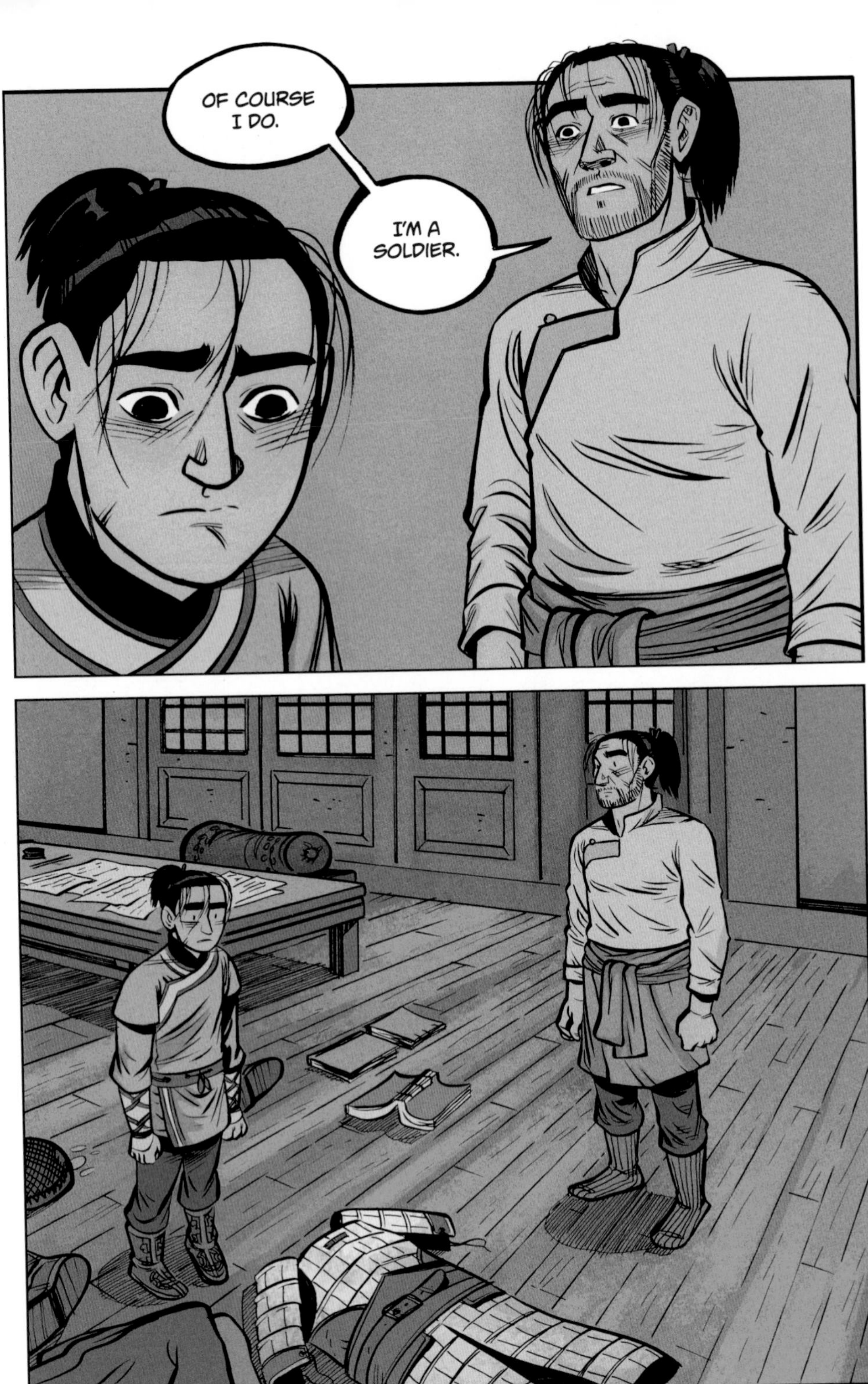
OF COURSE I DO.
I'M A SOLDIER.

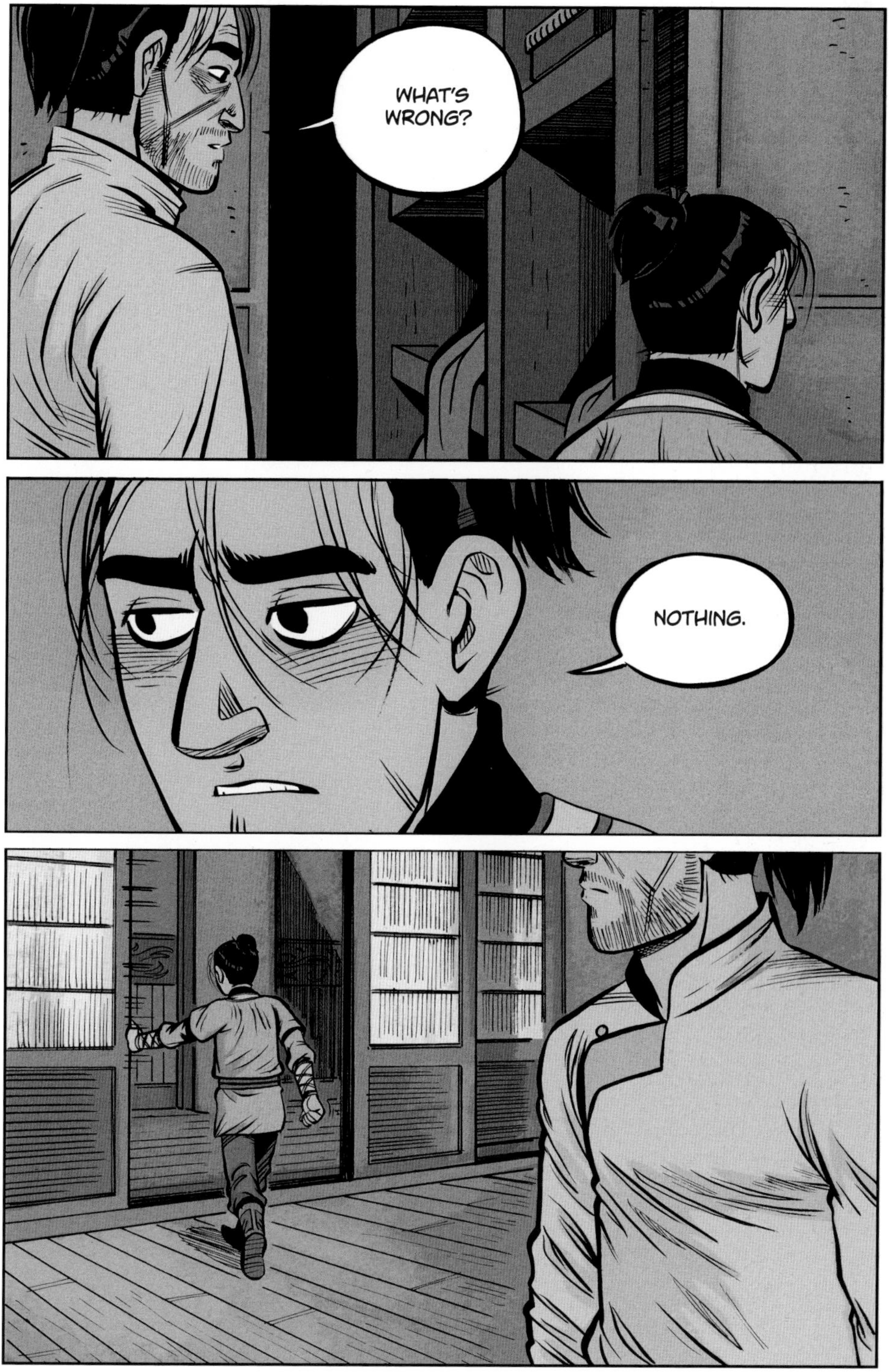
WHAT'S WRONG?
NOTHING.

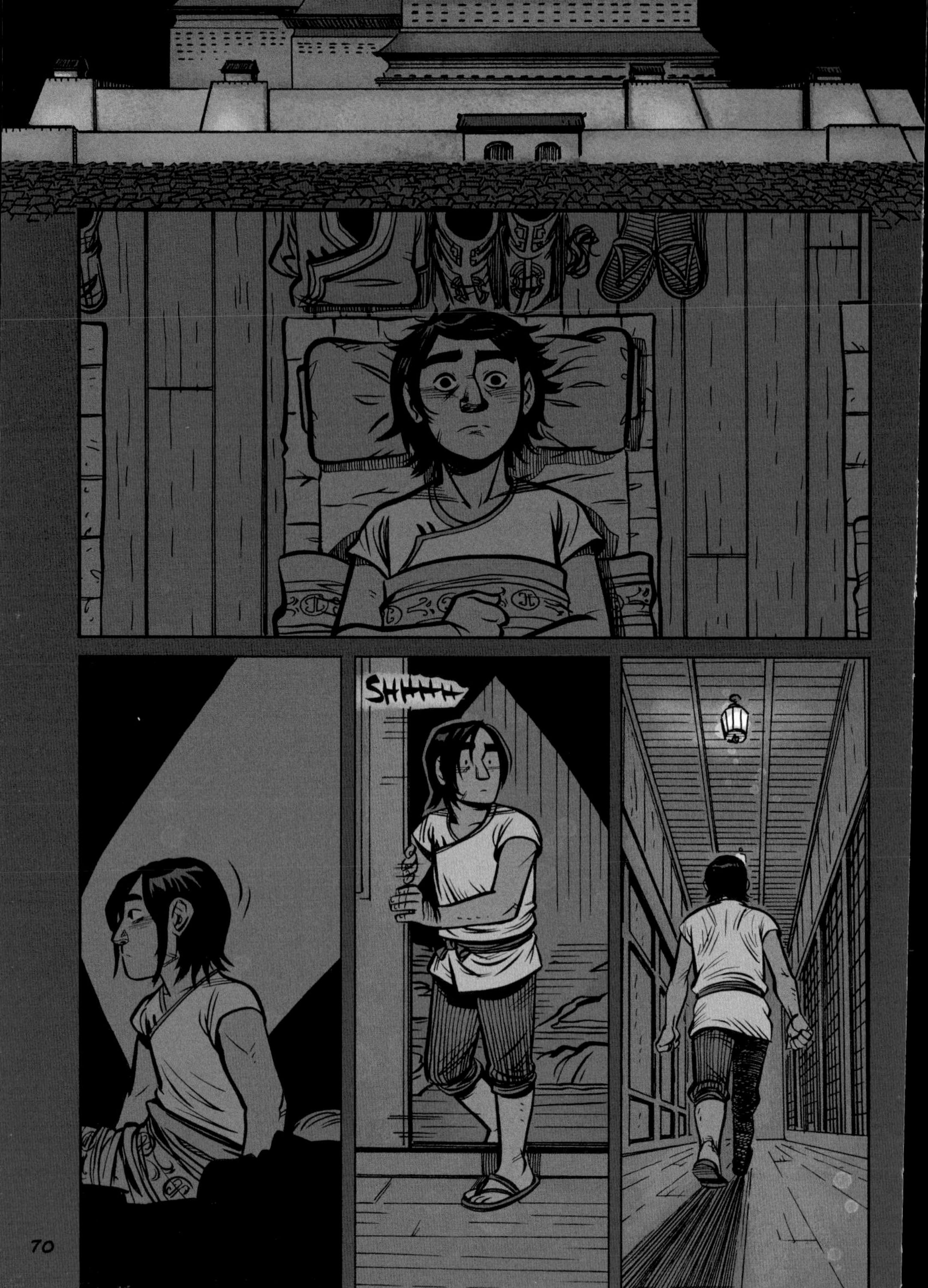
SHHHHH

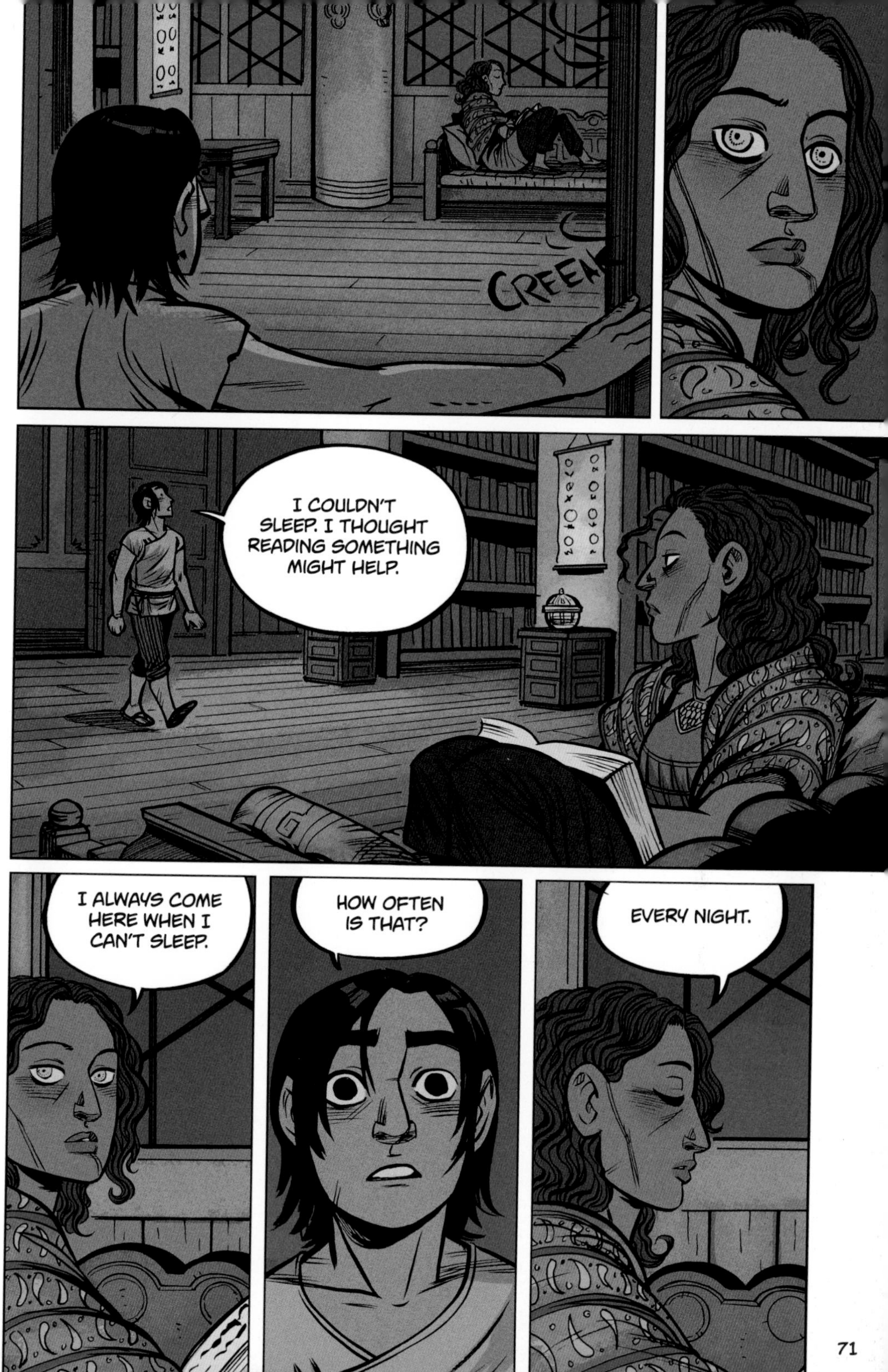
CREEAK
I COULDN'T SLEEP. I THOUGHT READING SOMETHING MIGHT HELP.
I ALWAYS COME HERE WHEN I CAN'T SLEEP.
HOW OFTEN IS THAT?
EVERY NIGHT.

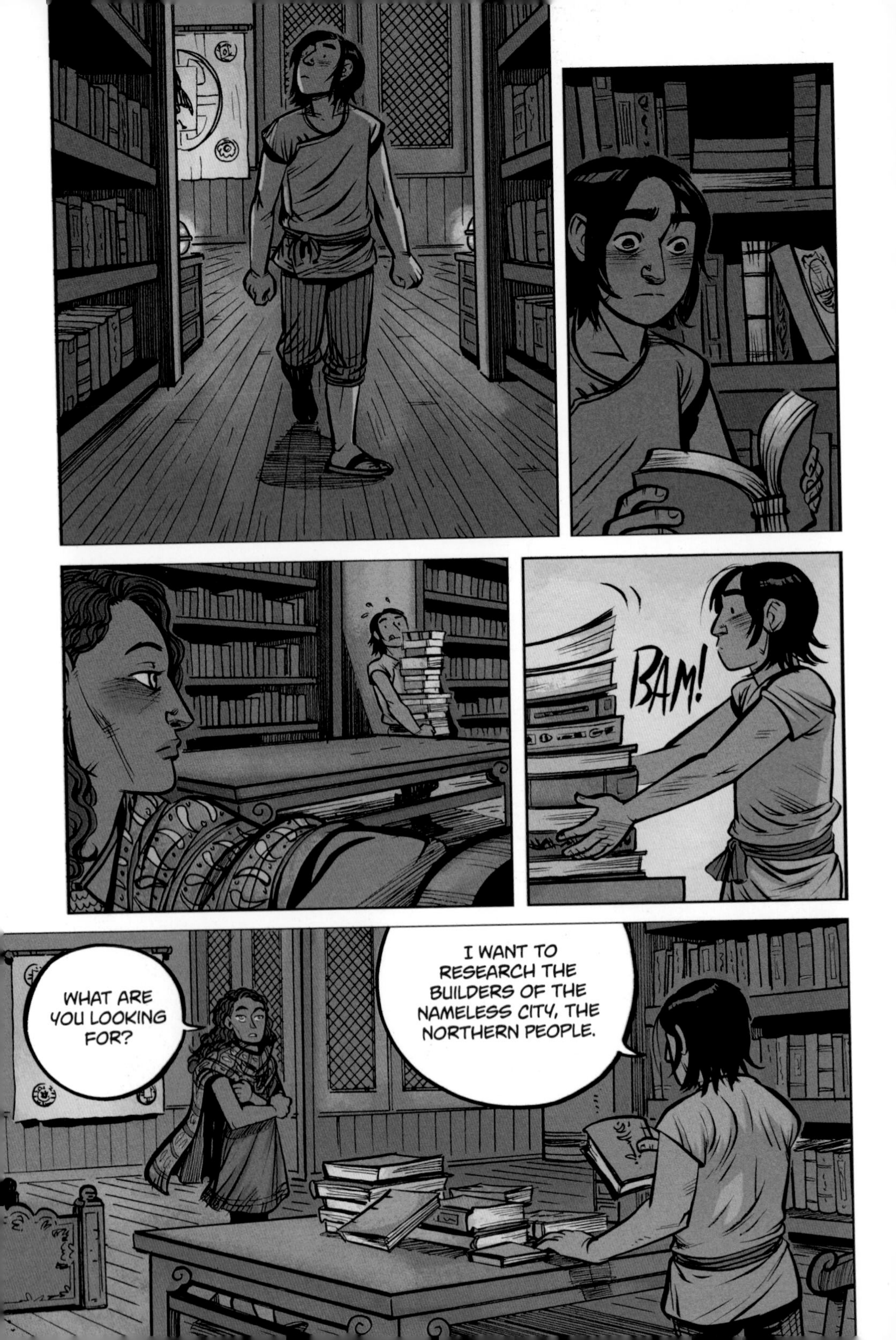
BAM!
WHAT ARE YOU LOOKING FOR?
I WANT TO RESEARCH THE BUILDERS OF THE NAMELESS CITY, THE NORTHERN PEOPLE.

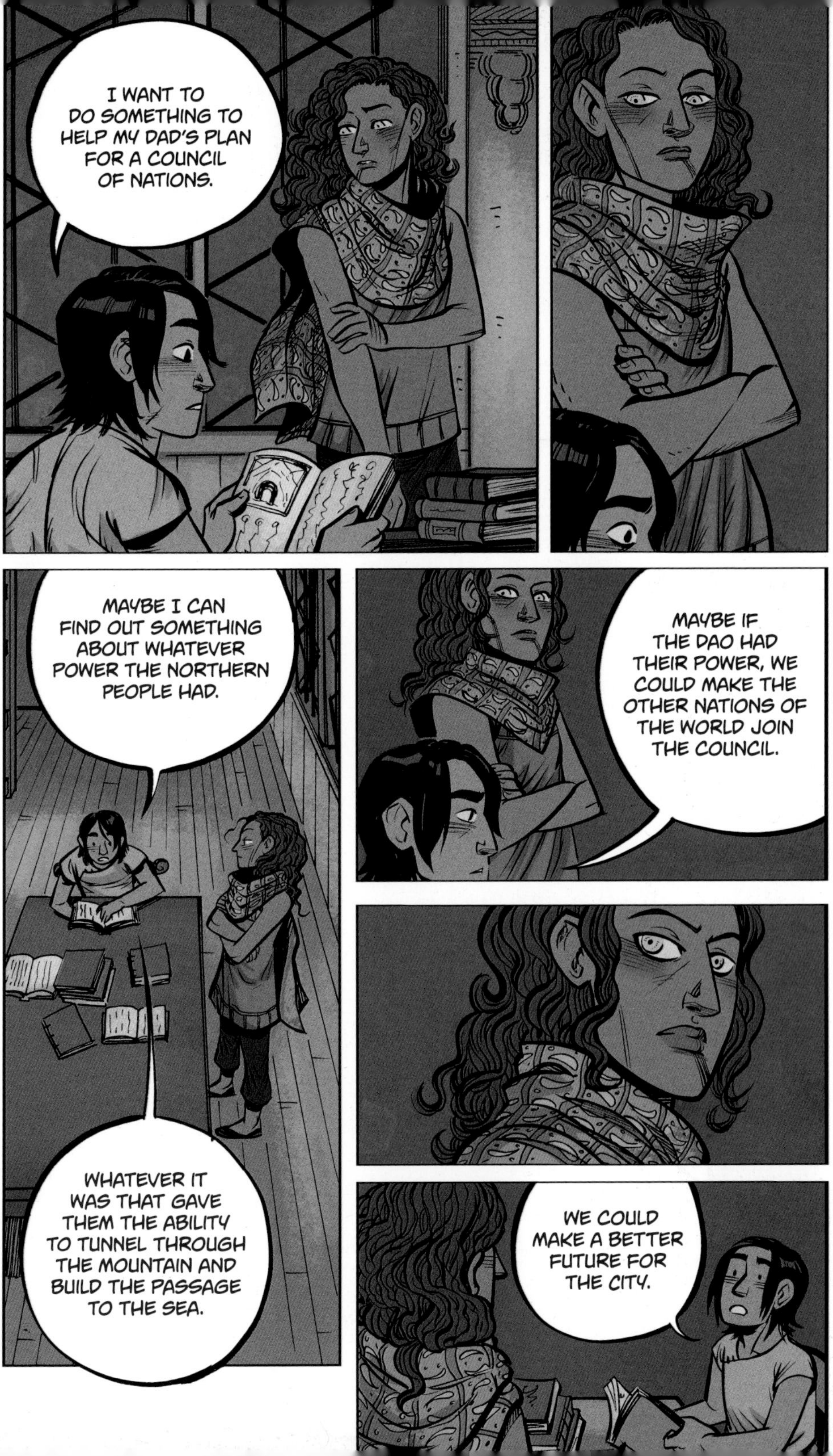
I WANT TO DO SOMETHING TO HELP MY DAD'S PLAN FOR A COUNCIL OF NATIONS.
MAYBE I CAN FIND OUT SOMETHING ABOUT WHATEVER POWER THE NORTHERN PEOPLE HAD.
WHATEVER IT WAS THAT GAVE THEM THE ABILITY TO TUNNEL THROUGH THE MOUNTAIN AND BUILD THE PASSAGE TO THE SEA.
MAYBE IF THE DAO HAD THEIR POWER, WE COULD MAKE THE OTHER NATIONS OF THE WORLD JOIN THE COUNCIL.
WE COULD MAKE A BETTER FUTURE FOR THE CITY.

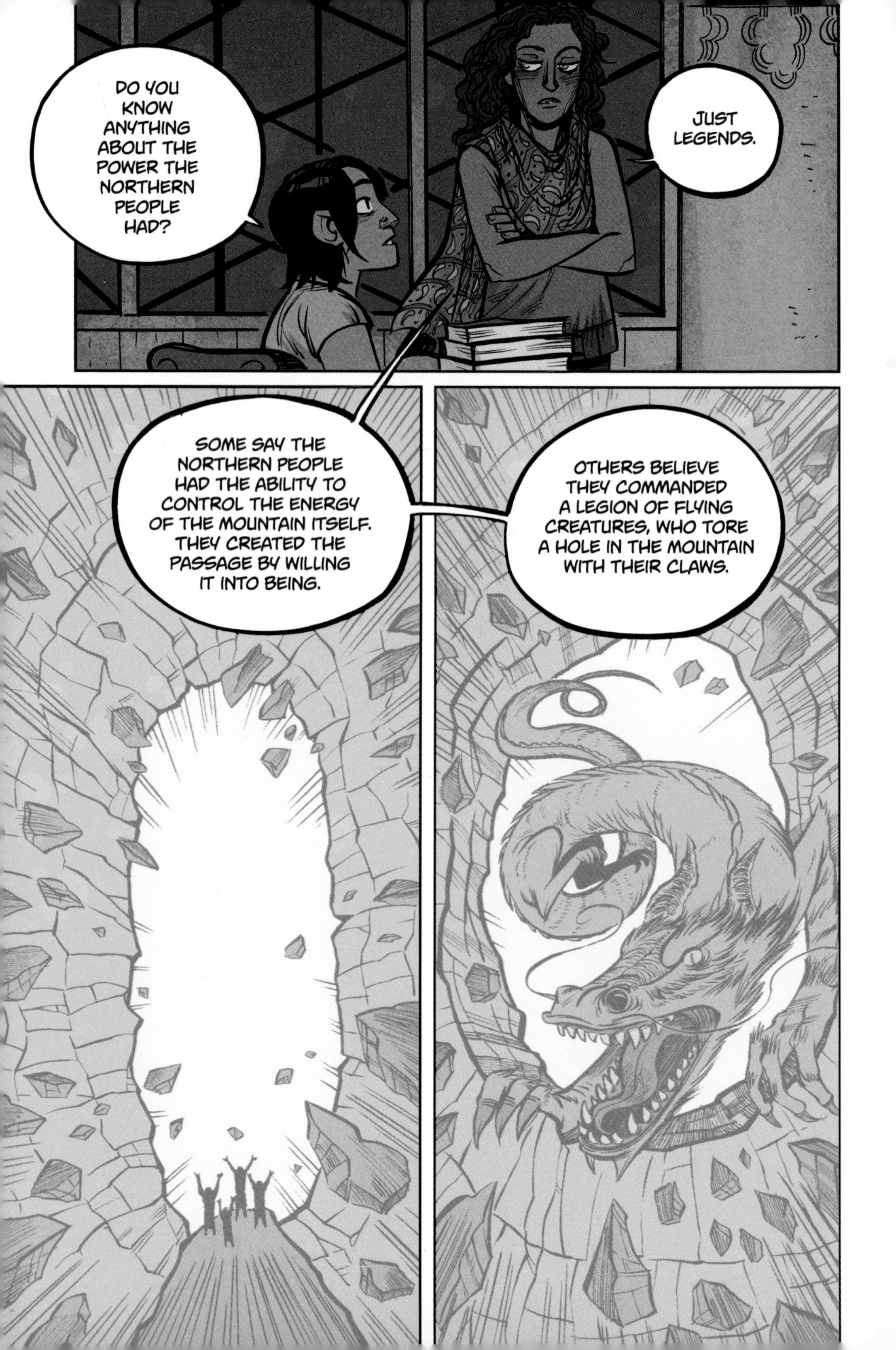
DO YOU KNOW ANYTHING ABOUT THE POWER THE NORTHERN PEOPLE HAD?
JUST LEGENDS.
SOME SAY THE NORTHERN PEOPLE HAD THE ABILITY TO CONTROL THE ENERGY OF THE MOUNTAIN ITSELF. THEY CREATED THE PASSAGE BY WILLING IT INTO BEING.
OTHERS BELIEVE THEY COMMANDED A LEGION OF FLYING CREATURES, WHO TORE A HOLE IN THE MOUNTAIN WITH THEIR CLAWS.

WHAT DO YOU BELIEVE THEIR POWER WAS?

FIRE AND DESTRUCTION.

I BELIEVE THE NORTHERN PEOPLE HAD A FORMULA THAT COULD SUMMON A TERRIBLE FIRE. A FIRE SO POWERFUL IT COULD BURN THROUGH STONE AND FLESH.

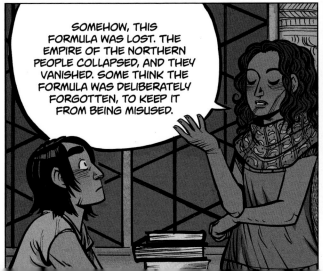

SOMEHOW, THIS FORMULA WAS LOST. THE EMPIRE OF THE NORTHERN PEOPLE COLLAPSED, AND THEY VANISHED. SOME THINK THE FORMULA WAS DELIBERATELY FORGOTTEN, TO KEEP IT FROM BEING MISUSED.

...HUH.

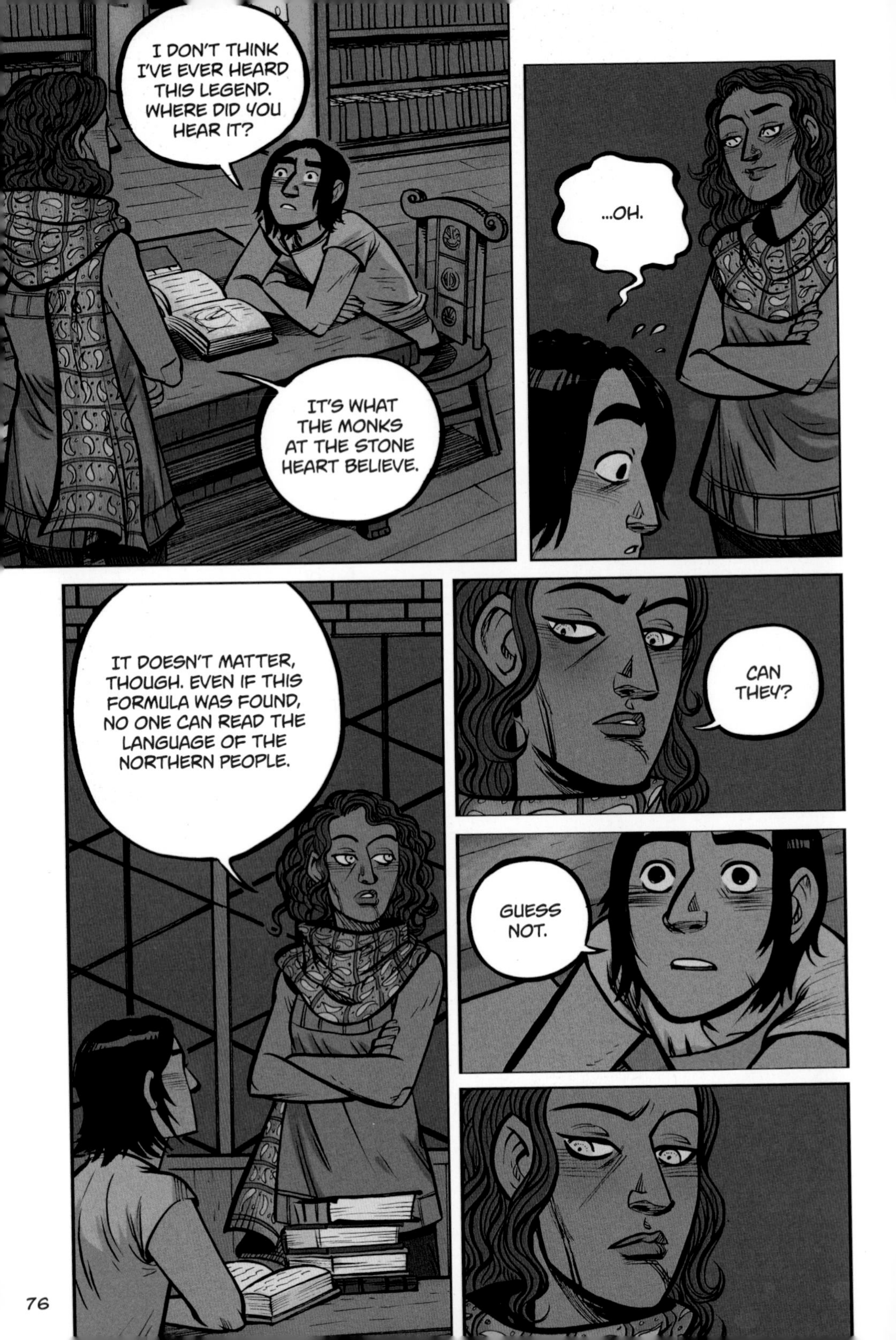

I DON'T THINK I'VE EVER HEARD THIS LEGEND. WHERE DID YOU HEAR IT?
IT'S WHAT THE MONKS AT THE STONE HEART BELIEVE.
...OH.
IT DOESN'T MATTER, THOUGH. EVEN IF THIS FORMULA WAS FOUND, NO ONE CAN READ THE LANGUAGE OF THE NORTHERN PEOPLE.
CAN THEY?
GUESS NOT.

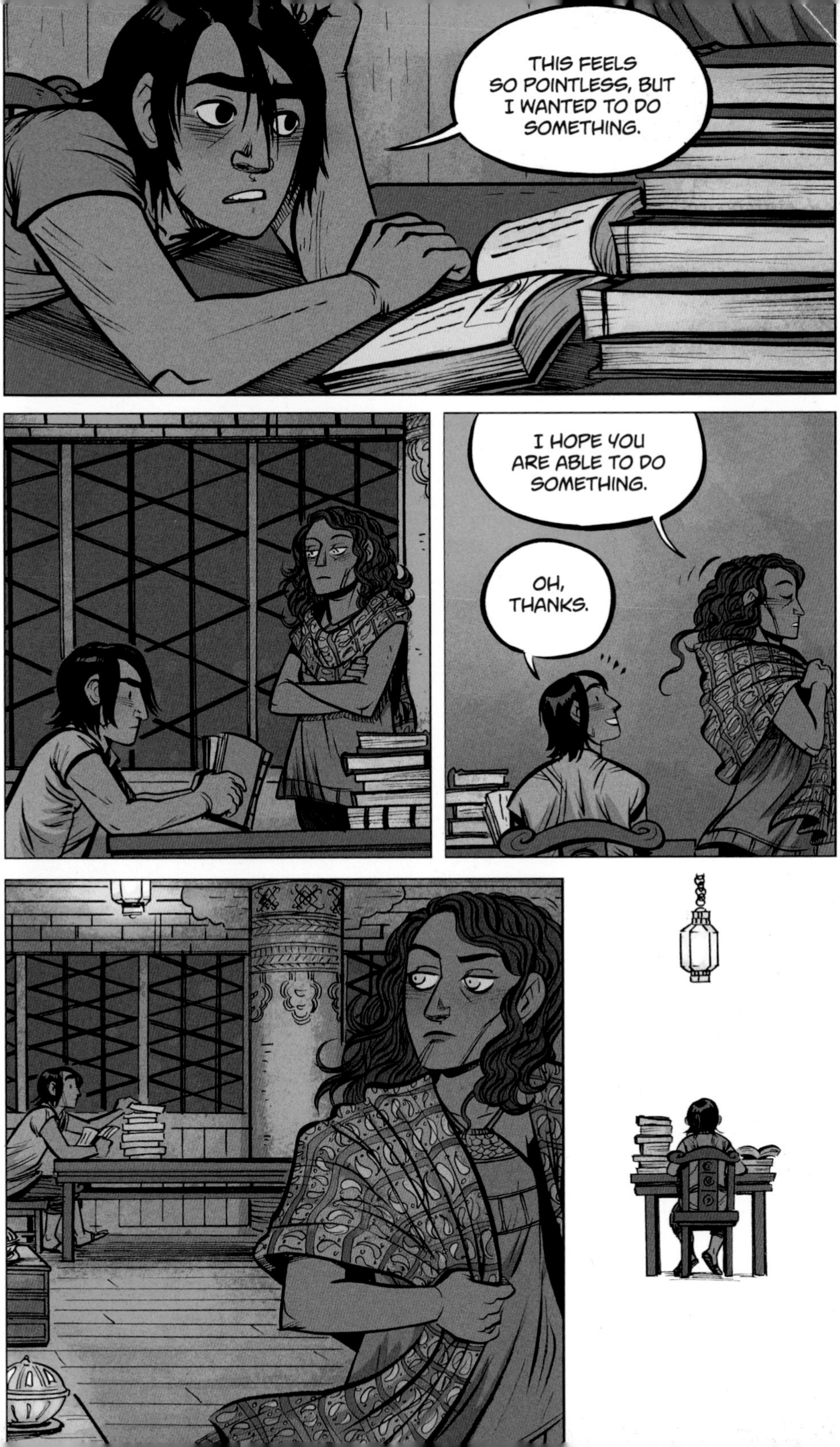
THIS FEELS SO POINTLESS, BUT I WANTED TO DO SOMETHING.
I HOPE YOU ARE ABLE TO DO SOMETHING.
OH, THANKS.

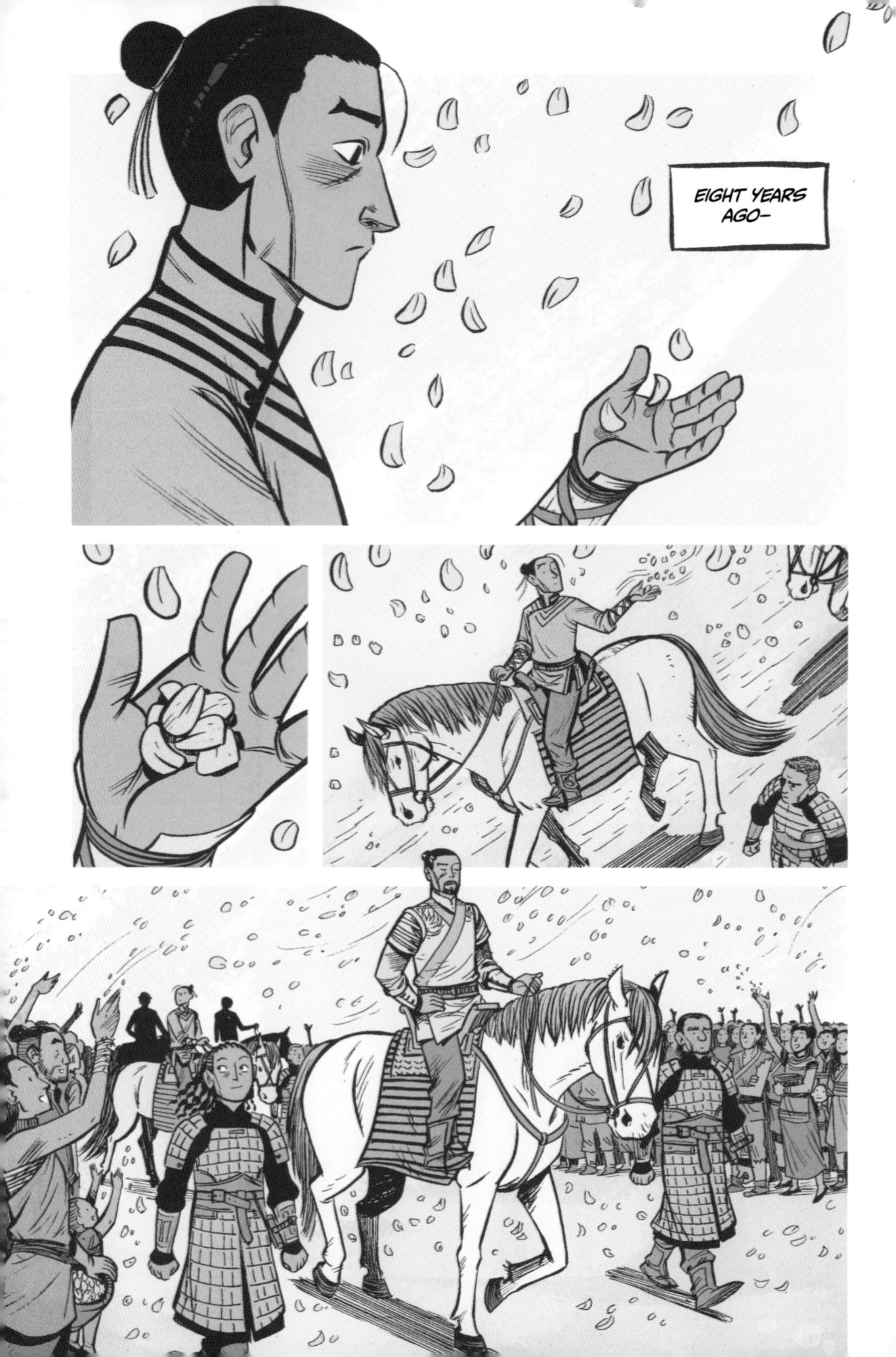
EIGHT YEARS AGO–

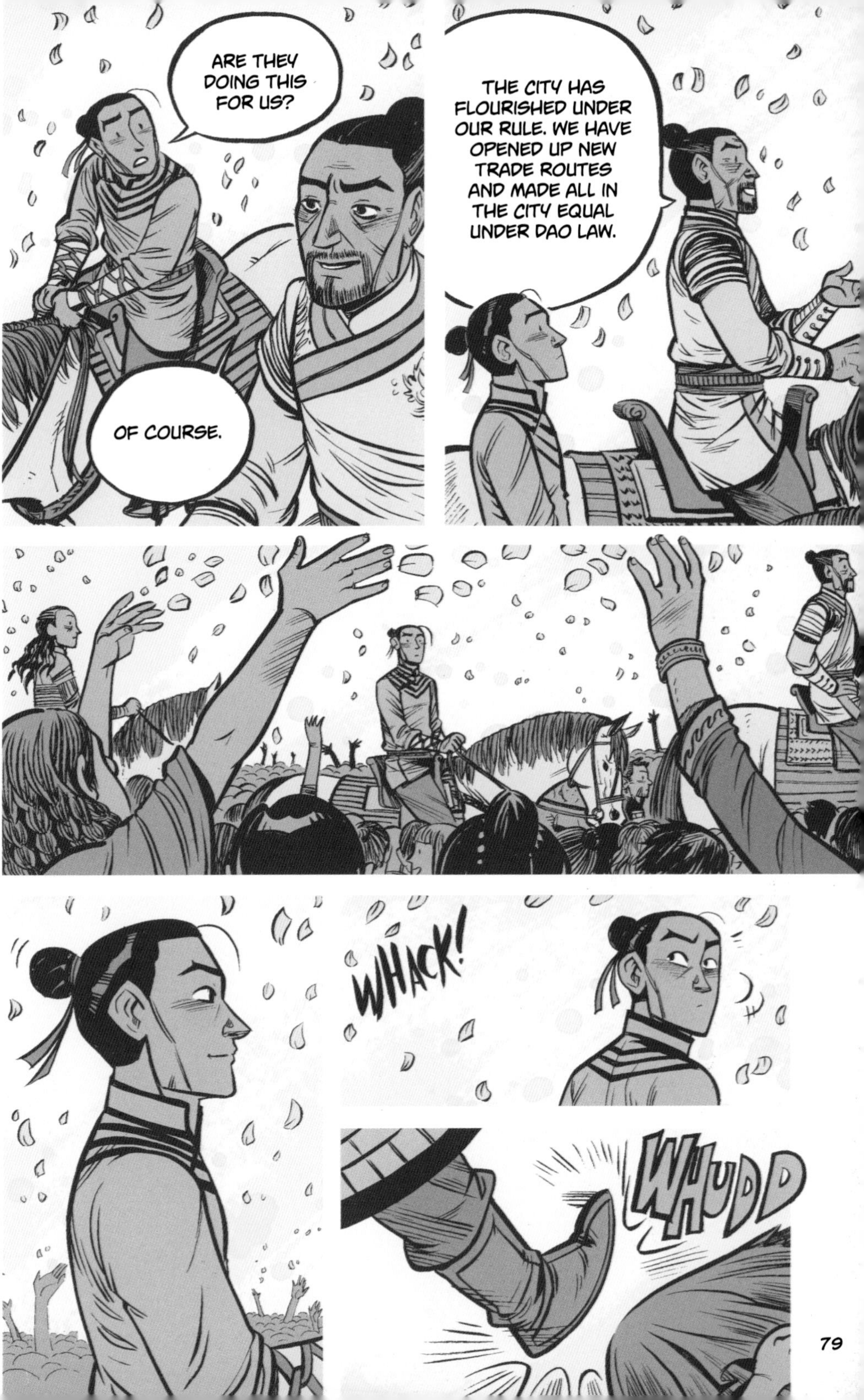
ARE THEY DOING THIS FOR US?
OF COURSE.
THE CITY HAS FLOURISHED UNDER OUR RULE. WE HAVE OPENED UP NEW TRADE ROUTES AND MADE ALL IN THE CITY EQUAL UNDER DAO LAW.
WHACK!
WHUDD

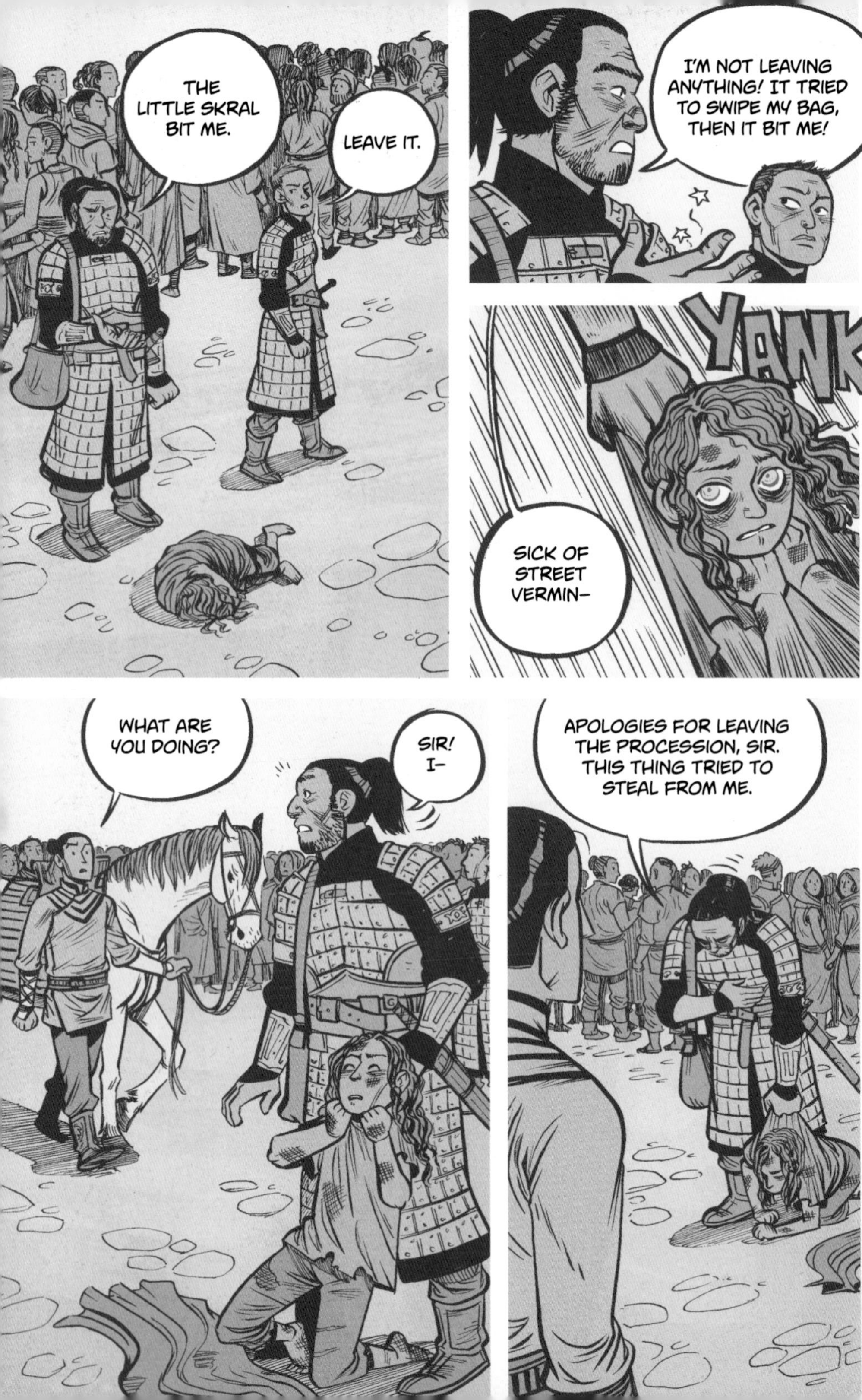
THE LITTLE SKRAL BIT ME.
LEAVE IT.
I'M NOT LEAVING ANYTHING! IT TRIED TO SWIPE MY BAG, THEN IT BIT ME!
YANK
SICK OF STREET VERMIN–
WHAT ARE YOU DOING?
SIR! I–
APOLOGIES FOR LEAVING THE PROCESSION, SIR. THIS THING TRIED TO STEAL FROM ME.

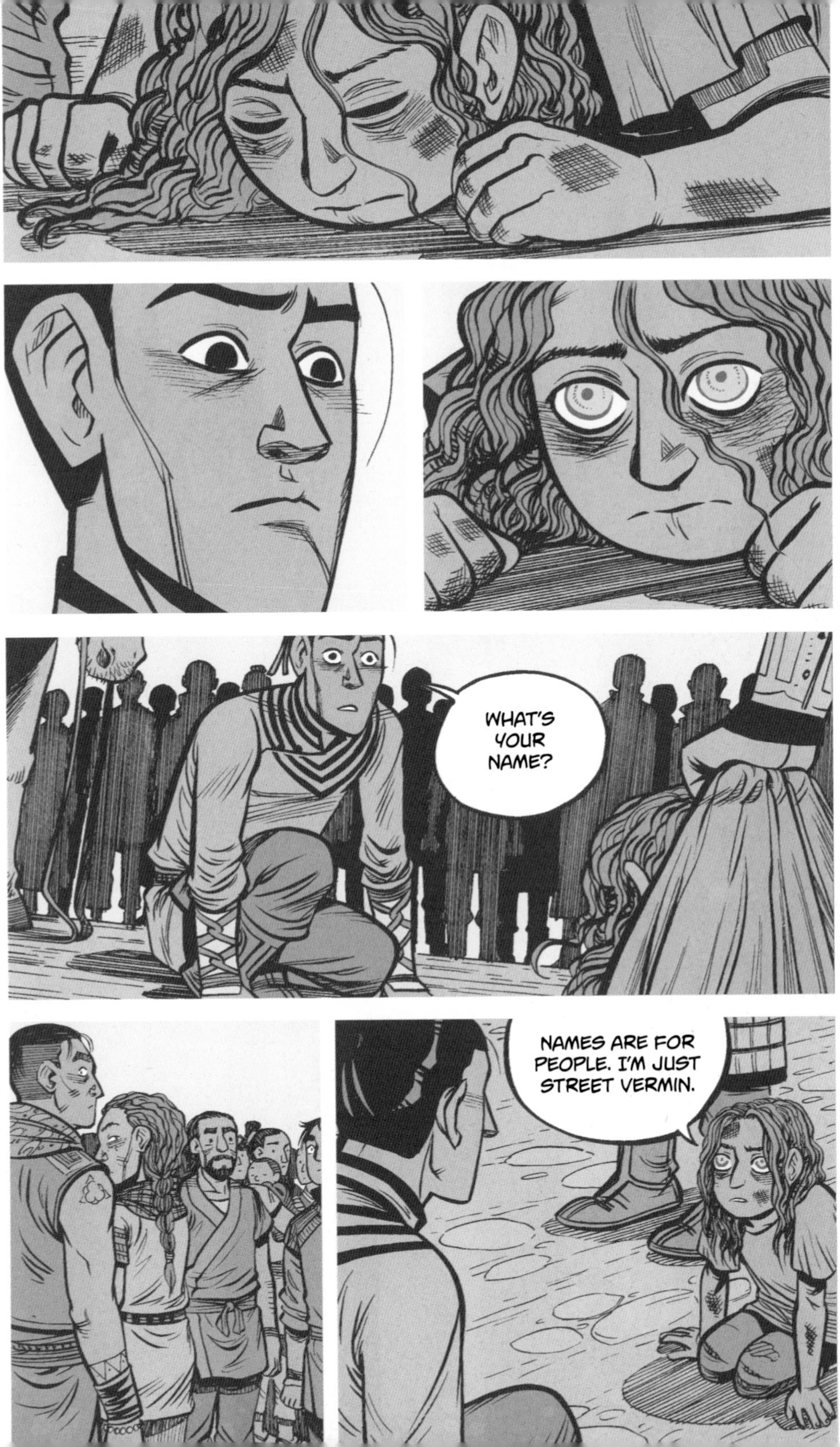
WHAT'S YOUR NAME?
NAMES ARE FOR PEOPLE. I'M JUST STREET VERMIN.

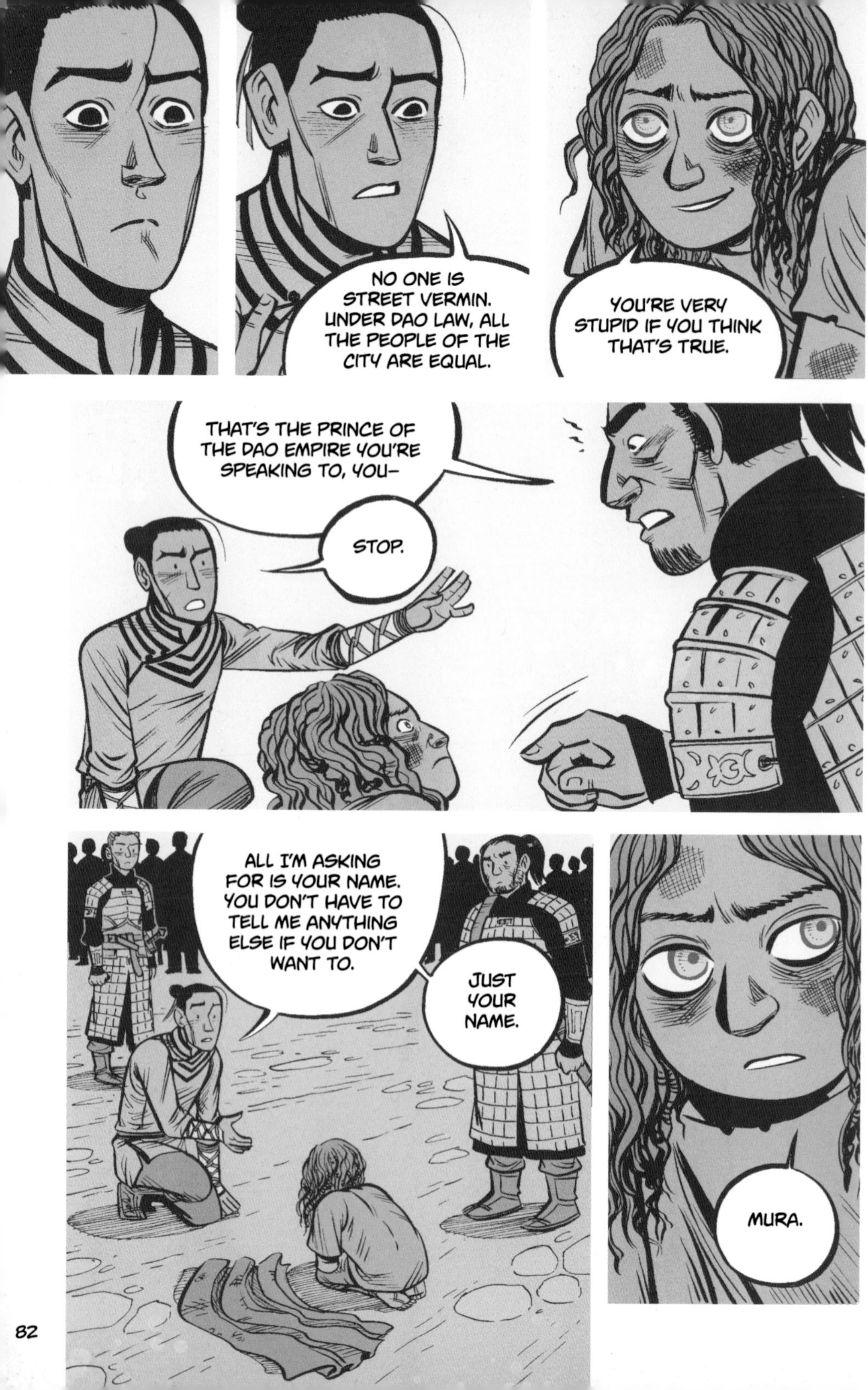
NO ONE IS STREET VERMIN. UNDER DAO LAW, ALL THE PEOPLE OF THE CITY ARE EQUAL.
YOU'RE VERY STUPID IF YOU THINK THAT'S TRUE.
THAT'S THE PRINCE OF THE DAO EMPIRE YOU'RE SPEAKING TO, YOU–
STOP.
ALL I'M ASKING FOR IS YOUR NAME. YOU DON'T HAVE TO TELL ME ANYTHING ELSE IF YOU DON'T WANT TO.
JUST YOUR NAME.
MURA.

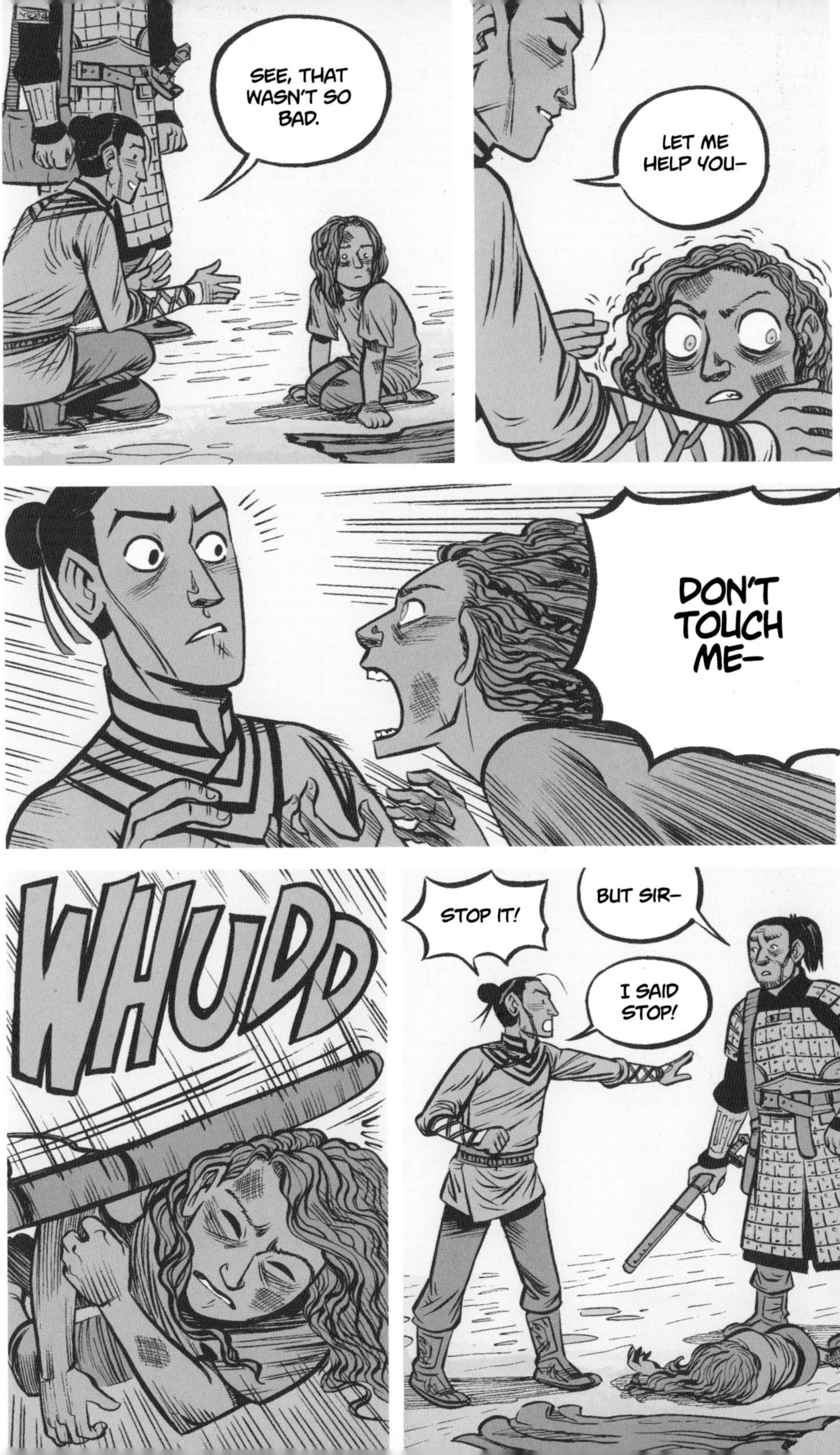
SEE, THAT WASN'T SO BAD.
LET ME HELP YOU–
DON'T TOUCH ME–
WHUDD
STOP IT!
BUT SIR–
I SAID STOP!

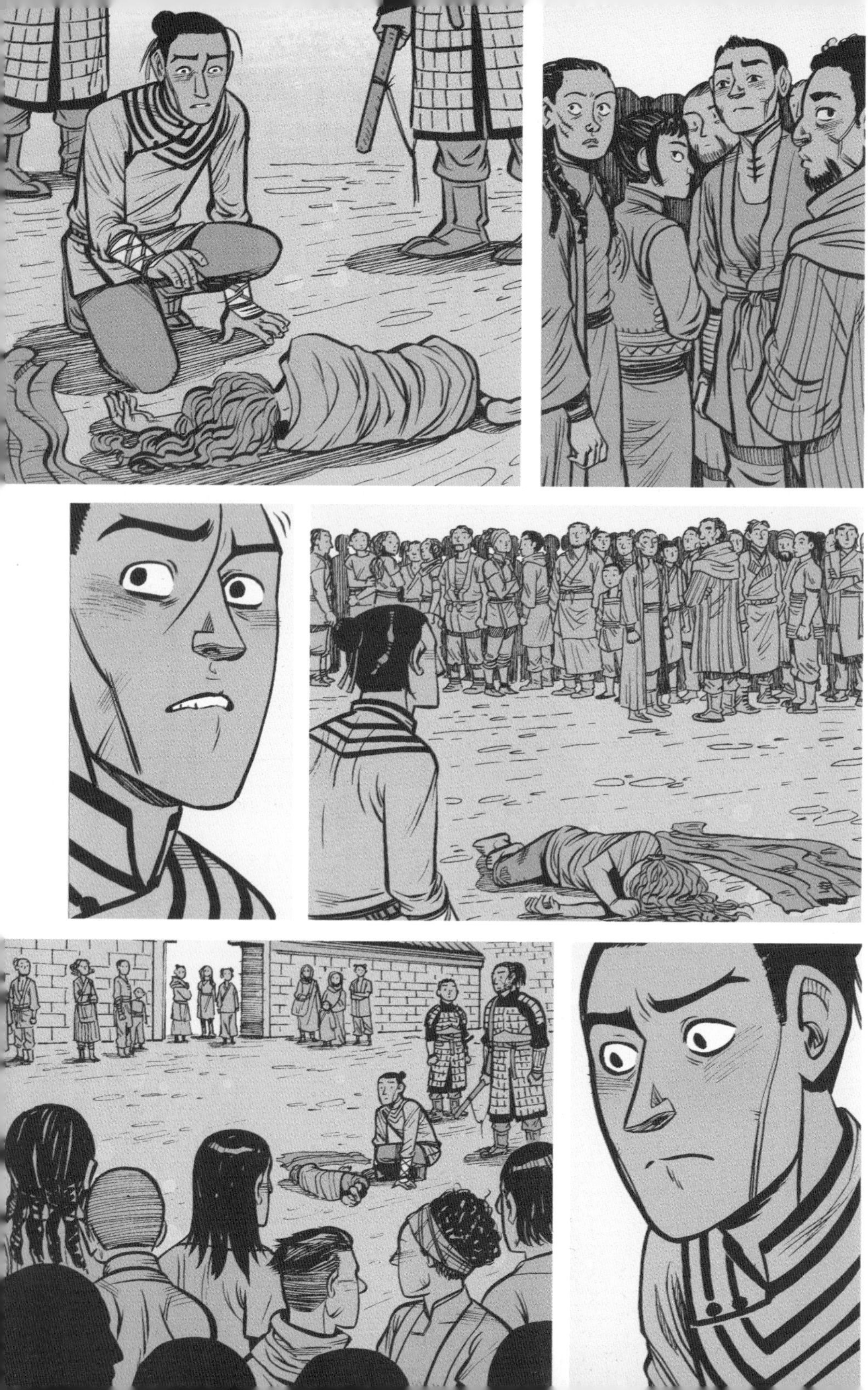

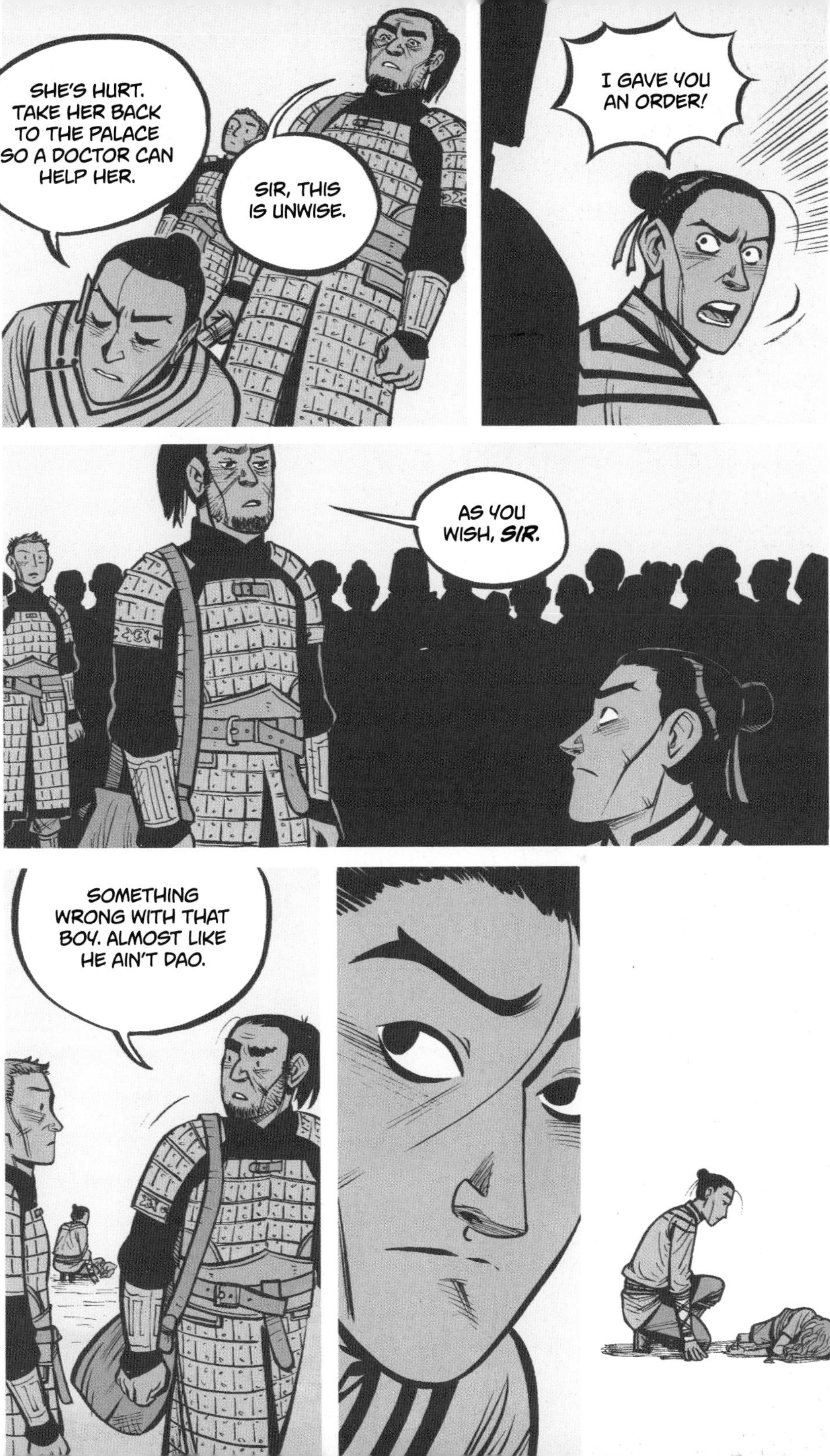
SHE'S HURT. TAKE HER BACK TO THE PALACE SO A DOCTOR CAN HELP HER.
SIR, THIS IS UNWISE.
I GAVE YOU AN ORDER!
AS YOU WISH, SIR.
SOMETHING WRONG WITH THAT BOY. ALMOST LIKE HE AIN'T DAO.

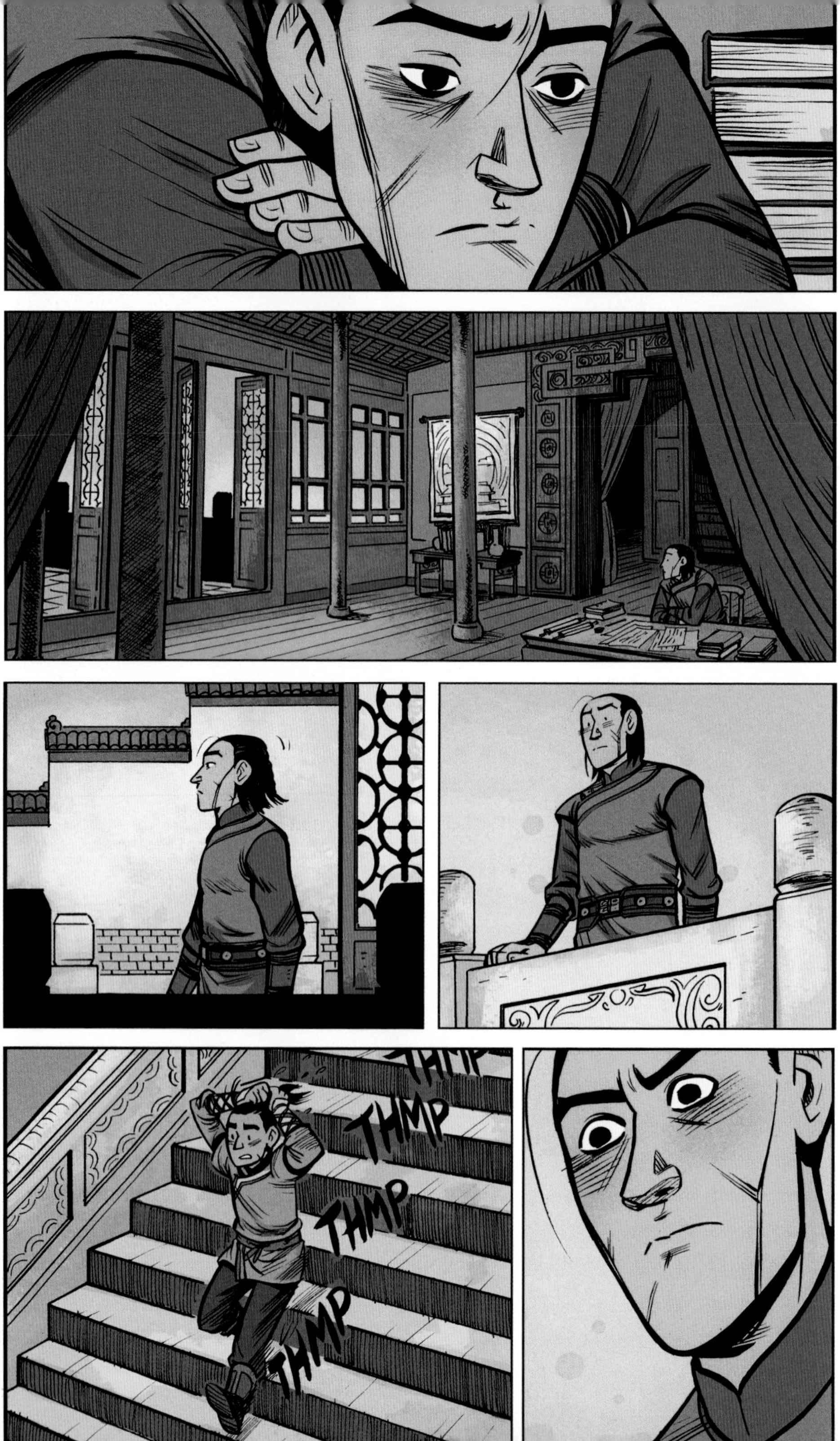
THMP
THMP
THMP
THMP
THMP

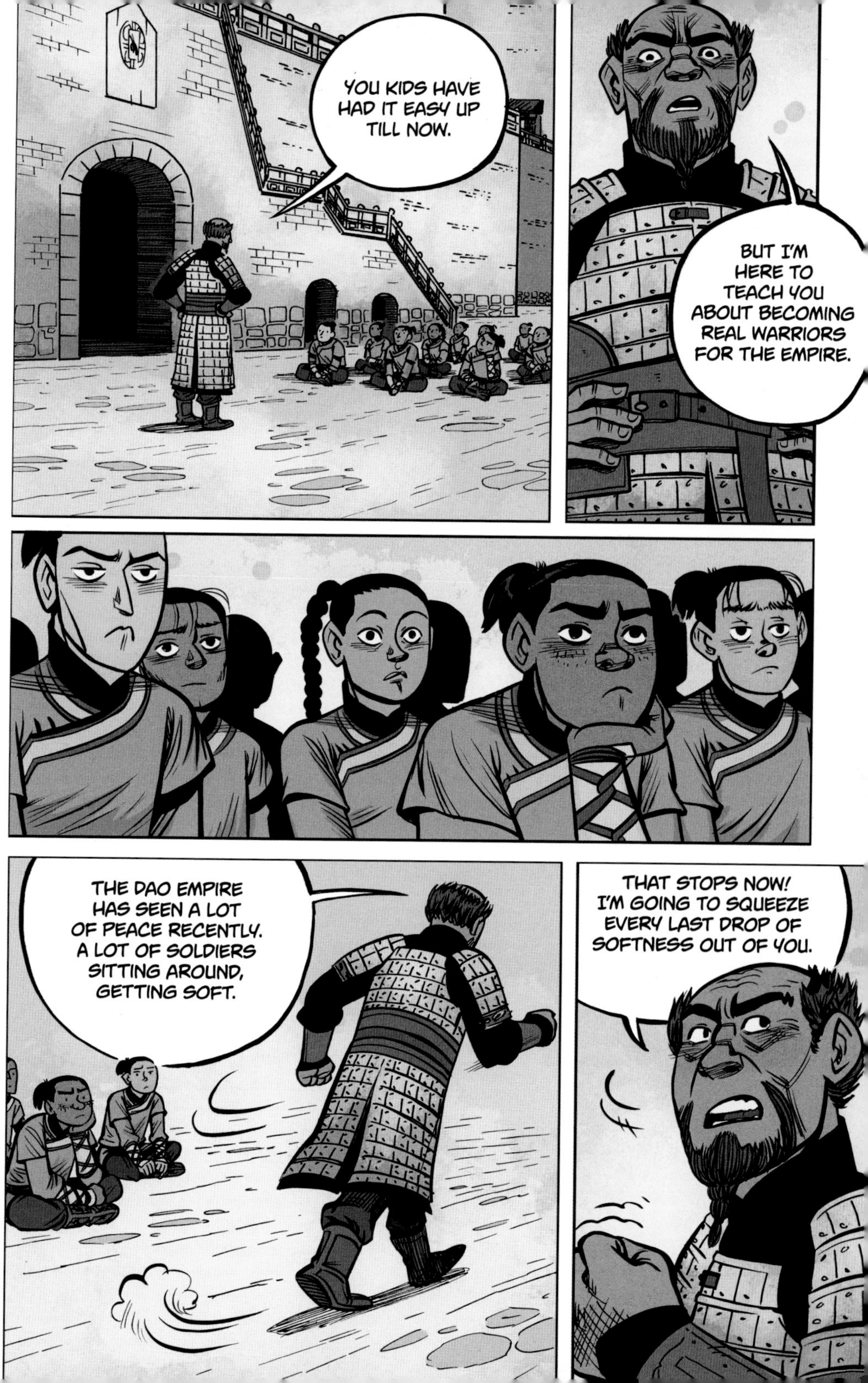
YOU KIDS HAVE HAD IT EASY UP TILL NOW.
BUT I'M HERE TO TEACH YOU ABOUT BECOMING REAL WARRIORS FOR THE EMPIRE.
THE DAO EMPIRE HAS SEEN A LOT OF PEACE RECENTLY. A LOT OF SOLDIERS SITTING AROUND, GETTING SOFT.
THAT STOPS NOW! I'M GOING TO SQUEEZE EVERY LAST DROP OF SOFTNESS OUT OF YOU.

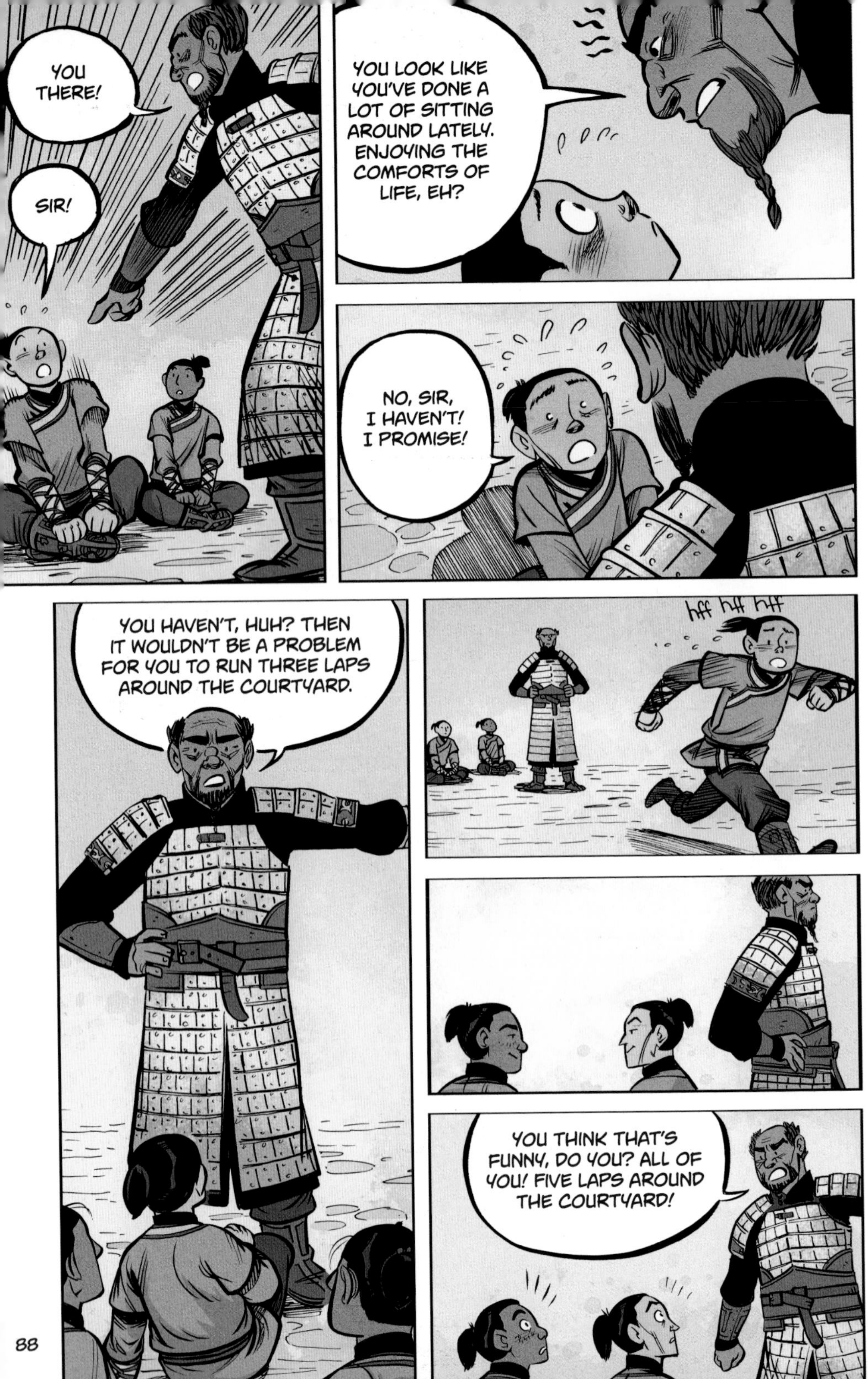
YOU THERE!
SIR!
YOU LOOK LIKE YOU'VE DONE A LOT OF SITTING AROUND LATELY. ENJOYING THE COMFORTS OF LIFE, EH?
NO, SIR, I HAVEN'T! I PROMISE!
YOU HAVEN'T, HUH? THEN IT WOULDN'T BE A PROBLEM FOR YOU TO RUN THREE LAPS AROUND THE COURTYARD.
hff hff hff
YOU THINK THAT'S FUNNY, DO YOU? ALL OF YOU! FIVE LAPS AROUND THE COURTYARD!

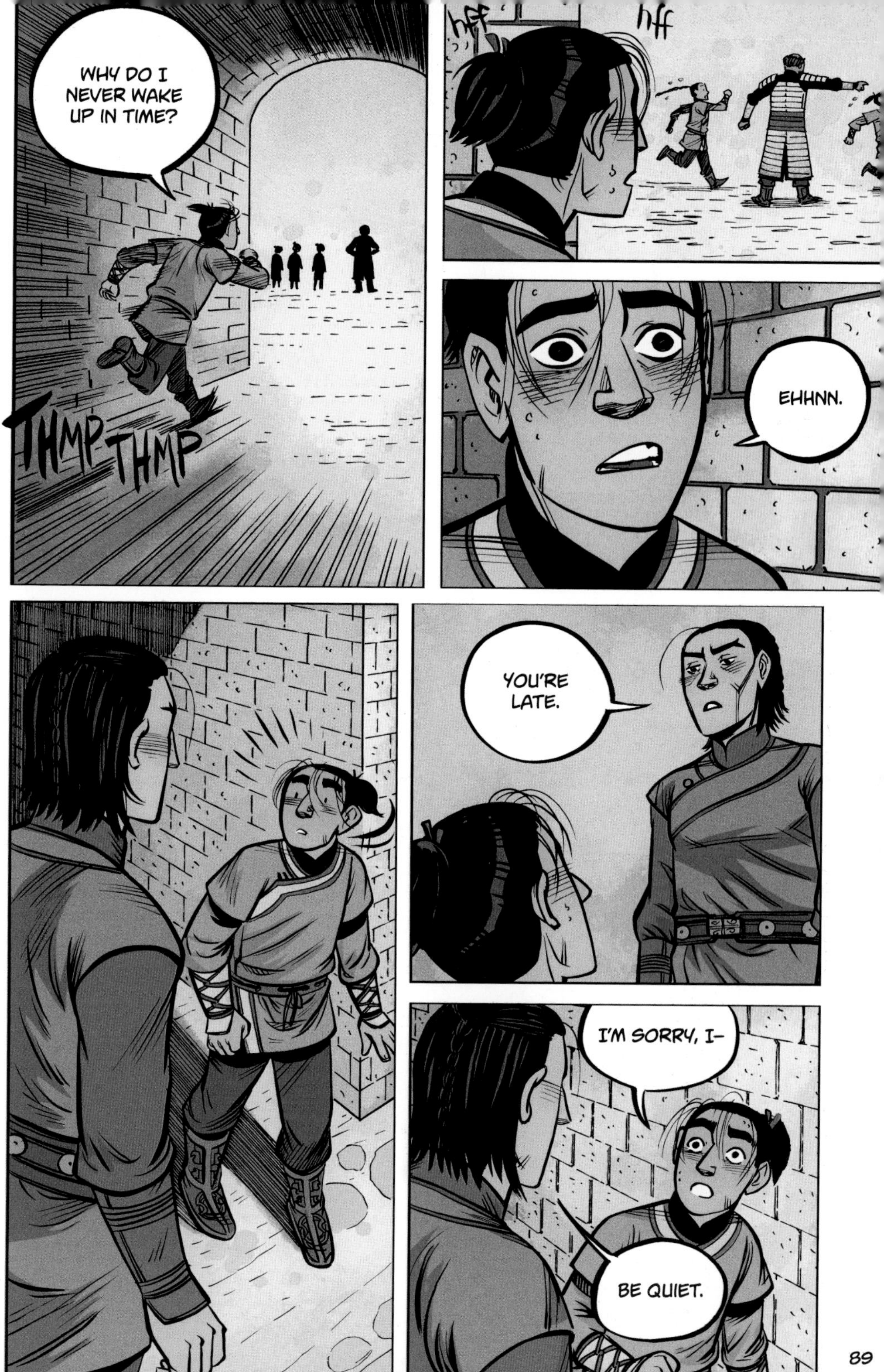
WHY DO I NEVER WAKE UP IN TIME?
THMP THMP
hff
hff
EHHNN.
YOU'RE LATE.
I'M SORRY, I–
BE QUIET.

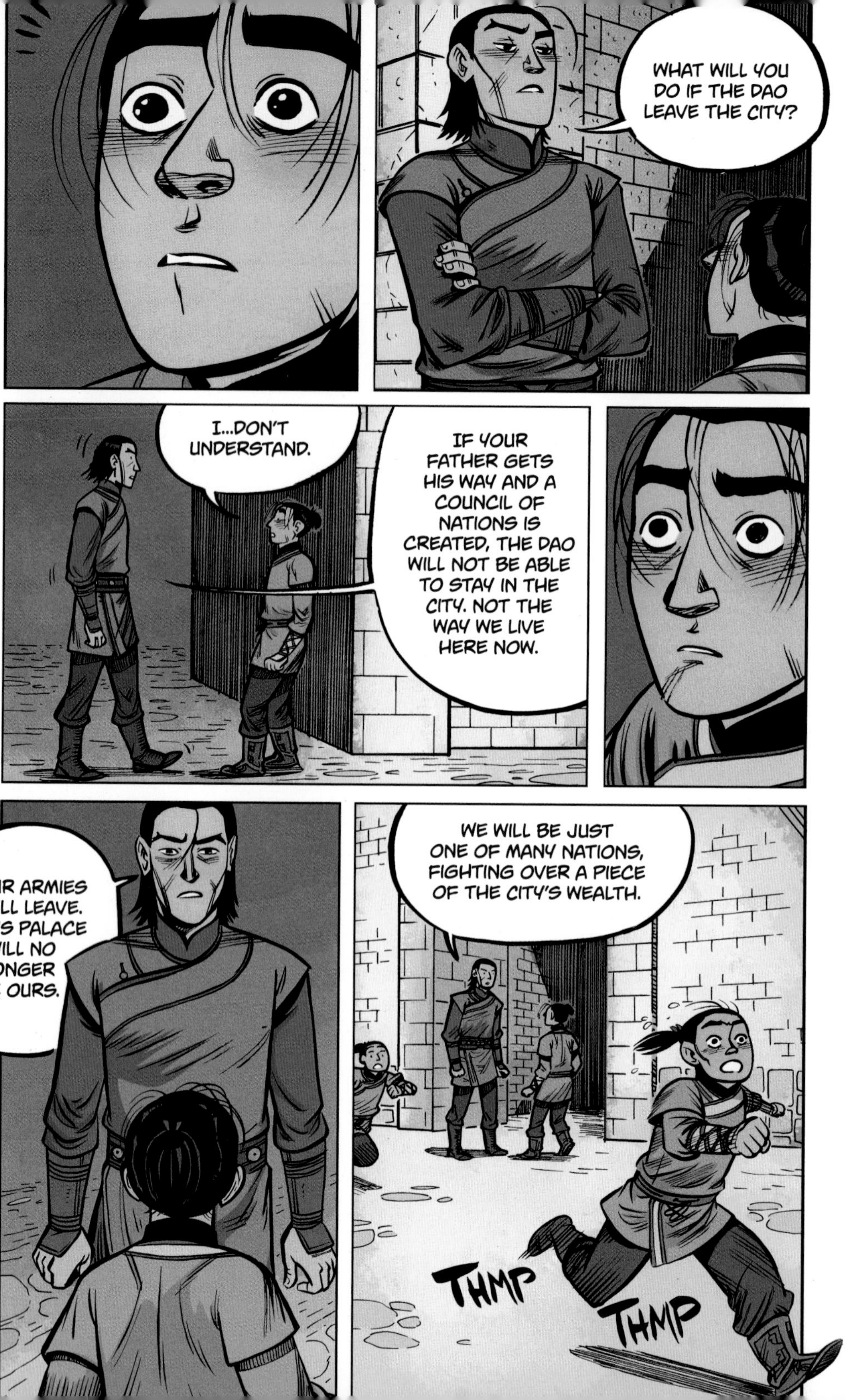
WHAT WILL YOU DO IF THE DAO LEAVE THE CITY?
I...DON'T UNDERSTAND.
IF YOUR FATHER GETS HIS WAY AND A COUNCIL OF NATIONS IS CREATED, THE DAO WILL NOT BE ABLE TO STAY IN THE CITY. NOT THE WAY WE LIVE HERE NOW.
OUR ARMIES WILL LEAVE. THIS PALACE WILL NO LONGER BE OURS.
WE WILL BE JUST ONE OF MANY NATIONS, FIGHTING OVER A PIECE OF THE CITY'S WEALTH.
THMP
THMP

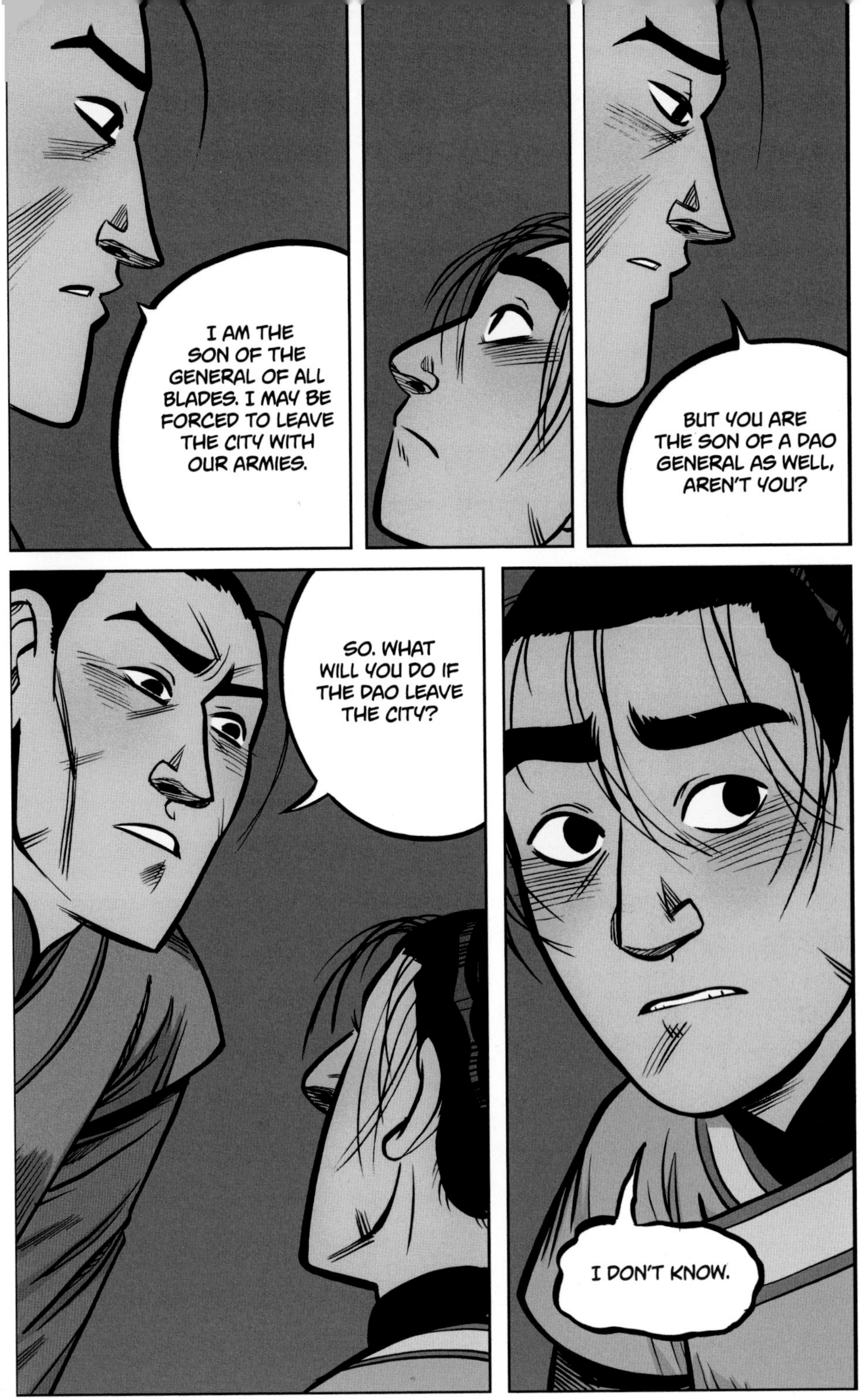
I AM THE SON OF THE GENERAL OF ALL BLADES. I MAY BE FORCED TO LEAVE THE CITY WITH OUR ARMIES.
BUT YOU ARE THE SON OF A DAO GENERAL AS WELL, AREN'T YOU?
SO. WHAT WILL YOU DO IF THE DAO LEAVE THE CITY?
I DON'T KNOW.

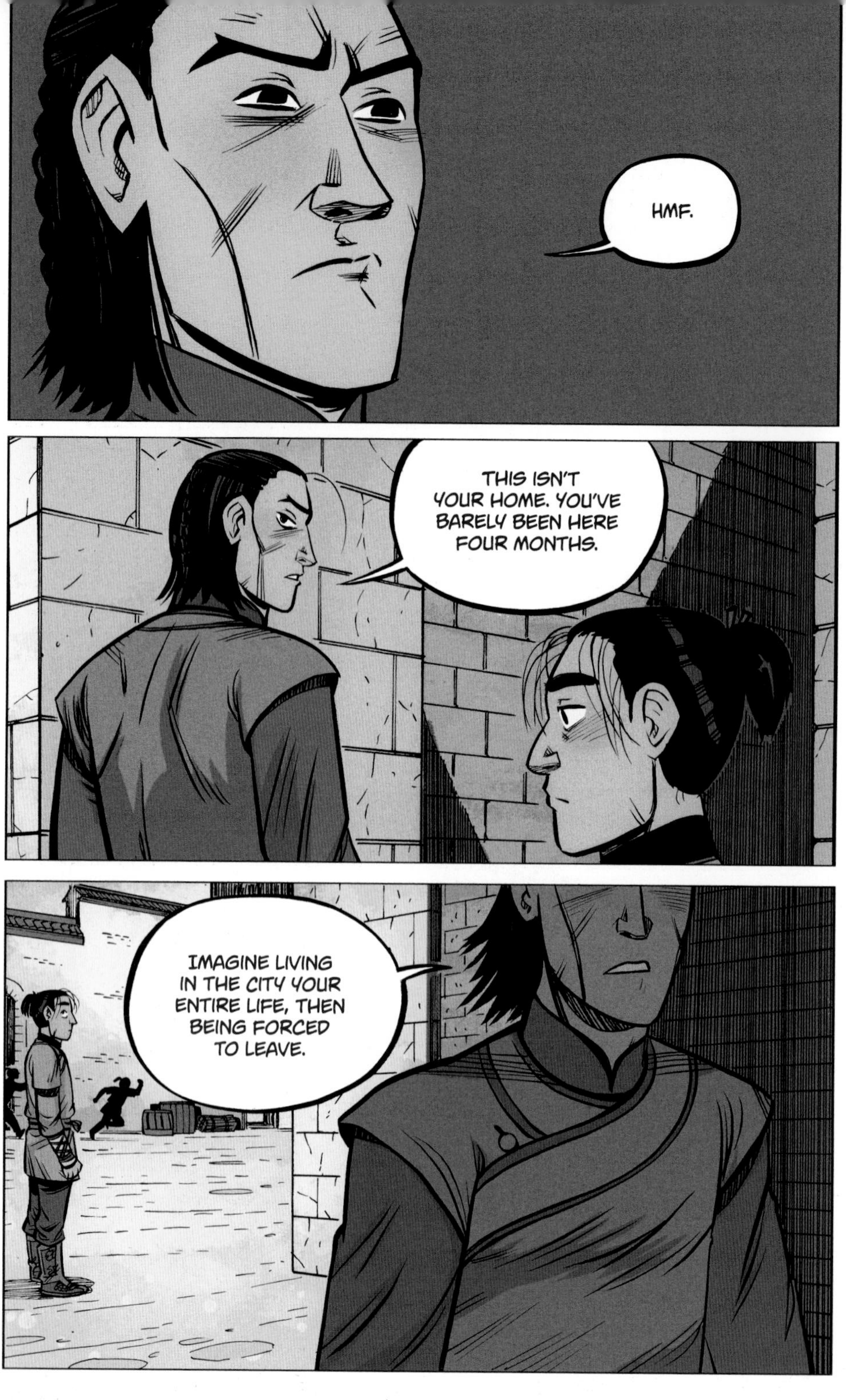
HMF.
THIS ISN'T YOUR HOME. YOU'VE BARELY BEEN HERE FOUR MONTHS.
IMAGINE LIVING IN THE CITY YOUR ENTIRE LIFE, THEN BEING FORCED TO LEAVE.

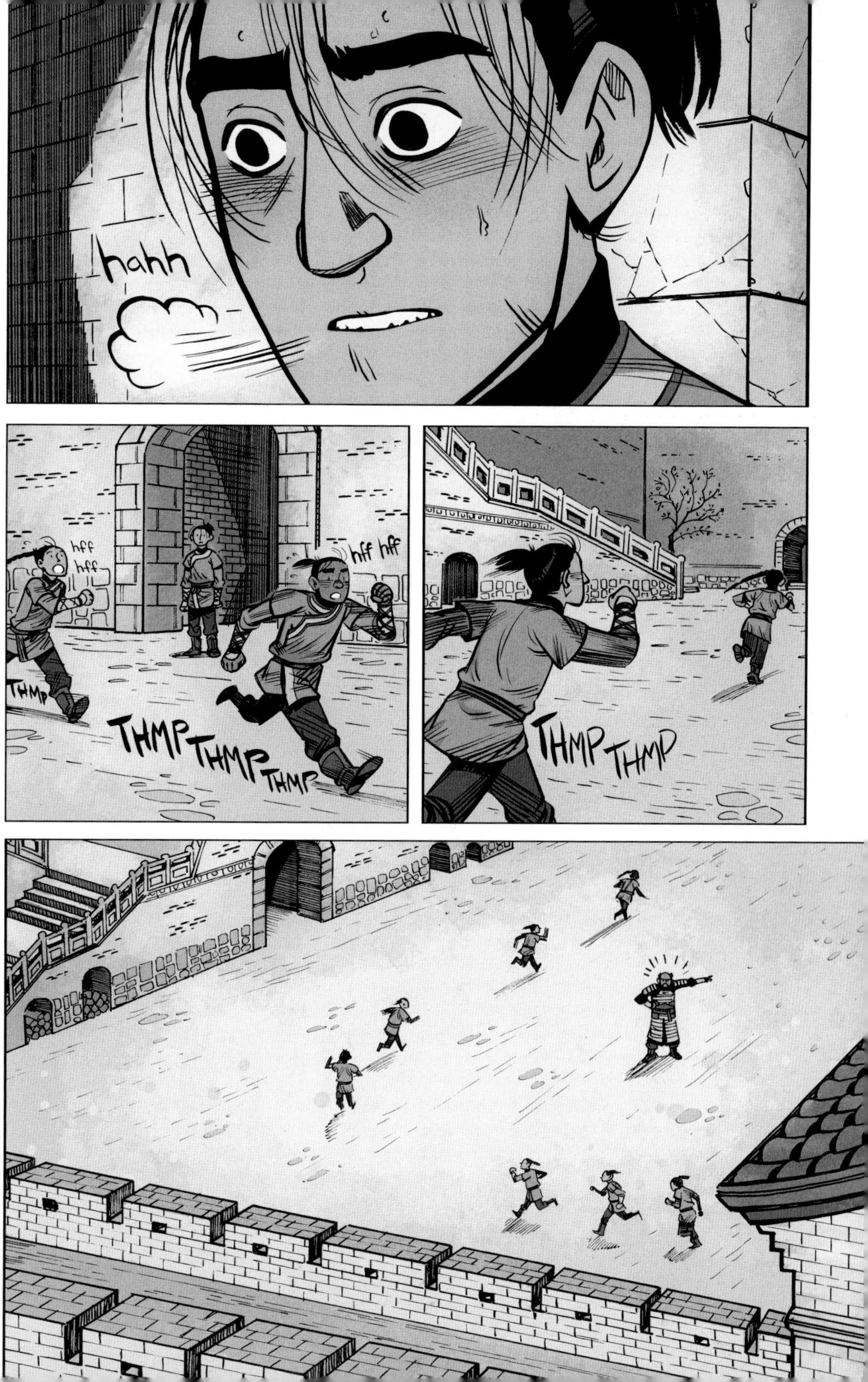
hahh
hff
hff
hff hff
THMP
THMP THMP THMP
THMP THMP

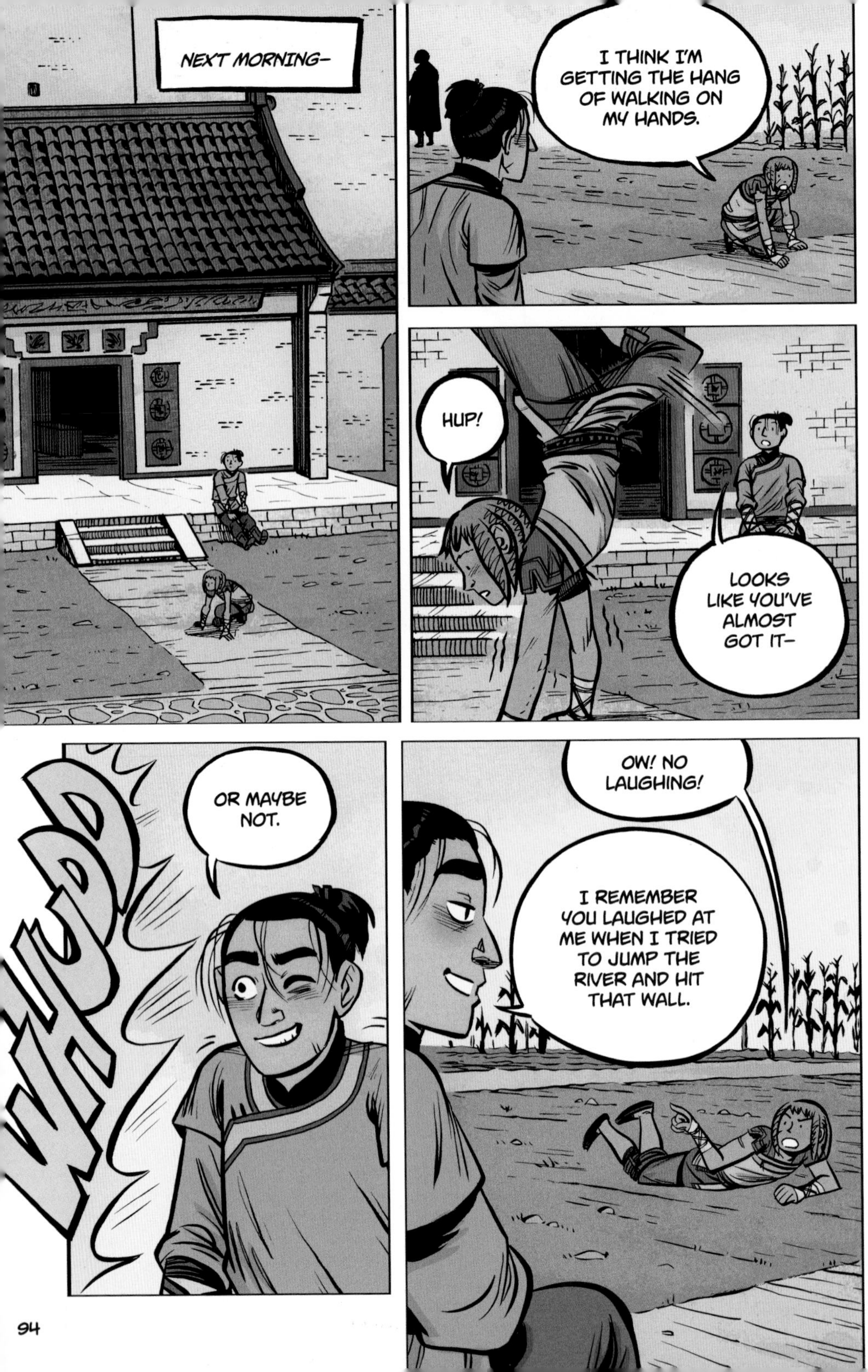
NEXT MORNING–
I THINK I'M GETTING THE HANG OF WALKING ON MY HANDS.
HUP!
LOOKS LIKE YOU'VE ALMOST GOT IT–
WHUD
OR MAYBE NOT.
OW! NO LAUGHING!
I REMEMBER YOU LAUGHED AT ME WHEN I TRIED TO JUMP THE RIVER AND HIT THAT WALL.

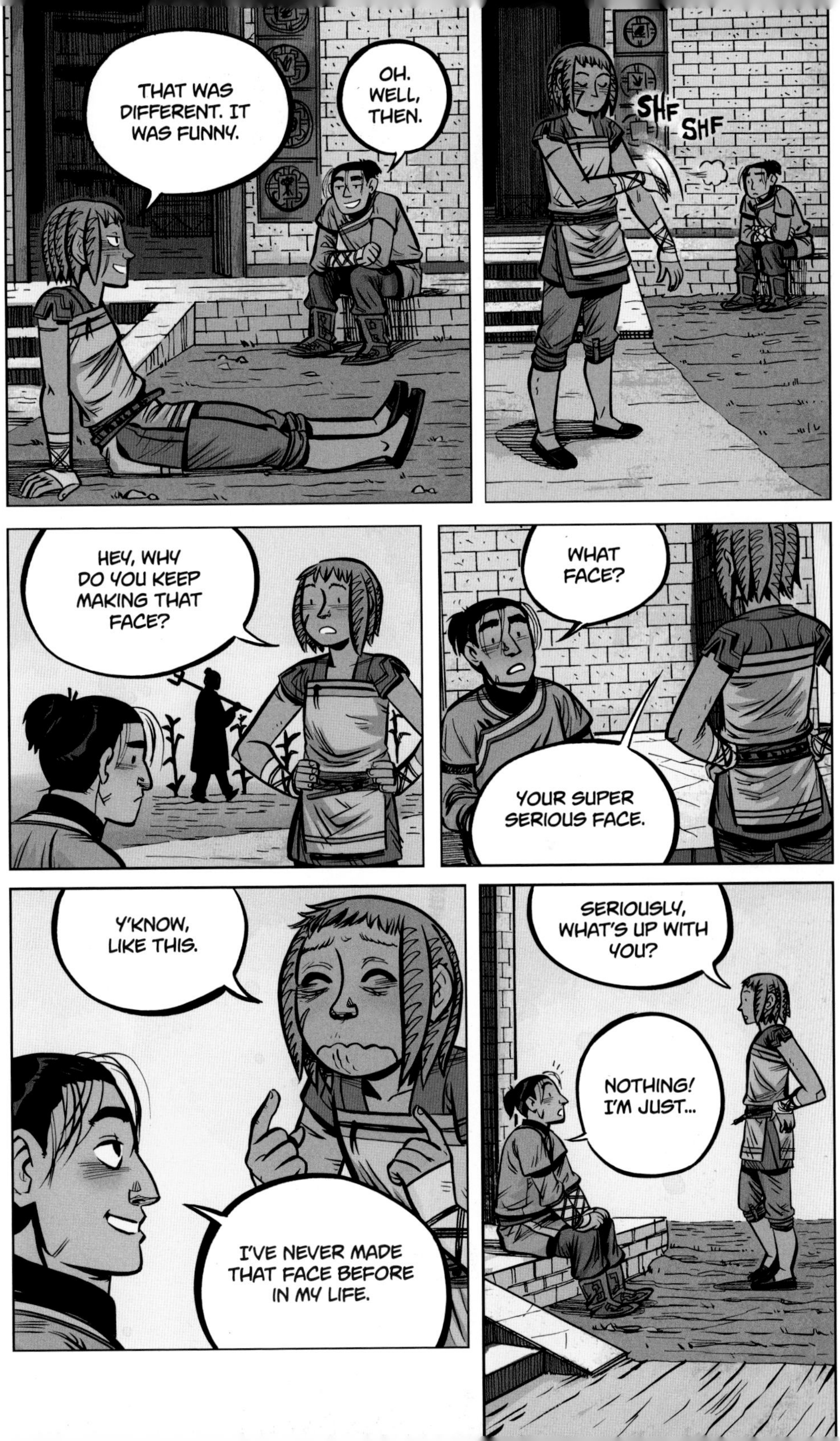
THAT WAS DIFFERENT. IT WAS FUNNY.
OH. WELL, THEN.
SHF SHF
HEY, WHY DO YOU KEEP MAKING THAT FACE?
WHAT FACE?
YOUR SUPER SERIOUS FACE.
Y'KNOW, LIKE THIS.
I'VE NEVER MADE THAT FACE BEFORE IN MY LIFE.
SERIOUSLY, WHAT'S UP WITH YOU?
NOTHING! I'M JUST...

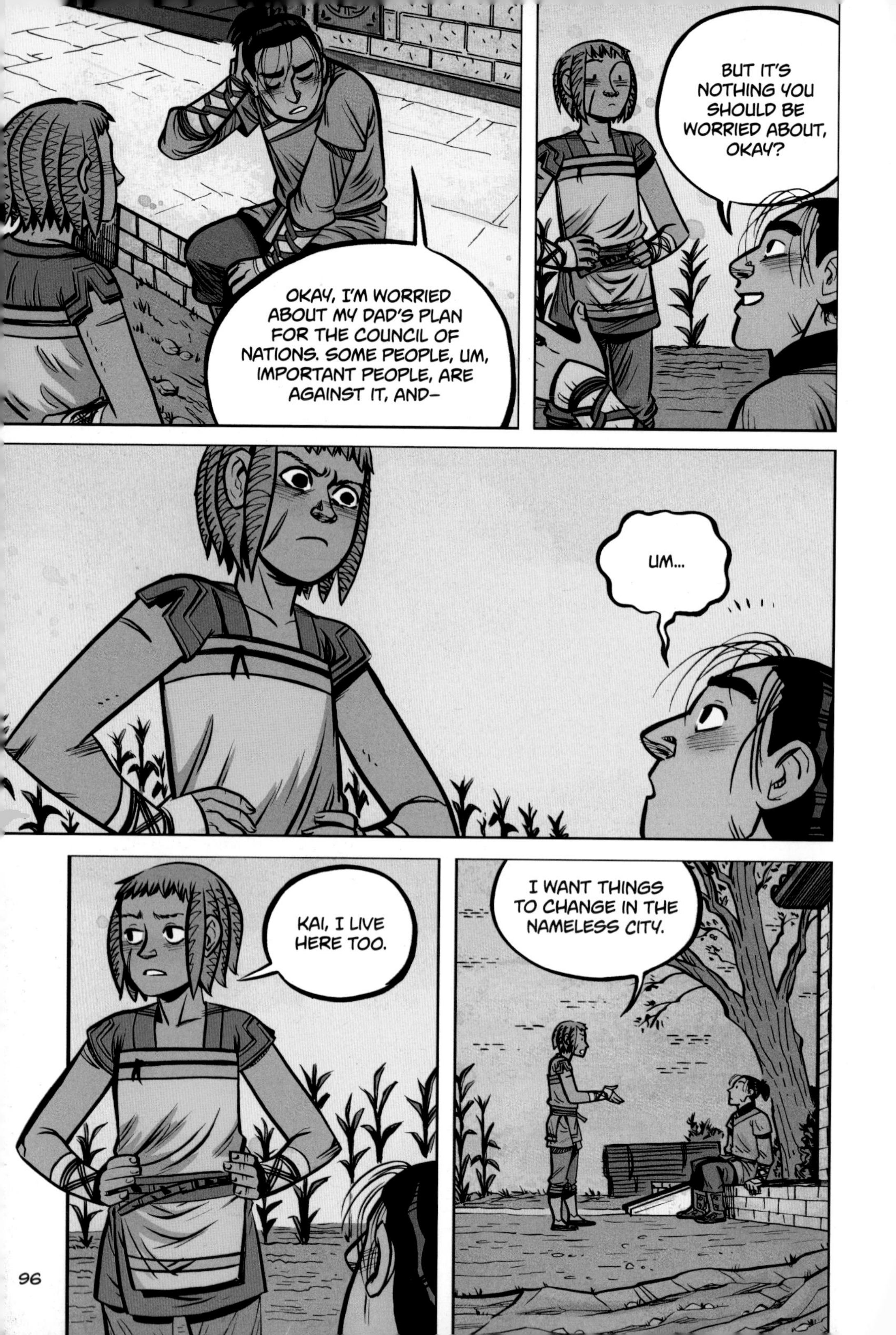
OKAY, I'M WORRIED ABOUT MY DAD'S PLAN FOR THE COUNCIL OF NATIONS. SOME PEOPLE, UM, IMPORTANT PEOPLE, ARE AGAINST IT, AND–
BUT IT'S NOTHING YOU SHOULD BE WORRIED ABOUT, OKAY?
UM...
KAI, I LIVE HERE TOO.
I WANT THINGS TO CHANGE IN THE NAMELESS CITY.

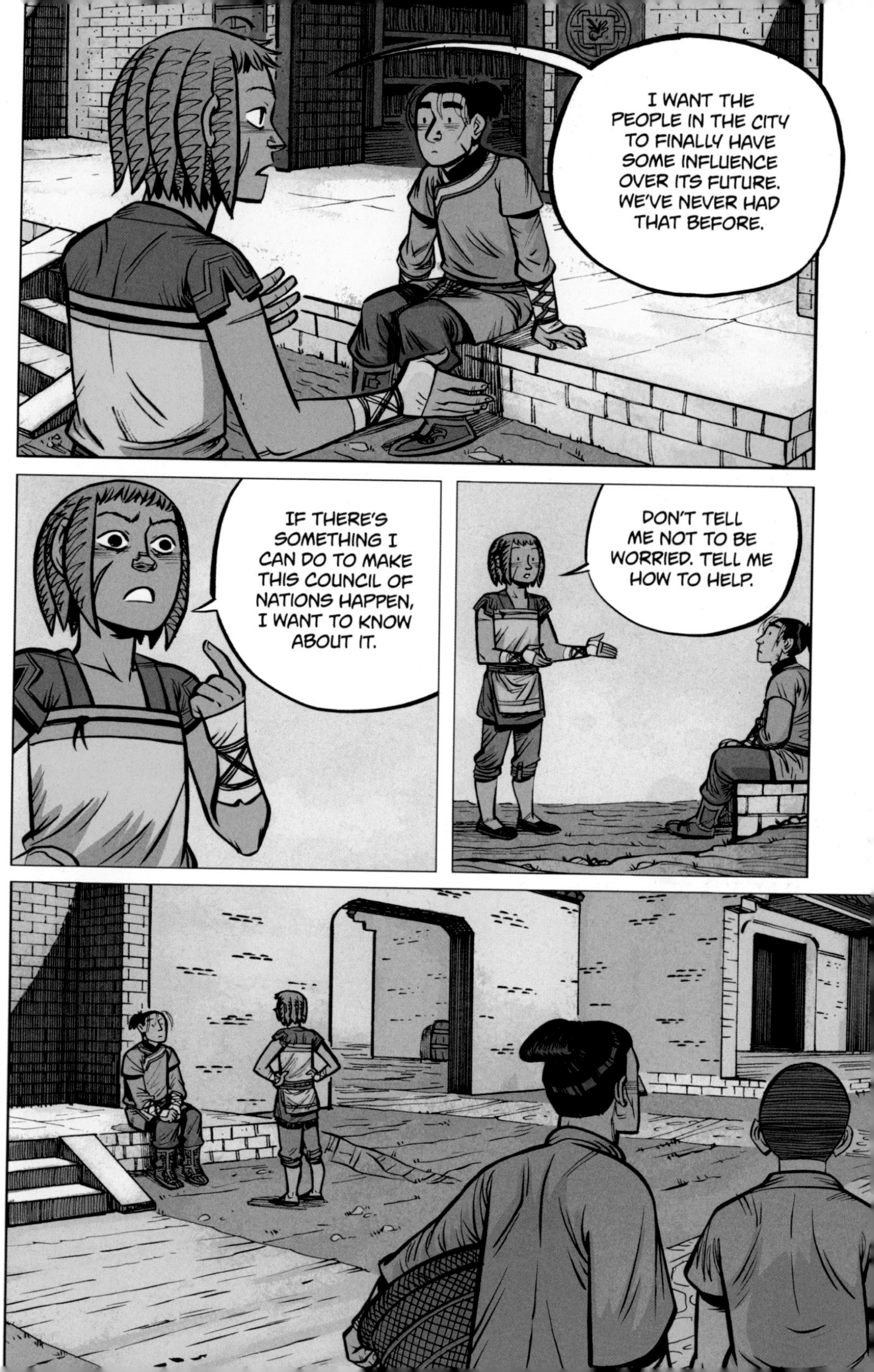
I WANT THE PEOPLE IN THE CITY TO FINALLY HAVE SOME INFLUENCE OVER ITS FUTURE. WE'VE NEVER HAD THAT BEFORE.
IF THERE'S SOMETHING I CAN DO TO MAKE THIS COUNCIL OF NATIONS HAPPEN, I WANT TO KNOW ABOUT IT.
DON'T TELL ME NOT TO BE WORRIED. TELL ME HOW TO HELP.

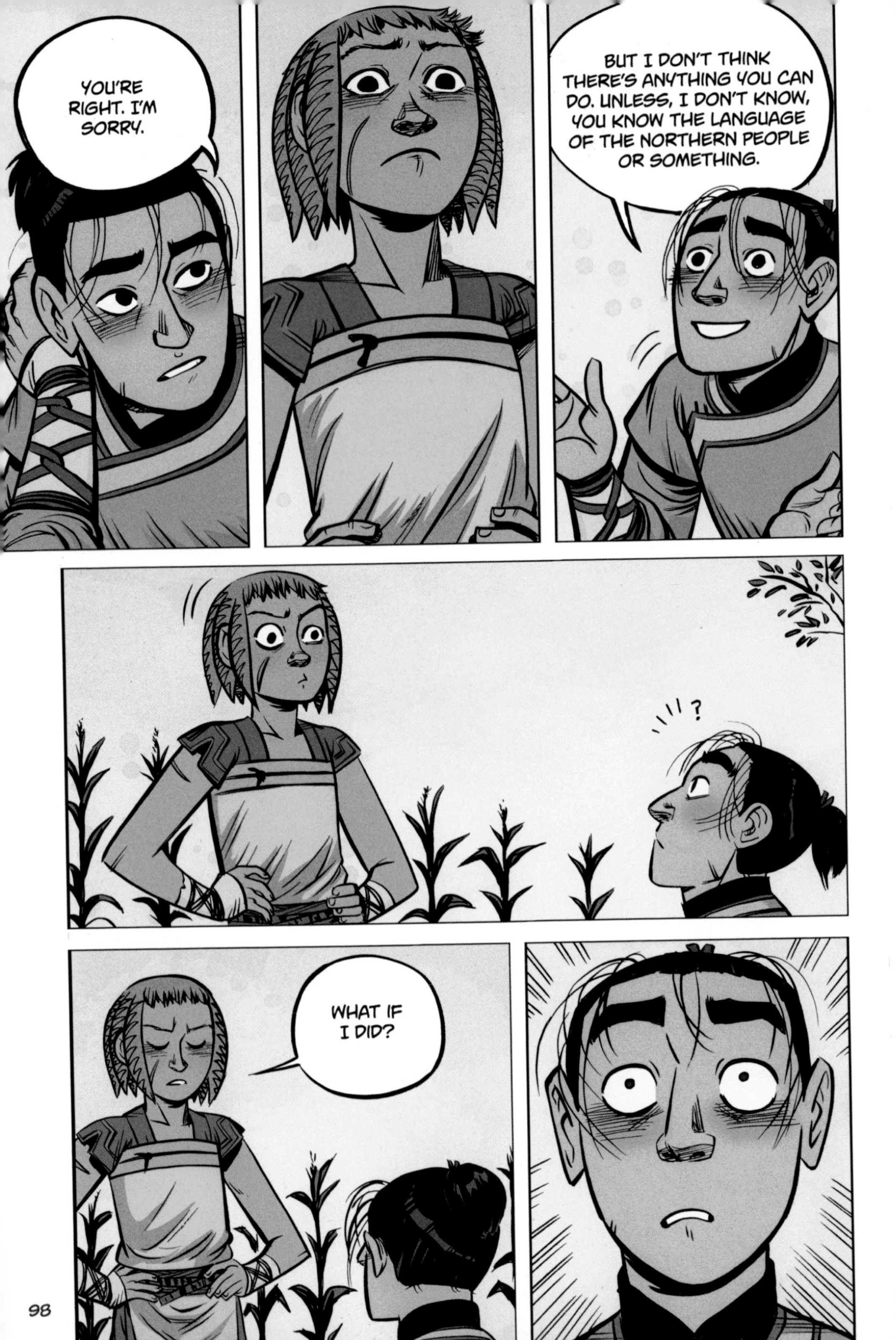
YOU'RE RIGHT. I'M SORRY.
BUT I DON'T THINK THERE'S ANYTHING YOU CAN DO. UNLESS, I DON'T KNOW, YOU KNOW THE LANGUAGE OF THE NORTHERN PEOPLE OR SOMETHING.
?
WHAT IF I DID?

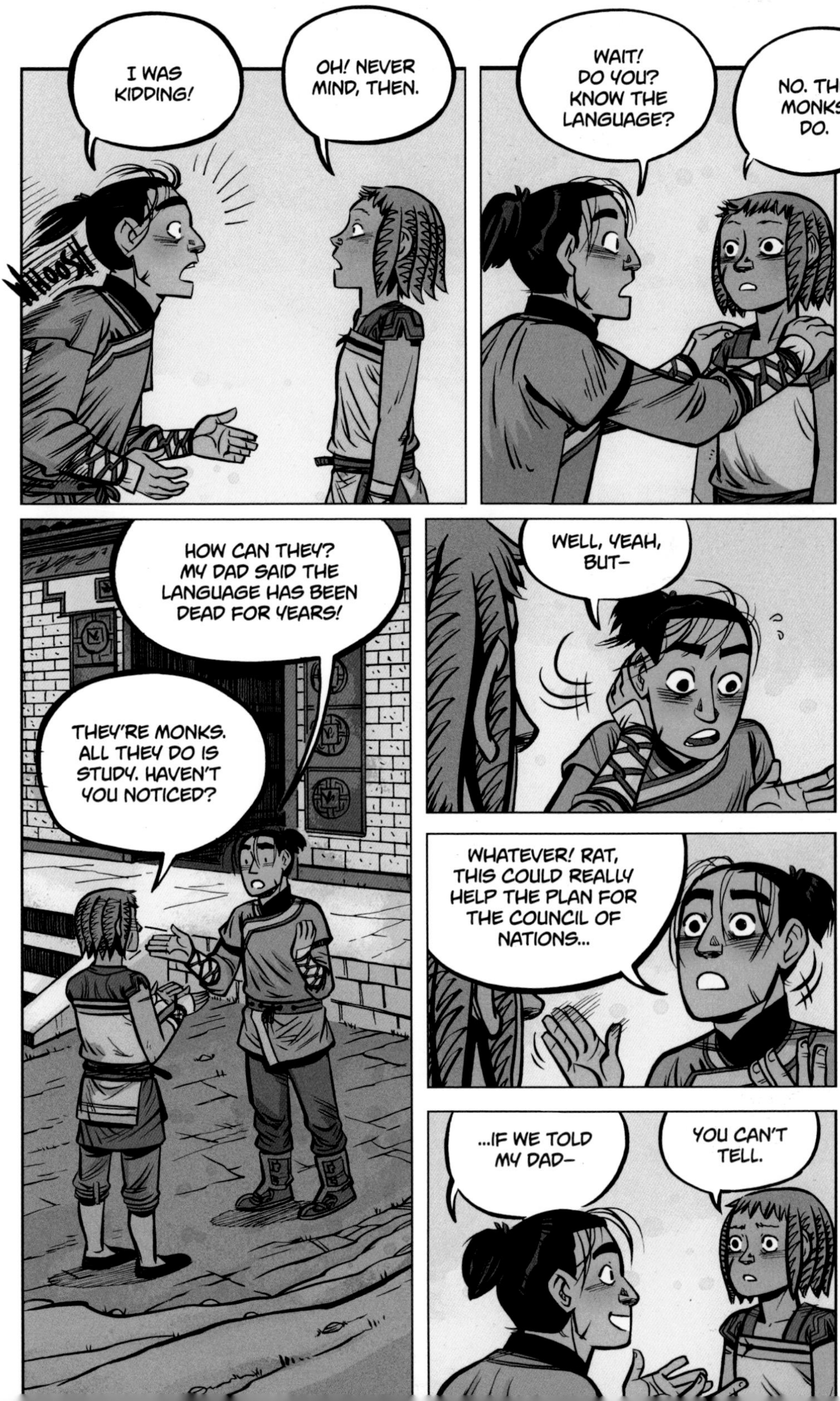
I WAS KIDDING!
WHOOSH
OH! NEVER MIND, THEN.
WAIT! DO YOU? KNOW THE LANGUAGE?
NO. THE MONKS DO.
HOW CAN THEY? MY DAD SAID THE LANGUAGE HAS BEEN DEAD FOR YEARS!
THEY'RE MONKS. ALL THEY DO IS STUDY. HAVEN'T YOU NOTICED?
WELL, YEAH, BUT–
WHATEVER! RAT, THIS COULD REALLY HELP THE PLAN FOR THE COUNCIL OF NATIONS...
...IF WE TOLD MY DAD–
YOU CAN'T TELL.

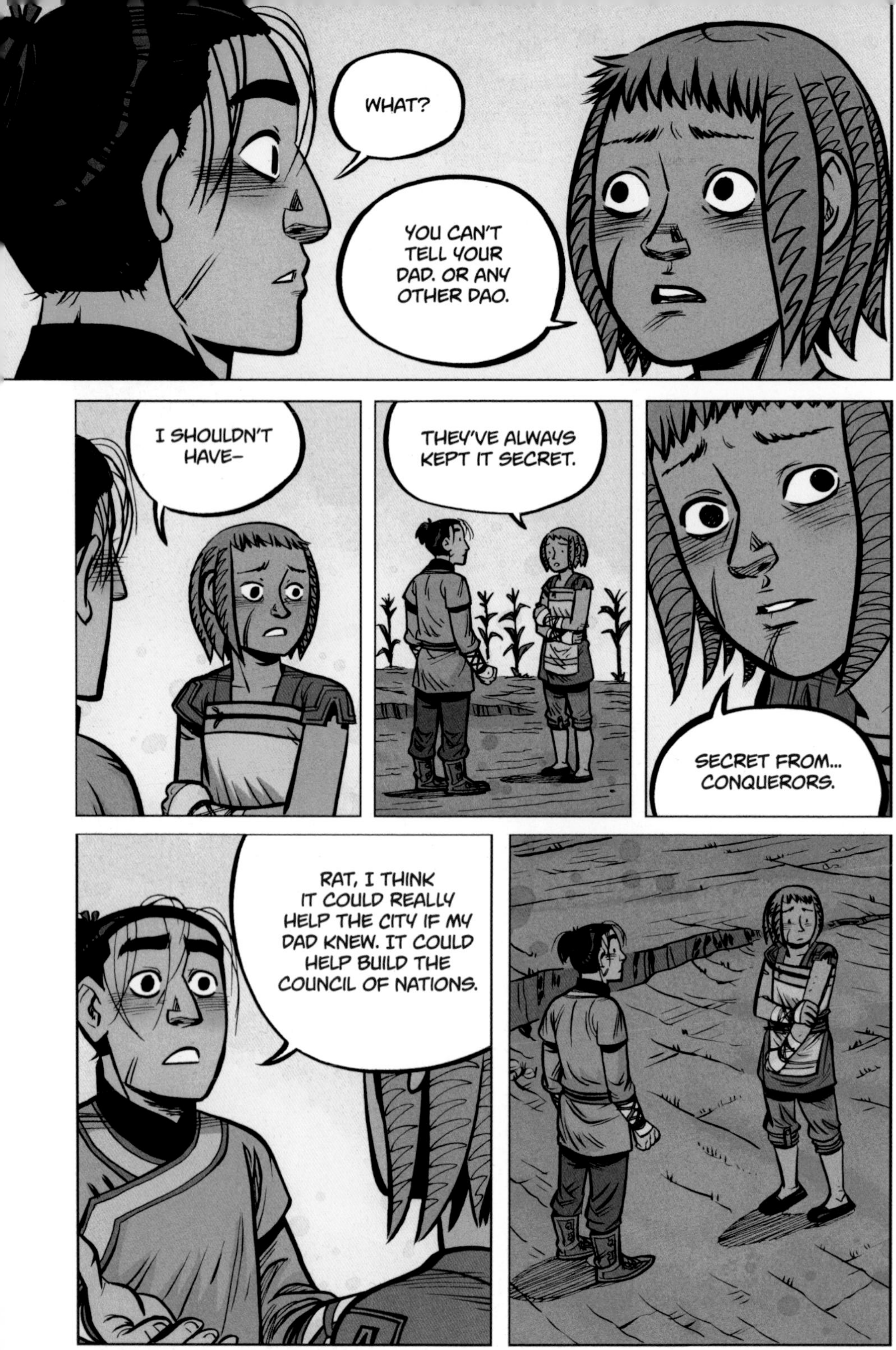
WHAT?
YOU CAN'T TELL YOUR DAD. OR ANY OTHER DAO.
I SHOULDN'T HAVE–
THEY'VE ALWAYS KEPT IT SECRET.
SECRET FROM... CONQUERORS.
RAT, I THINK IT COULD REALLY HELP THE CITY IF MY DAD KNEW. IT COULD HELP BUILD THE COUNCIL OF NATIONS.

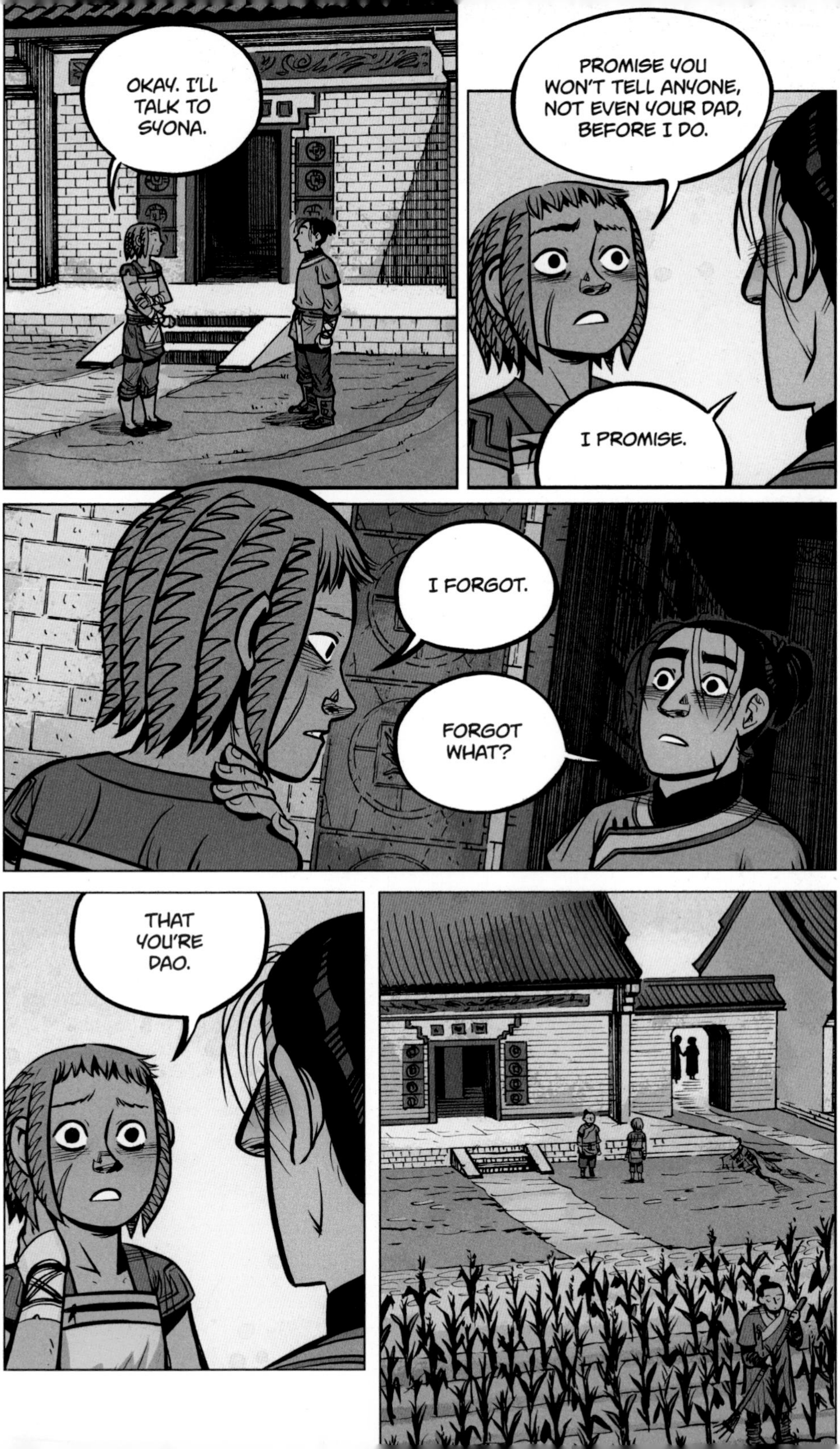
OKAY. I'LL TALK TO SYONA.
PROMISE YOU WON'T TELL ANYONE, NOT EVEN YOUR DAD, BEFORE I DO.
I PROMISE.
I FORGOT.
FORGOT WHAT?
THAT YOU'RE DAO.

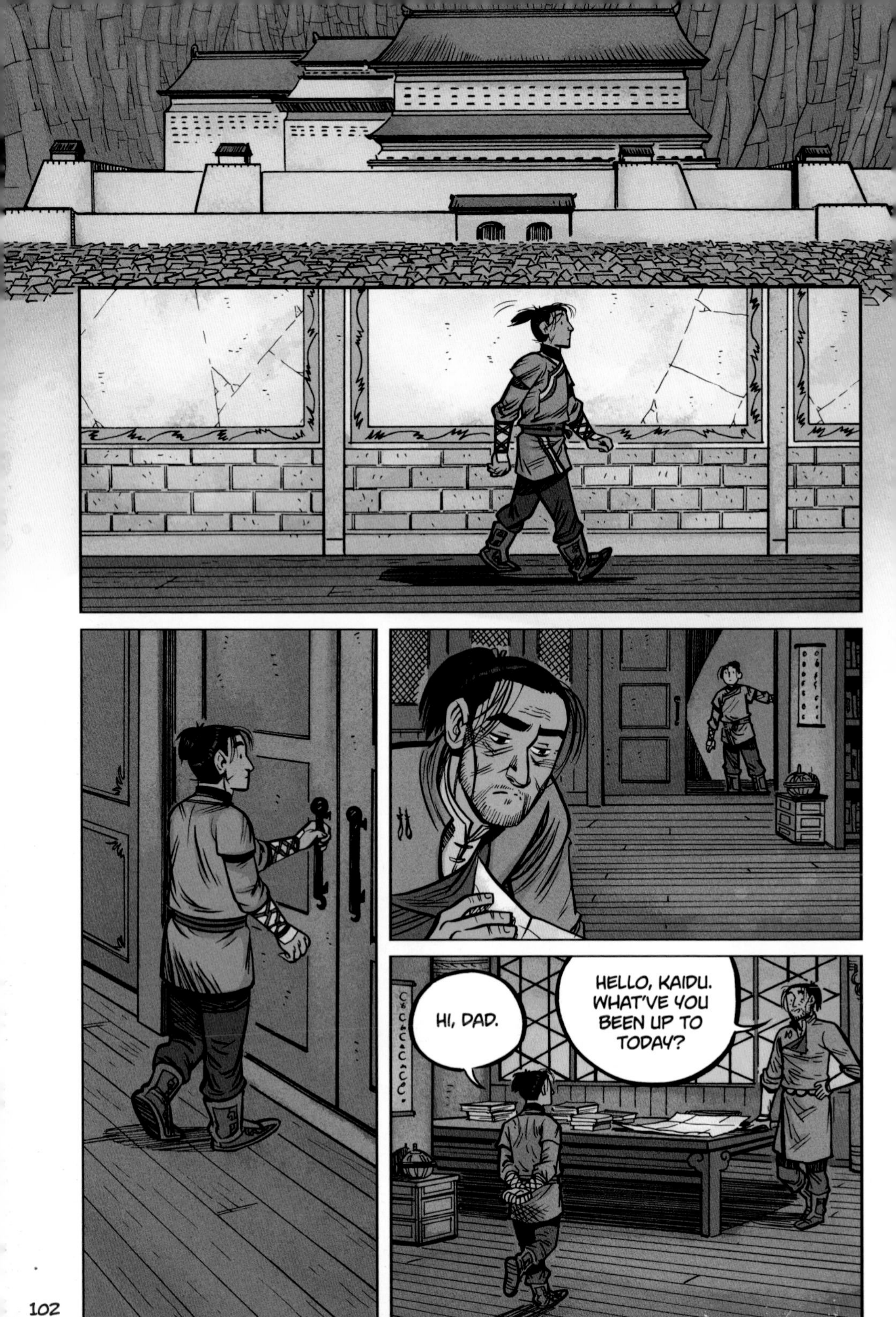
HI, DAD.
HELLO, KAIDU. WHAT'VE YOU BEEN UP TO TODAY?

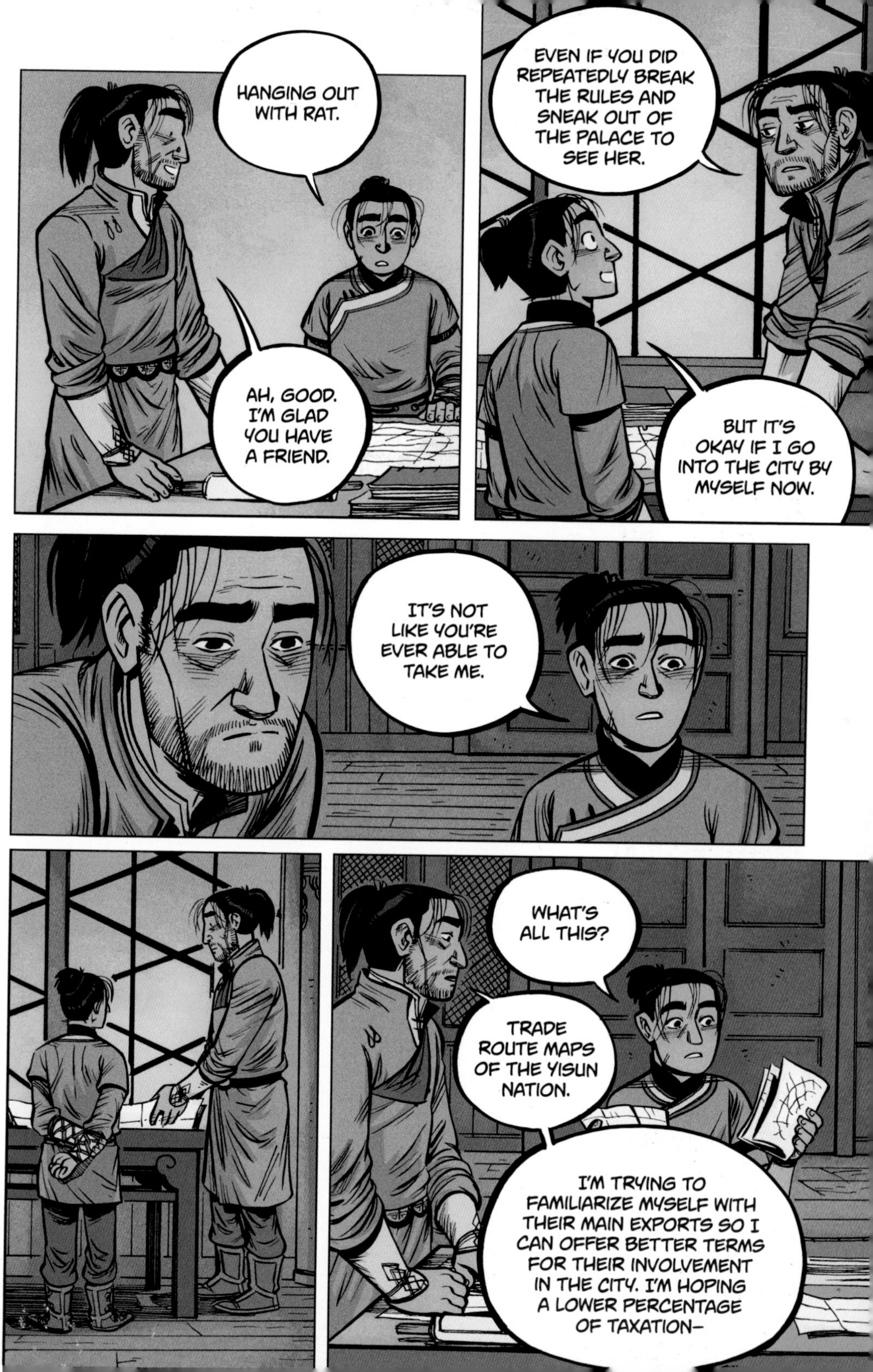
HANGING OUT WITH RAT.
AH, GOOD. I'M GLAD YOU HAVE A FRIEND.
EVEN IF YOU DID REPEATEDLY BREAK THE RULES AND SNEAK OUT OF THE PALACE TO SEE HER.
BUT IT'S OKAY IF I GO INTO THE CITY BY MYSELF NOW.
IT'S NOT LIKE YOU'RE EVER ABLE TO TAKE ME.
WHAT'S ALL THIS?
TRADE ROUTE MAPS OF THE YISUN NATION.
I'M TRYING TO FAMILIARIZE MYSELF WITH THEIR MAIN EXPORTS SO I CAN OFFER BETTER TERMS FOR THEIR INVOLVEMENT IN THE CITY. I'M HOPING A LOWER PERCENTAGE OF TAXATION—

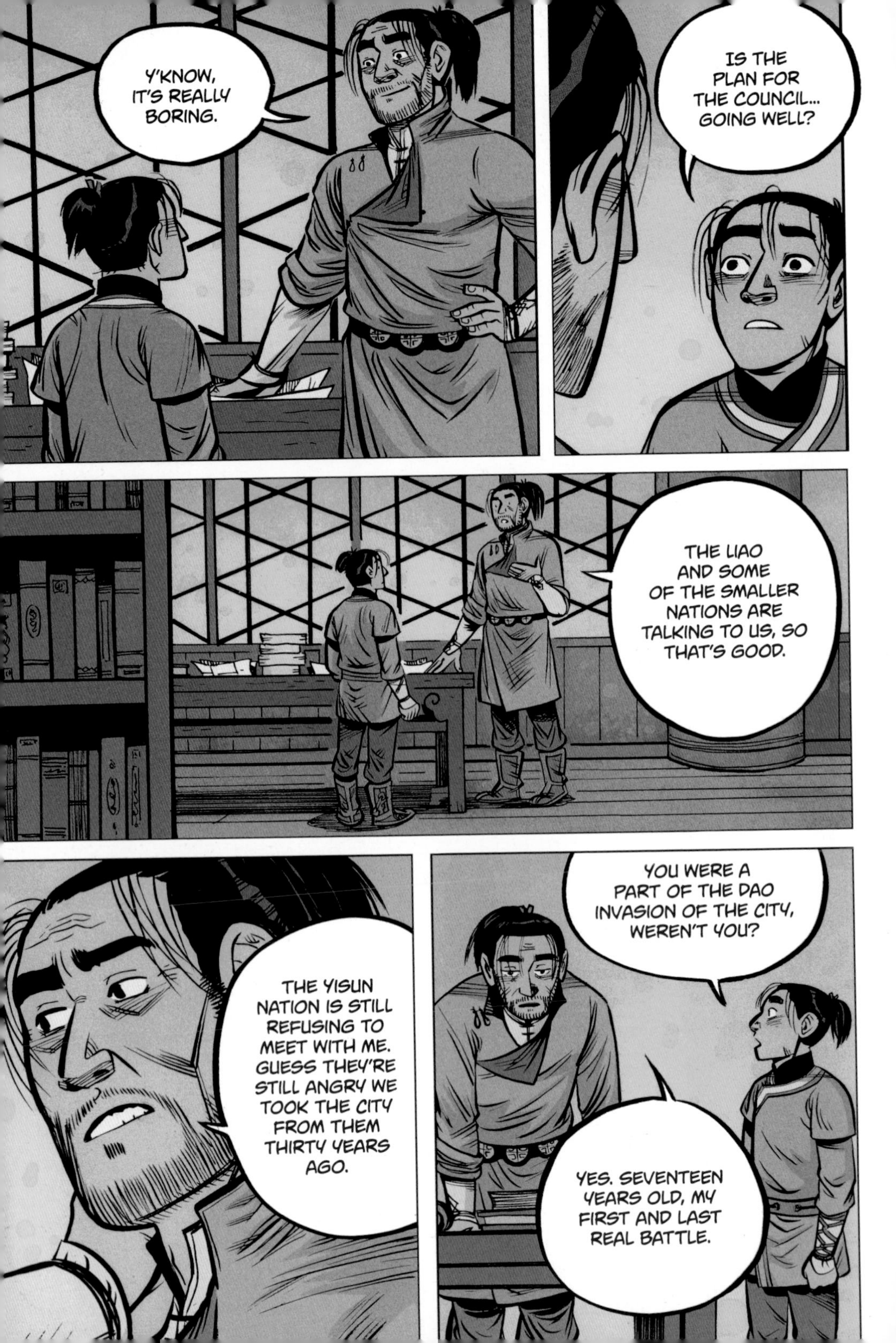
Y'KNOW, IT'S REALLY BORING.
IS THE PLAN FOR THE COUNCIL... GOING WELL?
THE LIAO AND SOME OF THE SMALLER NATIONS ARE TALKING TO US, SO THAT'S GOOD.
THE YISUN NATION IS STILL REFUSING TO MEET WITH ME. GUESS THEY'RE STILL ANGRY WE TOOK THE CITY FROM THEM THIRTY YEARS AGO.
YOU WERE A PART OF THE DAO INVASION OF THE CITY, WEREN'T YOU?
YES. SEVENTEEN YEARS OLD, MY FIRST AND LAST REAL BATTLE.

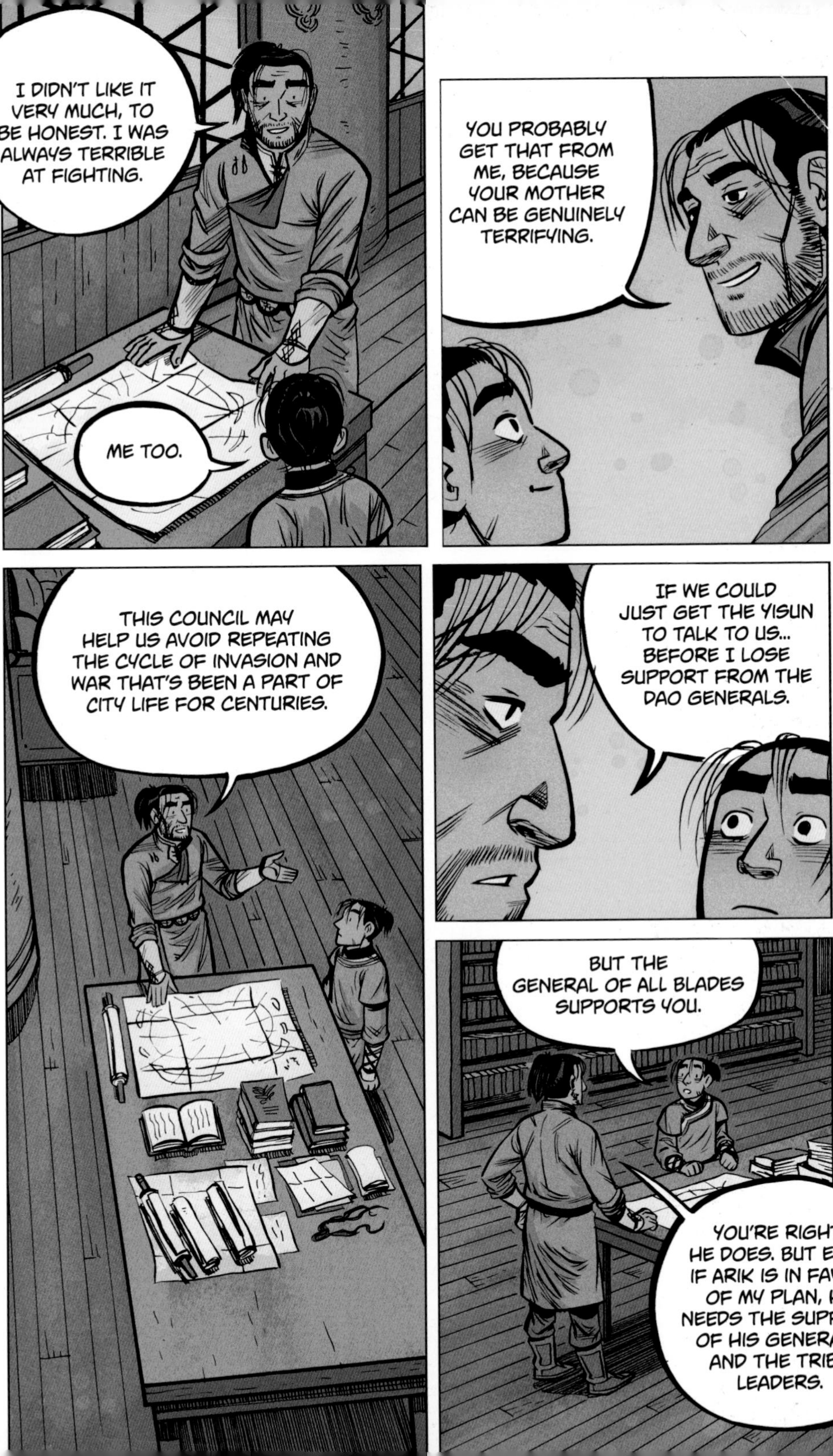
I DIDN'T LIKE IT VERY MUCH, TO BE HONEST. I WAS ALWAYS TERRIBLE AT FIGHTING.
ME TOO.
YOU PROBABLY GET THAT FROM ME, BECAUSE YOUR MOTHER CAN BE GENUINELY TERRIFYING.
THIS COUNCIL MAY HELP US AVOID REPEATING THE CYCLE OF INVASION AND WAR THAT'S BEEN A PART OF CITY LIFE FOR CENTURIES.
IF WE COULD JUST GET THE YISUN TO TALK TO US... BEFORE I LOSE SUPPORT FROM THE DAO GENERALS.
BUT THE GENERAL OF ALL BLADES SUPPORTS YOU.
YOU'RE RIGHT, HE DOES. BUT EVEN IF ARIK IS IN FAVOR OF MY PLAN, HE NEEDS THE SUPPORT OF HIS GENERALS AND THE TRIBE LEADERS.

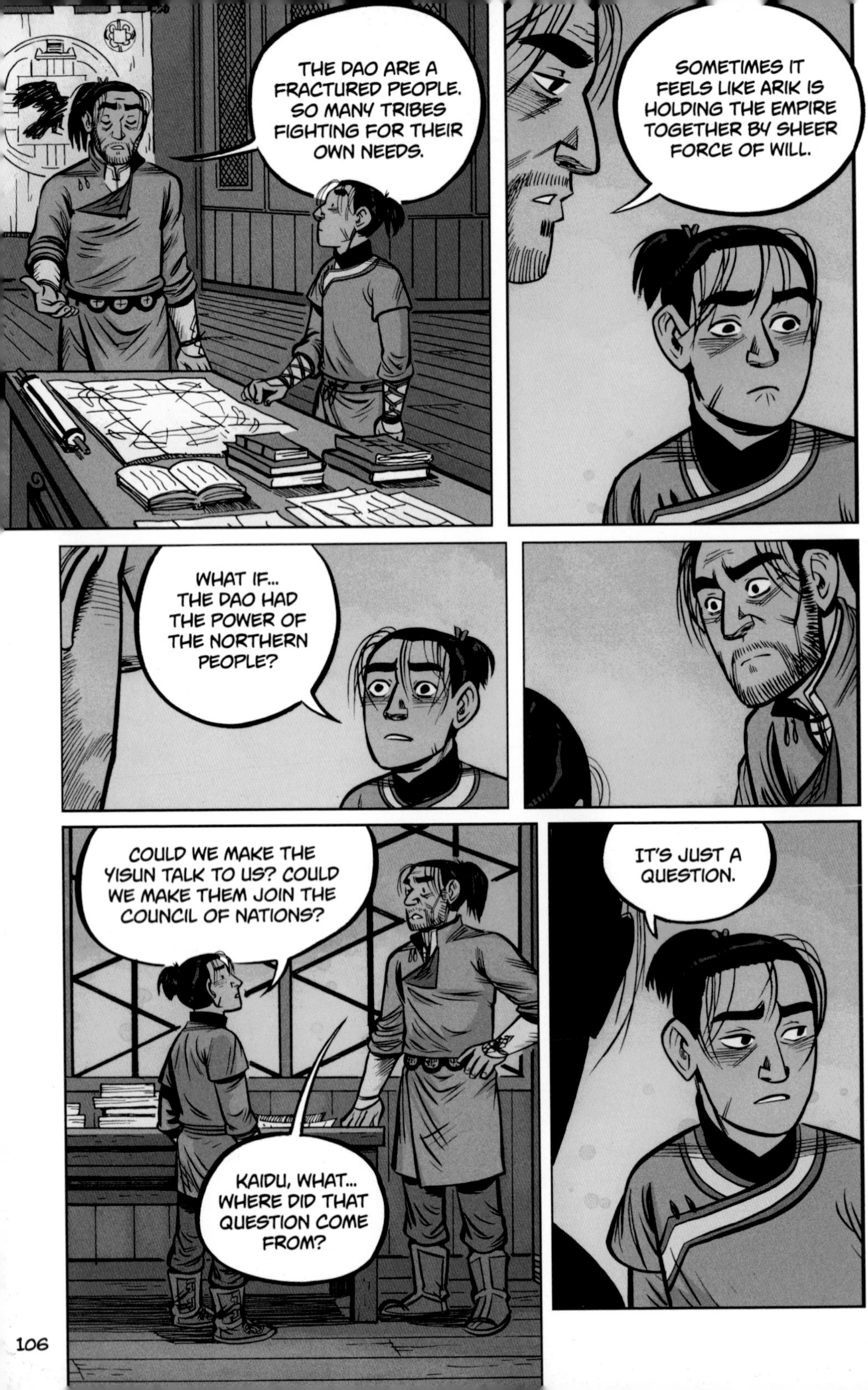
THE DAO ARE A FRACTURED PEOPLE. SO MANY TRIBES FIGHTING FOR THEIR OWN NEEDS.
SOMETIMES IT FEELS LIKE ARIK IS HOLDING THE EMPIRE TOGETHER BY SHEER FORCE OF WILL.
WHAT IF... THE DAO HAD THE POWER OF THE NORTHERN PEOPLE?
COULD WE MAKE THE YISUN TALK TO US? COULD WE MAKE THEM JOIN THE COUNCIL OF NATIONS?
KAIDU, WHAT... WHERE DID THAT QUESTION COME FROM?
IT'S JUST A QUESTION.

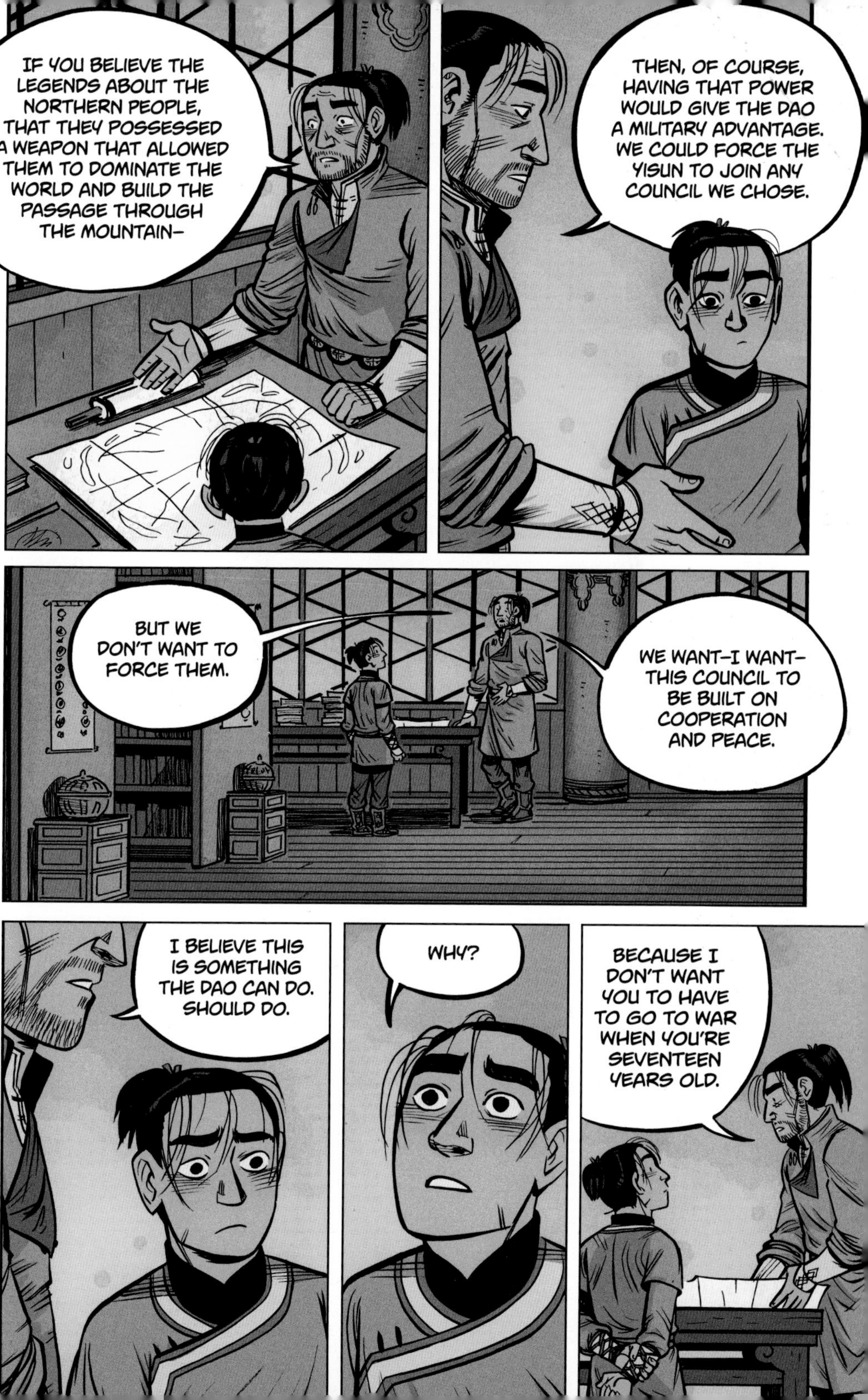
IF YOU BELIEVE THE LEGENDS ABOUT THE NORTHERN PEOPLE, THAT THEY POSSESSED A WEAPON THAT ALLOWED THEM TO DOMINATE THE WORLD AND BUILD THE PASSAGE THROUGH THE MOUNTAIN–
THEN, OF COURSE, HAVING THAT POWER WOULD GIVE THE DAO A MILITARY ADVANTAGE. WE COULD FORCE THE YISUN TO JOIN ANY COUNCIL WE CHOSE.
BUT WE DON'T WANT TO FORCE THEM.
WE WANT–I WANT–THIS COUNCIL TO BE BUILT ON COOPERATION AND PEACE.
I BELIEVE THIS IS SOMETHING THE DAO CAN DO. SHOULD DO.
WHY?
BECAUSE I DON'T WANT YOU TO HAVE TO GO TO WAR WHEN YOU'RE SEVENTEEN YEARS OLD.

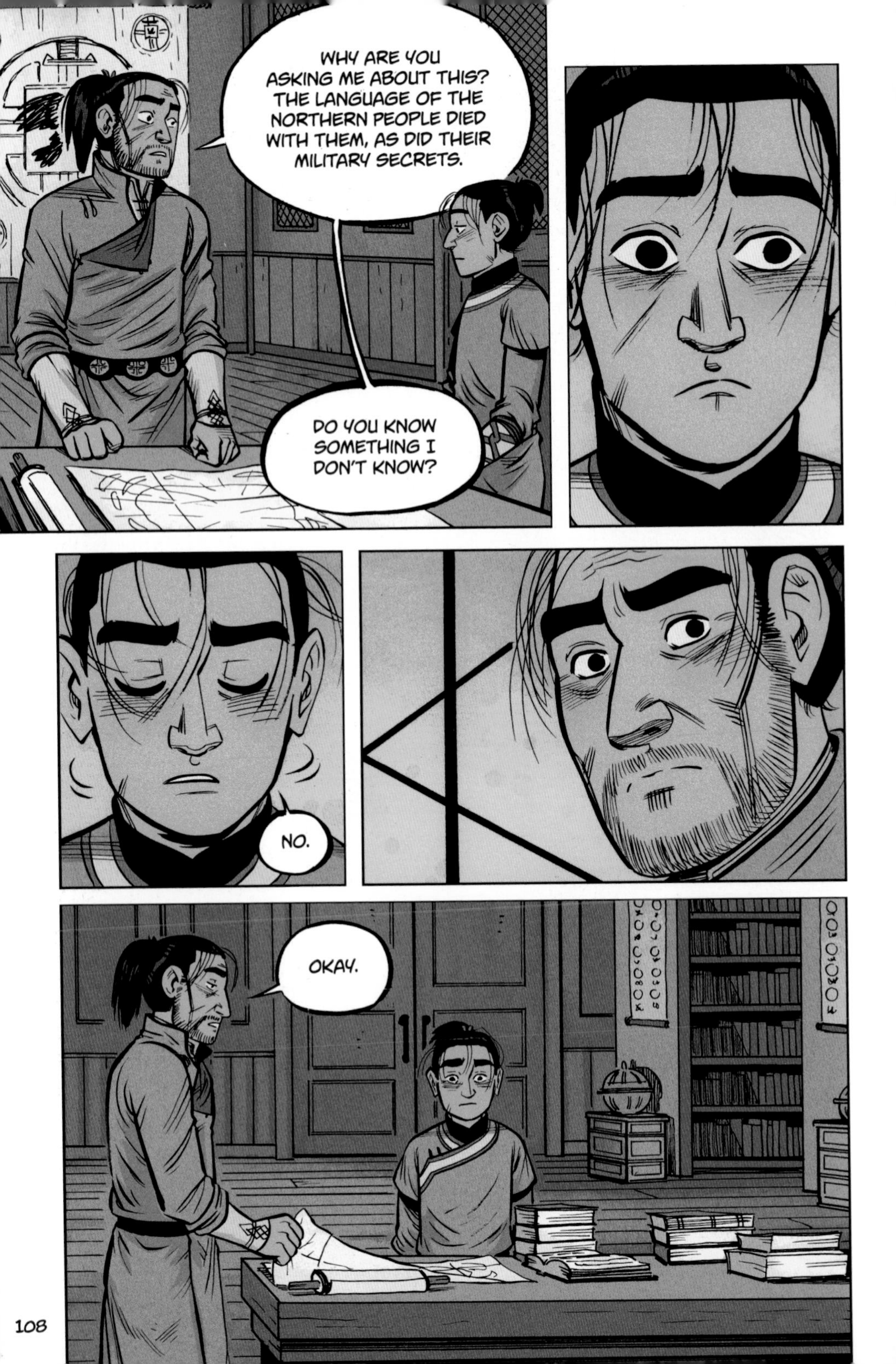
WHY ARE YOU ASKING ME ABOUT THIS? THE LANGUAGE OF THE NORTHERN PEOPLE DIED WITH THEM, AS DID THEIR MILITARY SECRETS.
DO YOU KNOW SOMETHING I DON'T KNOW?
NO.
OKAY.

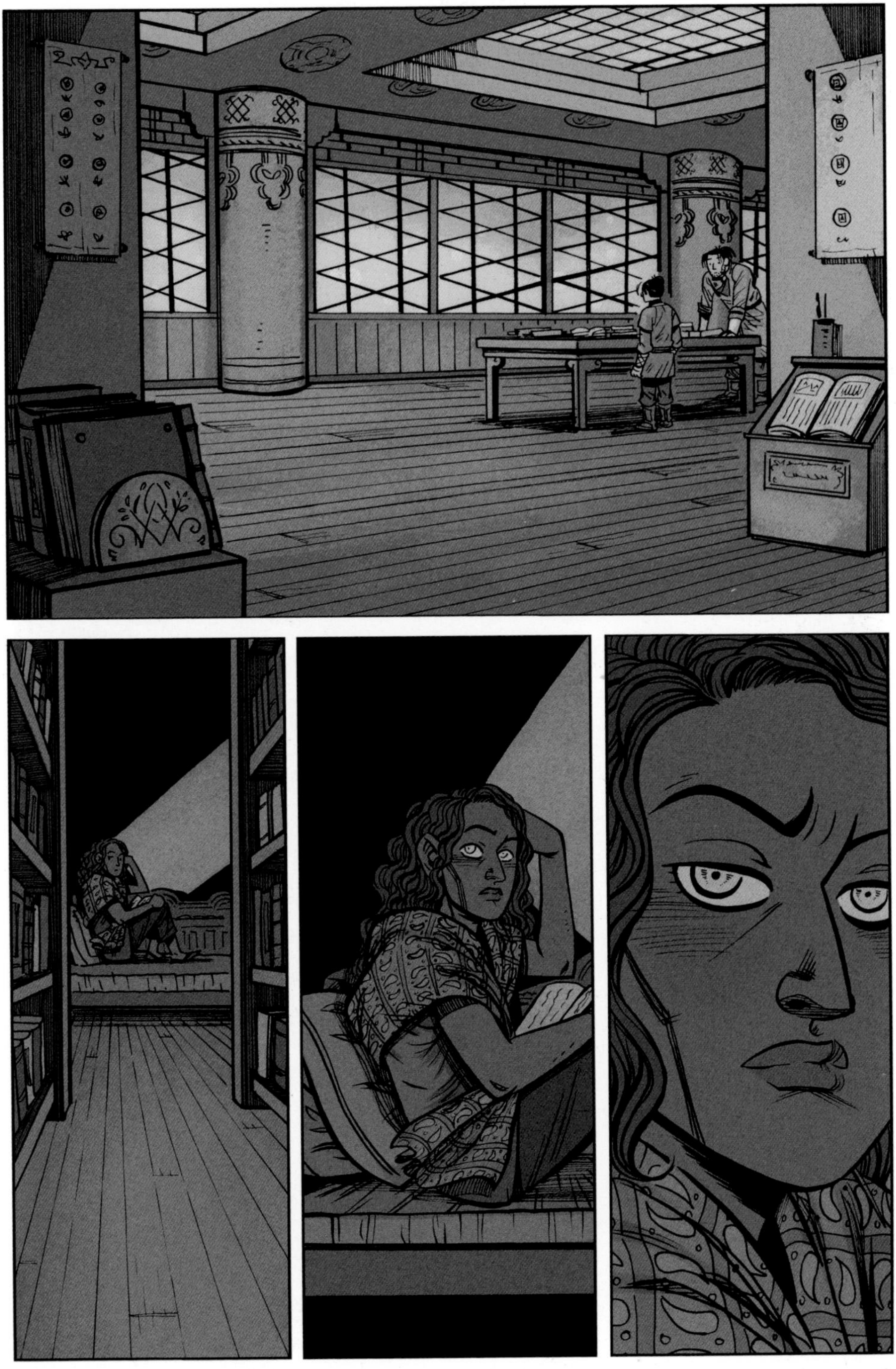

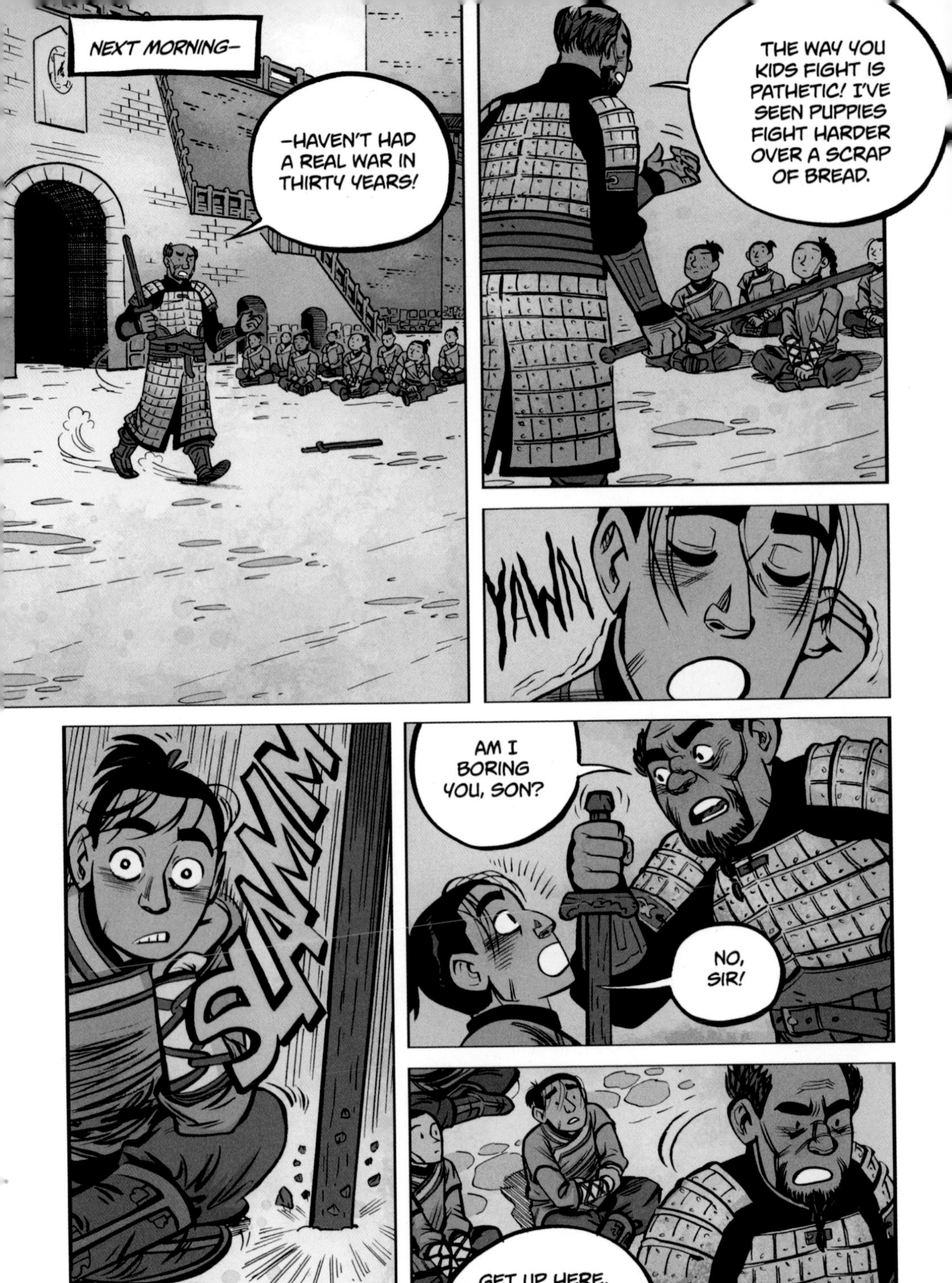
NEXT MORNING—
—HAVEN'T HAD A REAL WAR IN THIRTY YEARS!
THE WAY YOU KIDS FIGHT IS PATHETIC! I'VE SEEN PUPPIES FIGHT HARDER OVER A SCRAP OF BREAD.
YAWN
SLAMM
AM I BORING YOU, SON?
NO, SIR!
GET UP HERE, BOY. YOU GET TO BE MY SPARRING PARTNER TODAY.

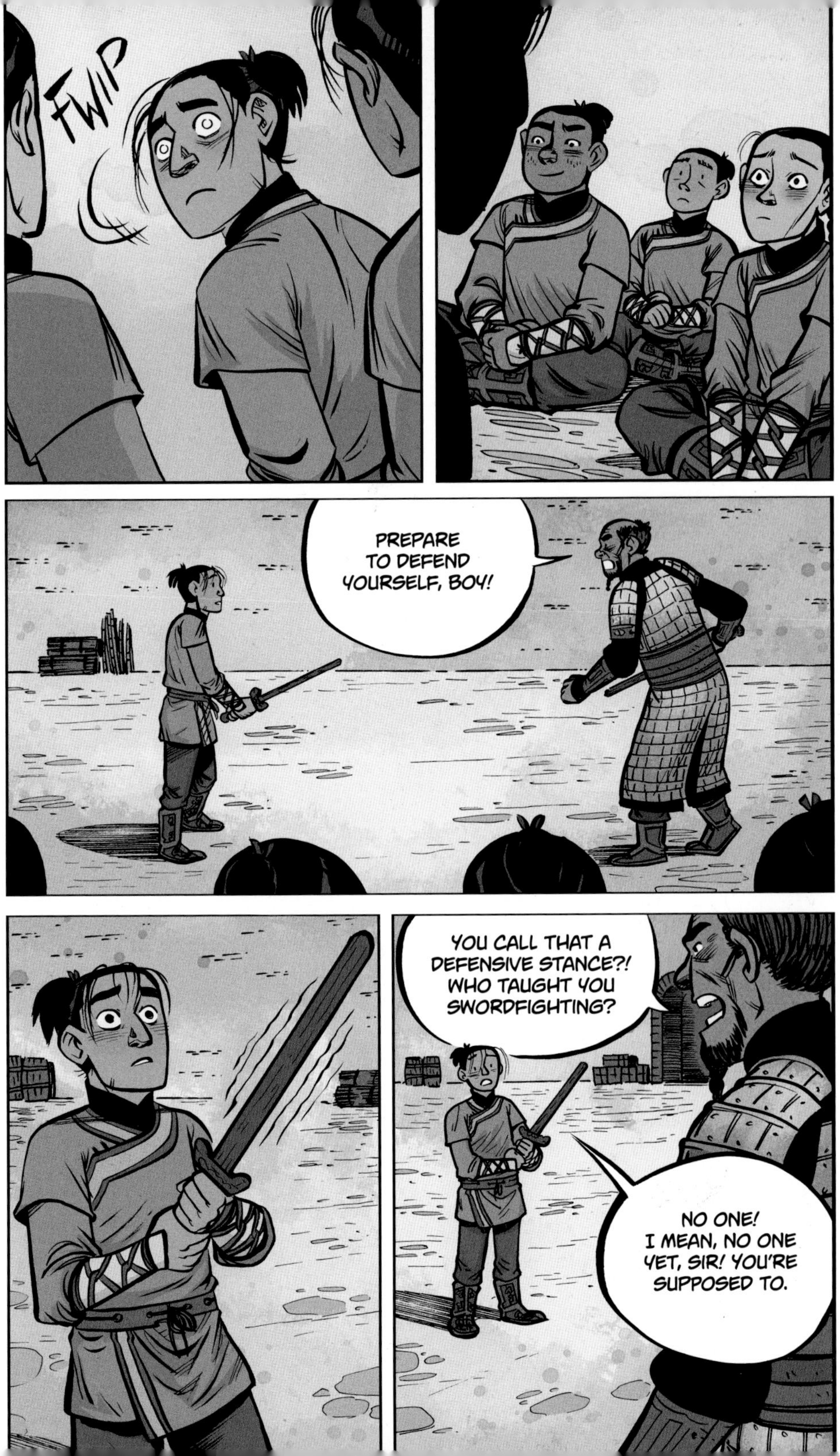
FWIP
PREPARE TO DEFEND YOURSELF, BOY!
YOU CALL THAT A DEFENSIVE STANCE?! WHO TAUGHT YOU SWORDFIGHTING?
NO ONE! I MEAN, NO ONE YET, SIR! YOU'RE SUPPOSED TO.

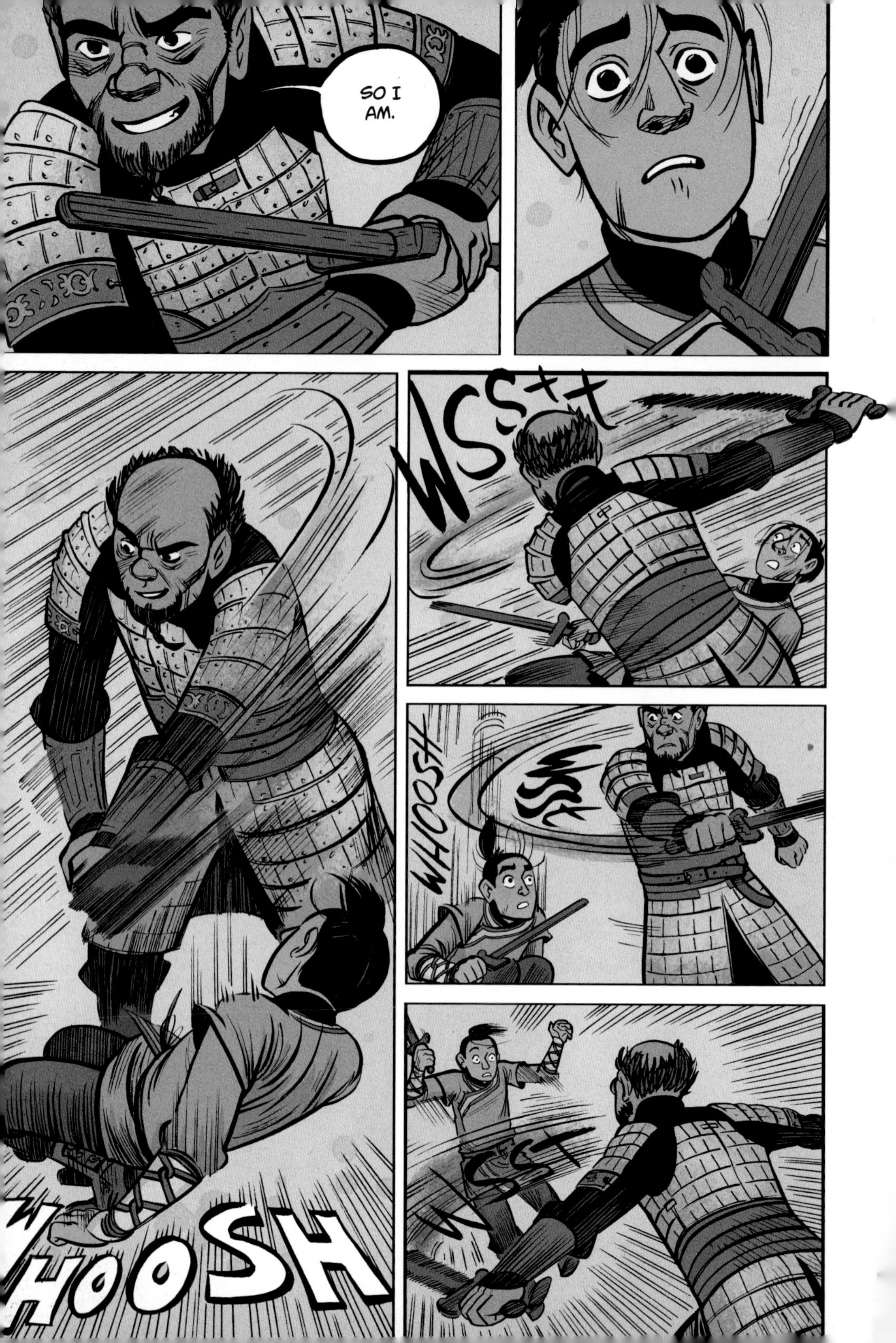
SO I AM.
WHOOSH
WSSttt
WHOOSH
WSSK
WSST

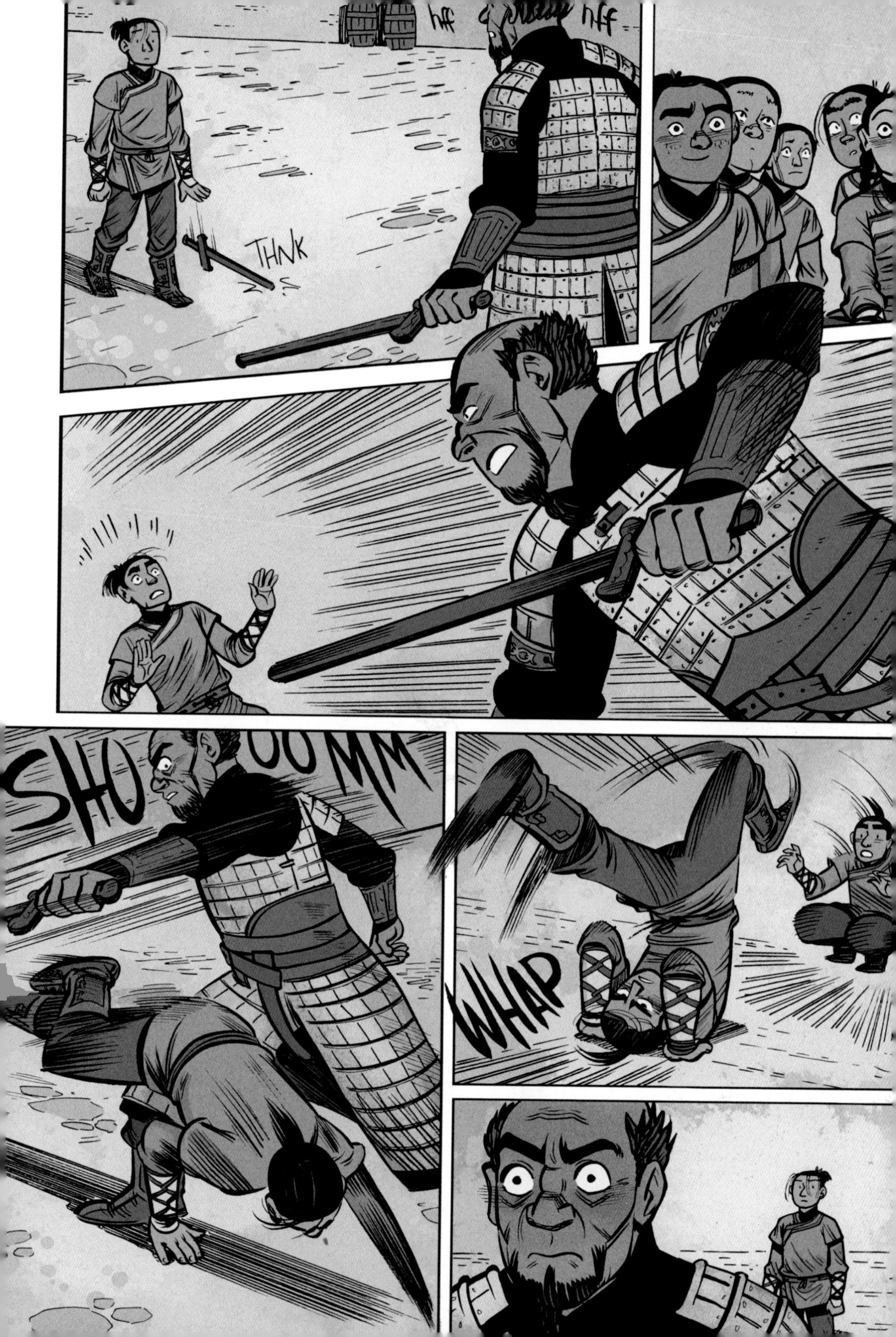

hff
hff
THNK
SHUOOMM
WHAP

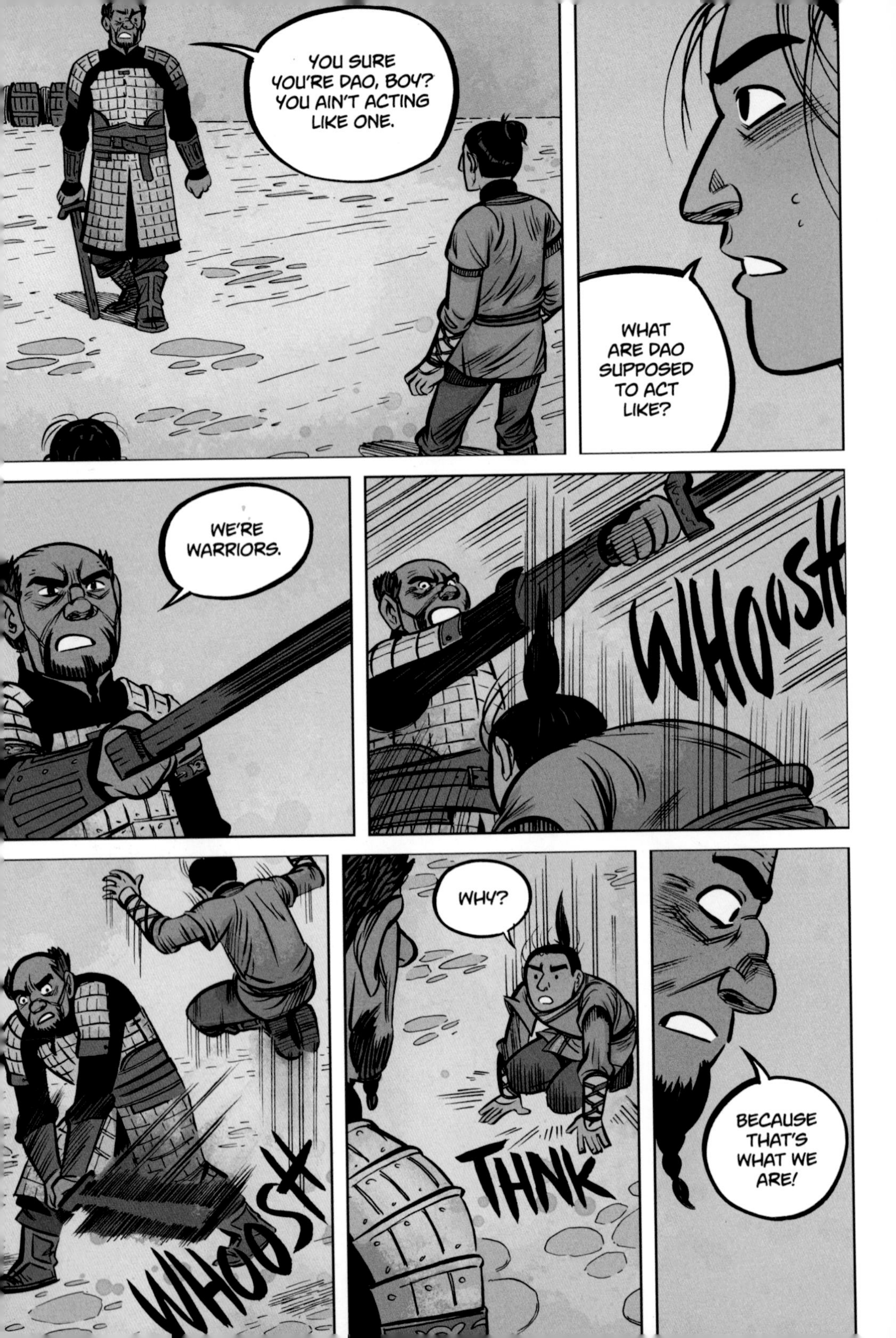
YOU SURE YOU'RE DAO, BOY? YOU AIN'T ACTING LIKE ONE.
WHAT ARE DAO SUPPOSED TO ACT LIKE?
WE'RE WARRIORS.
WHOOSH
WHOOSH
WHY?
THNK
BECAUSE THAT'S WHAT WE ARE!

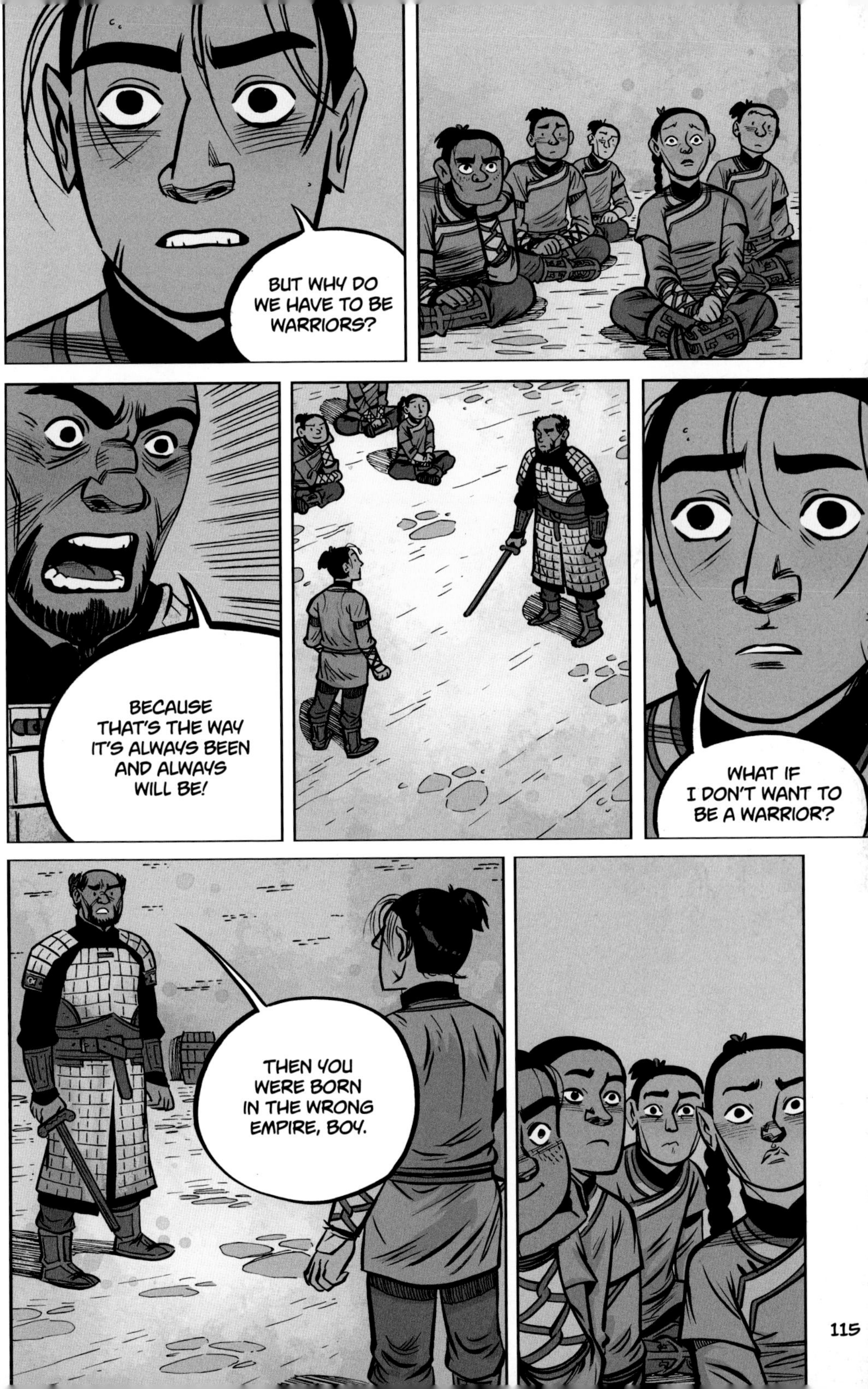
BUT WHY DO WE HAVE TO BE WARRIORS?
BECAUSE THAT'S THE WAY IT'S ALWAYS BEEN AND ALWAYS WILL BE!
WHAT IF I DON'T WANT TO BE A WARRIOR?
THEN YOU WERE BORN IN THE WRONG EMPIRE, BOY.

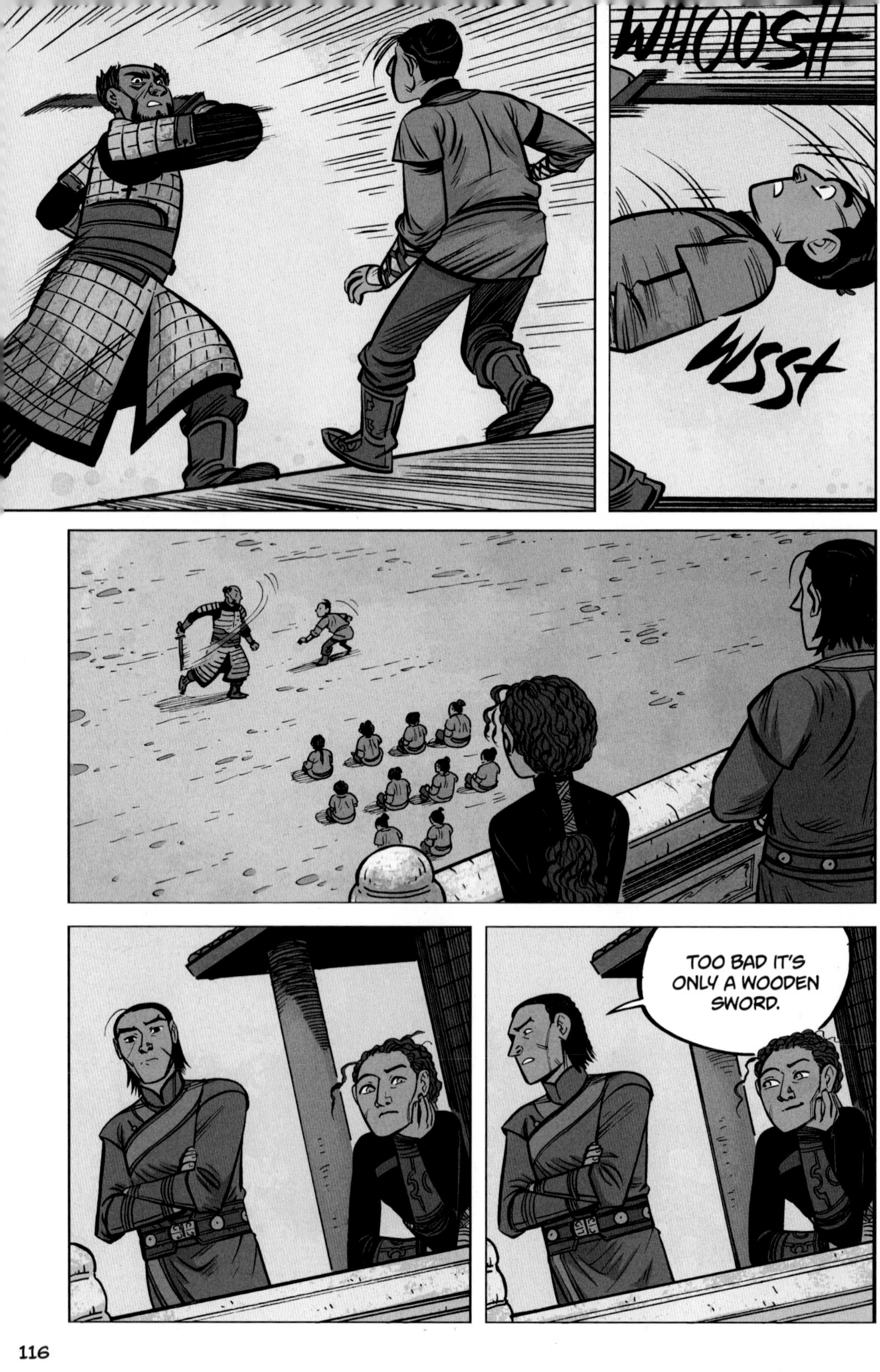
WHOOSH
WSSH
TOO BAD IT'S ONLY A WOODEN SWORD.

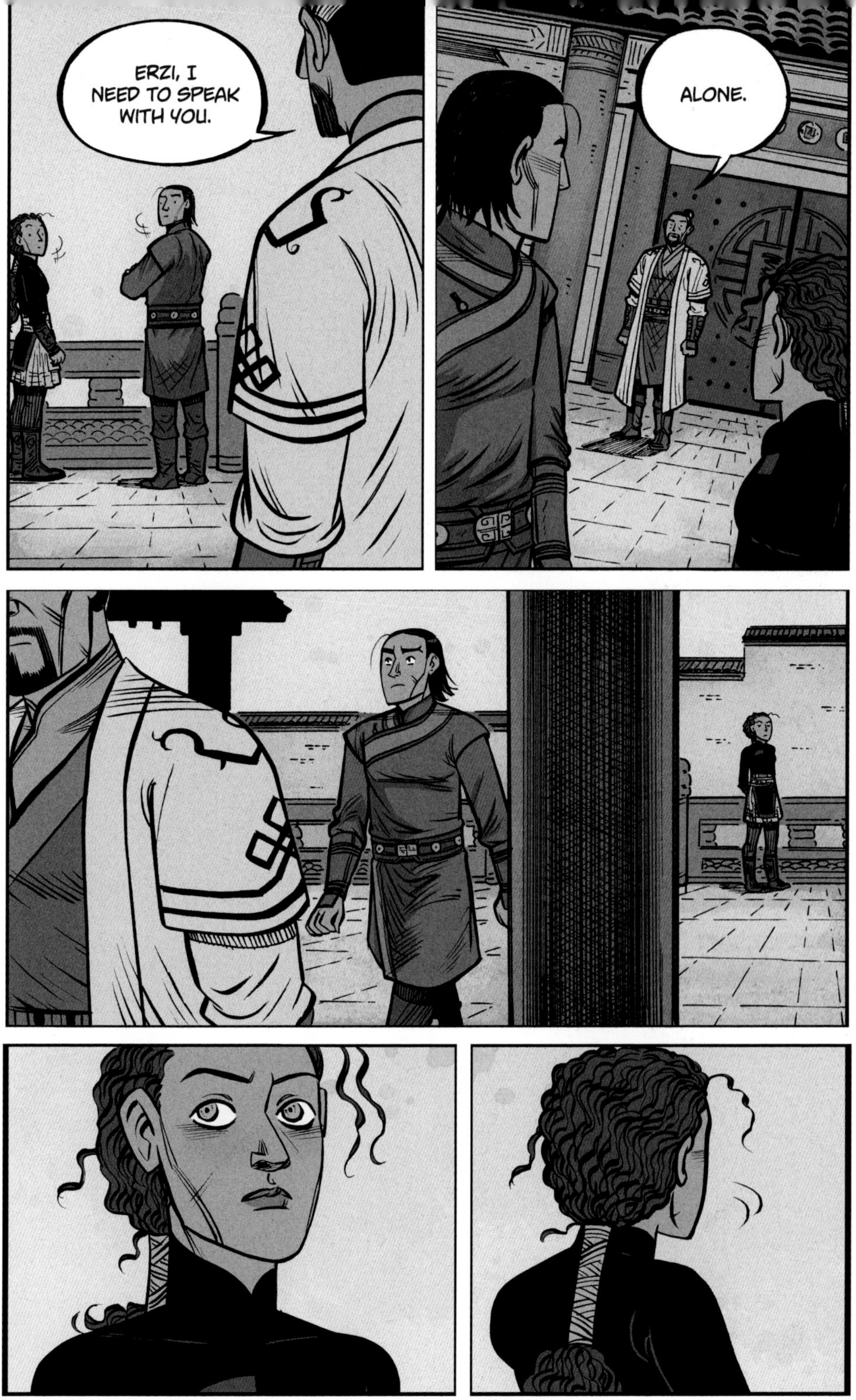
ERZI, I NEED TO SPEAK WITH YOU.
ALONE.

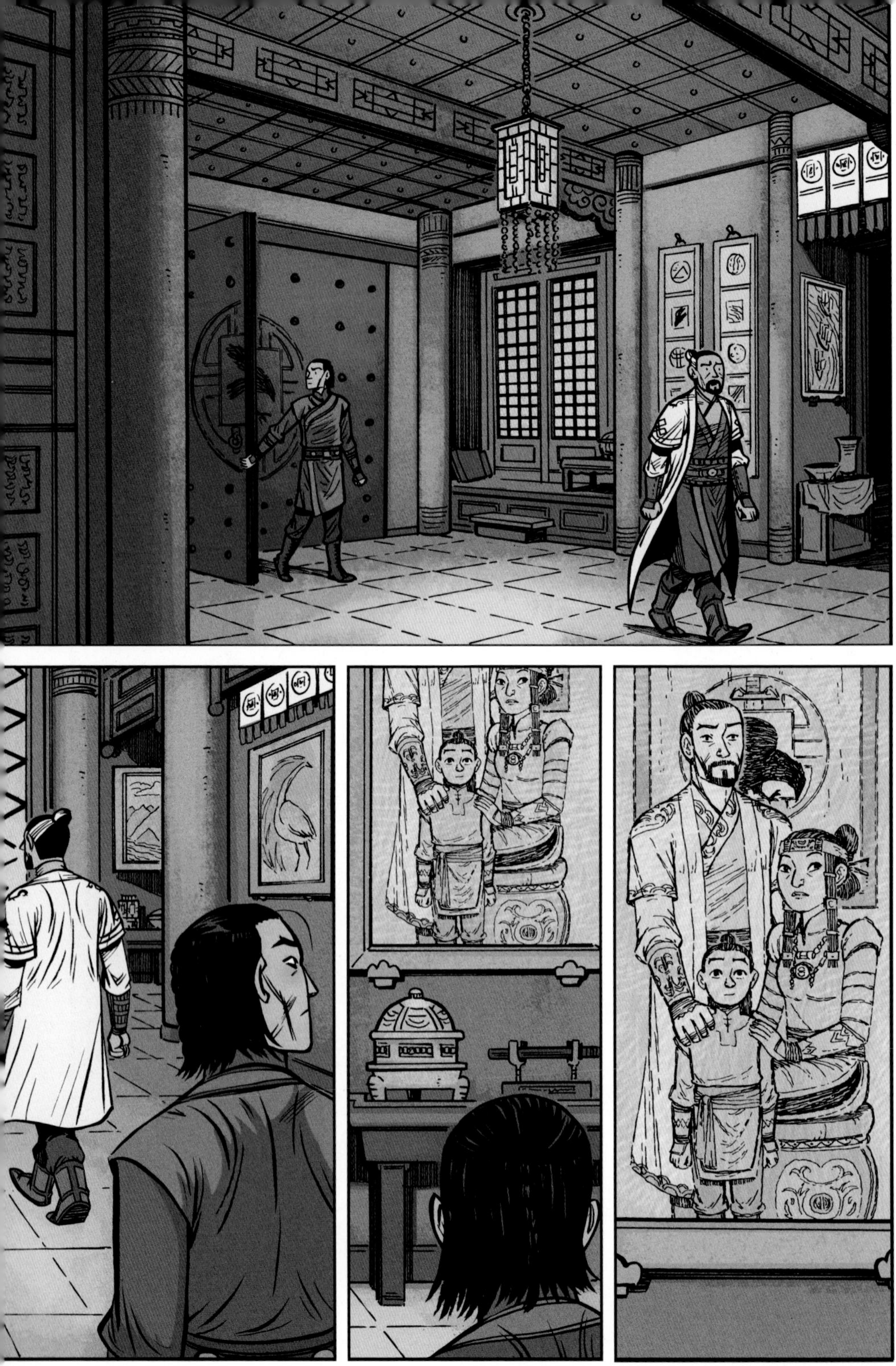

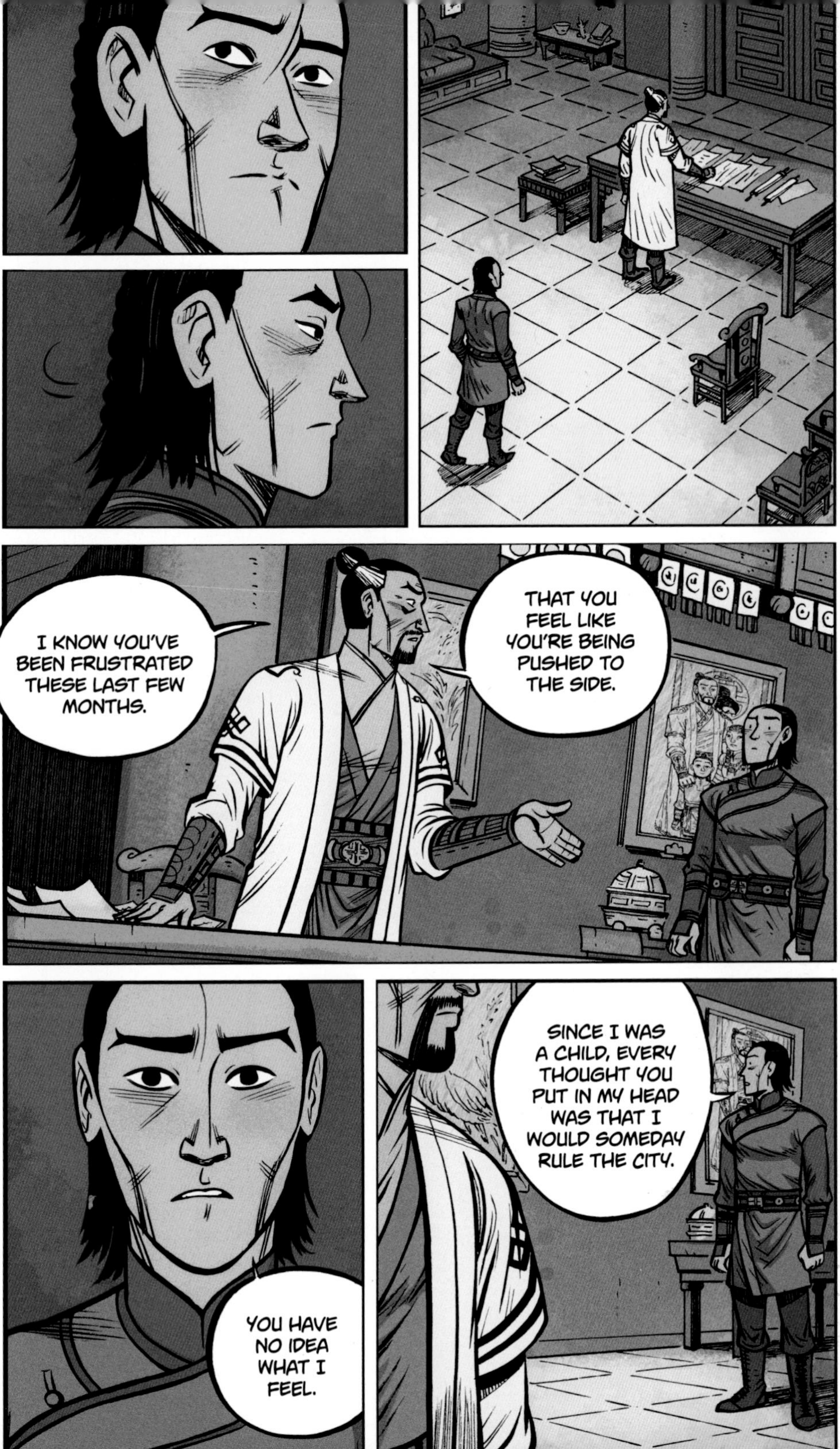
I KNOW YOU'VE BEEN FRUSTRATED THESE LAST FEW MONTHS.
THAT YOU FEEL LIKE YOU'RE BEING PUSHED TO THE SIDE.
YOU HAVE NO IDEA WHAT I FEEL.
SINCE I WAS A CHILD, EVERY THOUGHT YOU PUT IN MY HEAD WAS THAT I WOULD SOMEDAY RULE THE CITY.

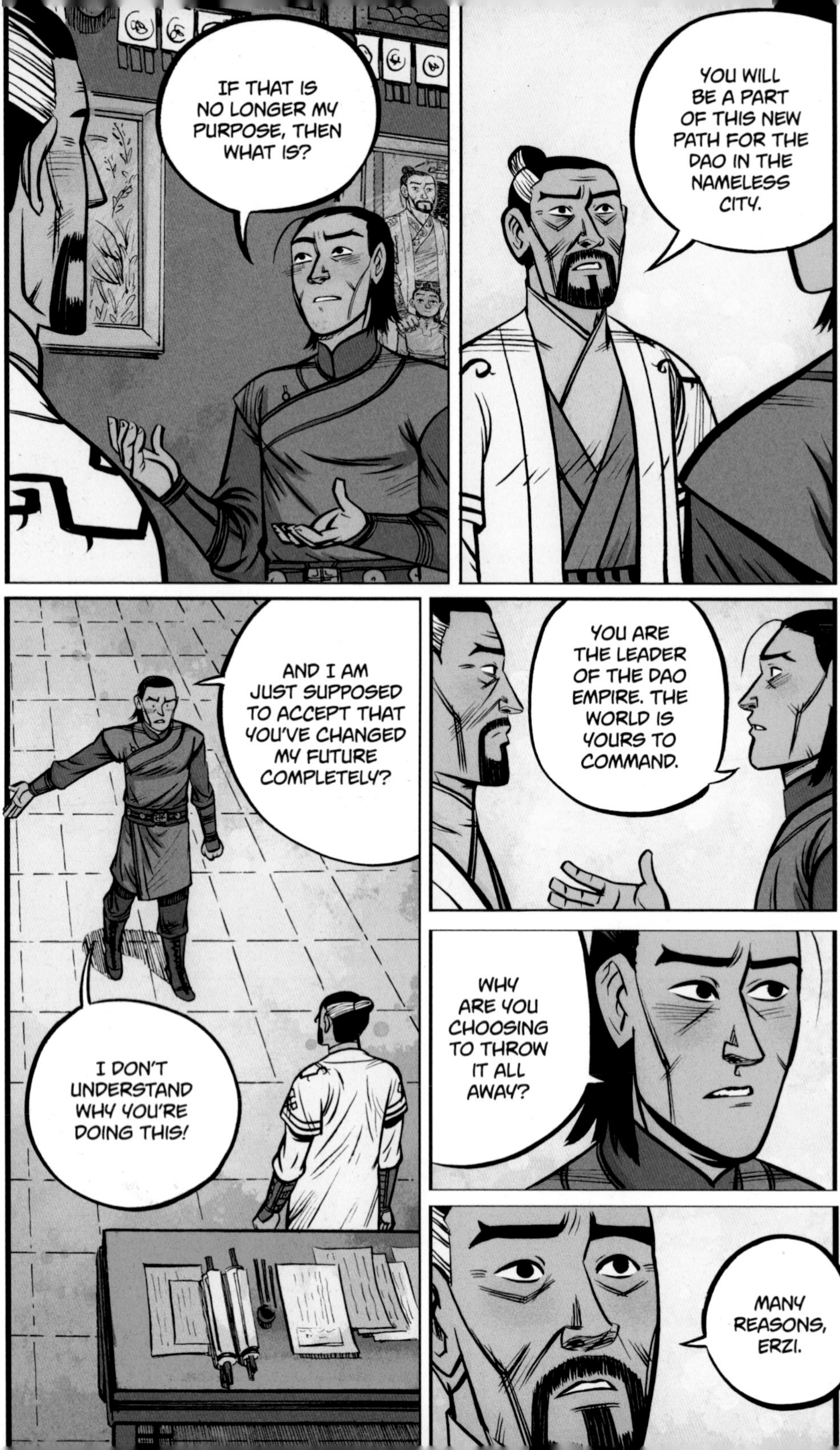
IF THAT IS NO LONGER MY PURPOSE, THEN WHAT IS?
YOU WILL BE A PART OF THIS NEW PATH FOR THE DAO IN THE NAMELESS CITY.
AND I AM JUST SUPPOSED TO ACCEPT THAT YOU'VE CHANGED MY FUTURE COMPLETELY?
I DON'T UNDERSTAND WHY YOU'RE DOING THIS!
YOU ARE THE LEADER OF THE DAO EMPIRE. THE WORLD IS YOURS TO COMMAND.
WHY ARE YOU CHOOSING TO THROW IT ALL AWAY?
MANY REASONS, ERZI.

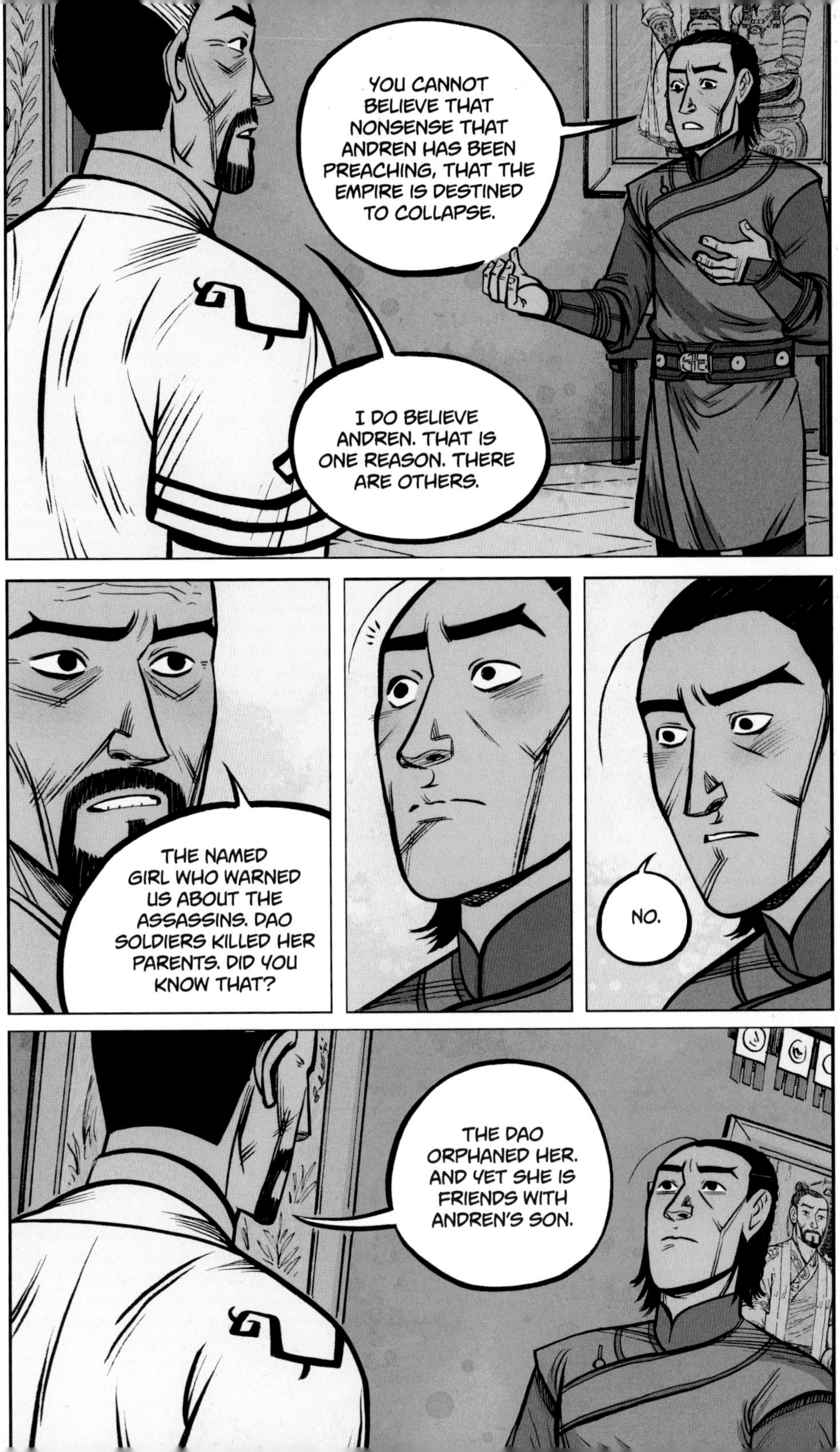
YOU CANNOT BELIEVE THAT NONSENSE THAT ANDREN HAS BEEN PREACHING, THAT THE EMPIRE IS DESTINED TO COLLAPSE.
I DO BELIEVE ANDREN. THAT IS ONE REASON. THERE ARE OTHERS.
THE NAMED GIRL WHO WARNED US ABOUT THE ASSASSINS. DAO SOLDIERS KILLED HER PARENTS. DID YOU KNOW THAT?
NO.
THE DAO ORPHANED HER. AND YET SHE IS FRIENDS WITH ANDREN'S SON.

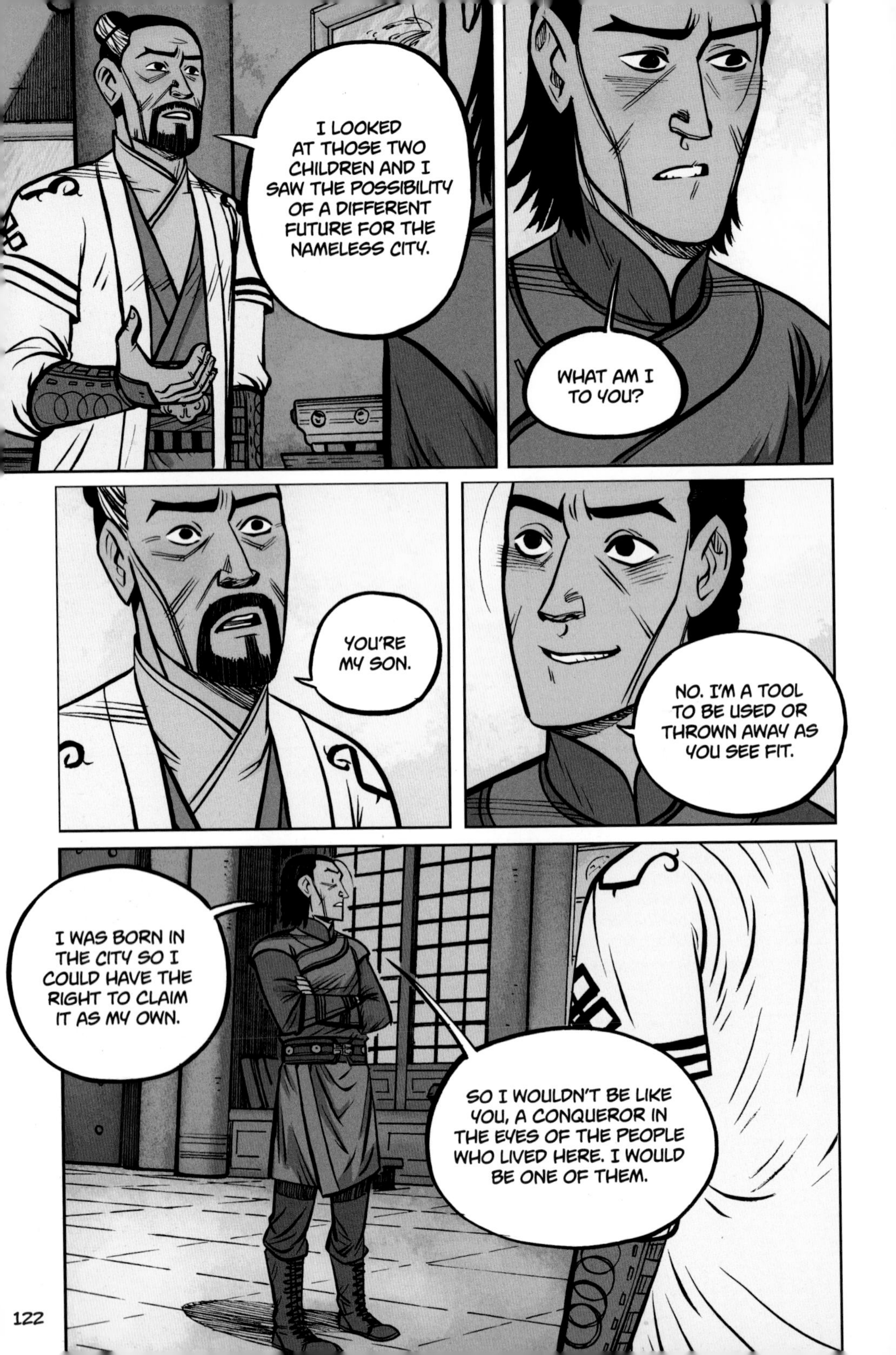
I LOOKED AT THOSE TWO CHILDREN AND I SAW THE POSSIBILITY OF A DIFFERENT FUTURE FOR THE NAMELESS CITY.
WHAT AM I TO YOU?
YOU'RE MY SON.
NO. I'M A TOOL TO BE USED OR THROWN AWAY AS YOU SEE FIT.
I WAS BORN IN THE CITY SO I COULD HAVE THE RIGHT TO CLAIM IT AS MY OWN.
SO I WOULDN'T BE LIKE YOU, A CONQUEROR IN THE EYES OF THE PEOPLE WHO LIVED HERE. I WOULD BE ONE OF THEM.

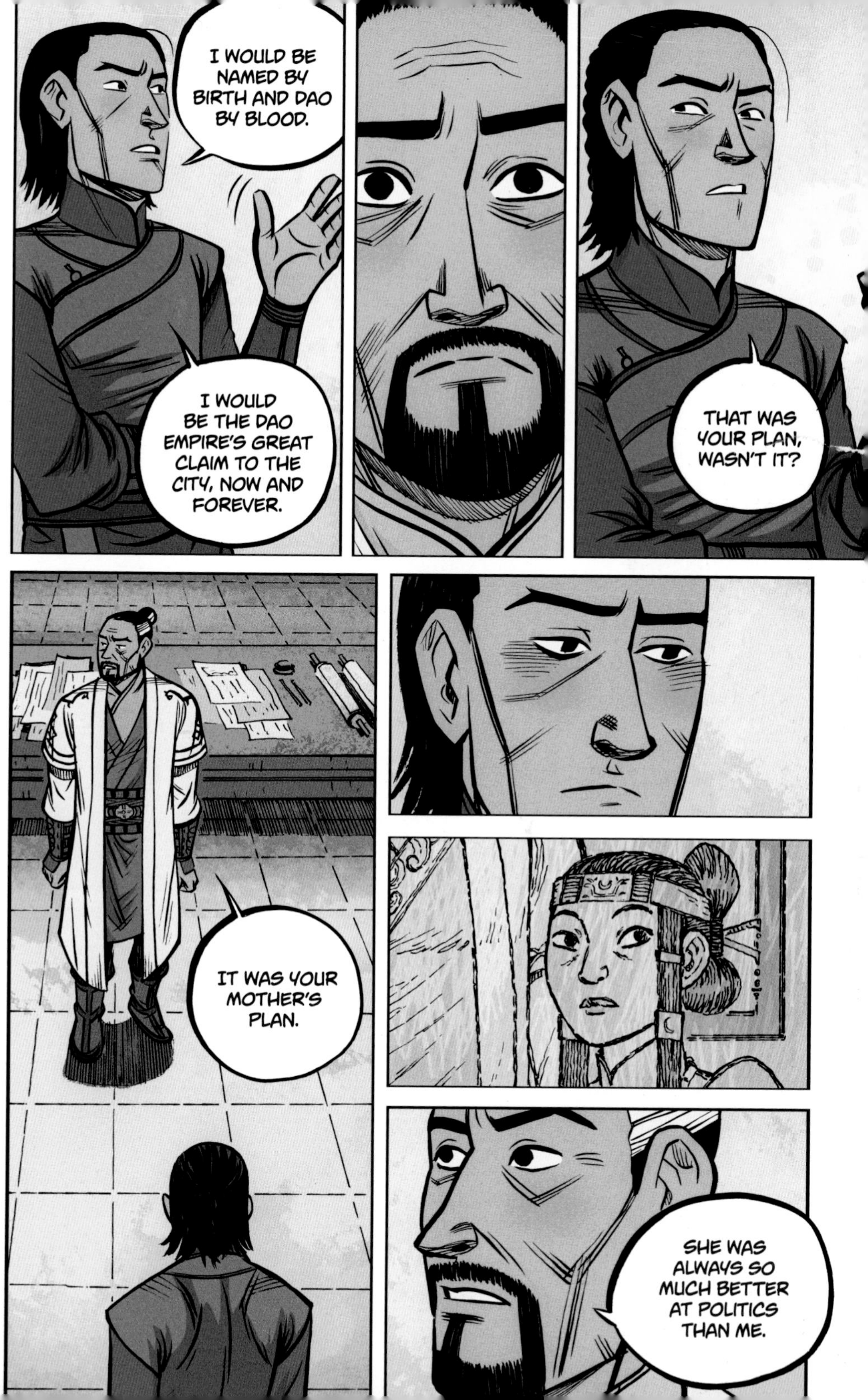
I WOULD BE NAMED BY BIRTH AND DAO BY BLOOD.
I WOULD BE THE DAO EMPIRE'S GREAT CLAIM TO THE CITY, NOW AND FOREVER.
THAT WAS YOUR PLAN, WASN'T IT?
IT WAS YOUR MOTHER'S PLAN.
SHE WAS ALWAYS SO MUCH BETTER AT POLITICS THAN ME.

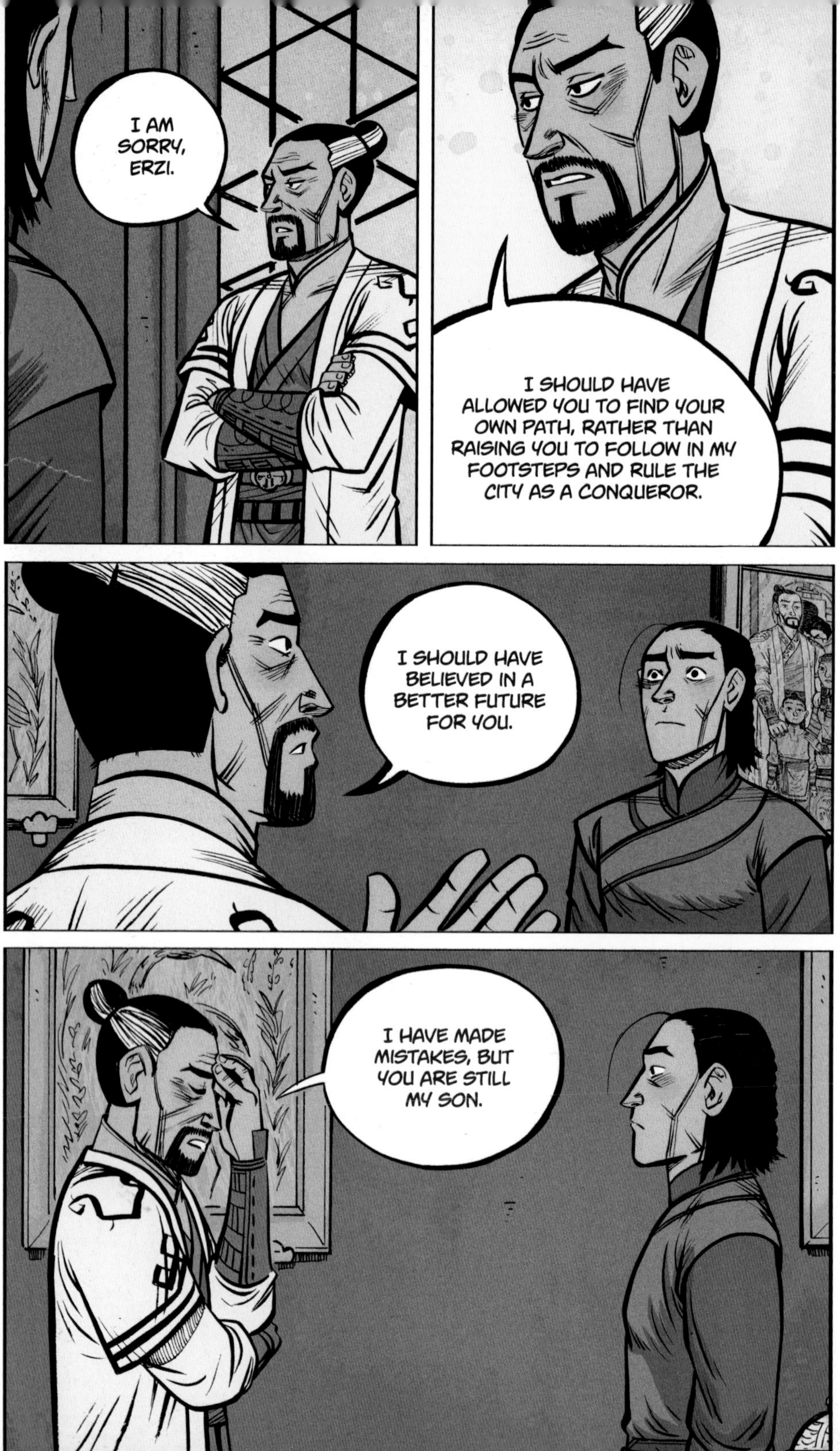
I AM SORRY, ERZI.
I SHOULD HAVE ALLOWED YOU TO FIND YOUR OWN PATH, RATHER THAN RAISING YOU TO FOLLOW IN MY FOOTSTEPS AND RULE THE CITY AS A CONQUEROR.
I SHOULD HAVE BELIEVED IN A BETTER FUTURE FOR YOU.
I HAVE MADE MISTAKES, BUT YOU ARE STILL MY SON.

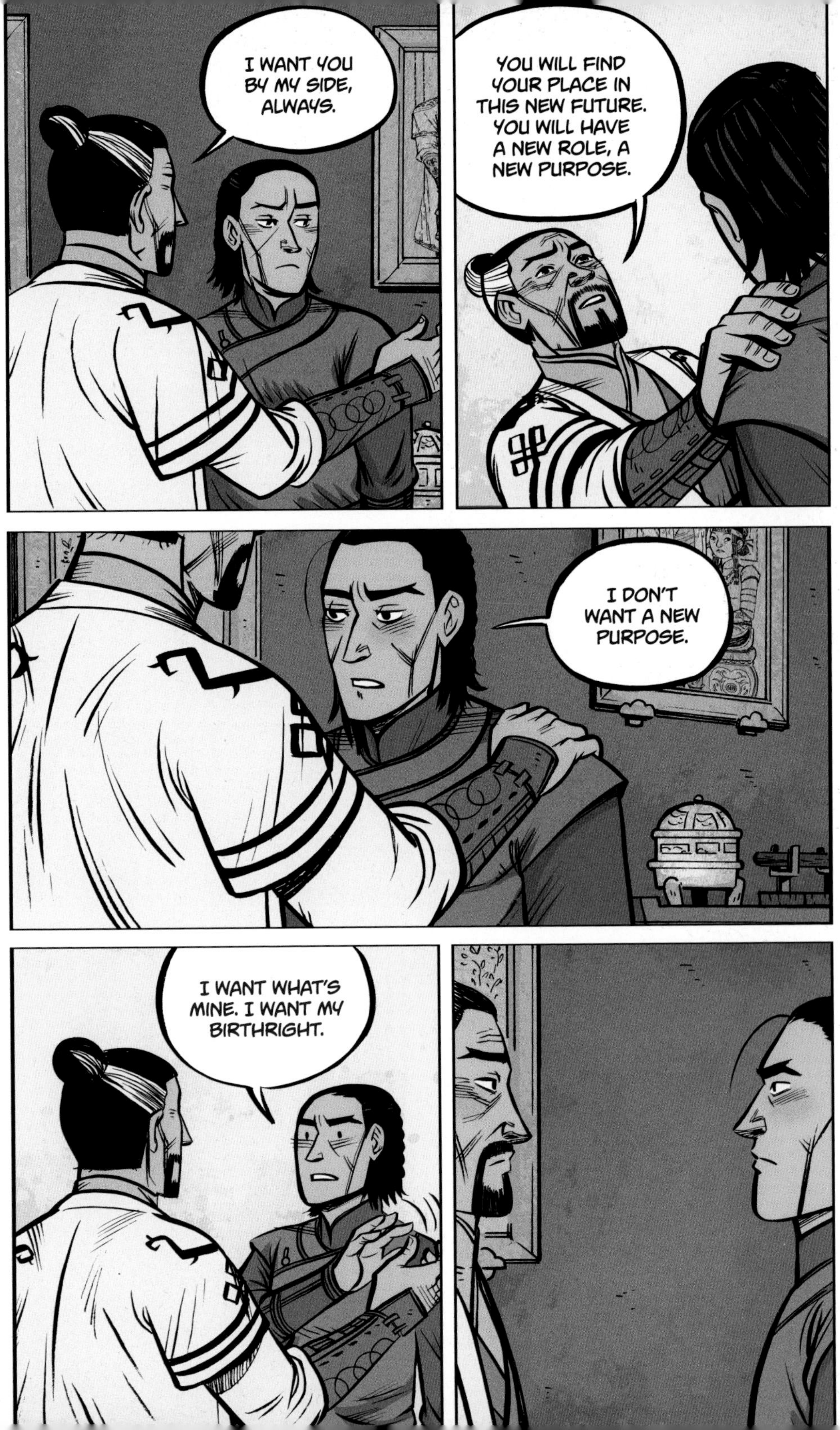
I WANT YOU BY MY SIDE, ALWAYS.
YOU WILL FIND YOUR PLACE IN THIS NEW FUTURE. YOU WILL HAVE A NEW ROLE, A NEW PURPOSE.
I DON'T WANT A NEW PURPOSE.
I WANT WHAT'S MINE. I WANT MY BIRTHRIGHT.

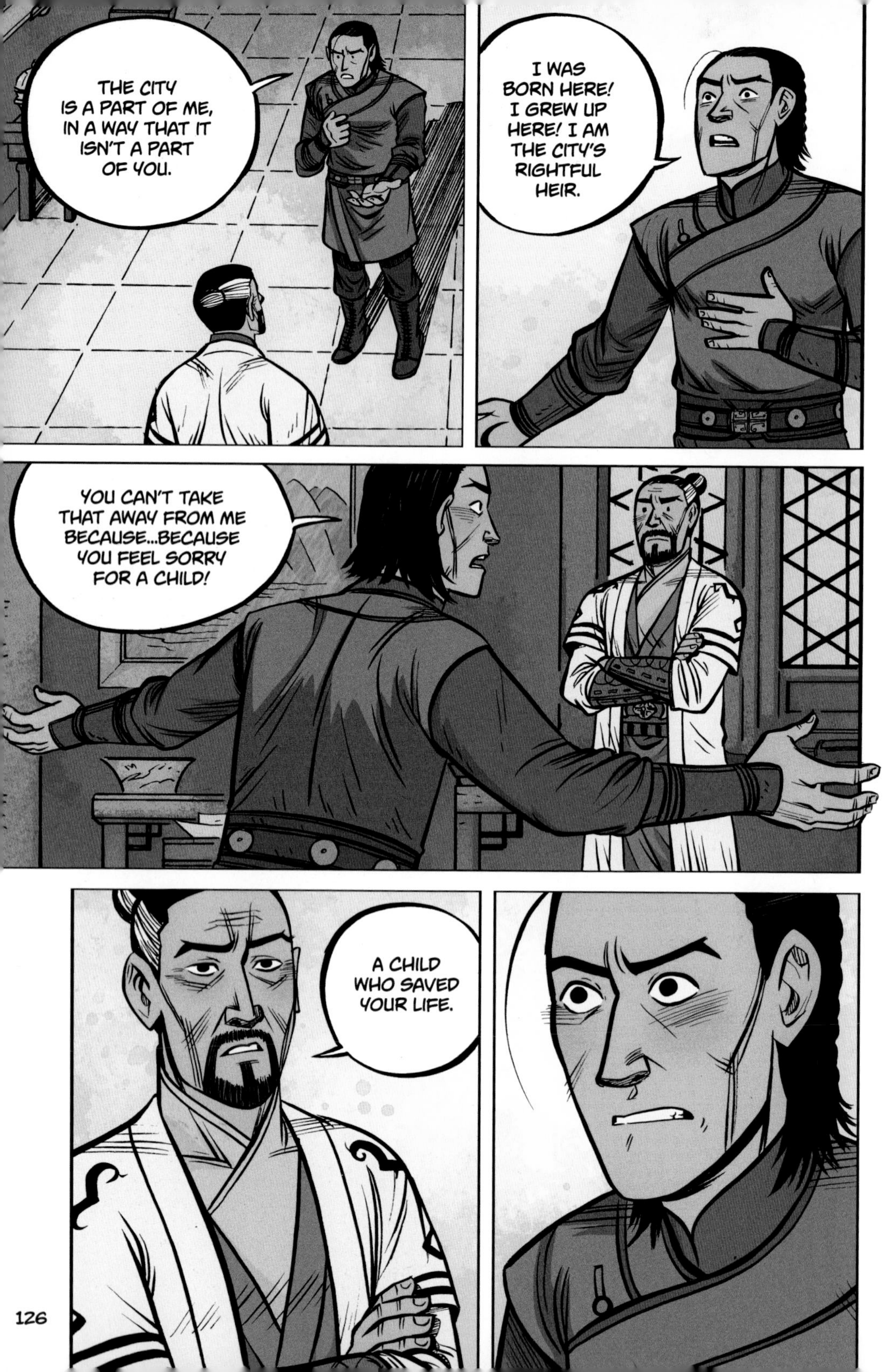
THE CITY IS A PART OF ME, IN A WAY THAT IT ISN'T A PART OF YOU.
I WAS BORN HERE! I GREW UP HERE! I AM THE CITY'S RIGHTFUL HEIR.
YOU CAN'T TAKE THAT AWAY FROM ME BECAUSE...BECAUSE YOU FEEL SORRY FOR A CHILD!
A CHILD WHO SAVED YOUR LIFE.

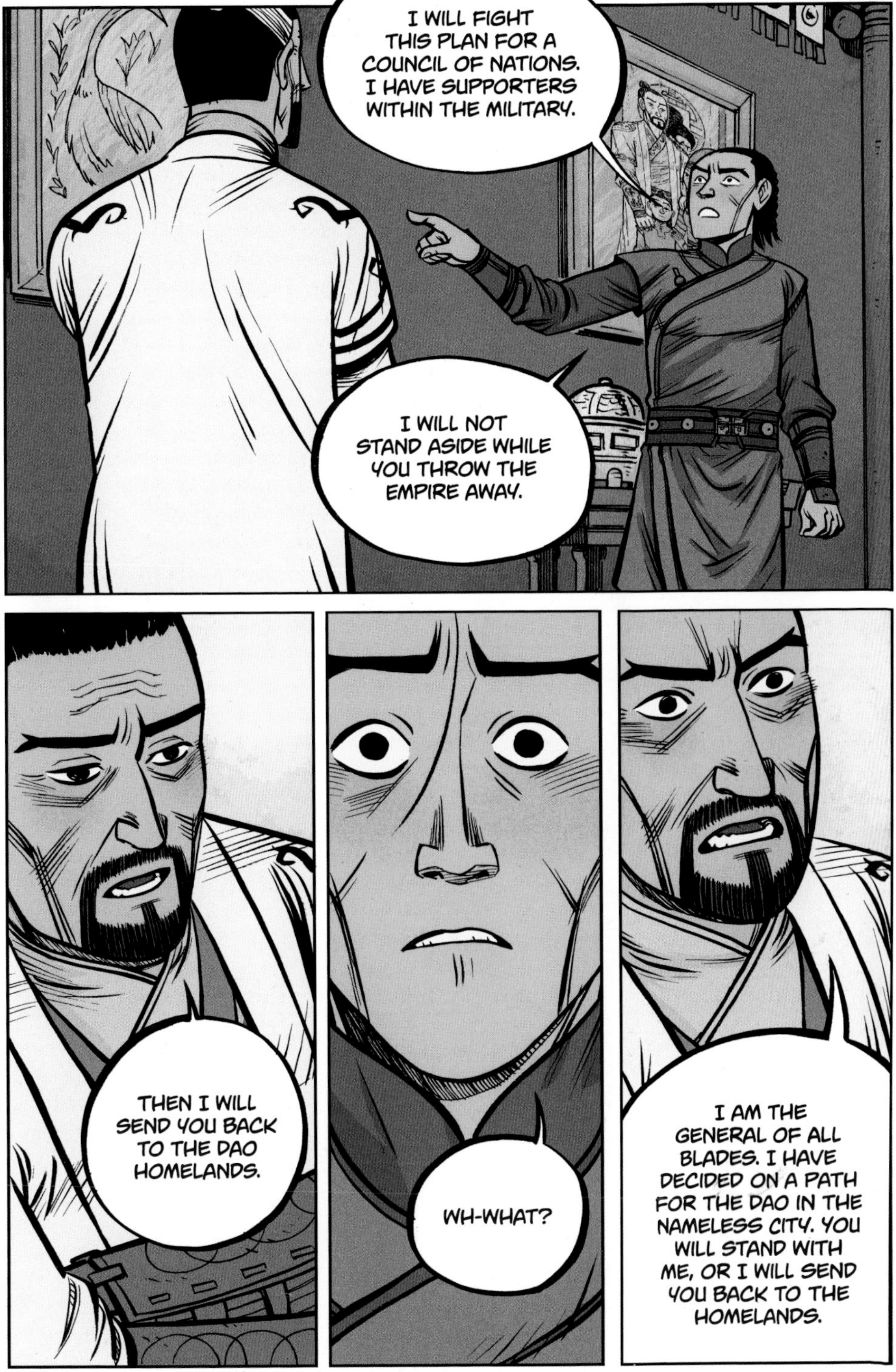
I WILL FIGHT THIS PLAN FOR A COUNCIL OF NATIONS. I HAVE SUPPORTERS WITHIN THE MILITARY.
I WILL NOT STAND ASIDE WHILE YOU THROW THE EMPIRE AWAY.
THEN I WILL SEND YOU BACK TO THE DAO HOMELANDS.
WH-WHAT?
I AM THE GENERAL OF ALL BLADES. I HAVE DECIDED ON A PATH FOR THE DAO IN THE NAMELESS CITY. YOU WILL STAND WITH ME, OR I WILL SEND YOU BACK TO THE HOMELANDS.

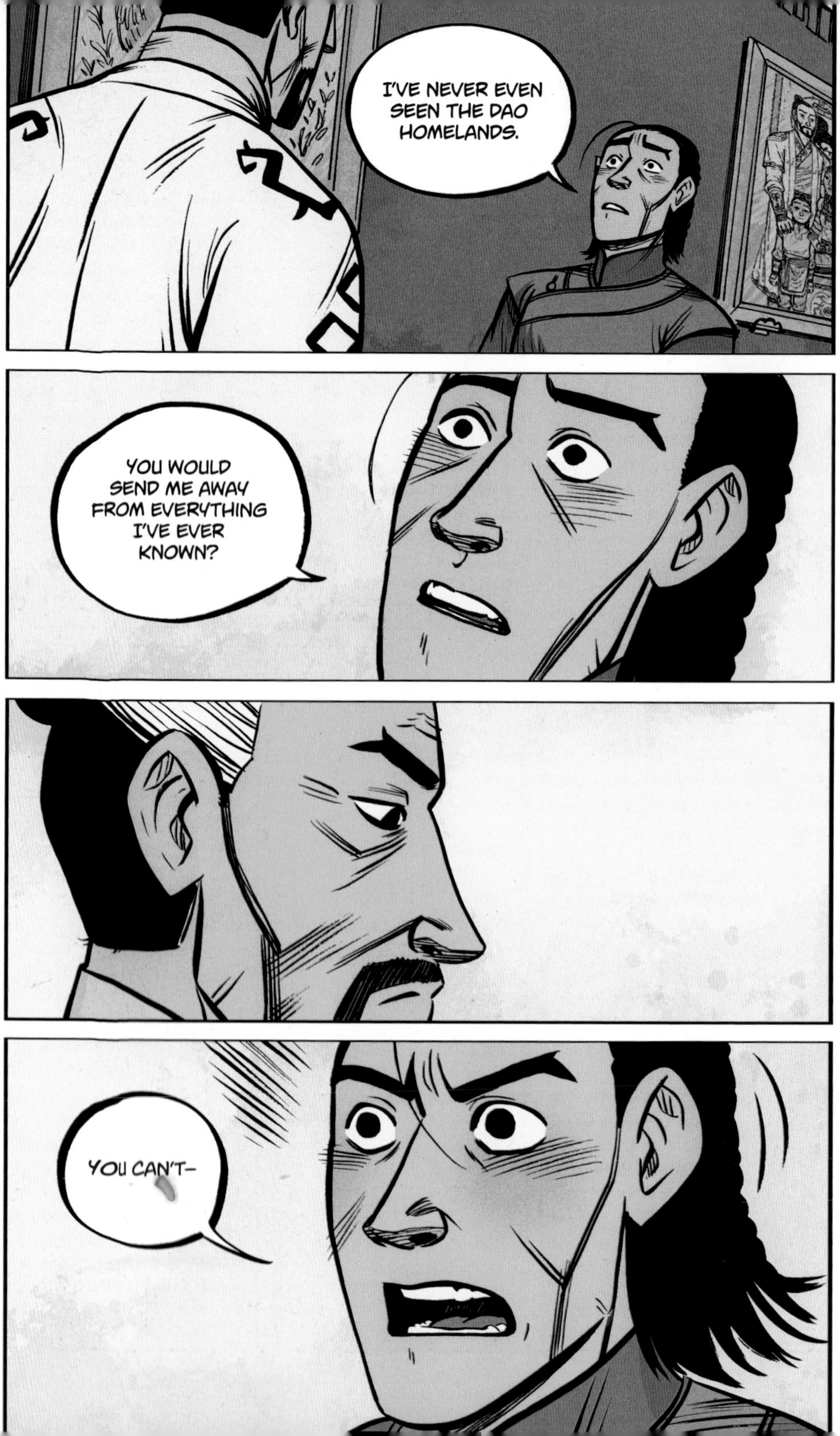

I'VE NEVER EVEN SEEN THE DAO HOMELANDS.
YOU WOULD SEND ME AWAY FROM EVERYTHING I'VE EVER KNOWN?
YOU CAN'T-

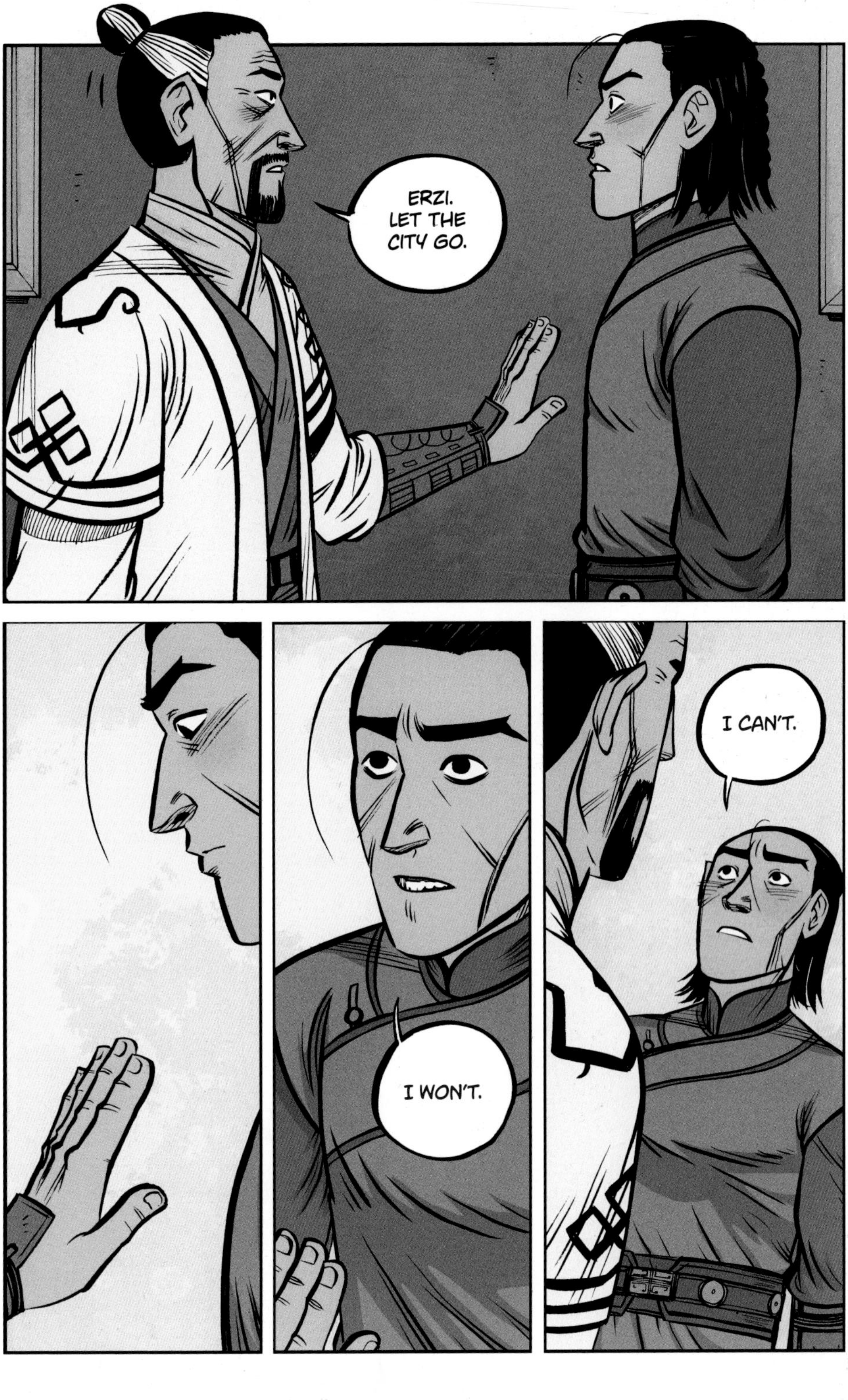
ERZI.
LET THE
CITY GO.
I WON'T.
I CAN'T.

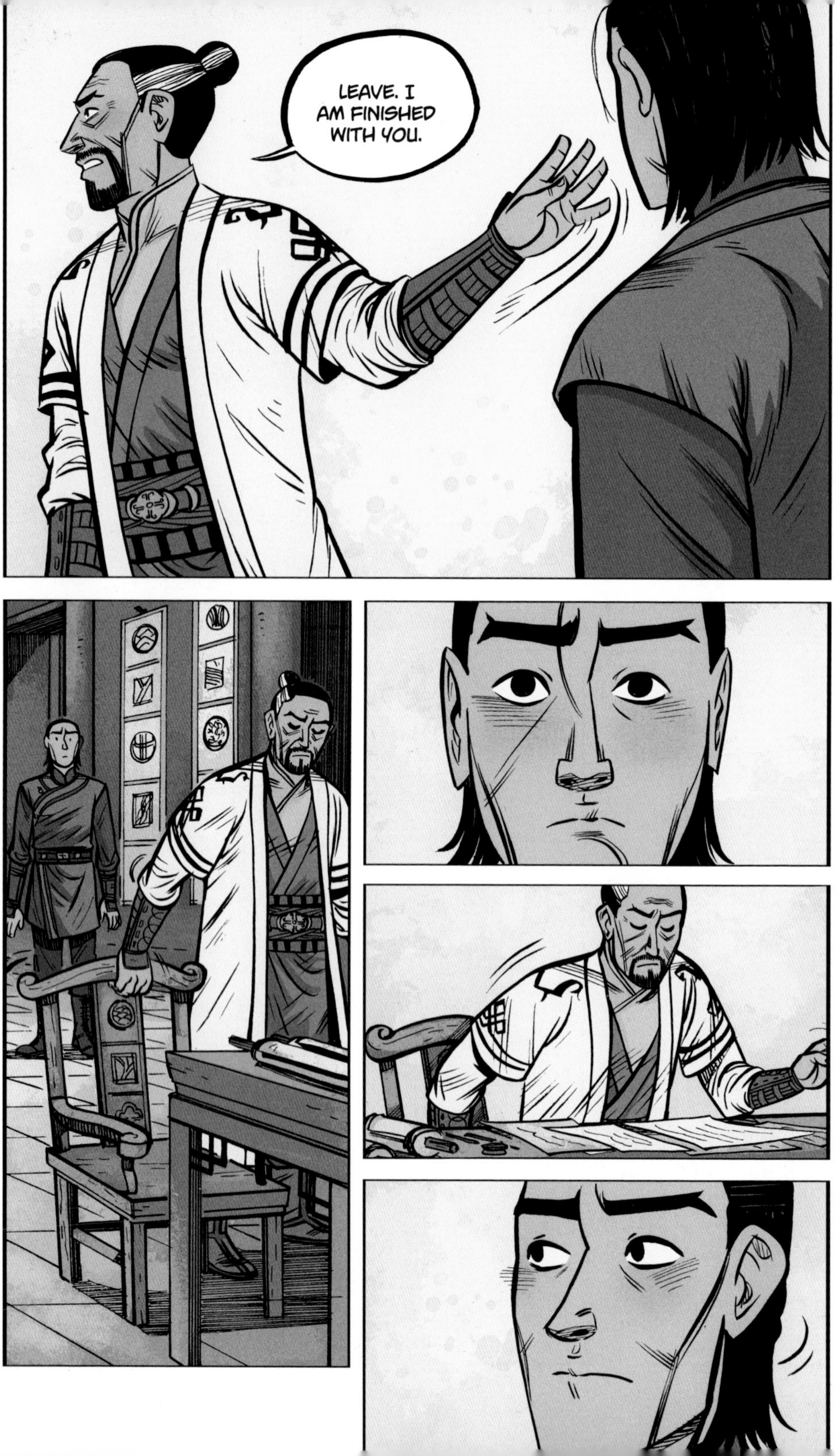
LEAVE. I AM FINISHED WITH YOU.

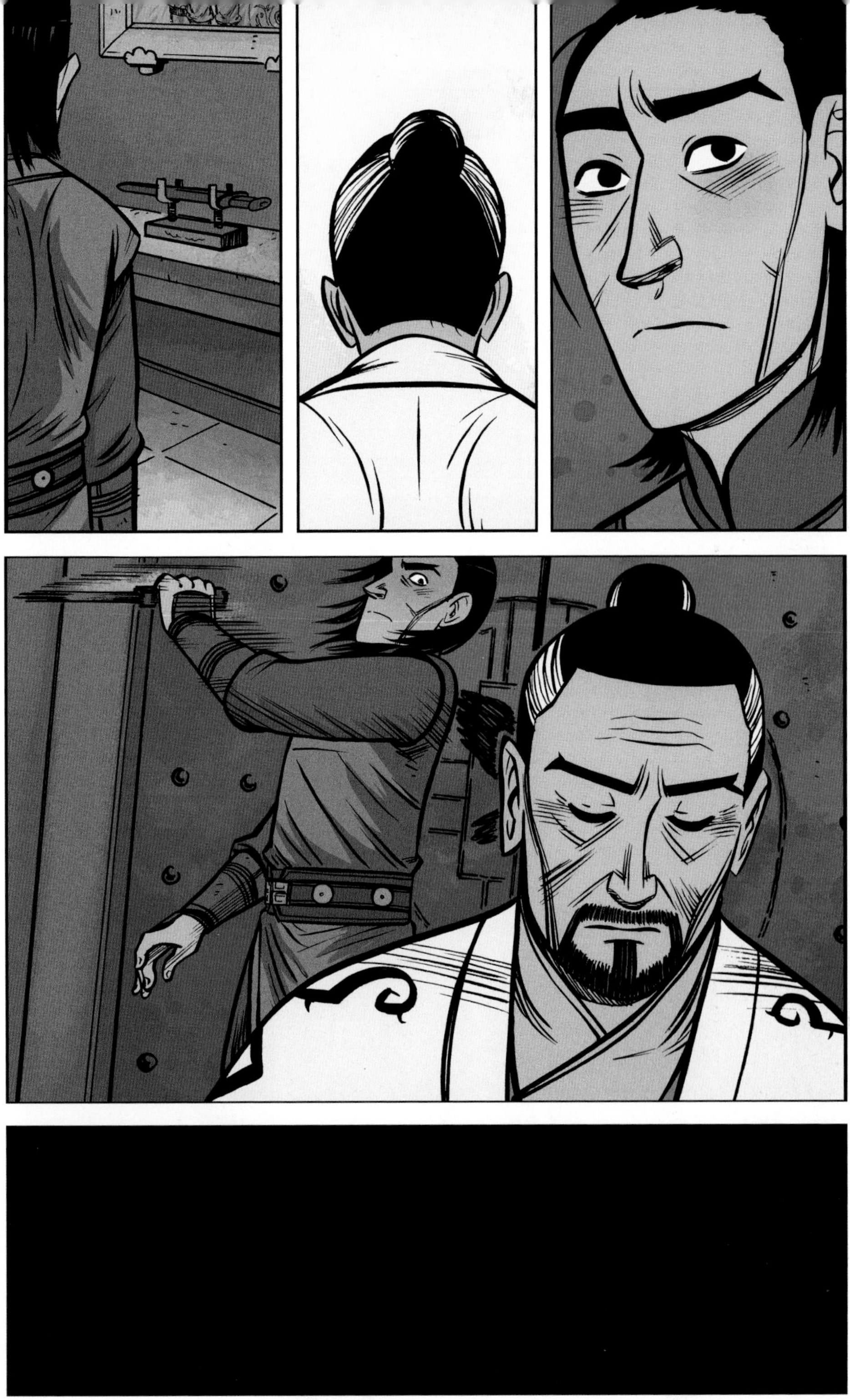

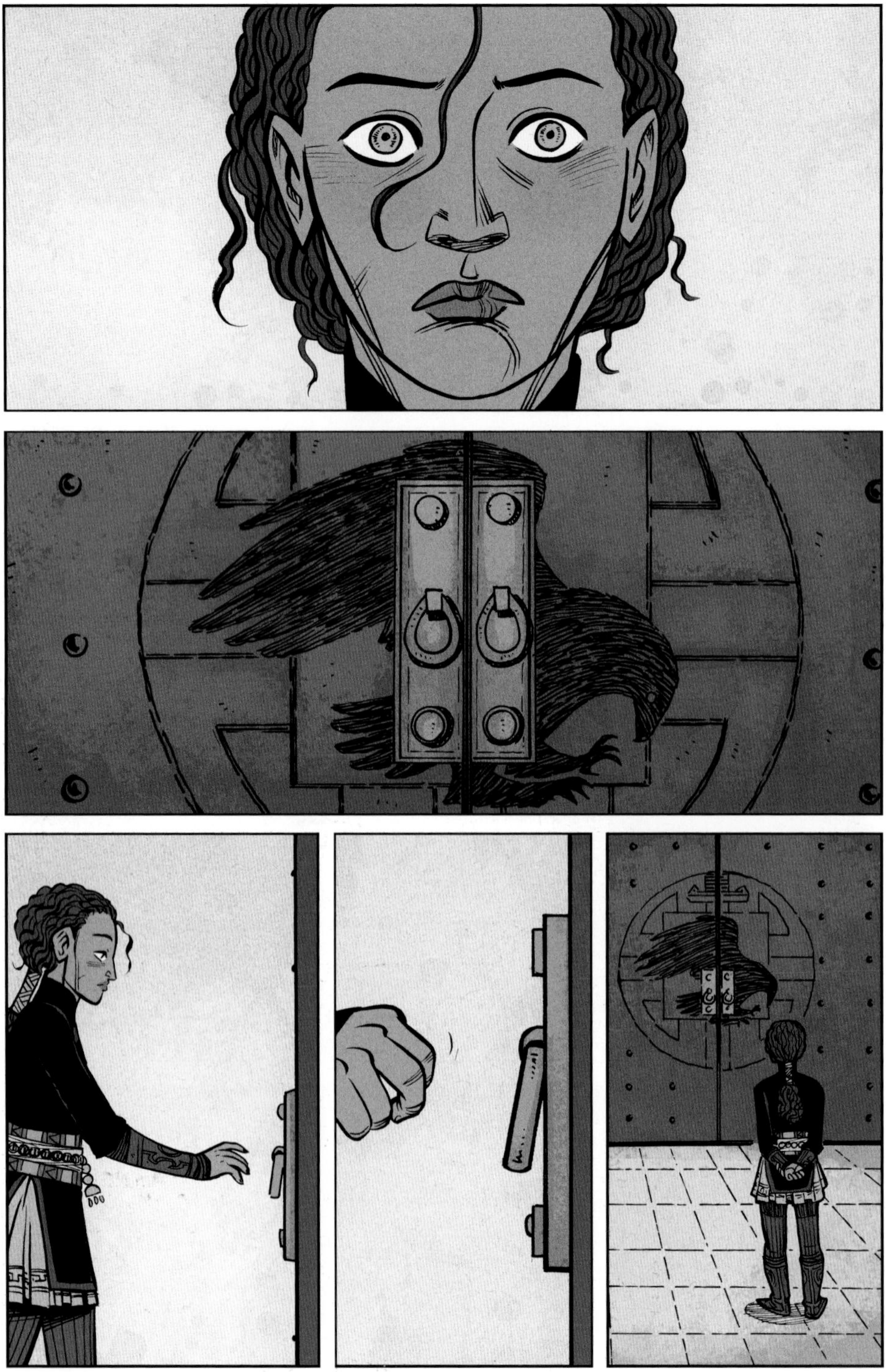

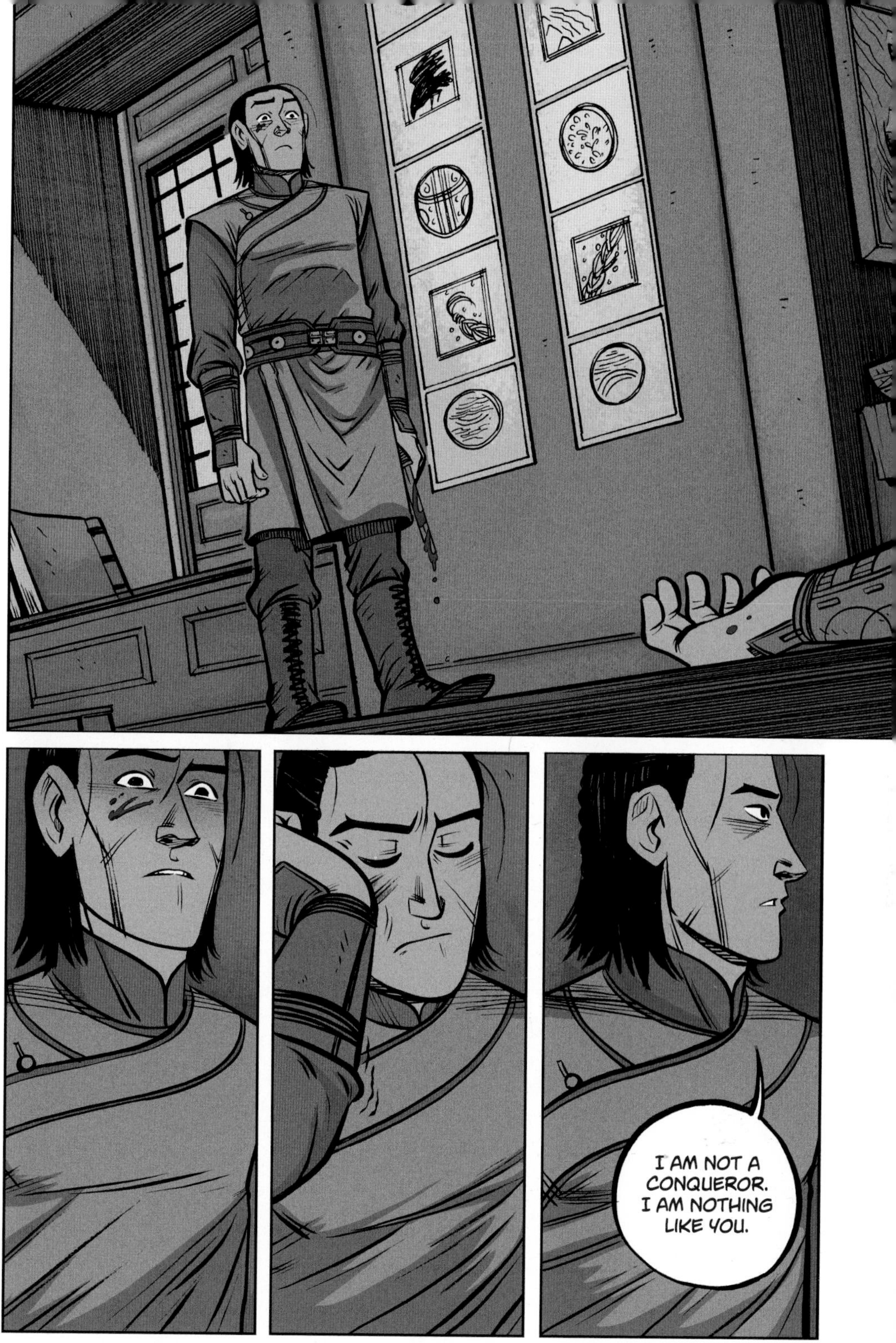
I AM NOT A CONQUEROR. I AM NOTHING LIKE YOU.

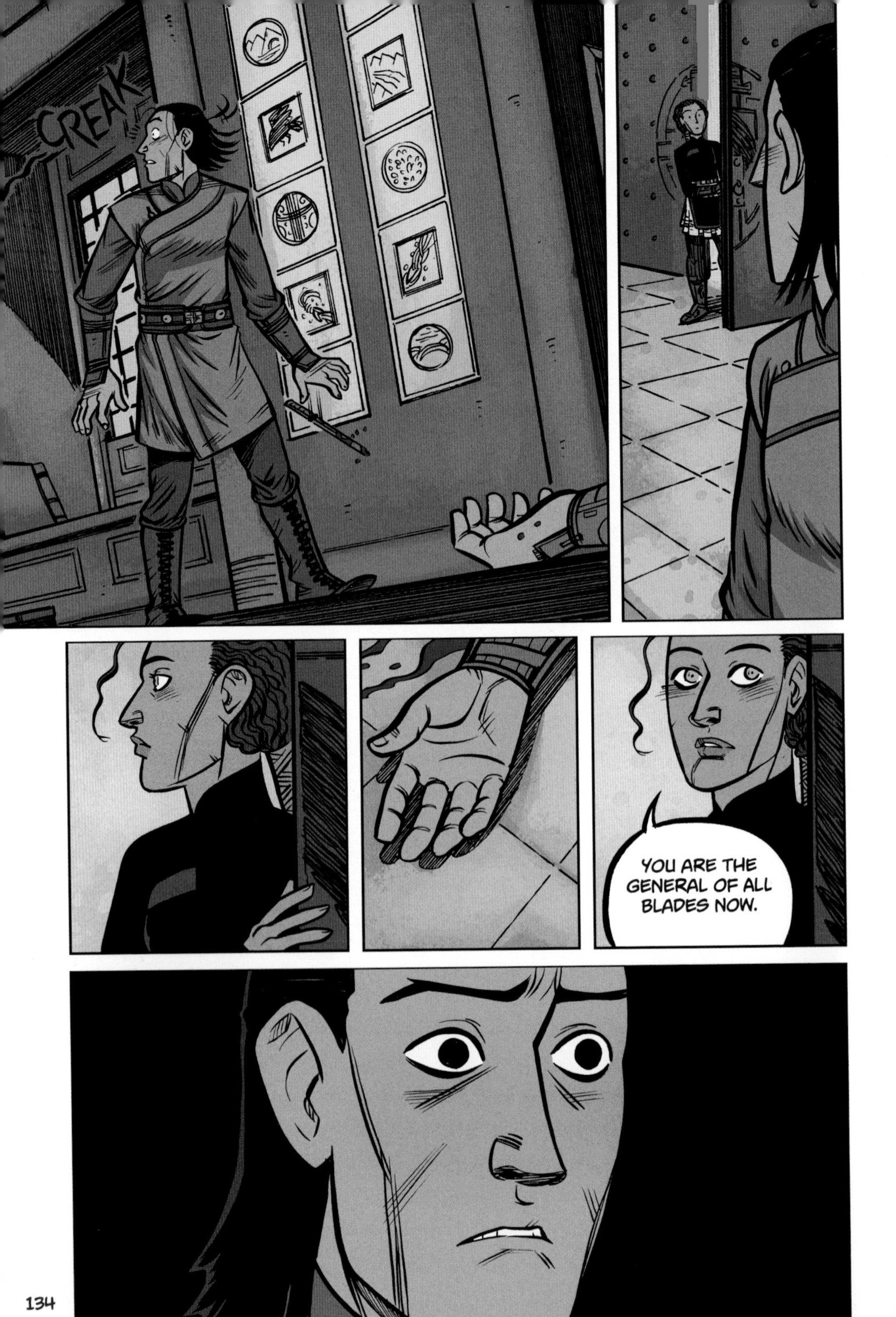
CREAK
YOU ARE THE GENERAL OF ALL BLADES NOW.

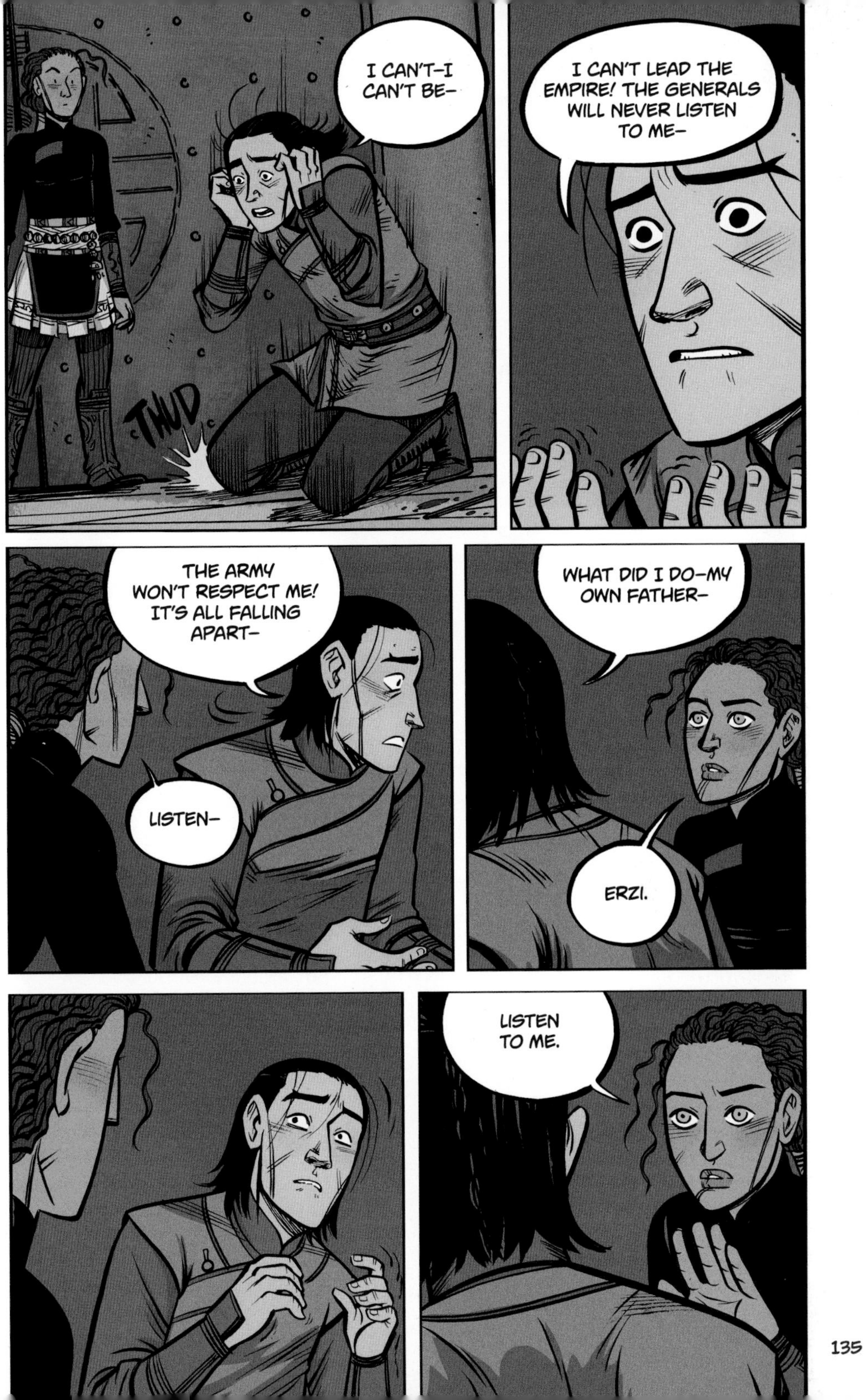
I CAN'T—I CAN'T BE—
THUD
I CAN'T LEAD THE EMPIRE! THE GENERALS WILL NEVER LISTEN TO ME—
THE ARMY WON'T RESPECT ME! IT'S ALL FALLING APART—
LISTEN—
WHAT DID I DO—MY OWN FATHER—
ERZI.
LISTEN TO ME.

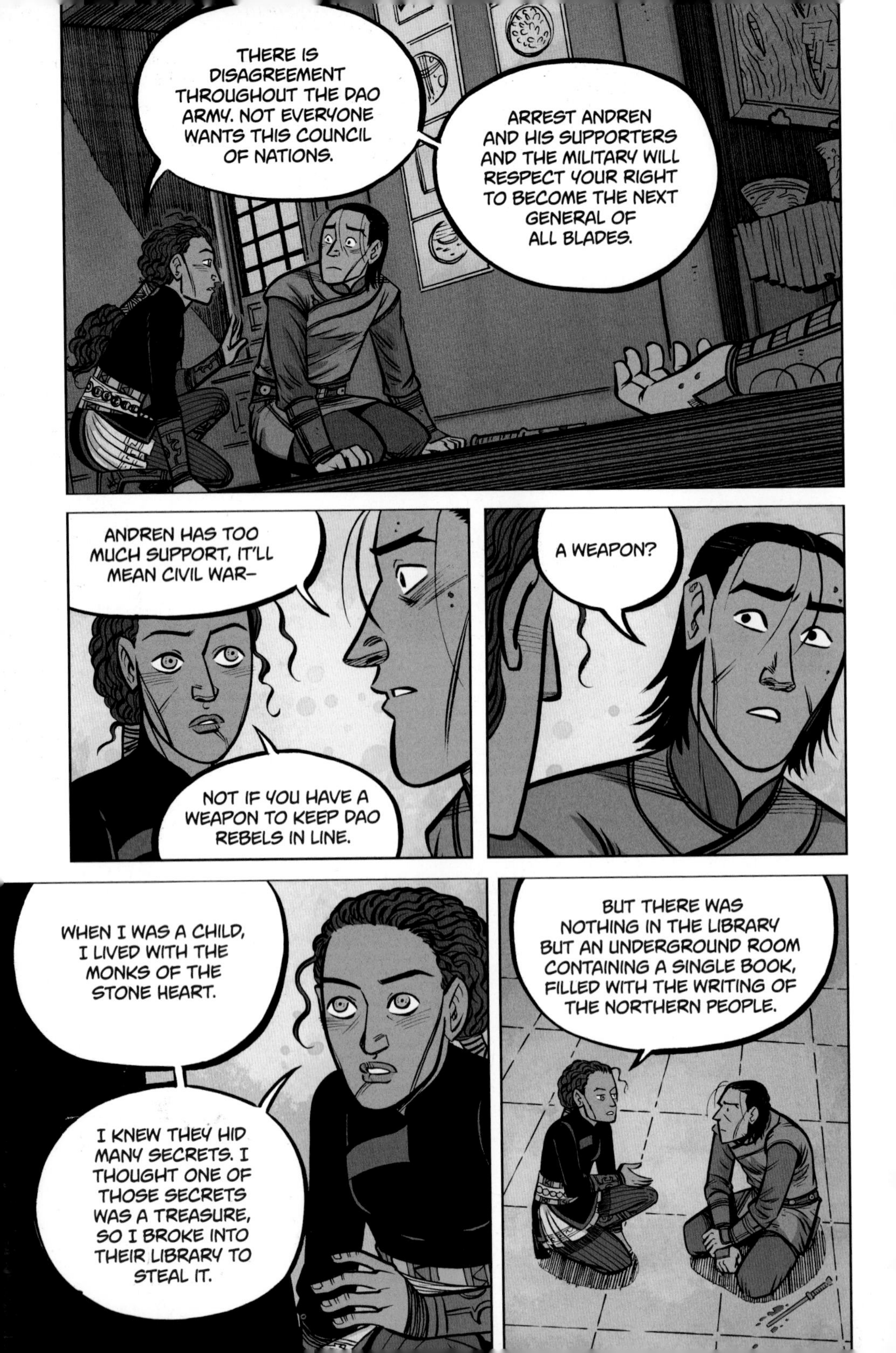
THERE IS DISAGREEMENT THROUGHOUT THE DAO ARMY. NOT EVERYONE WANTS THIS COUNCIL OF NATIONS.
ARREST ANDREN AND HIS SUPPORTERS AND THE MILITARY WILL RESPECT YOUR RIGHT TO BECOME THE NEXT GENERAL OF ALL BLADES.
ANDREN HAS TOO MUCH SUPPORT, IT'LL MEAN CIVIL WAR–
NOT IF YOU HAVE A WEAPON TO KEEP DAO REBELS IN LINE.
A WEAPON?
WHEN I WAS A CHILD, I LIVED WITH THE MONKS OF THE STONE HEART.
I KNEW THEY HID MANY SECRETS. I THOUGHT ONE OF THOSE SECRETS WAS A TREASURE, SO I BROKE INTO THEIR LIBRARY TO STEAL IT.
BUT THERE WAS NOTHING IN THE LIBRARY BUT AN UNDERGROUND ROOM CONTAINING A SINGLE BOOK, FILLED WITH THE WRITING OF THE NORTHERN PEOPLE.

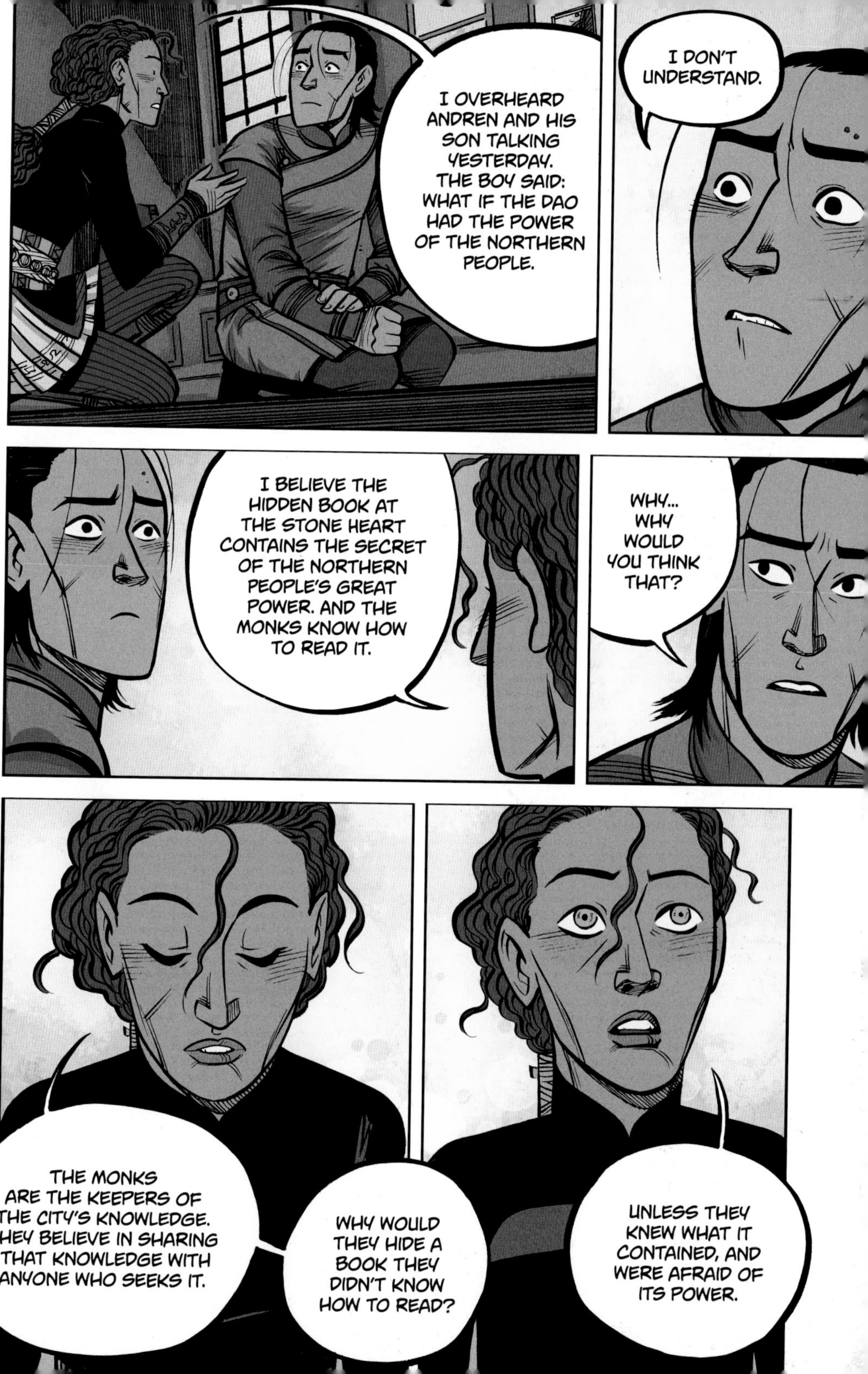
I OVERHEARD ANDREN AND HIS SON TALKING YESTERDAY. THE BOY SAID: WHAT IF THE DAO HAD THE POWER OF THE NORTHERN PEOPLE.
I DON'T UNDERSTAND.
I BELIEVE THE HIDDEN BOOK AT THE STONE HEART CONTAINS THE SECRET OF THE NORTHERN PEOPLE'S GREAT POWER. AND THE MONKS KNOW HOW TO READ IT.
WHY... WHY WOULD YOU THINK THAT?
THE MONKS ARE THE KEEPERS OF THE CITY'S KNOWLEDGE. THEY BELIEVE IN SHARING THAT KNOWLEDGE WITH ANYONE WHO SEEKS IT.
WHY WOULD THEY HIDE A BOOK THEY DIDN'T KNOW HOW TO READ?
UNLESS THEY KNEW WHAT IT CONTAINED, AND WERE AFRAID OF ITS POWER.

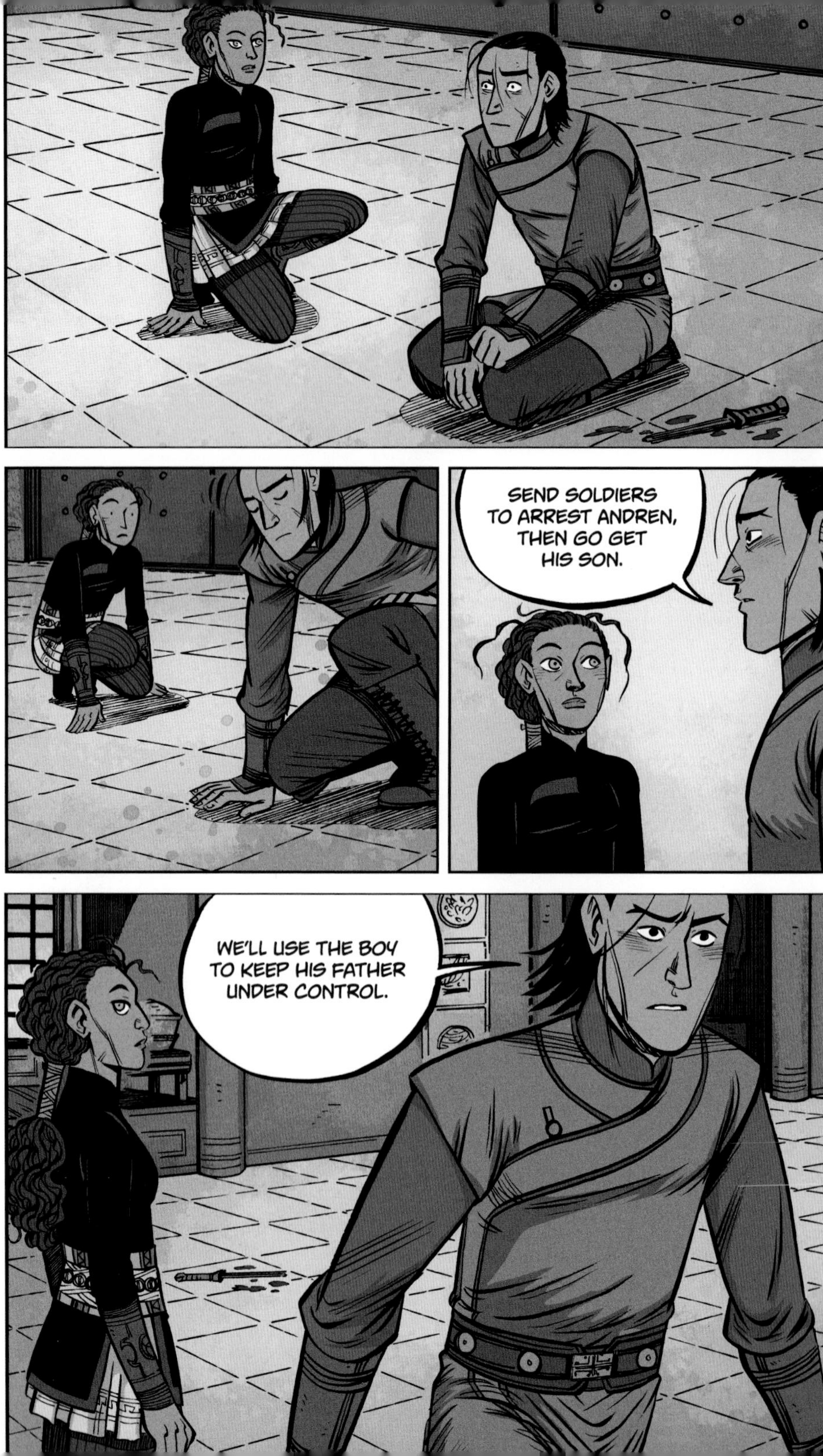
SEND SOLDIERS TO ARREST ANDREN, THEN GO GET HIS SON.
WE'LL USE THE BOY TO KEEP HIS FATHER UNDER CONTROL.

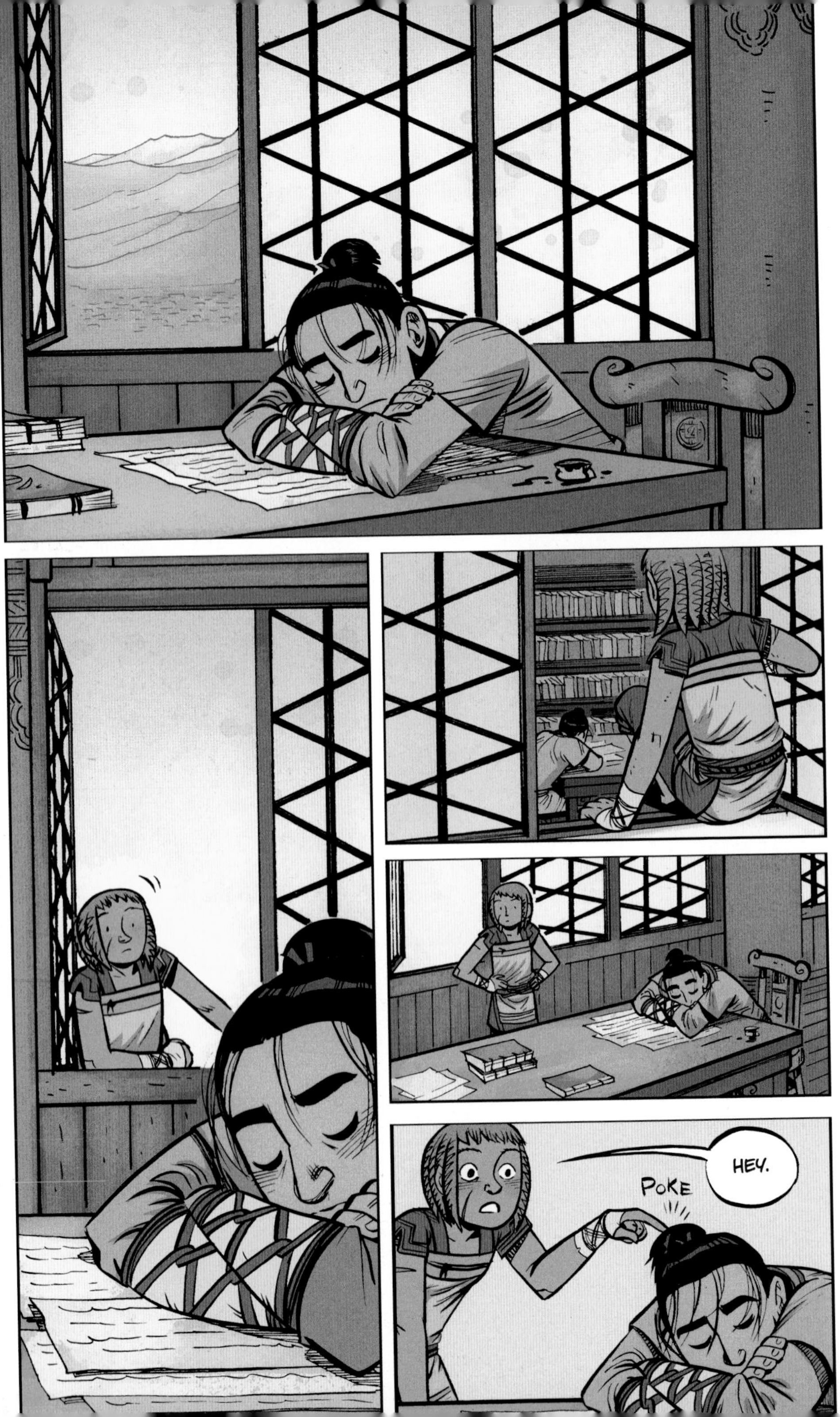
POKE
HEY.

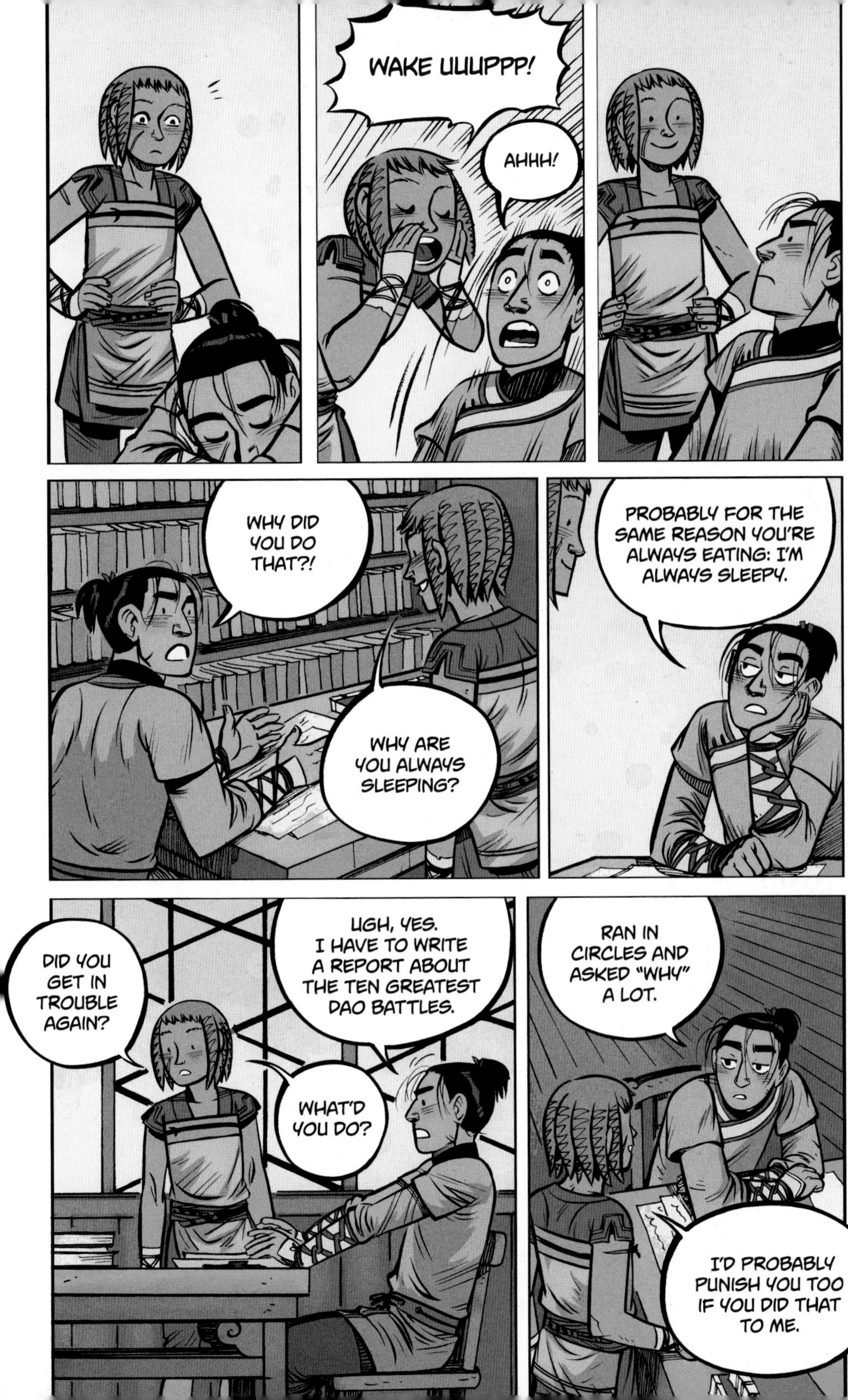
WAKE UUUPPP!
AHHH!
WHY DID YOU DO THAT?!
WHY ARE YOU ALWAYS SLEEPING?
PROBABLY FOR THE SAME REASON YOU'RE ALWAYS EATING: I'M ALWAYS SLEEPY.
DID YOU GET IN TROUBLE AGAIN?
UGH, YES. I HAVE TO WRITE A REPORT ABOUT THE TEN GREATEST DAO BATTLES.
WHAT'D YOU DO?
RAN IN CIRCLES AND ASKED "WHY" A LOT.
I'D PROBABLY PUNISH YOU TOO IF YOU DID THAT TO ME.

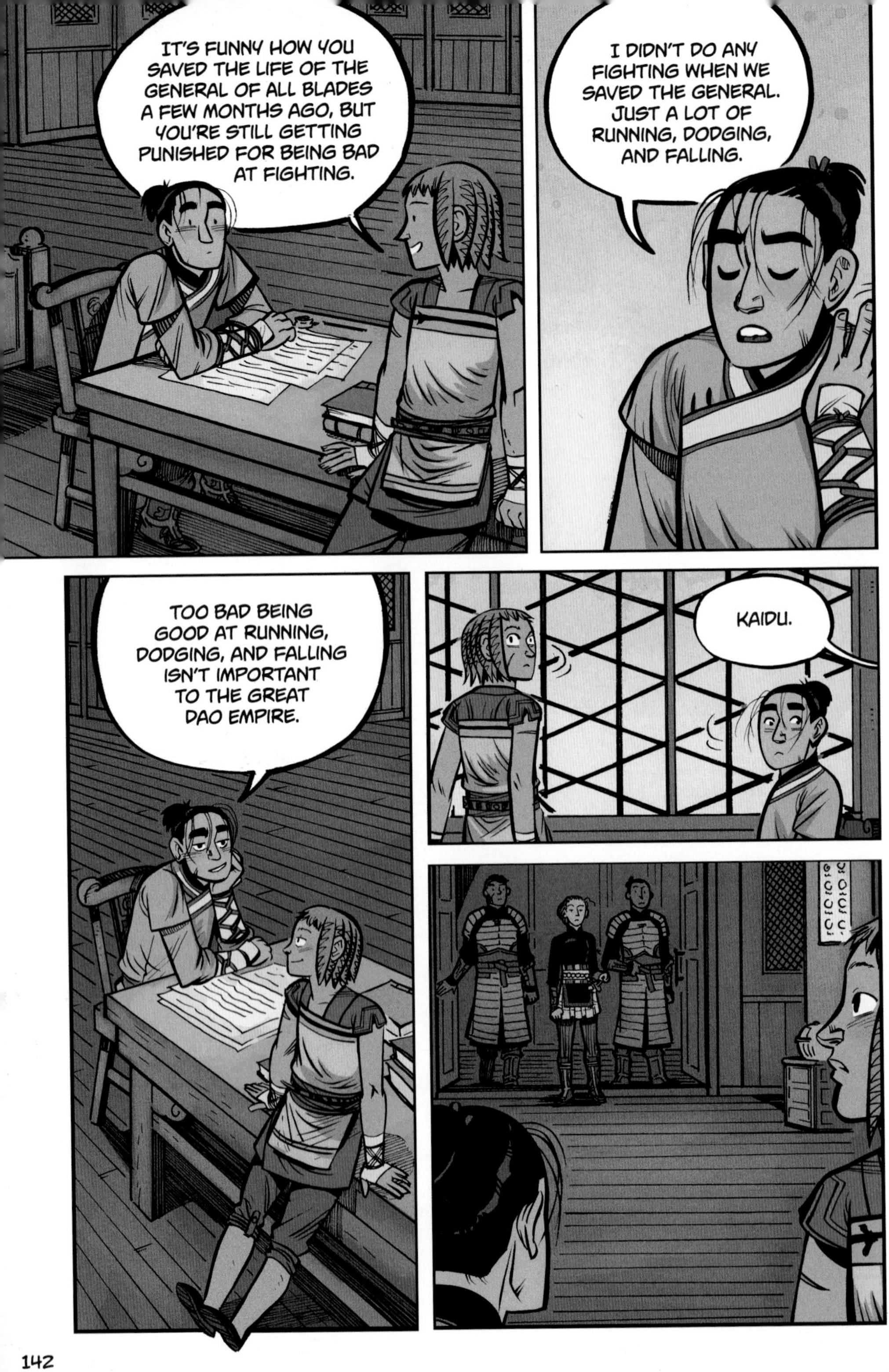
IT'S FUNNY HOW YOU SAVED THE LIFE OF THE GENERAL OF ALL BLADES A FEW MONTHS AGO, BUT YOU'RE STILL GETTING PUNISHED FOR BEING BAD AT FIGHTING.
I DIDN'T DO ANY FIGHTING WHEN WE SAVED THE GENERAL. JUST A LOT OF RUNNING, DODGING, AND FALLING.
TOO BAD BEING GOOD AT RUNNING, DODGING, AND FALLING ISN'T IMPORTANT TO THE GREAT DAO EMPIRE.
KAIDU.

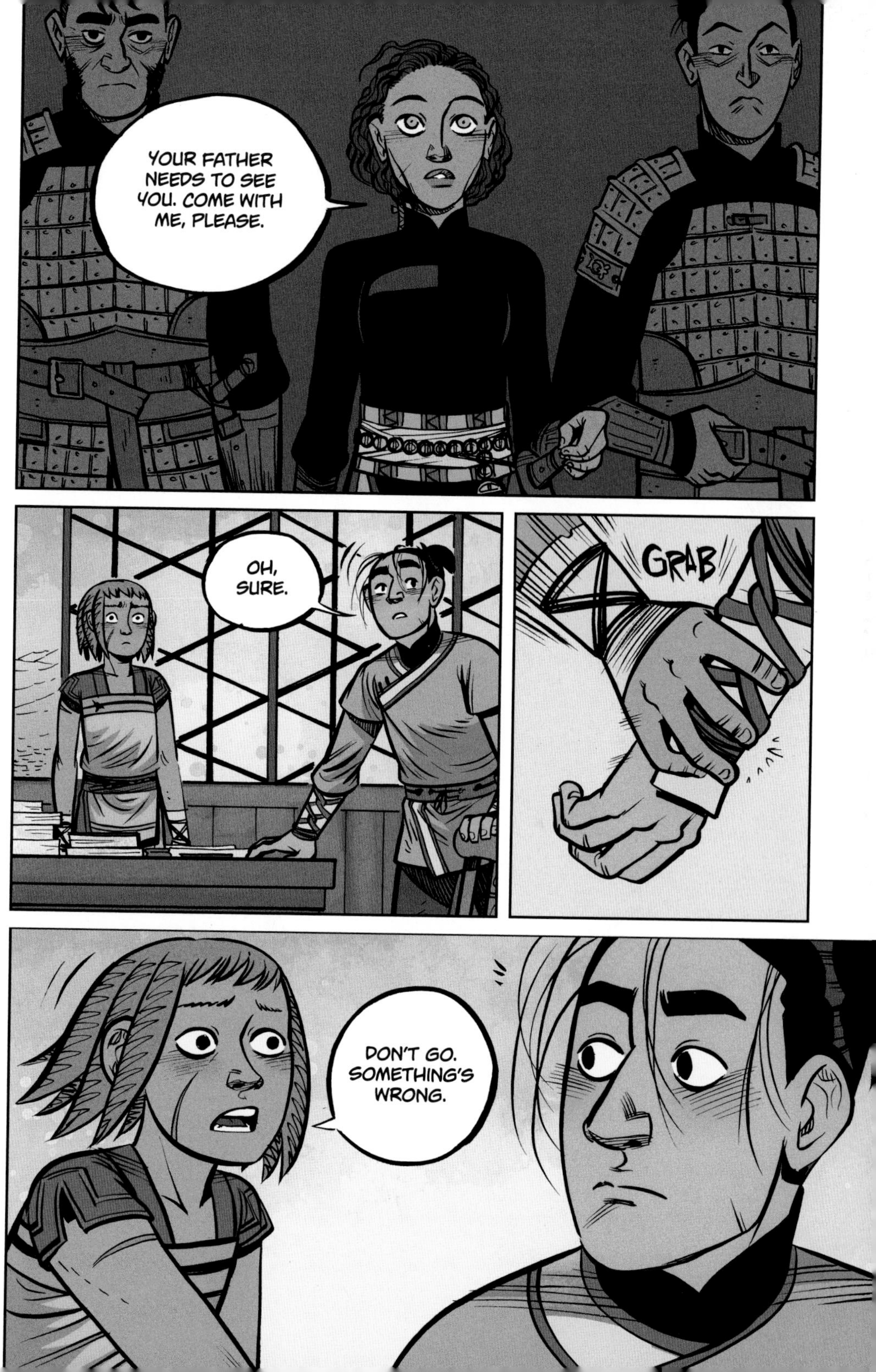
YOUR FATHER NEEDS TO SEE YOU. COME WITH ME, PLEASE.
OH, SURE.
GRAB
DON'T GO. SOMETHING'S WRONG.

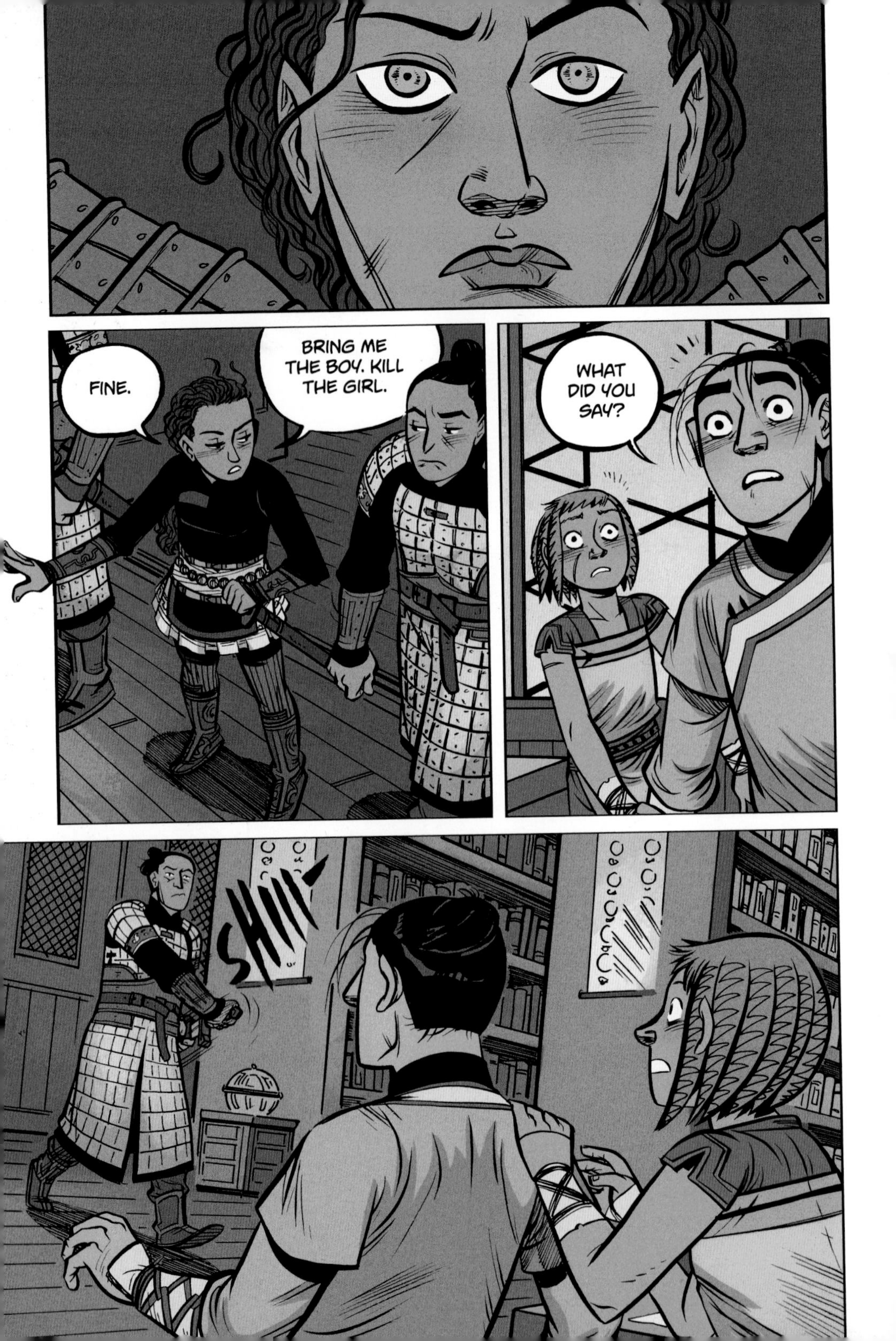
FINE.
BRING ME THE BOY. KILL THE GIRL.
WHAT DID YOU SAY?
SHIIING

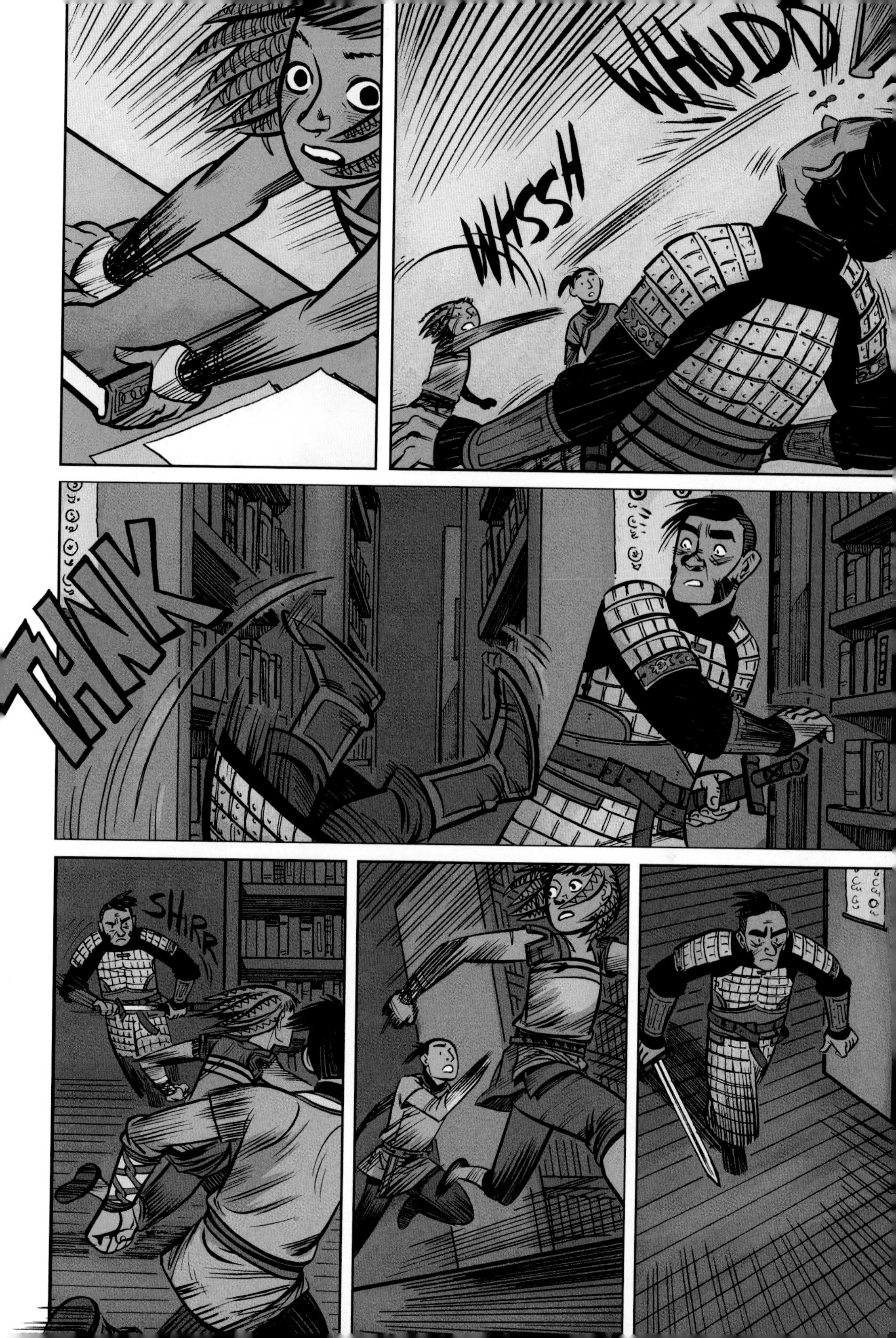
WHUDD
WHSSH
THNK
SHIRR

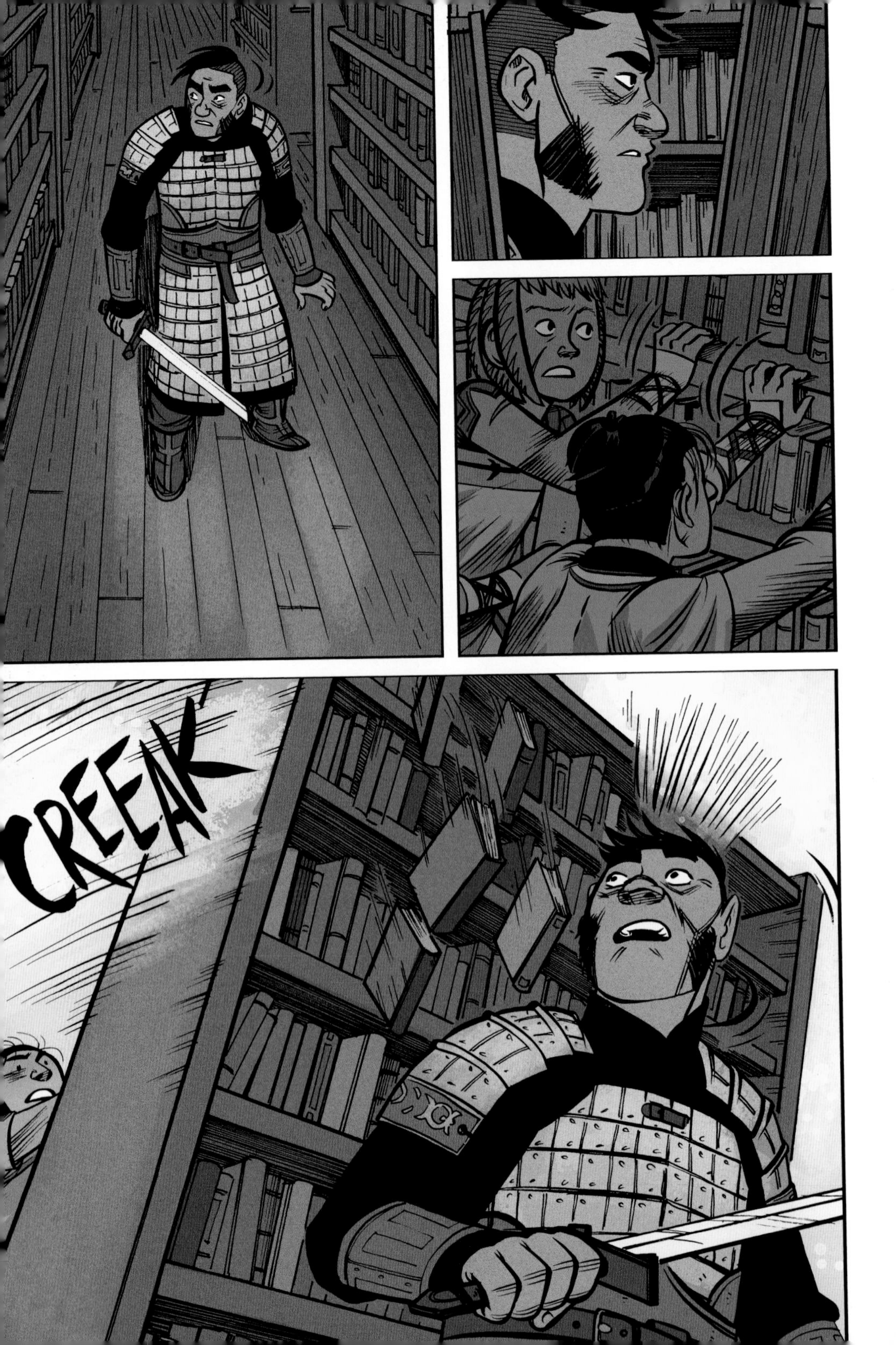
CREEAK

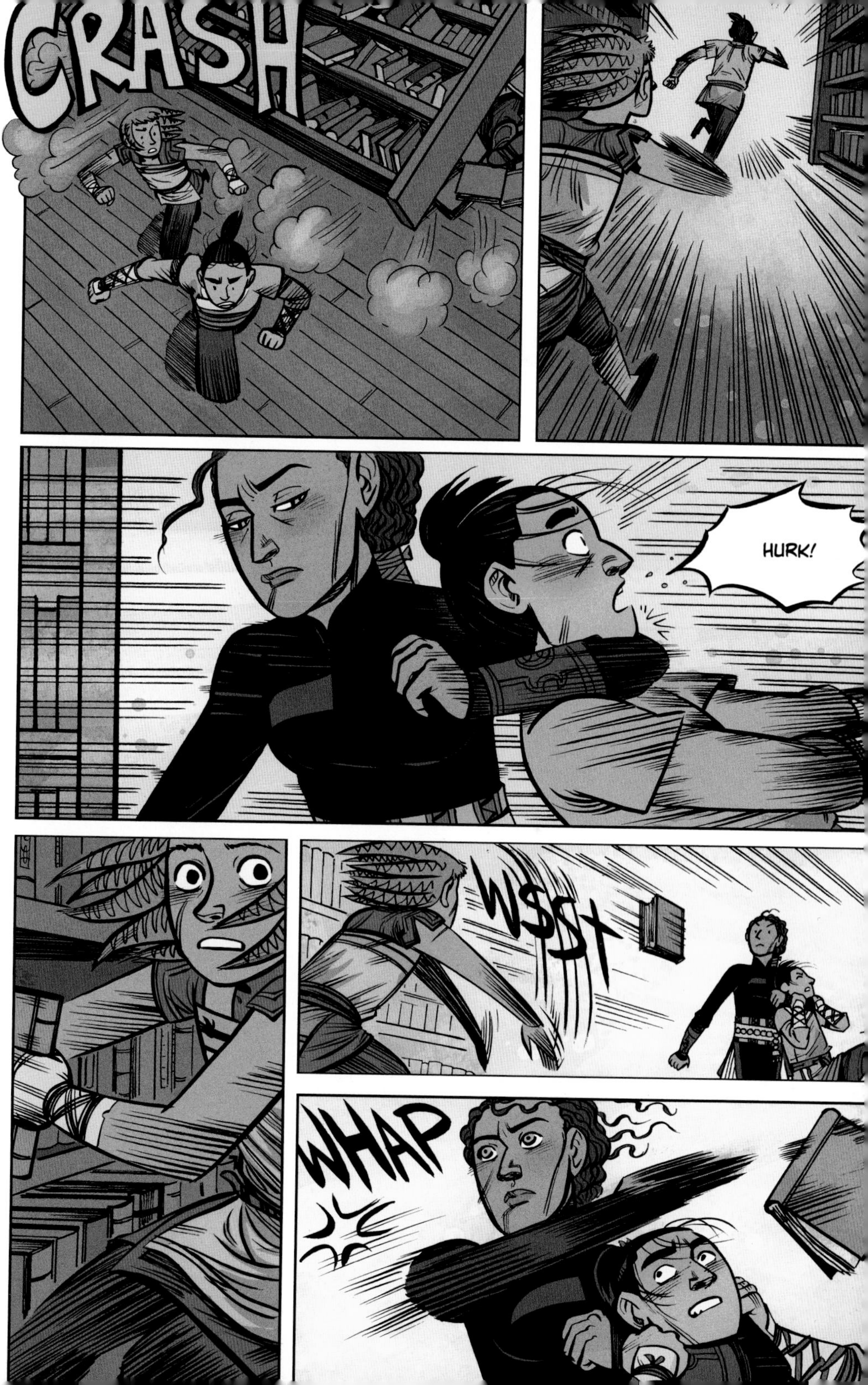
CRASH
HURK!
WSSSX
WHAP

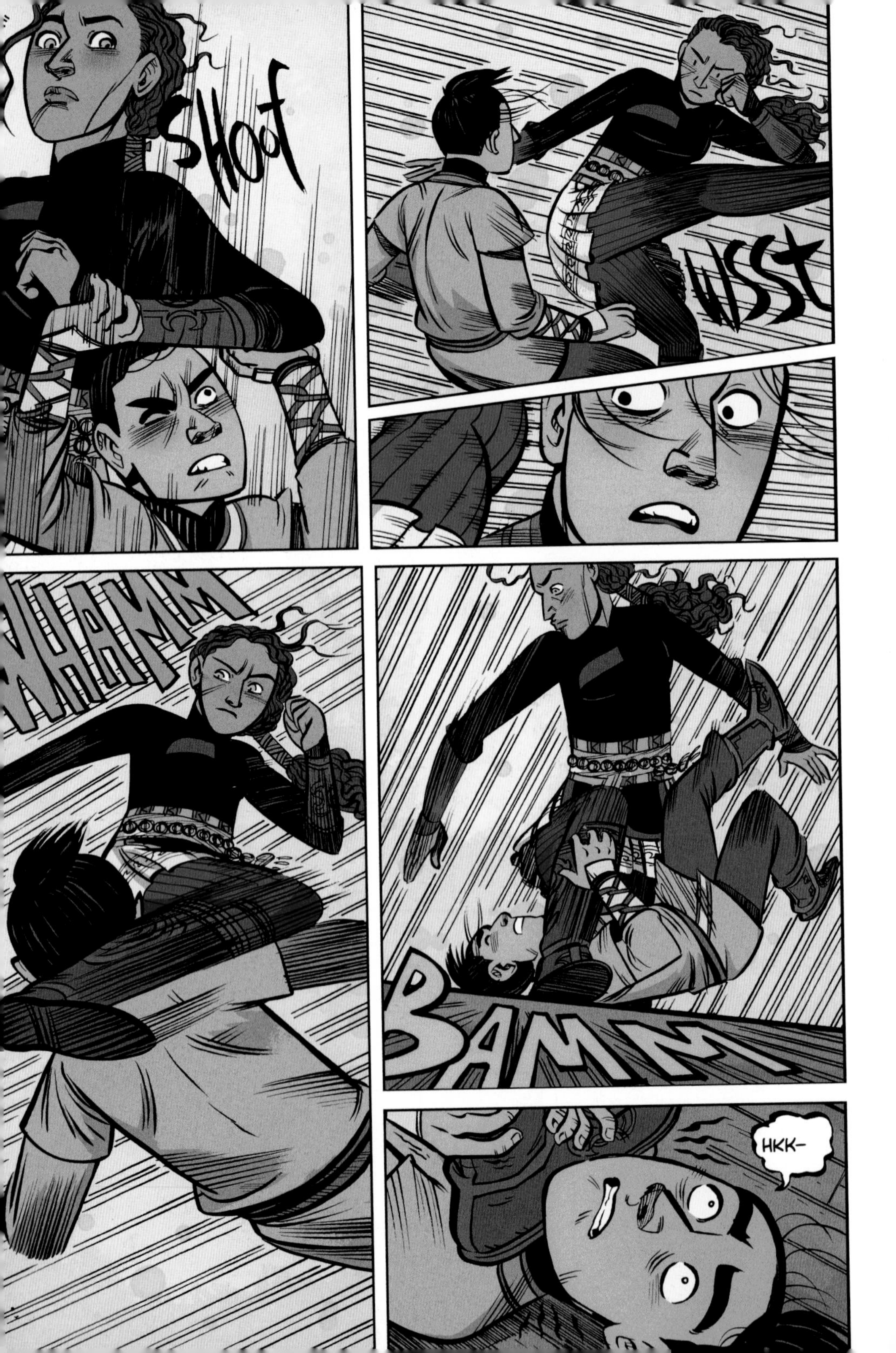
SHOOF
WSST
WHAMM
BAMM
HKK-

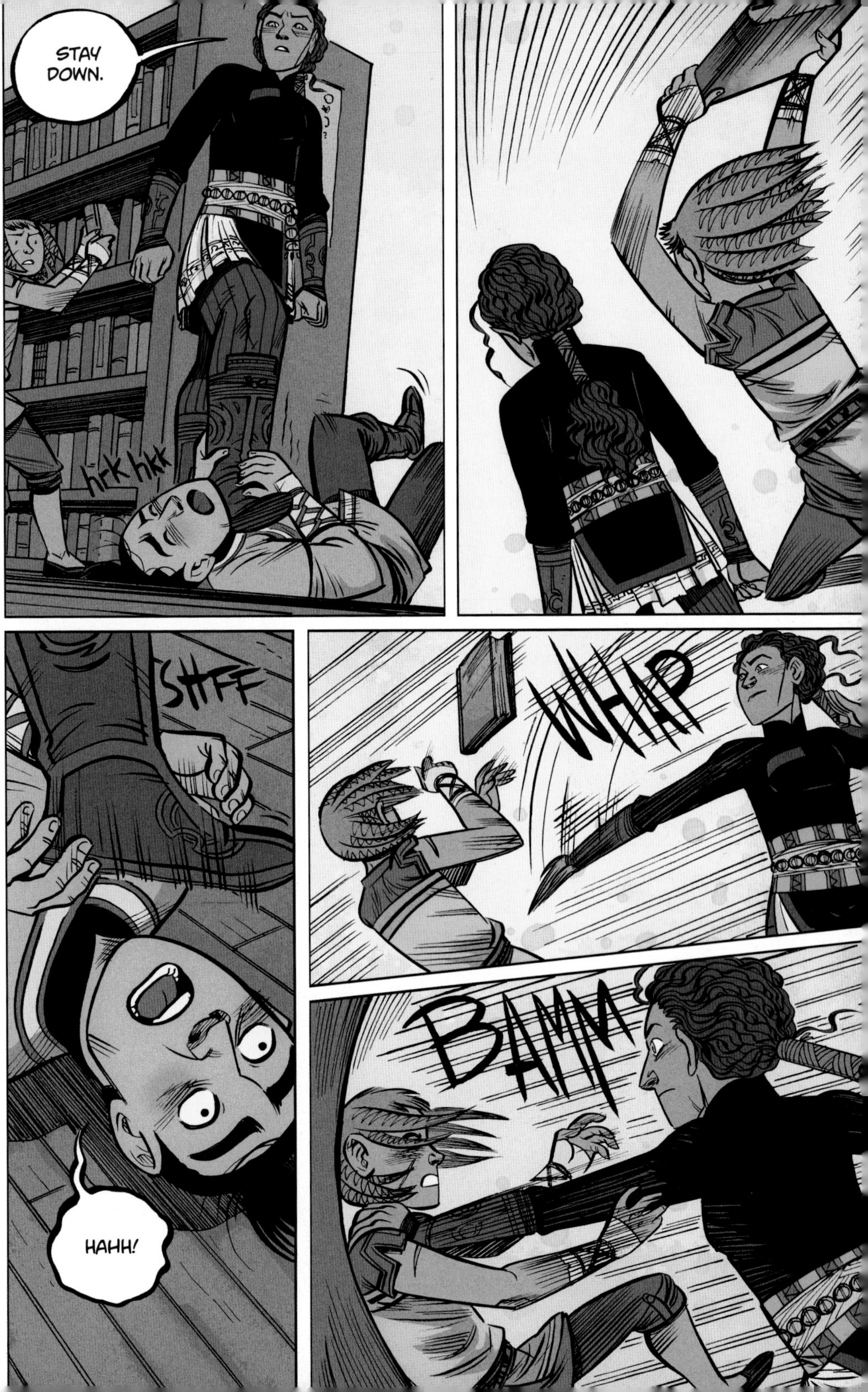
STAY DOWN.
hrk hkk
SHFF
HAHH!
WHAP
BAMM

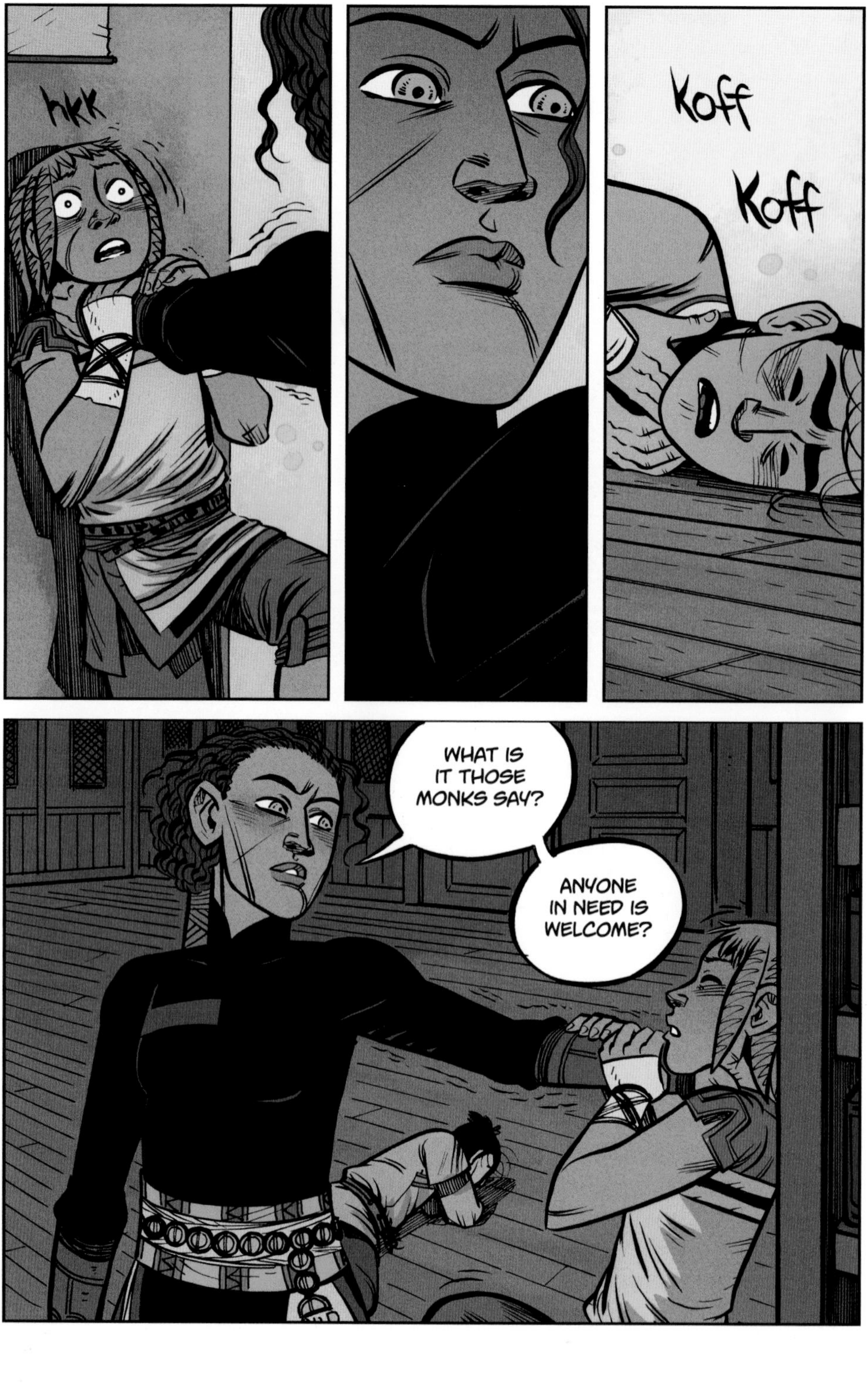
hkk
Koff
Koff
WHAT IS IT THOSE MONKS SAY?
ANYONE IN NEED IS WELCOME?

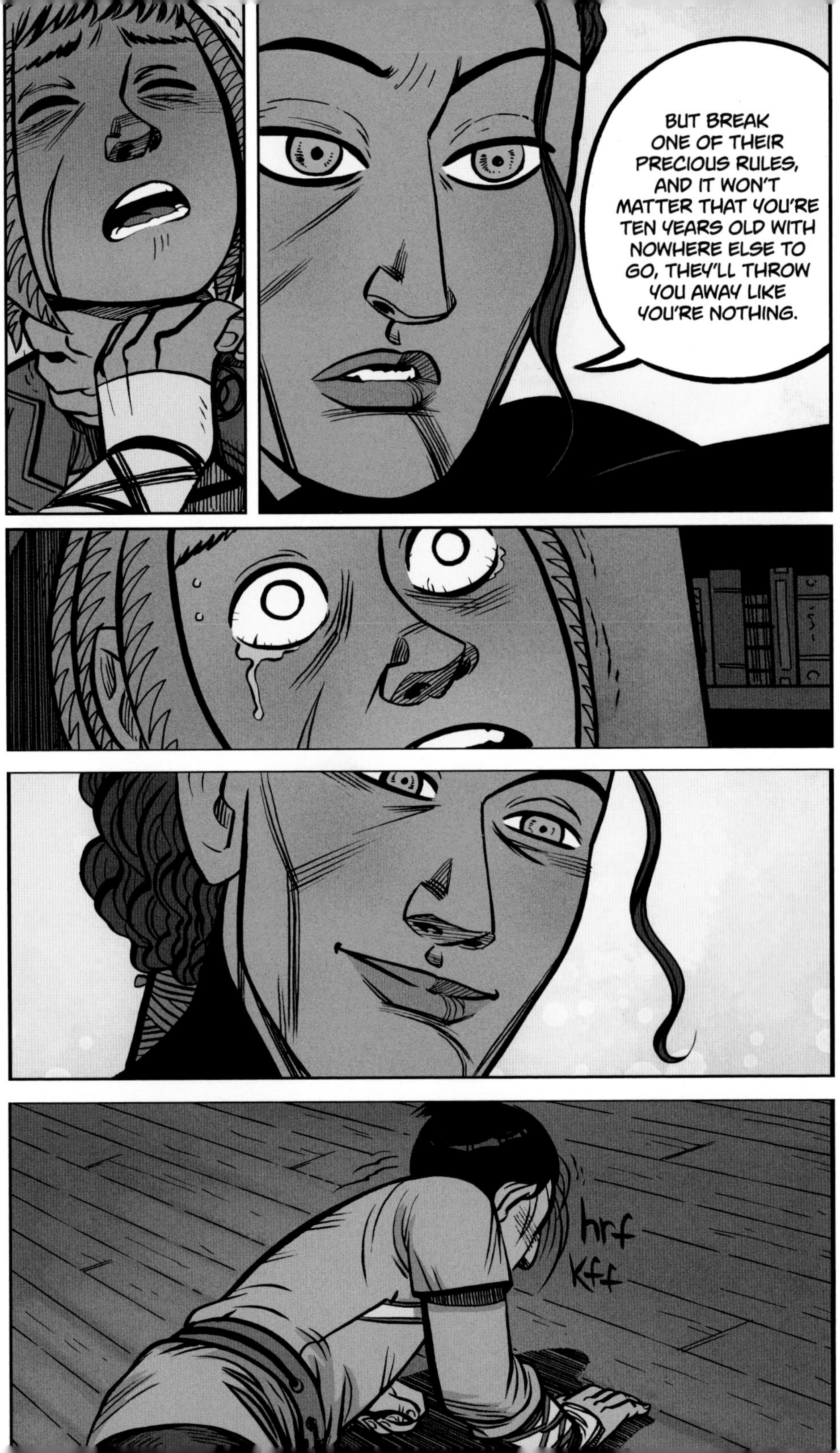
BUT BREAK ONE OF THEIR PRECIOUS RULES, AND IT WON'T MATTER THAT YOU'RE TEN YEARS OLD WITH NOWHERE ELSE TO GO, THEY'LL THROW YOU AWAY LIKE YOU'RE NOTHING.
hrf
kff

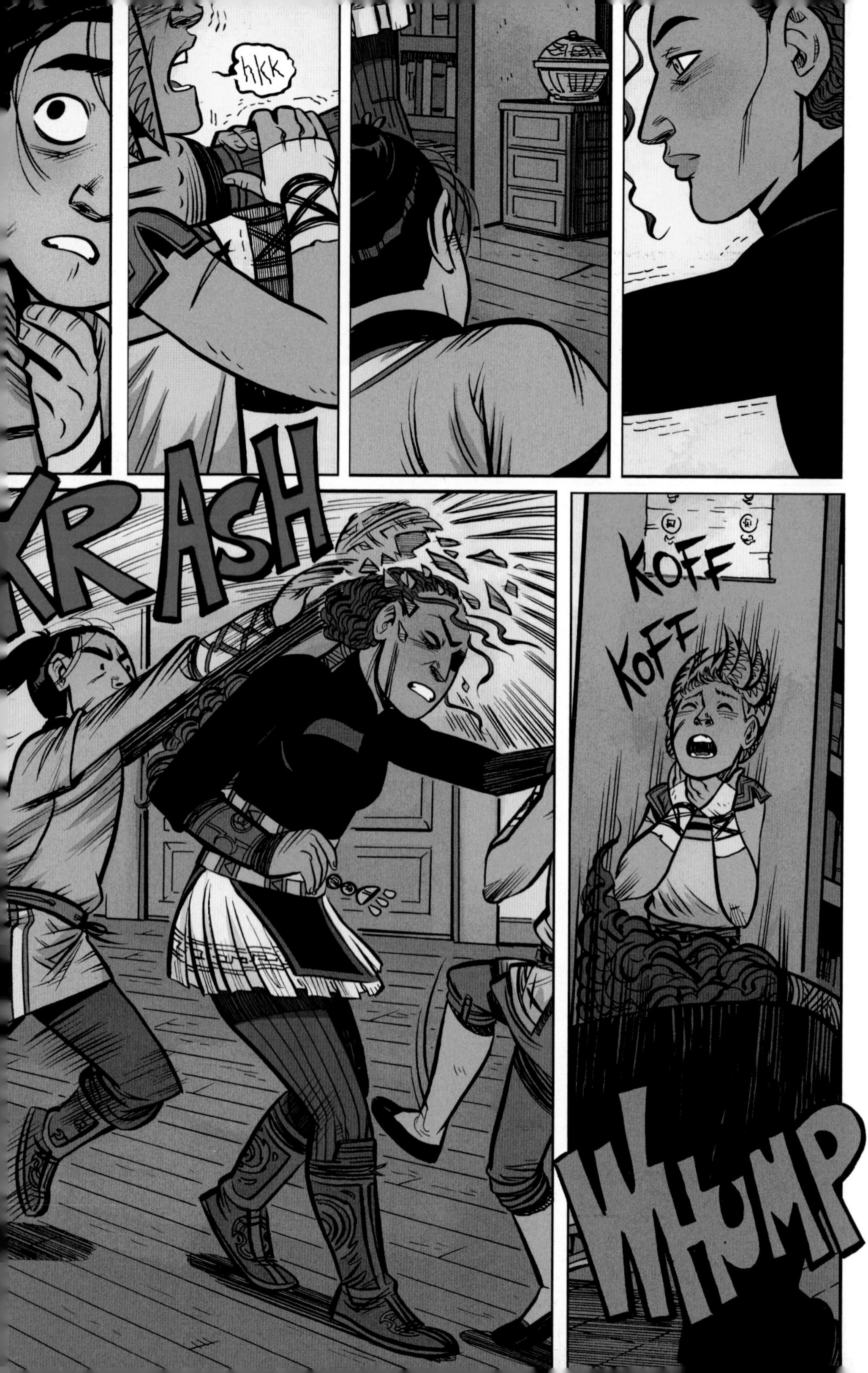
hkk
KRASH
KOFF
KOFF
WHUMP

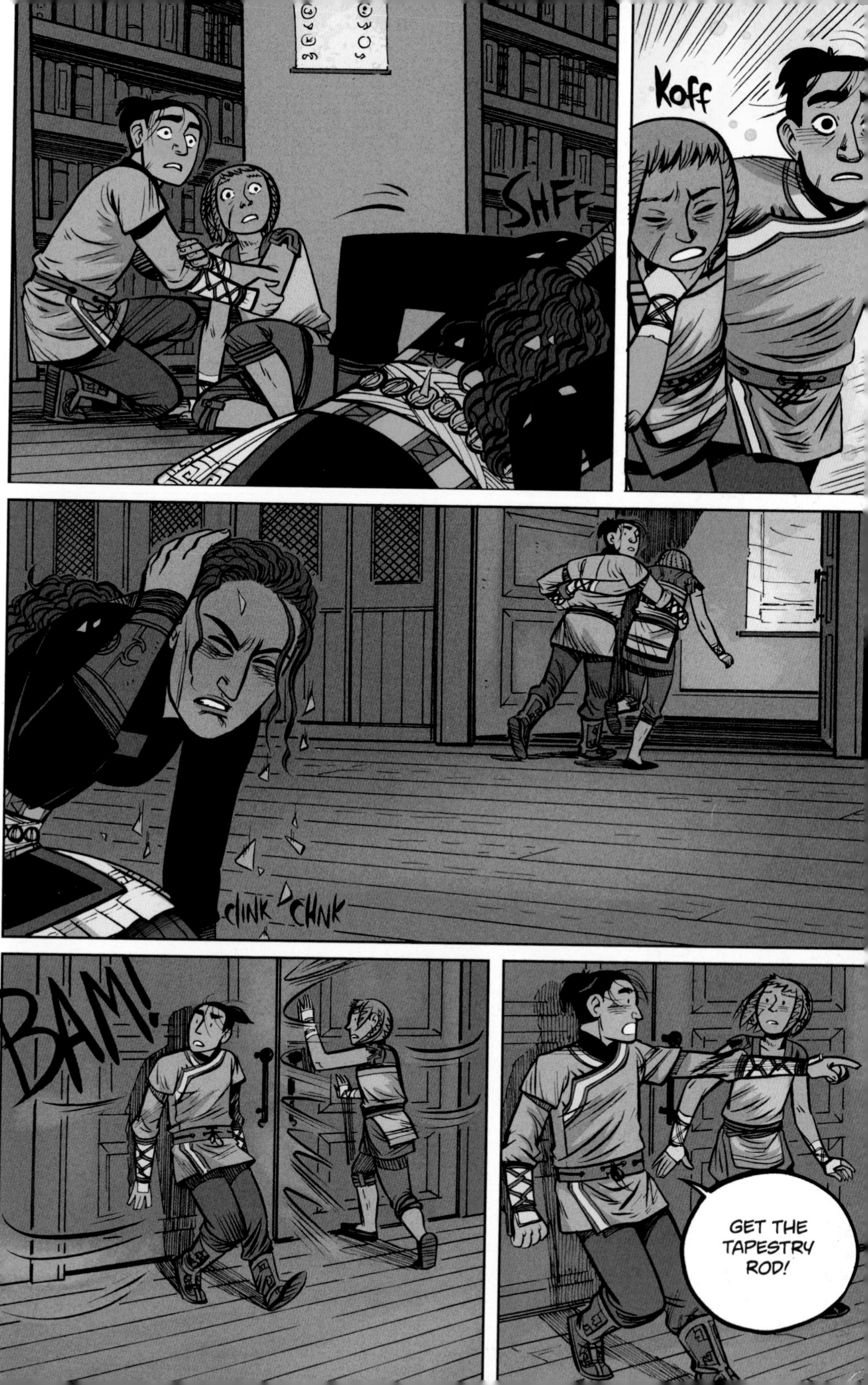
SHFF
Koff
CLINK CHNK
BAM!
GET THE TAPESTRY ROD!

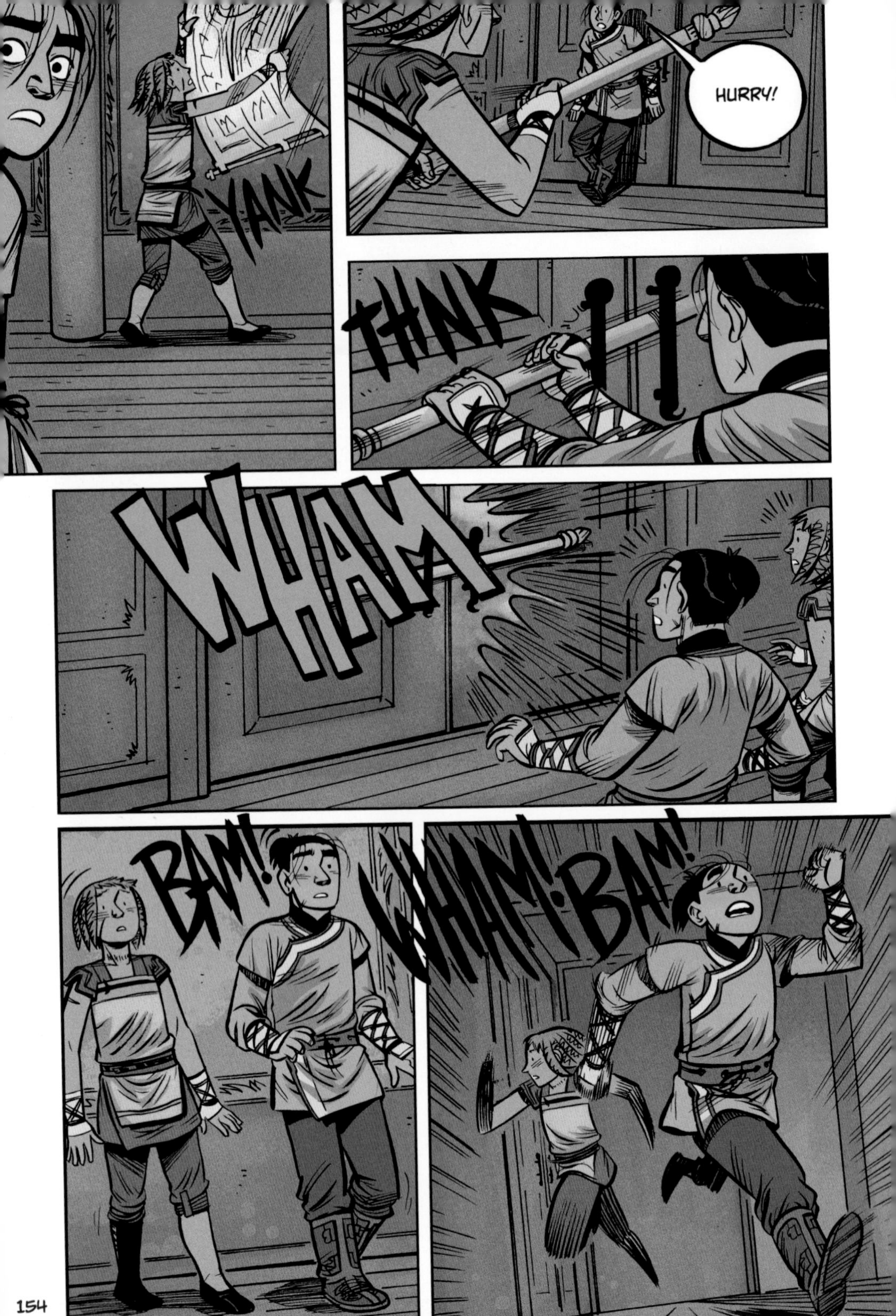
YANK
HURRY!
THNK
WHAM
BAM!
WHAM!
BAM!

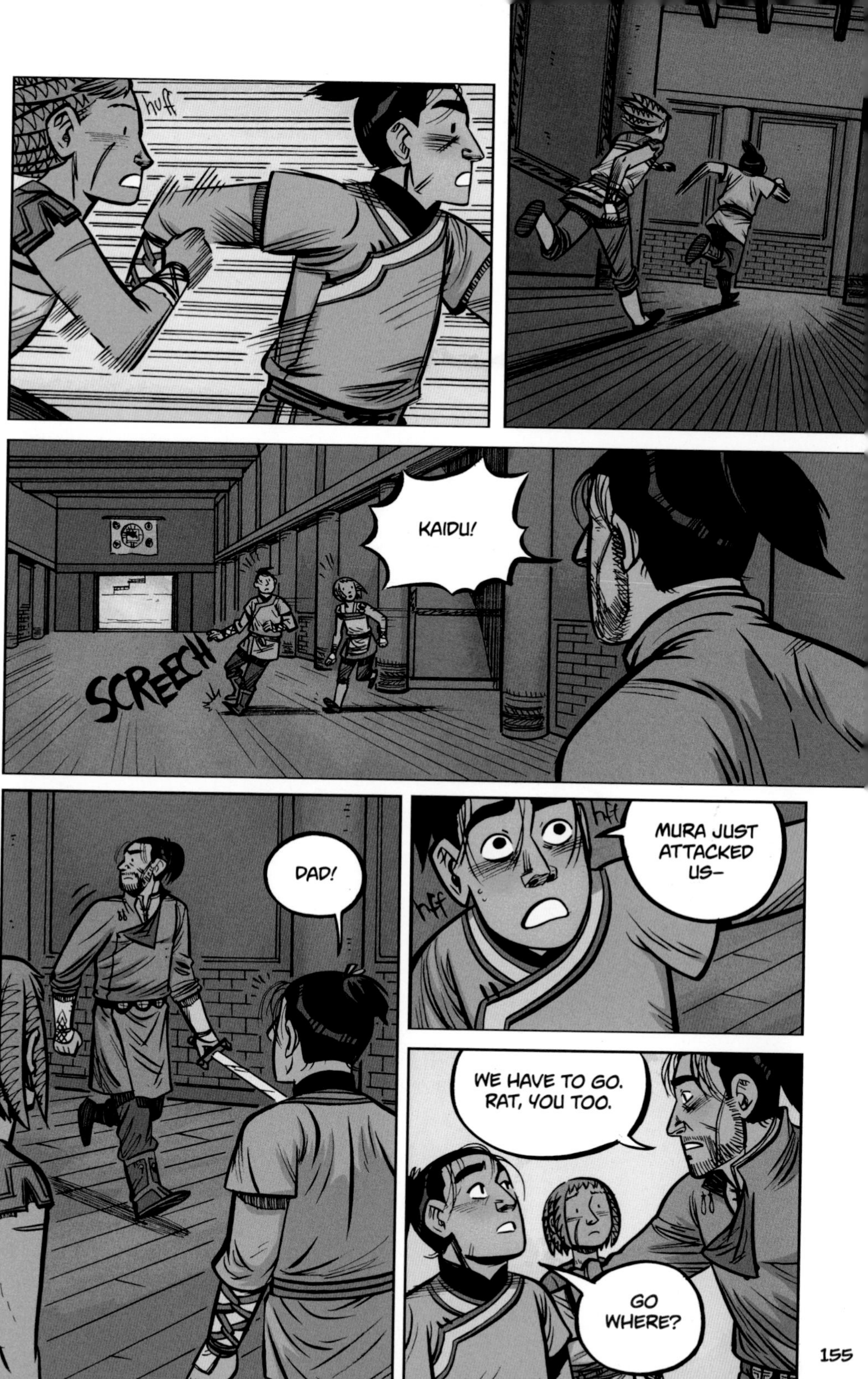
huff
KAIDU!
SCREECH
DAD!
MURA JUST ATTACKED US—
WE HAVE TO GO. RAT, YOU TOO.
GO WHERE?

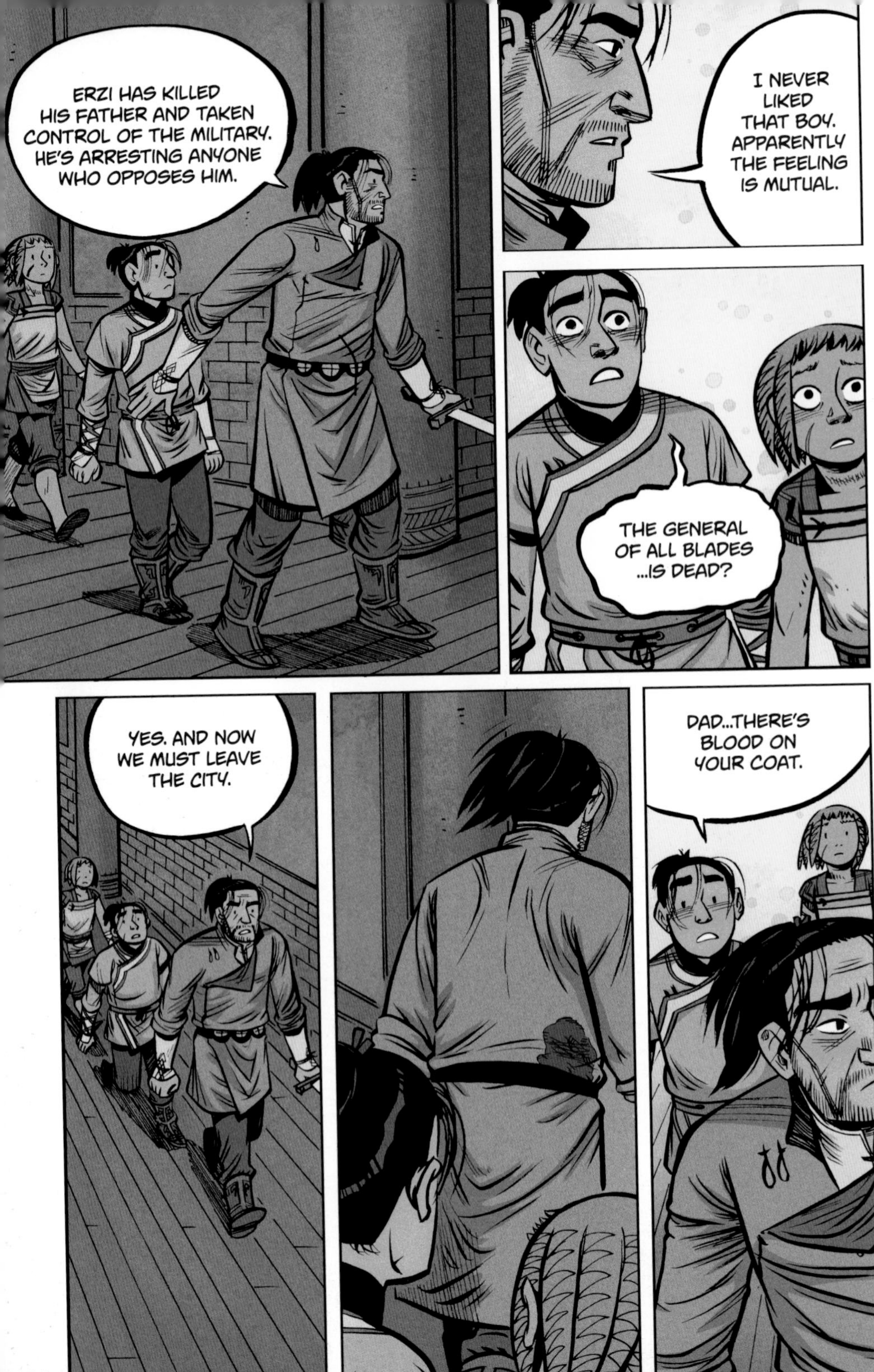
ERZI HAS KILLED HIS FATHER AND TAKEN CONTROL OF THE MILITARY. HE'S ARRESTING ANYONE WHO OPPOSES HIM.
I NEVER LIKED THAT BOY. APPARENTLY THE FEELING IS MUTUAL.
THE GENERAL OF ALL BLADES ...IS DEAD?
YES. AND NOW WE MUST LEAVE THE CITY.
DAD...THERE'S BLOOD ON YOUR COAT.

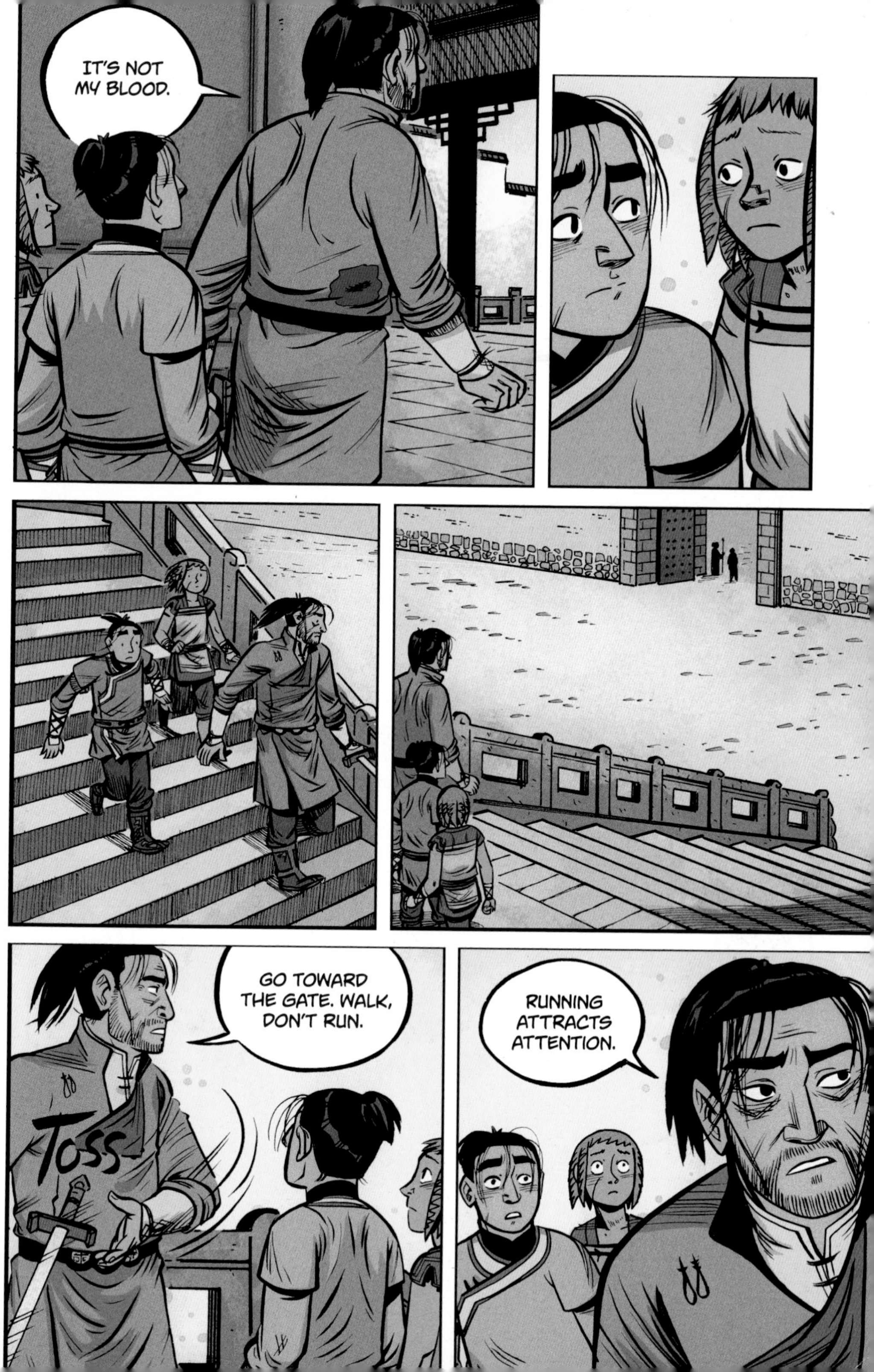
IT'S NOT MY BLOOD.
TOSS
GO TOWARD THE GATE. WALK, DON'T RUN.
RUNNING ATTRACTS ATTENTION.

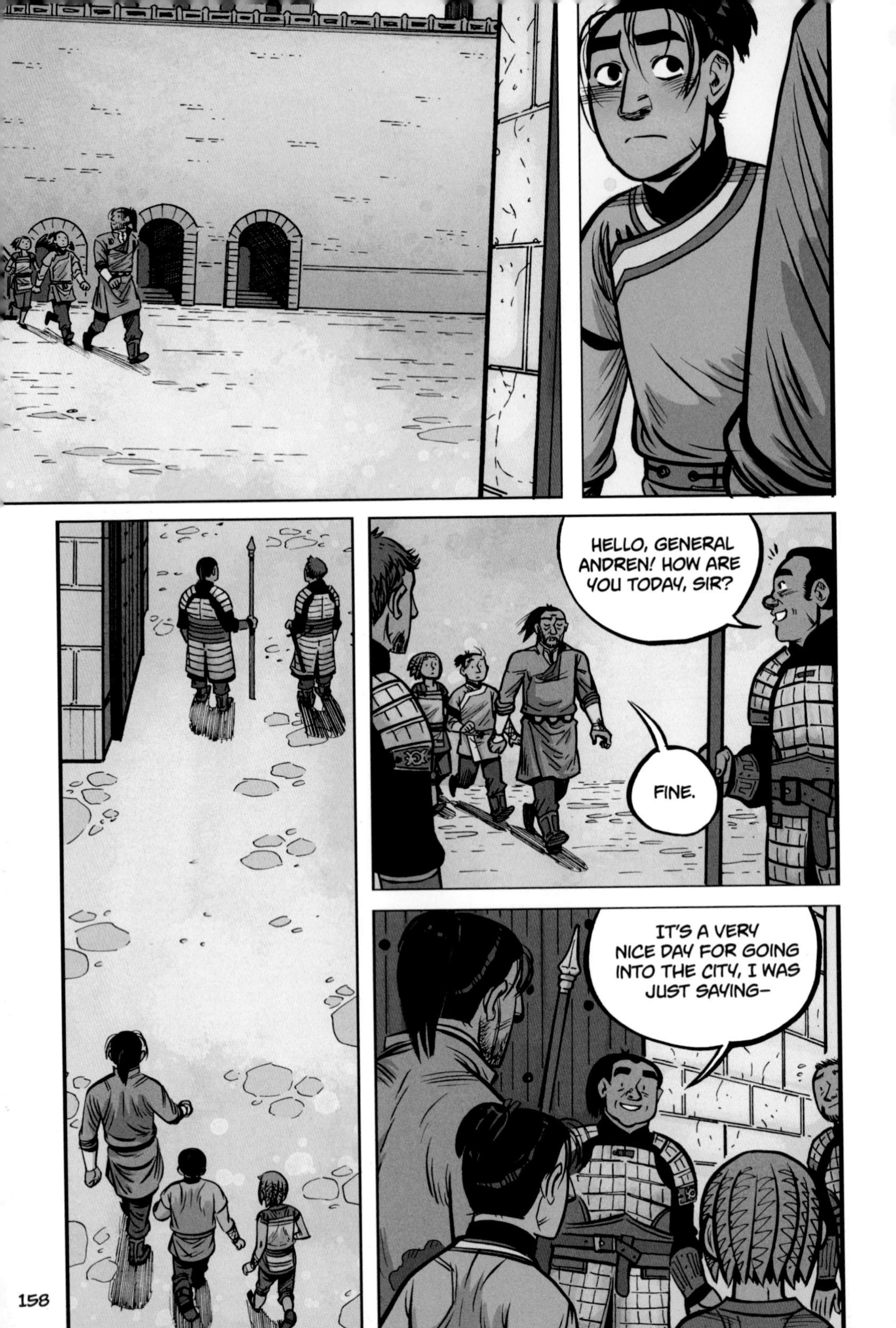
HELLO, GENERAL ANDREN! HOW ARE YOU TODAY, SIR?
FINE.
IT'S A VERY NICE DAY FOR GOING INTO THE CITY, I WAS JUST SAYING–

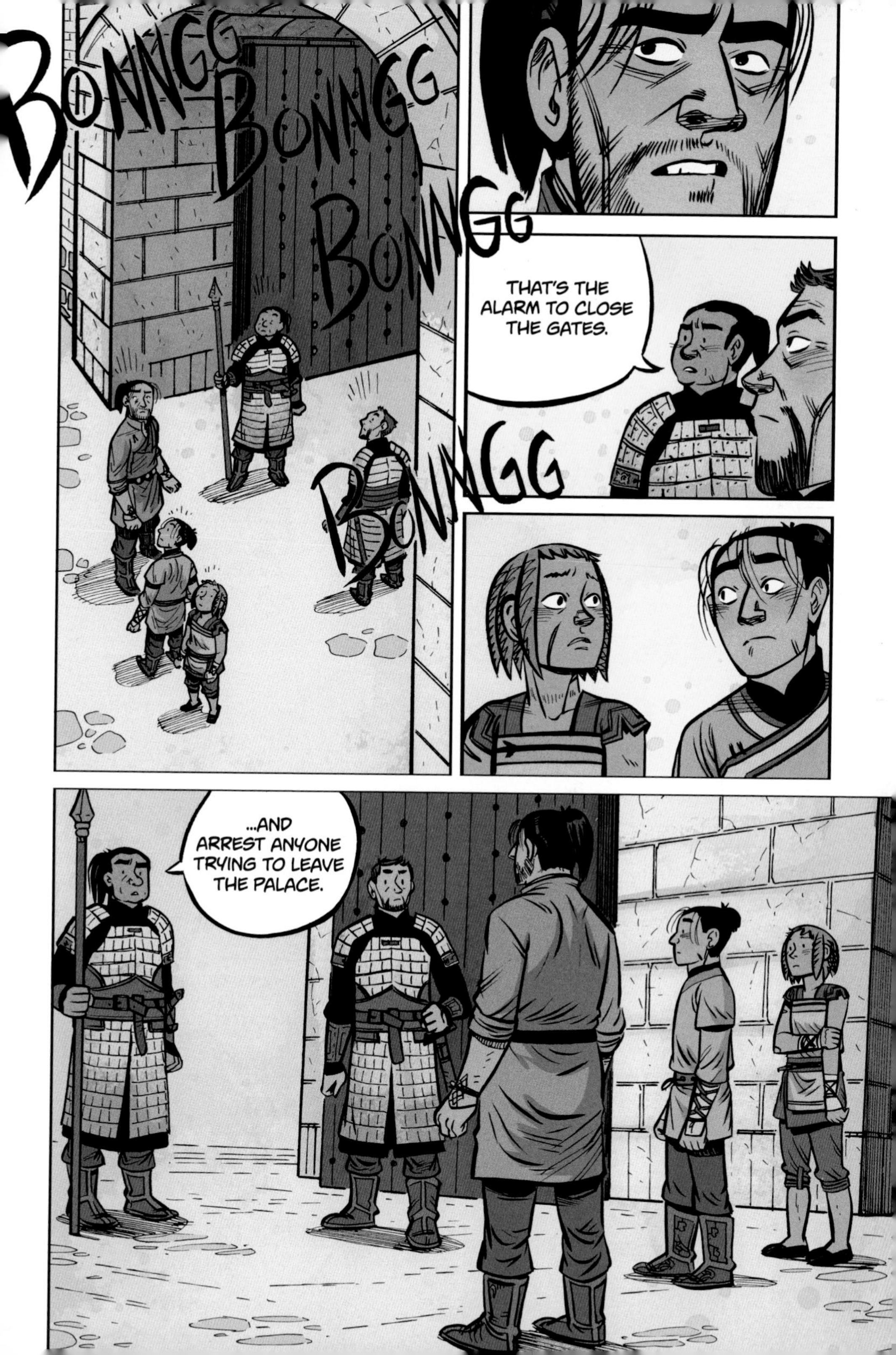
BONNGG
BONNGG
BONNGG
BONNGG
THAT'S THE ALARM TO CLOSE THE GATES.
...AND ARREST ANYONE TRYING TO LEAVE THE PALACE.

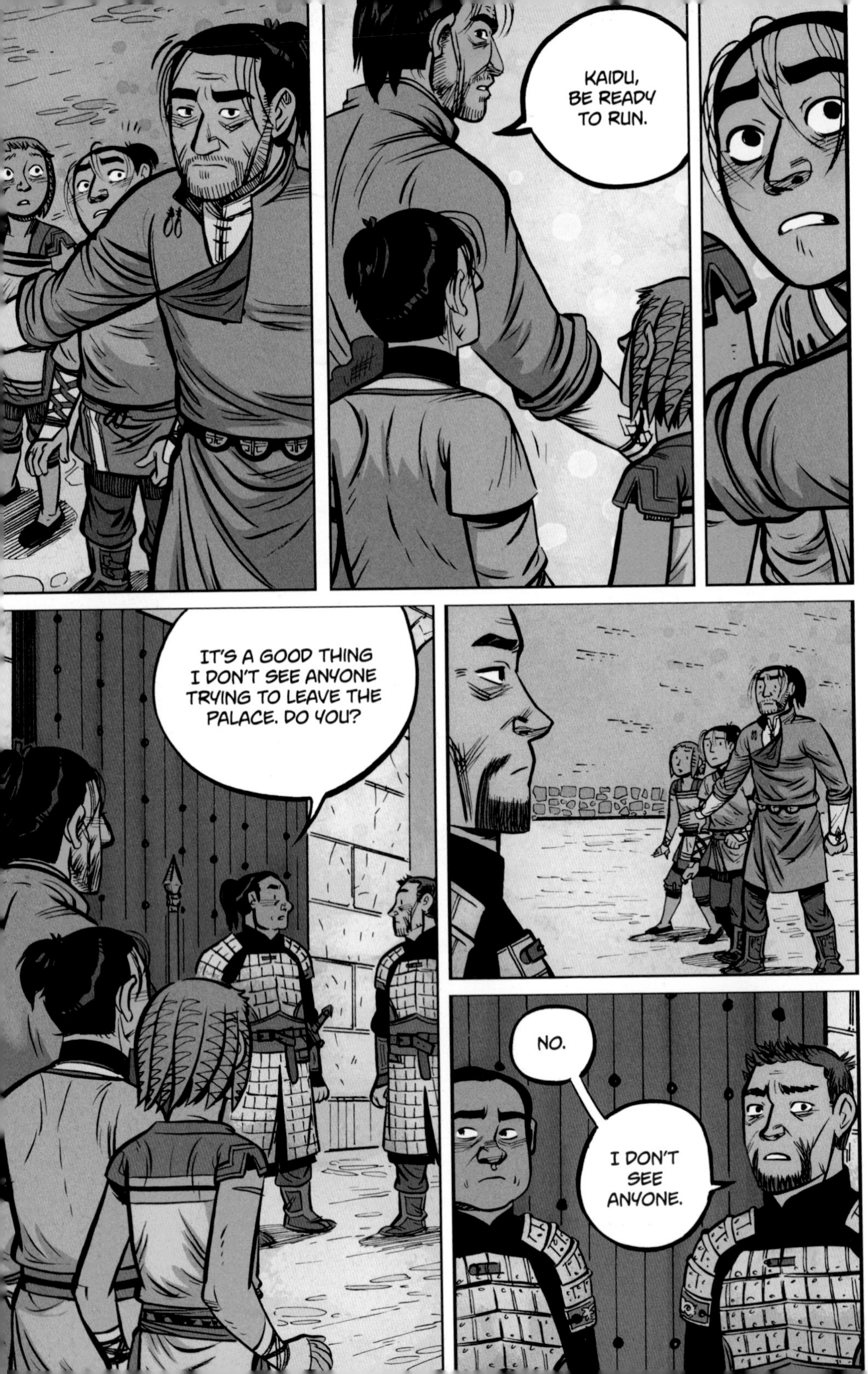
KAIDU, BE READY TO RUN.
IT'S A GOOD THING I DON'T SEE ANYONE TRYING TO LEAVE THE PALACE. DO YOU?
NO.
I DON'T SEE ANYONE.

THANK YOU.

CRREEEAK

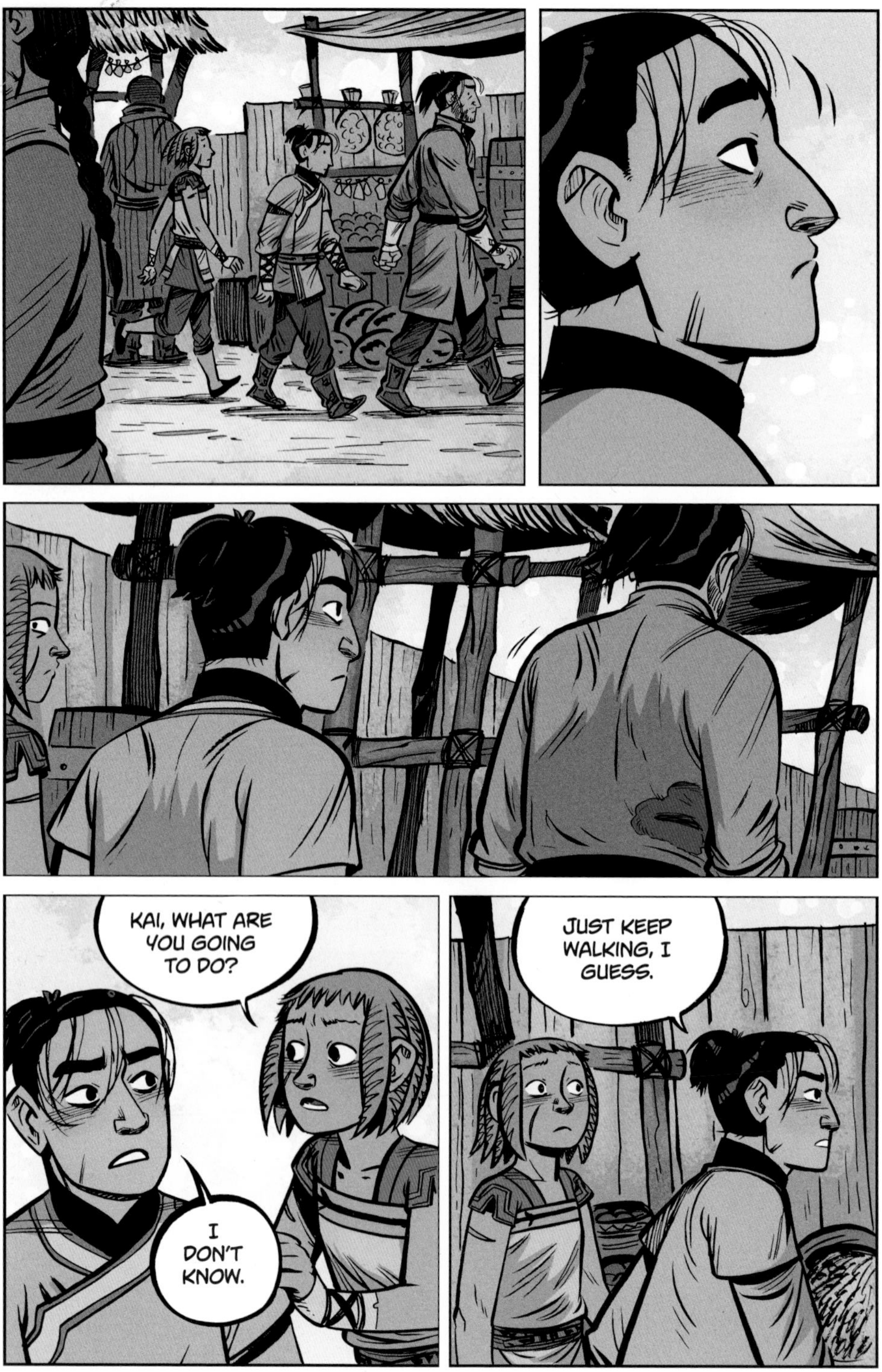
KAI, WHAT ARE YOU GOING TO DO?
I DON'T KNOW.
JUST KEEP WALKING, I GUESS.

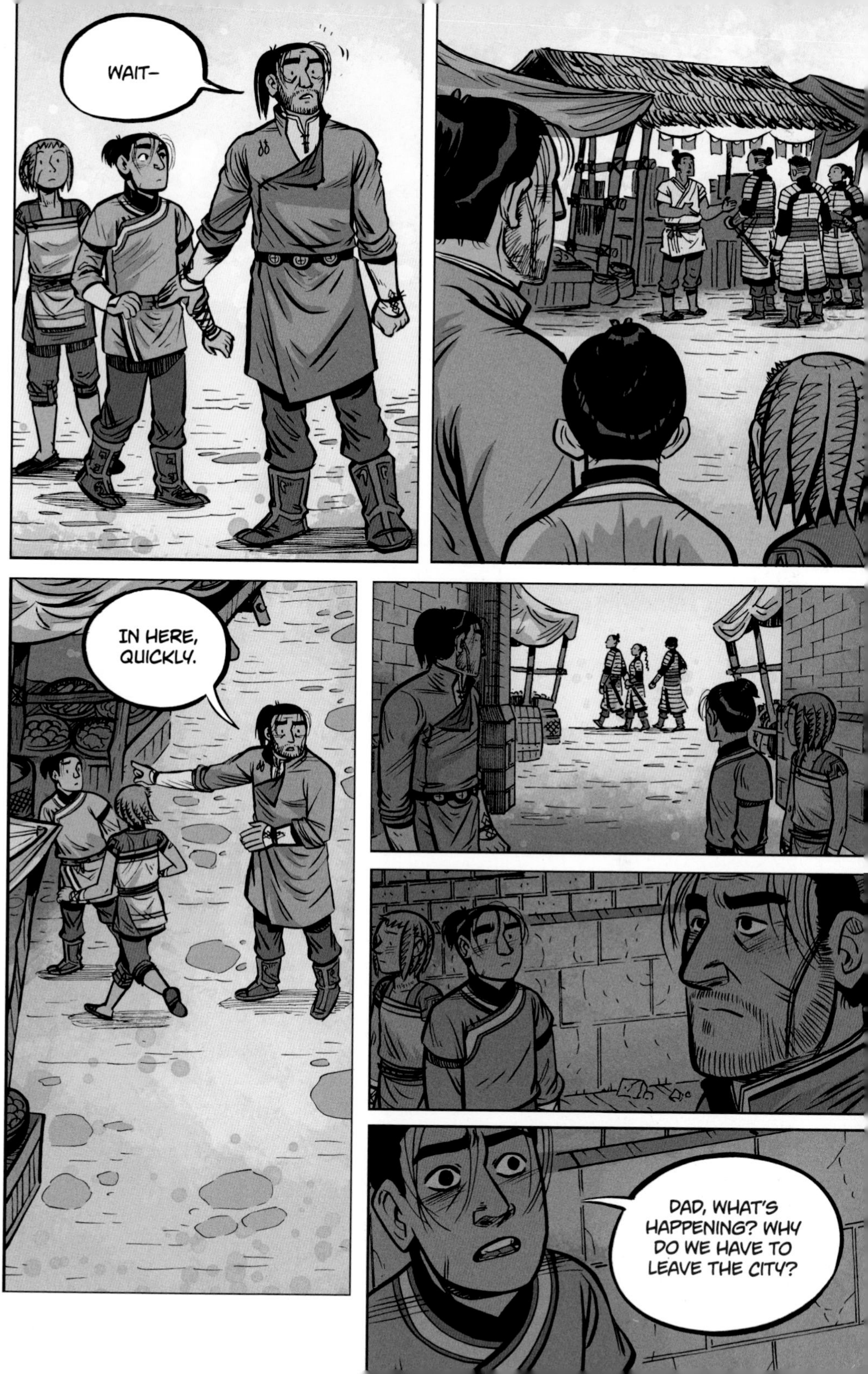
WAIT–
IN HERE, QUICKLY.
DAD, WHAT'S HAPPENING? WHY DO WE HAVE TO LEAVE THE CITY?

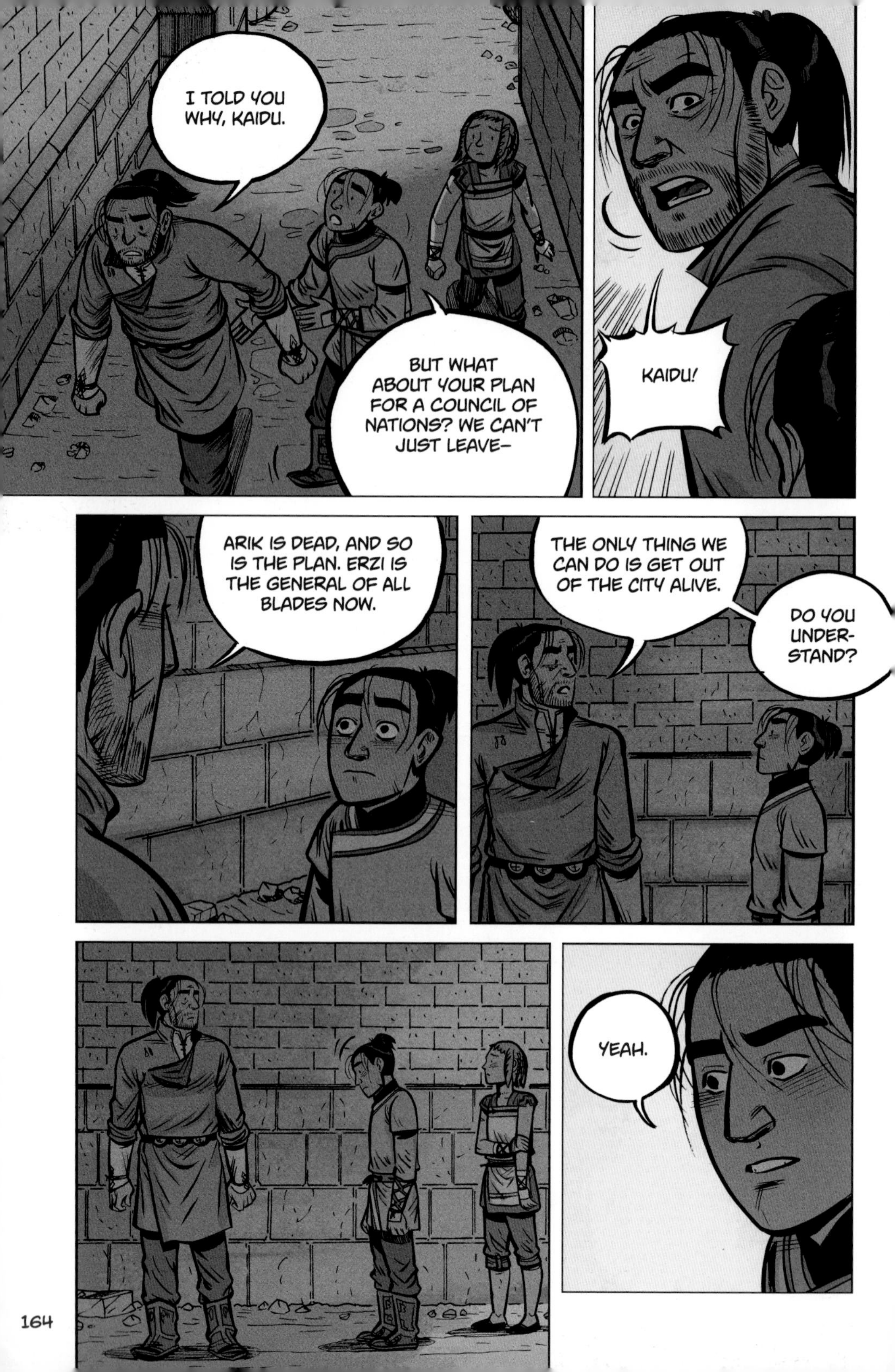
I TOLD YOU WHY, KAIDU.
BUT WHAT ABOUT YOUR PLAN FOR A COUNCIL OF NATIONS? WE CAN'T JUST LEAVE–
KAIDU!
ARIK IS DEAD, AND SO IS THE PLAN. ERZI IS THE GENERAL OF ALL BLADES NOW.
THE ONLY THING WE CAN DO IS GET OUT OF THE CITY ALIVE.
DO YOU UNDER-STAND?
YEAH.

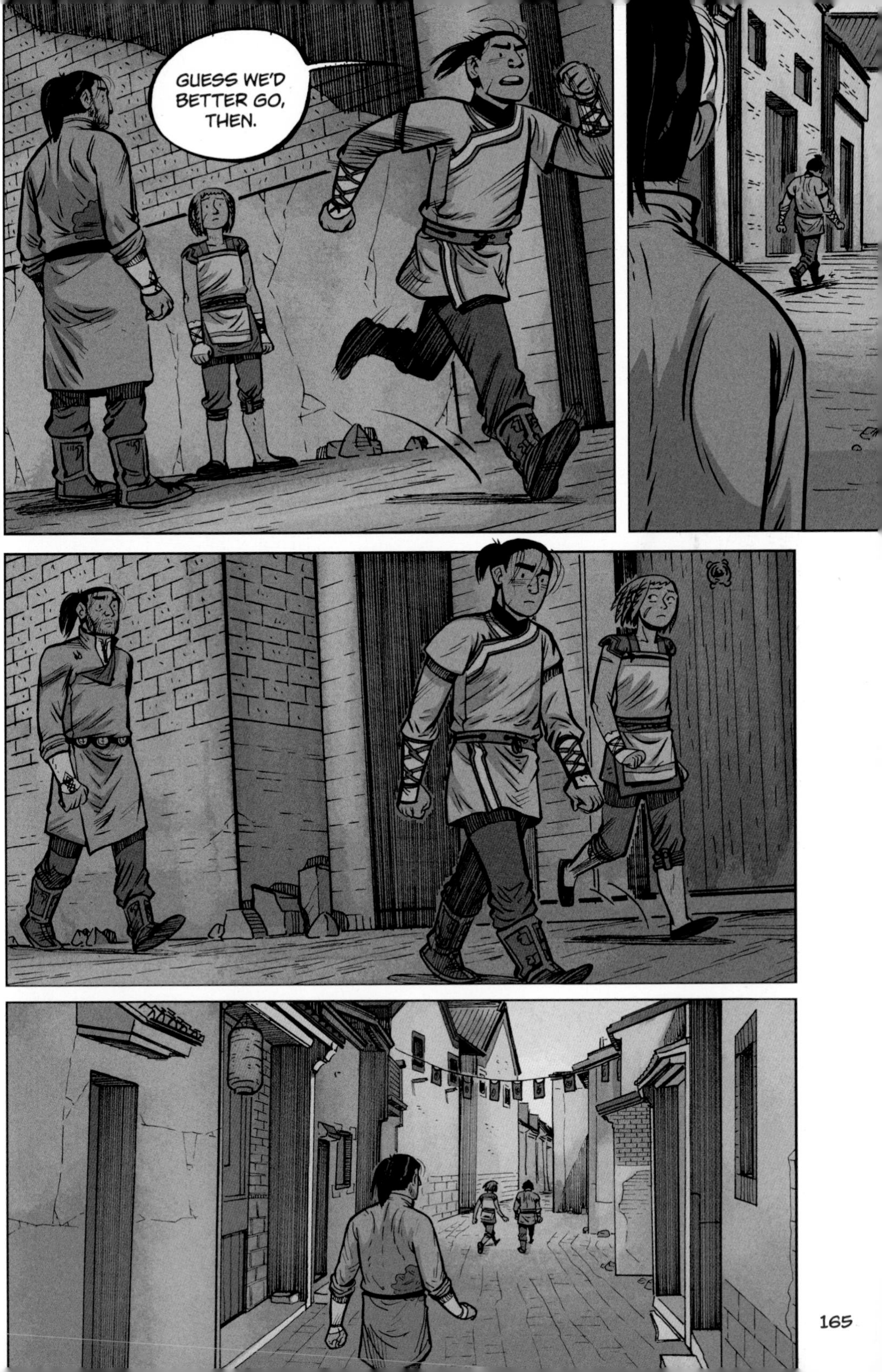
GUESS WE'D BETTER GO, THEN.

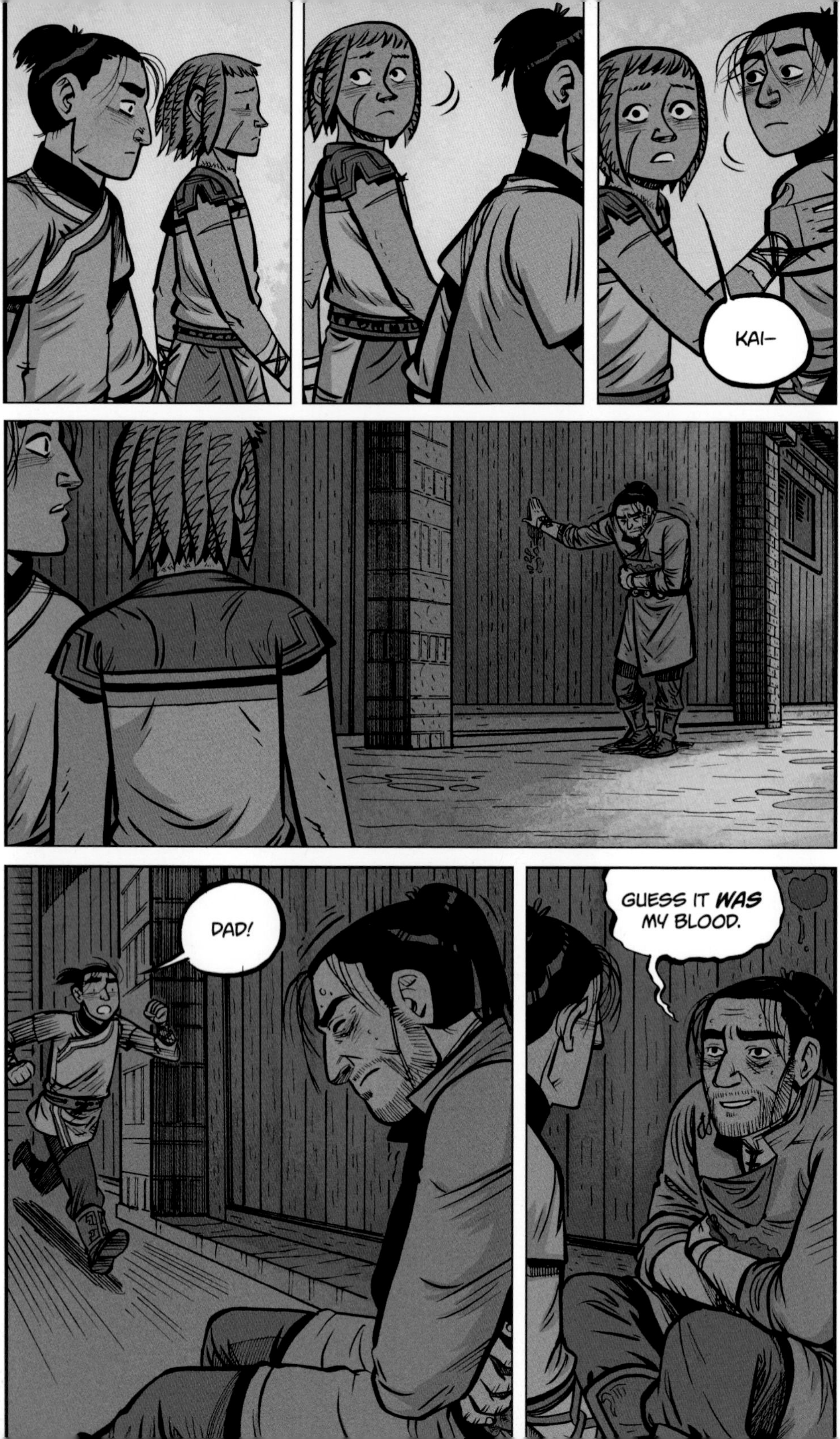
KAI-
DAD!
GUESS IT *WAS* MY BLOOD.

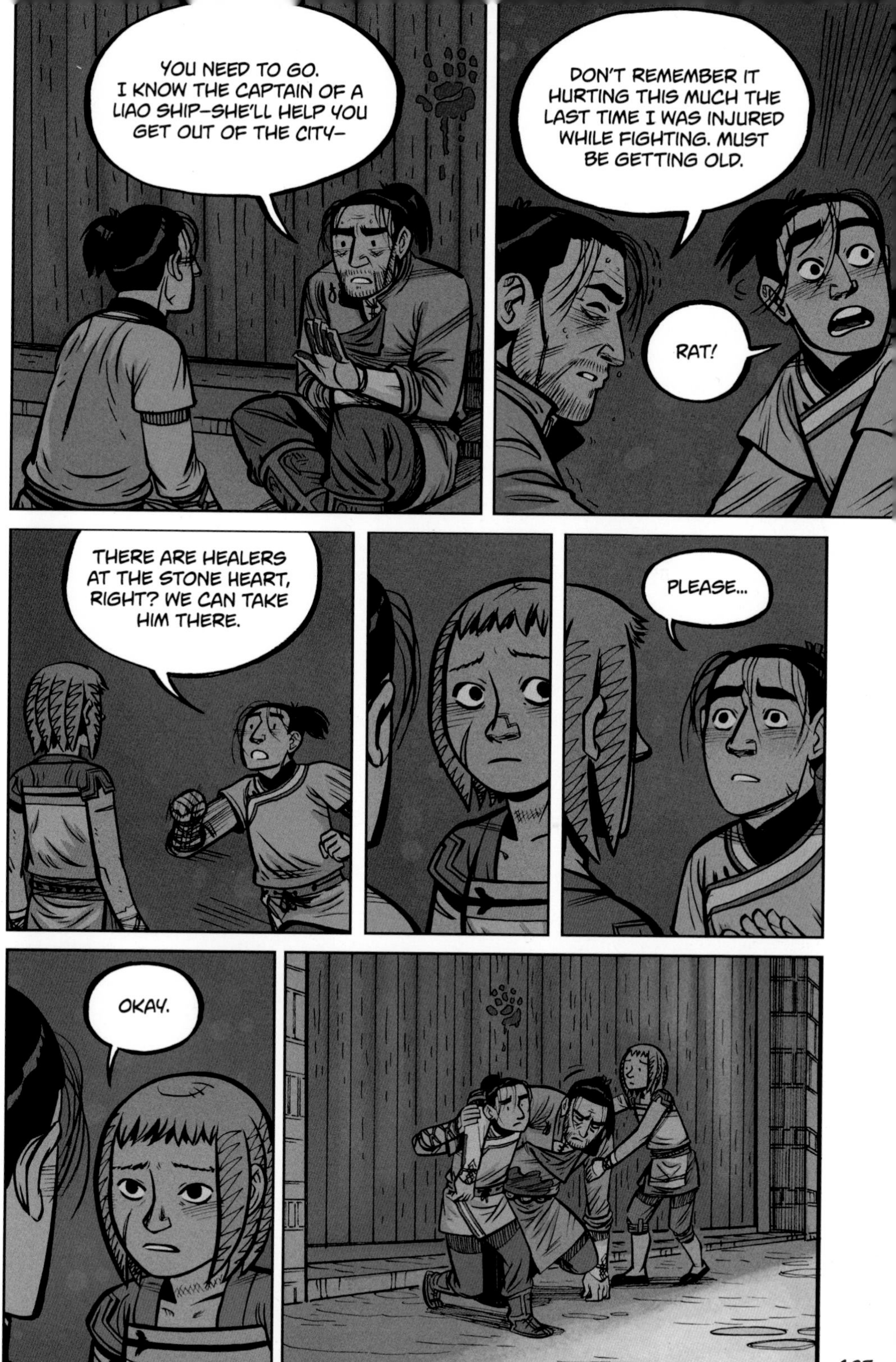
YOU NEED TO GO. I KNOW THE CAPTAIN OF A LIAO SHIP—SHE'LL HELP YOU GET OUT OF THE CITY—
DON'T REMEMBER IT HURTING THIS MUCH THE LAST TIME I WAS INJURED WHILE FIGHTING. MUST BE GETTING OLD.
RAT!
THERE ARE HEALERS AT THE STONE HEART, RIGHT? WE CAN TAKE HIM THERE.
PLEASE...
OKAY.

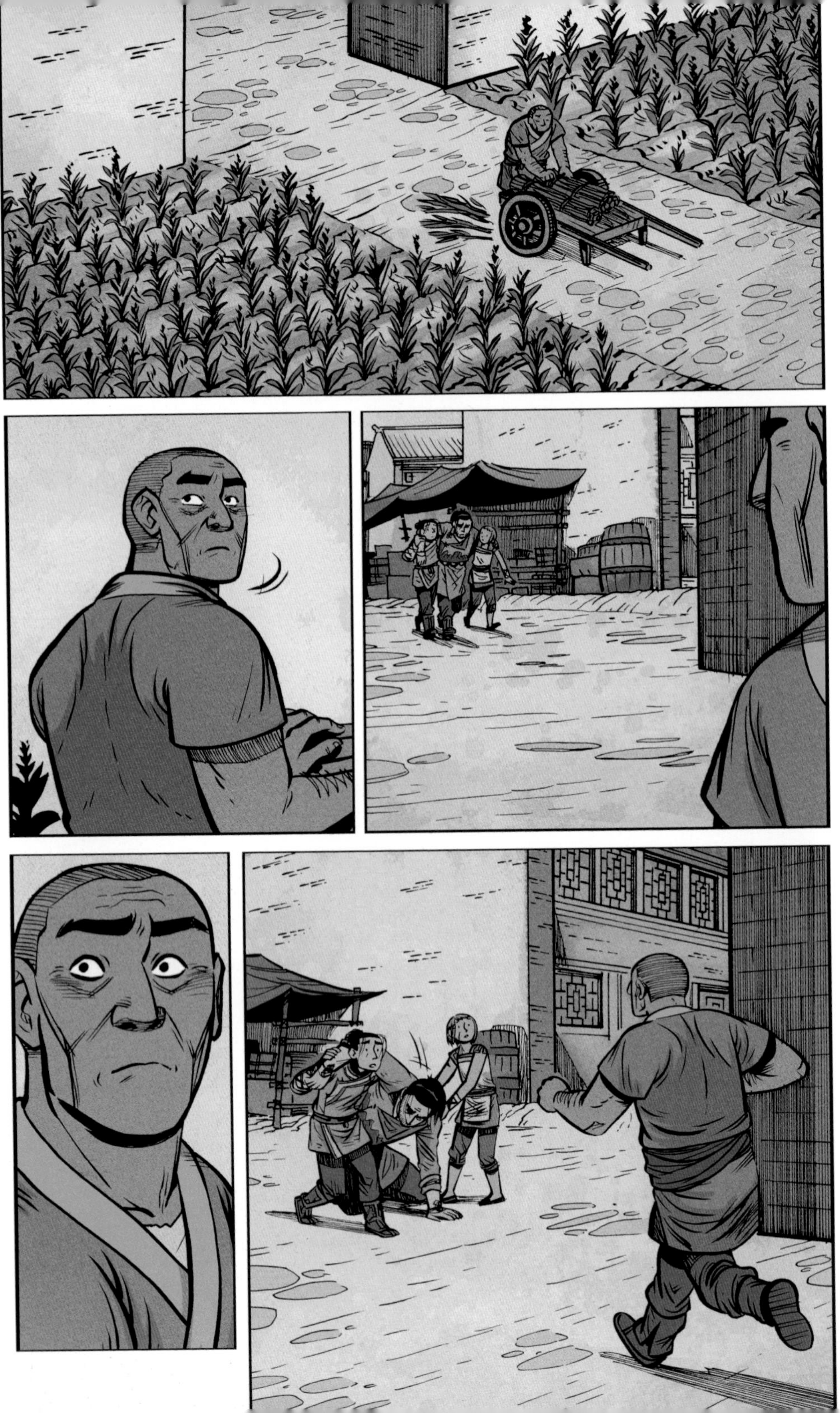

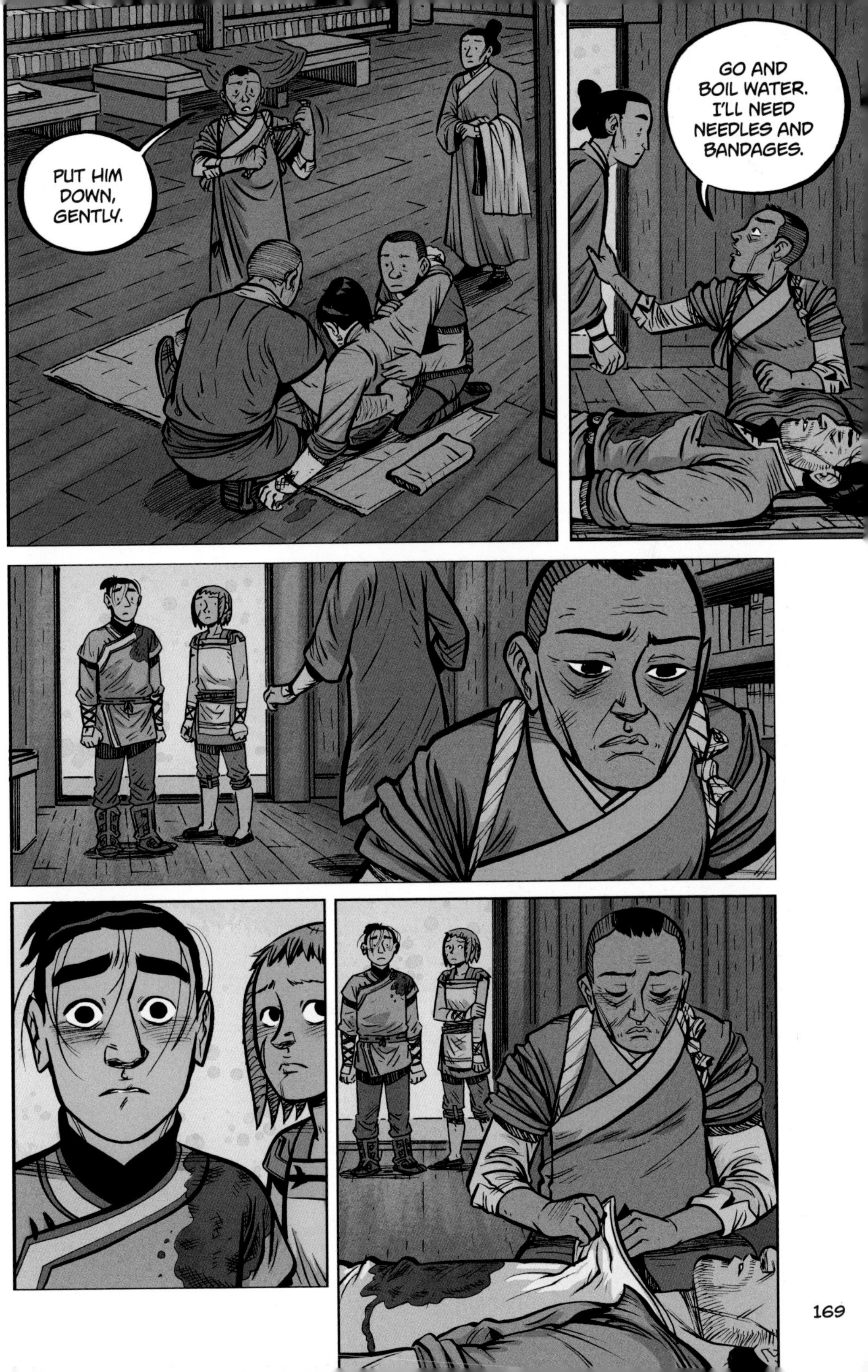
PUT HIM DOWN, GENTLY.
GO AND BOIL WATER. I'LL NEED NEEDLES AND BANDAGES.

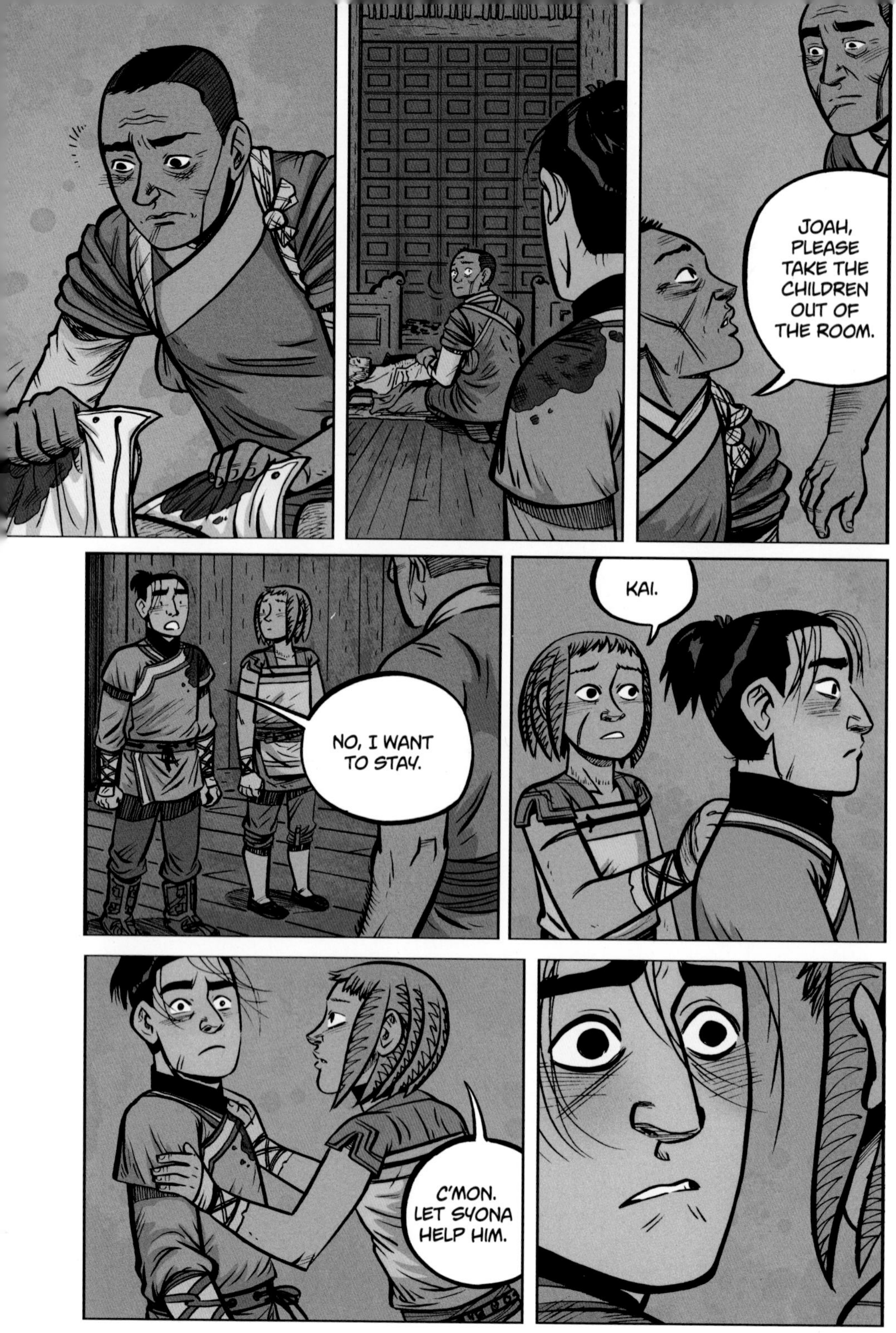
JOAH, PLEASE TAKE THE CHILDREN OUT OF THE ROOM.
NO, I WANT TO STAY.
KAI.
C'MON. LET SYONA HELP HIM.

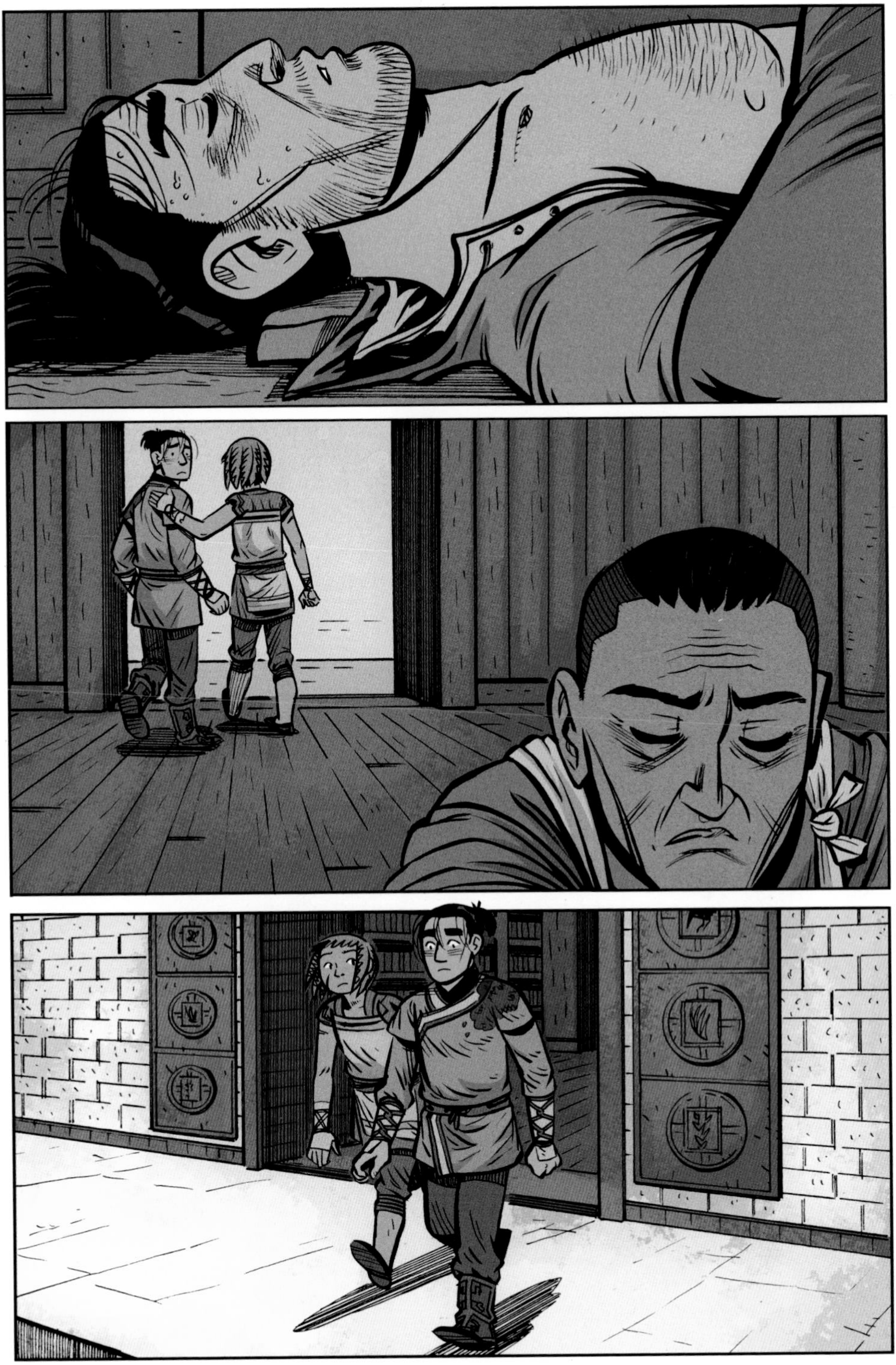

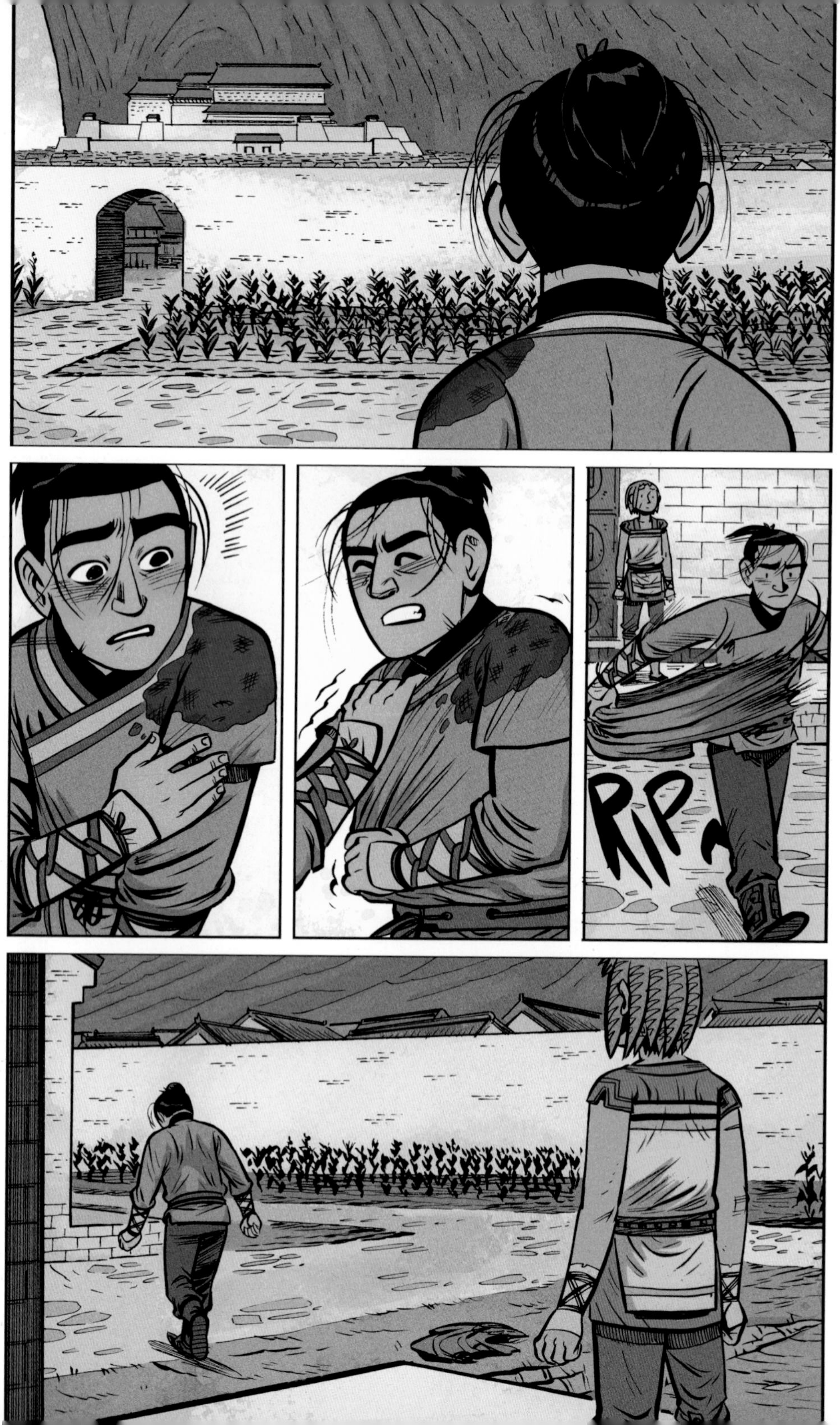
RIP

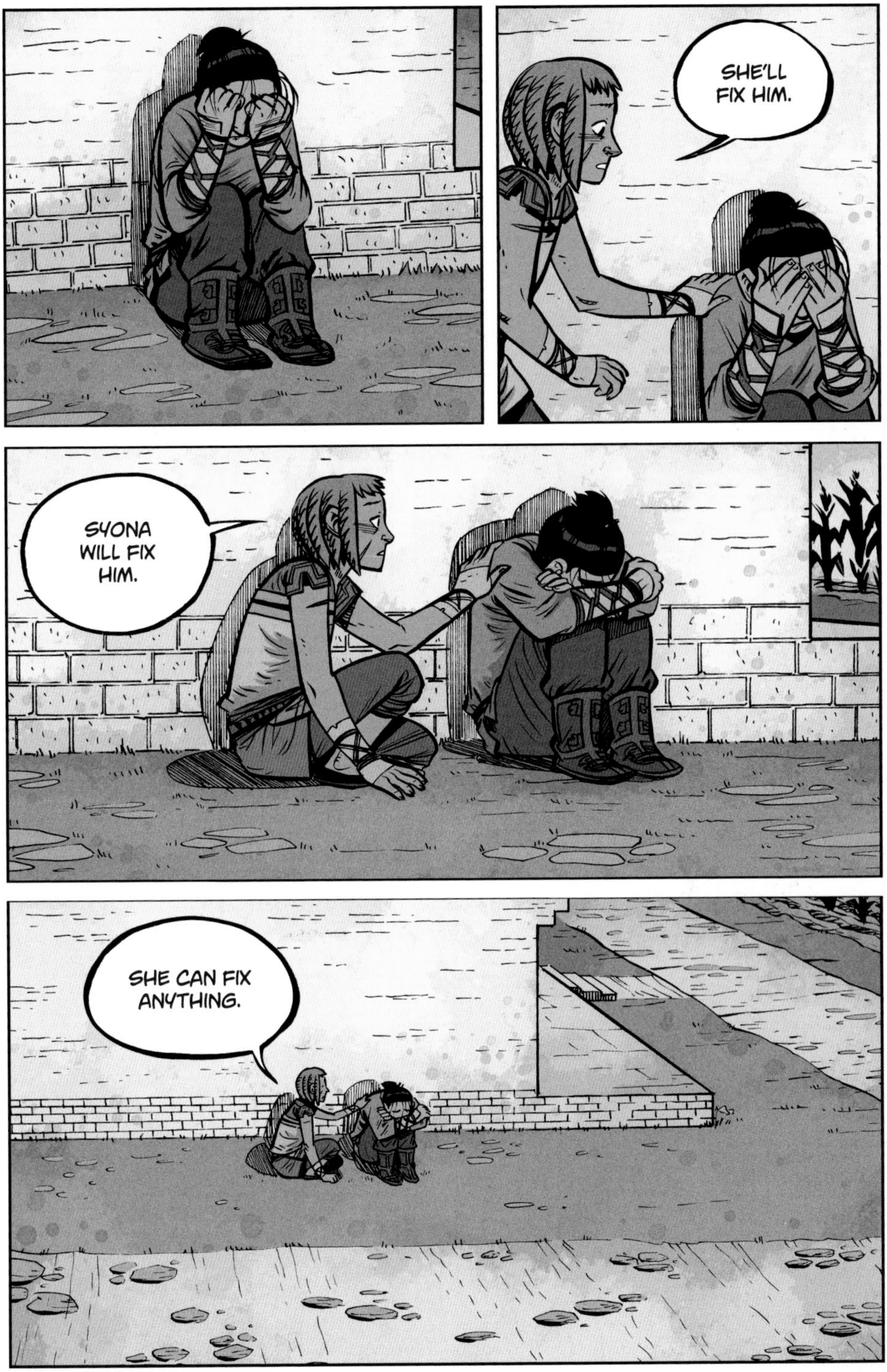

SHE'LL FIX HIM.
SYONA WILL FIX HIM.
SHE CAN FIX ANYTHING.

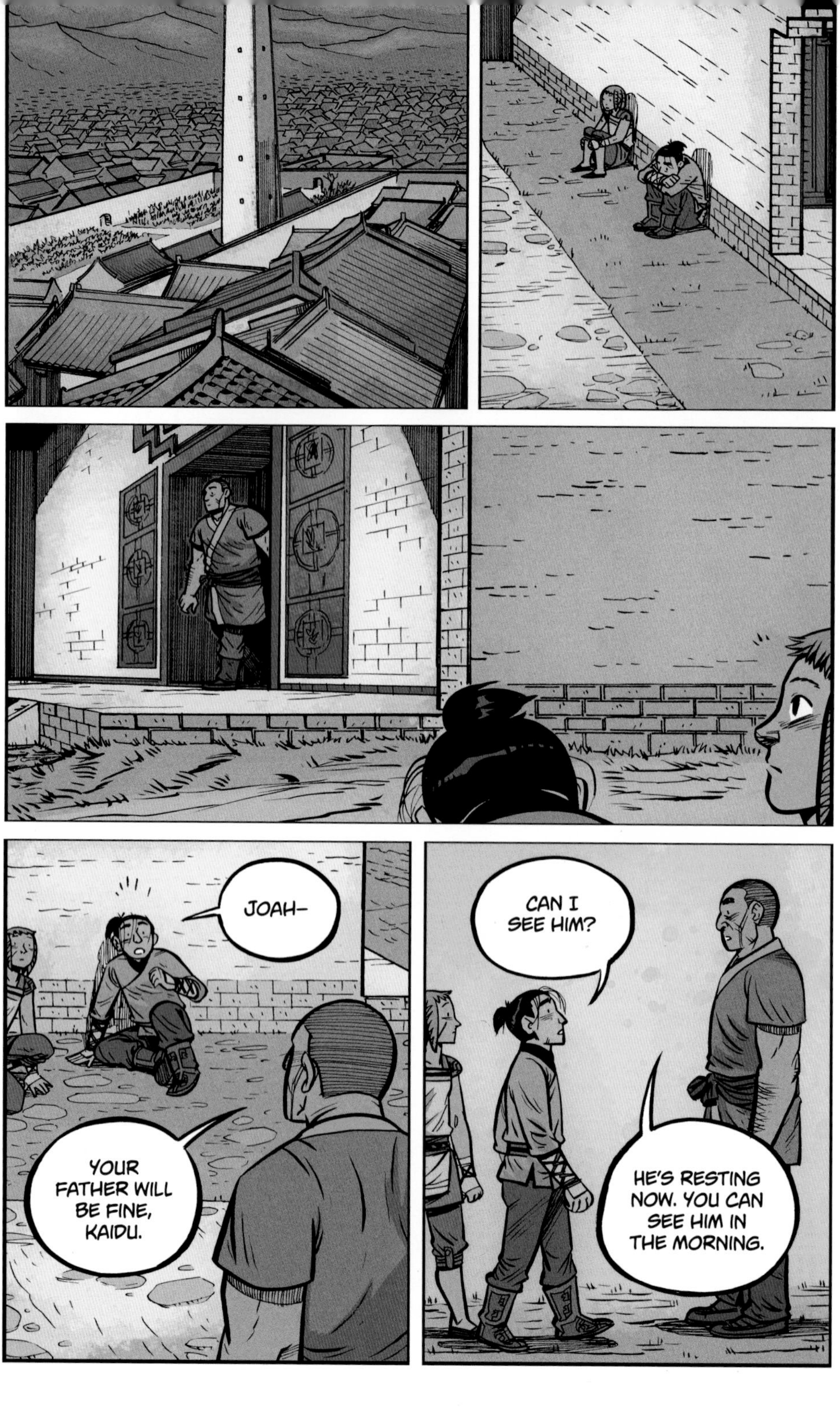
JOAH–
YOUR FATHER WILL BE FINE, KAIDU.
CAN I SEE HIM?
HE'S RESTING NOW. YOU CAN SEE HIM IN THE MORNING.

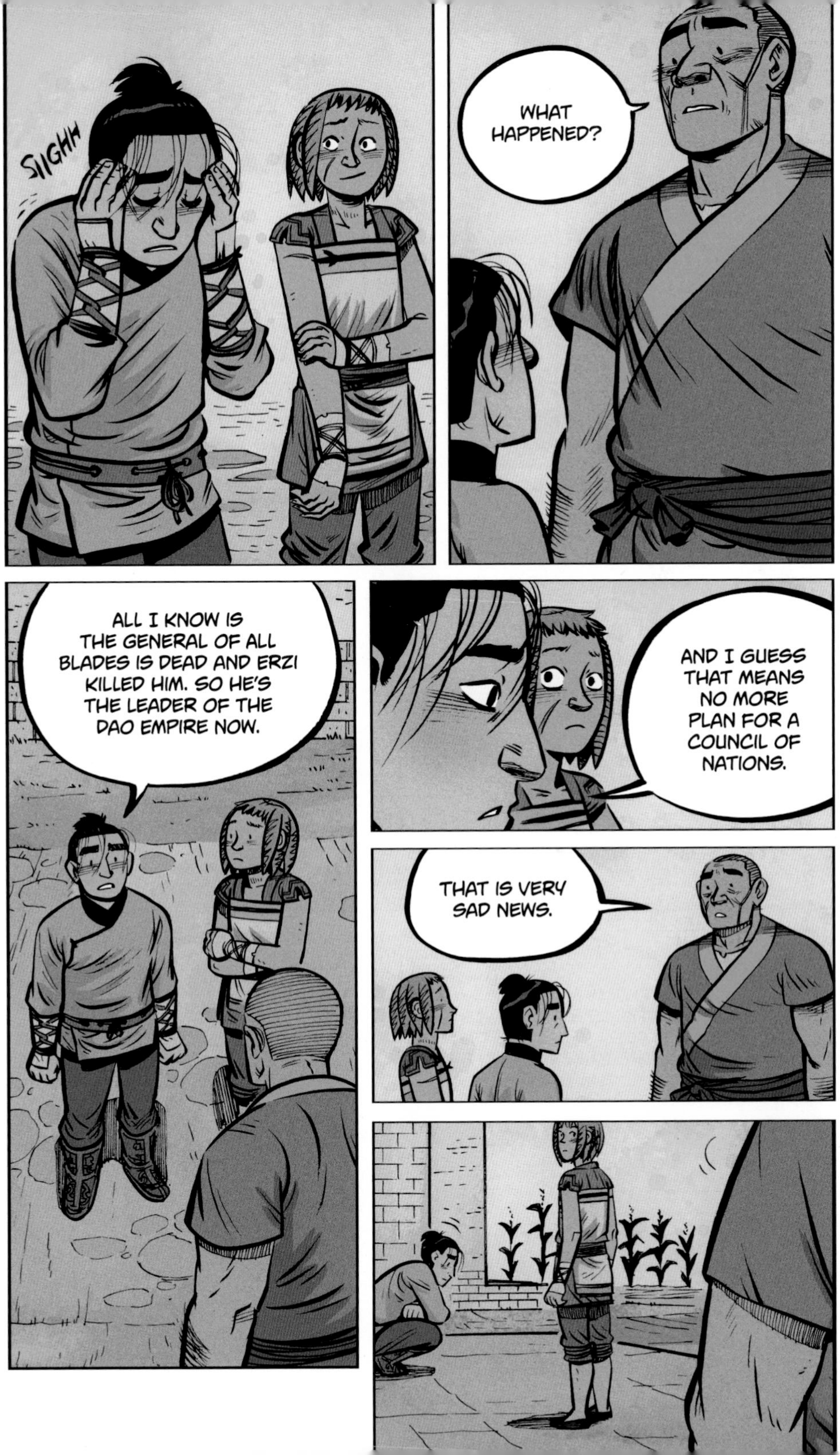
SIIGHH
WHAT HAPPENED?
ALL I KNOW IS THE GENERAL OF ALL BLADES IS DEAD AND ERZI KILLED HIM. SO HE'S THE LEADER OF THE DAO EMPIRE NOW.
AND I GUESS THAT MEANS NO MORE PLAN FOR A COUNCIL OF NATIONS.
THAT IS VERY SAD NEWS.

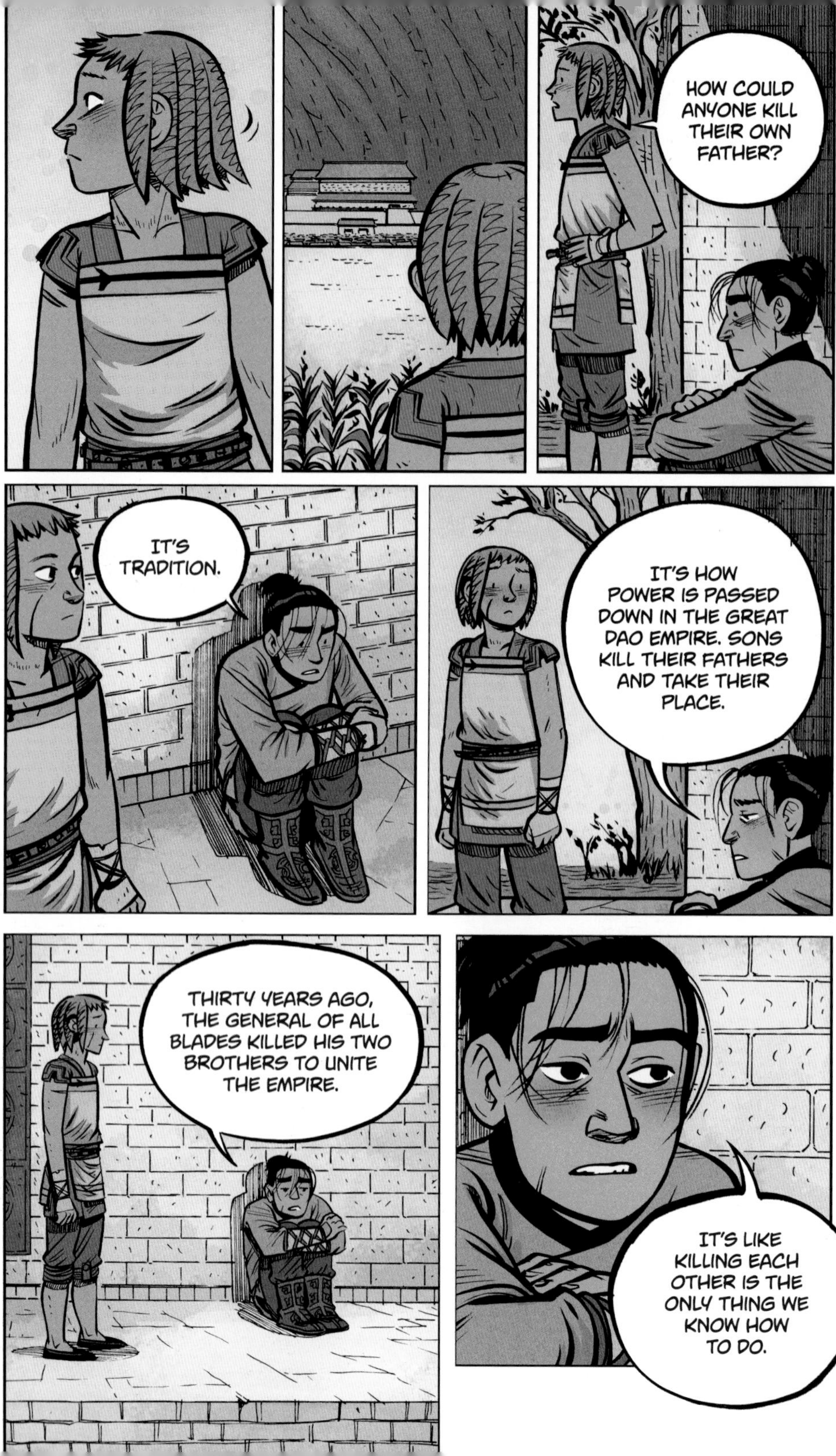
HOW COULD ANYONE KILL THEIR OWN FATHER?
IT'S TRADITION.
IT'S HOW POWER IS PASSED DOWN IN THE GREAT DAO EMPIRE. SONS KILL THEIR FATHERS AND TAKE THEIR PLACE.
THIRTY YEARS AGO, THE GENERAL OF ALL BLADES KILLED HIS TWO BROTHERS TO UNITE THE EMPIRE.
IT'S LIKE KILLING EACH OTHER IS THE ONLY THING WE KNOW HOW TO DO.

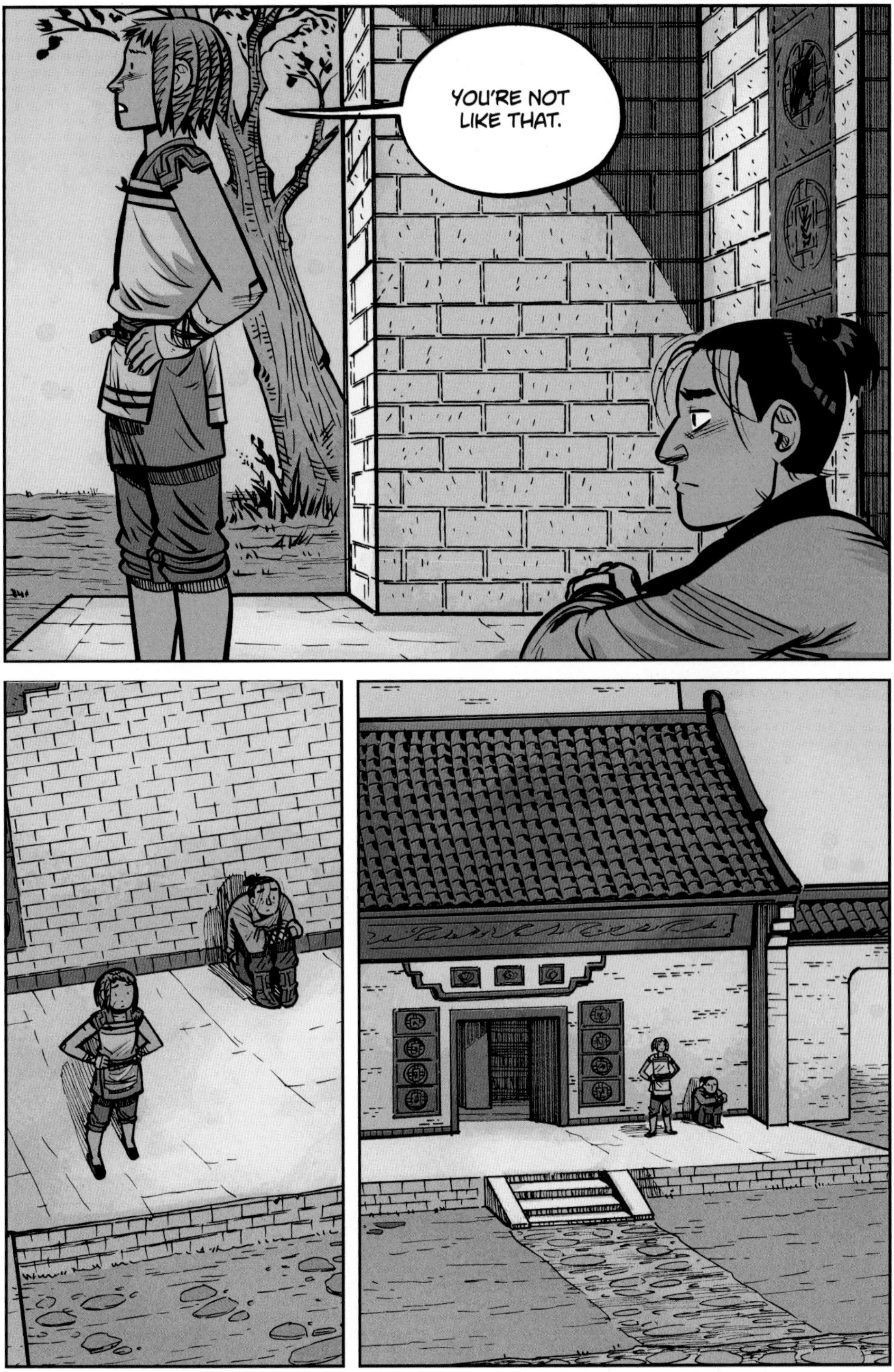
YOU'RE NOT LIKE THAT.

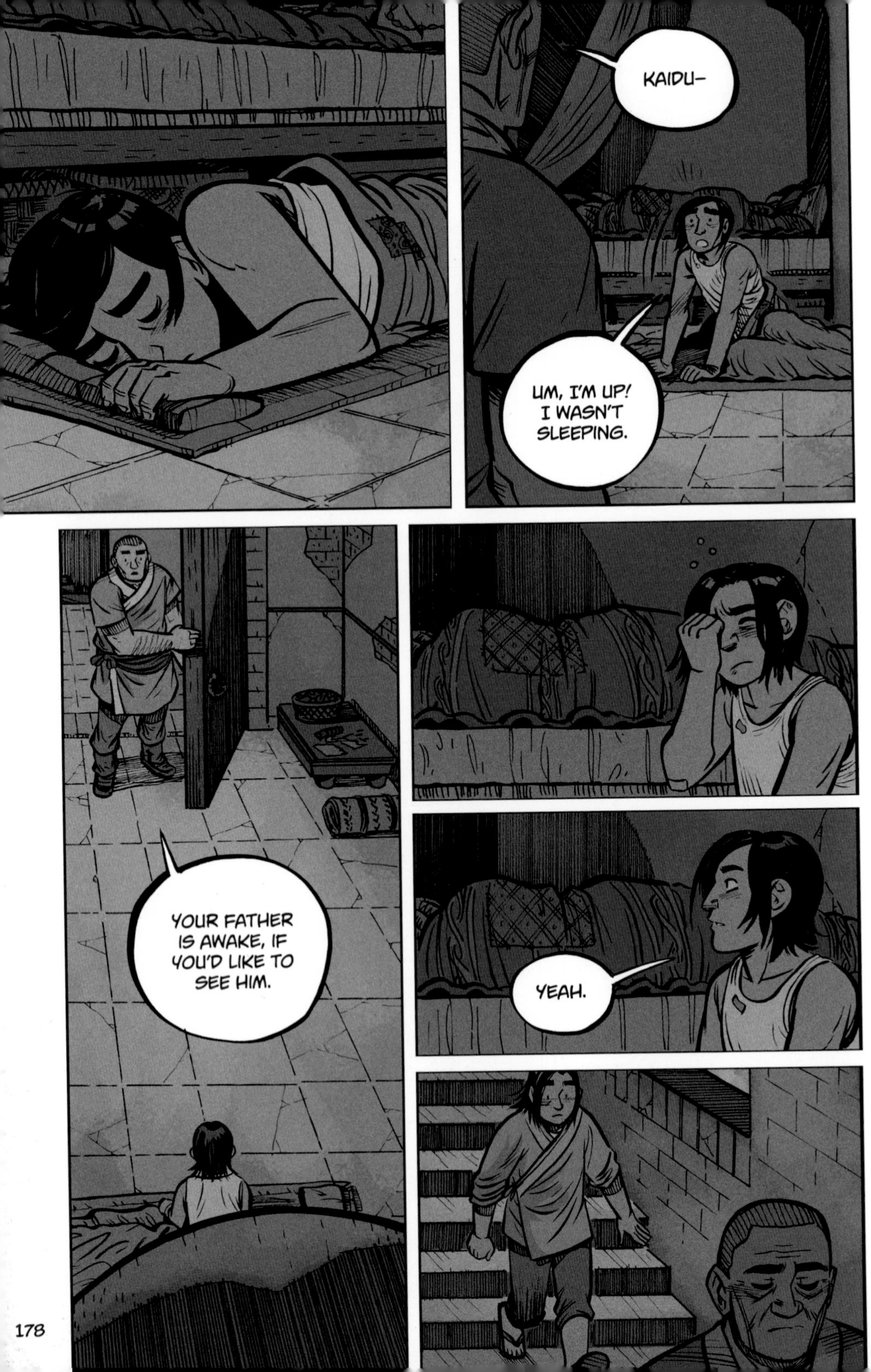
KAIDU–
UM, I'M UP! I WASN'T SLEEPING.
YOUR FATHER IS AWAKE, IF YOU'D LIKE TO SEE HIM.
YEAH.

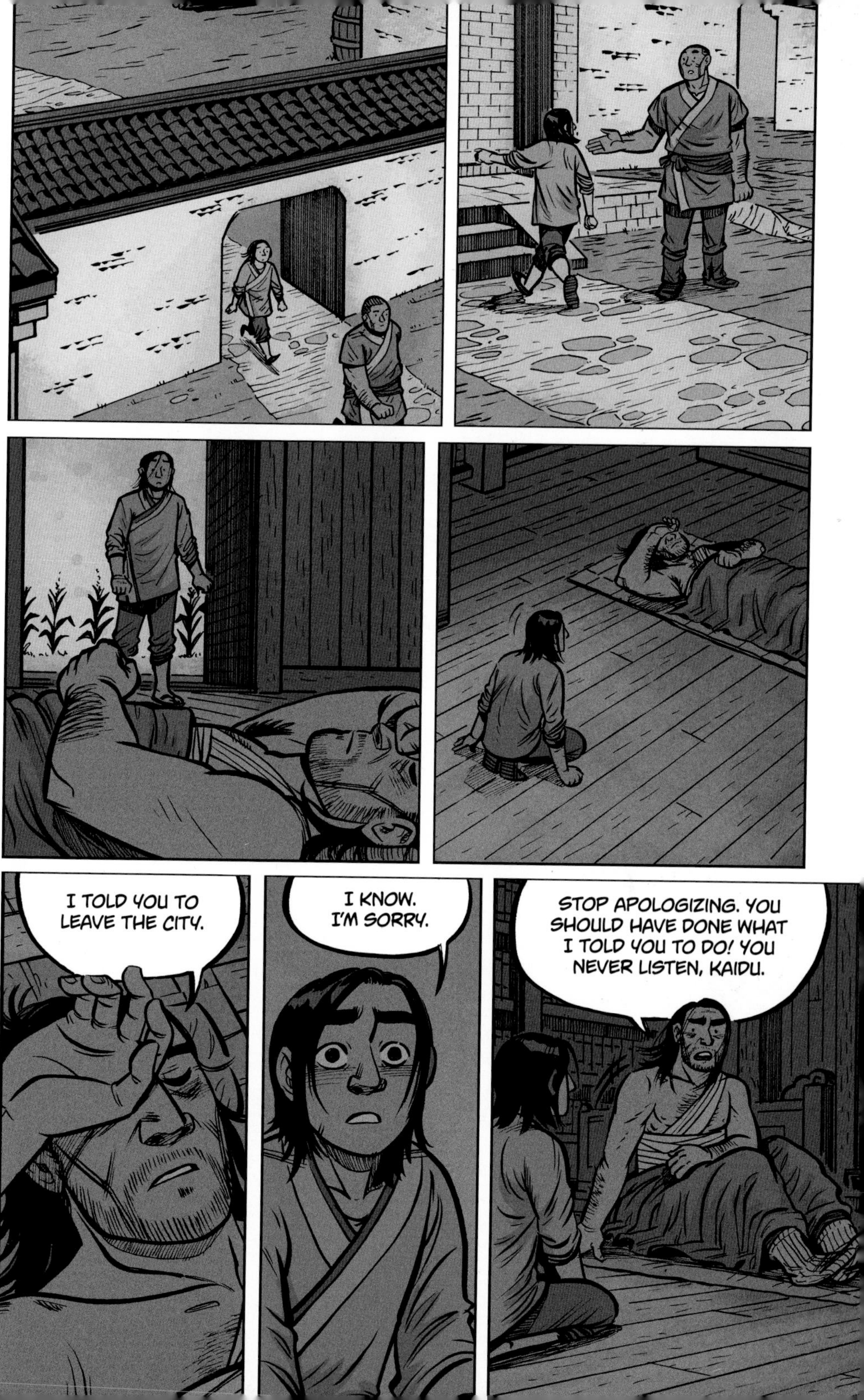
I TOLD YOU TO LEAVE THE CITY.
I KNOW. I'M SORRY.
STOP APOLOGIZING. YOU SHOULD HAVE DONE WHAT I TOLD YOU TO DO! YOU NEVER LISTEN, KAIDU.

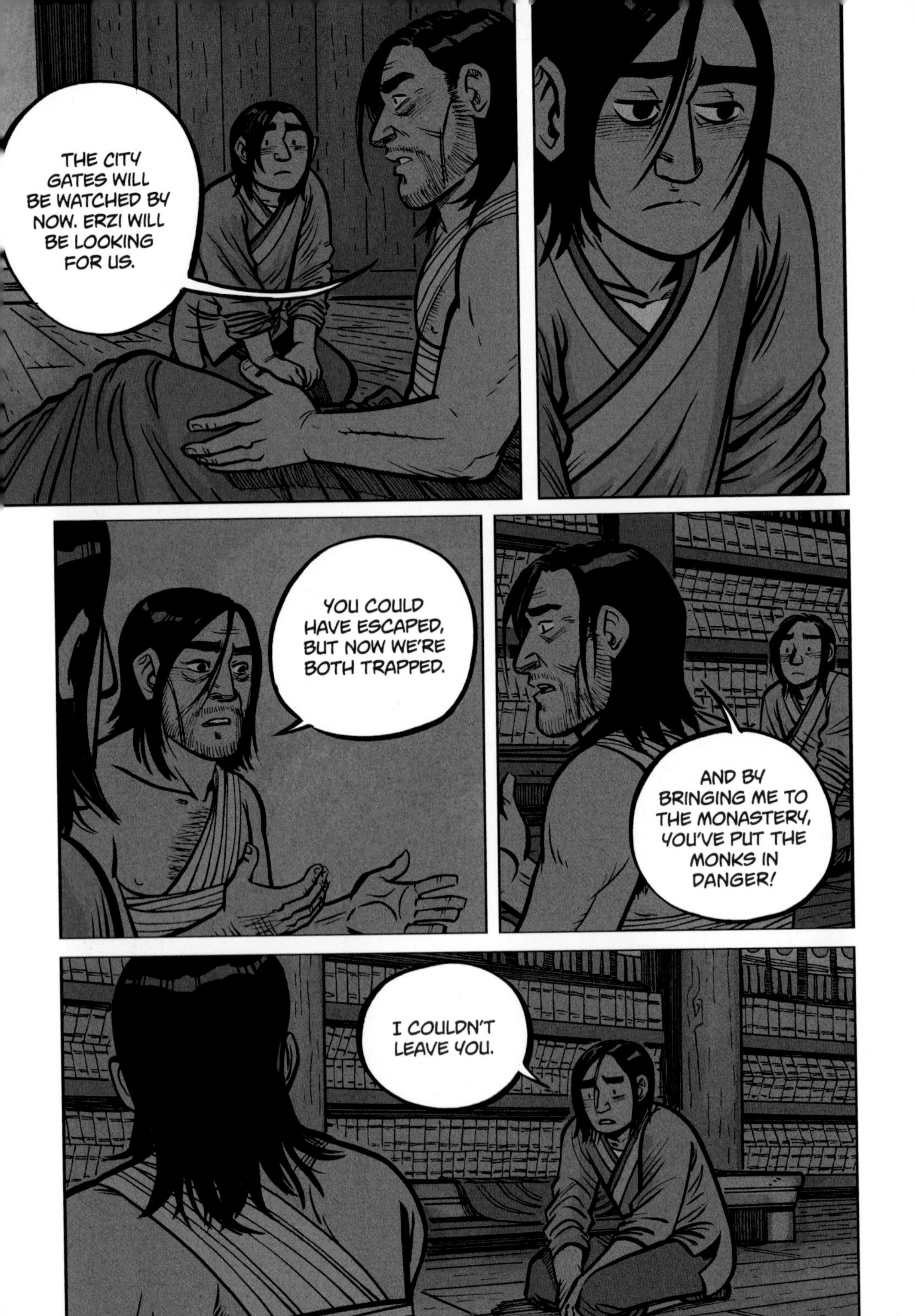
THE CITY GATES WILL BE WATCHED BY NOW. ERZI WILL BE LOOKING FOR US.
YOU COULD HAVE ESCAPED, BUT NOW WE'RE BOTH TRAPPED.
AND BY BRINGING ME TO THE MONASTERY, YOU'VE PUT THE MONKS IN DANGER!
I COULDN'T LEAVE YOU.

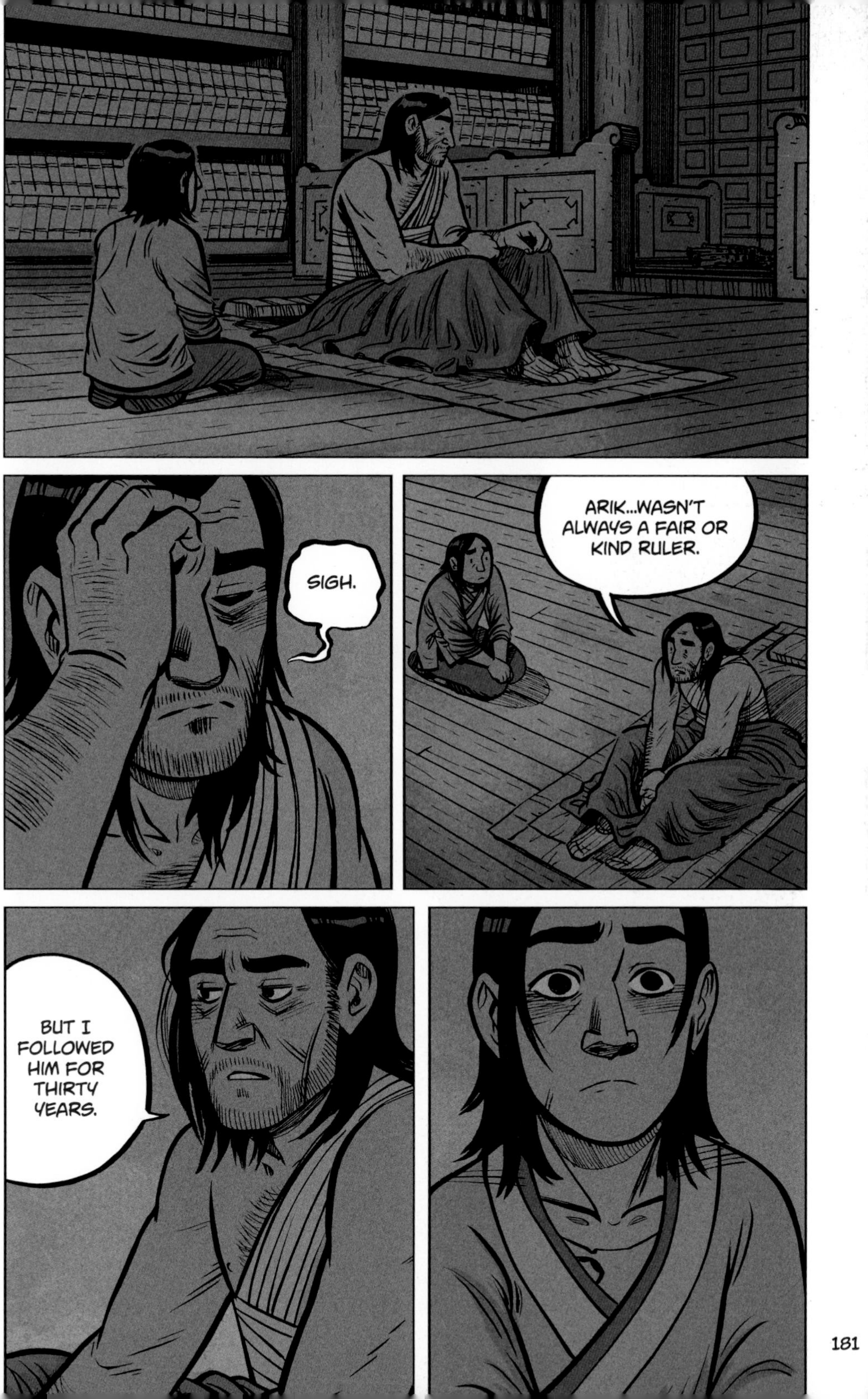
SIGH.
ARIK...WASN'T ALWAYS A FAIR OR KIND RULER.
BUT I FOLLOWED HIM FOR THIRTY YEARS.

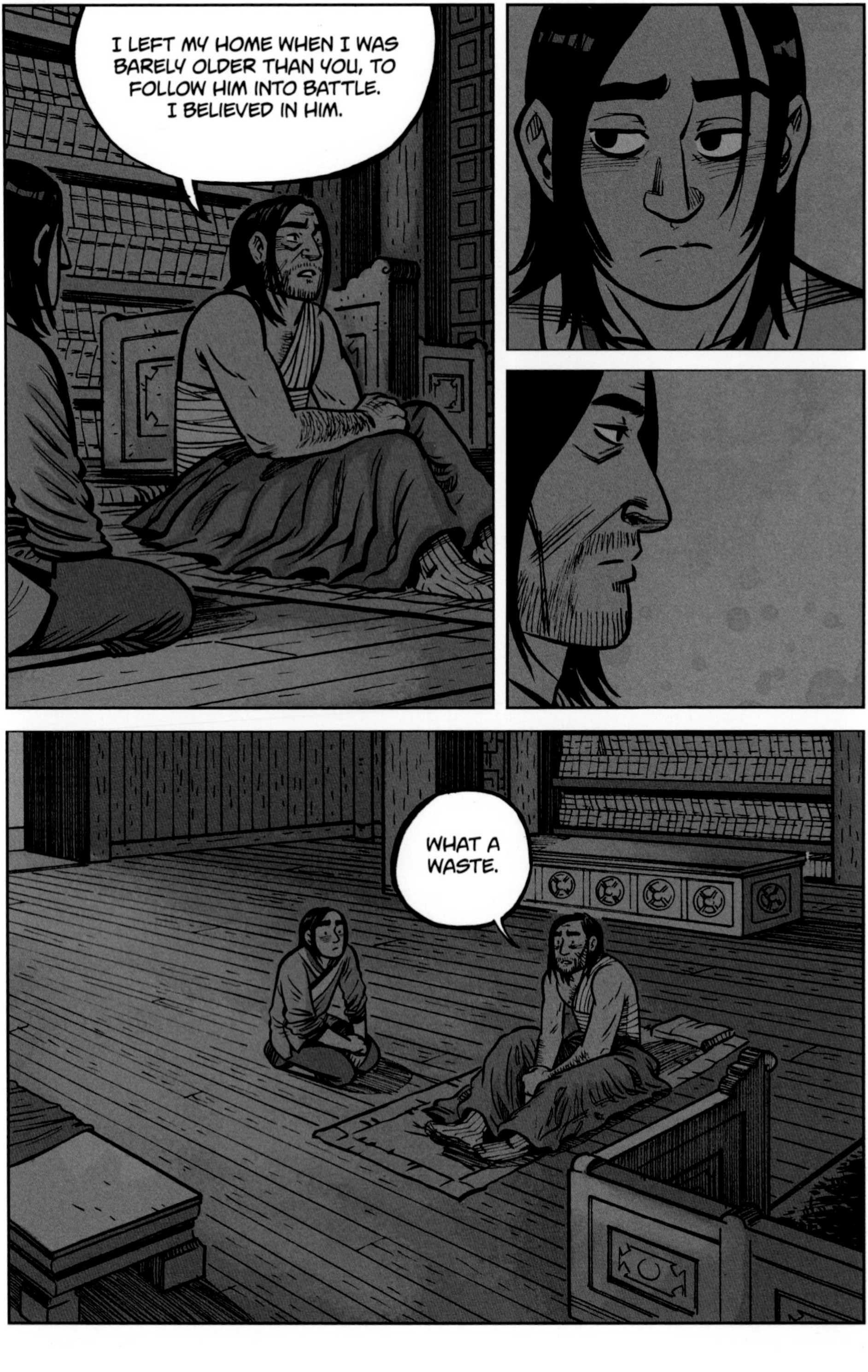
I LEFT MY HOME WHEN I WAS BARELY OLDER THAN YOU, TO FOLLOW HIM INTO BATTLE. I BELIEVED IN HIM.
WHAT A WASTE.

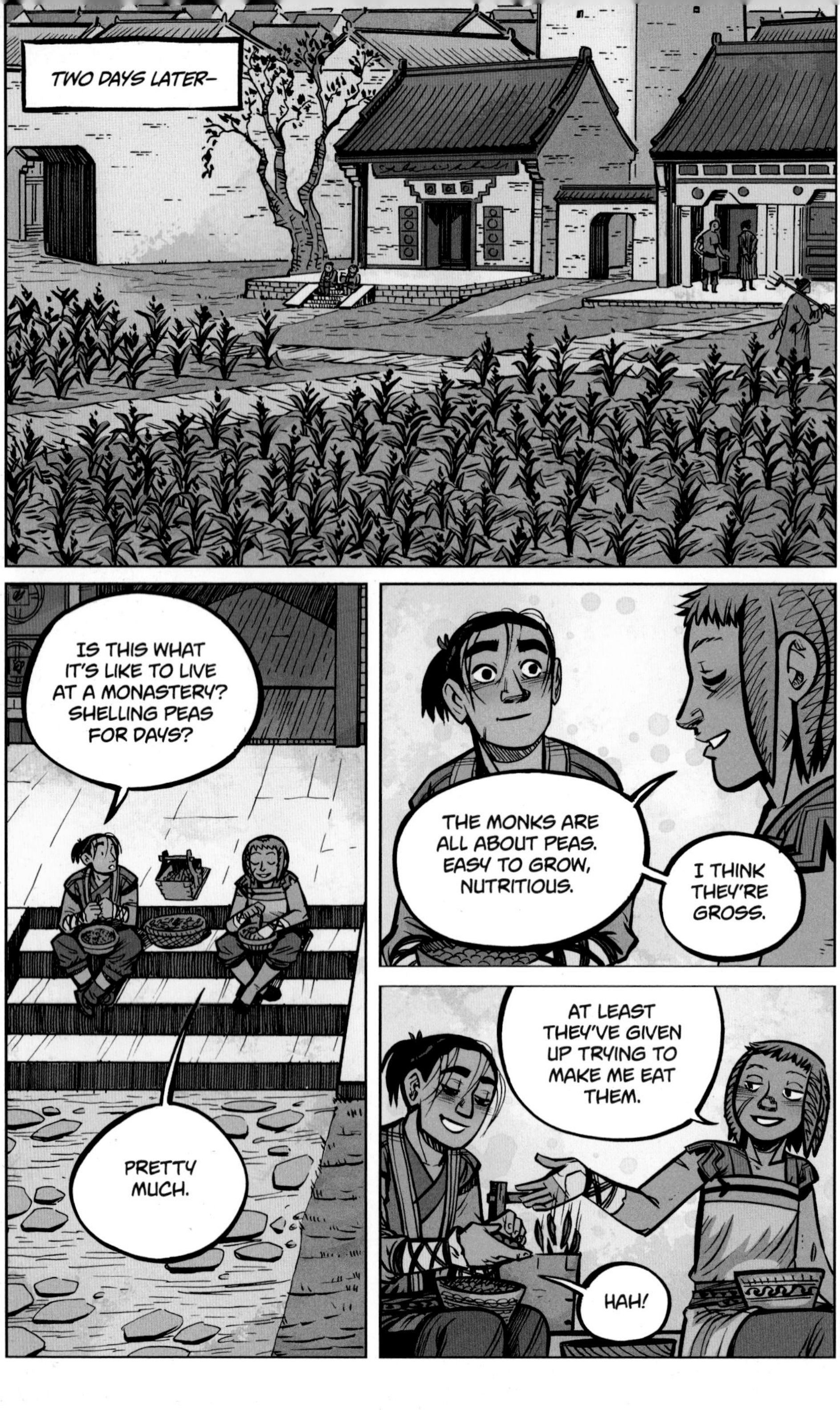
TWO DAYS LATER–
IS THIS WHAT IT'S LIKE TO LIVE AT A MONASTERY? SHELLING PEAS FOR DAYS?
PRETTY MUCH.
THE MONKS ARE ALL ABOUT PEAS. EASY TO GROW, NUTRITIOUS.
I THINK THEY'RE GROSS.
AT LEAST THEY'VE GIVEN UP TRYING TO MAKE ME EAT THEM.
HAH!

I HATE EATING FISH. BUT WHEN I LIVED WITH MY MOM, IF THAT'S WHAT WE HAD FOR SUPPER, I HAD TO EAT IT. NO ARGUMENTS.

Y'KNOW, "THERE ARE STARVING LIAO KIDS WHO'D LOVE FISH FOR SUPPER, SO CLEAN YOUR PLATE, KAIDU."

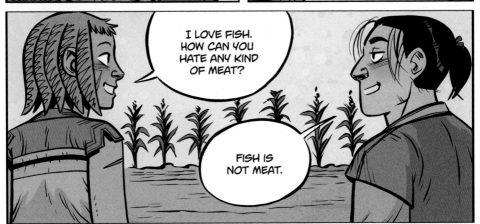

I LOVE FISH. HOW CAN YOU HATE ANY KIND OF MEAT?

FISH IS NOT MEAT.

WHAT'S YOUR MOM LIKE?

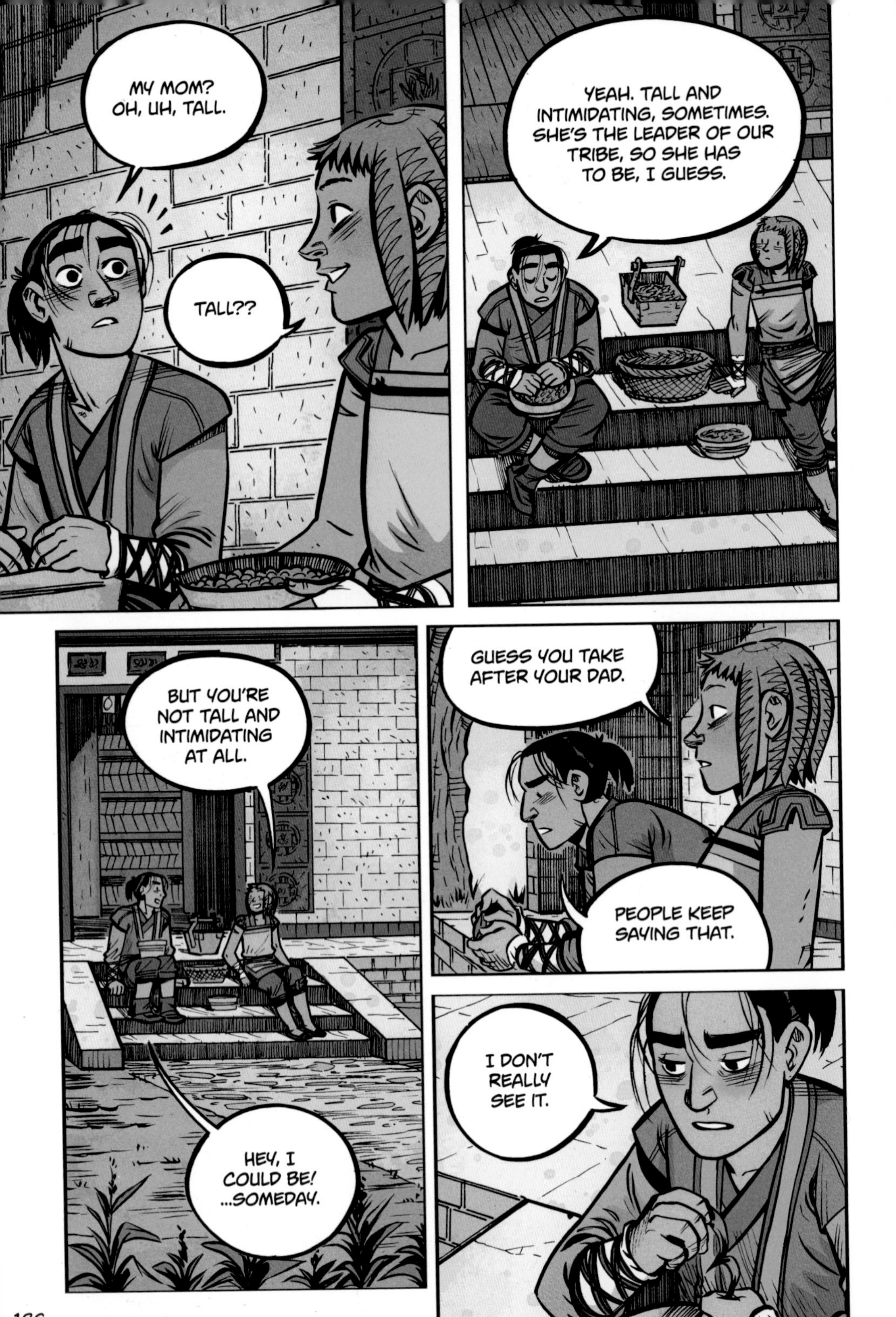
MY MOM?
OH, UH, TALL.
TALL??
YEAH. TALL AND INTIMIDATING, SOMETIMES. SHE'S THE LEADER OF OUR TRIBE, SO SHE HAS TO BE, I GUESS.
BUT YOU'RE NOT TALL AND INTIMIDATING AT ALL.
HEY, I COULD BE! ...SOMEDAY.
GUESS YOU TAKE AFTER YOUR DAD.
PEOPLE KEEP SAYING THAT.
I DON'T REALLY SEE IT.

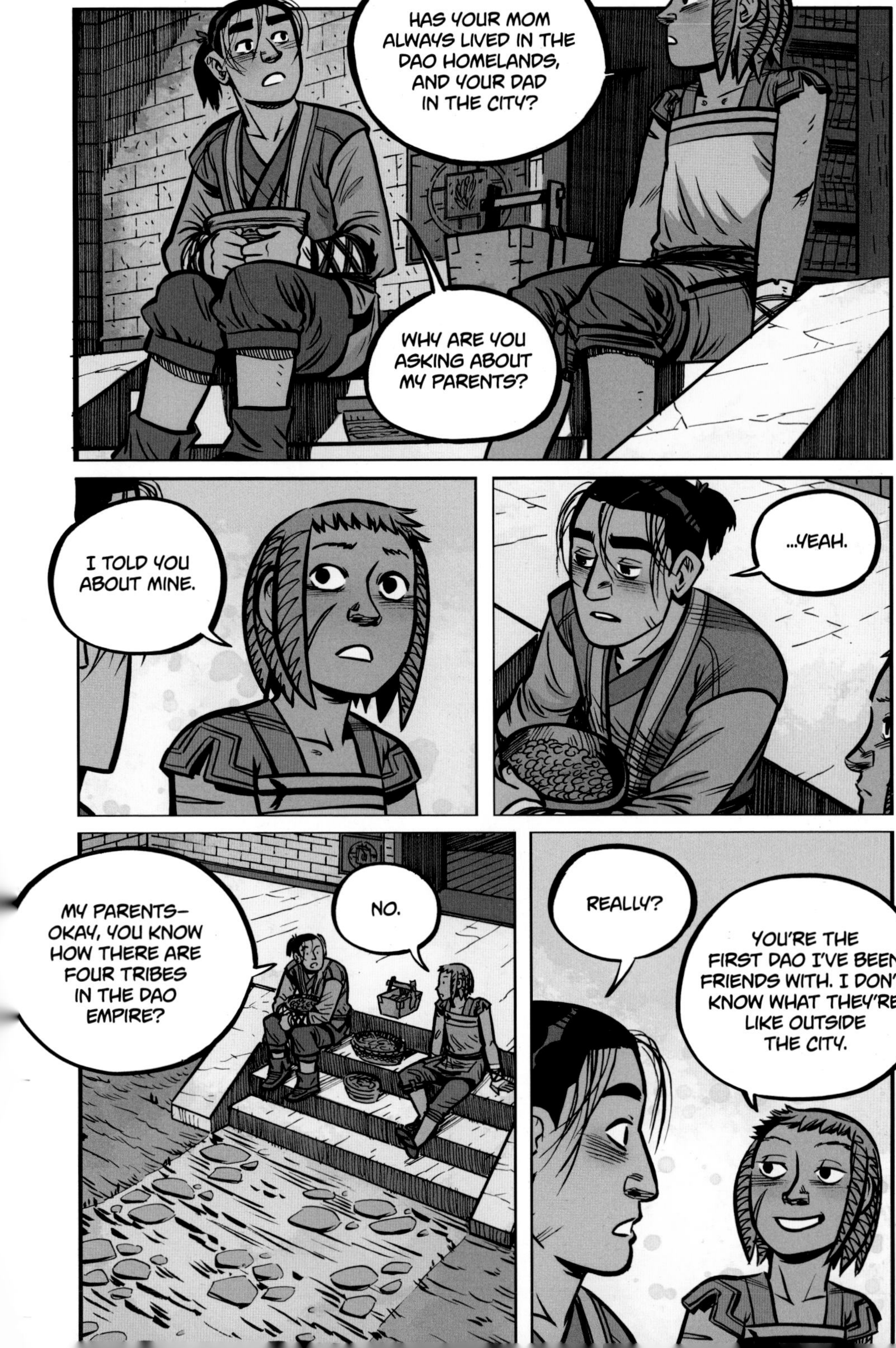
HAS YOUR MOM ALWAYS LIVED IN THE DAO HOMELANDS, AND YOUR DAD IN THE CITY?
WHY ARE YOU ASKING ABOUT MY PARENTS?
I TOLD YOU ABOUT MINE.
...YEAH.
MY PARENTS— OKAY, YOU KNOW HOW THERE ARE FOUR TRIBES IN THE DAO EMPIRE?
NO.
REALLY?
YOU'RE THE FIRST DAO I'VE BEEN FRIENDS WITH. I DON'T KNOW WHAT THEY'RE LIKE OUTSIDE THE CITY.

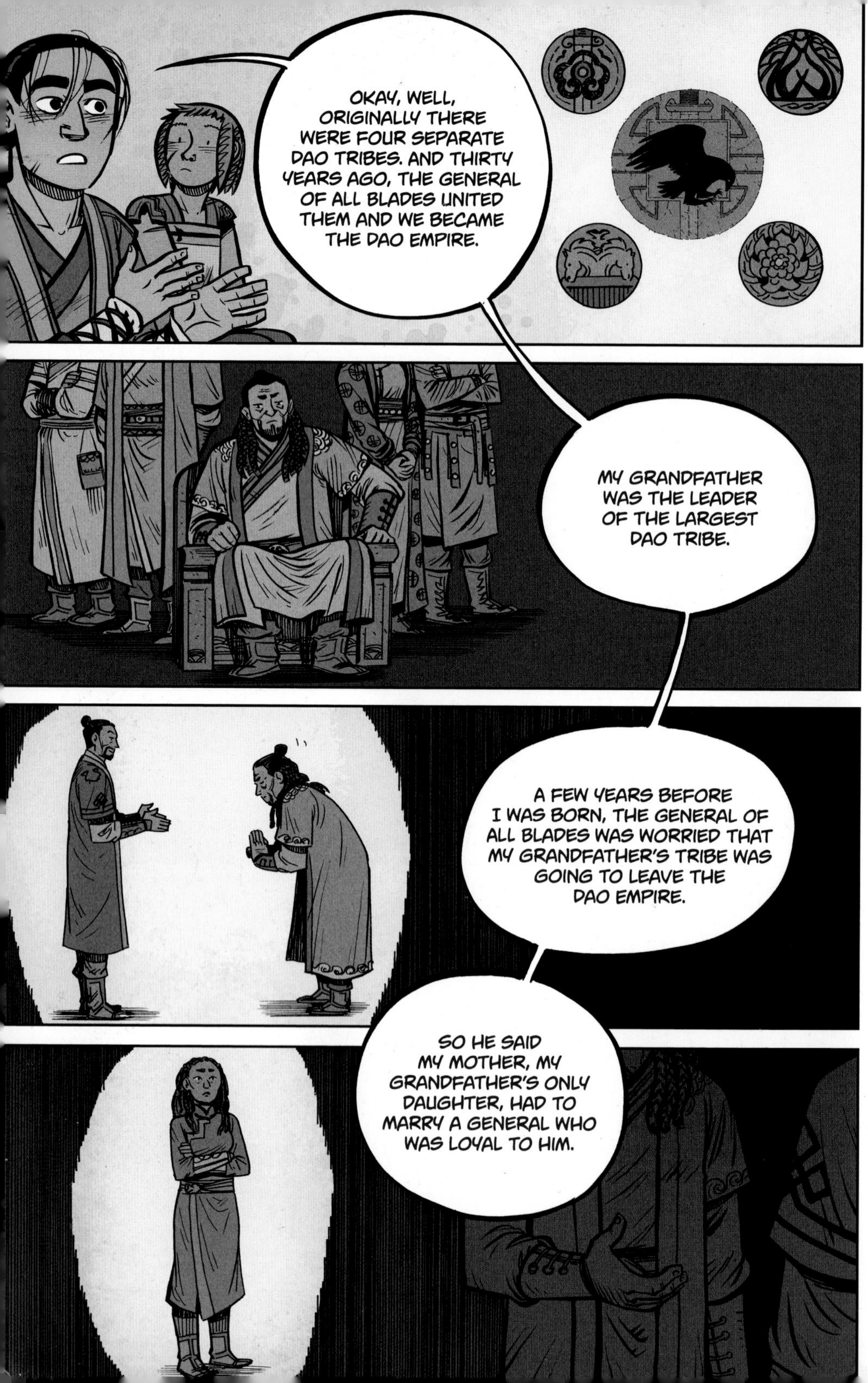
OKAY, WELL, ORIGINALLY THERE WERE FOUR SEPARATE DAO TRIBES. AND THIRTY YEARS AGO, THE GENERAL OF ALL BLADES UNITED THEM AND WE BECAME THE DAO EMPIRE.
MY GRANDFATHER WAS THE LEADER OF THE LARGEST DAO TRIBE.
A FEW YEARS BEFORE I WAS BORN, THE GENERAL OF ALL BLADES WAS WORRIED THAT MY GRANDFATHER'S TRIBE WAS GOING TO LEAVE THE DAO EMPIRE.
SO HE SAID MY MOTHER, MY GRANDFATHER'S ONLY DAUGHTER, HAD TO MARRY A GENERAL WHO WAS LOYAL TO HIM.

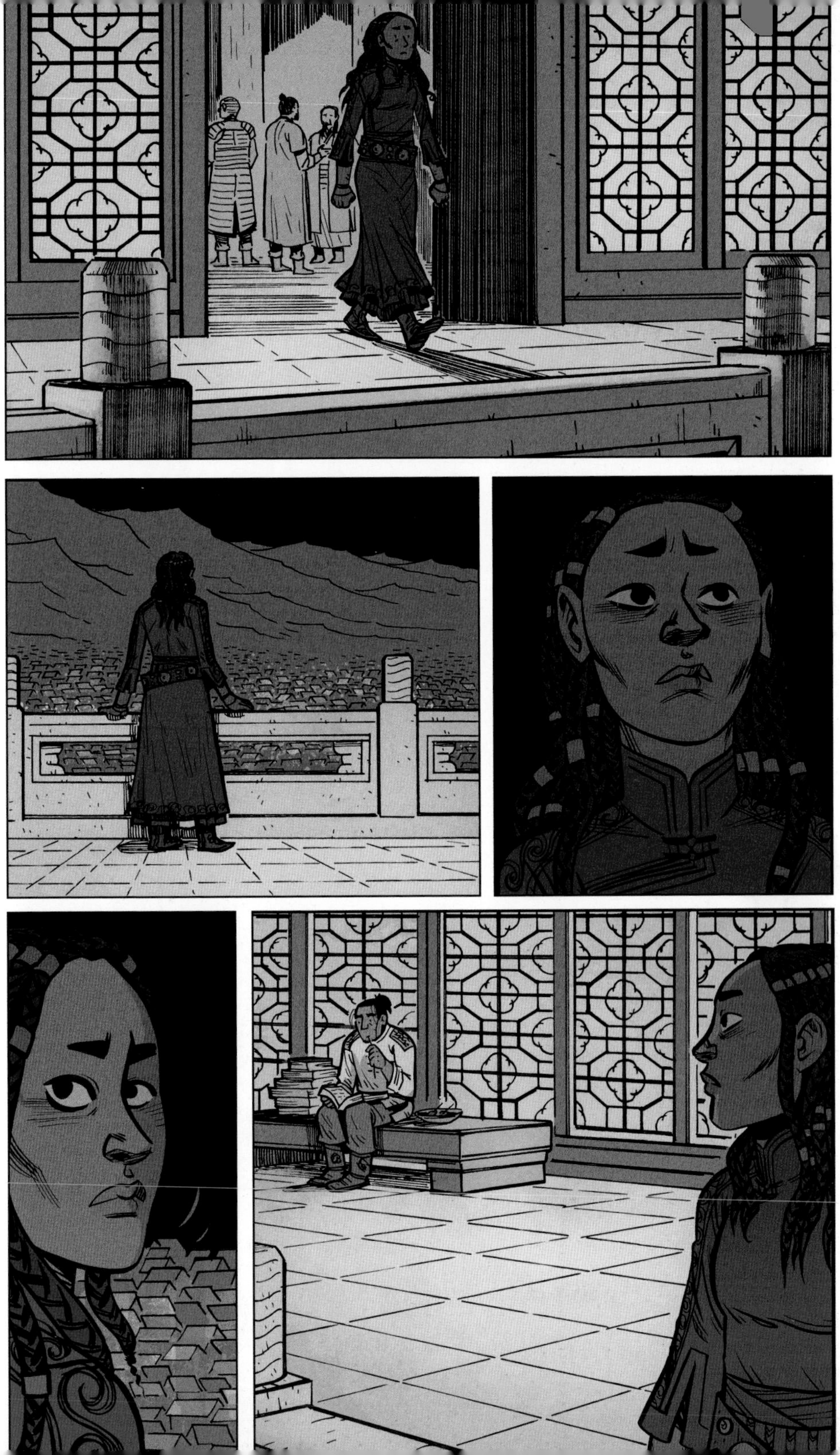

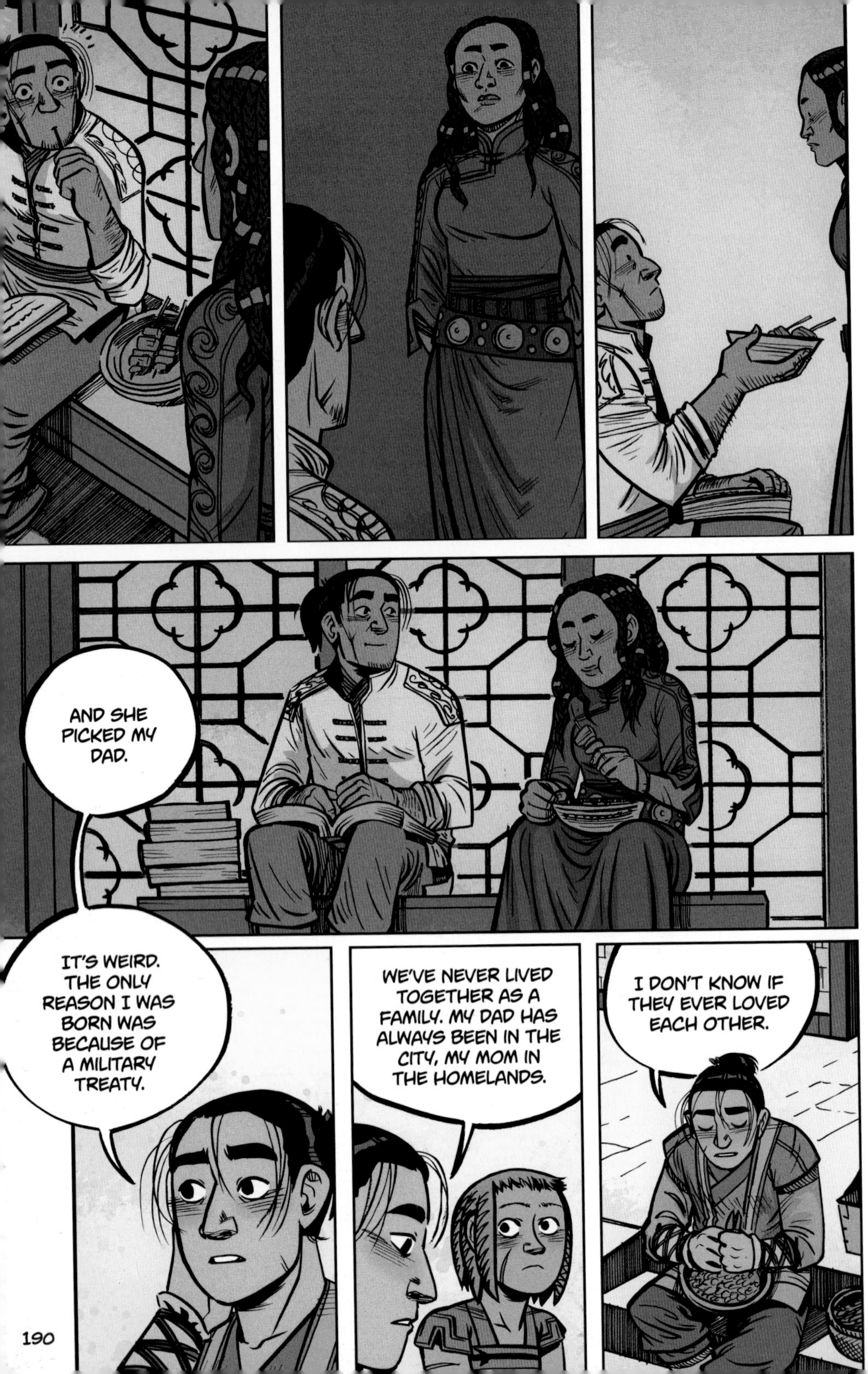
AND SHE PICKED MY DAD.
IT'S WEIRD. THE ONLY REASON I WAS BORN WAS BECAUSE OF A MILITARY TREATY.
WE'VE NEVER LIVED TOGETHER AS A FAMILY. MY DAD HAS ALWAYS BEEN IN THE CITY, MY MOM IN THE HOMELANDS.
I DON'T KNOW IF THEY EVER LOVED EACH OTHER.

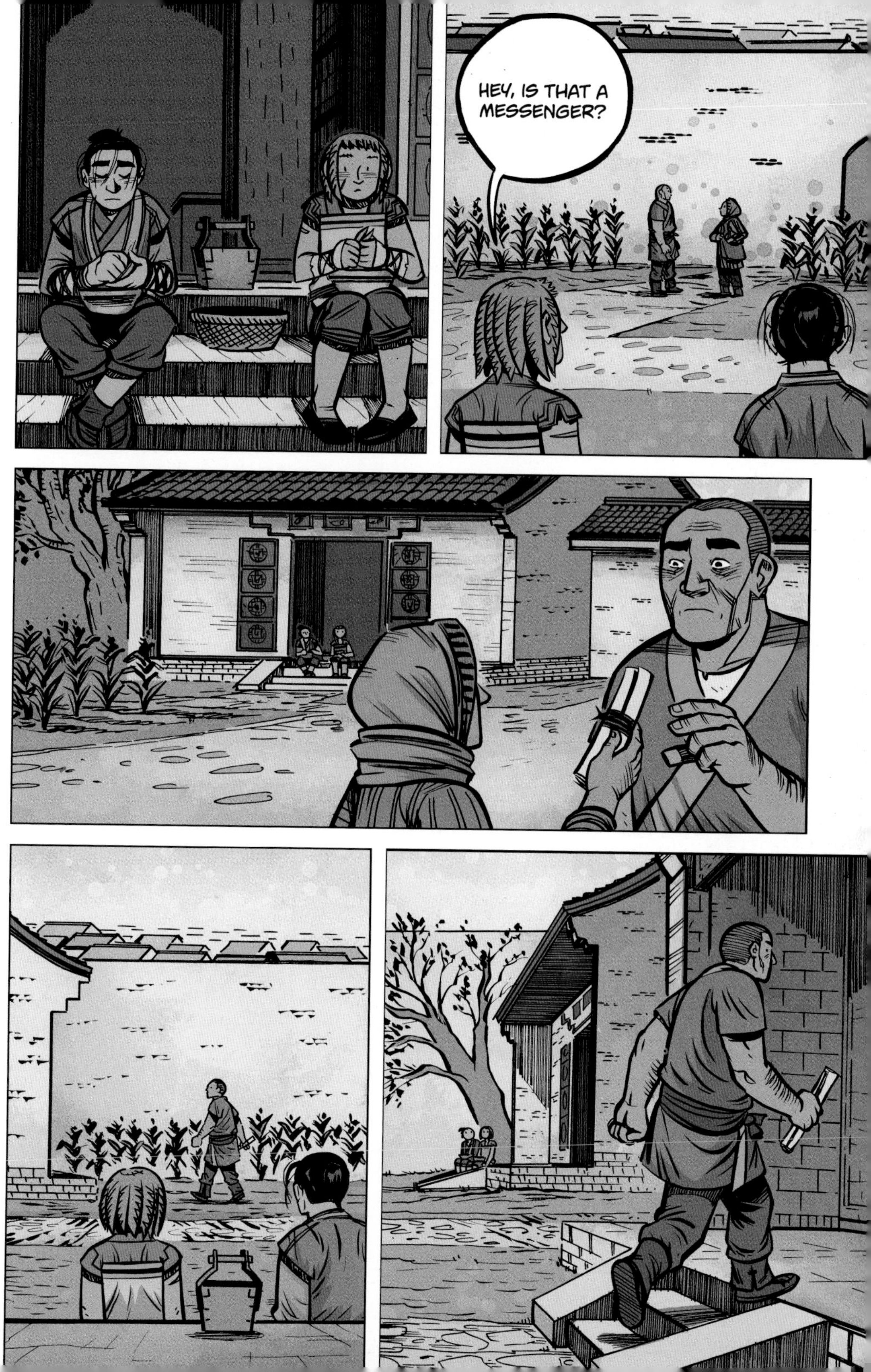
HEY, IS THAT A MESSENGER?

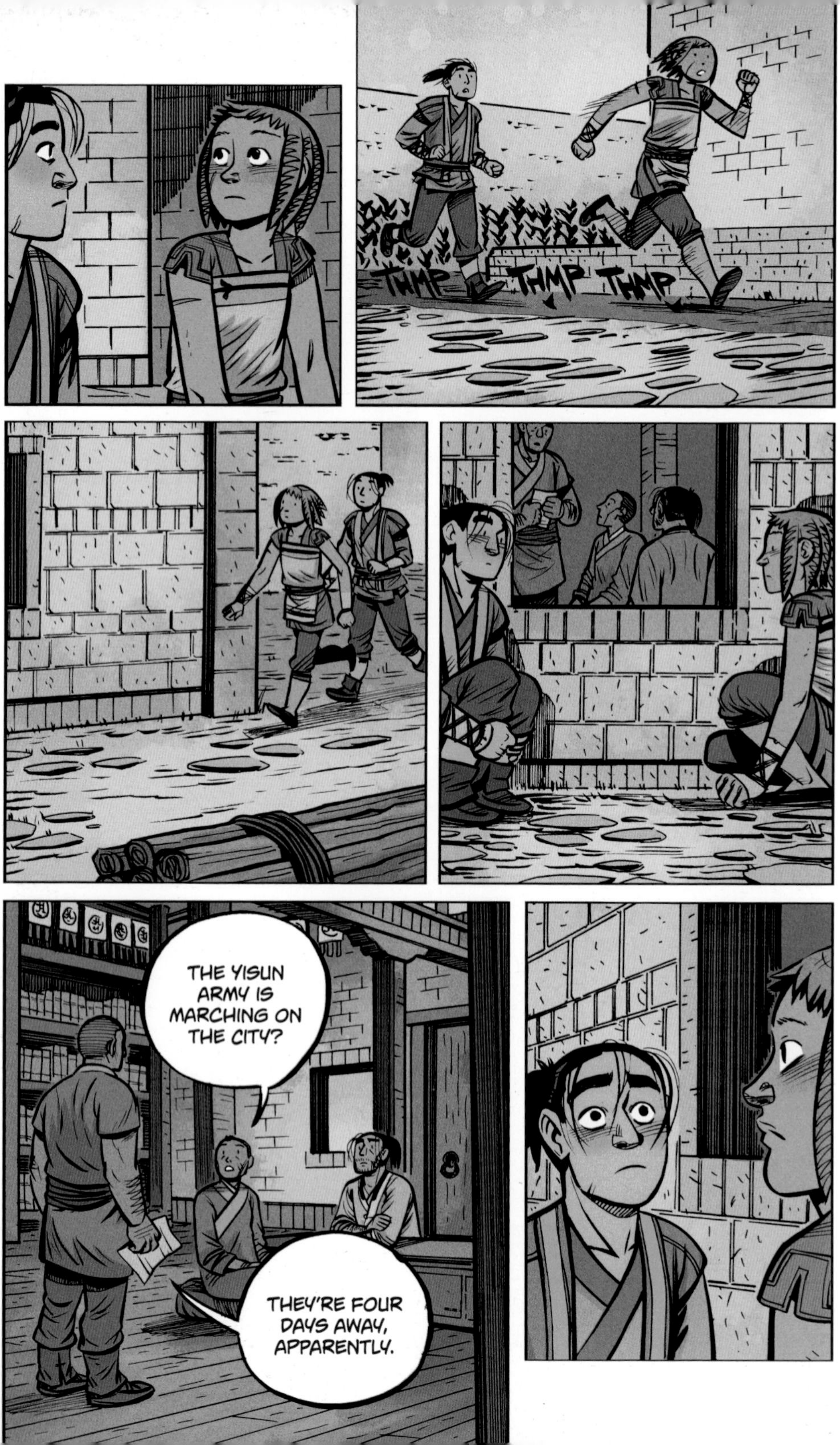
THMP THMP THMP
THE YISUN ARMY IS MARCHING ON THE CITY?
THEY'RE FOUR DAYS AWAY, APPARENTLY.

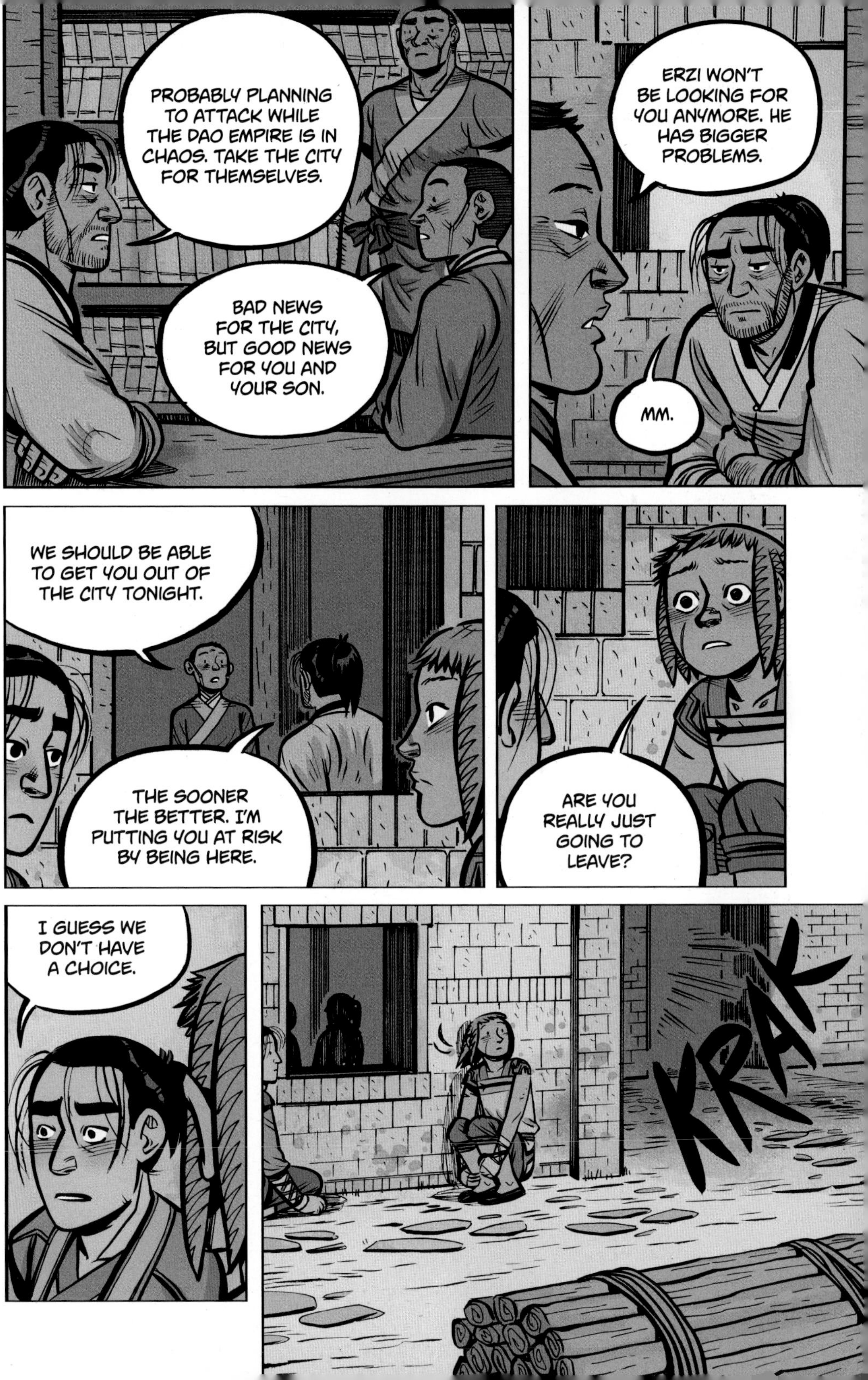
PROBABLY PLANNING TO ATTACK WHILE THE DAO EMPIRE IS IN CHAOS. TAKE THE CITY FOR THEMSELVES.
BAD NEWS FOR THE CITY, BUT GOOD NEWS FOR YOU AND YOUR SON.
ERZI WON'T BE LOOKING FOR YOU ANYMORE. HE HAS BIGGER PROBLEMS.
MM.
WE SHOULD BE ABLE TO GET YOU OUT OF THE CITY TONIGHT.
THE SOONER THE BETTER. I'M PUTTING YOU AT RISK BY BEING HERE.
ARE YOU REALLY JUST GOING TO LEAVE?
I GUESS WE DON'T HAVE A CHOICE.
KRAK

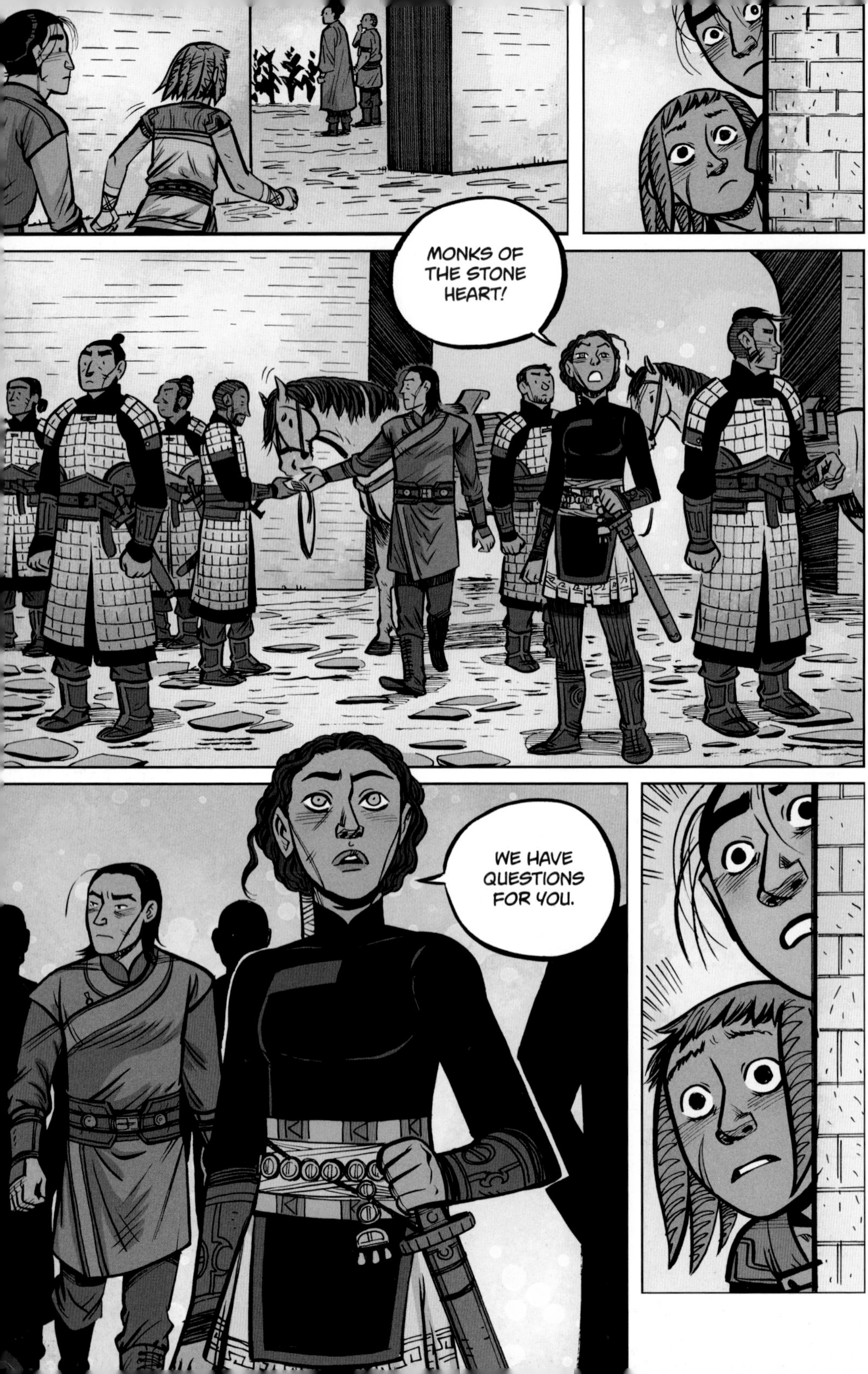
MONKS OF THE STONE HEART!
WE HAVE QUESTIONS FOR YOU.

THERE YOU ARE. QUICK, THIS WAY.

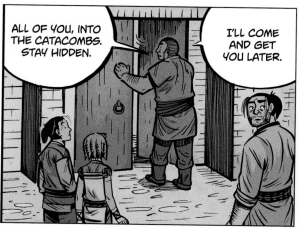

ALL OF YOU, INTO THE CATACOMBS. STAY HIDDEN.

I'LL COME AND GET YOU LATER.

I HAVE TO GO TOO?

YES, YOU TOO.

I WANT TO STAY WITH YOU!

RAT, IT'S SAFEST IF YOU'RE OUT OF SIGHT.

DO THIS FOR ME. SO I WON'T WORRY.

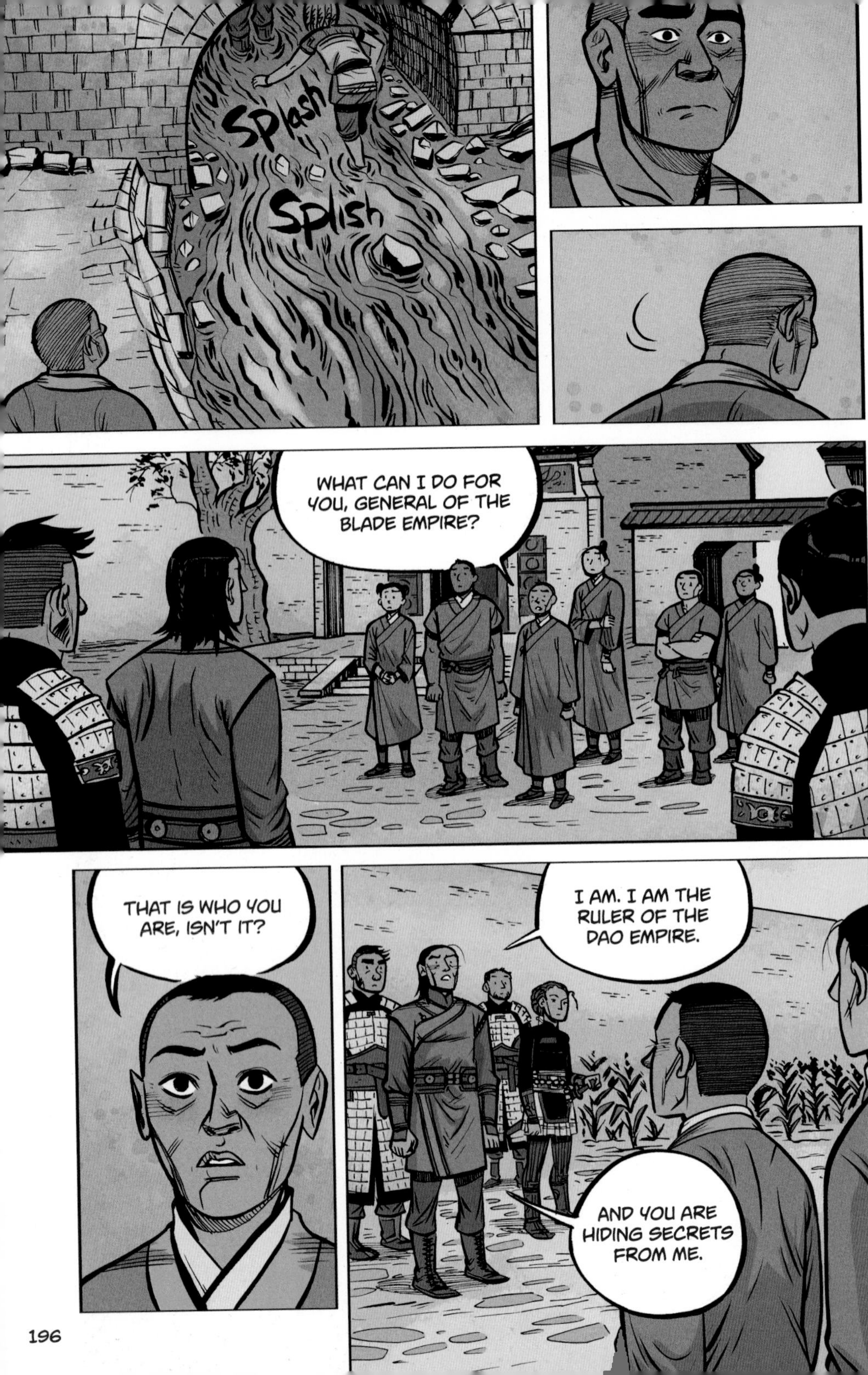
Splash
Splish
WHAT CAN I DO FOR YOU, GENERAL OF THE BLADE EMPIRE?
THAT IS WHO YOU ARE, ISN'T IT?
I AM. I AM THE RULER OF THE DAO EMPIRE.
AND YOU ARE HIDING SECRETS FROM ME.

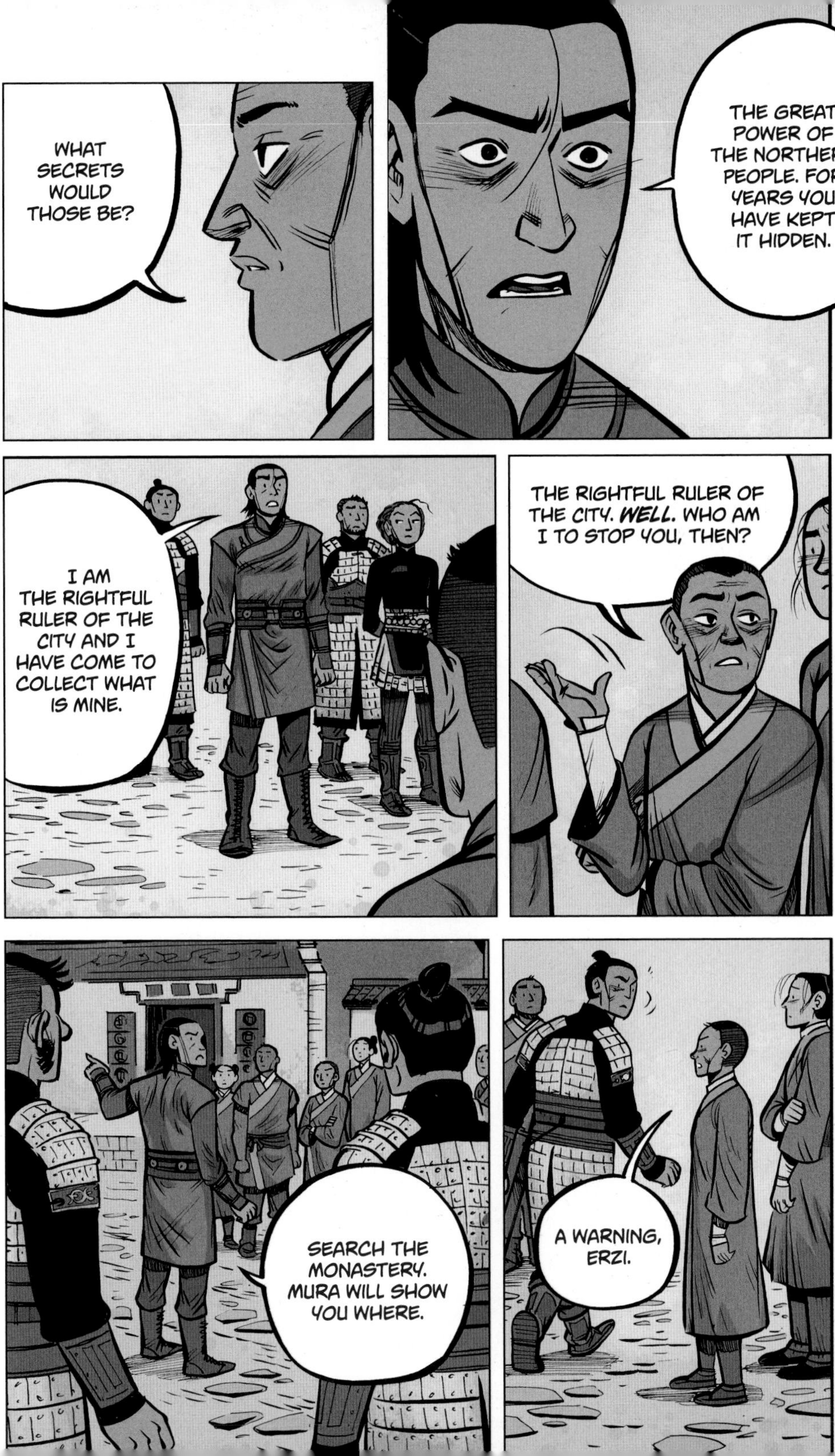
WHAT SECRETS WOULD THOSE BE?
THE GREAT POWER OF THE NORTHERN PEOPLE. FOR YEARS YOU HAVE KEPT IT HIDDEN.
I AM THE RIGHTFUL RULER OF THE CITY AND I HAVE COME TO COLLECT WHAT IS MINE.
THE RIGHTFUL RULER OF THE CITY. WELL. WHO AM I TO STOP YOU, THEN?
SEARCH THE MONASTERY. MURA WILL SHOW YOU WHERE.
A WARNING, ERZI.

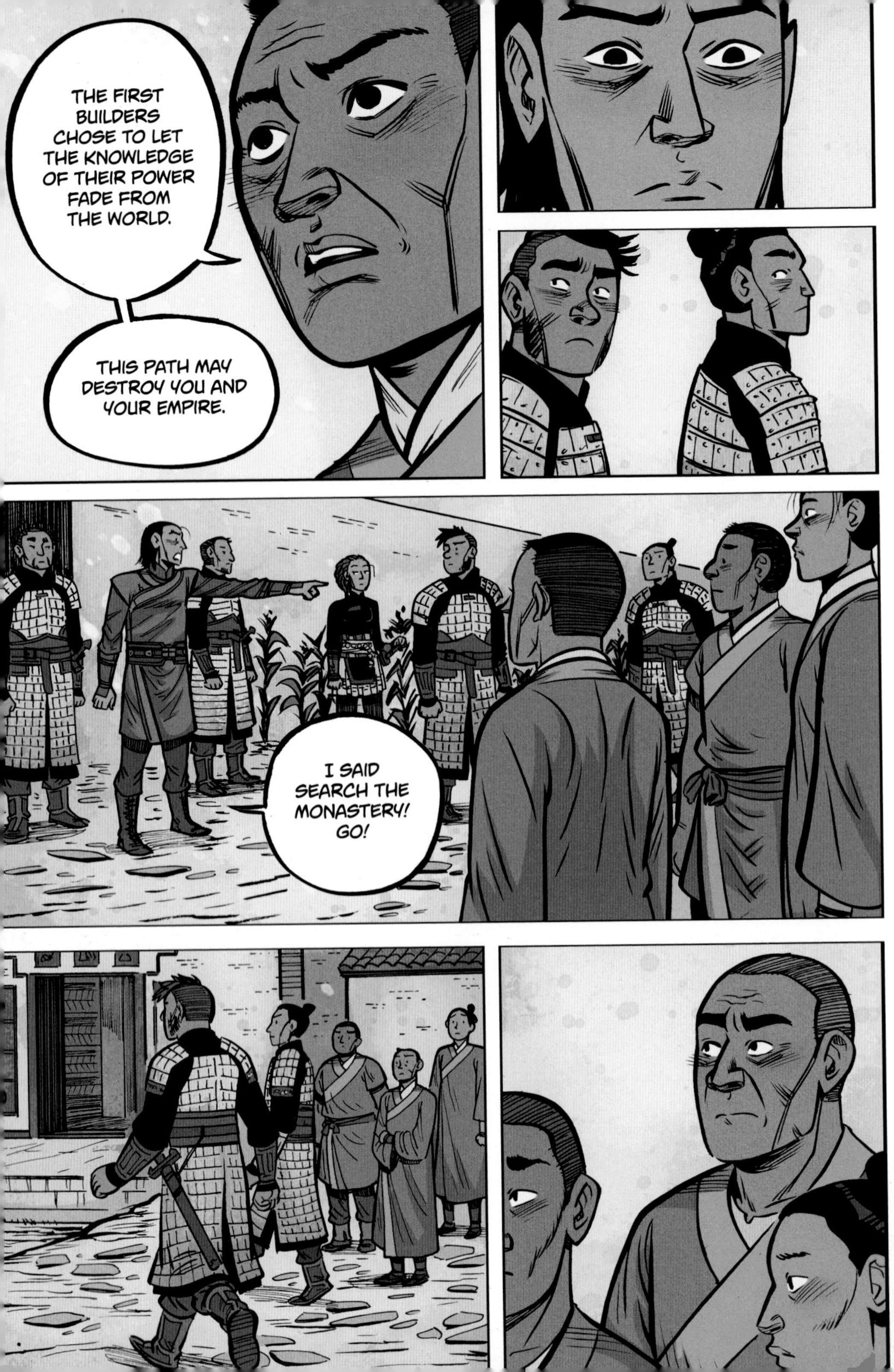
THE FIRST BUILDERS CHOSE TO LET THE KNOWLEDGE OF THEIR POWER FADE FROM THE WORLD.
THIS PATH MAY DESTROY YOU AND YOUR EMPIRE.
I SAID SEARCH THE MONASTERY! GO!

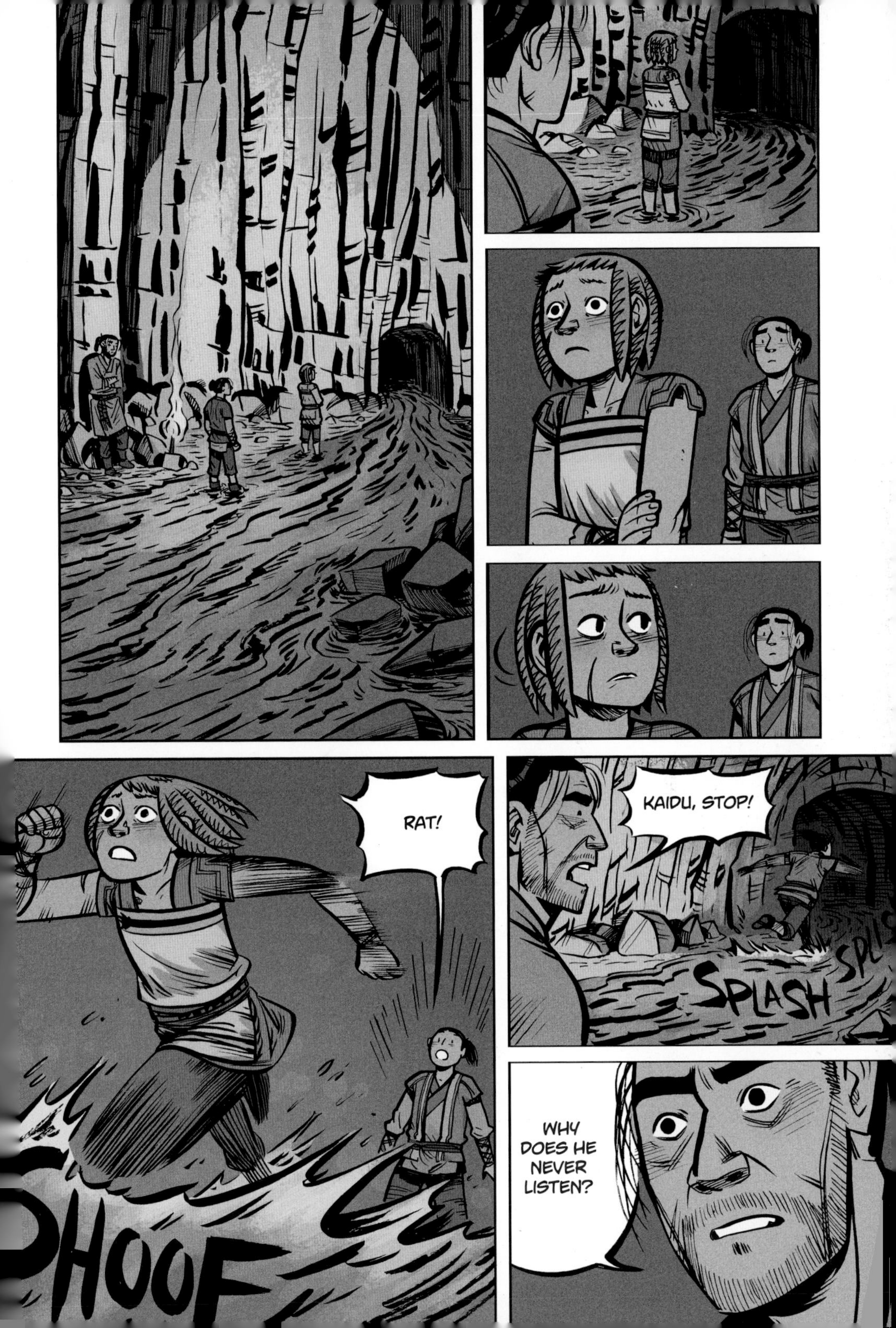

RAT!
SHOOF
KAIDU, STOP!
SPLASH
SPLASH
WHY DOES HE NEVER LISTEN?

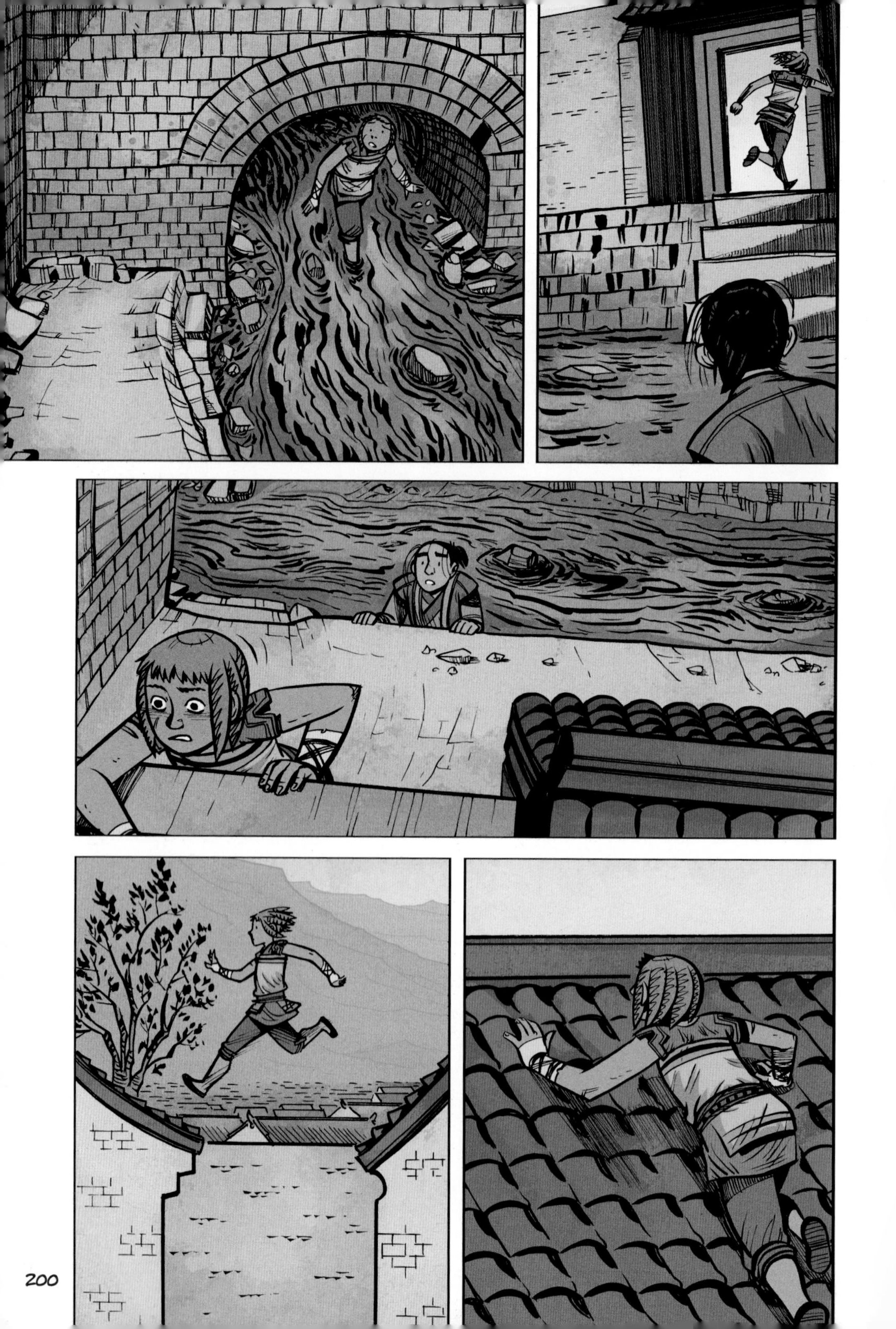

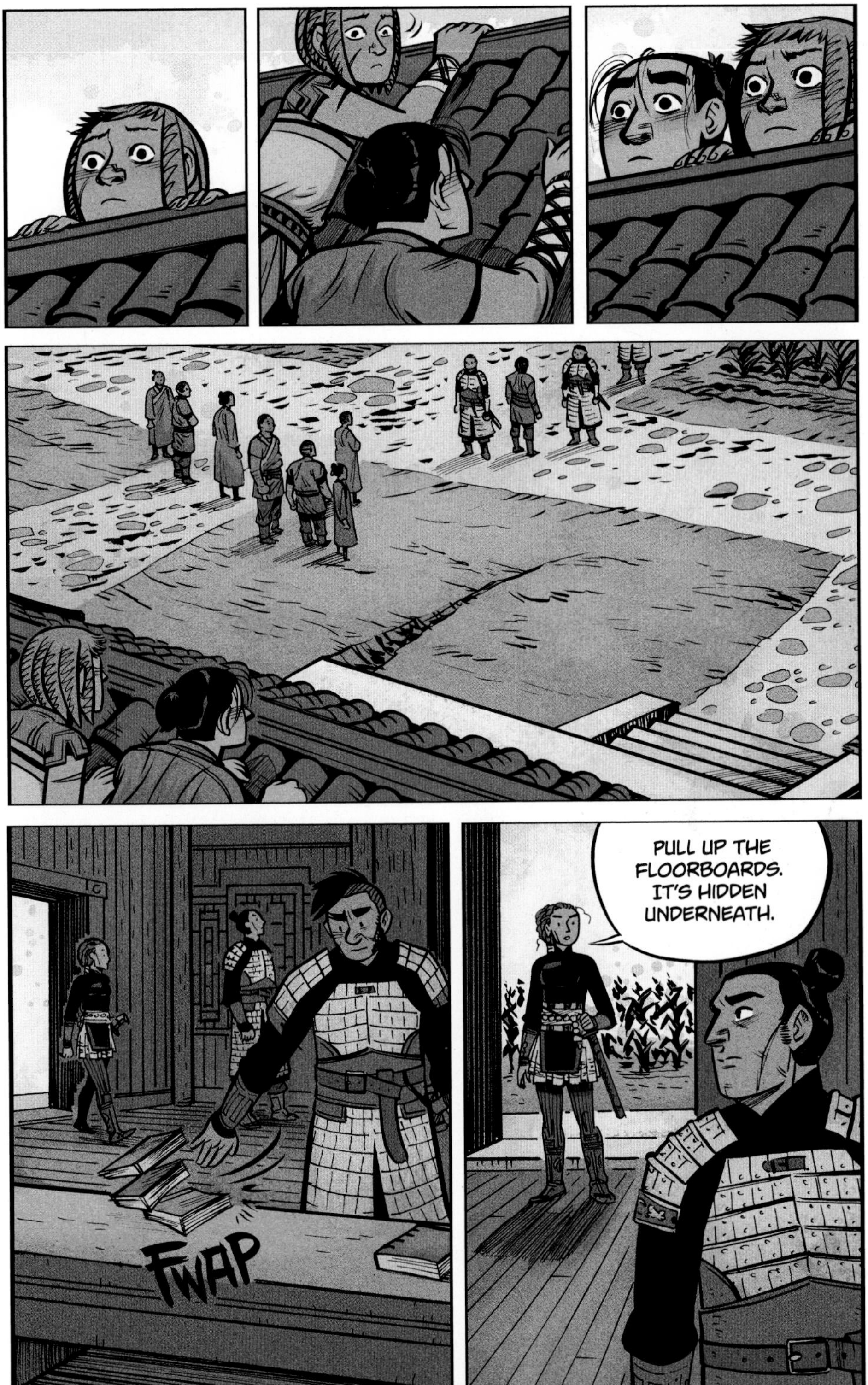
FWAP
PULL UP THE FLOORBOARDS. IT'S HIDDEN UNDERNEATH.

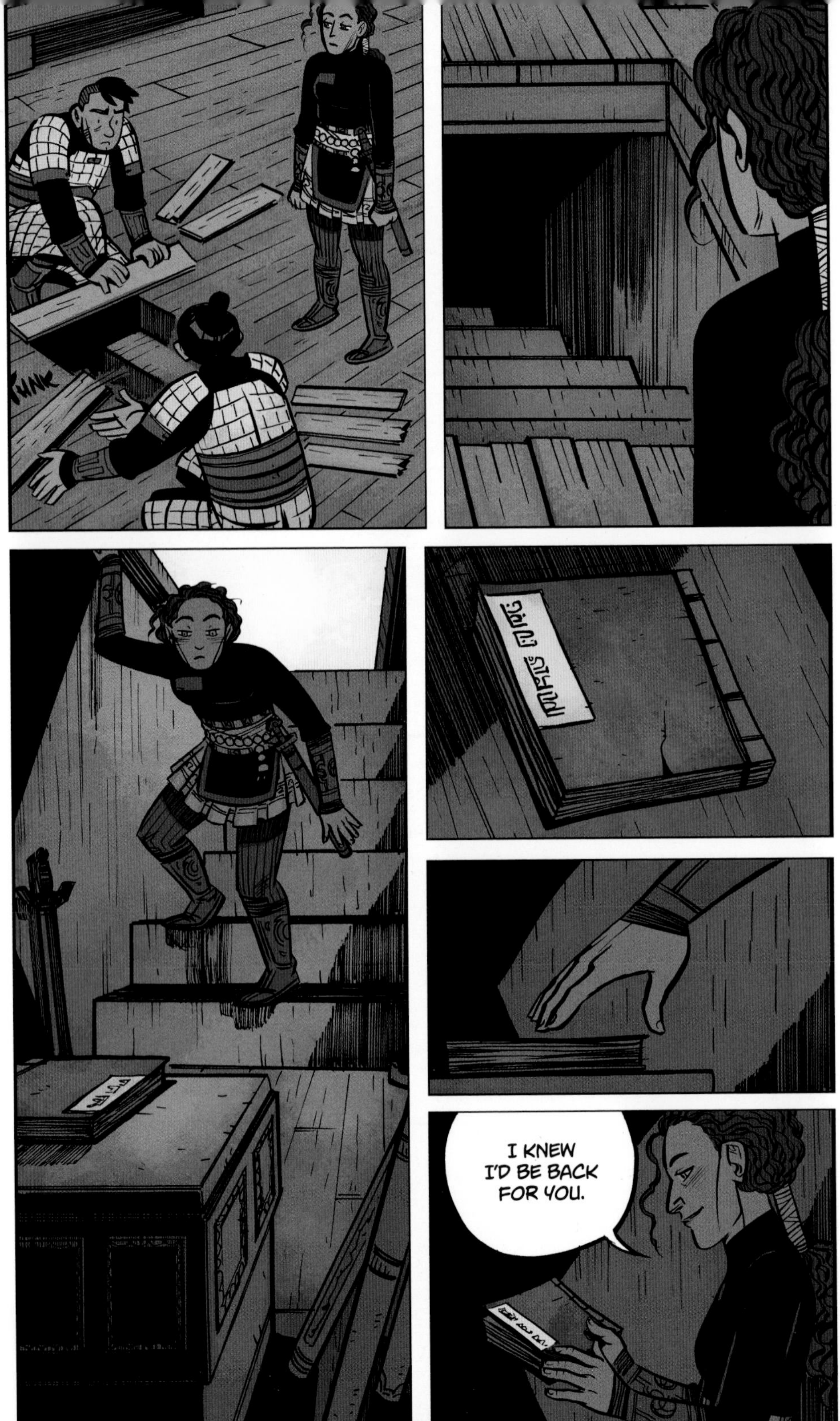
THUNK
I KNEW I'D BE BACK FOR YOU.

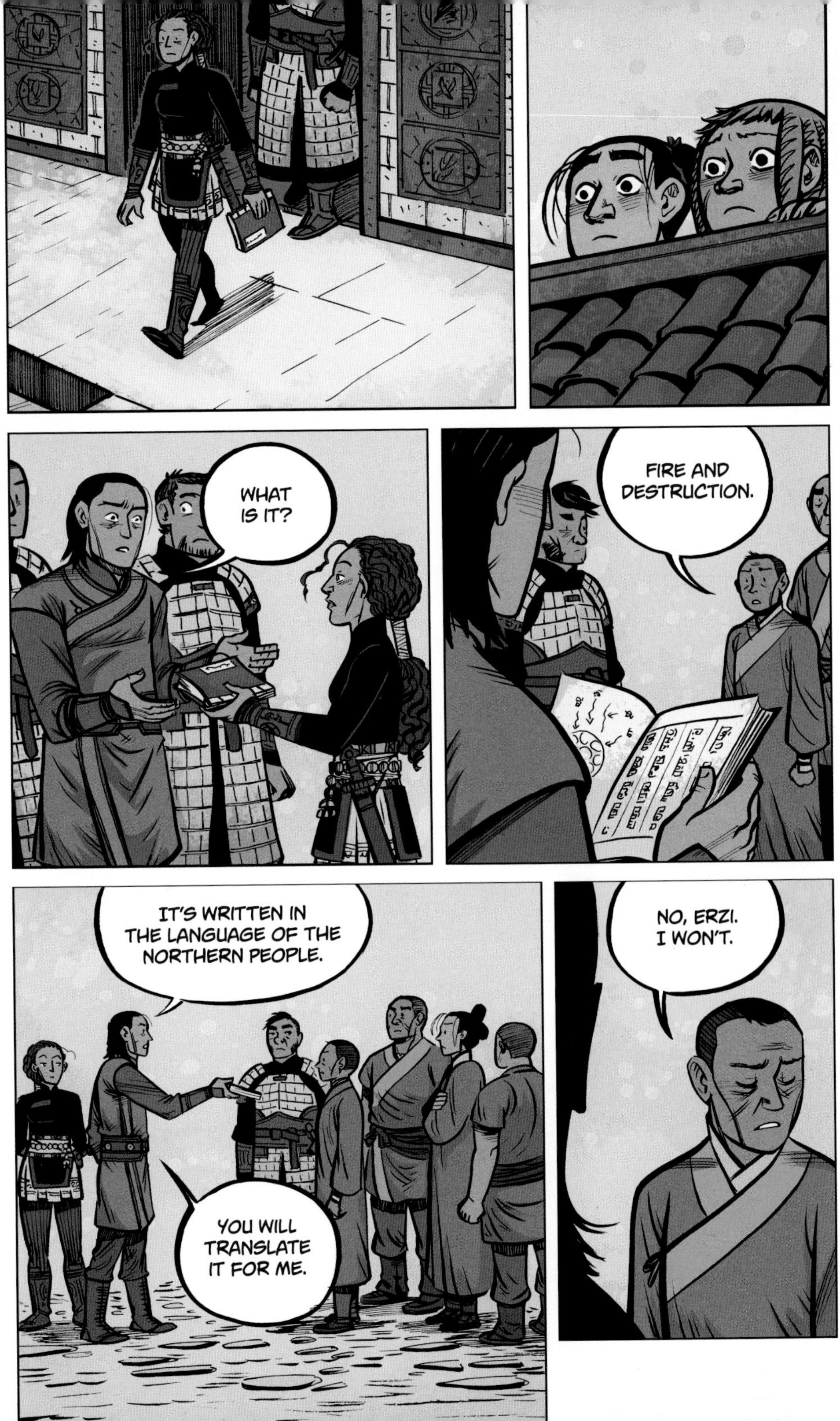
WHAT IS IT?
FIRE AND DESTRUCTION.
IT'S WRITTEN IN THE LANGUAGE OF THE NORTHERN PEOPLE.
YOU WILL TRANSLATE IT FOR ME.
NO, ERZI. I WON'T.

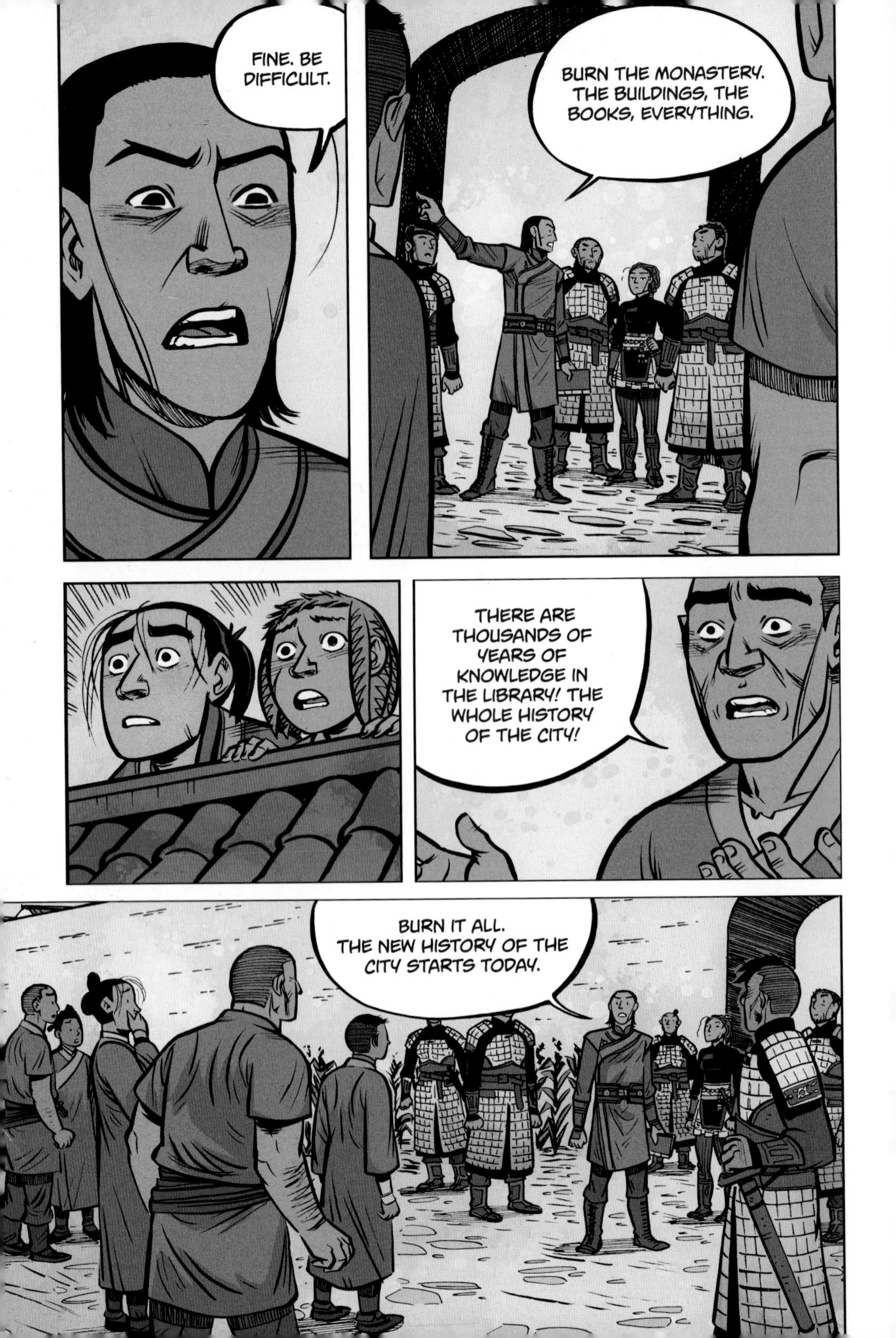
FINE. BE DIFFICULT.
BURN THE MONASTERY. THE BUILDINGS, THE BOOKS, EVERYTHING.
THERE ARE THOUSANDS OF YEARS OF KNOWLEDGE IN THE LIBRARY! THE WHOLE HISTORY OF THE CITY!
BURN IT ALL. THE NEW HISTORY OF THE CITY STARTS TODAY.

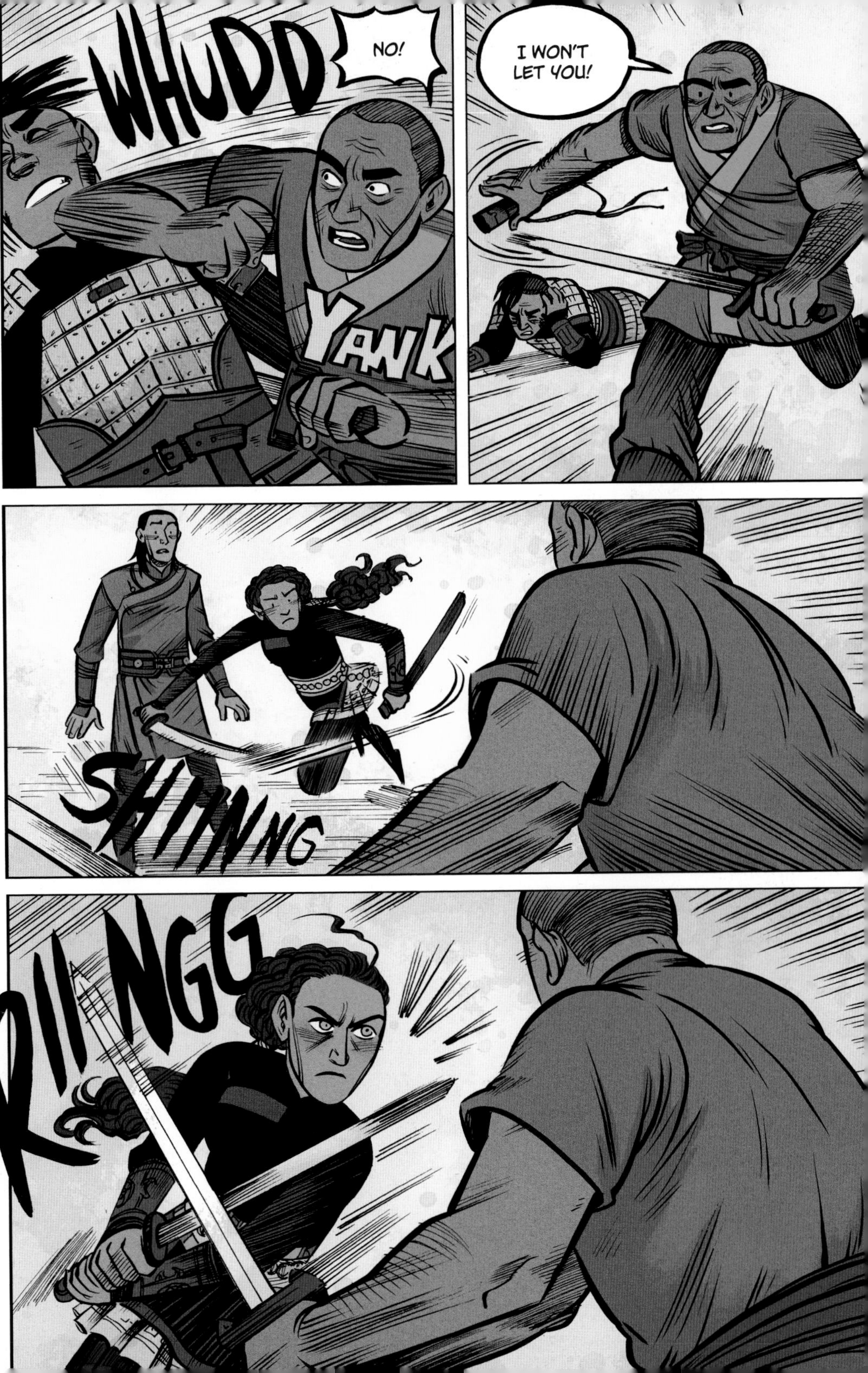
WHUDD
NO!
YANK
I WON'T LET YOU!
SHIIING
RIINGG

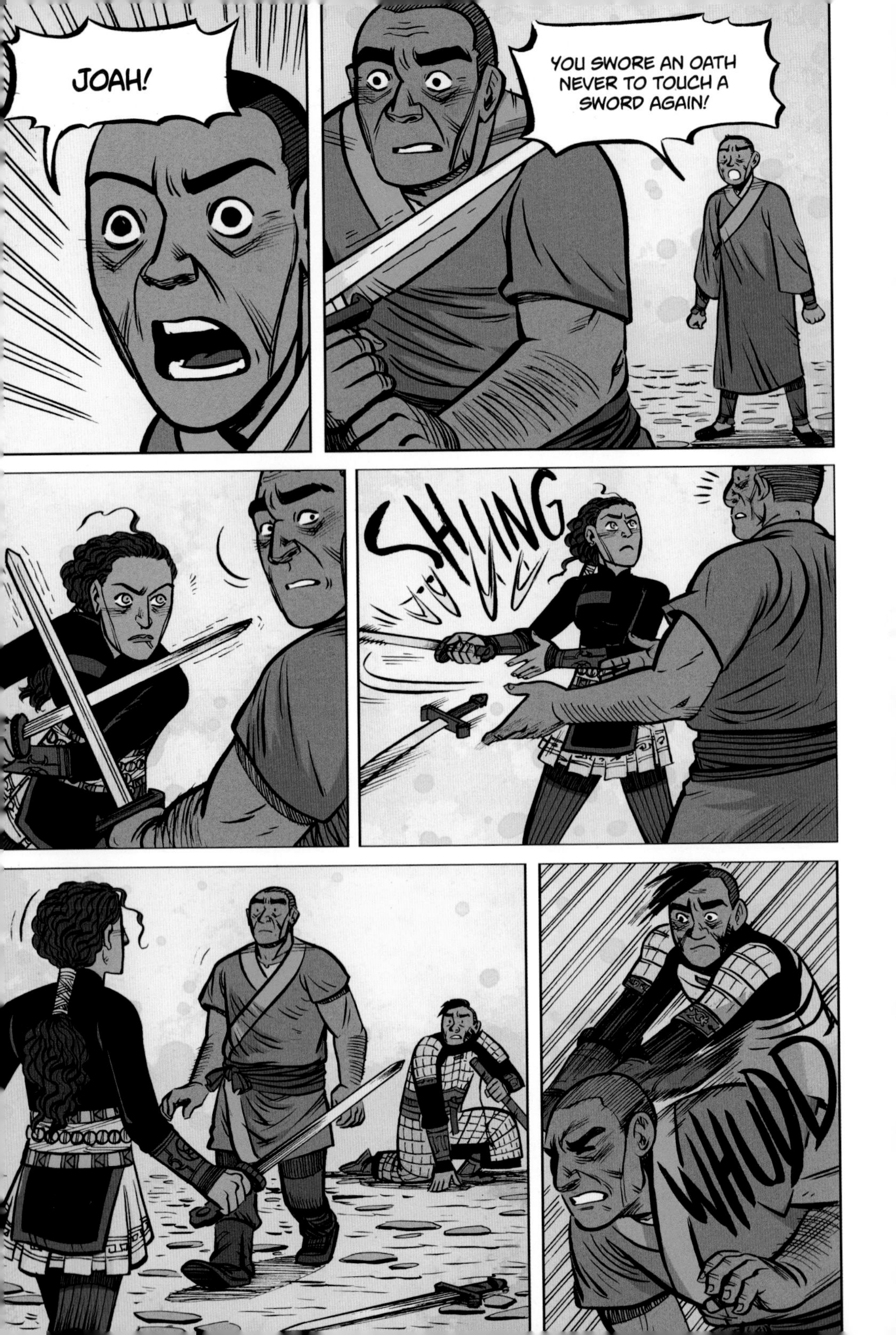
JOAH!
YOU SWORE AN OATH NEVER TO TOUCH A SWORD AGAIN!
SHING
WHUD

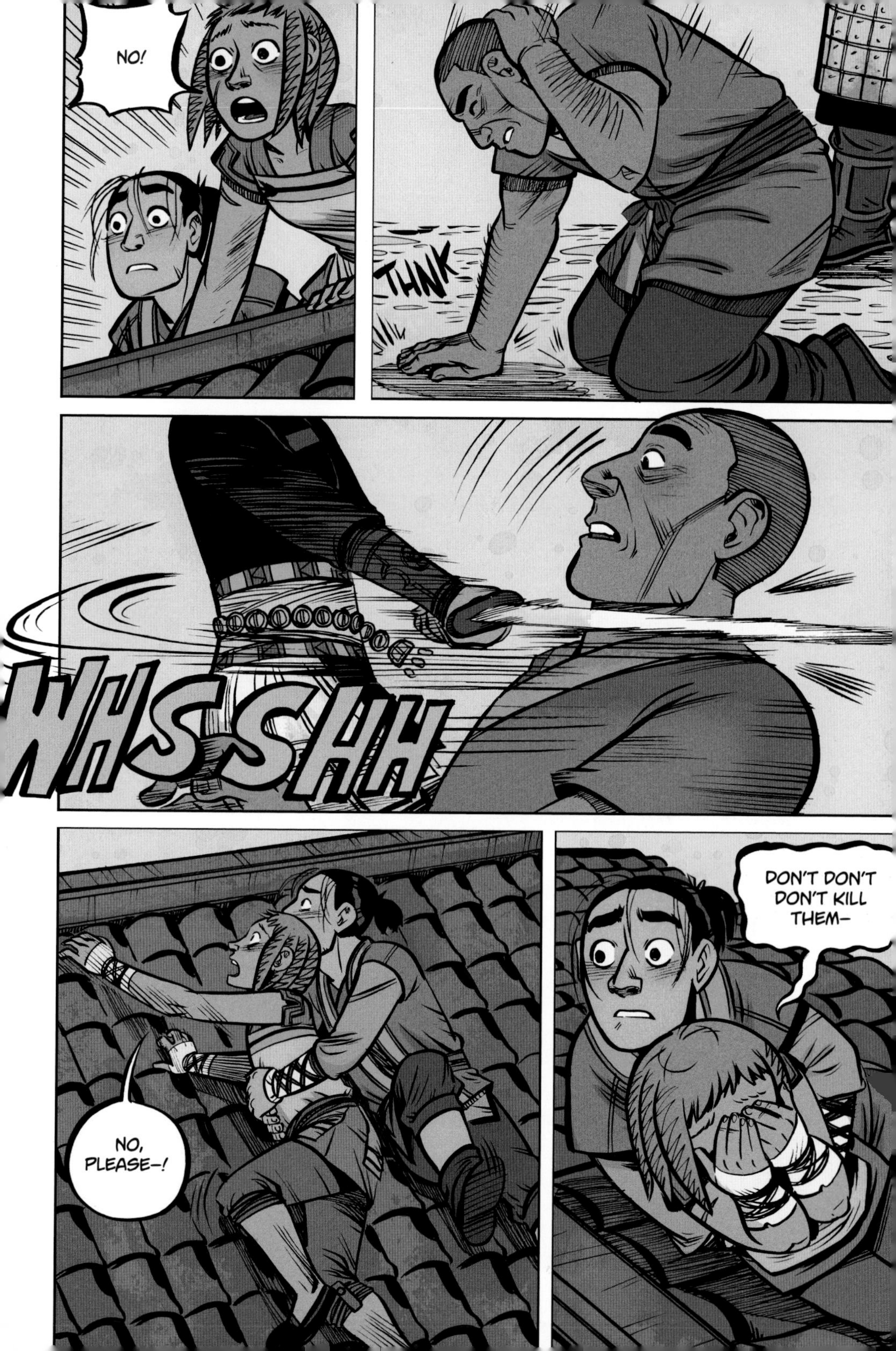
NO!
THNK
WHSSHH
NO, PLEASE–!
DON'T DON'T DON'T KILL THEM–

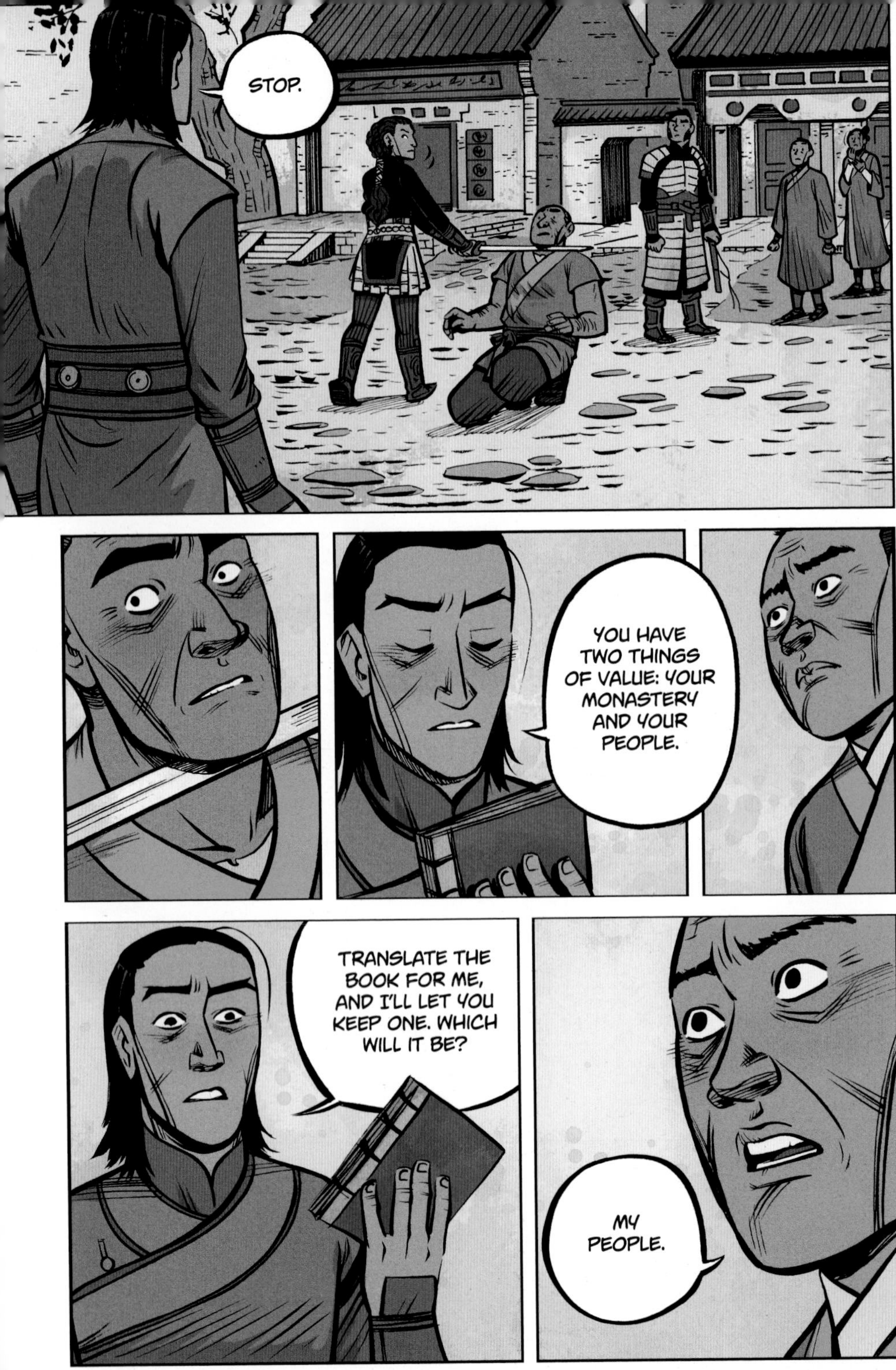
STOP.
YOU HAVE TWO THINGS OF VALUE: YOUR MONASTERY AND YOUR PEOPLE.
TRANSLATE THE BOOK FOR ME, AND I'LL LET YOU KEEP ONE. WHICH WILL IT BE?
MY PEOPLE.

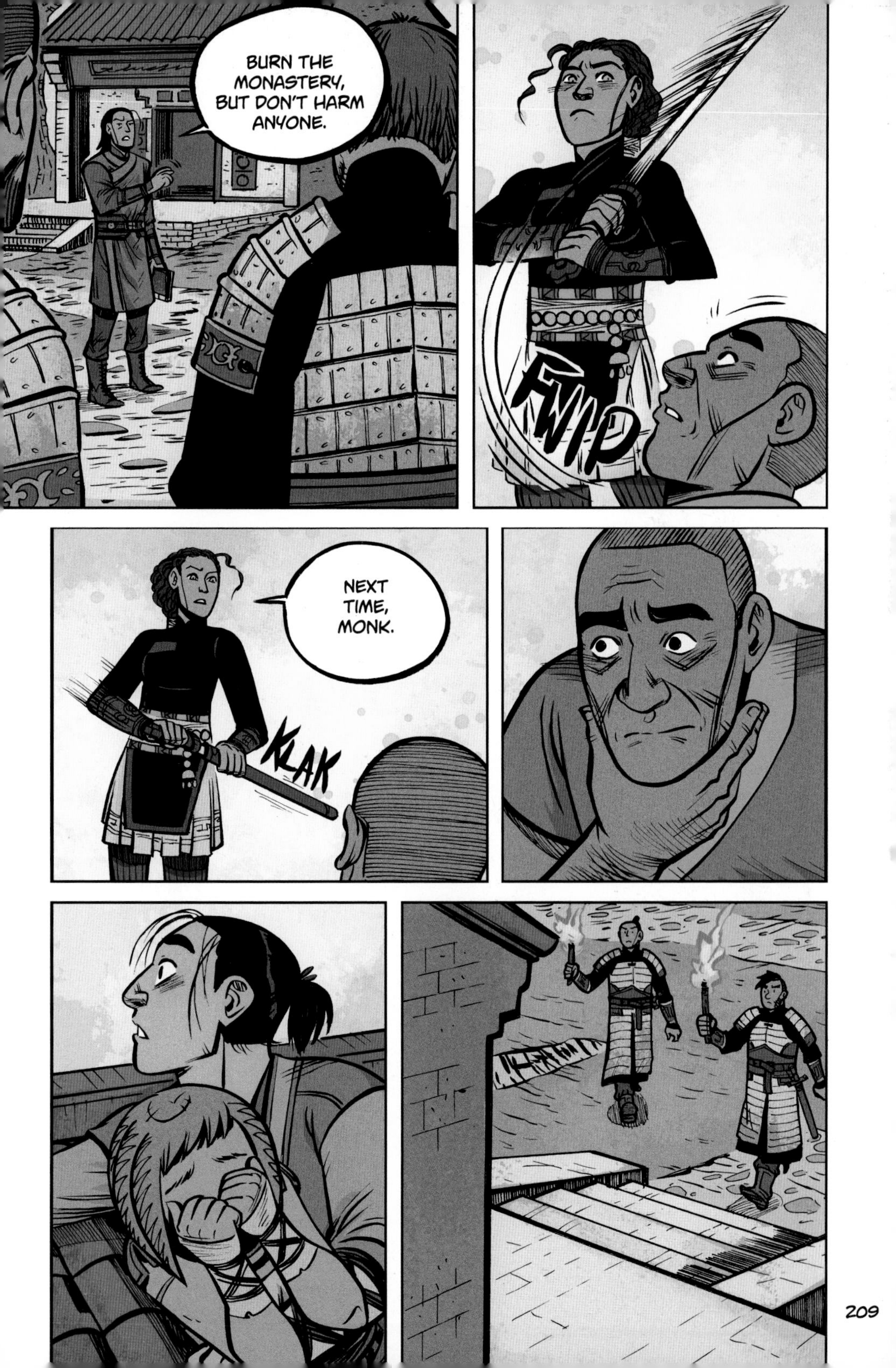
BURN THE MONASTERY, BUT DON'T HARM ANYONE.
FWIP
NEXT TIME, MONK.
KLAK

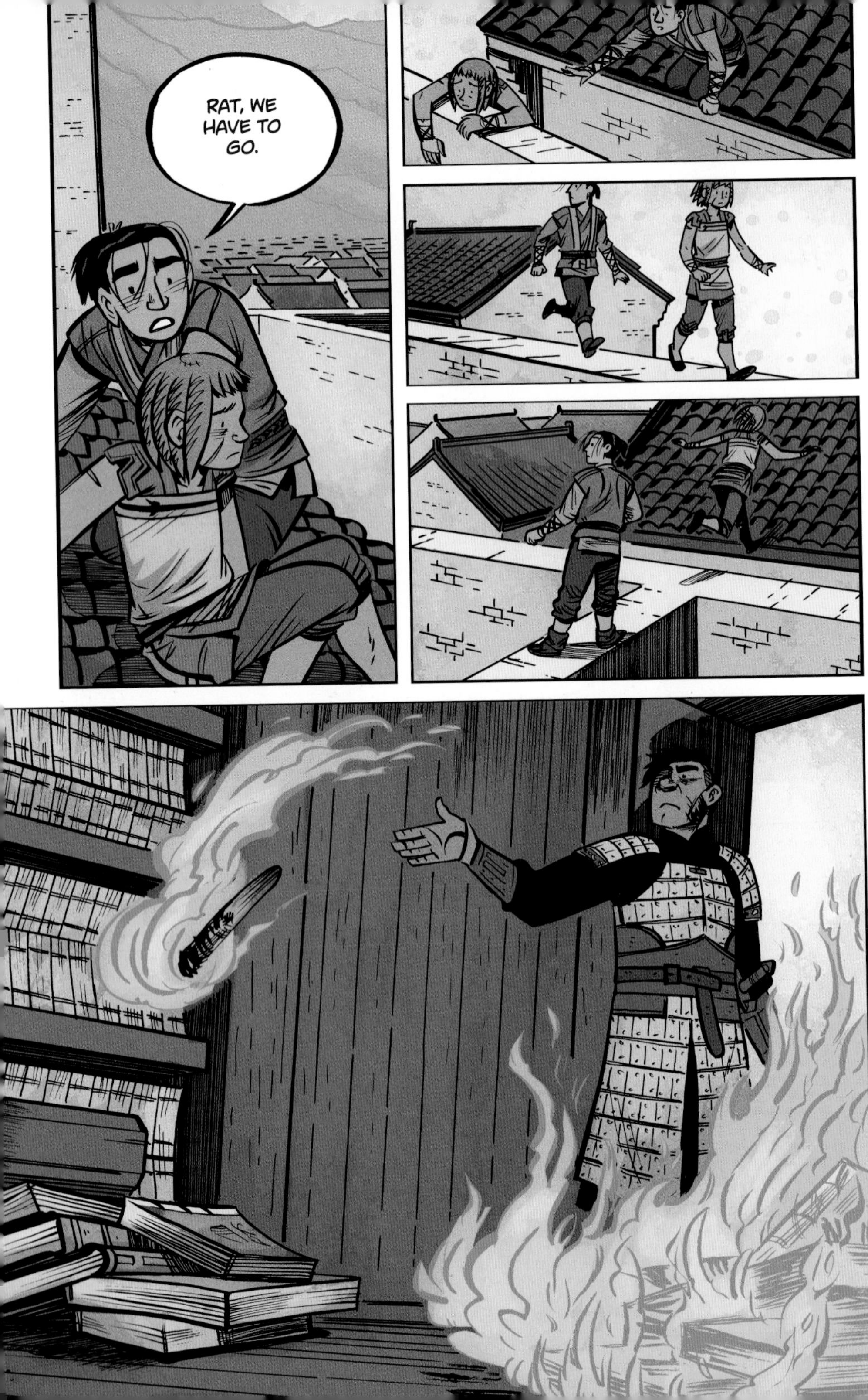
RAT, WE HAVE TO GO.

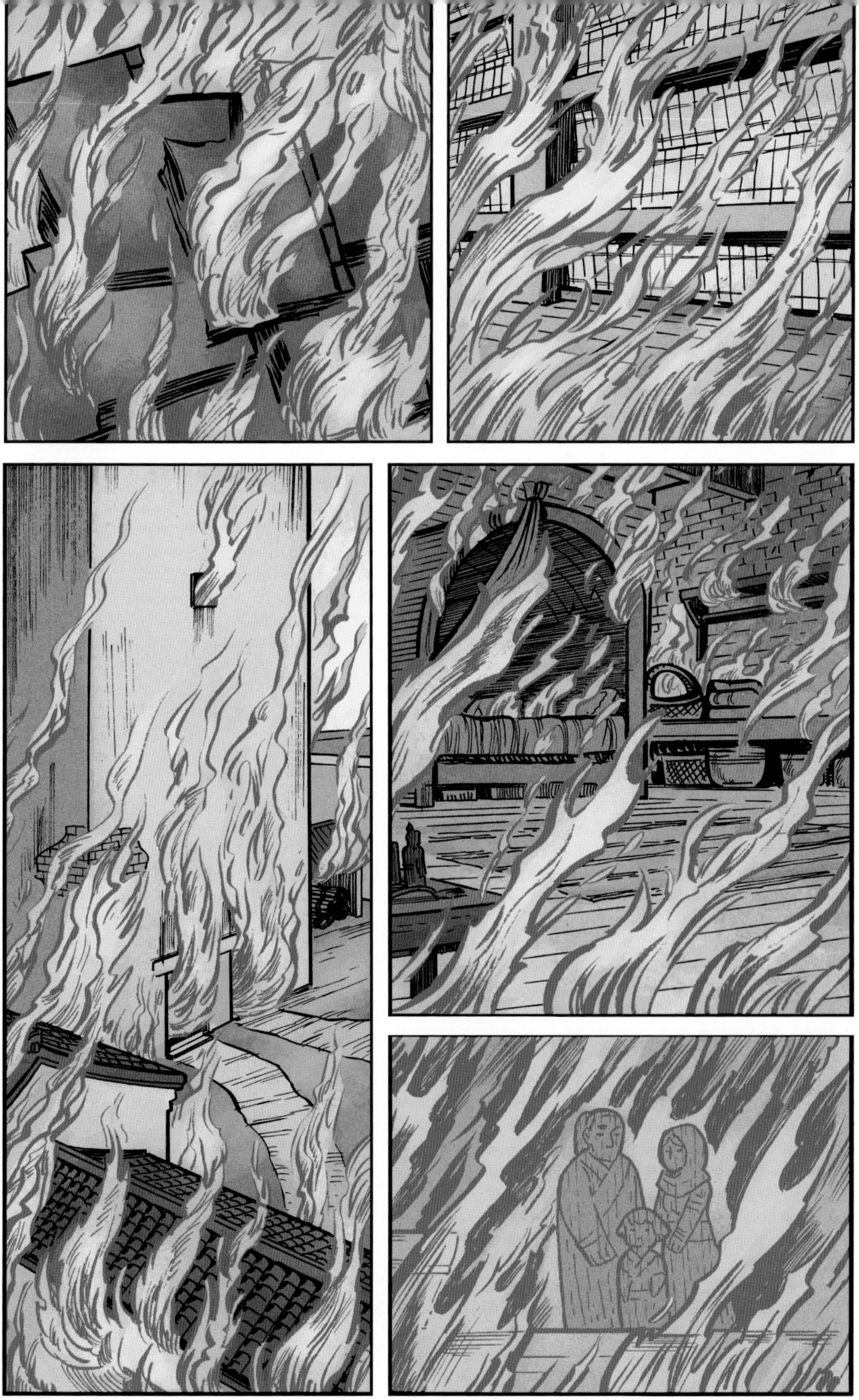

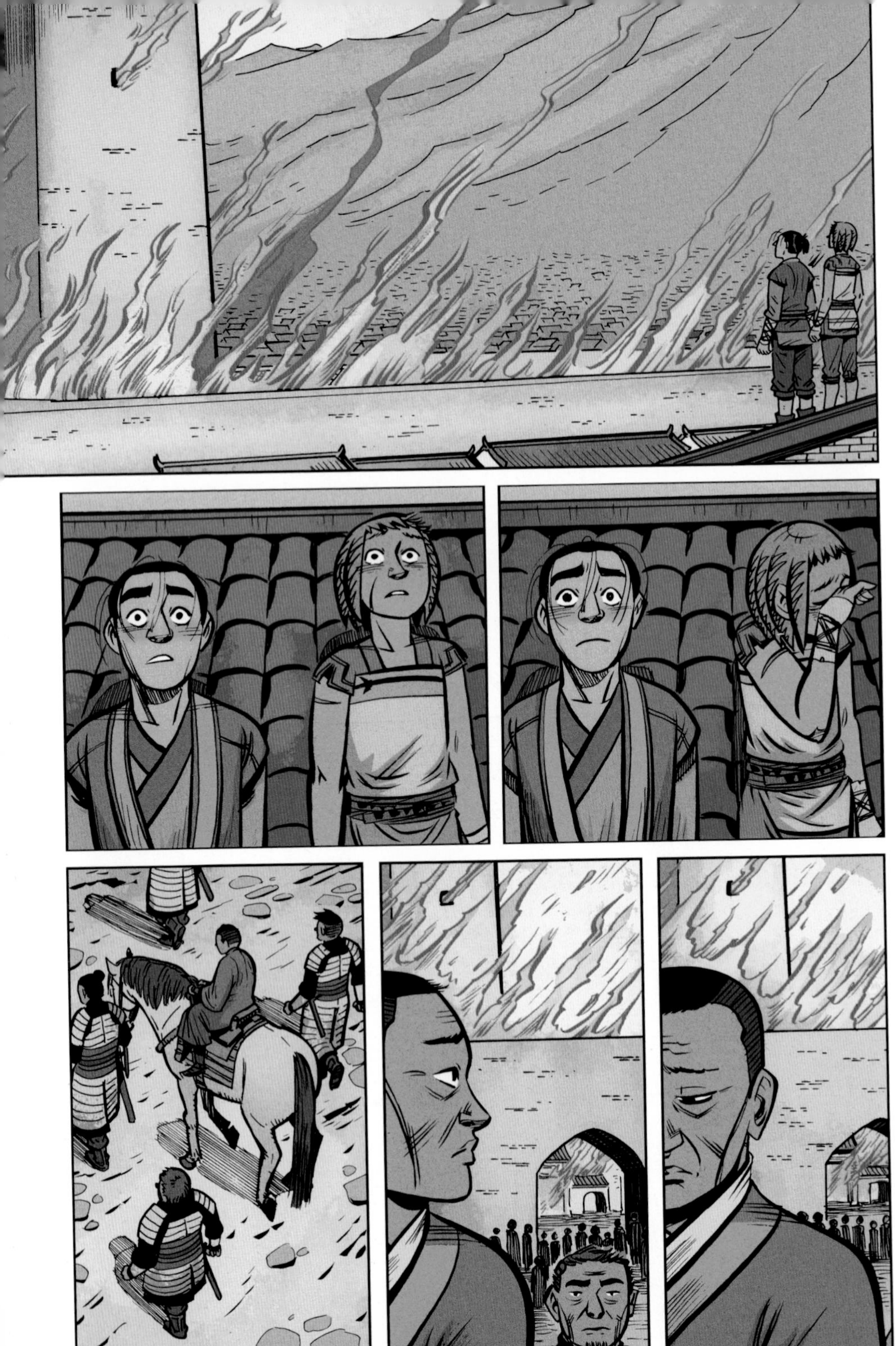

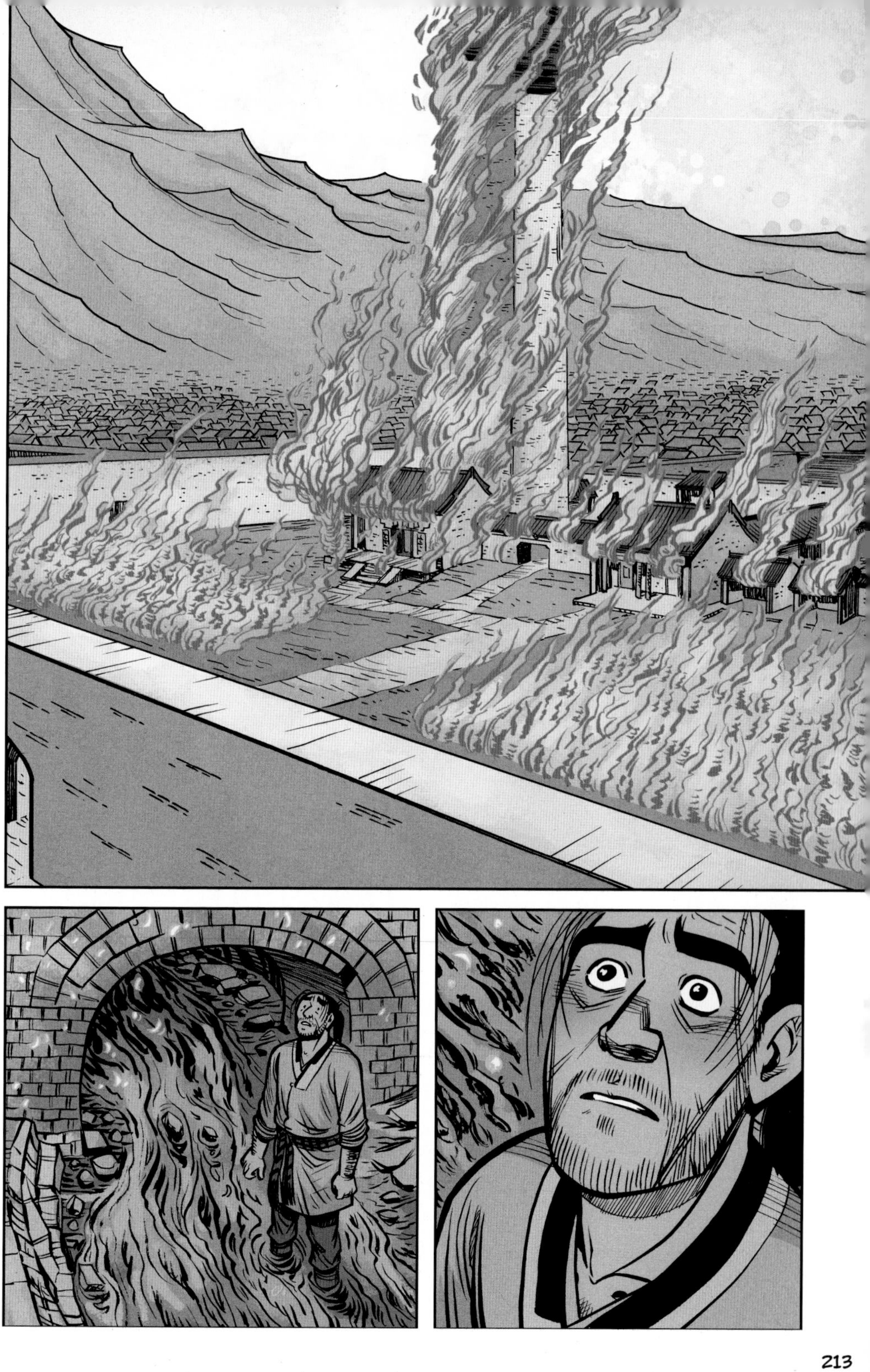

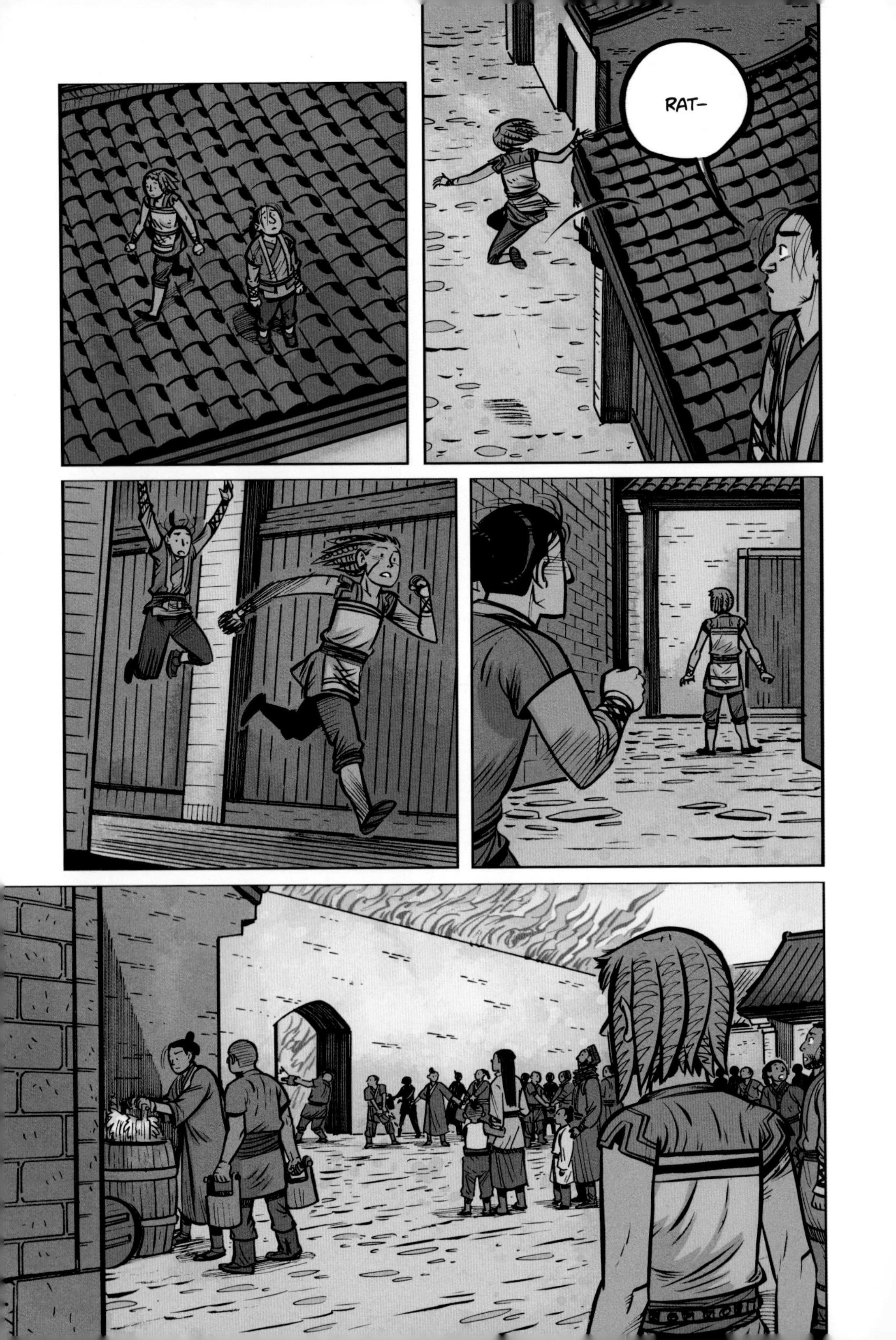
RAT-

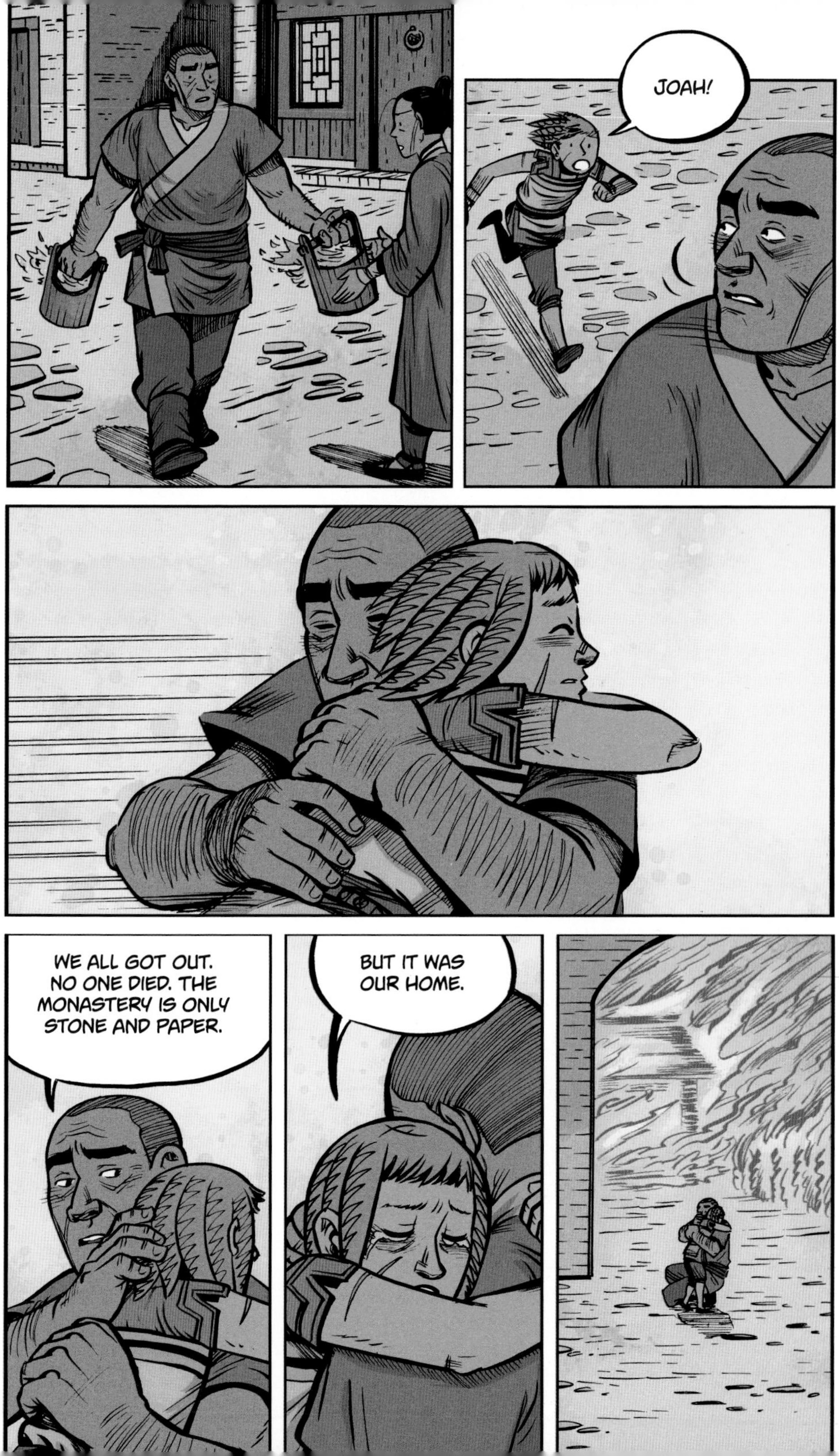
JOAH!
WE ALL GOT OUT. NO ONE DIED. THE MONASTERY IS ONLY STONE AND PAPER.
BUT IT WAS OUR HOME.

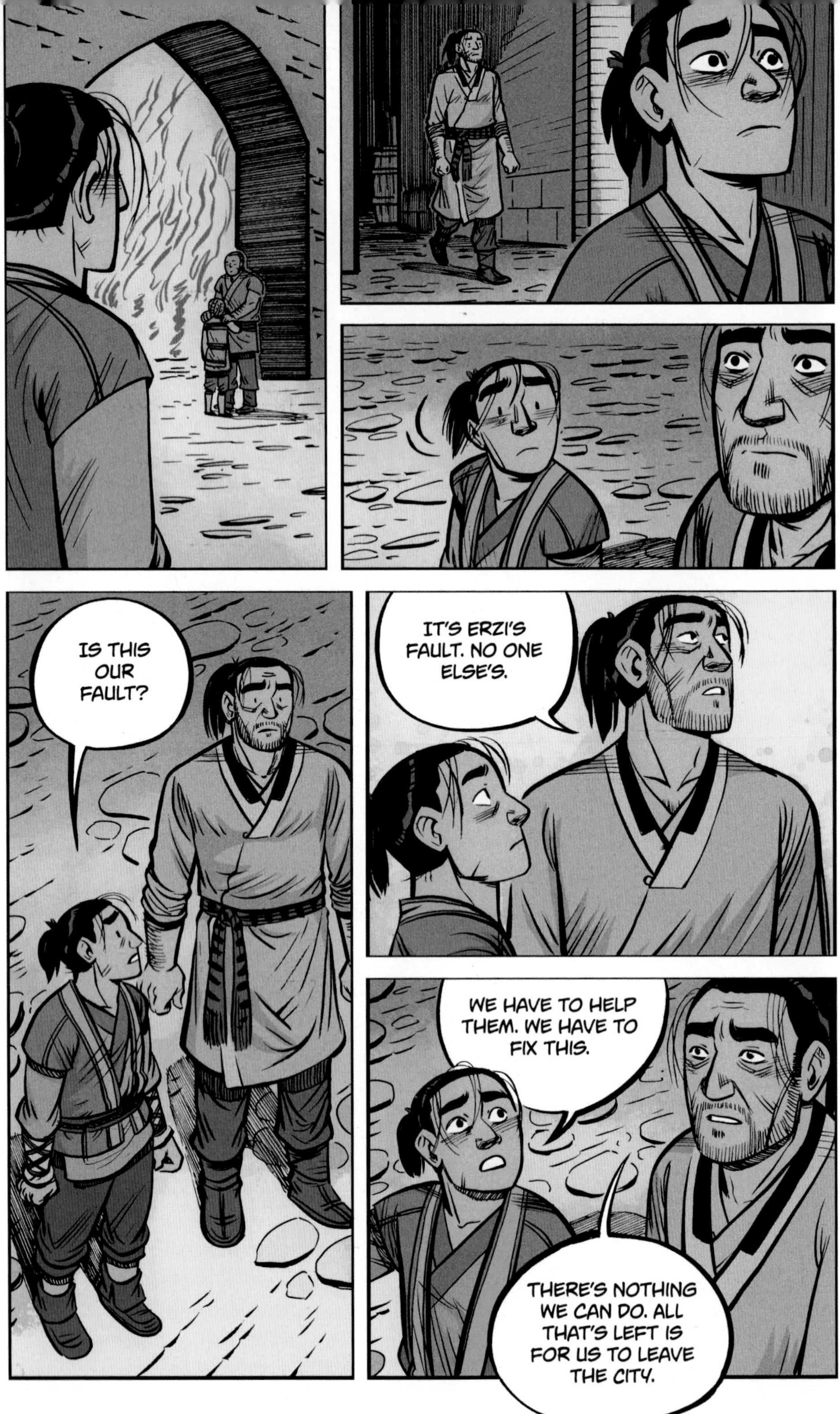
IS THIS OUR FAULT?
IT'S ERZI'S FAULT. NO ONE ELSE'S.
WE HAVE TO HELP THEM. WE HAVE TO FIX THIS.
THERE'S NOTHING WE CAN DO. ALL THAT'S LEFT IS FOR US TO LEAVE THE CITY.

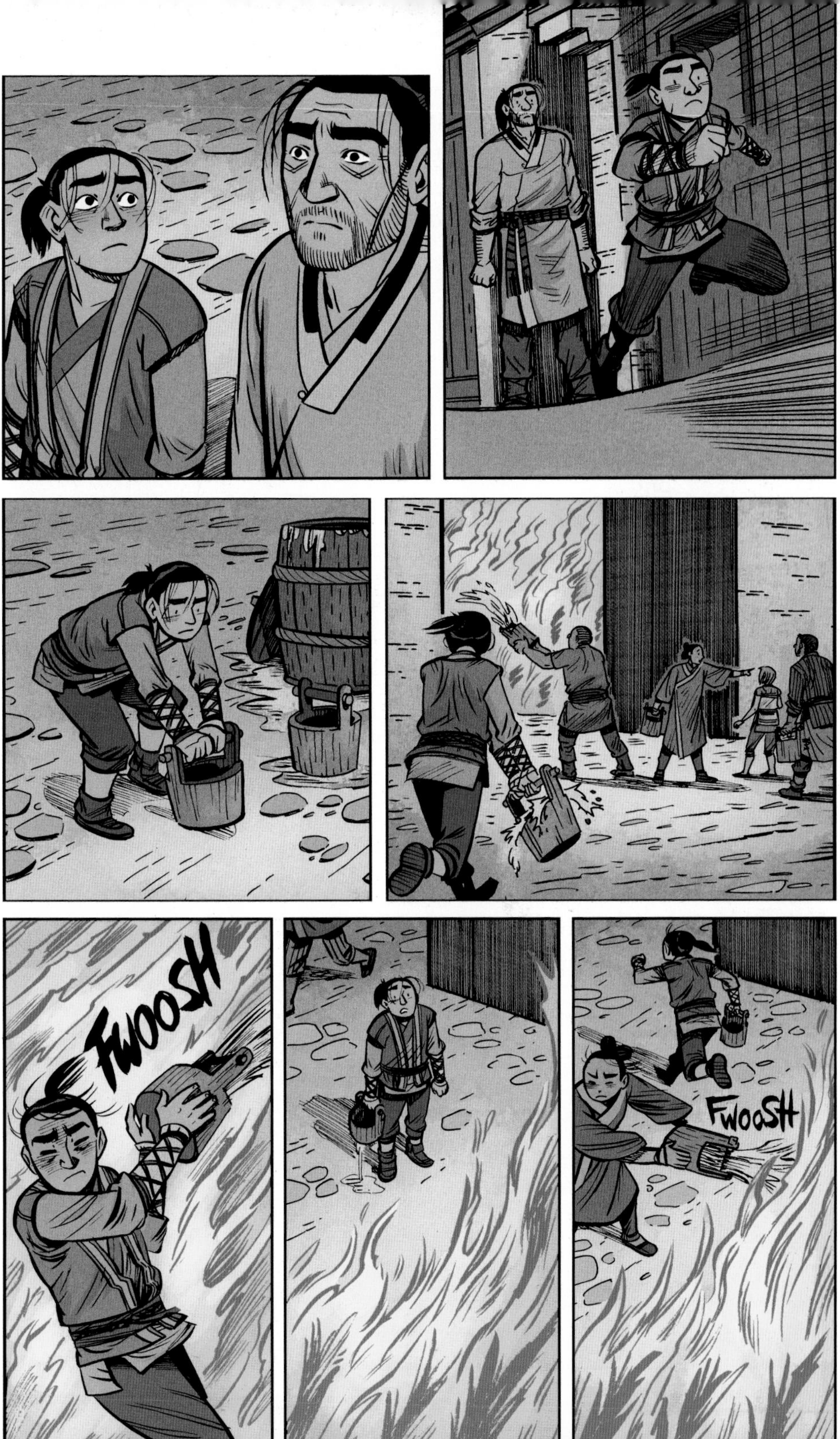
FWOOSH
FWOOSH

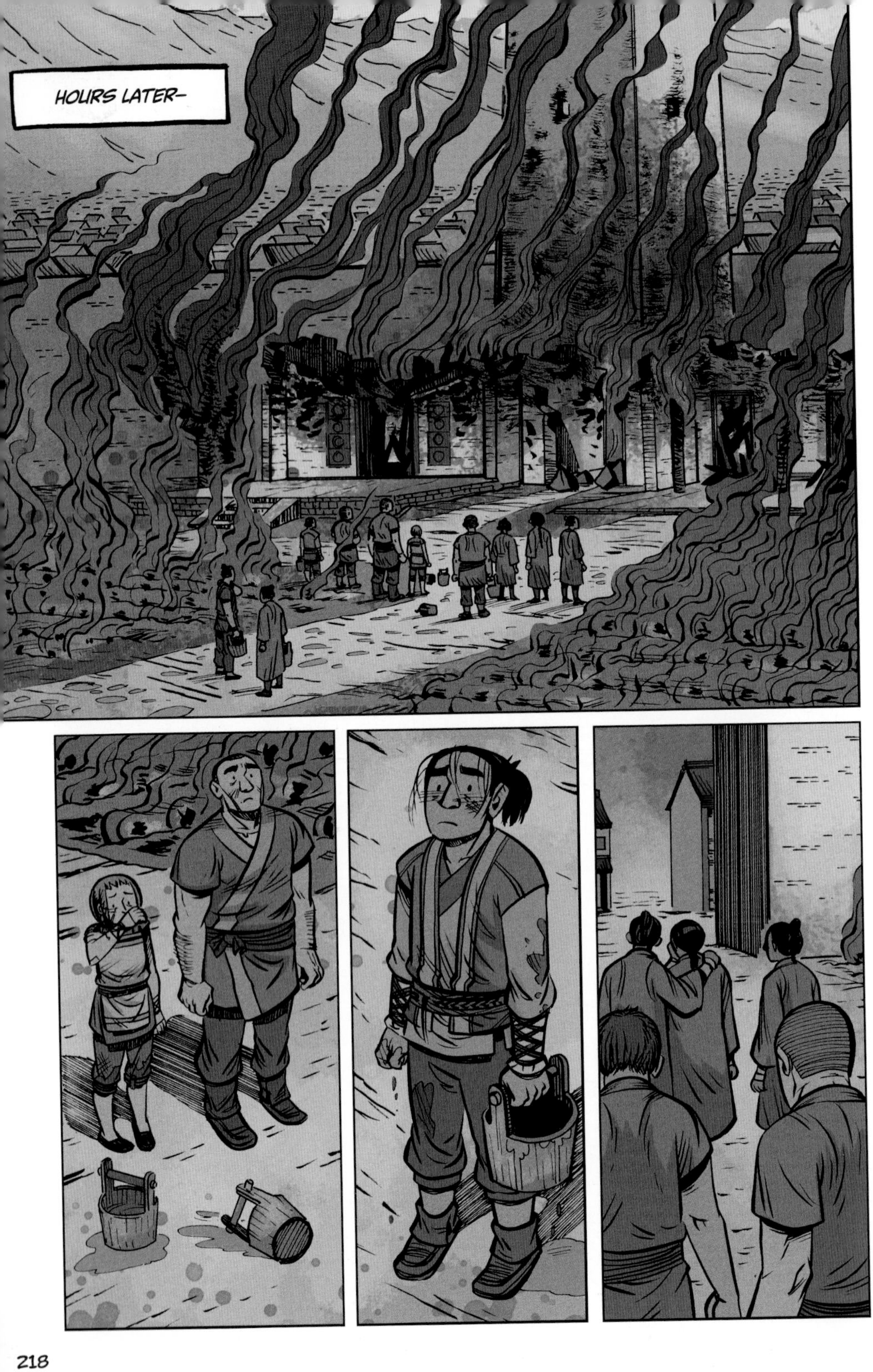
HOURS LATER–

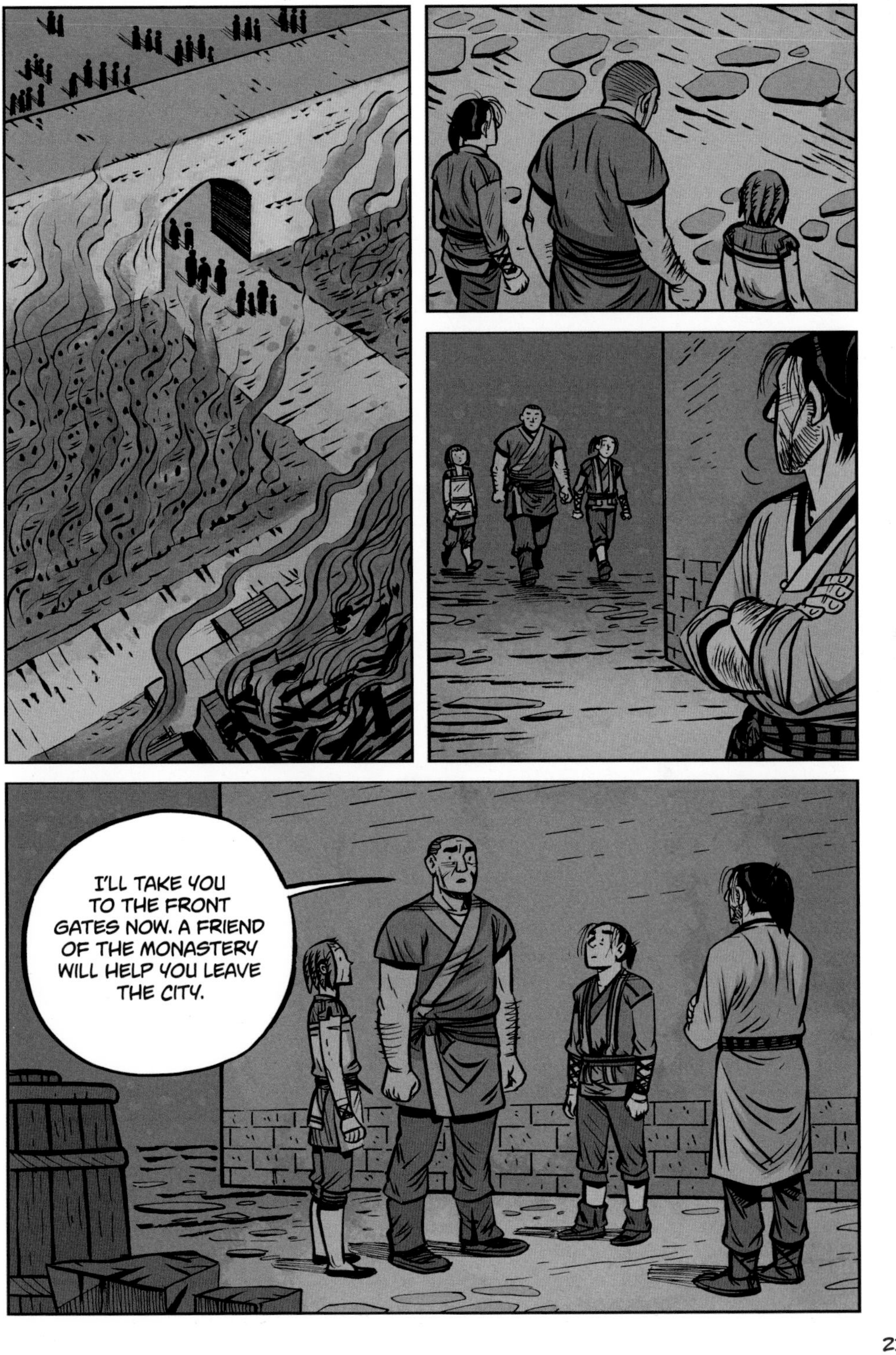
I'LL TAKE YOU TO THE FRONT GATES NOW. A FRIEND OF THE MONASTERY WILL HELP YOU LEAVE THE CITY.

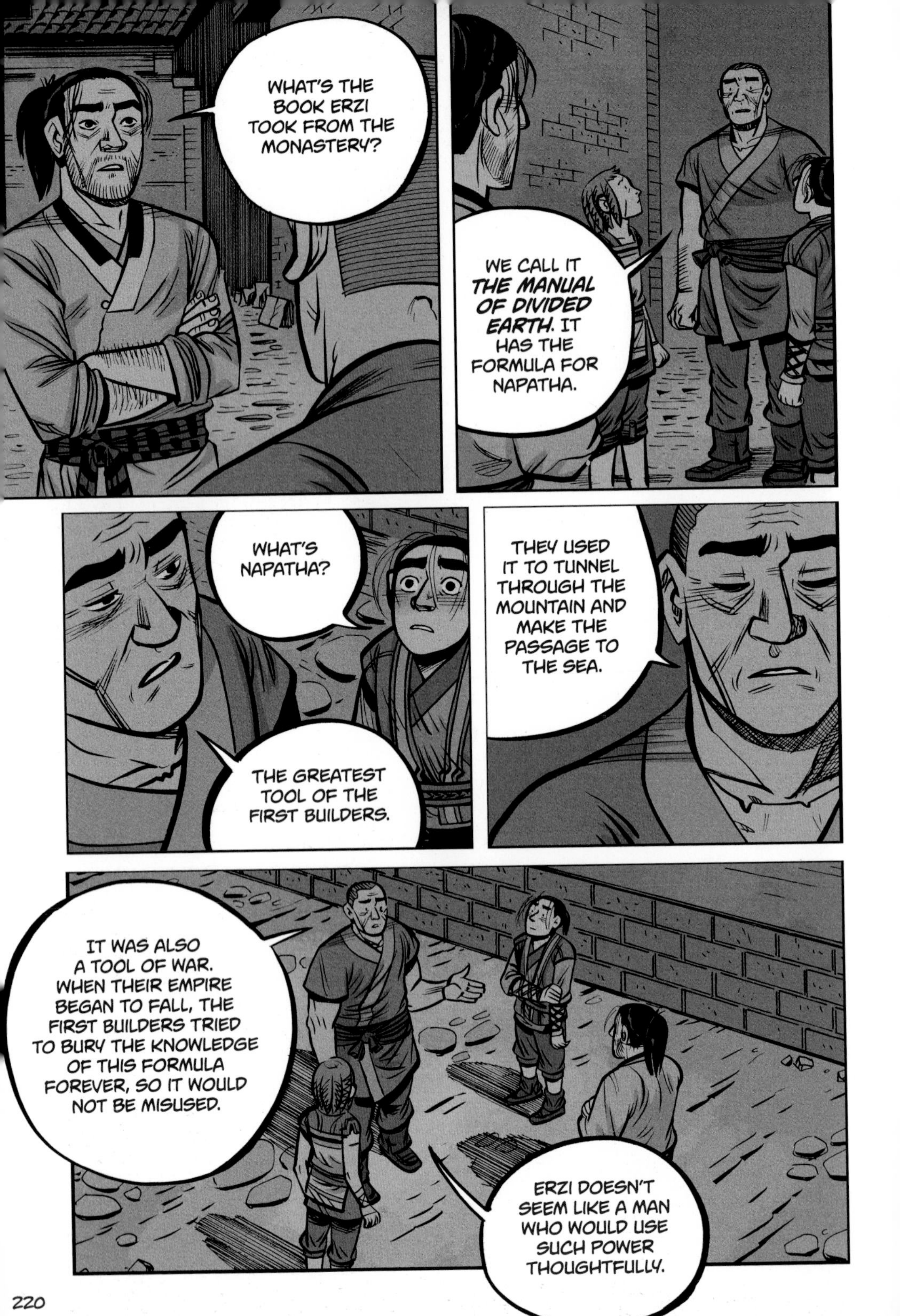
WHAT'S THE BOOK ERZI TOOK FROM THE MONASTERY?
WE CALL IT THE MANUAL OF DIVIDED EARTH. IT HAS THE FORMULA FOR NAPATHA.
WHAT'S NAPATHA?
THE GREATEST TOOL OF THE FIRST BUILDERS.
THEY USED IT TO TUNNEL THROUGH THE MOUNTAIN AND MAKE THE PASSAGE TO THE SEA.
IT WAS ALSO A TOOL OF WAR. WHEN THEIR EMPIRE BEGAN TO FALL, THE FIRST BUILDERS TRIED TO BURY THE KNOWLEDGE OF THIS FORMULA FOREVER, SO IT WOULD NOT BE MISUSED.
ERZI DOESN'T SEEM LIKE A MAN WHO WOULD USE SUCH POWER THOUGHTFULLY.

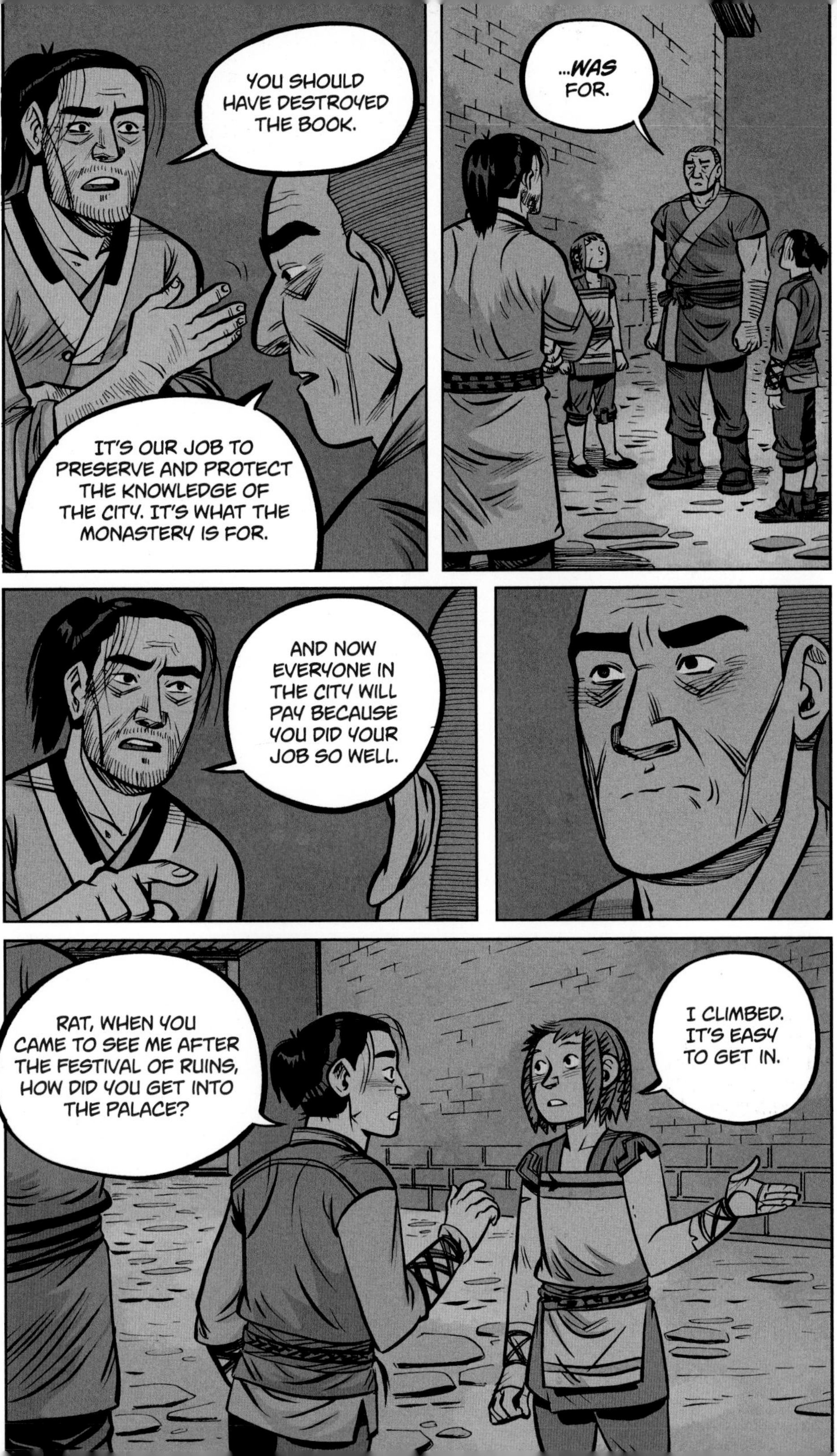
YOU SHOULD HAVE DESTROYED THE BOOK.
IT'S OUR JOB TO PRESERVE AND PROTECT THE KNOWLEDGE OF THE CITY. IT'S WHAT THE MONASTERY IS FOR.
...WAS FOR.
AND NOW EVERYONE IN THE CITY WILL PAY BECAUSE YOU DID YOUR JOB SO WELL.
RAT, WHEN YOU CAME TO SEE ME AFTER THE FESTIVAL OF RUINS, HOW DID YOU GET INTO THE PALACE?
I CLIMBED. IT'S EASY TO GET IN.

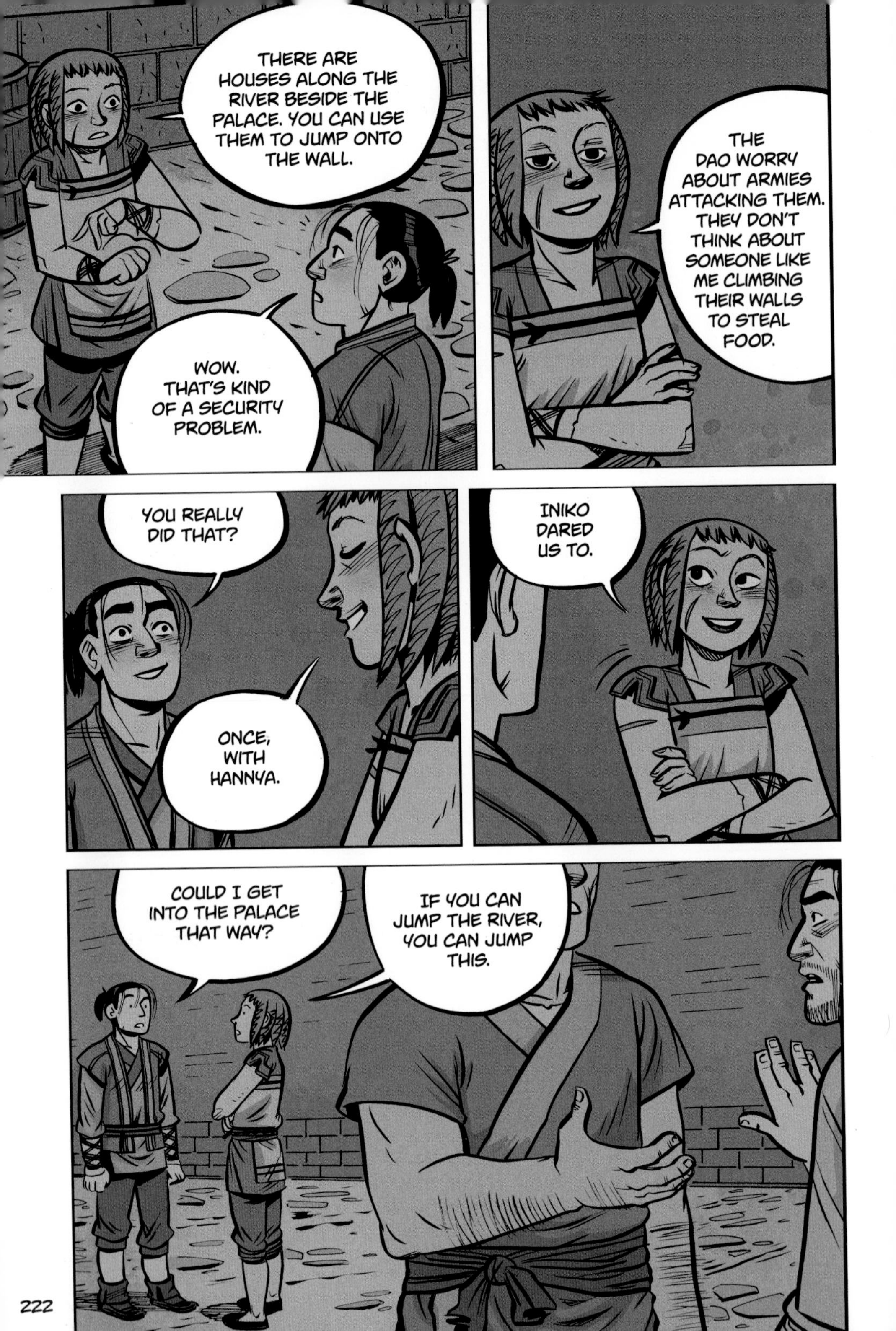
THERE ARE HOUSES ALONG THE RIVER BESIDE THE PALACE. YOU CAN USE THEM TO JUMP ONTO THE WALL.
WOW. THAT'S KIND OF A SECURITY PROBLEM.
THE DAO WORRY ABOUT ARMIES ATTACKING THEM. THEY DON'T THINK ABOUT SOMEONE LIKE ME CLIMBING THEIR WALLS TO STEAL FOOD.
YOU REALLY DID THAT?
ONCE, WITH HANNYA.
INIKO DARED US TO.
COULD I GET INTO THE PALACE THAT WAY?
IF YOU CAN JUMP THE RIVER, YOU CAN JUMP THIS.

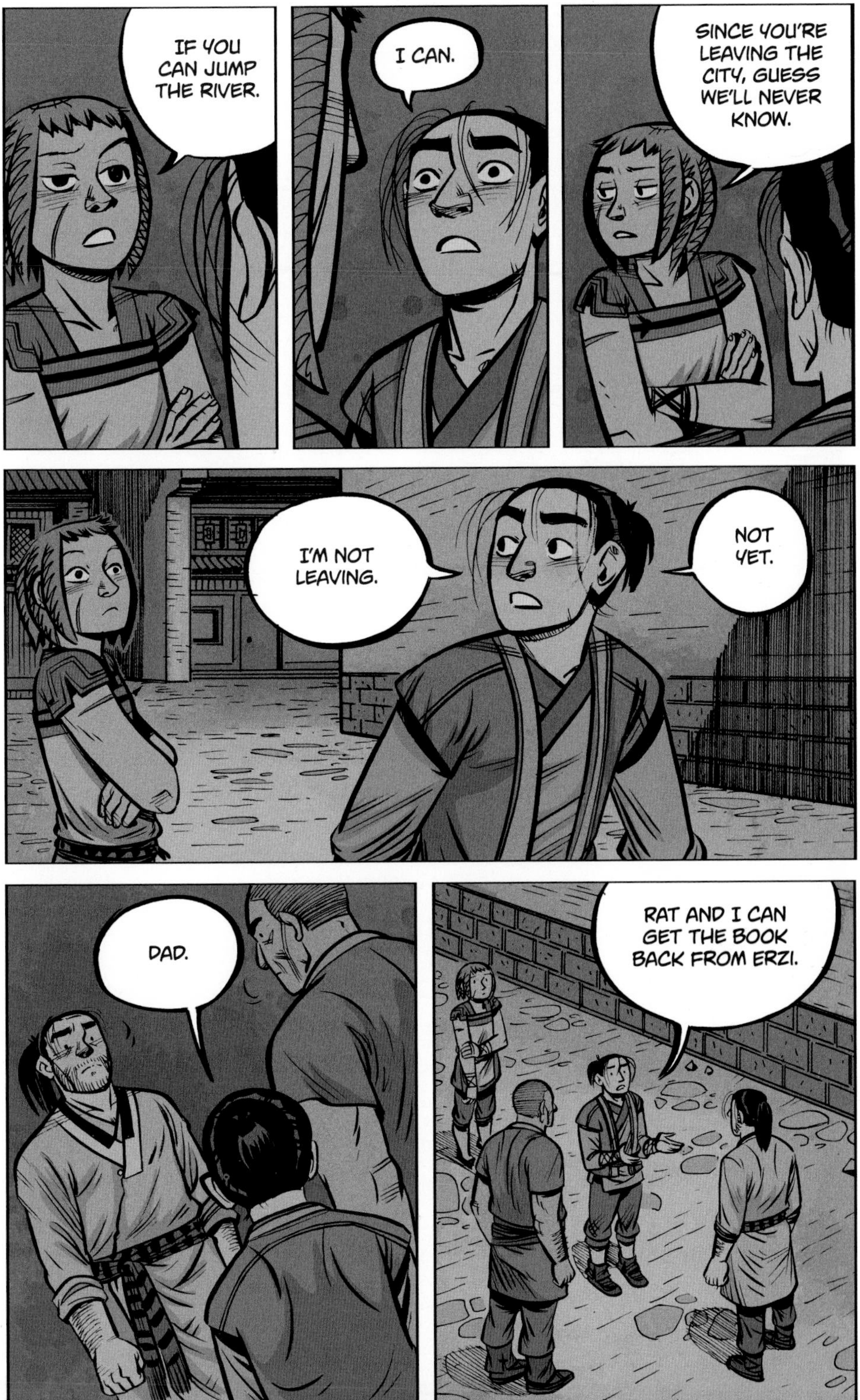
IF YOU CAN JUMP THE RIVER.
I CAN.
SINCE YOU'RE LEAVING THE CITY, GUESS WE'LL NEVER KNOW.
I'M NOT LEAVING.
NOT YET.
DAD.
RAT AND I CAN GET THE BOOK BACK FROM ERZI.

WHAT?

SHE CAN GET INTO THE PALACE. WE CAN GO IN AT NIGHT AND STEAL THE BOOK FROM HIM.

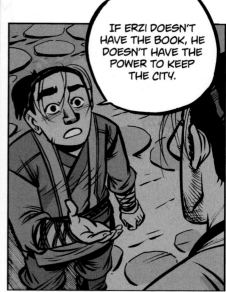

IF ERZI DOESN'T HAVE THE BOOK, HE DOESN'T HAVE THE POWER TO KEEP THE CITY.

YOU'LL HELP ME GET INTO THE PALACE, RIGHT? I'M SORRY, I SHOULD'VE ASKED.

YEAH. I CAN—

NO.

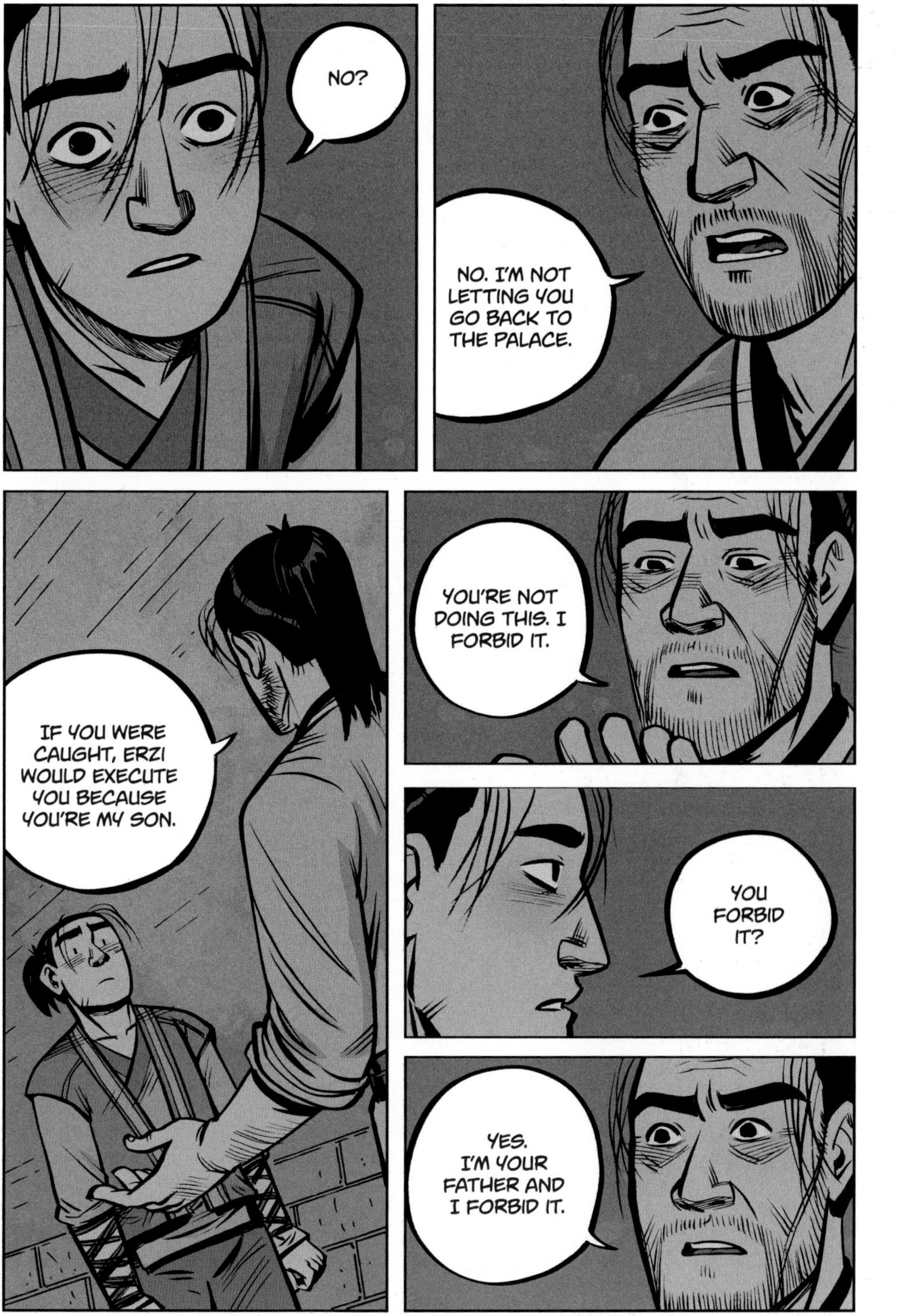
NO?
NO. I'M NOT LETTING YOU GO BACK TO THE PALACE.
IF YOU WERE CAUGHT, ERZI WOULD EXECUTE YOU BECAUSE YOU'RE MY SON.
YOU'RE NOT DOING THIS. I FORBID IT.
YOU FORBID IT?
YES. I'M YOUR FATHER AND I FORBID IT.

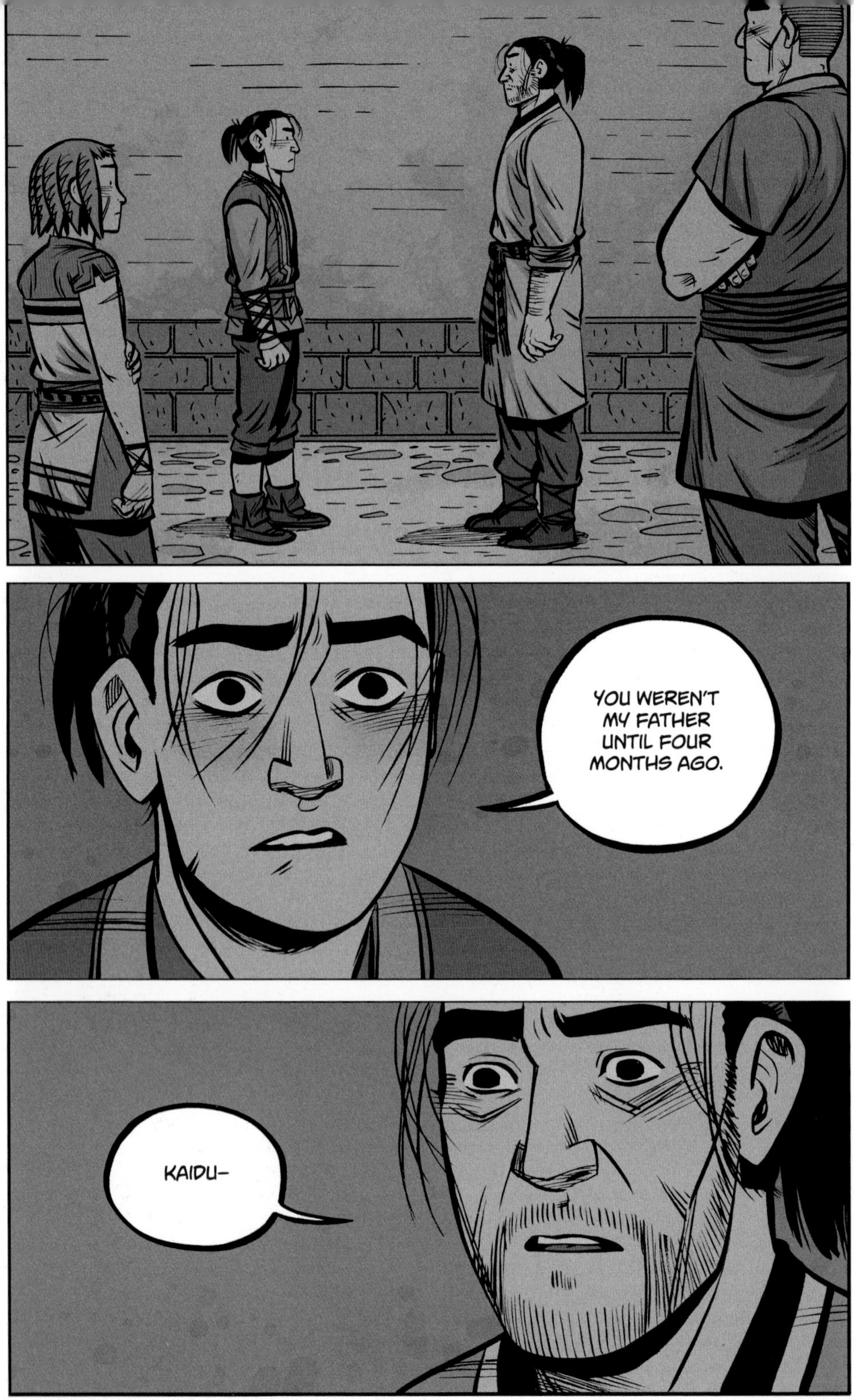
YOU WEREN'T MY FATHER UNTIL FOUR MONTHS AGO.
KAIDU-

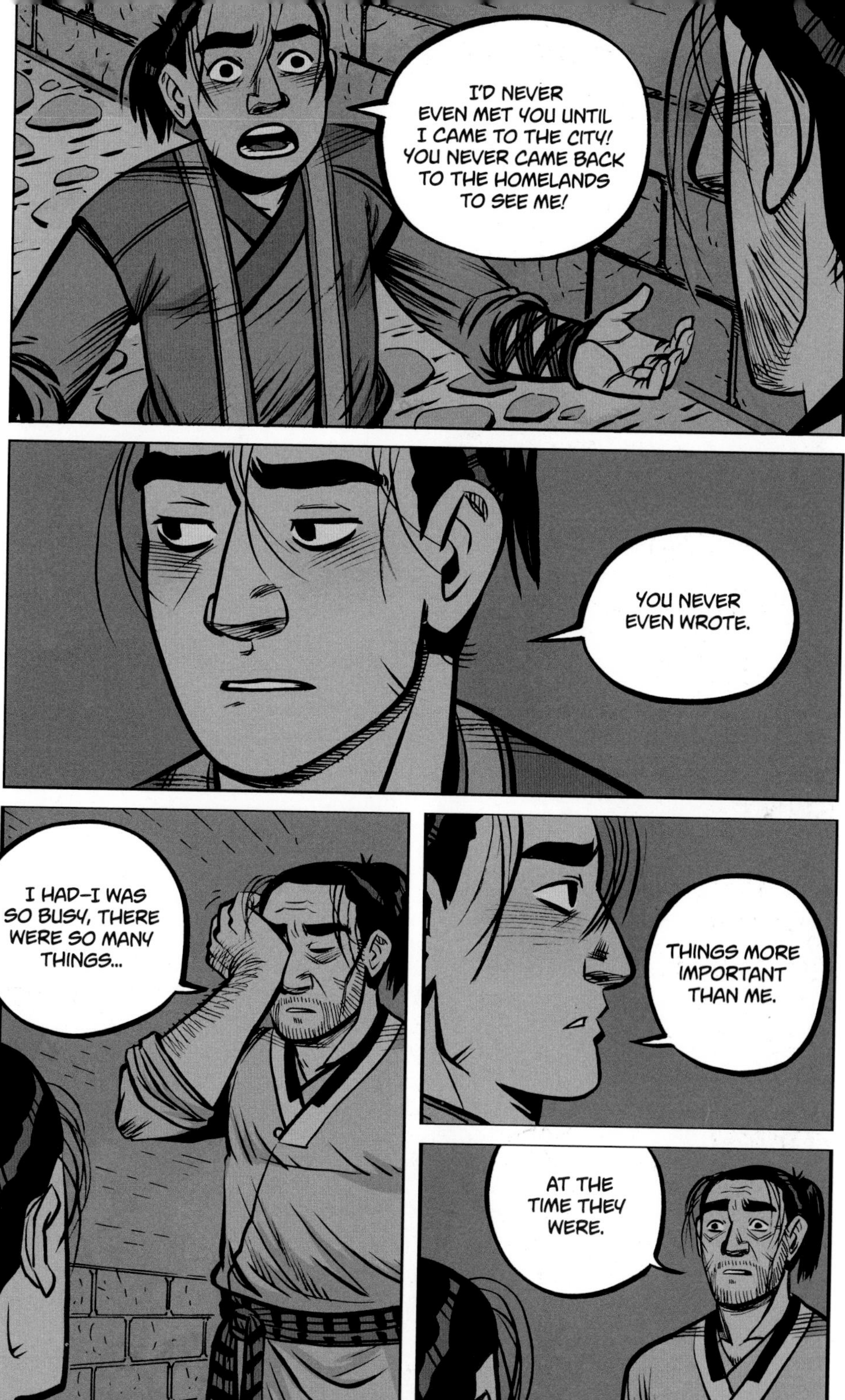
I'D NEVER EVEN MET YOU UNTIL I CAME TO THE CITY! YOU NEVER CAME BACK TO THE HOMELANDS TO SEE ME!
YOU NEVER EVEN WROTE.
I HAD–I WAS SO BUSY, THERE WERE SO MANY THINGS...
THINGS MORE IMPORTANT THAN ME.
AT THE TIME THEY WERE.

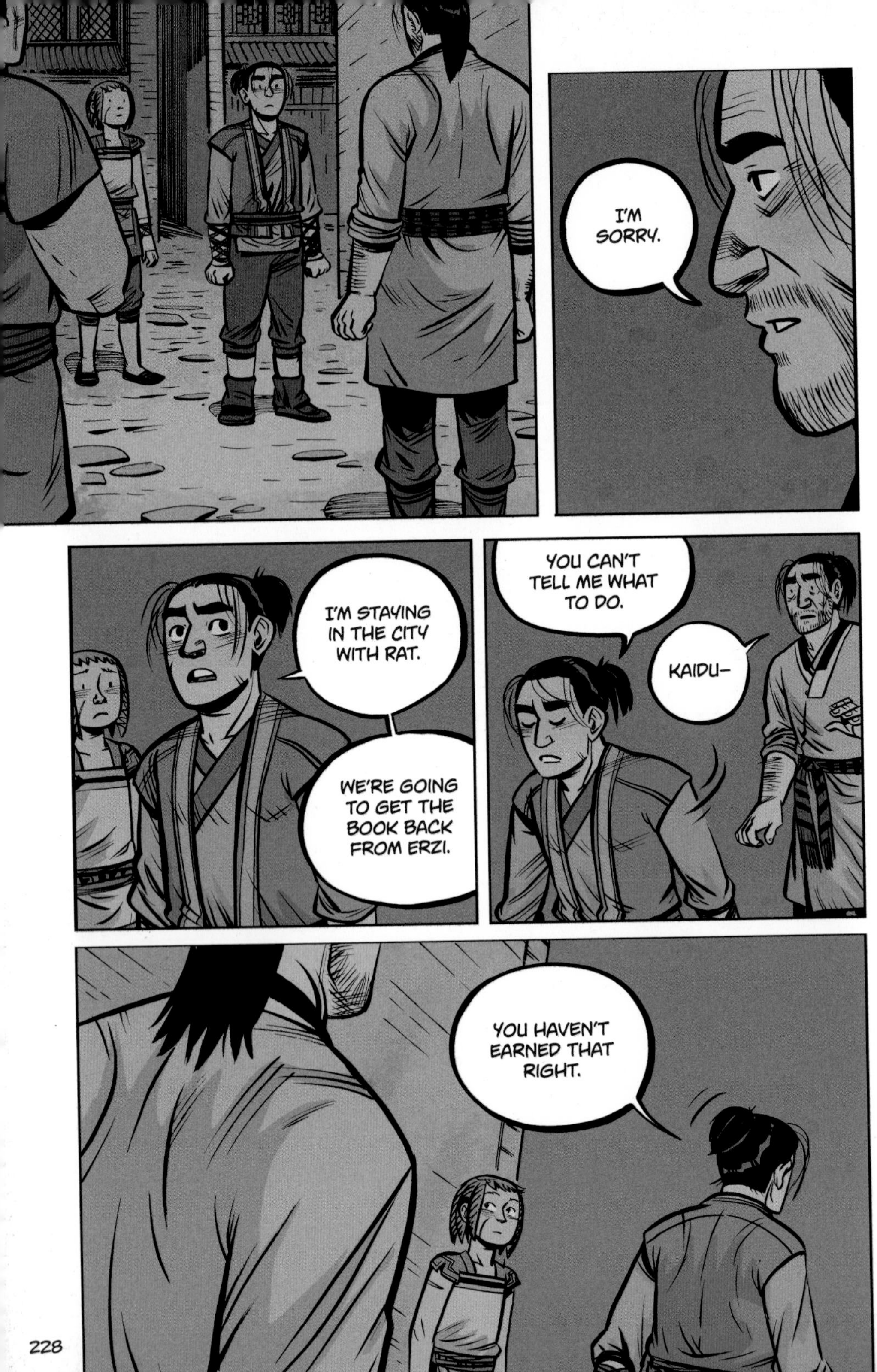
I'M SORRY.
I'M STAYING IN THE CITY WITH RAT.
WE'RE GOING TO GET THE BOOK BACK FROM ERZI.
YOU CAN'T TELL ME WHAT TO DO.
KAIDU-
YOU HAVEN'T EARNED THAT RIGHT.

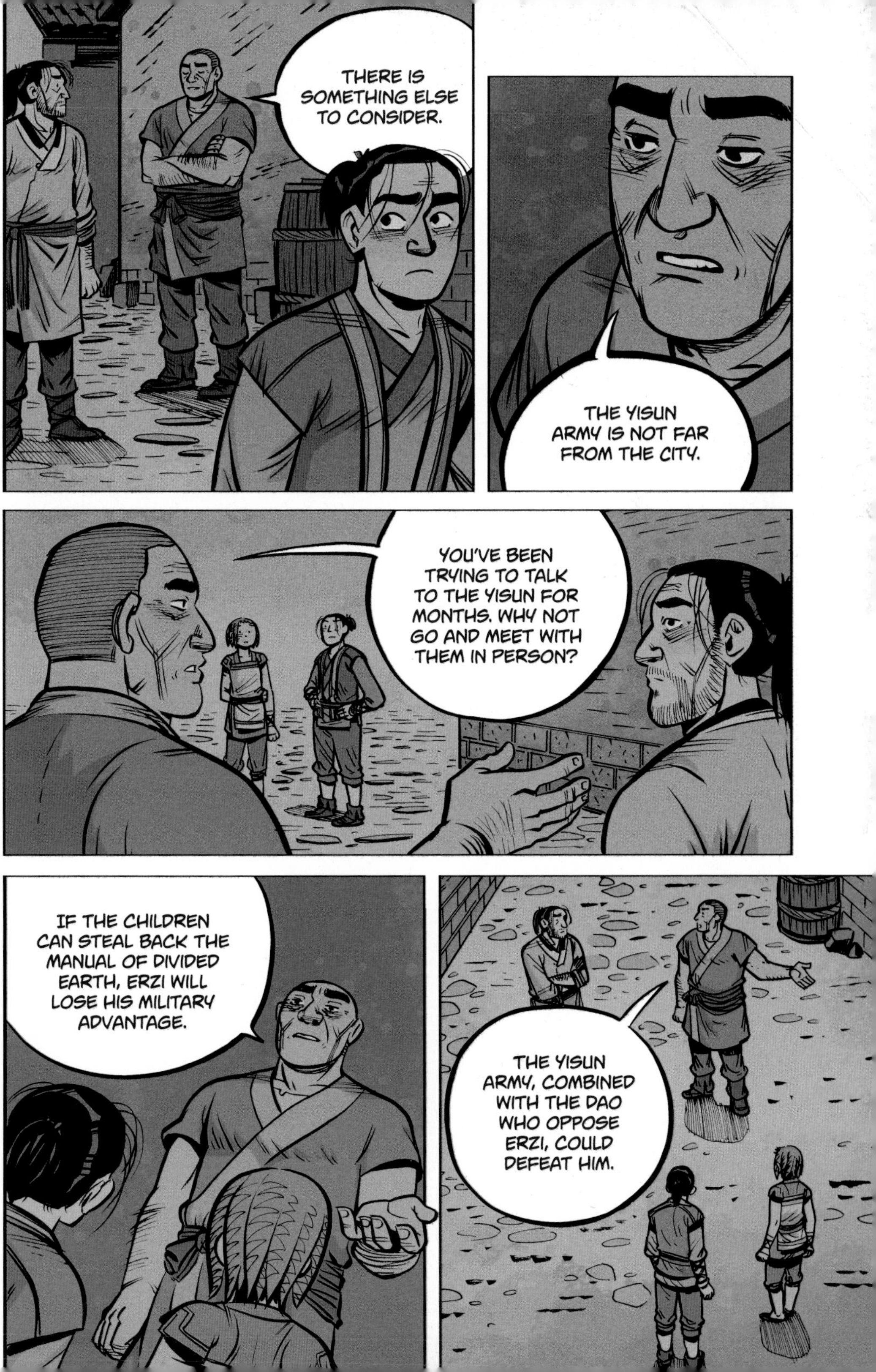
THERE IS SOMETHING ELSE TO CONSIDER.
THE YISUN ARMY IS NOT FAR FROM THE CITY.
YOU'VE BEEN TRYING TO TALK TO THE YISUN FOR MONTHS. WHY NOT GO AND MEET WITH THEM IN PERSON?
IF THE CHILDREN CAN STEAL BACK THE MANUAL OF DIVIDED EARTH, ERZI WILL LOSE HIS MILITARY ADVANTAGE.
THE YISUN ARMY, COMBINED WITH THE DAO WHO OPPOSE ERZI, COULD DEFEAT HIM.

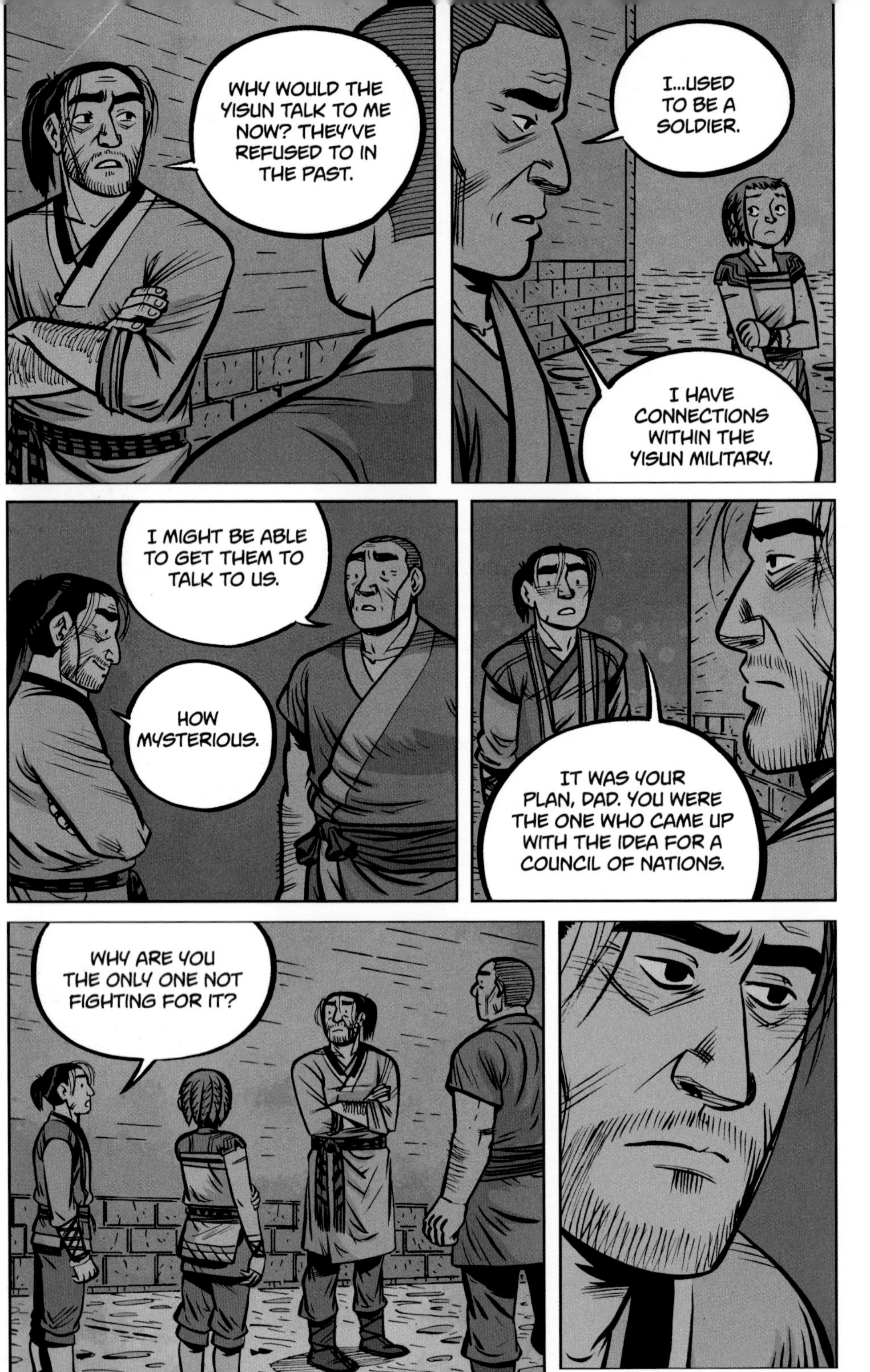
WHY WOULD THE YISUN TALK TO ME NOW? THEY'VE REFUSED TO IN THE PAST.
I...USED TO BE A SOLDIER.
I HAVE CONNECTIONS WITHIN THE YISUN MILITARY.
I MIGHT BE ABLE TO GET THEM TO TALK TO US.
HOW MYSTERIOUS.
IT WAS YOUR PLAN, DAD. YOU WERE THE ONE WHO CAME UP WITH THE IDEA FOR A COUNCIL OF NATIONS.
WHY ARE YOU THE ONLY ONE NOT FIGHTING FOR IT?

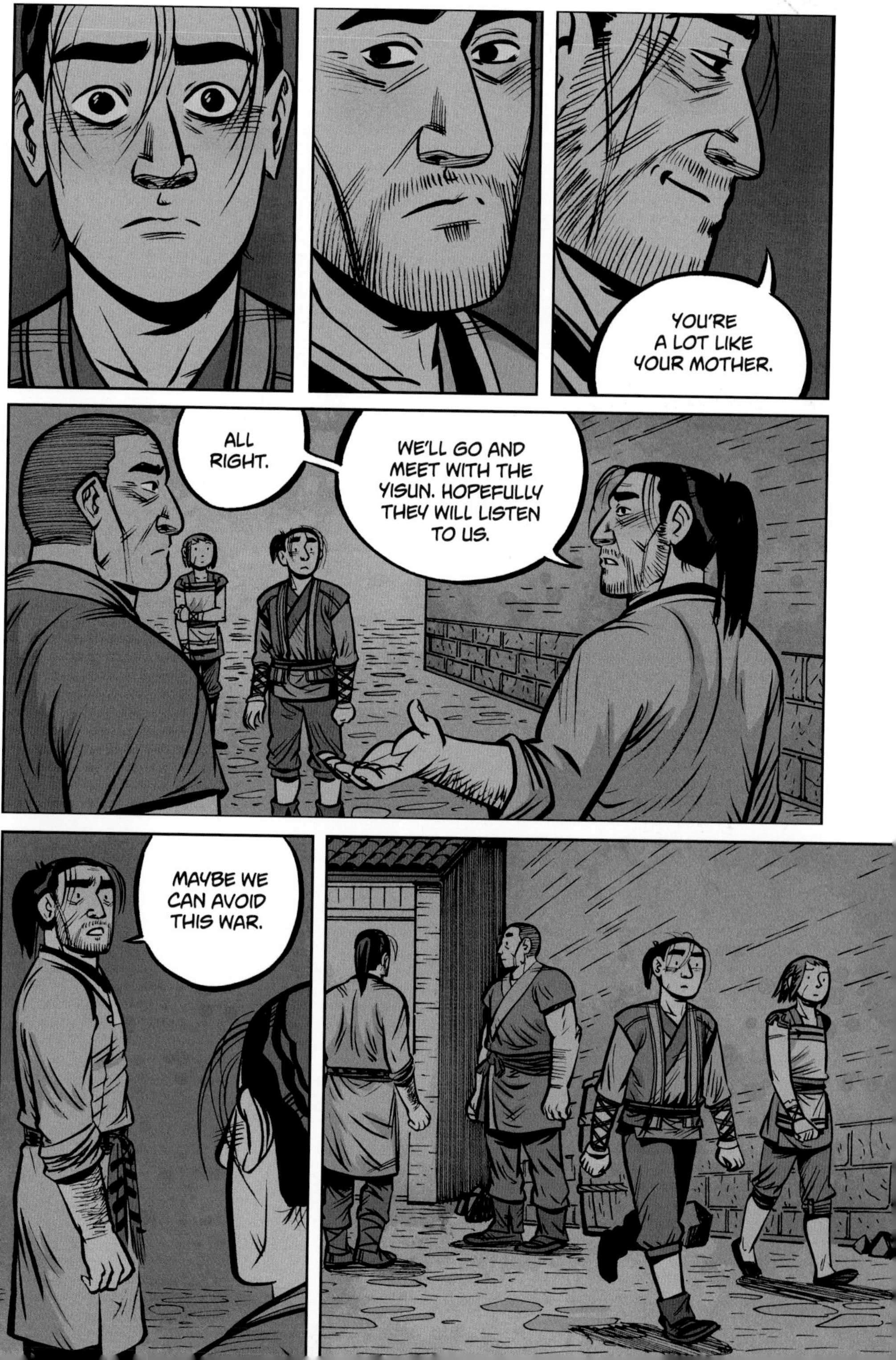
YOU'RE A LOT LIKE YOUR MOTHER.
ALL RIGHT.
WE'LL GO AND MEET WITH THE YISUN. HOPEFULLY THEY WILL LISTEN TO US.
MAYBE WE CAN AVOID THIS WAR.

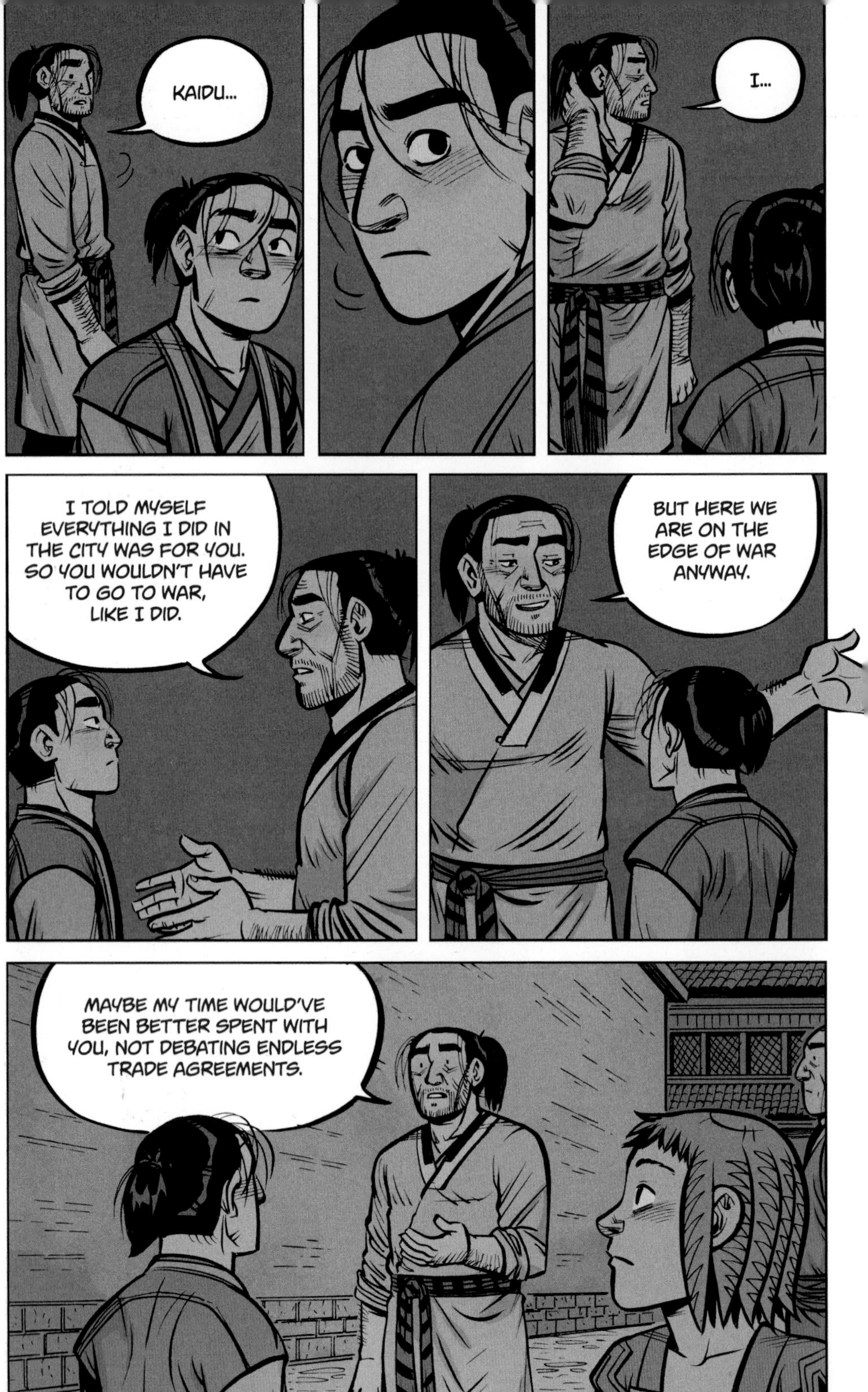
KAIDU...
I...
I TOLD MYSELF EVERYTHING I DID IN THE CITY WAS FOR YOU. SO YOU WOULDN'T HAVE TO GO TO WAR, LIKE I DID.
BUT HERE WE ARE ON THE EDGE OF WAR ANYWAY.
MAYBE MY TIME WOULD'VE BEEN BETTER SPENT WITH YOU, NOT DEBATING ENDLESS TRADE AGREEMENTS.

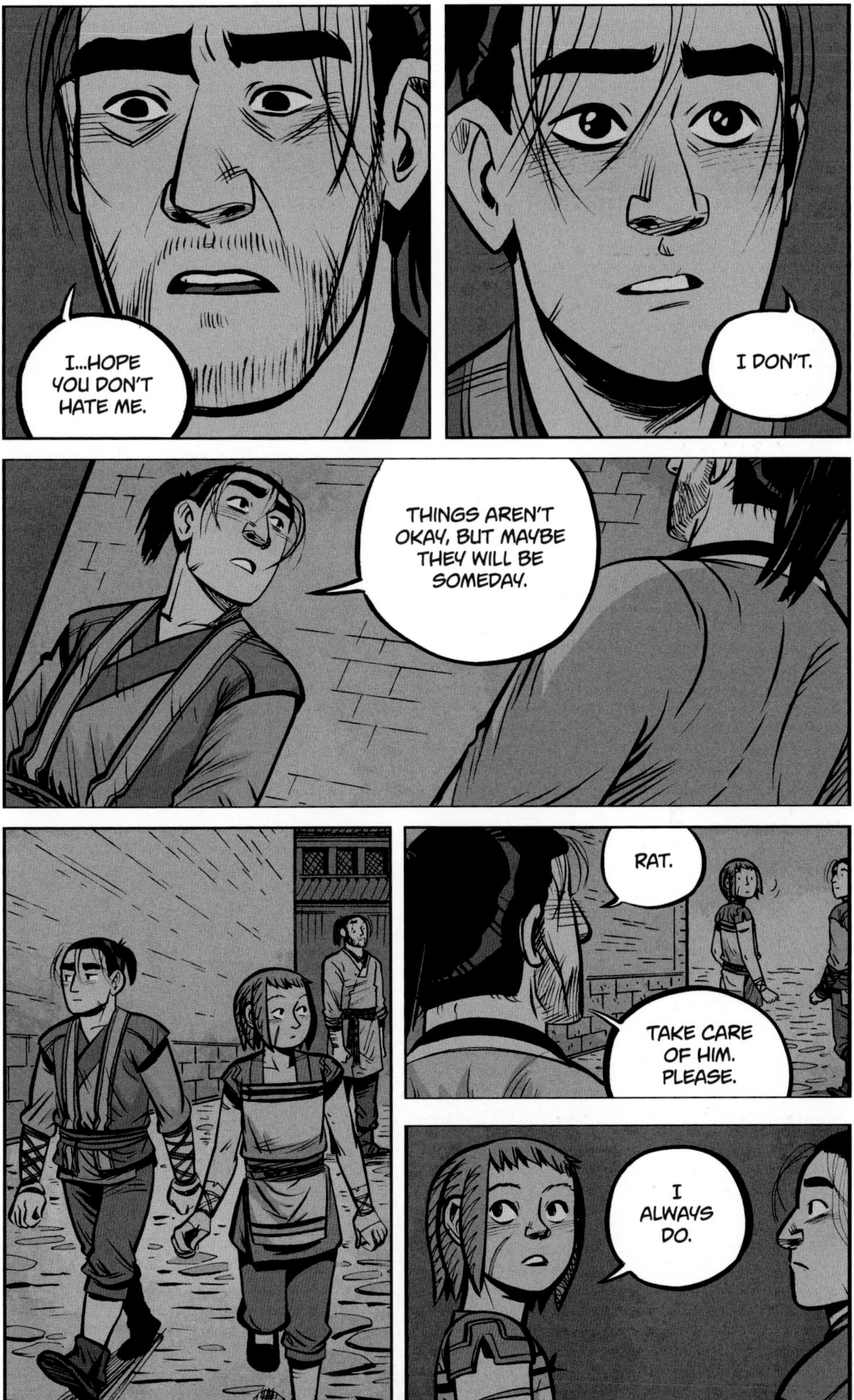
I...HOPE YOU DON'T HATE ME.
I DON'T.
THINGS AREN'T OKAY, BUT MAYBE THEY WILL BE SOMEDAY.
RAT.
TAKE CARE OF HIM. PLEASE.
I ALWAYS DO.

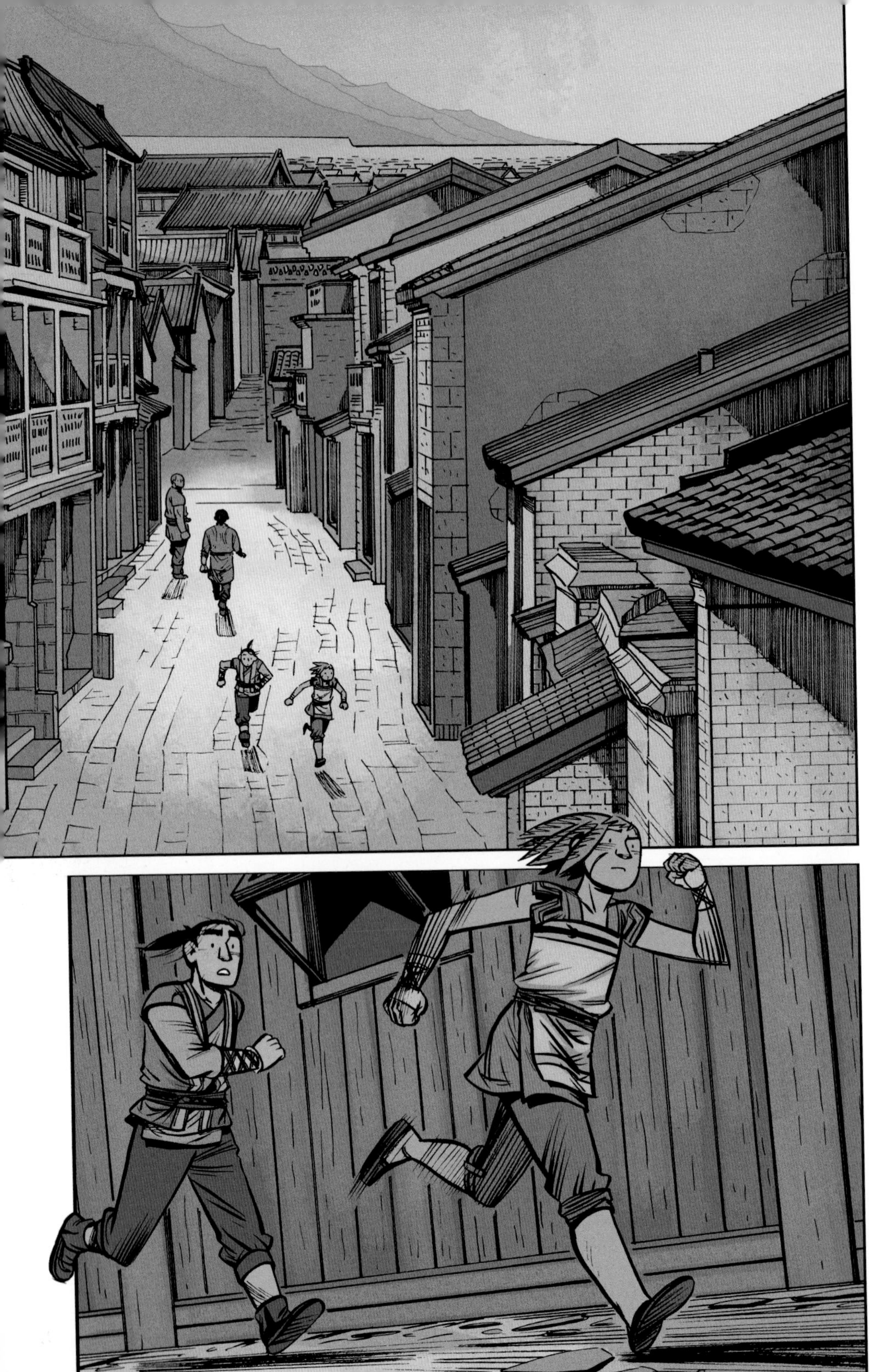

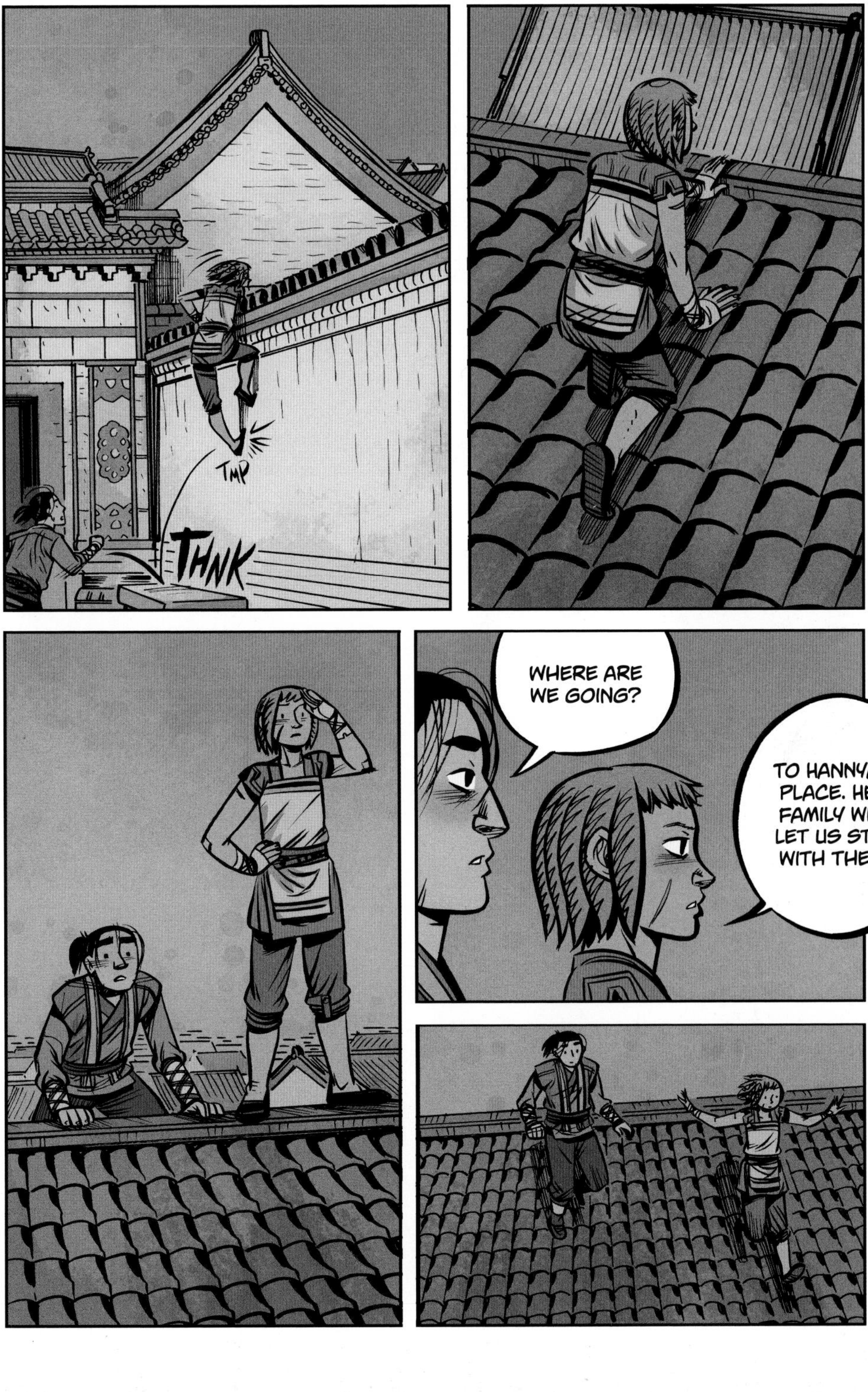
TMP
THNK
WHERE ARE WE GOING?
TO HANNYA'S PLACE. HER FAMILY WILL LET US STAY WITH THEM.

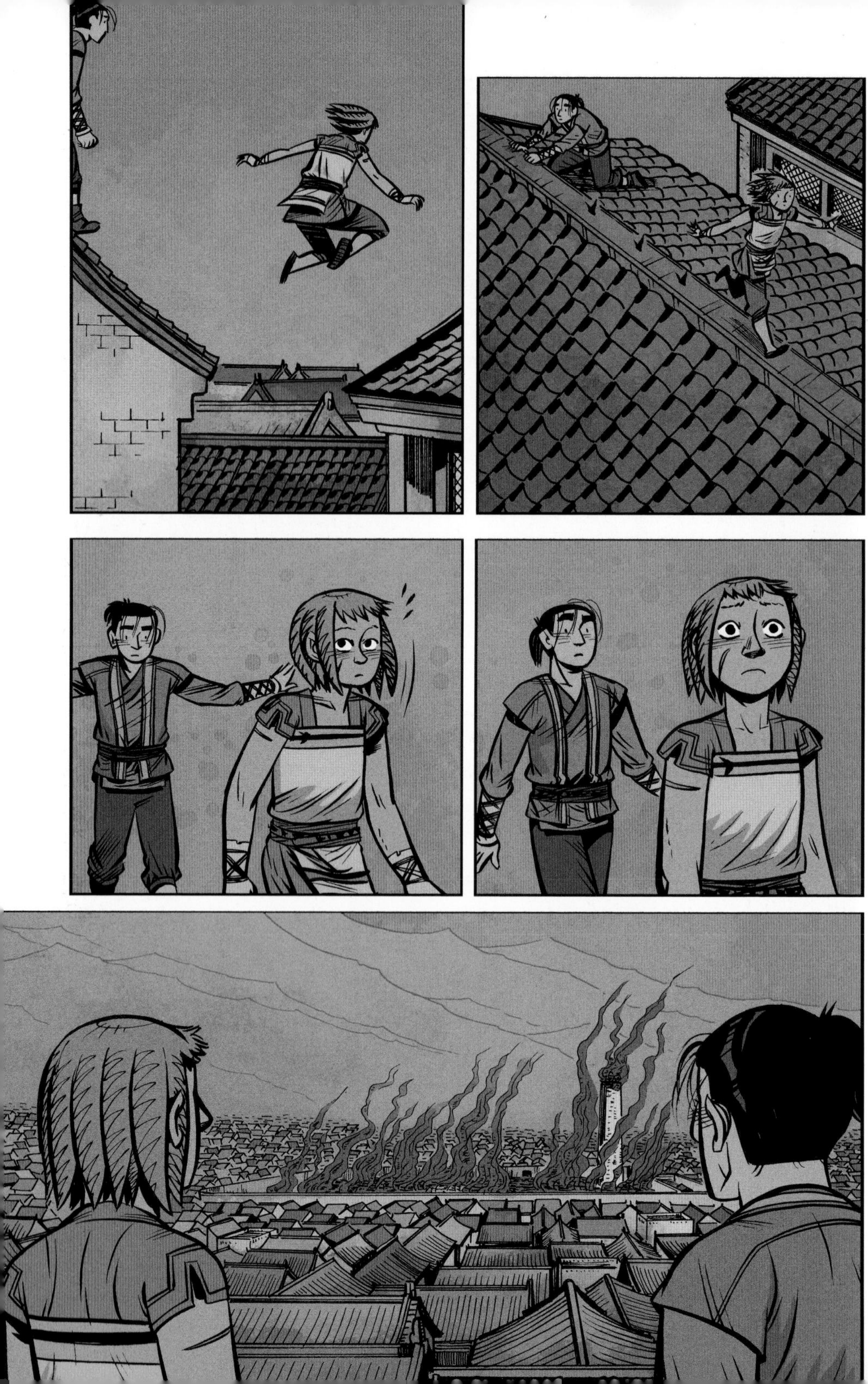

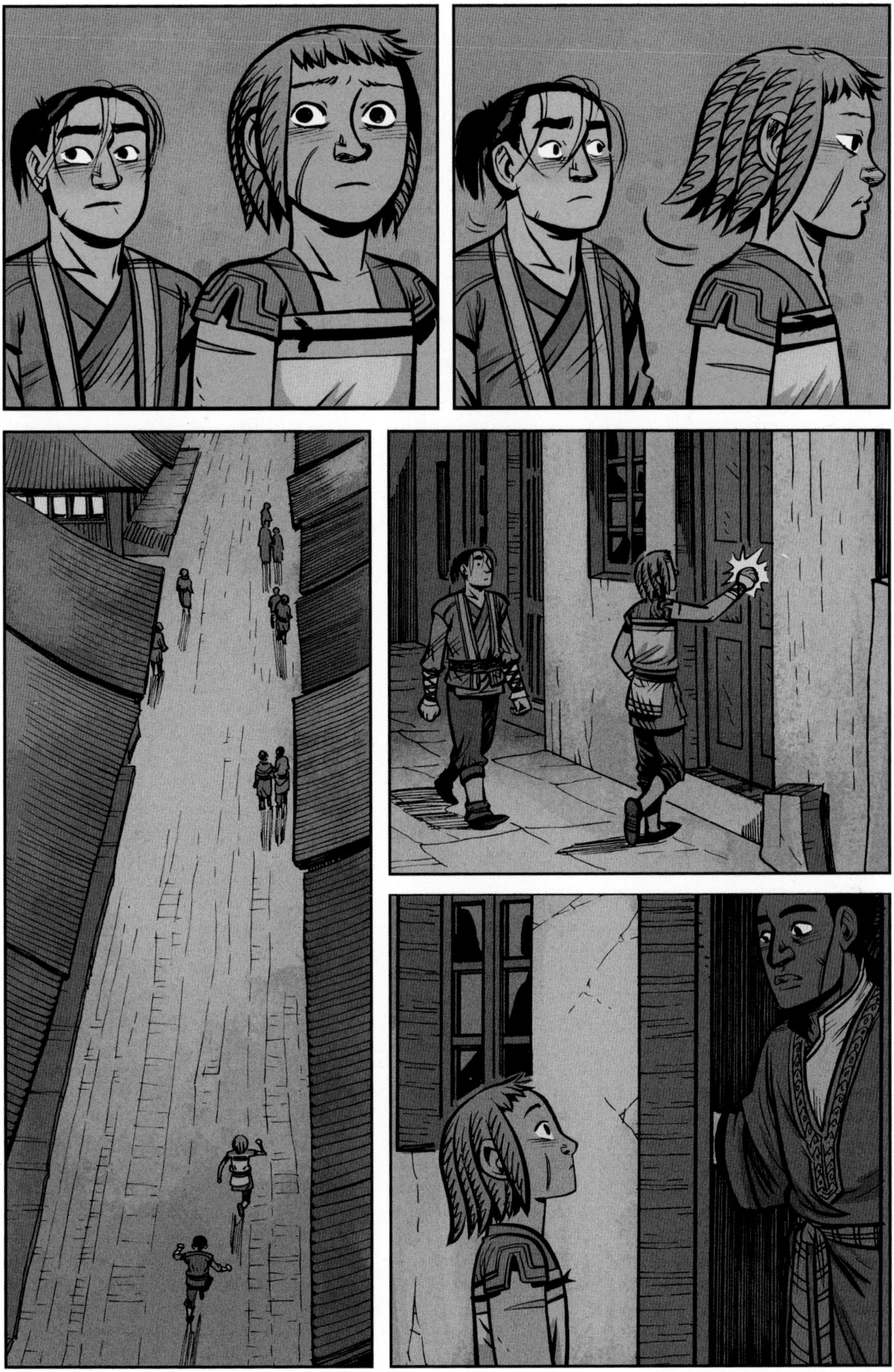

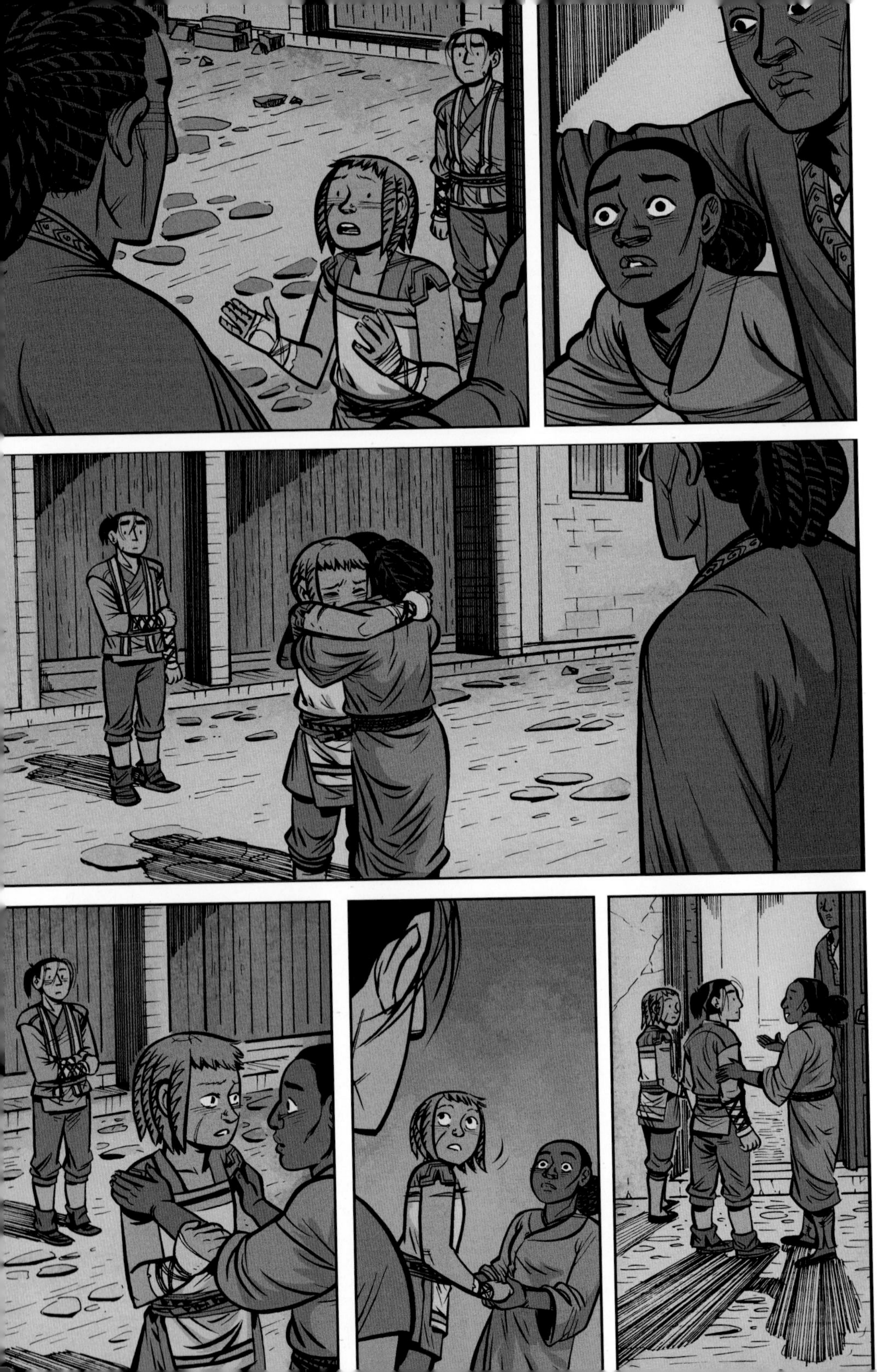

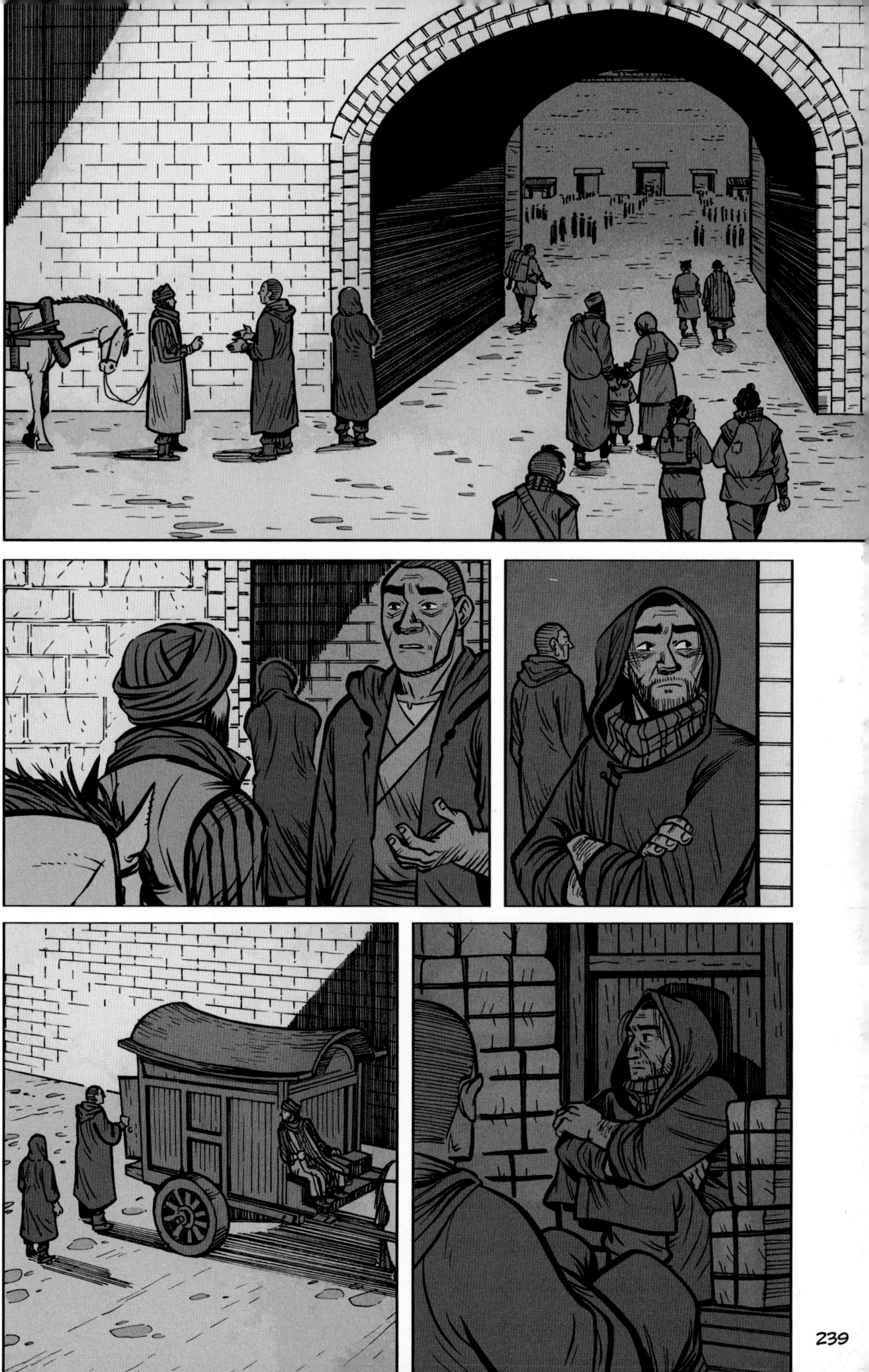

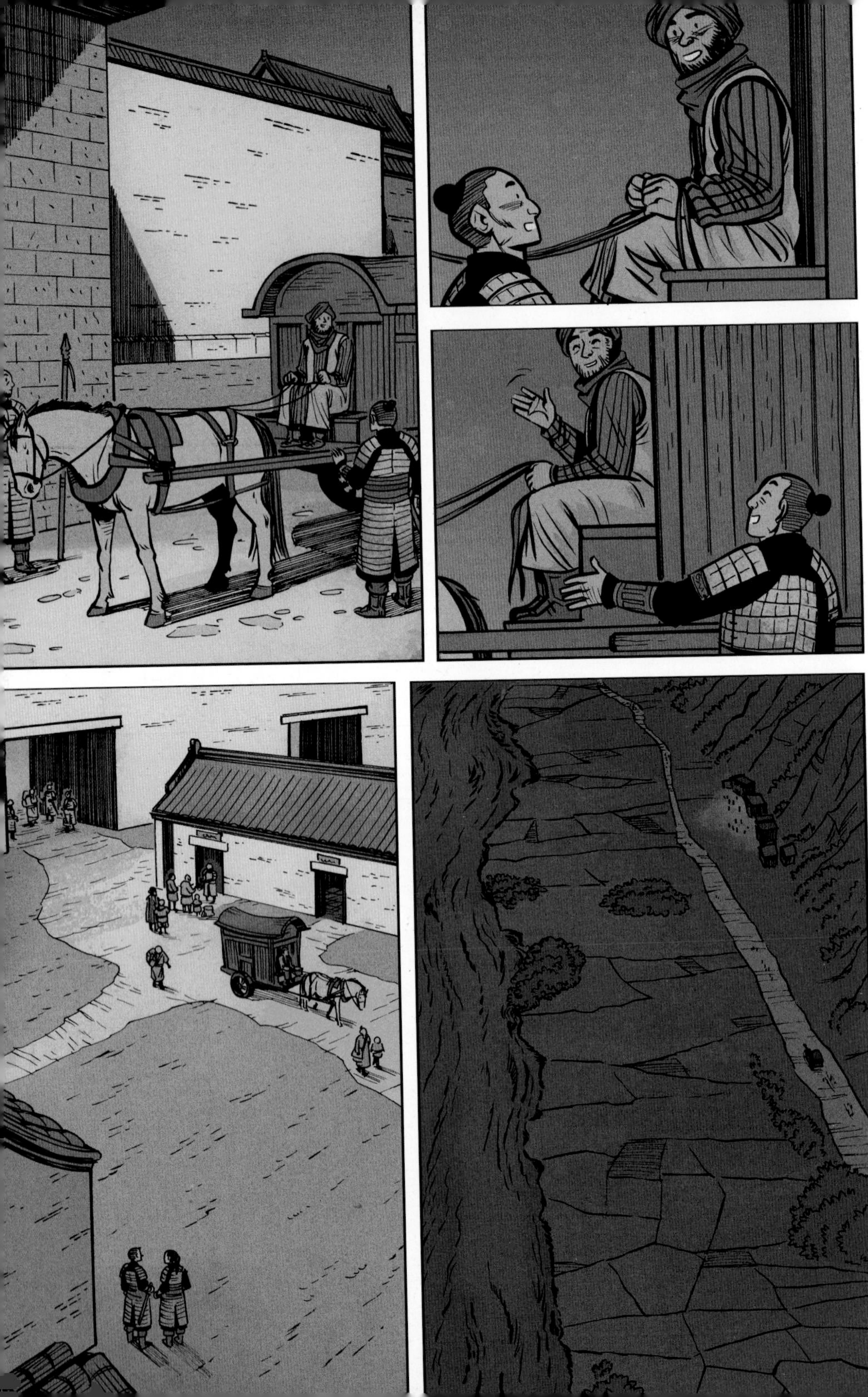

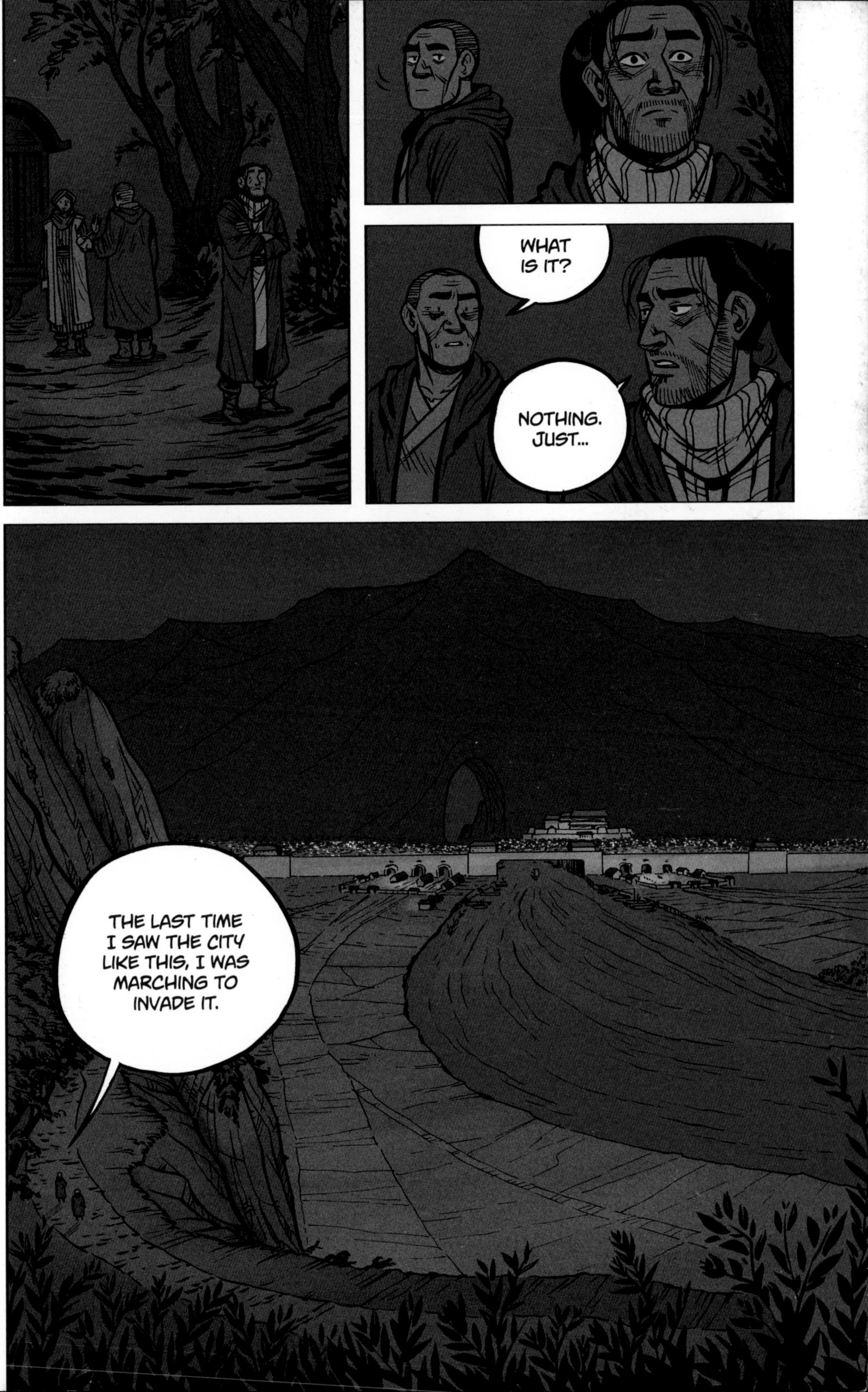
WHAT IS IT?
NOTHING. JUST...
THE LAST TIME I SAW THE CITY LIKE THIS, I WAS MARCHING TO INVADE IT.

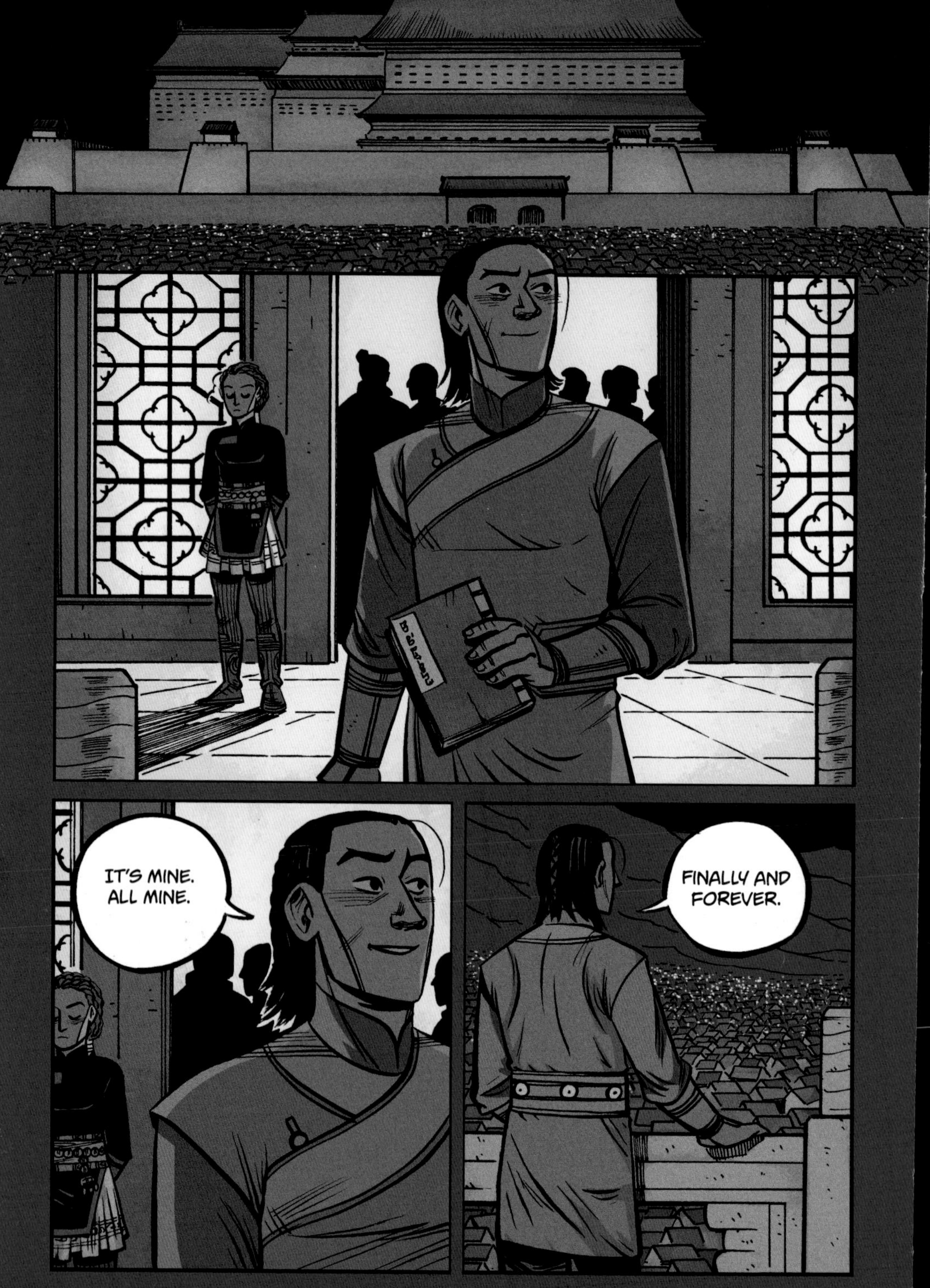
IT'S MINE. ALL MINE.
FINALLY AND FOREVER.

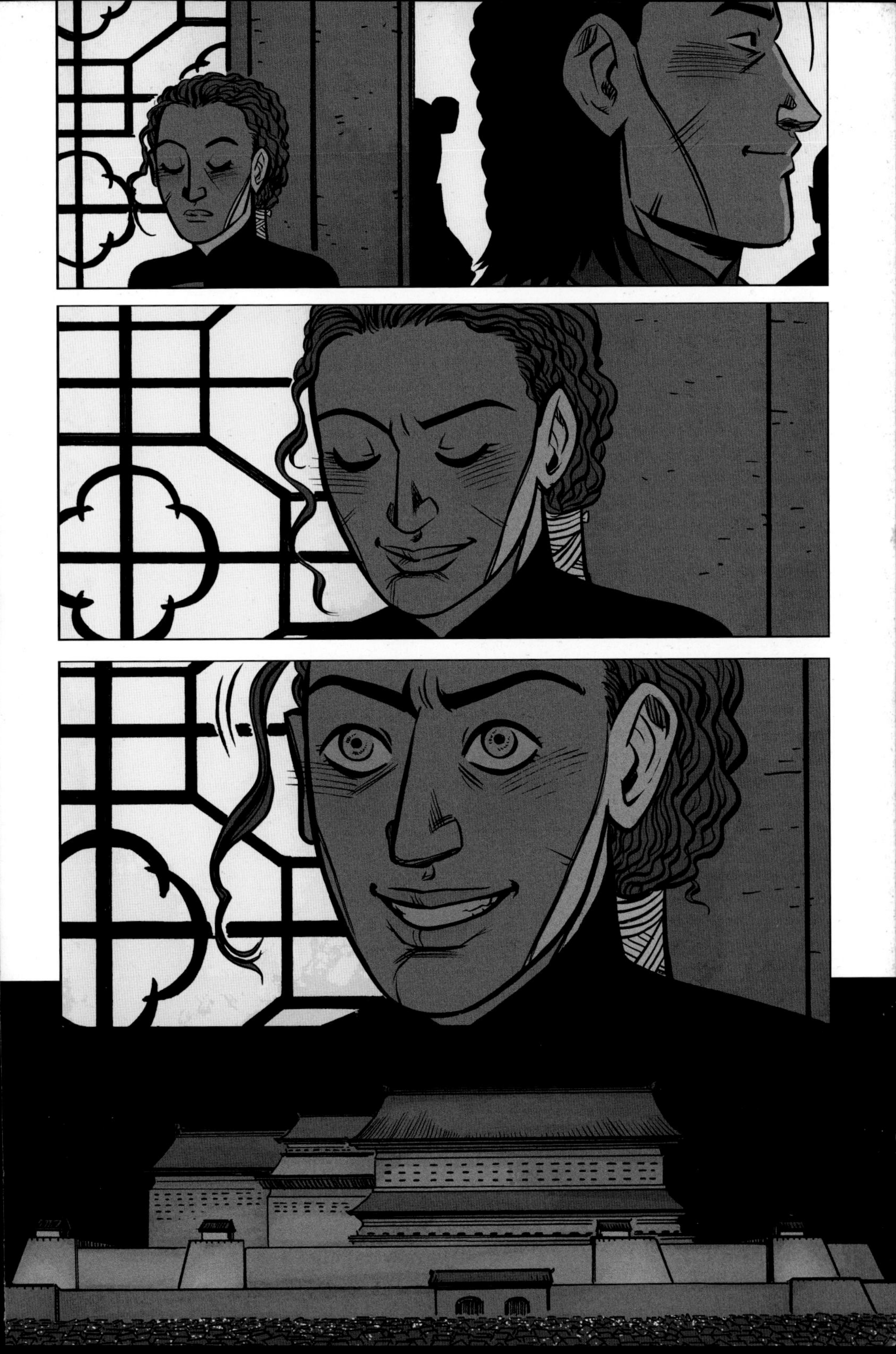

TO BE CONTINUED IN

THE DIVIDED EARTH

BOOK 3 OF THE NAMELESS CITY SERIES

AUTHOR'S NOTE

As of this writing, two books in The Nameless City trilogy are complete, and I will soon begin work on the third, where the story of Rat and Kai and the various characters introduced over the past 450-plus pages will (hopefully) find a satisfying ending. The Nameless City has been an unusual and challenging project for me: It's the first trilogy I've both written and drawn on my own and the first comic I've drawn that has not been set in present-day North America (or its post-apocalyptic future). After two graphic novels set in a modern high school (*Friends with Boys* and *Nothing Can Possibly Go Wrong*), I wanted to stretch my drawing muscles, and I settled on creating a comic with thousands of tiled Chinese rooftops. During my darkest times drawing these two (soon to be three) graphic novels, I may have had one or two moments regretting that choice and longing for the easy-to-draw lockers of a modern high school hallway. But they were only moments. For all its challenges, I've greatly enjoyed drawing the complicated world that Rat and Kai inhabit.

The world of The Nameless City is fictional, but its roots are based on thirteenth-century China. There is no "Nameless City" in history, but I drew from my research on the Yuan Dynasty and the Silk Road to create this vast, multicultural place where Kai and Rat live. Hopefully that research gives their home weight and substance. I have tried to create a world that is visually authentic, if not accurate to historical events of the time. There are differences between the real thirteenth-century China and the world of The Nameless City—the history, the language of its people—but I have tried to ground my artwork in that particular time and place. I am grateful to the historical clothing reference books available at the Halifax Public Library (where I did much of my research before moving all the way across Canada to Vancouver, British Columbia), as well as the online photo galleries of libraries across the US and Canada, all of which were a great asset in the years leading up to the creation of this trilogy. Libraries are, as always, a cartoonist's best friend.

CONCEPT ART FOR
THE NAMELESS CITY

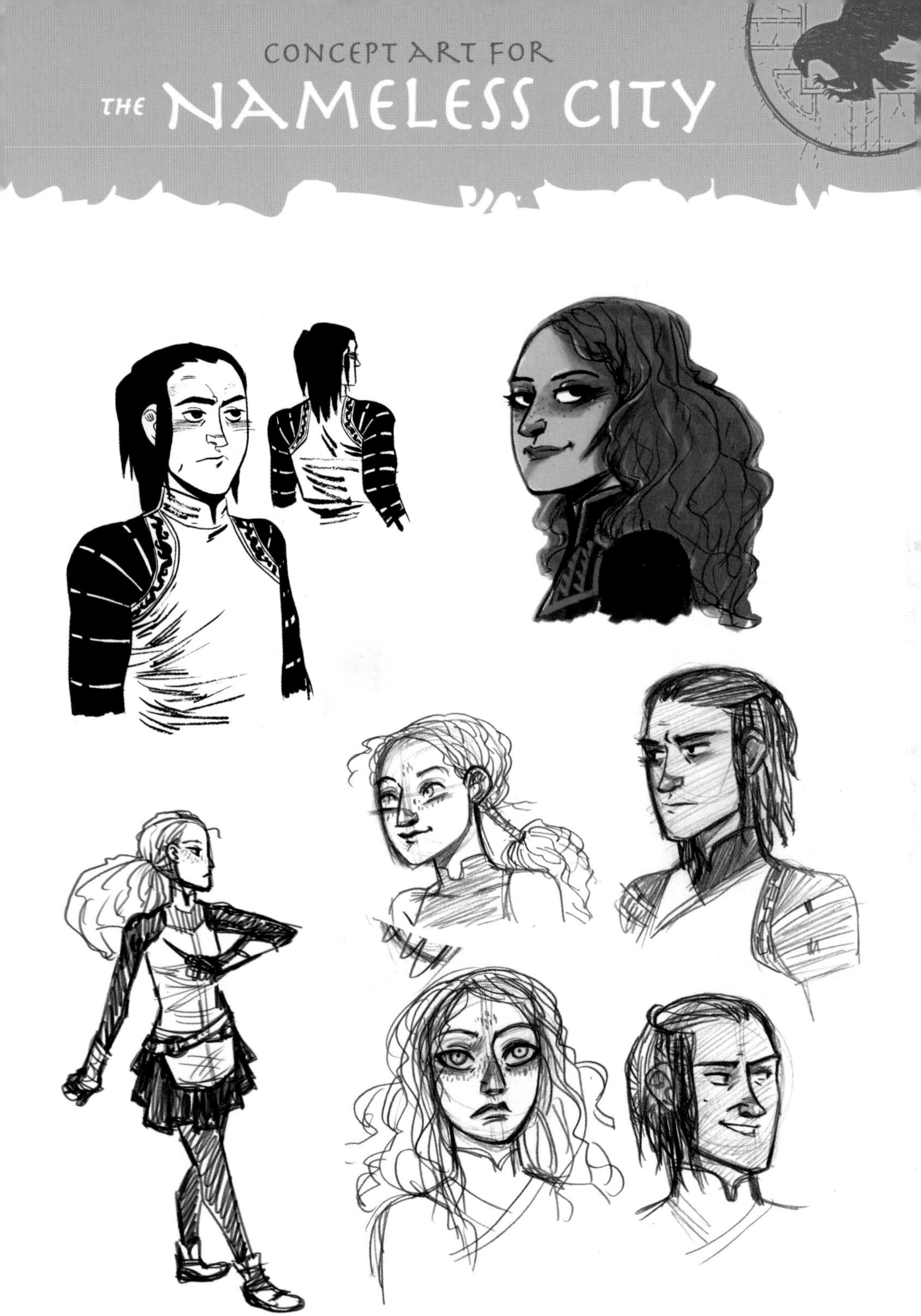

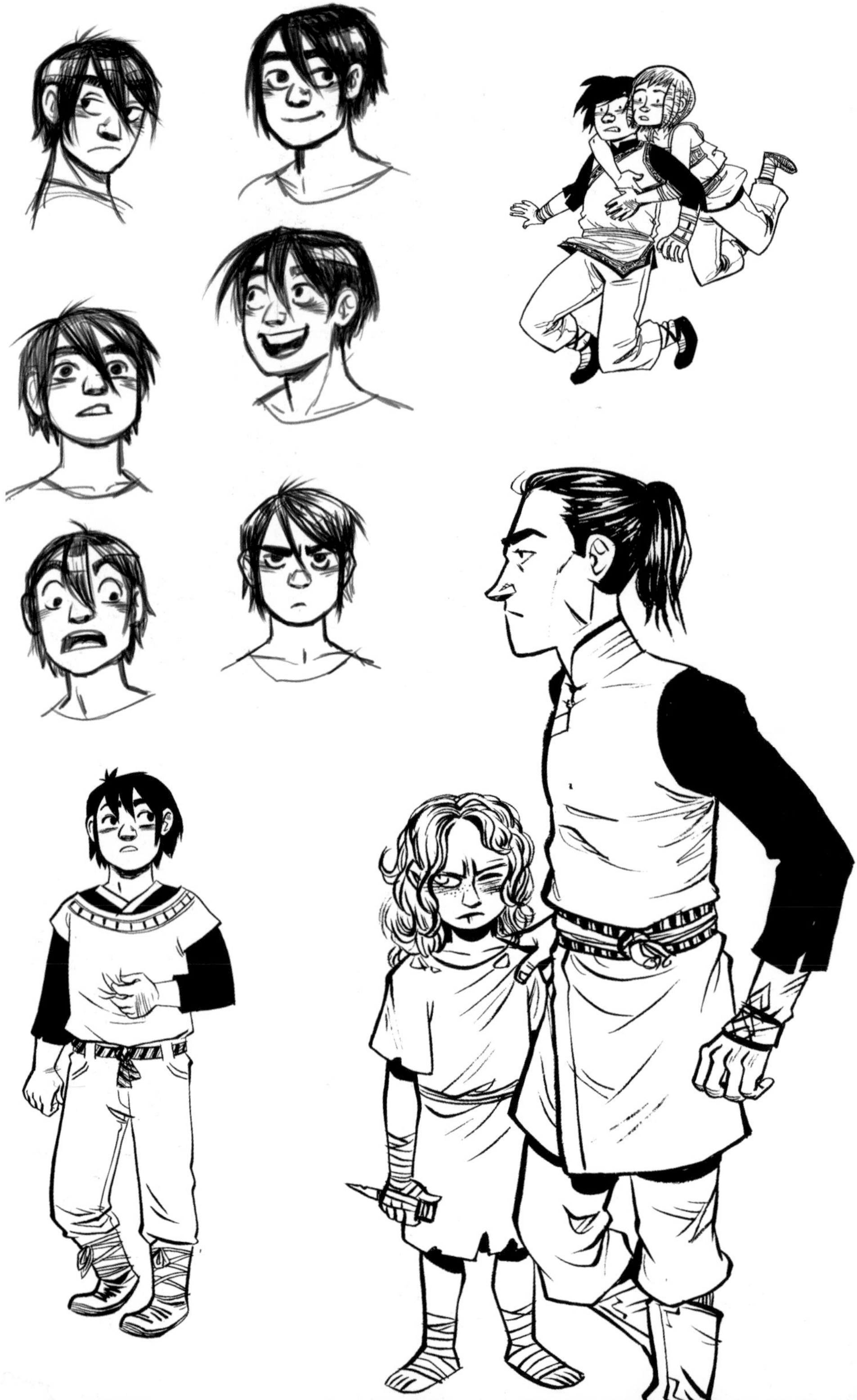

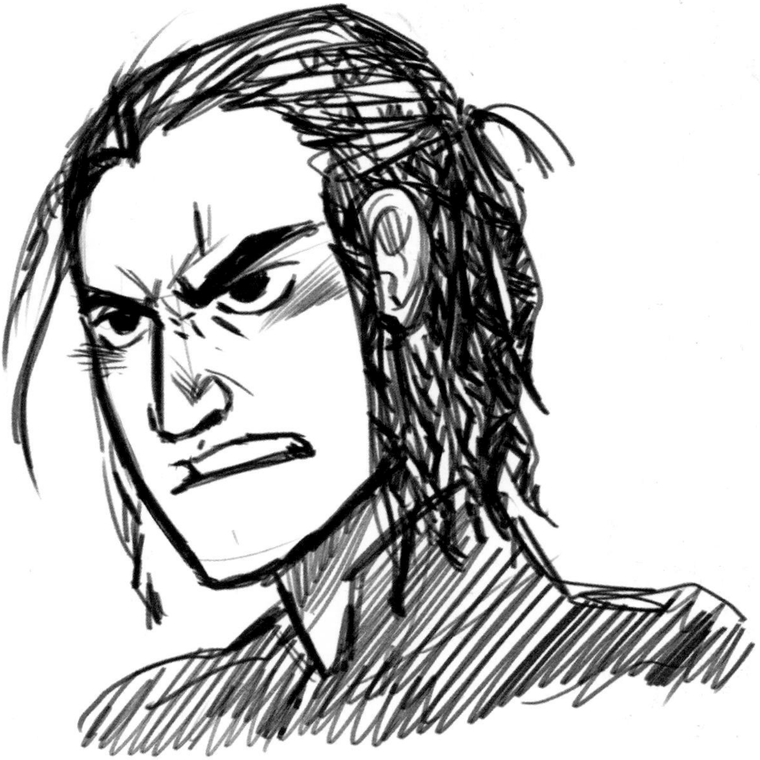

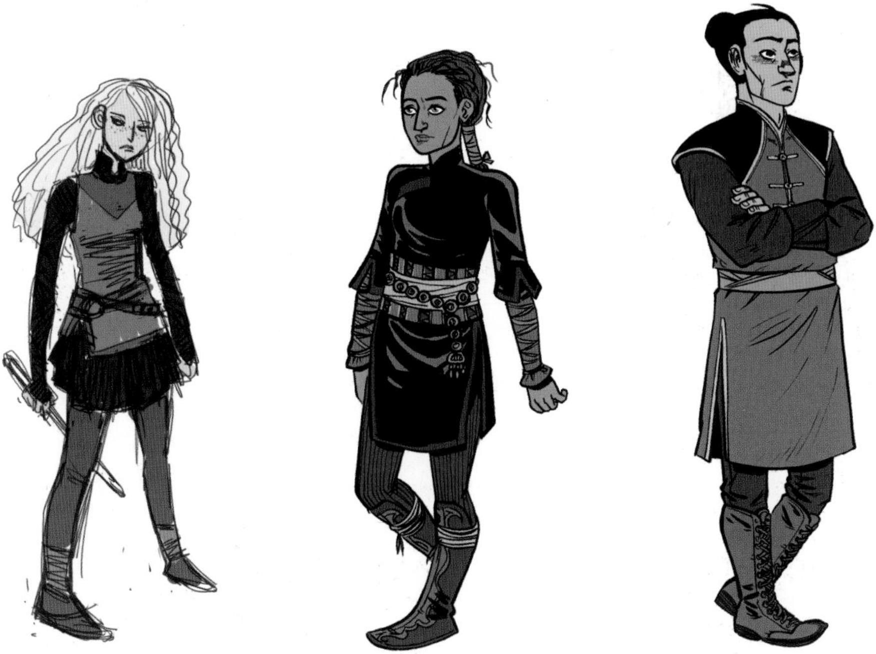

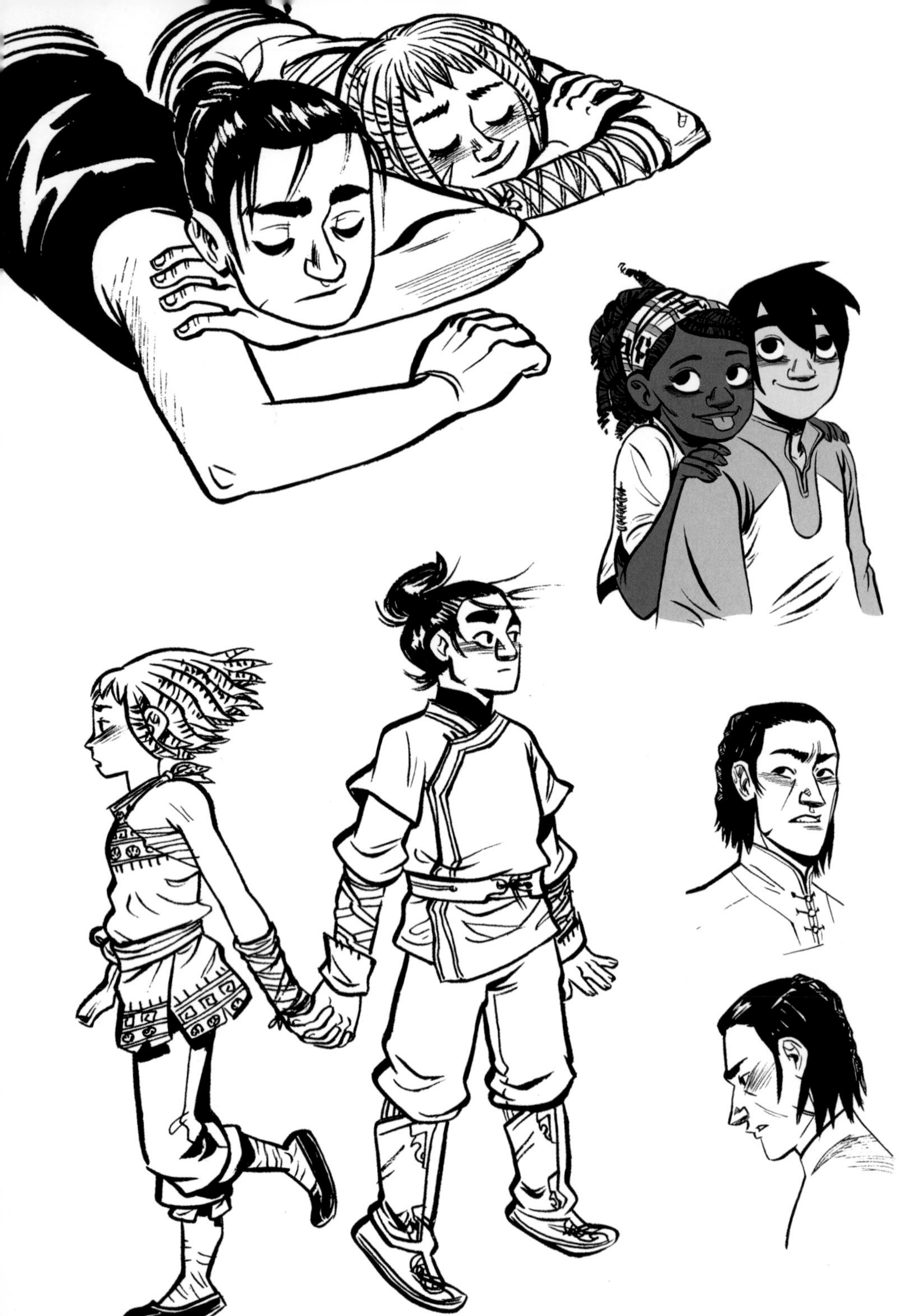

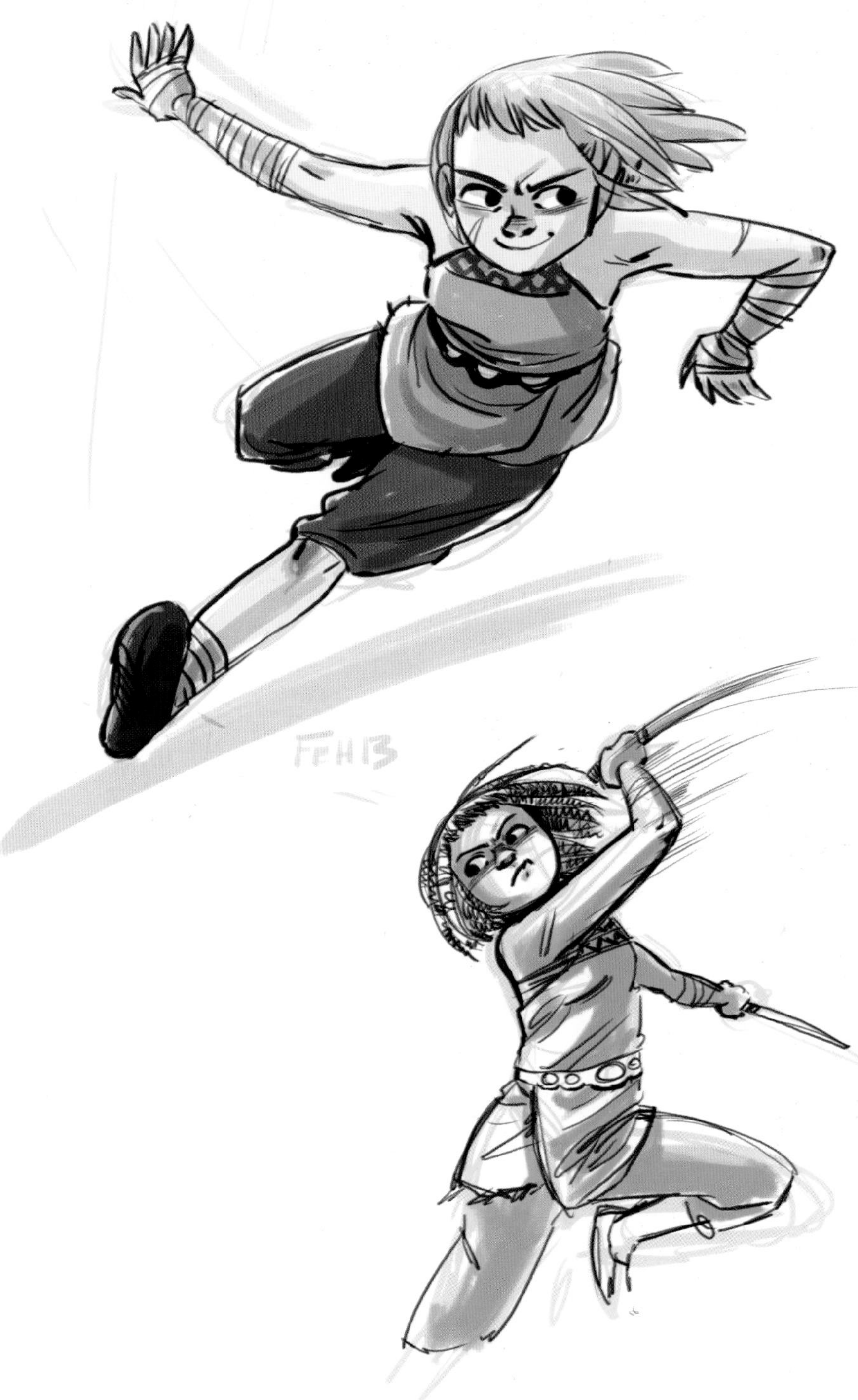
FFH13

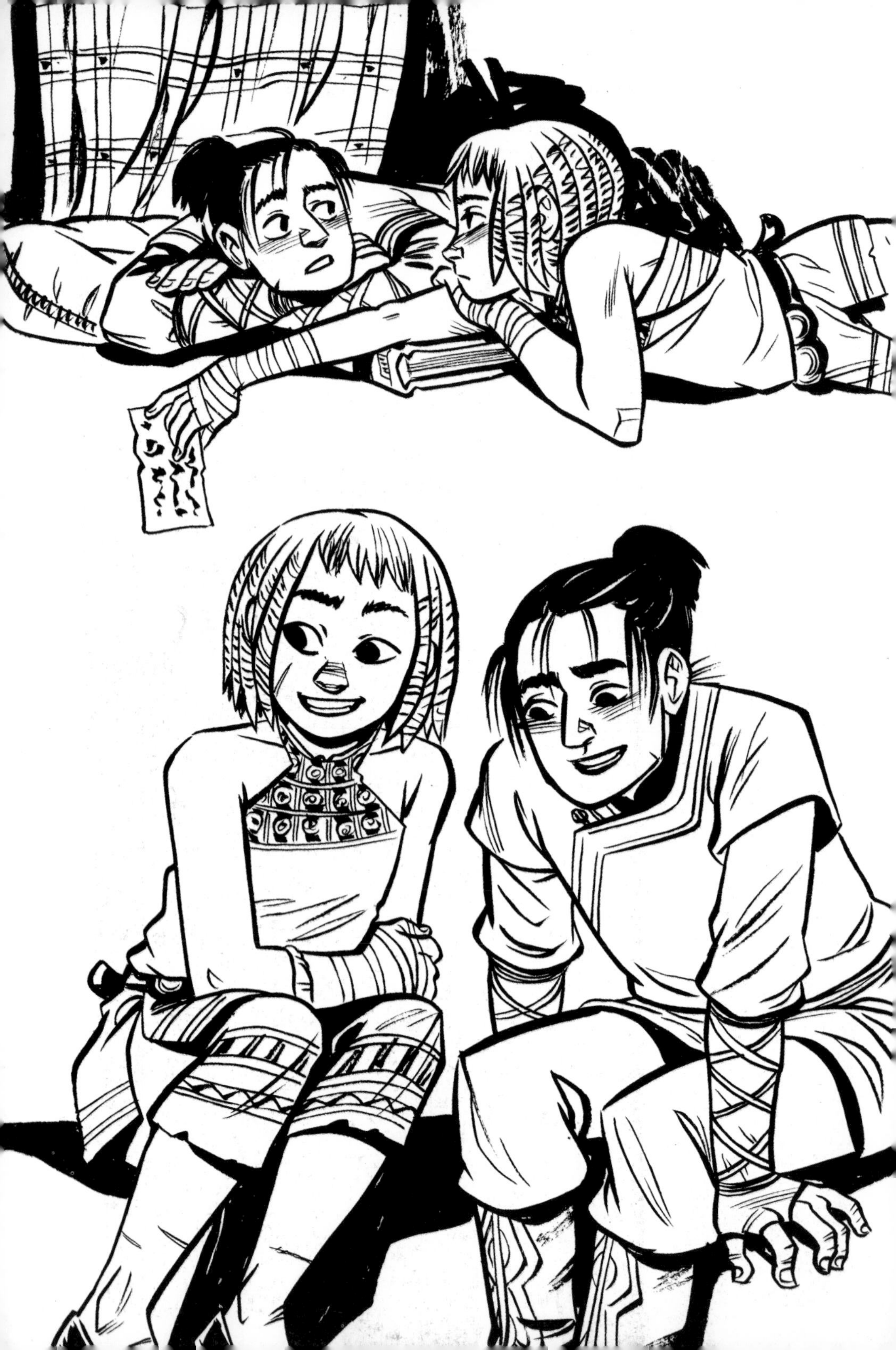

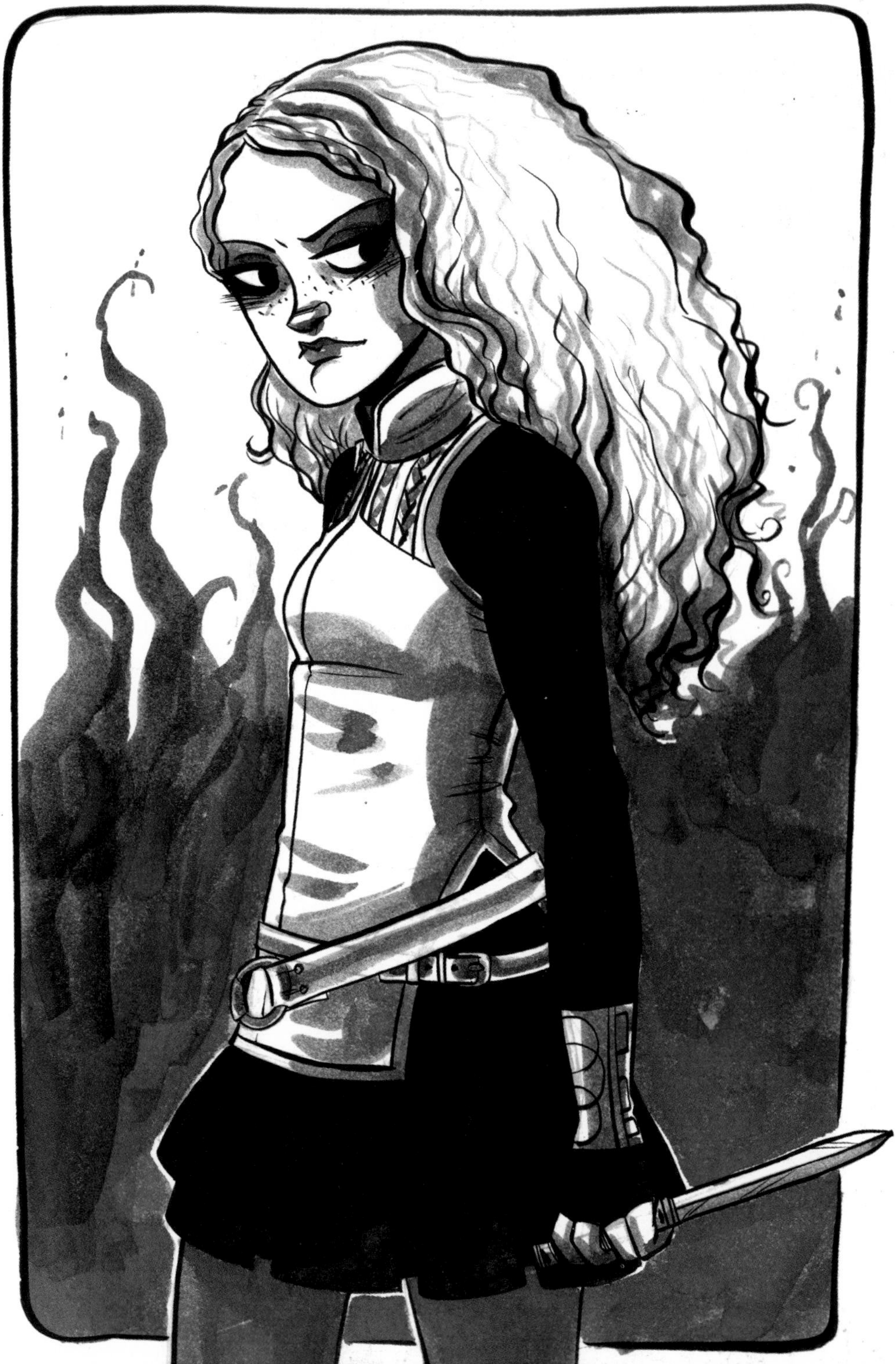

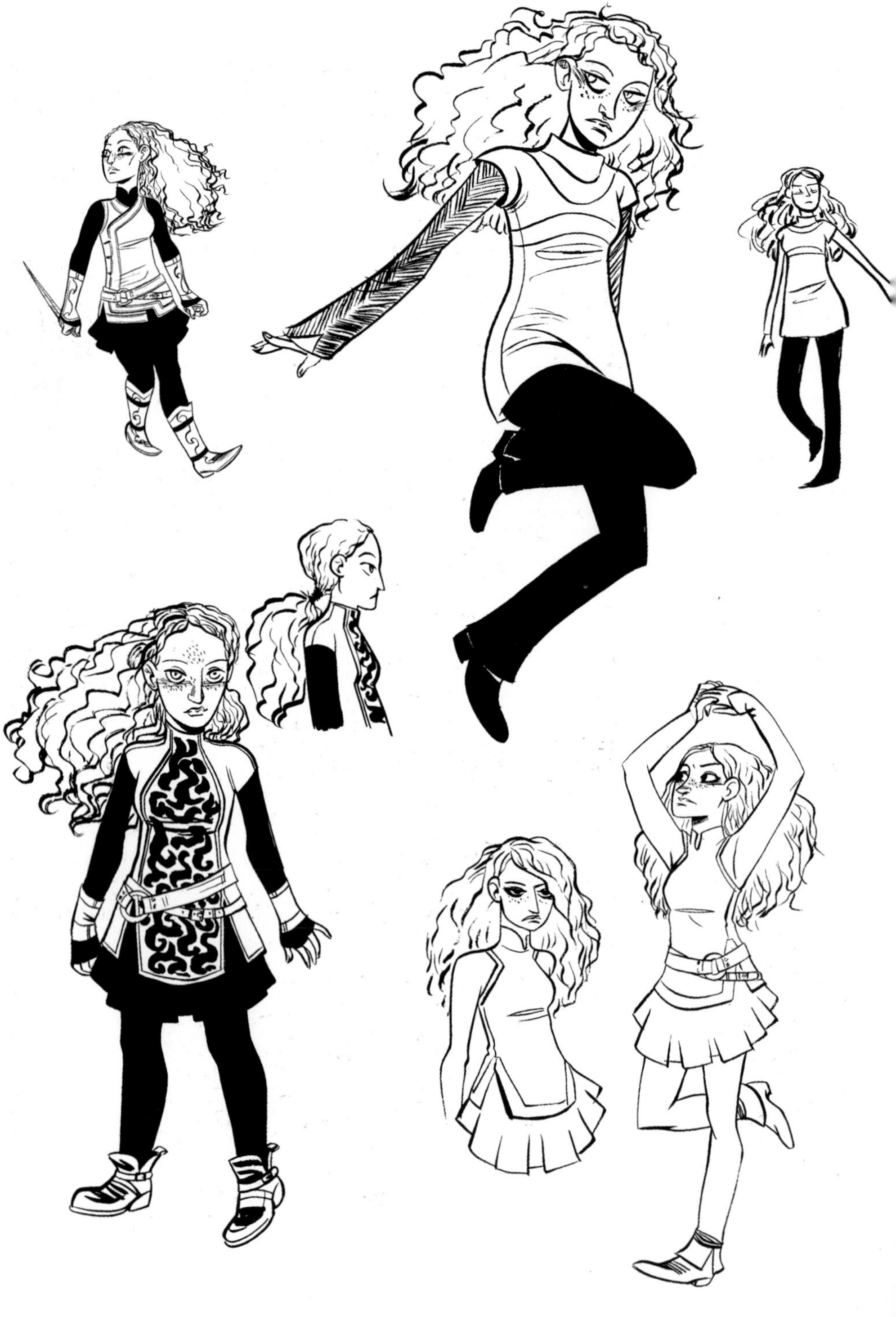

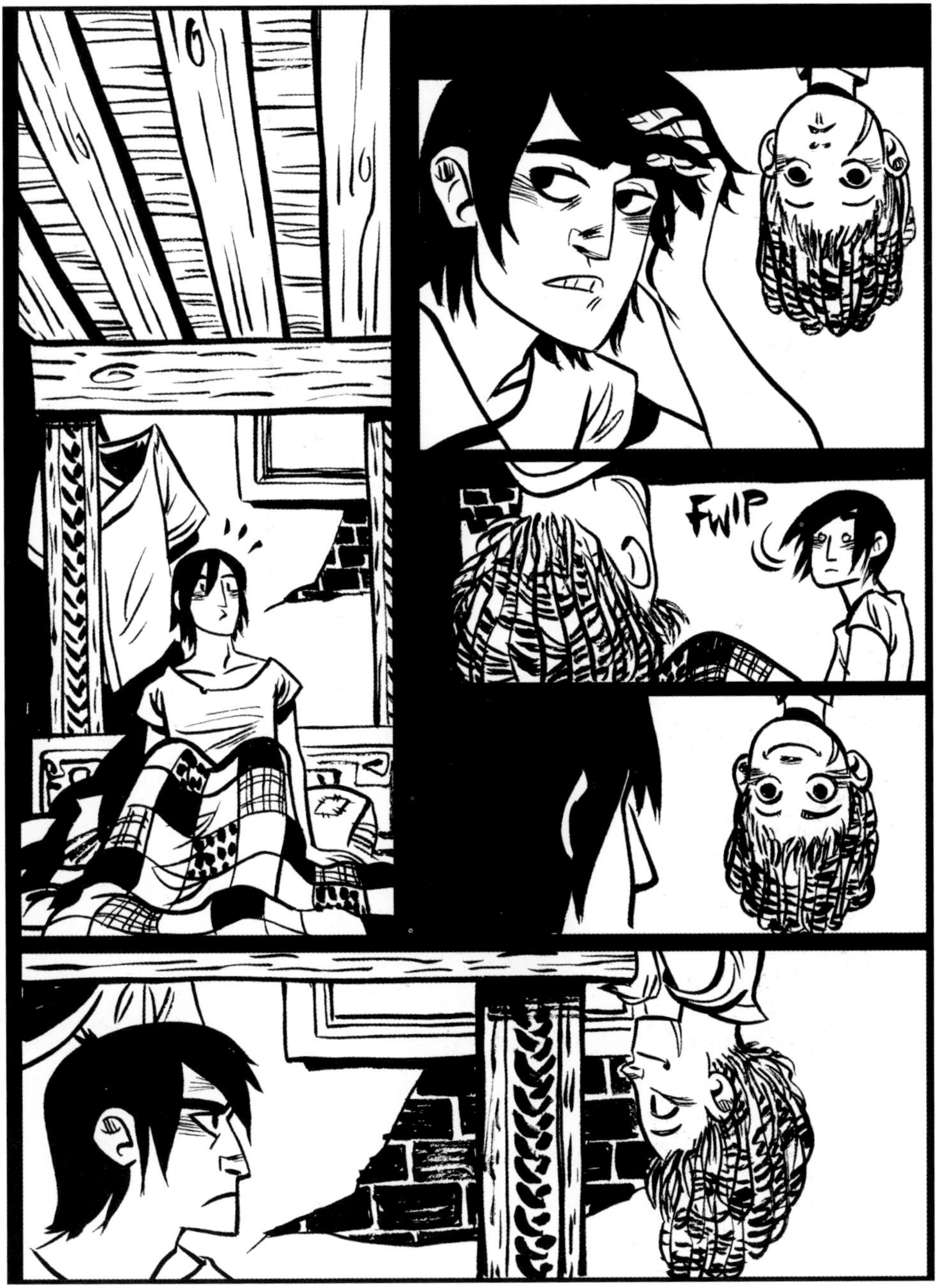
FWIP

Canada Council for the Arts Conseil des arts du Canada

Faith Erin Hicks acknowledges the support of the Canada Council for the Arts, which last year invested $153 million to bring the arts to Canadians throughout the country.

Faith Erin Hicks remercions le Conseil des arts du Canada de son soutien. L'an dernier, le Conseil a investi 153 millions de dollars pour mettre de l'art dans la vie des Canadiennes et des Canadiens de tout le pays.

:01 First Second

Published by First Second
First Second is an imprint of Roaring Brook Press, a division of
Holtzbrinck Publishing Holdings Limited Partnership
120 Broadway, New York, NY 10271

Library of Congress Control Number: 2016938731

Hardcover ISBN: 978-1-62672-159-3
Paperback ISBN: 978-1-62672-158-6

Our books may be purchased in bulk for promotional, educational, or business use. Please contact your local bookseller or the Macmillan Corporate and Premium Sales Department at (800) 221-7945 ext. 5442 or by e-mail at MacmillanSpecialMarkets@macmillan.com.

FIRST EDITION

First edition 2017

Interior art colored by Jordie Bellaire
Cover art colored by Braden Lamb and Shelli Paroline
Book design by Danielle Ceccolini
Printed in China by Toppan Leefung Printing Ltd., Dongguan City, Guangdong Province

Hardcover: 10 9 8 7 6 5 4 3 2
Paperback: 10 9 8 7

Penciled digitally in Manga Studio on a Wacom Cintiq. Inked traditionally with a Raphaël Kolinsky watercolor brush.

BY ART WE LIVE